Gaining Ground

The David and Mallory Anderson Trilogy: Volume 3

The way of the slothful man is as an hedge of thorns (a maze): but the way of the righteous shall be made plain.
Proverbs 15:19

Paula Rae Wallace

Order this book online at www.trafford.com
or email orders@trafford.com

Most Trafford titles are also available at major online book retailers.

The Arkansas map on the cover is provided courtesy of the Arkansas
State Highway and Transportation Department.

Printed in the United States of America.

ISBN: 978-1-4907-2817-9 (sc)
ISBN: 978-1-4907-2818-6 (hc)
ISBN: 978-1-4907-2819-3 (e)

Library of Congress Control Number: 2014903272

Trafford rev. 02/24/2014

Trafford PUBLISHING www.trafford.com

North America & international
toll-free: 1 888 232 4444 (USA & Canada)
fax: 812 355 4082

PREFACE

This book, its characters, institutions, and events are all fictitious!

TABLE OF CONTENTS

Chapter 1: GOLD

"Okay, slow down and be careful. I don't want you to fall and skin yourself up! And you need to keep an eye out for snakes." Beautiful Geologist, Mallory Anderson, watched as her small daughter, Amelia, toddled up the dry stream bed toward a hastily placed RV village. Smiling, she returned to her task, swinging a state-of-the art metal detector from side to side in the arroyo. Repeated beeps encouraged, but she didn't pause for close exploration; really no need to.

"You hunting for Diamonds?"

She whirled with a start at the sudden presence beside her. She paused, backing away and preparing to swing the instrument, should the intruder stepped nearer. Thoughts flashed through her brain with the speed of a DART A-train hurtling from the suburbs into Dallas. 'Why would she use a metal detector to look for Diamonds? Who is this, and how does he connect me to Diamonds? Where's David? Where's anyone? How did this guy gain access to our land?'

The old guy regarded her steadily before grinning. "Reckon I done scared ya a mite."

Her eyes flashed. "Reckon you did. You're on private property and there are trespassing signs posted."

He ran a gnarly hand through a straggly beard, before spitting a stream toward a rock. "Yeah, well I do no harm. Signs and fences don't mean nothin'. Everything belongs to the good Lord, anyhoo!"

"Uh-huh; so that's your angle if you find the *Lost Dutchman*? What are you, seriously, an old prospector? Or maybe there's a movie being produced, and the realtor forgot to mention that fact to us?"

He chuckled and wheezed. "Yeah, and I'm the star." He mentioned a prominent name.

Mallory frowned. "Yeah, the makeup people did a good job disguising you. Seriously, who are you and why are you on our land?"

"Look, Girlie, it's gettin' hot out. Why don't you go find a nice air-conditioned trailer house-"

Mallory backed farther. "Fine, I'll do that. But we better not catch you on our land again."

He held his ground and shrugged contemptuously. "Okay, reckon I won't letcha ketch me then."

Daniel Faulkner listened interestedly to the latest from David and Mallory. "Okay, that sounds amazing." His voice effervesced. "We're going to stop in Phoenix and have lunch with the attorney, just to be on the safe side with the land acquisition and mineral rights. We don't want to lose out on technicalities."

"Good idea," David agreed. "Is that water rights, too? And, try to be casual about it, but I think it would behoove us to obtain whatever else is on the market. Adjacent of course, is most convenient-"

"That good; huh?" Daniel's eyes met Diana's.

David laughed. "Yes, Sir; we think so! Of course, when a couple more Geologists get on site, we can get a better read."

Alexandra bounced up and down behind her dad's seat as when she was a little kid.

"Can't we please go to the property first?" she cajoled. "And you and Mom can get with the attorneys later on today?"

"Wish we could, Al." Daniel liked his daughter's eagerness as a Geology student, to get into the field. But if the first site was as promising as it sounded, they needed all of the legal *t*'s crossed, and the *i*'s dotted. No margin for error!

Mallory nodded slowly at the new development. "Well, Daniel's right, of course. If this place is the treasure trove the initial tests are showing, people will be looking for loopholes to take it away from us. But I was hoping they'd be here quicker, so someone could keep an eye open here while we go into town." She paused thoughtfully. "We really need more people here, anyway. There's security in numbers."

David nodded agreement as he set another wooden block in place on his tower. The baby, Avery, knocked it down gleefully, and he pretended to pout. "Well, you're right about security in numbers," he answered thoughtfully, "if the numbers are people you trust."

She nodded. "For some reason, I've been thinking about Katy and Jason! And Trayne!"

Against Avery's wailing protest, David hopped up from the pile of wooden blocks! "That is brilliant!" He paused to plant a kiss on Mallory's lips. "Do you want me to call them~"

She smiled brightly. "Yeah, go ahead. See how fast they can get here! Like on the next flight! We can get them whatever they'll need when they get here."

"You're right." David shot Mallory a sideways glance. They tailed the trespasser as he pulled into the assay office. David nodded the go ahead: "Call the police department."

She did, and found herself in an argument with a clerk.

David frowned. So much for that plan. "Hang up and dial 911." He reached for her phone, taking over the call.

"Yes, Ma'am, the nature of our emergency is that we encountered a trespasser on our property yesterday, and now he's stolen from us. We're at~" He pulled in, reading a fading sign: Dane Webster, Assayer, 218 West Main. "The address is 218 West Main."

"Is this an emergency?"

"It is! Have an officer respond!" He handed Mallory's phone back. "Okay, keep your gun handy and wait out here."

She nodded, ready to comply. But with both little girls in the SUV~ "Okay, you be careful, too!"

David strode into the aged structure and the assayer looked up briefly. "Be with you in a moment, Sir."

David nodded pleasantly. No rush; the police didn't seem to be responding quickly anyway.

"Man, Rudy," the assayer looked up sharply from the scale, "you got some good stuff here! You finally find the *Lost Dutchman*?

"S-hhhhh-t," the nappy-looking prospector hissed a warning, indicating the newcomer behind him. "Don't be askin' me no questions. Just weigh her out and pay me my money."

As the transaction neared completion, a police car finally rolled in. A lone officer rambled in.

"Mornin' Hank," the assayer greeted, "What brings you in here?"

"You haven't got a crime in progress, Dane? We received a 911 that some emergency was going down here. Glad to see you're okay."

David stepped forward. "Good morning, officer. My wife and I called in. This gentleman," he indicated the thief, "well, we caught him yesterday, trespassing on our land. He actually startled my wife. He's here now, selling gold that he stole when he returned during the night."

"Hey, you ain't got no proof of that-" The prospector's whiny voice grated.

"Easy, Rudy, I've got things under control," Hank's eyes bored into David. "Them's some pretty serious charges, Son!"

"Nevertheless, true!" Resenting the attempt at intimidation; David stepped closer rather than backing away. "My name is David Anderson, and we do have proof that the gold is ours."

Hank Darby crossed his arms importantly across his expansive chest.

"Like I said," David went on patiently. "My wife's a Geologist, and we've purchased a good-sized plot where we've begun exploration. Mr.-uh-Rudy, is it? He slipped up near an arroyo where she was taking tests with a metal detector. He heard the beeps and knew slipping back at night would be worth his while. Here, let me show you pictures we took on my phone. Here's where he dug in our arroyo, with his little folding shovel; the shovel that's in the back of his truck out there, now!"

Hank smirked. "Big deal- Lots of guys prospect with similar equipment."

"Probably, but Rudy here, wasn't prospecting! He knew straight where to come to grab a small fortune! But there's more proof! When we first arrived, we spread our place with organic fertilizer and grass seed. Those indicators are bound to be on his clothes and boots, as well as on his equipment-"

Forced into a corner, Hank capitulated. "Okay, Dane, you heard this fella's claim. I'm taking that gold into evidence. Rudy, looks like you're back in your same cell; we'll have ta send your clothes off to the state lab for testing."

"Organic fertilizer," the felon mumbled. "I wondered what smelled so rank." His words interspersed liberally with profanity.

The policeman didn't bother with cuffs, but indicated for the prisoner to precede him. "No kiddin', Rudy; we thought it was just you!"

Donovan Cline did one more email check prior to leaving his office for the day. The missive quickened his pulse and flushed his face with color. Permission from foreign authorities to place his salvage operation at the Straits of Tiran to explore with a submersible! Part of him wished he had considered the more extensive operation from the outset; but he knew that the first attempt, though not accomplishing his immediate goals, was what was now giving him favor and the go-ahead! Sitting back down at his ornate desk, he sent a group email to the friends who were as eager for word as he was. This was absolutely thrilling!

Nina Garcia followed slowly behind a group of excited tourists. Taking in a day excursion from the cruise ship, she strolled alone. Feeling shy and inadequate about both her poor English and her impoverished upbringing, she didn't mingle easily with the well-heeled cruise crowd. She was happy, though, taking note of warm sunshine tempered with a capricious breeze. She was on Malta! She strolled among the vendors along the Valletta waterfront, admiring crafts and eager for ideas. She paused in her meandering to find a table at an outdoor café for a pastry and coffee. She smiled easily when the proprietor requested that she share the table. Nothing strange for Nina! People in most countries were more amenable to crowding together and sharing space than were Americans. She smiled timidly as she pulled out her crochet work.

The couple at her table conversed softly with one another as they placed their order and waited for their food.

"Very pretty; your handbag," Nina smiled, pointing at the newcomer's exclusive bag. "Is Italian?"

"Yes, as a matter of fact! We like Italian leather better than any place in the world."

"Nina nodded, "Yes, very fine quality! Do you try Spain?"

The lady became suddenly loquacious. "You know, I think it's so odd that you should mention that! One of my dear friends recently returned from Spain, and she brought the most adorable shoes back with her! I had no idea! What is that beautiful item you're crocheting?"

Nina blushed, "Is dress!" She stated the obvious. "I make for my niece's company, and her beautiful friend." Nina timidly offered a business card and showed a sketch of Mallory modeling the product of the moment. Feeling suddenly brave in the other woman's openness, she offered. "Also, I am very good cook! You ever go Miami?"

"Why Dear, we live in Miami!"

"You come buy from my truck! You like!" She pointed to the elegant seafood sandwich being placed carefully by a server! "Is better! Honduran! You ever eat?"

"I don't believe we ever have! But we always love new adventures, don't we Taylor?"

Taylor looked up from his *Wall Street Journal*, "Yes, Dear!"

"There! David!" Mallory's voice broke the silence so suddenly that he jumped. "That looks perfect!"

He laughed, always amazed by her ability to see what others missed. "You know, I read a passage this morning that reminded me of you!

> *Joshua 6:1&2 Now Jericho was straitly shut up because of the children of Israel: none went out, and none came in.*
>
> *And the LORD said unto Joshua, See, I have given into thine hand Jericho, and the king thereof, and the mighty men of valor.*

Joshua was looking at a fortified and impenetrable city, and the Lord told him, that regardless of how hopeless things looked from a human standpoint, that He could do the impossible, and bring great victory." He turned his blinker on for a left turn and waited for a few oncoming vehicles, before pulling in to the derelict property.

Mallory simply gazed around, her excitement growing. "Can you make out the phone number?"

He frowned. The aged building defied description for pitiful. "Mallory, that for sale sign must be at least twenty years old! It's been used for target practice, and it's rusty! No, I can't read the number, and it probably wouldn't be a valid number by now. But let's check the building out." He unlocked his truck door.

"No, wait. I need to call Kerry and have him acquire it for us. Without the locals knowing we're interested. That could make them assume it holds vast riches, which it may-"

He nodded. "Yeah, it's been here empty so long, and it's such an eyesore, that we should be able to get a good deal. We don't want the owner to 'see us coming' and jack up the price. Still, I'd like to see what we're making an offer on."

She laughed. "Uh, pretty sure what we see is what we get. Let's assume it's a total wreck, and if anything's still usable, we'll consider it a plus."

"Yeah, but look at the foundation. We might be ahead by razing the building and starting over on the lot."

"Well, it doesn't say it's condemned. You can make it workable!"

Katy and Jason, accompanied by Trayne and their kids, loaded into the sixteen passenger van and headed northeast from Phoenix on 60, Superstition Freeway.

"I'm excited to see David and Mallory again. I'm dying to see their kids!" Katy glowed with anticipation.

Jason nodded absently as he studied an article in a journal of nursing. He looked up. "Yeah, I hope they aren't bringing us down for the purpose of treating the wounded in a gold camp war."

"Come on, Jason, you know better. We're bringing our kids, and the Faulkners are in and out with theirs. It's sad when law enforcement people are sympathetic to the local populace more than in over-all law and order. David and Mallory are rushing to make everything they're doing, state-of-the-art secure!"

Still, Jason frowned thoughtfully. "Isn't your dad pretty good friends with that Arabian Horse rancher and his *SOC Foundation*?"

"He is, Jason; but I don't want dad and mom to get on the warpath about the kids. They didn't have to let us bring them. But, what we can do is remind David about the Hansons and the power of the people!" She smiled brightly. "That's a great idea!"

David bobbed in at their Dallas home. No one seemed in proximity except for Mallory's raucous Hyacinth Mackaws. "Hey, is anyone home?" His voice echoed in the foyer, echoed again by the birds: "Hey, is anyone home?"

"We're coming!" Amelia's bright smile and curly hair appeared at the top of the stairs. "Watch, Daddy! Catch me!" She climbed onto the swirling banister and swooshed toward him.

"Does Mommy let you do that?" David, possessed with a riotous sense of fun, hated to be a killjoy.

"Uh-huh! Mommy teached me!"

He laughed, and tucking her beneath one arm, jogged up the staircase.

"Almost ready," Mallory apologized, somewhat breathless and ruffled. "Things have kept coming up-"

"Really, have the girls minded?"

She laughed. "Yeah, about like usual. Other things have presented challenges besides their escapades. Look what came a couple of hours ago!"

His gaze followed the sweep of her manicured hand. "That's nice; who'd it come from?"

Amelia pulled up onto their king sized bed and started jumping energetically. "It comed from Noah"!

"Okay, Amelia; stop jumping and put your toothpaste and toothbrush in your suitcase," Mallory instructed. "And you say, 'it came', not 'it comed'."

"Who's Noah?" David's question, more of habit than curiosity!

Mallory's auburn tresses swung around her shoulders and she sighed. "Amar bin Saaye! Now Amelia's convinced that since he wasn't Moses, and he had a large yacht, that he was Noah! And his pets were all in their cages out of sight-"

David frowned. "See, that's why I wasn't sure about sending him the candy- He was already sweet on you."

She laughed and shoved her way into his arms. "Well, his intercession basically saved our lives; candy was actually a pretty paltry token of gratitude. And the chest isn't a gift to me, as much as a sample to show us this craft! I noticed similar, smaller pieces in the tourist shops on the way from Amman to Petra. They're made from inlaid camel bone." She raised the lid on the glistening white piece, to reveal cedar wood veneer lining the trunk's floor and lid. "I think these are the reason he approached us to begin with! Somehow he was aware of the fact that we promote some of the Turkish bazaar wares. I think he wanted us to partner in bringing these to the American market."

As a craftsman, himself, David admired the workmanship in the piece of furniture. "So, did you call him and work a deal?"

She shook her head. "Actually, I've been trying to get packed up and ready to leave for Arizona. But Trayne and Cade have both called to ask me questions. And then David Higgins ran into problems with the drill rig. Typical morning! How's your skyscraper? Sorry I forgot to ask when you first came in."

He pressed his mouth on hers. "It's actually still a deep hole in the ground. When there's a little bit more to see, I'll bring you with me."

She smiled. "I can't wait! So, anyway, no, I haven't tried to contact the Sheik. I thought maybe in all your spare time-"

Mallory laughed with delight as they drove through the main gate of the Arizona property! With the well water and their seed-sowing, the grass looked nearly verdant! She laughed, too, at her mother's handiwork! In addition to her usual floral landscaping, she had also made use of an abundance of wide, sprawling cactus plants. A month's worth of work by a motivated and talented crew evidenced itself!

"This looks amazing, David!"

He nodded, not taking it as a personal compliment, so much as agreeing with the progress. "Yes, with the big generator being delivered later today, we can finally electrify the fences, at least at night! Meanwhile, we've gone kinda crazy with 'bob war'. He laughed as he placed little Amelia's Texas drawl on the term, 'barbed wire'.

"Well, 'bob war' works as a deterrent for me," Mallory agreed, surveying angry-looking scars on her legs. "And the new property above this one: it's fenced, too?"

He nodded, satisfaction etched in handsome features.

Organic chemist, Cade Holman, watched the jet's shadow on the ground below as seatbelt lights dinged on, and the flight attendant made the usual announcements. Once at the gate, he turned his phone on to check for messages. He grinned at the one he sought. "Go get em, Tiger!" From his wife of a month, and since there was the usual logjám waiting to deplane, he responded. "Keep praying, Baby! As you know, this is already beyond my wildest dreams!"

Grabbing his carry-on, he gained freedom at last and sprinted for the terminal exit! A few yards beyond the exit, he spotted the gleaming new SUV, neatly lettered: *Holman, Corporation.* Even as a happy feeling of pride surged, he refrained from snapping a picture to forward to Catrina. There would be time for that. He extended his hand, "Hello, Cade Holman."

The other man nodded pleasantly. "I go by Trayne. I'm pleased to meet you. Listen, David really hates it-"

Cade laughed easily, "Pleased to meet you at last, Trayne. David's not being able to meet me is no problem."

A jovial laugh, "Okay, Man, from this point forward, I'm just along for the ride. Do you want to drive your new company vehicle; or do you have stuff to work on? And then I can drive you?"

"Hey, since I don't have a clue where we're going, why don't you drive, if you don't mind?" He pulled his laptop free from his backpack and pulled long legs in on the passenger's side.

"Well, there you go," David gestured proudly as Mallory surveyed the amazing transformation! She sat, taking it in before she asked him to circle the building. He eased forward slowly, emerging at the front of the building once more. He beheld it proudly. The decades'-long-empty Gibson's store was alive once more! The old graffiti'd bricks wore a new soft, sandstone-red coat of paint, trimmed with gray that bordered on sage. The sandstone bluffs sloping upward at the rear of the lot seemed the perfect frame. New blacktop, precisely painted; and brimming flower beds, lent a special life-breathing appeal. New, young conifers lined the front, and the neatly lettered sign read: *Holman Corporation*!

"And, best of all, here's the CO! Want to take a tour?" David's features shone as he waved the important document.

"I'm dying to take the tour!" She hesitated.

"But you want to wait for Holman?"

"Yeah; kinda. Wish Catrina could have come with him. Look, there they are."

The interior renovation made Mallory gasp with wonder! She took in the small but luxurious office spaces, the break room and restrooms, the loading dock, and the gleaming, efficient labs!

Cade emerged from his daze to accept the sets of keys. "Wow! Wow! This is amazing! Tell your dad I said thanks for everything!"

David frowned! He had kind of busted his crew to accomplish the impossible! And Holman was thanking his dad?

Mallory giggled.

"Woops, guess that didn't come out just right," Cade apologized. "Thanks to both of you, too! The reason-"

David nodded. "Yeah, we get it! You were a very determined atheist! And you got saved at my dad's church, and the blessings have rained down on you ever since!"

"Yeah, you know, I wanted to be a Chemist because I understood Chemistry and figured I could make pretty good money! And then, I graduated with honors and the whole nine yards, and couldn't even get an entry-level job-Then I found the Lord, and Catrina! I talked her into marrying me, we own our own company, and I'm hiring chemists rather than begging for a job!"

David nodded understanding. "Luke and some of his guys will be here first thing Monday morning to orient and train your staff. By Thursday, we'll deliver the first of our core samples. We're eager to find out what we have, hopefully without the whole world's finding out at the same time! That's the problem with state run labs; that, and the backlog! You and Catrina already signed CDA's and Luke's crew addresses it for the others in the training. Why don't you follow us to the *Enclave*? Trayne is staying to oversee the security set-up here. There are already some nosy and harassing neighbors, sad to say."

A stunning palette of colors stained the sky, deepening the richness of the earth tones as the gates to the Enclave swung open automatically. "Smile for all the cameras," David reminded Mallory good-naturedly. "If we get mad at one another, word will get around quick!" He pulled in, followed by Cade in his company car. The gates closed, and David hopped out to open the double-wide, readied for the new executive's use.

Chapter 2: GRABBING

"Why don't y'all come stay with us in Tulsa for the Holidays?" Diana invited. "We know David drops in and out of Tulsa checking on his mansion project."

"Okay, thank you for the offer. We can't exactly decide what to do. We like Arkansas the best for Christmas, and Amelia really misses Mocha and her cria, Jasmine. I mean, when do you let your kids drive your decisions-" Mallory paused, embarrassed.

Daniel laughed. "Probably from the moment they enter the world. You know, you become a family entity and you try to accommodate each member as much as you can. We love the Christmasy atmosphere there, too. It's just, I've let things slide at *GeoHy* while I've been so engrossed down here. My dad does a good job, but he's pretty much been chained to the place for the past couple of months! Of course, having most of the accounting farmed out now, is a huge boost!"

Mallory gazed around. Beyond the cultivated *Enclave*, wild, barren, beauty prevailed! But the cluster of RV's and double-wides lacked the atmosphere of their sumptuous homes. She acquiesced. "But we should still make this place as joyous as possible!"

"Maybe next year," David cautioned. "For this year, with so many trespassers and curiosity seekers, I don't want to set up a Christmas light display that will bring more gawkers out here!"

The Faulkner mansion glowed resplendently through soft snowfall.

"A white Christmas"! Diana's joyous laugh! "It doesn't happen very often! I love it! On the mission field in Africa, we never saw snow except in pictures! Why don't you let the kids go out and play with our kids? While they're all bundled up"! She reached for Avery, planting kisses on both girls. "Alexandra loves the snow, too; so she's keeping an eye on all the little ones. This makes me want to ski!"

"Well, let's plan for Aspen in March," Mallory agreed readily. "If your baby cooperates and comes on time, it should work out!"

"Okay, tentatively. Of course, that's kind of a big 'if'! Have you seen the pictures Donovan Cline sent out?"

Mallory nodded. "Yes, Ma'am; they looked clear as mud to me! And the Saudi side seems even more dismal. The Saudis contacted us to return to drill and operate the GPR."

Diana's eyes registered her surprise! "Are you going to?"

"Uh! No Ma'am! I had more than enough of that place!"

"Well, you could enter into the contract and send David Higgins! You and your David wouldn't need to get near the place!"

"Yes; but there's always such a radical element! Even if the government is acting in good faith, what's to keep crazies from kidnapping Higgins? I mean, David and I left a couple of dead bodies behind there! I don't trust the whole creepy thing!"

"Probably wisest"!

Lilly paced impatiently. Not like herself, at all! Well, not like her regenerated self. Sighing, she opened her Bible! She couldn't figure out why she was having such a tough time focusing! Her phone made her jump! Not recognizing the number, she answered suspiciously, "Hello, this is Lilly Cowan."

"Cousin Lilly"! Nick Moa'a'loa's exuberant tone lifted her spirits immediately.

"Hello, Nick. How are you and Jennifer doing? And little Jason"?

"Pleased to say, we've never been better! We've been too long-uh-thanking-"

Lilly interrupted. "Well, there's nothing to thank me for. It's good to hear your voices. What do you hear from people?"

"Uh-you mean about Cassandra Faulkner?"

Lilly coughed to hide emotions. "Well, I hardly hear from anyone."

A long pause before Nick laughed. "Apologies, Mrs. Cowan. I guess since we all know you know everything, we don't call you like we should."

Lilly tapped a pencil eraser on her blotter, but for some reason couldn't think of a clever comeback. When the awkward silence continued, Nick attempted to fill the space.

"Well, we don't hear from people either, not as much as we'd like. We feel like Jennifer and Jason are safer now, but we still haven't ventured far. We-uh-hear that Cassandra's pursuing nursing!"

Disconnecting, Lilly burst into tears.

"Okay, that was a merry Christmas, I guess!" Mallory's eyes met David's as they exited the Faulkner estate en route to the Arkansas Ranch. "I love this!" She lifted her hand to show off the new Claddagh jewelry, Christmas gifts from him. "And the kids are so much fun! Watching their excitement"!

He reached over and caught hold of her hand, laughing. "Yeah, it was interesting! Wonder what plans our kids will have that they'll be afraid to tell us."

Mallory glanced back at the girls, each playing with a new Christmas toy, from the confinement of their car seats. "Yeah, maybe the Lord will rapture us before we have to deal with adolescence."

His eyes danced. "Yeah, my mom and dad prayed the same thing! And they've had to deal with all five us going through the maturation process. Maybe you'll be as perceptive with our kids as you've been with the Faulkners'."

She sighed. "Maybe so! To me it was obvious that Alexandra wanted to be a Geologist and not a nurse! And that kind of crushed Diana! And now, Cassandra's interest in nursing has been a blow to Daniel. He figured violin would be enough for her. Which, it hasn't been for him!"

"Yeah, let's agree that we won't pick for our kids; you know living vicariously through their lives."

She frowned. "Well, Daniel and Diana haven't really done that. I mean their lives are exciting and meaningful; it's not like they don't have a life. I guess they just thought they had it figured out. What do you think about a ski trip to Aspen in March? Diana mentioned it, and I thought it sounded like fun. The plan hinges on when their baby arrives."

He nodded, "Sounds good."

Cade Holman caught a glimpse of the sheriff's car as it pulled onto the *Holman, Corporation* parking lot. He frowned and made his way to the outer office. "Morning, Sheriff, can I help you?"

"Sheriff Red Radcliffe! Yeah, you can explain to me just exactly what kind of a company you're running here."

Cade studied him carefully. Big guy with sandy-colored hair turning gray! Eyes so pale as to seem colorless! Intimidating!

"We have a web site that explains as much as the public needs to know. Have you received any complaints? Exactly why are you out here?"

"I keep tabs on what goes down in my county! And folks are real curious what kind of loads you receive in the middle of the nights!"

"Well, I'm not in the business of satisfying the curiosities of mindless gossips. Trust me. We're legal and above-board. Our business is based in confidentiality. Thank you for stopping by. Would you like a cup of coffee to take along with you?"

The officer spluttered. "Trust me, Son; I'll figure out what you're up to. It'll go better if you come clean up front."

Cade leaned forward ever so slightly. "I'm glad to hear that you keep tabs on county stuff. We're depending on that. Nice of you to come by"!

Rattled by the unpleasant interview, Holman watched the county vehicle turn left across the road before he slipped back into his office and placed a call to his attorney.

Mallory napped while the girls slept, then offered to drive.

"I'm good!" David's winks still sent thrills through her. "Why don't you call Lilly and wish her a Merry Christmas?"

"Uh, because I'm afraid she's probably found out about Cassandra's interest in nursing. And I'm not the bad person, here, David! That made Cassandra lean her own direction!"

He laughed teasingly. “Yeah maybe, but you’re the one that decided to air it all out!”

Tears sparkled suddenly. “You think I should have kept my mouth shut?”

He laughed again. “I didn’t say that! What I said is, that you should call Lilly and wish her a merry Christmas! Because she’s a very good friend to you, to us! And I’m sure that even though she keeps in the information loop, it’s not the same to her as you calling!”

She pulled her phone free. “It’s kind of late there. Hello, Lilly, I hope I didn’t-are you okay?”

Lilly’s voice came through angry tears. “Why are you calling me, Mallory?”

“Well, to wish you a somewhat late, Merry Christmas! What’s going on? Are you doing okay? David just reprimanded me for not calling you oftener; I apologize-I should call-I appreciate you, and I’ve been terribly careless-”

“Snooping is my job, Mallory!”

Mallory laughed. “Yes, I know it is, and I’ve gotten used to it, and almost count on it. I don’t resent your guidance about the stones-”

“Shhhhh! Not on the phone!”

Mallory laughed. “See, that’s why I don’t call more! We love you, Lilly! Merry Christmas! When can you come visit?”

David made a slitting-his-throat gesture as Lilly promised to visit soon.

Mallory clasped David’s arm in alarm. “Is that Frank and Linda Gilmore? I hope they haven’t changed their minds about the financing!”

He pulled beyond the other car and pressed the remote to swing the gate open. Frank and Linda pulled in behind them.

“Merry Christmas”! Franks’ voice carried through the crisp evening air. “We know you’re just pulling in, but we have exciting news! Well, we think so!”

“Awesome, come on in.” David and Mallory each pulled a daughter free as they led the way into the kitchen. “I’ll start some coffee.”

“No need for that. And we weren’t waiting out there to waylay you. We just took a run by to see if you were back. We’re on our way to Little Rock!” Frank drew an envelope from his pocket and held it out.

"What's this?" David took it with some trepidation.

Frank laughed out loud. "Come on; it's not a snake."

A long, plain, white envelope showed his name on the front, in Linda's pretty hand. He pulled the check, out, questioningly. "What's this for?"

Frank grinned smugly. "We might drink one cup of coffee."

Over steaming mugs, he divulged his story. "Well, I took a lesson from y'all about hiring a PI! So, I hired a fella to check things out about the lumber mill that was processing that expensive wood you found. Remember you mentioned that we should be getting more board feet out of it? And that the small pieces were also valuable? Well, the PI found you were right, and based on his findings, we filed suit! They got scared and settled out of court. That's your eighty per cent! We already kept our twenty!"

David was speechless. "Well, you went to a lot of trouble."

"Yeah, we don't want more than we're entitled to, but we don't take a liking to getting cheated. They were forced to cover court costs. The PI fees, we deducted already. Oh, and thank you for the big box of toffee. We've gotten hooked on it, and look forward to getting it. Have you ever visited this *Enstrom's Fine Candies* in Grand Junction, Colorado?"

They laughed and Mallory responded, "No, not yet; I saw one of their brochures the first time we ever went to Aspen. I want to go there, though." Truly spoken, because it was a site pinned on her Geological exploration map!

"Judge, there's no telling what they're receiving in the dead of night! It's probably drugs, or guns, or both. Please, just sign the search warrant. I'll nail this guy for something. He's an arrogant, young punk."

Judge Hawthorne sighed. "The last law book I read didn't say it's against the law to be an arrogant, young punk. When it is, I reckon everyone I know will about be going to jail. "'Cept you! You're not young. You have no probable cause, Red. I already heard from the *Holman, Corporation* attorney. You overstepped by showing up out there. Let's assume they're innocent, just doing work that they figure isn't everybody's business who wants to know! You ever hear of corporate espionage? If they were defense contractors, we wouldn't be able to sail in and demand sensitive material! Stay away from them."

Deborah paused at Ruben's for the café specialty; cheese blintzes. Laughingly, she tried to scoop up the last bits of cream cheese and powdered sugar.

"Would you like another order?" Ruben's eyes twinkled.

"I would, but I better not! I have work to do, the reason for being here. And I need to stay where I can fit into my clothes. I'm ready for my check, but could I get a coffee to go, please?"

The newly-prosperous restaurateur held his hands up, refusing to present the check. He poured special blend coffee into a large Styrofoam cup and snapped the lid securely. "I hope your business is doing as well as mine!"

She nodded vaguely. "You have the advantage on me, of being already established. I hope it's safe to say that mine is coming along."

He nodded knowingly! "Yes, his restaurant was established-lonnnng established, until it was run-down and boring, remaining in a declining neighborhood! And then Deborah Rodriguez and her business brought the Andersons on scene!

He stood, watching her retreat until she disappeared behind the large, solid doors of her factory! Now, his business was far healthier! People didn't fear gang activity, and properties gained new tenants each day, bringing business owners and clients into his establishment. Well, people enjoyed options, with the various foodie trucks and cheery outdoor space! And, even though those choices kept people from being forced to his café as the only option, all of the new life served to give the neighborhood a safe, lively energy. Not certain how better to help the fledgling business; he posted her site once again on his Facebook page. Curious, he opened her site! He called his daughter-in-law, Françesca. "Please, go online to this site. Pick something nice, if you like, and I'll buy it for you." He disconnected. It wasn't much, but he hoped it would make a little difference. Meanwhile, some of his Facebook friends shared the *Rodriguez* link. Then a friend of a friend somehow got his email and asked him if he knew if *Rodriguez* was hiring experienced seamstresses. Trying to be upbeat, he helped the job-seeker connect with a thrilled Deborah. Later in the afternoon, one of the Miami magazines called, asking to feature him and the new life of the restaurant on the revitalized street. Maybe it was true, that if you helped others in what way you could, that help would come to you. He called in extra workers to service the clientele while others polished the restaurant up for the pending interview.

> *Proverbs 25:3 The heaven for height, and the **earth for depth**, and the heart of kings is unsearchable.*

Mallory studied the first *Holman* report with interest. All of the elements indicated by the metal detector were present; plus more. She closed her eyes, allowing her mind to wander. It took her back to a stormy night in early spring, her junior year. She meditated upon the terrifying event! Having just lost her father; no phone, no power; her mother in Hope looking for a job! Prowlers on the property, adding unbelievably to her distress! Back in the present, she opened her Bible to the same text she had opened, panic-driven, on that fateful night!

> *Psalm 104:24 O Lord, how manifold are thy works! in wisdom hast thou made them all: the **earth** is **full** of thy **riches**.*

Tears sparkled on her lashes. It wasn't just Pike County, Arkansas, that was filled with His riches! Although that certainly had proven true! The **whole** earth! The whole **earth!** The whole earth was **filled** with His riches! The earth was filled with **His** riches! The earth was filled with His **riches!!!** She chuckled to herself. And people thought being a Christian was dull! Her breath caught with excitement! On to doing research! She loved doing research! Because everything was so interesting! And it always paid off. She remembered a high school bulletin board, the significance of which escaped her at the time. She giggled inwardly: probably because all she ever thought about back then was David. The message on the bulletin board: KNOWLEDGE IS POWER!

Now, nearly eight years later, and with advanced degrees in Geology and Hydrology, she was more convinced of the truths shown her that night, than ever! "The earth is literally and truly filled with Your riches, just as You said! And they are not depleted, and the US Geological Survey certainly hasn't located everything there is! They haven't scratched the surface! It's all as infinite, like the verse states, as the heaven for height and the earth for depth!

She placed a call to Catrina. "Hey, I just looked over the first report."

"Yes, and-" Catrina's tone showed uncertainty. "Cade figured you'd be really disappointed."

Mallory laughed. "Well, I might be, if my hopes were for a vein of some type of concentrated, precious metal deposit. Drilling these arroyos simply yields samples of what has washed from higher elevations. I think it makes the mountains look intriguing. Since I'm not a Chemist like you, I'm delving into what each of these elements actually does, and how much value they have."

"Well, not a bad plan, but if it would simplify things for you, we can attach thumbnails about the major traces we find."

"Okay, and then I can still research the minor ones."

Catrina laughed at the other executive's determination. "Or we can supply thumbnails of every grain we analyze!"

"Now you're talking!" Mallory disconnected and made her way cautiously to the arroyo. She frowned to see Rudy approach from behind a pile of rocks. Curious, she wondered why he was out of jail trespassing again.

"Mornin'," he greeted. "You findin' anything of great value?" He pulled his battered hat from stringy hair and gestured sarcastically with it.

Mallory referenced the *Holman* report she held. "Uh, Hydrogen, Oxygen-"

He frowned, "Them there's gases, ain't they?"

Wide eyes met his. "I guess they can be, but when they combine, they form a liquid. You're standing in it, and it's quite rare and valuable out here in the desert." Her words were true, and the water, though a great blessing in one sense, complicated drilling and getting good core samples. He made her nervous.

Disgusted with her answer he took a step forward, "Here, Girlie, why don't ya let me see what yer paper there says?"

She stepped backwards. "No! Bad idea! Why are you on our land again?"

"I done tol' ya; it ain't yers! What I want to know is, when yer metal detector was beeping so strong, why wasn't there more gold there?"

"Well, if it's any of your business, the frequency wasn't set on gold the day you heard the machine. You're the one that assumed there was a gold mine here. You did snatch some, that's hung up now in evidence~thank you very much." She whistled sharply and a muscular German shepherd galloped toward them, barking frenziedly.

Rudy made the miscalculation of trying to run for it. "Call 'im off, please." The whine would have been pitiful, but the dog only had him by a scuffed up boot. Mallory whistled again and the dog moved obediently to her side. The trespasser's worst woe from the ordeal was the cactus spines sticking out from pretty much everywhere!

"Okay, 'Pin Cushion'! Get off our land, and don't come back! Let's go, Hero!" Dog at her side, they watched until the sleazy guy hitched his way out through the main gates.

Deborah faced down her aunt Rose across her aged desk. Deborah planned to improve her office and its furnishings, but she stayed a little strapped. Supplies, payroll, materials! Nearly daunting expenses to someone not yet twenty! "Tia," she strove for a reasonable tone, hopefully hiding her panic! "Tia, you are not working to make me rich! You are working to make yourself rich! When did you ever make so much money?"

The belligerent response was simply that Deborah and her immediate family were making more.

"Yes, Tia, a little more; but we take the risks and deal with all the headaches. I can't give you what you ask; and if I do, then all the others~"

Her aunt Rose broke in impatiently. "The others are not as valuable to you; you should compensate according to value!"

Deborah rose and paced, trying to decide what Mallory and Diana would do. And her aunt was right, about her value to the company. She paused and beamed brightly. The solution to the problem caused her to gasp with wonder. "Tia, you should start your own company!"

Rose was somewhat taken aback. When she thought she had her niece against the wall~ "You are letting me go, then?"

Deborah laughed. "Yes, to be blunt! The same way that Mallory and Diana let me go! When they found it difficult to pay me more, due to taxes and regulations, they helped set this up!" She waved around her at the Miami plant.

"You want me to start another sewing business?" Rose, genuinely confused.

Ideas tripped over one another in the young entrepreneur's mind. But she had to get Rose on board with her plan! "Let's go for blintzes."

Situated at a patio table with coffee poured, Deborah doctored her brew as she tried to marshal her pin wheeling thoughts. She knew Mallory and Diana would pray before a meeting like this, because they were different kinds of Christians than she was, and she wasn't real devout. Like, she didn't own a rosary. So, she plunged ahead, trying to channel her torrent of thoughts into a gentle stream her aunt could grasp without being overwhelmed.

"I never ate here, Deborah, and you eat here all of the time, because you are so rich. I am too poor to do anything but bring left-over tamales from home."

Deborah frowned. "You could afford to eat here, but you waste your money; especially on the lottery. Mr. Faulkner says that's a tax on poor people, is all it is. And, even though the lunches here cost money, it isn't wasted money. If I eat reheated tamales at the factory, who sees my cute outfits we make? Only the ones who make them and see them all of the time! And so these lunches where I make business contacts are deductions, because I am incorporated." They paused long enough for Deborah to order the specialty for both of them. When they were alone again, she continued. "See that large building? It's empty. Picture your name on a sign there."

Suspicious, dark eyes drilled into her, but she laughed, undeterred. Because she was right, and her new plan was brilliant! "*Rose Reynosa, Corporation*! You like best the cutting out, and supervising the cutters; yes, Tia?"

Rose nodded as she sipped coffee. "Well, yes, but it must all be done; the sewing, pressing. You have to do all the parts, whether you like them as much, or not!"

"Well, yes," Deborah agreed. "But many of the others like to sew, and hate the cutting. We can specialize more. You can start a corporation that cuts out. Then, I and Señora Diana and anyone else who wants the service can contract for cut out pieces ready for sewing."

Rose's face was a study in doubt. "You think that would work?"

"Well, Tia, that is up to you! I know it can work! You must apply for a loan; but since you're a minority woman, it's practically approved before you start. So then, you'll have operating capital for renting space, refurbishing, and maybe you can purchase some of the fabrics."

Rose considered. "So, in a sense, I can design, too? I can order fabric and cut my designs, and contract with your company to sew and finish?"

Deborah paused thoughtfully. "I don't know why not."

"Should we ask the Andersons and Faulkners? What they think?"

"No!" Deborah's response was swift. "We can do this! Once the building is rented, my brother can get a team to renovate. I'll make an appointment for us to see the banker."

Mallory slid from her mount, somewhat perilously, trying to keep a grasp on Avery.

"Mommy, I want to keep riding some more," Amelia's pouting announcement. "When's daddy coming? He said he'd be right out."

"Yeah, I know, Baby. Maybe he got tied up with a phone call." Grasping both Mocha and Ginger's reins, she approached the double-wide that comprised their Arizona home. Alarms jangled at the scene that confronted her. She whistled sharply for Hero. When there was no response, her panic skyrocketed. Trying to be calm, she pulled her pistol from her saddlebag. Securing both sets of reins, she whispered for Amelia to remain mounted on her pony. Cautiously, she moved into the quiet of the shining kitchen. "David? David?" She crept in farther, keeping an eye on Amelia through the living room windows! David's laptop was open on his desk with his cell phone beside it. She knew it! Something was wrong! She scooped up his phone and speed dialed Erik. When he didn't answer, she left a terse message.

Diana paced. Two days past due, and she was beyond ready for her new baby's debut. She paused to rub the small of her back before sitting back down in her studio. She guessed her focus on the pending labor and delivery and hoping the ski trip would work out, were serving to stall out her creativity. Frustrated, she decided to phone Mallory. Usually Mallory could come up with fantastic inspiration. Surprised to get no answer, she redialed. Worry crowded her thoughts. 'That's odd, she told me to contact her when labor started. She should answer.' Suddenly concerned, she phoned Daniel.

David's pounding head thwacked again and again against the bed of an aged pickup truck. And he was pretty well powerless to brace himself. Regaining consciousness, he realized that a thorough job with duct tape made him into something akin to a mummy. His attempts to stretch the restricting cocoon only resulted in wasting energy and driving the pains more sharply into his head. He moaned and thumped, helpless as a rag doll, as the protesting truck climbed a steep, rocky road toward a destination that surely wouldn't be good. At one point, he became aware of Hero in the truck bed with him, also rendered helpless by similar restrictive bonds.

Back in the yard, Mallory released the reins and led Mocha to where Cap'n stood, saddled and ready for David to ride. She had never tried David's big gelding, but there was a first time for everything. She pulled him next to the corral, and with Avery grasped tightly in one arm, she hoisted herself up the corral so she could mount. Steady as a rock, he barely twitched. Relieved, she settled in, wishing the stirrups were adjusted better for her height. Still, grasping the little pony's reins firmly, she wheeled the big horse around and crossed the yard, picking up a trail she had noticed.

She clicked and the horse broke into a trot.

"Mommy"! Amelia's terrified voice.

"What? You always say you want to ride faster. Hang on tight. Besides, you're strapped in and have your helmet." Which was true. With David leaving little to chance, he had devised a pony car seat, so to speak. She picked the pace up yet more, trying to figure out how someone had managed to spirit David away! She guessed she must have been so focused on the girls. Suddenly, she realized that whoever held David might have been planning to grab all of them! Well, she planned to make then sorry for messing with them! She frowned thoughtfully as she reached the upper boundary of their land. Real slick! Cutting the fence! She checked both phones. No response at all from Erik. Maybe he was in a meeting with his phone off. And she didn't trust any of the local law enforcement people. Well, maybe they were okay; just kind of partial to the locals. She kicked harder against Cap'n's side and he surged forward. The only problem was that little Mocha needed to keep up. Mallory fought frustrated tears.

A couple of rocky, barely discernable roads veered apart. She followed the correct one. She knew it was the correct one, because the truck with the nearly bald tires was leaking some kind of fluid. Still, just because they seemed goofy, was no reason for her to think she wouldn't encounter a formidable foe. 'After all, who could get the drop on David?'

Her phone buzzed again, and she didn't answer. Both Diana and Daniel! She hoped they were worried about her, and not just caught up with their baby's arrival.

She reined in, studying Mocha carefully. She wasn't trail-ride stock, and their ride around the pasture was about what she was accustomed to for endurance. Desert stretched all the way to foothills of the *Superstitions*. There was bottled water in the saddle bags, but none for the equines. "Lord, what am I doing? Please protect us! Please be with David." She prayed he wasn't already dead. There was only one little smear of blood, but~

Erik's phone lit up. He answered. "Yeah, I know! I'm on it, quick as I can. I'm trying to get mobilized out of Phoenix."

There was silence, then Daniel's voice. "So they are in trouble? I hoped we were jumping to conclusions."

"Yeah, I was in a meeting, and when I checked my phone~" Erik's voice cracked in spite of his efforts, "Just a short message from Mallory. That she thought David was in trouble, so she was taking the girls and going out~ We're heading for a chopper, so hope to get in with a posse."

Diana's blue eyes brimmed with tears. "She's out looking by herself? And she has the girls with her? Oh no"!

The truck stopped with one final tromp on the brakes! The worn engine turned off. David stifled a moan, hoping he could play 'unconscious'. Hero struggled next to him. David didn't have a clue how this scenario started, or if Mallory and the girls were in peril. But he was scared.

"Mommeee"! Amelia's plaintive voice! "Let's go home. I'm cold, and I need to go potty."

Mallory reined up and drew the pony nearer. "I know, Baby. But we've got to keep going! And help Daddy."

"He's big; he's okay. I'm scared." Her little hands fumbled for the buckle that restrained her.

Mallory's tone turned sharp. "No, Amelia! Don't unbuckle! Stop crying. Here, take a drink of water." She checked Avery, sleeping straddled in front of her. She was probably getting dehydrated, too. The wind picked up, pelting them with stinging bits of sand and causing a distinct chill. "Okay, Amelia, listen to Mommy. I need you to be a big girl. We need to keep going." As she spoke, she was concerned about the little pony. She figured it would be impossible to keep both of her little girls in the saddle with her, astride David's horse. The pony had to keep going! They all did! Fighting total discouragement, she dug her boots into Cap'n's sides once more.

"Keep digging, Rudy!"

"Man, this here ground's hard," the whining response. "Why don't you guys help me? How'r ya gonna dispatch Mr. Anderson? Shoot 'im?"

"Well, if you get the hole deep enough, and we throw the dirt in on top of him, that should take care of it! He'll stop breathing!" The words, accompanied by a hard laugh! "Make it big enough to throw the dog in too!"

"Gladly! Mutt nearly took off my foot and drug me through the cacti! I think I'm on bedrock here, though. This isn't giving a'tall!"

David heard every word and every clanging shovel blow against the unyielding rock. Still, he tried not to struggle, wasting energy. But try as he might, he couldn't come up with a plan!

Chapter 3: GORGE

Trent Morrison slapped his reins, getting sluggish response. Several encounters with rattlers along the trails caused the entire search party to be at a standstill. He studied a 'wanted poster', once again feeling an uncanny sense of urgency. In the rugged, unforgiving terrain, a mounted search had seemed like a sound enough approach.

"Agent Morrison; this isn't working out." Rob Addington's words, spoken at his elbow. "Rudy Sunquist goes into town all the time. Let's just set a stake-out to catch him then."

Trent dismounted before responding. "Good enough idea, Rob; except that may be too late. I want to press forward with this. I'm not even sure why."

Addington frowned. As the Southwestern Division Head of Law Enforcement in the National Forest System, he knew this territory and the pitfalls. His opinion was that Morrison should have stayed behind his desk in DC.

Trent often encountered this sentiment. He was boss, whether Addington was onboard, or not. Still, he hated to cause unnecessary friction. "You said he spends a lot of time in town? Do you know anything else about him?"

"Not much. Just, kind of a sleazy, theological nut! He's tried a lot of the 'abused American freedoms' rhetoric. About hunting and fishing, mainly. The animals belong to God and everybody else, so why should a few force the majority to 'buy' licenses? He's tried underground newspapers and stuff to spread his garbage, but he's so extreme that he runs off the other extremes!"

Trent gazed at the division head, trying to penetrate mirrored sunglass lenses. "So, he breaks laws, and encourages others to follow suit-"

Rob shrugged. "He's annoying as all get out, but he's hardly a Unabomber!"

"As far as we know! Colorado has some pretty unsettling stories about him. Him and his loosely organized group of associates-" Trent paused; there was nothing definite enough for him to put a finger on.

"Look, didn't you say a private investigator brought him to your attention? I have more respect for Rudy than I do for PI's."

"Sunquist's an arsonist and a murderer!" Morrison was losing patience.

"Says your PI, and since the old people didn't die, it's only attempted murder."

"Holy Cow, Rob"! One of the other Southwestern Division agents entered the conversation. "Listen to yourself. When did we start tolerating crime? I mean, poaching's bad, but attempted murder. And just because that couple escaped the fire, well that was no thanks to the arsonist."

Addington was slow to back down. "Alleged arson and attempted murder. Don't get in an uproar, Dean. Innocent, until proven guilty"!

"Well, I agree with Agent Morrison. We need to find him and look into it. We'll have to move on foot, just being wary of the snakes."

The division head bowed up. "That isn't your call, Dean."

Trent's voice was calm. "No, it isn't; it's mine! We're wasting time!"

"Mommmeee"! Amelia's petulant tone halted Mallory.

"Okay, Baby, okay. I hear you. Let's ride over to that stack of rocks, and we'll take a break." She figured by nearing the formation, she could dismount, and then clamber back on. She quickened the pace, frantic at the thought of delay. "We can't stop for long, though."

"Okay," the little voice showed exhaustion "When are we finding Daddy?"

"Soon, I hope. You've been so brave and good." She slid down, limping gingerly, from the uncomfortable ride. Maybe taking time to adjust the stirrups would be time well spent. She unbuckled Amelia and pulled her free, still holding onto the protesting Avery. If David was okay, he was going to be really ticked at her for pulling this crazy stunt. She knew Mocha wasn't going to survive- She tried to push the troubling thought away. If David was fine, she could get out of the doghouse. She hoped he was fine. But a stone tied to her heart told her dully that he wasn't fine. Holding both sets of reins, she found a smooth spot behind the rocks for the nature-calling break. No snakes in view.

As Mallory turned back toward the horses, Amelia broke free, running toward a tall Saguaro Cactus and pointing, "Look, Mommy; is that a security camera?"

Mallory started to laugh, even through her distress. Her daughter was accustomed to the ever present security measures at their homes. But as she followed the little pointing finger, she gasped in astonishment. Terror clamped down harder than ever on her heart. It was quite clever, placed securely within a knot in the cactus! She eased farther around the pile of stones, looking anxiously for any others. Approaching determinedly, she thrust with a sharp stick, driving the lens downward into the fleshy plant. Probably too late! Because by now, they knew she was coming! And what weapons she had! And that both girls were with her. So much for taking anyone by surprise!

"This ain't workin' Let's just put a bullet in 'im and leave 'im here. The vultures and coyotes'll drag him away and finish 'im off." Rudy Sunquist's voice held a troubling assurance. "There ain't no grave gettin' dug here."

Dane Webster licked his lips nervously. He had never done anything criminal in his life! Until now! And things were already way past what he had bargained for. His understanding was that Rudy would lead him and Hank to the source of the gold; and they were all going to carry out heaps of wealth within a couple of hours' time. Gold like what Rudy had brought into the assay office earlier in the year. He watched eagerly for some sign that Hank was ready to fold. The two of them could overpower Rudy, and-

An electronic beep brought Rudy from his grave-digging attempts, to open a tablet and leer evilly at the small screen. "Well, well, now, lookee what we got comin' here! Since we missed the missus this morning', it's really good of her to come callin' back!"

"Yeah, looks bad to me, Sunshine!" Hank's voice filled with rage as he made fun of Sunquist's name. "She's not alone; that would be stupid! How'd she follow us straight here? You said no one can find this place!" His hard gaze traveled around the prospector's shack, lighting on greasy, greenish spots soaked into the thin layer of sand. "Moron! Your truck's leaking transmission fluid!"

"Well, now, it's a broken seal; been leakin' fer awhile, but ya keep addin' fluid-"

Mallory tied Cap'n to the cactus, removing the saddle with its saddle bags and grasping a deer rifle. She settled both girls carefully on the saddle blanket. A further search of the saddle bags provided her hand gun, water, trail mix, plenty of ammo, and a broken scope.

"Okay, stay here, and don't move!" With that word of instruction, she advanced forward cautiously! Did the security camera's presence mean she was close? Were cameras all along the trail, and she had missed them? 'Who's watching me?' she wondered. 'Maybe good guys'?

She stopped suddenly, perhaps fifty yards beyond where the girls sat watching her. Before her lay a sudden change in terrain! The high desert dropped straight down, perhaps twenty-five feet, and then a deep gorge sloped back upwards toward the far end, where a tumble-down shack nestled against a soaring, sandstone cliff. Her gaze sought eagerly for signs of David, and then she choked a sob. One worn boot protruded from beneath a tarp in the pickup bed, and Rudy, leaning on a shovel, was gesturing toward a shallow hole. 'David was dead, and they were burying him?' Remembering they were aware of her approach, she lowered herself prone, watching, wishing for a pair of field glasses. Struggling against tears and blowing sand, she watched, pulling the powerful rifle closer. She couldn't accurately gauge the distance. Beyond range for an accurate shot; especially with the wind velocity over the gorge! The chamber was empty, and as she reached into the saddle bag for shells, she felt the scope. 'Yes!' Hoping the lens wouldn't reflect sunlight and reveal her vantage point, she sighted in the distant scene. It looked as though the boot in the truck bed wasn't moving. If she was too late to help David, was it wise to put the girls at more risk? He wouldn't want them-

Trent hated snakes more than any of them! Evidently! The reason he lived and worked in Washington DC, and they worked in the wilds of

the National Forests and Grasslands in northern Arizona. And if they all wished he weren't here, he wished it a hundredfold more! "How much farther?" he mouthed the words.

David's anguish deepened. Every word the men spoke made him more desperate to spring from his helpless state and shut their yaps for them. From the words he could understand, Mallory, on a one-woman search for him, was about to wander into their clutches. He listened, straining.

"She put your camera out of business. Now we don't have a clue what she's up to, or who else is coming. Up yonder's the only way out of here, since your place is a dead end," Hank's voice; worried, but not desperate. "If she wanders in alone-"

"If she wanders in alone, I got plans fer that purty little miss!"

Rudy's pure evil sent chills through Dane. "Look, let's not do anything to women and children. As a matter of fact, let's just climb the wall, and-"

Hank's voice cut in. "Yeah, you climb the wall- what are you, crazy? We're in this together." He paused and batted at a hornet. "Rudy, you should get rid of that nest."

"They don't hurt ya none; long as ya don't rile 'em," came the stupid response.

With a disgusted shake of his head, Hank continued, "Listen, Mrs. Anderson and her kids, well-they're kind of a treasure-with some people-if you know what I mean-"

Sadly, Dane did know what the other man meant. Human Trafficking! His stomach contents launched, and he bent over the rotting rail of the front porch!

Mallory turned her head, checking on the girls. Strangely, they were still sitting, per her orders. She scanned back and forth again with the scope; the boot remained motionless. Training the scope on the three men, she watched. One vomited, and they seemed to be arguing. "Lord, let them all kill each other," she breathed. "Because, I'm pretty sure I don't have a shot! Not even to take out one; let alone all three! It's too long of a range."

She dropped her face into her arms and sobbed in defeat. But after a few seconds, she knew she couldn't give up. With only Cap'n she was pretty sure she couldn't get back home with her babies. Avery, without even a clean diaper! Disjointed thoughts made her wonder if she was losing her grip. 'Diapers; gold nuggets captured in the rocky outcropping of her vantage point; if she was ruining her clothes!' She needed to focus on David!

She trained the scope once more. The argument seemed more heated, and the one who was the policeman, Hank, kept making the same brushing motion. Her breath caught! That was it! The brushing motion! She tried harder to focus her gaze, wishing the scope possessed just one more level of magnification so she could be sure! Then, she saw it, barely visible beneath the decaying wood of the porch roof! Pulling the rifle against her shoulder, she squeezed the trigger. The kick with the accompanying report against her ear stunned her, almost causing her to lose the weapon onto the rocks below. As her stunned gaze traveled back toward her girls, she was aware of men rushing toward them. It was over!

David jerked involuntarily as the rifle report echoed around him! With no clue of who was shooting at whom, he trembled beneath the tarp. He listened. No further shots, but he was aware of confused and terrified screams coming from his abductors. Then, as he strained his ears, he heard it! An angry and intense hum! Like the buzz of a very angry nest of hornets!

Sophia, Jay, and Brandon Vincent sat in a weak puddle of sunlight. Philadelphia didn't yield easily to springtime's warmth. "Look at that, Jay." She thrust a copy of a newspaper at him.

"What does it say?"

"Okay, Sophie, the story's been bumped to a smaller article on page two; no picture!" He read it in its entirety.

"That's all?" Sophia's sigh, "What took the front page?"

"A bomb threat and evacuation of one of the high schools"!

She scoffed softly, feeling for her orange juice glass. "Well, at one time, a bomb threat and evacuation at a public high school would have sent more Philadelphians scrambling to the safer haven of my dear alma mater. That's all the article said; that they brought him in for questioning? He was actually under arrest; was he not?"

"That was my understanding." He gazed at the front-page article, and again at the nearly insignificant second page story about Sophia's disappearance, and the strange actions of her school's headmaster at the time of her kidnapping!

"You know-" he paused to sip coffee as he considered whether his suspicions were valid enough to mention. "What you just said, about- I wonder. Would you think it possible that your school's board of regents-"

"What are you getting at, Jay?" Sophia did a precise job of finding her slice of toast.

"I think I know!" Brandon's voice boomed exuberantly, "The board of Regents! They know about all the bad publicity and loss of income the school will sustain, if there's a front-page story on the head master!"

Sophia laughed, "So-uh-what? They phone a bomb threat in to one of the public schools-"

"Yeah, Sophia; and not just one of the schools, but the largest"! Jay's confidence rising, convinced that the possibility was real. "Its evacuation and all of the bomb-sniffing dogs create a big enough story to bury their dirty laundry on the second page! And send frightened parents inquiring into the private sector."

"Well, that would be diabolically clever. Who could think of anything like that?"

"People whose wealth and social positions are at stake!" As ludicrous as it seemed when the thought first occurred to him, Brandon's jumping to the same conclusion lessened Jay's self-doubt.

"Do you think anyone will listen to us about it? It may sound a little far-fetched." Sophia pulled her sweater more tightly as a capricious breeze scooted clouds, obliterating the small circle of sunshine.

Jay laughed and planted a kiss on her cheek. "What do you think?"

She nodded, "Back to our faithful private investigator!"

"It's worked for us before." He settled his jacket around her shoulders, too. Like her grandfather, if it wasn't snowing, she thought it was spring!

"Mallory! Mallory! Take it easy! It's Trent! These guys are all Forestry-" Trent paused as the 30.06 remained trained on him, "Mallory! We're here to help-where's David"?

Trent moved cautiously to remove his broad-brimmed hat and sunglasses.

With the appearance of the familiar face, she relaxed, nearly to the point of collapsing. She turned her gaze from Trent back up along the gorge. She couldn't figure out where the rifle scope was; perhaps fallen to the ledge below. Her eyes took in the fallen bodies of her adversaries, still being attacked by vicious hordes of insects. She wasn't sure if they were dead; they probably would die.

Trent's hand on her shoulder startled her. His lips were moving, but her ears roared from the blast. Dazed, she massaged the inside of her shoulder.

Anguished, she spoke. "David! I think he's-" She waved her hand toward the spectacle unfolding beyond. She couldn't bring herself to speak the word.

Her stunned eyes met Trent's. "You-you came! Where's Erik? Is he-"

Trent squatted next to her, holding a bottle of water. "I'm not sure where he is. We're just out on a mission trying to find this guy; didn't have a clue you were in trouble out here."

Ignoring the water, she reached for the poster. "Rudy the Prospector, or the movie star; take your pick!"

"Yeah, drink! You're dehydrated! We're calling in a couple of choppers to get you evacked!"

Dutifully, Mallory sipped, but the warm water caused her to gag. She fought nausea. When she could speak, it was to borrow his field glasses. She trained in once again on the battered pickup. The tarp was still in place, but the boot was gone! "I-I thought David was down in the bed of that pickup; because it looked like one of his boots-" Figuring she wasn't making sense, she started to cry.

Not sure how to comfort the distraught victim, he simply took back the glasses and dialed in on the truck. "Mallory, it is David. He's trying to sit up! Looks like he's mummified in twenty rolls of duct tape! What went down here?"

Still helpless, David eased back down, trying to shelter himself beneath the tarp, from the frenzied insects. He sensed a surge of triumph! (Mallory must have shot at the hornet's nest from her distant position! Pretty genius!) Now, if the enraged hornets didn't attack him, too~ Cries of the three men had ceased, leaving sighing wind and the coming and going of the still angrily swarming hornets. Nervously, he wondered how long it took them to calm down and rebuild, or move along, or whatever it was they did.

Trent sent a protesting Mallory and her little girls via chopper to the nearest medical facility, placing Dean Schaeffer in charge of her protection. As soon as the chopper lifted and headed away, they put down the suffering, little pony. Keeping Rob and three others with him, he sent the other agents back to headquarters in the other bird. From Mallory's former vantage point, he watched the scene below. It seemed evident that the three felons were dead. There was no further movement from David either, but hopefully he was lying still to avoid the attention of the swarm.

Rob strode around Trent, kicking and scuffing at the scrabble of desert grass and loose earth. Trent noticed when he bent and picked something up.

He glanced up, meeting the Division Head's sunglass lenses, once more. "Put it down, Agent."

"What's up with you?" Rob's voice erupted, angry at being caught. "According to Arizona law, it's okay to just pick up gold nuggets when you find them."

"According to Federal law, as a federal employee, you can't prospect on government time! We're still on a mission! And it isn't about you lining your pockets! Put it down, and focus on your job!"

From the curtained cubicle of the small hospital, Mallory answered Erik's call.

"Where are you? Are you okay?" He strove for a steady tone of voice "We've been trying to get to your position; almost made it, and then you headed lickety-split~"

She laughed, "Yeah, in a helicopter. Trent Morrison and some Forestry Service personnel~ They're still waiting to check on David." Tears and sobs forced their way to the surface. "I wasn't sure David's~I mean, I hope he's okay~he was all trussed up tight with tape~"

"Any word"? Daniel moved quickly to the maternity waiting room for a progress report.

"Yes, Sir; Agent Bransom finally heard from Mallory." Jeremiah's answer provided some relief. "She and the girls are okay, transported to a hospital to get checked out. They think David's going to be okay, but I guess they can't get to him for a while to make sure. How's Mom?"

Daniel sank down, suddenly weak-kneed. "Uh, she's fine! They finally decided on an emergency C-section! Your new little sister's beautiful! Elysia Dannae. You can see them both in a few minutes."

The other kids took his words in philosophically.

The forestry law enforcement officers seemed slow to respond to Trent's requests. The property was actually outside of the National Forest. Which, Morrison was aware of that. But since the felons had no problem with going back and forth across the arbitrarily decreed boundaries, and there was a victim still out there~

The hornets didn't seem to be settling down. The destruction of the nest seemed to leave them disoriented and mad as hornets. He could see now where that overworked expression came from. After placing phone calls, and getting little useful information on the best way to deal with the insects, they formed a battle plan. At last, armed with beekeepers' garb, a flame-thrower, and cans of powerful spray; Trent and his contingency made their way! Following the greasy spots, they descended a steep, stony trail that led across to the cabin. No wonder the truck leaked!

"Easy," Trent cautioned. "Don't burn the cabin down. There may be evidence." Trent grew more aggravated with the Division Head as the hours went on.

"Don't think we're going to need evidence. I think he's deader 'n a hammer."

"That doesn't mean there haven't been other victims or accomplices. Just use the spray cans, please?"

Cap'n snorted suddenly, straining slightly against the reins Trent held.

"Yeah, boy; go find David." He released the reins and watched the big horse make its way toward the pickup, pausing to watch the swarms warily. Trent followed, hoping any new attack would be directed against the horse, and that he, as the smaller target, could use the range of the spray cans to drive the hornets back. To the truck bed, at last, he laid down a covering of insecticide on the tarp. Then jerking it aside, he gazed at last into David's terrified eyes.

"Okay, keep us covered," he instructed Addington and the others. Emptying a nearly full can of the spray into the cab, he scooted in and turned the key. He raised the windows and maneuvered toward the trail and safety. Once atop, he went to work on the tape, waiting for another air evacuation. He was worried; David showed little interest in the water he should be dying for. He hopped into the chopper, giving instructions to the Division Head and his men. "Recover the other bodies and finish your reports. Don't make any move on this gold."

"Planning to get it for yourself?" Rob Addington's furious voice!

"If I were, I'd take it now, because I'm not planning to come back here!" Trent's frayed nerves caused his temper to flare. "We could've just spent the afternoon picking up all the bright, shiny little pieces we could find, and let people die! You need to make a career choice before the week's out!"

As the chopper rose, bearing toward town and the trauma center, Trent took in the bodies of the three men sprawled in the gorge below. It made him think of a verse he showed often to his kids: a verse that apparently Rob should consider:

> *Proverbs 1:19 So are the ways of every one that is greedy of gain; which taketh away the life of the owners thereof.*

Chapter 4: GREED

Trent was shocked at David's condition! Barely responsive, hypothermic, and moaning in pain! The tape pulled away from his mouth with relative ease, degraded by saliva, tears, and stomach acid. Trent wasn't sure whether the blue tinge around the mouth was due to hypothermia or oxygen deprivation. The layers of tape could be restricting his breathing. The German shepherd was dead, fully in rigor mortis, and also encased in duct tape! Trent surmised that both the dog and David must have been rendered unconscious before being securely trussed. He suspected a powerful tranquilizer of some sort. He phoned Addington, instructing him to secure the dog's remains, as well as those of the three criminals.

Since the chopper was not actually an air ambulance, David basically lacked immediate treatment. To Trent, the twenty minute flight seemed endless. He prayed the small, local trauma center would be adequate.

Diana's eager eyes met her husband's. He stepped into the room and took her hand. "The baby's beautiful, and she's fine! I'm not sure why she decided to give you such a hard time."

"I guess it serves me right for having been so hard on Mallory! I've never had labor like that, even with Alexandra! Speaking of Mallory; what's the latest?"

He sank into the large chair. "Well, Mallory and the girls are fine: sun and wind-burned, and dehydrated. David just now arrived and they're evaluating his condition. They told Mallory, 'Guarded' which has her nearly in hysterics."

Horror showed on Diana's features. "We should be there!"

"Okay, take it easy. Maybe we should be, but we can't! Your C-section is going to cause more down time than you're used to. And I'm absolutely insisting that we take care of you, and make you a priority! We can pray from here, and that's the best we can do." He took her hand, wording a prayer.

Erik wasn't sure when he had been more frustrated. For having a precise coordinate, gleaned from David and Mallory's cell phones, the spot was a demon to get in to.

"Since the Forestry guys are already on site and recovering the bodies, maybe we should forget this," spoke Dan Wells, head agent of the Phoenix office, and not usually one to give up."

Erik was tempted to agree. He was eager to get to David and Mallory and the girls, but- Even after Forestry recovered the bodies, Erik wanted to be on site! Taking pictures, going over the pickup truck, everything in the pitiful cabin! There was work to be done, and the Forestry guys didn't have the same expertise.

Danna Ames ran a critical eye over David as he was rolled into the ER.

"He got pretty cold out there, what with the wind and the hour getting late. We tried to warm him up some in the helicopter, but that was the best we could do for him," Trent's words and expression were anxious.

Ames nodded at the quick rundown before turning her attention to David. "We're ready for you, Mr. Anderson, and we're going to get straight down to business, but first, you have some people dying to see you."

"Any chance I can clean up a little, first?" David's words came out, hard to understand, between clenched teeth and a tenuous hold on consciousness.

"Your condition is nothing you could have helped. It's a defense mechanism the body has for resisting infection. They want to see you, stat!"

Tears of frustration welled up, but the nurse moved to the curtain to beckon Mallory.

His tears created an automatic response from her.

She leaned over, kissing him gently. "Hey, Miss Ames said they need to get busy on you. We're praying! We love you."

Anguished terror in deep brown eyes was the only response.

"Love ya, Katy. Go sit with Mallory. Look, she's here alone. Mrs. Faulkner just gave birth again, and who knows where Mrs. Bransom is?"

Katy's face registered resistance to her husband's words. "Jason, the kids will be too wild for the hospital waiting room. Give me the keys, and we'll all go to the *Enclave*. You can call when you're finished, and I'll come get you."

Jason surveyed her steadily. With David Anderson's serious condition, the hospital had contacted auxiliary medical personnel to be on standby. He was always eager to share his skills, but he felt an extra obligation to David and Mallory. And Katy did, too. She was simply always a little overwhelmed at Mallory's presence. And, he felt some guilt for David's current condition. Like if he and Katy hadn't taken a day for a little family jaunt, he would have been at the Enclave to help ward off the bad guys.

"Okay," Katy capitulated. "But give me the keys, so that if I think we're getting on her nerves, more than we're helping-"

He brushed her lips with his, and slid the key ring into her hand before sprinting past doors which warned: 'Do Not Enter!'

"Hello, Mrs. Anderson?" Mallory glanced up in response to her name, to see a couple of nicely dressed, middle-aged men. She rose and moved toward them.

"Yes, Sir, that's right. Can I help you?"

"Dr. William Stringer, from Phoenix; this is Dr. Dean Hammond, an anesthesiologist."

She extended her hand. "Pleased to meet you; is my husband-"

"We just arrived. The center here wanted to transport your husband, but the wind-well, choppers aren't flying-"

"Oh? Then, how did y'all get here?"

Dr. Stringer smiled, even in the grave situation. "Well, I guess you could say that we're a couple of nuts that don't believe people about the wind and choppers! At any rate, we're here now. You're aware that your husband's condition is serious?"

Mallory summoned all of her resolve to control threadbare emotions. "Yes, I am; thank you both for coming! David's family members are en route, and lots of people are praying for him; and for you, too."

The anesthesiologist seemed comfortable with the faith-filled words, but the neurosurgeon responded with a sardonic smile. "I guess it can't hurt!"

Mallory finished with fourteen phone calls; all of them pressing. Forcing a brave smile, she went in search of Cassandra Faulkner, on loan to help her with Amelia and Avery. Running everything without David was incredibly tough.

"Were the phone calls okay?" Cassandra's stunning features registered distress.

Mallory grinned. "I guess I got a little loud?"

"A couple of times," Cassandra admitted. "Mallory, if you need my dad and mom to help you with more-"

"I know, Cass, and they're already helping with so much! I need to do as much as I can. It helps me when I have other things to focus on. Maybe I should have prayed more, for wisdom, before I placed a couple of those calls." She was grateful for all of her friends and relatives; many calls and notes from people she had never heard of, who encouraged and offered help. And her words were true, that Cassandra's entire family was working overtime, assisting with all the various angles of the multi-faceted business. Parts of it, though, were confidential, even from them. She knew David wouldn't like it if privileged information leaked out.

"Mommmeee," Amelia's petulant voice penetrated her thoughts.

"Don't whine, Amelia, please! What do you want?"

Guilt struck her as Amelia's little face puckered and her chin quivered.

"I'm sorry, Baby; Mommy didn't mean to sound cross!"

Helpless, Cassandra wandered from the room. She tried to help, but it was all too sad!

Mallory followed her. "Cassandra-"

"It's okay, Mallory." Cassandra struggled with holding her own emotions in check.

"I know, but you've gone above and beyond. And you're missing spending time with your new baby sister. I called Pastor and Lana last night, and they've agreed to let Janni come help. I'll take you to the airport tomorrow to send you home, and she can take over. And you know Katy and the kids help a lot."

Cassandra simply nodded. It seemed as if the plan was made. She wasn't sure if she should protest, but the retreat of home suddenly appealed to her.

Mallory's tone changed, "We're getting fried chicken for lunch. Jason and Katy and the kids are coming; we'll have a picnic, and y'all can play in the park while I go visit David."

Cassandra nodded. "That sounds like fun." She wasn't sure if Mallory even realized that it was Arizona summertime, and the playground equipment would be blistering. If she felt as though she were dwelling in the midst of a nightmare, she couldn't imagine Mallory's feelings!

Mallory drove numbly to the long term care facility, oblivious to the stark beauty and brilliant blue canopy of the Arizona afternoon. She worried about Cassandra. She should probably take the girls and accompany Cass on the flight home, and return with Janni. Not that the Andersons had really agreed to that. They seemed to blame Mallory for David's condition! No problem there! It was all her fault! She mopped at her eyes out of habit. But there were no tears! They were all cried out! Thoughts inserted themselves. Maybe she should look into moving David to a facility in Dallas. There were bound to be more and better choices. Or maybe Little Rock, where his family could visit him more easily. Not that they seemed able to. Seeing him just lying like, that, as motionless, almost, as death itself-

Dawson's voice made Erik jump. "Sorry, Jed;" Eric apologized sheepishly. "I guess I was lost in thought. Didn't hear you coming! So much for all of my finely-honed FBI Agent senses."

Jed Dawson laughed mirthlessly. "Hey, man, not surprised you're jumpy. Any changes"?

"Nah! At least, I guess he isn't losing ground. And everybody in that stinkin' town still thinks that Hank and Dane were the two most stellar citizens ever to grace this earth."

"Well, maybe the prospector had them under duress, too," Dawson suggested.

"Mallory said they were all in on the abduction together!"

"From what she could tell through a scope, from a half-mile away! And she hasn't been her usual, rational, thinking self."

Erik swirled his chair and gave it a shove toward the coffee pot. He figured Mallory knew what she saw. And maybe the two men in question had been good guys- past tense. He wished David would wake up and give his statement. How crazy was that? He wished and prayed that constantly! For far more reasons than a statement!

"Mallory can't figure out why they even abducted him. She says that Sunquist's haunt up there virtually sparkled with gold! She's never seen so much, nuggets, just lying around, easily visible. I guess Morrison nearly got in a fight with his Southwestern Division Head, for being more interested in picking up gold nuggets than trying to halt a crime in progress!"

Dawson accepted a mug full of the hours-old brew, making a face as he took a swig. "If that's true, and I find out that those actions further delayed David Anderson's medical treatment-" The senior agent's eyes flashed dangerously, "I'll put the guy in prison, personally!"

"Okay, Lord," Mallory removed the key and paused to apply lip gloss. "Please give me the oil of gladness above my fellows." She laughed at the strange-sounding wording: King James for 'Lord, help me get my game-face on!' Surveying her gaunt features, she slid from the truck and reached the ornate front doors. That was where ambience died, and a nursing home, stark and smelly, emerged. Smiling and offering warm greetings to elderly people who grabbed at her, she moved to Corridor A and paused at the closed door. She opened it softly, not sure why! Maybe she should bang it! As if any noise she might make could penetrate to where he was. She frowned. From the doorway she could tell that the catheter lacked for attention; the heavy stubble's meaning he hadn't been bathed yet, or shaved.

Hope held out its hand! 'Yes, she would move him to Dallas! How could a move hurt him anymore?' She went into the bathroom and dampened a ridiculously thin washcloth to sponge him, then gasped with amazement when he jerked his hand back. His eyes opened, and from the depth, a spark of recognition flashed! He mumbled something and his eyes closed again!

"David, it's Mallory! David, can you hear me?" she moved closer, watching eagerly for another glimmer of hope. When no further response came, hot tears spilled down her cheeks! Just when she was accepting what was- Sobs rose. She lost it once more, to the overwhelming grief!

When she recovered slightly and began the sponging process once more, his dark eyes opened, meeting hers with a probing, puzzled, stare.

"You-you got hurt-Uh, Rudy-and-"

His face contorted, remembering- the abduction? Trying to understand her stammering words? Trying to figure out who he was? Who she was"?

Dr. Stringer's words echoed in her mind, following the long and arduous surgery: that if he ever regained consciousness, he would more than likely be a vegetable.

"You're David," she tried. "I'm Mallory!"

A smile tugged upwards around the ventilator, and his deep eyes held a surprisingly normal mischievousness. She knew what he was thinking! They often knew each other's thoughts.

She laughed at her own absurdity of explaining to him who they were, "You Tarzan! Me Jane"!

He nodded, holding her gaze! Fumbling for her hand, he squeezed gently.

Trent scowled at Erik's update. Aware for several days of the miraculous news of David's reemergence, he had been eager to hear David's account of what happened. "Does he remember what happened to him?"

"Yeah, in searing detail," Erik's voice remained emotional. "It's about what we thought, but with a couple of sadistic twists. First, they planned to bury him alive, but their choice of a place to dig a grave was another miracle. About the only place out there where bed rock was nearly exposed. Rudy couldn't get the grave dug. But while they were all chatting, Rudy suggested that they forget burying him, saying something to the effect that coyotes would drag his body off and the vultures would finish what was left. David insists that Rudy sounded sure of his facts, like that had worked for him before. You know-"

Trent's voice cut in. "Yeah, hikers and prospectors disappear up in that area in alarming numbers, feeding the 'curse' myths about the *Flying Dutchman*! Maybe the 'curse' has been Sunquist for a long time."

"Maybe," Erik didn't sound convinced. "Here's a couple of other disturbing facts about him. Mallory encountered him trespassing from nearly the first day they set up there; being stealth and watching her work the metal detector. She thinks the beeps that day spawned his first interest ever in gold prospecting! He was scouting her, and not gold. She told me that even a really amateur prospector couldn't have missed all the gold nuggets right on the surface out there at that old cabin. Then she told me that his not being a prospector, must mean he was a movie star-some kind of inside joke. He asked her if she was hunting diamonds, and she felt that was an absurd question; since metal detectors don't beep at diamonds. But it was disconcerting to her, that he connected her to diamonds. He knew who she was!"

"Well, we may never find out now, why they grabbed David. I'll contact Southwest Division and tell them to mount an in-depth search out there for additional human remains. What put me on Sunquist to start with was a Private Investigator, hired by Mallory. The investigator was working the arson at the Colorado cabin, and Sunquist kept popping up next to him, 'out of nowhere', startling him, and asking questions, being a pest. The PI started to wonder if he was the arsonist. And my LEI in the region said he wouldn't leave Nanci Burnside alone, either. Then, suddenly, he's out of Colorado and in Arizona, coincidentally, on top of another of Mallory's properties. At least he's out of the picture for good!"

"Come home," Lana cajoled plaintively. "*The Ranch* is the most comfortable and the most secure of all of your places."

David usually found it tough to resist his mom, but since he sensed his Dad's coaching behind her, the arguments rolled out. "Yes, Mom, but it's also the place that's running the most smoothly without us there. Jeff is-"

"Don't change the subject! You don't have to sell me on Jeff! But at least until you get your feet underneath you and finish your recovery!"

"See, Mom, that's another reason why we should hang here. Dr. Stringer's in Phoenix and I have an appointment in ten days. Look, Mom, I know you and Dad worry, and I can't tell you how much difference I think your prayers for me made. But this is our home, too. We love it, and we have lots going on!"

"You're too busy, Honey. Are you resting at all? We just hate the way Mallory drags you around after all of her hair-brained schemes! She seemed so grounded, you know, in the Word-"

"Okay, see Mom, I'm done talking. You don't know the first thing about either of us and what we're doing. Tell Dad I know he's listening and coaching you."

He disconnected as Mallory appeared. "I'm taking it easy; that was my mom. You know, I've been thinking about the care facility-"

Mallory nodded miserably. "I know, David; it was horrid. I should have moved you! I-I just couldn't even think." Tears started again, and he pulled her down onto the sofa next to him.

"When you didn't wake up-day-after-day-after-day-" She continued, dabbing her eyes, "I thought nothing could get worse, and then Dana Ames and the chief of staff at the medical center said we had to relocate you from the hospital to another facility-"

His heart wrenched at having put her through so much. He tucked his index finger beneath her chin so she would meet his gaze. "I wasn't thinking bad thoughts about it, per se; except, it wouldn't really take a whole lot to give it a facelift. I'm out, but a lot of other people have to finish out their days there. You know, I can call a team in-"

"We don't even know who owns it, or if they would sanction a renovation. I'm not sure we can afford to do it, just for sympathy's sake-" Something in his expression silenced her. "Okay, bringing your laptop now. Maybe you can unearth who the ownership is, and you can also start your plan."

He grinned triumphantly. "I'm getting some ice cream; want some?"

Trent galloped up the stairs in the Forestry Department office building in downtown DC, whistling as usual. "Morning, Maureen," he greeted his receptionist. Then noting her strained expression, he paused. "What's up?"

"Uh-you have an FBI task force waiting for you."

Stunned, he opened the door to his office. Yep, she was right. "Gentlemen, to what do I owe the pleasure?"

Badges flashed and he laughed a rolling, infectious, relaxed laugh. "Yeah, I get that part. FBI! But what brings you to my doorstep so bright and early?"

He relaxed even more. At least, he wasn't being accused of wrongdoing; well, in a way he was. Of not being as conscientious about his job as they felt he should be. The whole thing struck him more than crazy. He wasn't sure the Justice Department had any jurisdiction snooping into the Department of Agriculture's Forestry Division. At any rate, they seemed to have sniffed out quite a bit of helpful information, so he heard them out. He frowned. "So, you have all of the phone calls verified?"

"We do. While you frantically made phone calls to everyone you could think of about the best way to deal with the wasps, the others weren't making the calls you ordered. Rob Addington called his secretary to rewrite the schedule, giving him the next day off-presumably to beat the others back to grab the big nuggets. Another guy called an equipment rental place to reserve a metal detector. It seems as though, in spite of your orders to forget about the loot and concentrate on their jobs, they became distracted and irresponsible, further delaying critical treatment for David Anderson. Your actions were nothing short of heroic- Why didn't you delve into their actions further, when you returned to the city?"

"I don't know. Why does the FBI give their agents the benefit of the doubt? Finding qualified people is always a challenge. I thought I'd wait and see if they get back to doing their jobs in ways I find acceptable, and prospect in their spare time. Thank you for your phone snooping. My powers aren't as vast as yours. And I must say, I'm almost glad that they aren't. You're right! Time was critical for David! I didn't know they disobeyed orders."

Chapter 5: GRAPPLING

"Let's all go out for dinner." David appeared in the kitchen doorway as Mallory surveyed contents of pantry and fridge.

"I can scrounge us up something. Go out to eat where? This does make me appreciate the chow hall; I miss it, probably more than anything."

"The pancake place!" was his response. "That's practically all there is. Tomorrow, I'll ask Jason and Katy to pick some groceries up for us. And I'm getting better."

"Pancakes"! Amelia's face alight, she ran to find Avery. "Avery! We get pancakes!"

Deborah checked her phone when an email alert pinged. David's checkup was good, but his total healing was a long way off. There were still concerns about the little fractures, blood clots, and possible bleeding. At least, the situation in the past two weeks was greatly improved. She opened a spreadsheet and took the facts in, satisfied. In addition, *Rose Reynosa, Incorporated* was almost up and running. She was proud of being able to put it together; who would ever have guessed? But now, she felt a little guilty that the Faulkners and Andersons didn't know yet, about the new division of labor. There seemed to have been no opportune moment to share the change.

Her mother knocked at her open office door; "Deborah, the cruise company called. All of your leads panned out, so they are sending a couple of complimentary VIP fares."

Deborah beamed! Not that she wanted to go on another cruise right away. It was the satisfaction of promoting some other entity, and finding that good usually boomeranged back to her.

"Do you and Papa-"

Nita laughed. "No, Pocita; we are still on diets from last cruises. And we have much work to do! And it's work that, well, that pays, and for the most part, is so enjoyable. The fares are good for six months. We can keep for incentive-"

Deborah nodded. "Gracias, thank you, Mommy!"

Sleeping Beauty Turquoise™, the benchmark for the highest quality turquoise in the world, came from the *Sleeping Beauty* mine in Arizona. At the moment, the sky appeared to have been artfully chiseled from the bright blue material; not a cloud, nor a jet contrail, broke the blue.

"I'm hungry!" Came Amelia's voice from her car seat. "Where are my pancakes? I want my pancakes!"

Mallory met her daughter's gaze in a special mirror invented for spying on kids in back seats. "Shhhh; Amelia, Daddy's sleeping. Just watch the movie. It's still a little ways yet."

She gazed nervously at David's pallor, hoping the outing wouldn't in any way set back his progress.

"I've seen this movie, Mommeeee!"

"Amelia!" One word from David was all it ever took.

"Yes, Sir"! The subdued response.

"I guess I let her get a little out of hand," Mallory apologized.

"Would you take it easy on yourself? You've done great! If it's apology time-"

She laughed. "It isn't, and you've already apologized for being unconscious-"

The deep blue afternoon sky melded into violet with an orange glow on the western horizon. One bright star shimmered in the atmosphere. "Pretty evening"! David's husky voice as Mallory pulled into a parking space at the popular, one and only, eatery.

She nodded, matching the depths of his emotions. "Now the girls are both asleep. Are you sure you're up for this? They'll be out of sorts, if we wake them the minute they've conked out."

"No, now that we're here. It'll be okay." He winced as he turned his head to rouse Avery.

With both daughters awake and protesting, they headed for the entrance.

"Hey, Anderson"!

Mallory moved lightning fast, without even thinking! Just an automatic response! The fist swinging toward David sent her sprawling. Dazed, she struggled to get up and reclaim her dignity.

David's pistol trained quickly on the drunk assailant.

"Whoa, whoa, I don't want no trouble." Dark, wild eyes showed shock that the young couple was armed.

"Okay, if you don't want any trouble, why'd you hit my wife?"

"You know I was swinging at you! Some man, hides behind his wife!"

David held the gun unwaveringly, trying to think of an answer to defuse the situation. To his relief, the police chief pulled in beside them.

"You kids sure stir up trouble," he grumbled. "Crazy Feather, what's going down here?"

David holstered his gun, hoping Jim Dunlap had the situation under control. Since the policeman had directed his question to the assailant, David turned his attention to Mallory. "Are you okay?"

Always quick to shake things off, she answered quickly. "Ye-eah, I think so." She raised her right forearm to see a long scrape starting to bleed; and a lump forming. "I guess I hit my arm on the curb." She rubbed her jaw gingerly, too.

Trying to decide the best way to spin his story, the man addressed as Crazy Feather, at last found his voice. "Look, Jim, I don't make a habit to hit women! I was swinging at him, and she got in the way."

"You're drunk again. Why were you trying to hit anyone? You usually don't get violent." The patient police officer turned toward David and Mallory. "Are you sure you're okay, Ma'am?"

I-I think so." Mallory sounded stunned. Then to make things worse, both girls recovered from the initial shock and terror, to scream in unison.

"Look, let's just go inside. We can get a better look at this and patch you up, while I get to the bottom of things. Did y'all say some kinda racial slight to him? That riles him up."

"No, Sir," David strove for calm, although his head hurt, and thinking straight with both girls crying at their loudest made it hurt more. "We never saw him. We got the girls awake and were starting toward the door.

He screamed, 'Hey, Anderson,' and he was already swinging a wicked, right upper-cut. Mallory blocked the blow-because-"

"Yeah; because you sustained a nearly-fatal brain injury, that put you in a coma for four months! I'm sorry for what I said about y'all stirring up trouble."

"Well, we're sure that's how it must seem," Mallory's words of understanding "Would y'all care to join us; our treat?"

"Well, I appreciate that and all, but I guess I need to go book Crazy Feather in-again. And once more try to explain to him that his actions have ramifications."

"Well, would you be violating any protocols by all of us eating first?" David didn't want the police chief to get in trouble, but he was curious what he might have done to raise the Native American's ire. "I'd like to find out what we've done-"

"Like you don't know-" The inebriated scrapper roused quickly from his subdued state.

"Can it, Brown!" The Chief glared at his prisoner. "Do you want to eat and work things out, or not? I'm hungry, and you know how cranky that can make me."

Mallory crossed the small café with both daughters! The normal potty/diaper change routine. She replaced her bloody tissue with a paper towel soaked in cool water. The lump was already going back down. She was pretty sure no bones were broken.

Jason and Katy Simmons greeted her brother and his family at the airport in Phoenix.

"How's David doing?" Were Billy's first words after all around hugs!

Chad, Richy, and Amy loved their cousins, Ivan and Samantha. Katy and Jason were excited, too, about Billy and Johnna coming to start a church.

"Uh, okay; we hope!" Katy answered the question about David. "It's been really tough, like you couldn't believe! Don't quit praying for him just because he's trying to act like he's fine."

"Duly noted! Wow, Kate, you look fabulous!"

"Don't call me Kate!" Katy tried to look stern at her older sibling. "I feel fabulous! When I see what a drastic difference there is between serving the Lord and fighting against Him, I wonder why it took me so long to surrender. We're really excited that y'all are here! Uh, the church is a little behind schedule, though."

"So, what's first?" Johnna Blaire's voice always sounded breathless and fretful.

"Well, first, McDonalds!" Jason's response; "And then on the way out of the city, we need to stock up on plenty of groceries! For y'all, us, and the Andersons! Your double-wide is ready, pretty complete with all you'll need, once we shop for groceries. You can unpack your other stuff tomorrow."

"When do you think the church will be ready?" Again Johnna's concern, as if her previous worry were not already solved.

"Handsome bracelet!" Mallory tried unsuccessfully to make conversation with the taciturn Native American.

Dark, hate-filled eyes met hers.

David helped Amelia with chocolate milk, but she spilled it anyway. As he bent to mop at the mess, he noted a huge knife sheathed in Crazy Feather's boot. Since bending down caused his head to hammer harder, he pulled the weapon free and straightened up. Someone else would have to clean up the milk.

Jim met David's stare, frankly embarrassed. He knew the drunk always carried the weapon, and knew how to use it, too! He couldn't count the times he had confiscated it when arresting the guy.

Mallory apologized to the disgusted waitress for the spilled milk and requested another one, before returning her attention to the striking silver and turquoise bracelet. "Did you buy that here locally?"

"You buy it?" He slid it from his muscular forearm and shoved it at her.

"Where'd you get it?" she asked again. "It's beautiful!" She studied the piece closely! Definitely masculine with its large proportions! Heavy, heavy silver, with large irregularly shaped cabochons of greenish turquoise veined with dark matrix. Inlaid mother-of-pearl and coral created thunderbirds between the large stones. The piece looked old and well-worn, with some of the tooled design wearing away.

"You wanna buy?" Cash-strapped, he hoped she would make a generous offer.

She handed it back. "Is it a family heirloom? You still haven't told me who made it. I don't want to buy yours, but if-"

"My grandfather made it. He's gone! There's no more."

Mallory's sincere admiration seemed to be crumbling his resistance.

"Well, then it would certainly be a shame for you to sell it. Wow, it's too bad no one's making this anymore!"

"Silver's expensive!" He shoved it back onto his wrist and attacked a stack of pancakes almost before the plate touched the table.

Mallory turned her attention to David and the girls, and they prayed before attacking the delectable stacks, themselves.

When the second and third orders had disappeared, the establishment had emptied out, and the still disgruntled server swept around them, Mallory tried again. "Listen, Crazy Feather, I'm aware of how the price of precious metals has sky-rocketed! Still, we have a customer base that would pay a king's ransom for something that beautiful, if anyone still knows the craft!"

"Many still retain the knowledge. This is not good turquoise, though!"

Mallory nodded. "Right; is it found in this area? I know it's a lot different than *Sleeping Beauty*. Personally, I love this soft, ocean green color with lots of veining. To me, it has more character. The *Sleeping Beauty* is so perfect, that to me it looks like plastic. Well, that's because costume jewelry makers make the plastic stuff to look like *Sleeping Beauty*. I'm probably not making much sense. My Uncle Herb, a really talented craftsman, disagrees with me about *Sleeping Beauty*. He always prefers the 'finest' of anything."

"Herbert Carlton, yes, I know of the man and his talent."

Mallory nodded. "I'm sorry, Sir, but you said we should know why you'd try to attack us. But, what's obvious to you, has us lost in the sauce. How are we stepping on people's toes? Are we settling on land that's considered sacred?"

He shrugged. "On land that's valuable. What's considered valuable is the 'new sacred', is it not? And it's only valuable because of what you have discovered there, or what the rumors say has been discovered there."

Jim sipped slowly at the thick dregs in his mug. "If I may, and I could be totally off-base, but are you importing work crews for your projects?"

"Trying to," David acknowledged. "I'm scrambling! I have so many jobs to get done, and I'm kind of hamstrung."

"Is it entirely safe here, now?" Johnna seemed to miss the loveliness of the high-end double wide, and the abundance of groceries crammed into cupboards, pantry, and refrigerator.

"Look, Hon," Billy tried, "Our own washer and dryer! We've never had that! No more Laundromat."

"Well, yeah, but look what happened to David and Mallory-"

Jason's apprehensive gaze met Katy's. The Anderson's double-wide was dark, and their truck was gone! And it was late! "Try to get some rest, and we'll give you a tour tomorrow. You got our cell numbers and land line. Give us a shout if you need anything."

"Dad?" Chad's caressing of the word always made Jason's heart ache.

He laughed. "Chad, we know what you're going to ask, and not tonight. There'll be lots of chances for sleepovers!" He could barely stand to ever disappoint any of the kids, but if he had to go hunting David and Mallory, he didn't want to alarm the newest *Enclave* residents, more than they already were!

Rhonna Abbott hummed happily as she cleaned and dusted her house. She paused at the large bathroom mirror to talk to her reflection. "Yes, Self, I can talk to you anytime, but right now, Girl, I need to look you straight in the eye!" She laughed. "You listenin' to me? Pay attention now, ya hear?" She laughed again. "See, this here? This is a dream sheet!" She held up the tattered notebook sheet, crammed full with no margins remaining. "Okay, are ya listenin' to me? I said to look!" She grew silent as she traveled backward in time to her school days in Murfreesboro, Arkansas. 'Mallory O'Shaughnessy! Lived in a junky, run-down place right outside of town, but always nice as could be! Kind of had that inner glow that didn't go out! Being poor didn't seem to bother her, and even when people acted mean toward her, she never acted mean back. And she was always nice to me, even though I was just a little, black, middle-school girl!' She remembered the shock in the little town at the sudden death of Mallory's father, and then Mallory hardly ever returning to school. Instead, a big fancy family from Tulsa arrived one spring week end, and moved her to Dallas. Rhonna recalled the blur of hearing about Mallory's brush with death at the hands of a beautician; and then after that, Mallory was confined to a big motorized wheel chair. She graduated from Murfreesboro high school, ridin' in that big chair. And then, Mallory started hirin' kids from Murfreesboro. That was where Rhonna came in; and her 'Dream Sheet', now crowded full, got its start. She waved good-bye to her reflection, and grabbing her phone, moved beneath her high-stilted bed to the sliding doors of the patio. Sliding the door behind her, she sank down in a deck chair and placed a call.

"Hey, Girlfriend! What about goin' out for a big steak?" She laughed and chatted, aware of the soft fragrance of roses filling the warm afternoon air

An amazed thought shot through David's head with one of the arrows of pain. That through the craziness of Crazy Feather and his drunken assault, the world was righting itself in an amazing way. Well, if Mallory and the baby were okay.

Sobering up with the stacks of pancakes and lots of strong coffee, the Navajo's surly anger turned into animated hope.

And David's hope soared in turn! Wow, this guy knew everyone in six counties, skilled guys needing work as desperately as David needed workers. "Okay," he clarified. "We run tight operations, doing surprise inspections like OSHA does. We adhere to their standards, but tighter. Safety matters to us. No one can come to work under the influence of anything, and no drugs or alcohol on site. We start with drug testing-"

"Yeah, I'll pass the word. Guess I'm spending the rest of the night in jail," he apologized as his gaze met that of the police chief.

Jim nodded. "Yeah, what's gonna be left of it by the time Mrs. Anderson finishes up getting checked over. And you're paying whatever out of pocket expenses there may be, that their insurance doesn't cover. Just so you know, if that blow had landed where you intended, and David ended up back in his coma, you would be liable for damages you could never see over, while doing an assault stint in prison! And if you'd killed him, it'd be twenty-five to life for involuntary manslaughter. I know you and lots of area men need jobs, and you're used to labor disputes, but-"

"You know, it's no secret, I do have a record," Crazy Feather admitted sadly to David. "So do some of the others. And one of the roofers, well he got a dishonorable-but it wasn't fair."

Jim shook his head. "It was, too."

David nodded seriously. “We’ll still give them a chance. People make mistakes.” He pushed his chair back and extended his hand. “Thanks, Chief Dunlap, but we’re just going to get home. Our girls have done lots of hospital and waiting room time.”

“Well, thank Crazy Feather here, that now they have to do more. I’m insisting! The last thing you need is to get out there to your place, and have her hemorrhage or something.”

“Yeah, Jason, any problems with getting Billy and his family situated?” David answered his cell as they pulled into an ER parking space and moved through the hissing automatic doors of the trauma center.

He listened to the update before responding. “Yeah, we’re fine! Didn’t mean to alarm y’all! Glad the flight was on time. We came into town for a pancake dinner, and we met a guy who can assemble work crews for us.”

Jason frowned. “Thought you said you’re fine. Why do I hear an intercom paging a doctor?”

“Well, we’re fine. Mallory fell, and we’re just making sure she’s okay; ya know? See you in the morning, and I’ll fill you in! It’s great!”

Dana Ames frowned. “Hello, Mr. Anderson, I’m not happy to see you back here. What are your symptoms?”

He protested as she scooted a wheel chair behind him. “Sorry, I don’t remember you. But if you saved my life, I’m forever in your debt. My wife fell earlier, and we wanted to make sure she’s okay, and the baby-”

Ames nodded. “We’ll take care of her. You, have a seat! We heard that you came to; you were in bad shape when they brought you in!” She showed Mallory to a cubicle and offered her the ubiquitous gown.

Mallory held it up, regarding it with a critical air. “This looks like last season’s. Do you have anything that’s a little more ‘with it’?”

Ames laughed. “I can tell you’re behind in reading *Vogue*! That’s the latest! From Paris on this afternoon’s flight”!

Mallory laughed. “Oh; my bad! I guess this contrast binding-”

“Yep, that’s how you tell. Okay, sonogram first. No bleeding? Then we’ll tend your arm. Clean it up and bandage. How did you fall?” Then, noting the slightest purple hint of a bruise along the patient’s jaw line- “Did he hit you? Did he ever abuse you before his brain injury?”

"Uh, no, Ma'am, it wasn't David that hit me! It's kind of one of those fluke things-"

The nurse stood back with folded arms that indicated she wasn't buying the story. "Let me guess! You just fell!"

Diana listened to Jason Simmons, concerned. "Okay, well, I'll give Mallory a call. I think if David was back in with complications, he'd tell you. At least he can talk again. Thanks for your call. Do you think Katy's brother's going to like it there?"

Jason considered. "Well, he will. He's been dying to pastor, and his dad will hardly let him lead in silent prayer. Now Johnna's kind of different. I'm not sure she'd be happy if she was a clam at high tide. Well, I shouldn't say that. Listen, I'm going to be up for awhile. Would you call me when you know more about David and Mallory?"

"Another little girl; did you know that?" Ames stuck her head in as the sonogram got underway. "Everything looks good, too. I'm sure that's a relief!"

Mallory nodded, trying to quell tears of disappointment. "Oh, yes, Ma'am, a big relief!" She forced her voice to sound cheerier than she felt! She loved her girls, but was hoping for a son this time. "Am I finished? Can I get dressed? Are the girls dismantling the place one brick at a time?"

"No, ten at a time"! She laughed. "Actually, they obey your husband."

"Hi, Diana, you're calling late. Is everything okay?" Mallory tried to sound perky, but she was concerned that something might be wrong; either with one of the Faulkners or something business-related.

"We're fine. It's nearly our bedtime, but Jason called. He got his brother-in-law settled in, but then when there was no sign of you guys, he got concerned."

"Well, we're doing great! Stupendous, actually, but while we worked out some details, it got late."

"Mmmm-hmm. Working details out back at the local hospital?"

Mallory sighed. She and David loved the Arizona adventure, but the Faulkners didn't share the enthusiasm. Kind of like David's parents, they wished the 'kids' would rein in, and do business from a safer venue. Like Mallory wanted David's head beaten into mush, and appreciated attacks by the crazy and greedy criminal element. She figured someone needed to stand up to it and fight back, at some point in time!

Yes, Ma'am, I fell and skinned my forearm, it raised up a lump, which quickly went back down. I'm sure I'll have a big scab and a bright, colorful bruise in a day or two. The Chief of Police wanted us, insisted that we, get the baby checked out before we went all the way back home. We're fine."

"Mmmmm-hmmm! You don't sound fine, Mallory."

Mallory laughed. "Actually, everything is really good. I guess I'm just a little bummed that we're having another girl. And, please don't lecture me because I am glad I haven't had any complications and that the girls are healthy. And then the trauma nurse just hurt my feelings about the way the girls act."

Diana laughed. "Welcome to parenthood. Okaay, so we'll wait to hear from you. Just something else has been on my mind. It seems like Deborah and all of the Rodriguez' have been silent."

"Hmmm," Mallory's thoughtful response! "I thought she was just trying to leave me alone since I've had so much other stuff to deal with. I figured that meant you were doing double-duty with helping them. I'll call tomorrow."

Mallory disconnected, satisfied. A late-night email, evidently catching the attention of an experienced salesman, created results. She watched her computer screen for confirmation and printed the order and payment agreement. Progress! She was relieved that both daughters were still asleep following the late night. David was getting dressed.

"Did you come to bed at all?" His deep eyes searched her expression.

"I did, but then I got right back up when I couldn't sleep! Inspiration was fired up. My first and most important order of business was getting more modular buildings on site!"

He sighed. "Wow, there are so many vacant properties that we can lease cheap."

She nodded, not dissuaded at his input. "There are! You're right! But everything's so far away! I'm just thinking we should expand our little village here. There's safety in greater numbers. You need an office from which to run all of your jobs. Free of the girls and their noise. But not that entails a thirty minute drive each way. And then, tools and equipment-"

He laughed and kissed her. "Good thinking! Show me what ya got. And of course, you're brilliant to think of keeping tools and equipment on site here; things can walk away. And not only are they expensive to replace, but it wastes time, when you're ready to use something, and discover it's missing."

Cade and Catrina stood on the loading dock of the *Chandler* part of *Sanders-Chandler*, melting in the heat.

Cat mopped with a soggy tissue. "You know, it's cooler and fallish in some places."

Cade nodded. "Yeah, and in Arizona it's still quite warm most days, but it's at least dry heat. Why don't you go back inside where the air is? I'll finish checking in the samples."

The workers seemed to be moving more and more slowly, but in the stifling heat, it was hard to blame them. At last, the final core sample made its way into the chemical plant. Cade signed off and went in search of his wife.

She looked up from her monitor. "You have to hand it to Mallory for caginess! She's taking 'secretive' to a whole new level. Not only does she not want state labs analyzing her samples, but this-" She extended her hand toward the monitor. Arkansas samples travel to the Arizona lab, Arizona samples may go to Hope or here. So, even if the analysts blab about what they find, they don't know the origin of the minerals."

He nodded. "Yeah, but they still better not blab. The CDA's are tough, with tough consequences for violations!"

Cat nodded. "Yeah, Mom and Dad have toughened up their stance, too, with everyone at *Sanders-Chandler*. You know, my dad's such a good Christian that he hates to even sound tough. So he's been badly taken advantage of. It's better to spell everything out in black and white as much as possible. The Bible is clear about 'not being slothful in business', and yet lackadaisical employees think he should endlessly overlook their shortcomings, or they say he isn't the Christian man he claims to be."

Cade was a newer Christian, "You're right! And yet, the Lord has blessed his business in an amazing way. Maybe because he manages to find a middle ground between hard-core, no nonsense, heartless management, and his more compassionate angle."

She nodded, flashing him one of her brightest smiles. "Are you ready to call it a day and go home?"

"Almost, I'll go check the lab and make sure the Chemists are off to a good start. I'm eager to see the results, too. Although that will take a few days"!

Trent disconnected from Sonia. Seemed as though he was, once again, on the hot seat! Welcome to Washington! After more than a decade in the jungliest jungle of them all, he wondered why anything surprised him. He laughed at the first complaint! Lodged by a professor who was contacted the afternoon David Anderson was in danger. He gazed out his office window, noting dust and dead flies accumulated on the sill. (That made him wonder what the federal cleaning crews actually did here all night. Well, at least, they emptied the trashcans.) He returned his gaze to the document. He remembered talking to the professor who couldn't give him an iota of information about how to calm an enraged swarm. Talking like he was lecturing in a classroom, he simply reasserted that, 'at nightfall, they would all return to their nest'. Trent remembered his anguished thoughts. 'What if David doesn't have 'til nightfall? And there's NO nest for the flying bugs to hole back up in! Hence! Why they were so mad, and why he was placing this call, to begin with. So, the guy was no help, whatsoever, but now he'd taken time to write Washington, the Forestry Service, specifically, to say he was terribly disappointed to learn that Forest Rangers didn't know that the insects were wasps; that hornets weren't indigenous anywhere in the Western Hemisphere. But ignorant people mistook bald-faced wasps for hornets. Okay, so who was ignorant? His introduction of himself was that he was a law enforcement officer with the National Forestry Service, a position totally different from that of the Ranger Service. The prof was apparently as ignorant about where his tax dollars went, as most people were about the difference between wasps and hornets!

The other strongly worded recommendations might have been humorous. Well, the gist of them was that evidently, he spent too much time in DC, and consequently, didn't have a feel for his field agents. That was kind of crazy, since, when he did take trips and spent money delving into wrongdoing within his department, they called him on the carpet for wasting federal resources! He felt like screaming, "Make up your mind!" But this was DC, which meant that there was no mind at all! Or that there were too many, with no consensus!

"Okay, Lord," he breathed. "Thank you for helping me use the brain that You've given me. Help this blow over, and help me run my department in a knowledgeable and equitable manner. And thank you for the nature lesson, even though You know my degrees are in criminal justice."

David was stunned. "Hey, uh, Mallory?"

She appeared in the doorway of the small office they shared.

"I printed off all your emails! You really were busy all night! I thought we talked about all this stuff!"

She stood there, uneasily. "Well, we didn't really. You just vetoed everything without listening."

"That's not true. I listened, and said, 'Not now'. What are we going to do with all this stuff? Well, I know what we can do with it; but how are we paying for it? Where's all this commercial kitchen stuff going? I said we can't do a chow hall here!"

She moved in and perched on the edge of a chair. "Well, yes, and I asked why not, and you told me this isn't Arkansas! Which, I knew that, but it wasn't really a valid argument!"

He stared at her in disbelief. "Okay, so what is this? You were hoping I'd die so no one would be in your way? And now since I didn't, you figure you'll do whatever you want anyway?"

Tears sprang to her eyes! "Hoping you'd die? How can you-How-? How can you say anything like that to me?"

He shook his throbbing head and dropped it into both hands. "Yeah, you know what? I'm sorry! I guess I'm trying to get a handle on everything that's happened! And why some guy I've never crossed paths with, comes swinging at me. And I'm relieved when you took the brunt of it so my lights don't get put back out!" He stared at the stack of documents in his hand. "Why are you so insistent on a chow hall? It isn't that much trouble for us to fix our food."

"Yeah, David, it is."

"I fix my own, most of the time!" He was determined.

"Yeah, and make a mess and leave everything out, and then I fix breakfast for the girls, and it's more stuff out, more mess, more dishes. And I barely accomplish anything, and they want lunch."

"We're using disposable stuff."

"Okay, listen to me because I make sense! But if you still disagree, I'll cancel the order!"

"Cancelling will still cost us."

She nodded. "Okay, let's say it takes one of us forty-five minutes to fix something, eat it, and clean up; both after breakfast and lunch. Dinner takes more like an hour and fifteen minutes. And these time-frames are fairly conservative. That's three hours per day, six days per week, figuring eating out on Sundays. That's eighteen hours a week. David, I'm not a little happy-to-be-a-home-maker type. And I think my strengths and abilities lie in doing other things. David, I'm not your mom!"

"Well, I thought being here and doing the homesteader thing was what you wanted."

"I'm a Geologist! And I thought you were on board with this. Your mom and dad want us to come back to Arkansas, but you told me you want to keep carving a place out here, too. Okay, back to the chow hall issue! I wish you'd let me finish one fight before you sidetrack me into another!"

He sighed. "Win one, you mean." But he couldn't help grinning. "Okay, hit me again with the chow hall!"

"Okay, eighteen hours a week of doing something I hate, seems like, not the wisest use of a resource. You know, in the Bible, the soldiers were allowed to cut trees to make tools and implements of war, but not if it was a food-bearing tree. Because bearing food trumped making implements! And we're not being efficient. Because if I'm spending eighteen hours a week in these tasks, so are Johnna and Katy. Eighteen times three of us equals fifty-four hours, and in a year~ And it will multiply even faster with any of the other wives we bring in! And, your eating a loaf of bread doesn't equate to fixing yourself something!"

He glanced down again at the sheaf before looking up and meeting her gaze. "Okay, well we need to have a prayer meeting about where all the money's coming from. You're right! I do want to stay and accomplish some things here, and I don't want to go back to Arkansas right now. But the reason you got up and did all this was that you were upset! We need to talk about the baby!"

Her expression flashed quickly, showing her hesitancy to address the issue. "What about her?" she hedged.

His dark eyes met hers squarely. "Okay, let's go back to the fateful day. You did a pregnancy test, and then just hid it; it was positive. Why not tell me?"

She felt trapped. "Well, because we were planning to ride."

His jaw dropped, incredulous. "That's it?"

"Yeah, the baby's so tiny that early, that I figured it would be safe, even if I fell off. But since we were taking a really gentle ride with the girls-I was going to tell you as soon as-" She started crying again. "But then there was no chance!"

He nodded understanding. "I was in a coma for four months. As soon as I actually was aware of you the day I regained consciousness, I knew I'd been conked out for quite a while. Because you were really showing"! He scooted next to her, taking her hand in his. "Admit it; you couldn't get to sleep because you were upset she's not a boy!"

"Well, it's just-" Emotion rendered her unable to speak. "They told me-you weren't going to make it-" She sobbed. "But then, you survived the surgery. And in that time period, when I thought you would never live-uh-the thought comforted me, that I might at least have your son-uh-to carry your name, and I wanted that part of you."

He pulled her into the circle of his arms. "But a daughter is just as much part of me. It's in God's hands, and He knows best about our family; the same as He knows best about our businesses. And I don't know what my mom and dad are lobbying for, but there isn't going to be a Jonathan David Anderson, III! I don't mind having my dad's name! But I'm not crazy about it, either! You told me once all the names you picked out for our kids back in junior high! They all had the initials; *AEA!*"

She sprang away, embarrassed and horrified. "I never told you about that!"

His mischievous giggle caused him to clasp his sides helplessly. At last, he gasped out, "Maybe it was Tammi that told me, then!"

Chapter 6: GIFTS

Ella Hamilton stared glumly from her office window, not sure why she bothered showing up today! The *Shady Grove Retirement Home* she administrated was once again under new ownership. And, not surprisingly, the narcotic and meds inventory was way off! She rose from the broken desk chair to check out a flurry of sudden activity out back. Hmmm, tall, chain-link fence going in; something she had lobbied unsuccessfully for during her entire tenure here. She sank back down, pushing a Styrofoam cup of cold coffee aside. Not that she would benefit from anything happening now. She was torn between turning in her resignation and waiting to be canned! Resigning would look better on her résumé, but being fired would qualify her for unemployment. She could collect that for a while as she considered options. Maybe she could take a cruise. She scoffed softly at herself. No use blowing her little nest egg.

A gentle tap at her door roused her from her reverie. She responded, to see Mallory Anderson.

"Oh no; what happened"? Her first thought was that David was being readmitted! But, that couldn't be it! The facility was over-crowded, and the Andersons hadn't reapplied for a bed!

David appeared beside her, and he extended a hand. "Good morning; is it okay if we call you Ella? We're David and Mallory. We just finished closing at the title company!"

"Great!" A bitter response! "So; what? This is payback for not having kept you cleaned up better? Let me guess; you want my resignation!"

David laughed, although references to his not being able to take care of his own needs embarrassed him. "Can we come in?"

She stood back. Her office was a disaster, but what difference~

Settled into a metal folding chair across from her, David began. "Let's make a deal; okay? I won't mention that the staff didn't keep me cleaner, if you won't mention it either. And believe me we don't want you to resign. See, we bought this place, but we actually don't know anything about the nursing home industry."

Still bitter; "What? You just have piles of money to burn?"

"Actually, we don't;" Mallory came in smoothly, "we need a success story here, and we need your expertise. We may not know this industry, but we know management. We helped turn a machine shop in Houston around, not because we know about machining, but because-"

Ella gazed skeptically at the two youthful, shining visages. They didn't look like they could know much about much. She laughed. "I'm sorry, but if you know as much about management as you're claiming, you would have given this place a wide berth!"

"Actually, our attorney and research department have completed a lot of due diligence." David again! "There is so much money in the nursing home business. I know many of the large, nursing home corporations get into trouble because it's so easy to defraud the social security system, Medicare, Medicaid, and insurance companies. But we can keep this profitable very easily and honestly And it has been yielding a huge profit! A surprise to you, we know, because everyone here's salaries are substandard!"

Ella knew her jaw dropped. Trying to recover herself, she demanded, "Okay, if it's such a prize, why did they sell?"

Mallory smiled broadly. "Well, it's kind of crazy. We're both Christians, and we put the Lord first. Well, when David got out of here, and started thinking about his experience-well, he was in a coma, and didn't even know he was in a really depressing situation. But he started thinking about all of the people who are still here. So, he wanted to do a facelift and make everything much nicer. We would have donated whatever was necessary, but when we contacted the owner, I guess he was spooked that we were suing! So, he put it on the market! He has other businesses, and he didn't want to deal with this deteriorated property and a possible law suit! When we started looking into purchasing it, we were amazed at the opportunity!"

Ella crossed her arms, refusing to allow hope to take wing. "So you're going to use the profit that's in it, to remodel?"

"Partially"! David's deep eyes smoldered, and the administrator marveled at the way the couple presented their narrative, like they understood one another and were on the same page, even finishing each other's sentences. "But it wouldn't make sense to fix one problem and leave everything else broken."

"So, the problems rest on my shoulders?"

"No, this is a tough business; we know that! It's filled with guilt and hopelessness. The patrons reach a point where they lose their independence and ability to function. And maybe their kids try to look after them. You know that can be a strain, and so when they wear out, they seek out a facility like this. So they're sad and guilty, but what are the options? So they make as many visits as they can, and they find out the staff is impatient, sometimes to the point of meanness. So, they complain, making the staff more frustrated than ever. We know you're tired and probably pretty beat up!"

To Ella's horror, tears flowed at Mallory's sympathetic words.

"So, you're taking a paid vacation, starting tomorrow." David rose as he spoke. "We need to have you answer as many of our questions as possible today, first, though! Your assistant can keep things going, and I'll be on and off-site with the remodel. We're still working on the benefit packages we're offering, but, we need you to stay on, and we'll reward you fairly for your contribution to everyone's overall success. I have in my hand, two VIP fares for a seven day, Scandinavian Cruise. Can you think of anyone who might enjoy-"

She nodded, not certain yet, exactly what he was saying. "Well, anyone I know would jump at a-is there a catch?"

"Kind of," Mallory admitted. "We really like it if people who work for us wear our fashion and jewelry lines so they can share our products with other people they meet!"

Mallory checked final interior touches at the *Enclave* guest house. It was beautiful. Two doublewides, placed end-to-end, and joined by a foyer should house the Faulkners' visit very nicely. One end featured kitchen, living, dining, bath, and three bedrooms. The other housed a spacious master-suite, nursery, and office. Beautiful Irish linen created a special ambiance atop brand new beds and billowed at windows and French doors. David and his crews could work wonders with pre-builts. Tucking in books, gifts, toys, and fruit basket, she gave one more satisfied look around and hurried to the chow hall.

David strode toward her. "What do you think?"

She welcomed his kiss. "I think it's gorgeous! Perfect! I'm so excited they're coming back! How did your day go?"

He released her. "Well, let's just say I have good news, and bad news. The bad news is that we hit a bunch of snags at the church facility, so there's no way to have a CO in time for church Sunday!"

Dismay registered in her expressive eyes. "Okaaa-a-y; and what's the good news?"

"Well, the good news is that we rented a big pavilion from a place in Phoenix. The weather for the rest of the week is supposed to be ideal, so I have a bunch of guys setting up chairs and a dais for the pulpit and instruments. That means we'll have to make do with a keyboard rather than a piano. I wangled a temporary CO so people can use the rest rooms in the building at Sunday service times only."

She inclined her head thoughtfully. "Maybe we should delay the Faulkners' coming for a week or so."

His eyes shone with mischief. "Or maybe, the Lord is really in this. Pretty sure the music will carry. Hey, remember in Hawaii?"

A smile lit her countenance. "Oh, yeah, enter Nick into our lives! Why haven't we asked him and Jennifer to come?"

"Uh, I don't know; the last time you and Jennifer were together down here-"

Her eyes blazed suddenly. "That wasn't our fault! Listen, Nick just brings something so special-"

He nodded. "Okay, I'll bounce it off Erik first. If he thinks it's an okay idea-" He paused as Katy appeared with the *Enclave* kids in tow. "Hey, Katy; we'll take a couple of kiddoes off your hands. Have they minded?"

"Always," Katy responded brightly!

David was amazed. Not that he should be, but Mallory's new division of labor was brilliant! Johnna loved overseeing the chow hall responsibilities, and she immediately produced recipes for feeding large crowds economically and fairly simply. Even now, the enticing aromas revved up his appetite. And Katy was a charmer of the kids. Well, it didn't hurt that Mallory had ordered a small, barebones modular for a game room. A Wii, TV, toys, games, and books filled the space, leaving more room in the individual families' doublewides, and giving Katy a place to supervise all of the kids together. Kids, who for the most part, were bonded friends across the age and gender differences.

Ella wakened early and gazed over at her mother who was still fast asleep. Pulling on a robe, she brewed a coffee single and moved out to the balcony of the first-class cabin. The surrounding view from the fjord stole her breath as she raised her camera. Wow! What a difference a few days could make! Carefully, she framed each shot. She considered herself a pretty good photographer, but the landscape was so spectacular~ Her phone chimed; probably more questions from David and Mallory. The message was from David, but rather than his usual bevy of questions about the home, this was some type of financial report. Not exactly her thing! Yada, yada! Closing out the books to start a new fiscal year~the CPA suggested~. She bogged down, wondering if this text possibly was intended for someone else. She took a sip and gazed around again before scrolling to view more of the message. Her eyes widened and she found herself fighting tears, once again!

"Bad news, Dear?" her mother stood in the doorway watching her.

"No, Mom. Very good news! Fix a coffee and join me."

"Okay, I can handle good news before I have my morning coffee!"

Ella laughed at her mother. "Okay, here goes~uh, I told you about David and Mallory when David first arrived at *Shady Grove*?"

"Uh-huh; if you ask me, that place is more 'shady', than it is 'grove'! Yeah, he regained consciousness, and that's who currently owns the place! And, sent us on this cruise! I'm still suspicious what they're really up to! No one's nice, just for the sake of being nice. They have an agenda! Trust me!"

Ella nodded, agreeing. "Yes, Mom, they do. And they're upfront about what it is. Their aim is growing their businesses and making money! And they aren't ashamed to say so! It's just that they're also savvy enough to know that 'No man is an island' and so they need good help and are willing to compensate appropriately!"

"Ah, is that you quoting Shakespeare? Or was it David? He's certainly a nice-looking young man!"

Ella laughed. "Yeah, you keep mentioning that, Mom. Actually it was Mallory that referenced the 'No man is an island,' thing. And she didn't know it was the 'Bard'. It's a verse in the Bible, further proving that Shakespeare wasn't original!"

Margaret Janson simply nodded. Retired from years of teaching high-school English-literature, she admired all of the classics. If William

Shakespeare was indeed a plagiarist, as was so often claimed, the works still, for the most part charmed her. "Don't try to start a fight with me, today, Dear! It's much too beautiful to spend time arguing. I need to dress so I can go peruse yet another buffet!"

"Okay, I'm with you there, but I haven't told you the good news yet. The good news is that they closed the books and started a new fiscal year. They're paying me a bonus! Which is great, but they've taken time to itemize why, and what I did right! Like, every time we inventory the medicine-"

"Yeah, you always call me in tears. Like you can be on site night and day-"

Ella nodded earnestly. "And of course, there was shrinkage with the narcotics again! But by industry standards, our loss, percentage-wise, was nearly negligible. I got a bonus on that for doing a good job, instead of catching 'Hail Columbia'!"

"Yeah, Martin treated you like you were the criminal."

Ella sat, dazed. "Because he thought I was! You know, David and Mallory told me they were good at management. And I'm sittin' there thinkin', 'Yeah, right'!"

Margaret nodded sagely; quick to catch on. "Martin didn't know enough about the business to know the trends industry-wide. Your little kids do their homework."

Ella nodded. "Yeah, the total bonus is seven thousand, after taxes. When I get back they want a CPA to meet with me to help lessen my tax bite. He wired the money to the purser, so all I have to do is present my ID and I'll get a debit card. We can do a couple more shore excursions and shop for souvenirs, too."

"Yeah, and don't forget that we also get to wear these pretty clothes!"

The *Enclave* hummed with activity. Various work crews appeared to check out tools and receive assignments. Mallory urged the girls to finish breakfast so they could go with Katy and the other kids. She glanced up as Crazy Feather appeared beside her.

"Could I ask a favor of you?"

"Uhhh, you can ask, I guess." She met his intense eyes as she took in the man standing next to him.

"My father; Charles! He's been a little sick, and the weather's supposed to be cool."

Mallory extended her hand. "It's nice to meet you. I'm Mallory." For some reason she liked the bronzed, dignified man. He wore deep green, crushed velvet and lots of silver and turquoise Navajo jewelry. Loosely plaited braids framed his face, and his expression crinkled into a broad smile, showing strong, even teeth.

"This is probably the best place for you to be out of the elements." She indicated the 'chow hall'. "I mean, it isn't the most comfortable for hanging out all day, but there's coffee." She reached for the remote to bring a large plasma TV to life. "Would you like to watch TV?"

"No, I'd rather watch you!"

Mallory laughed. "I'm flattered, but I'm afraid the chores I'm embarking on will be pretty dull. Make yourself as comfortable as you can in here." She stared after Crazy Feather as he stranded her to go join his crew.

Charles chuckled. "I guess this means you're stuck with me. I'll get coffee and we can visit."

Mallory was unsure why she didn't insist on leaving him so she could make her phone calls. Instead, she fixed another mug for herself and wiped the girls' hands and faces as she released them from their high chairs. Settled across from him, she plunged in. "What's on your mind?"

"Suspicion"! He admitted plainly. "These guys are all excited that you've come to help us. Sorry to be 'Chief Rain Cloud'; I can say that! But we always get-I suppose I should stick with polite language-"

Mallory nodded, completing his thought. "-Left in the lurch! I'm sure, Mr. Brown, is it?"

"Charles William Brown; but please, call me Charles. Yeah, we always get stung bad! To phrase it gently"!

"Okay, Charles, we aren't here for the purpose of helping you! We're here to help ourselves! I'm not sure how we've created the wrong impression! These guys being willing and eager to work, are a literal Godsend to us, and we want to make sure it's equitably beneficial! But we're not looking for someone to help for the sake of helping them! We need what they bring to the table!"

He sat quietly, considering her words. "This is good. This shows us respect. You and David showed respect and trust when you supplied the foremen with phones and laptops."

Mallory nodded. "We always do that, and for the most part, it creates more pluses than minuses." She paused to see what the girls were into. "Amelia, what are you doing?"

Charles laughed. "That one's a fiery little one! I'll call her 'Fire Spirit'."

Mallory frowned, liking her daughter's name. And then, she was doubly chagrined when Amelia fell in love with her new nickname, and also with Charles.

"Okay, girls, it's time to go. Katy'll be wondering where ya'll are."

Avery toddled directly to her, but Amelia's lip went out, and she clung to her new friend. So much for teaching her not to speak to strangers!

"I'll be right back!" Clasping Avery and the diaper bag, she sprinted to the playroom building. On the way back to the chow hall, she grabbed her laptop. She returned in time to see Charles draw out a huge pocket knife and open the blade.

"Mr. Charles is making me a toy."

Amelia's explanation halted Mallory's panicked, "What are you doing?" demand, and she backed down, hoping he hadn't noticed. A sly grin, however, assured her that he didn't miss much!

"Okay, Amelia, don't chatter his ears off," she cautioned. She was amazed at his patience, and at the toy materializing from a piece of fire wood.

"You just tend to your business, and leave us to ours," Charles rejoined good-naturedly. "I like talking with Fire Spirit. I get lonely sometimes."

Amazed, Mallory went to work, aware of Amelia's high-pitched questions and Charles' patient responses. The first two emails, she forwarded to David. Then, she received one from him; from the project where the crew quarried sandstone from the cliff face beyond Sunquist's cabin. She looked at photos of the work. One of the younger guys was worrying about the environment and the plan to quarry the cliff face back several feet. Mallory frowned. It was really a remote place, where few people would ever enjoy the pristine situation, either way. And the plan was to leave it looking basically the same. David planned to use the stone for landscaping and in the building of a permanent home here. Not surprisingly, the protestor was Little Feather Brown. She emailed back, "That's okay; what would he rather do?"

She smiled. She was dying to get inquisitive about the jewelry making skills, and David was determined to keep every able-bodied man building or quarrying. But everyone wasn't born to that end, and unhappy people made poor workers! It reminded her of a passage of Scripture:

> *Isaiah 41:6&7 They helped every one his neighbor; and every one said to his brother, Be of good courage.*
>
> *So the carpenter encouraged the goldsmith, and him that smootheth with the hammer, him that smote the anvil, saying, It is ready for the sodering,: and he fastened it with nails, that it should not be moved.*

"Excuse me, Mr. Brown?" she interrupted.

"Please call me Charles. What can I do for you?"

"Tell me a little bit about your grandson. What kind of work does he like? What are his hobbies?"

Charles' brows drew together. "Look, he needs to do whatever your husband wants him to do. What he enjoys is sleeping! I'll tell him to get his lazy self in gear!"

Mallory's turn to frown! "Does he know how to make jewelry like yours?"

"No, and they turn it out on machines now, anyway. He needs to work like a strong man. He can draw in his spare time!"

Rising for more coffee, she offered him a refill. He nodded, but when the carving halted while he sipped, Amelia stamped her foot.

"Watch it there, Fire Spirit," Mallory warned. "You do not stomp your feet at people! Apologize to Mr. Brown."

"I can call him Mr. Charles."

"Amelia! You can say you're sorry!"

"Wow, this place is transformed!"

Mallory nodded eagerly at Daniel's approval. "Yes, in spite of what happened to David! It's amazing! Here's the guest house." She made her way along a narrow asphalt road, watching for the occasional snake. Unlocking the door, she stood back.

"This is gorgeous!" Diana's quick response to the inviting space! Where is David? Is he okay?"

Mallory shrugged uncertainly. "Well, we hope so. He gets tremendous headaches, still. Trying to avoid narcotics, he pops lots of aspirin. I'm afraid they might cause him to bleed, but~ anyway, his last x-rays and MRI showed improvement." She held out her hands for the baby, and Diana handed her over.

"She's adorable."

"I'm eager to see your girls!"

Mallory shook her head, defeated. "They're something else! I've been hoping Lilly would come snatch them~" She paused, suddenly uncertain if the Faulkners would find that funny.

Actually, they did, and when they managed to stop laughing, they assured her she was doing a great job as a mom.

"Well, I think things got away from me, when David was hurt~"

Diana slid an arm around her. "Maybe they did, but, Mallory, it's just the age. Little ones are a challenge. They cry and fight and whine incessantly!"

"Well, ours never did," Daniel reminded.

Diana turned big, blue, indignant eyes on him. "Well, no, not when you were around! They were always smarter than that!"

Mallory laughed, starting to see over her hopeless discouragement! "That's exactly how Amelia and Avery do! David walks in the door; they're angels: and I'm the bad person!"

Diana strummed an air guitar, crooning *Welcome to My World.*

"You're kidding!" David's eyes blazed. "Crazy Feather asked you to baby sit his dad all day? Why did you agree?"

Mallory shrugged. "I'm not sure; the man is not without his charms. He entertained Amelia all day, and they're fast friends. He carved her a cute little baby on a papoose board. She yacked at him the whole time, and he must have taught her everything through the third grade. He told me that Little Feather's an artist. Why don't you take him back up to the quarry tomorrow and let him sketch or paint?"

"Mallory, that'll be a morale buster! What if everyone decides they'd rather sit and paint than work?"

"I don't know! Personally, I'd rather be cutting stones than trying to paint anything decent-looking. I'm just saying let's give him a chance at what his niche might be. We can get Phil and Risa's opinion about whether there's talent, and anything commercially viable. We're agreed about the commercially viable thing. And if he isn't working, he isn't getting paid. So he better hope his art's that good!"

To David's chagrin, Mallory's niche-finding plucked worker after worker from his crews. This one makes jewelry, this one carves sculptures; this one draws, tends sheep, spins wool, or weaves blankets and rugs.

Blessedly, there were stacks of applicants, and so his quarry and building projects steamed steadily along. The nursing home project, his pride and joy, satisfied him immensely! The clients enjoyed the broad, new, landscaped outdoors space. Smooth lawn, outdoor furniture, and abounding flowers delighted the senses. Electric fans; or tall, gas heaters; fended against either heat or cold. The largest screen TVs available played assorted entertainment venues in different assembly areas, each with the volume on loud and showing the closed captions. It was amazing how much interest people showed in the entertainment when they could follow what was going on. Two dogs and myriads of cats roamed the outside areas, and beyond the fence were horses and a little pony.

In addition to that, he supplied two computers with large, brightly lit keyboards. A grouchy patron informed him that all of the electronic novices would keep them fouled up.

David laughed. "Okay, Mike, how good are you?"

Mike's response was so knowledgeable and coherent that David wondered why he was even there. "Okay, well then, Mike, can I put you in charge? Now, you can't just be bossy and keep the others run off. But maybe you can help everybody, and if something gets loused up, I'm counting on you to make the fixes. Do a good job and I'll pay you a little bit."

Heading back toward his truck, he noticed an aged lady on her knees next to the largest flower bed. He approached, mostly to satisfy himself that she was okay. A stack of weeds lay beside her, and she handled a blossom's drooping head tenderly.

He knelt next to her and introduced himself, adding "I can't figure out what the problem is with that particular flower. I thought maybe they weren't getting enough water."

Her faint, crackly voice reminded him of rustling Bible pages. "Yes, when I saw these going in, I worried. The soil around here is too alkaline; they actually thrive on the acidic side."

He didn't understand why he felt so amazed. "Okay, what can we replace them with that might fare better?"

"Oh, well nearly anything." She spouted quite a list of species he'd never heard of. "These will die, though. Pity"!

"Okay, well, what do you think if we bring in window boxes filled with potting soil? Will they revive?"

"Well, you could try, I guess. Window boxes full of flowers would look nice. I love flowers!"

He pulled out his phone and brought up the notes ap. "Okay, spell out for me, one of the ones you said thrive in alkaline." He punched it in so he could contact Suzanne about replacements.

On the way back to the *Enclave* he received a call from Steb Hanson.

"Wow, I'm hearing good stuff about you guys."

"Really?" David's voice registered surprise.

"Well the *SOC Foundation* is getting some new followers in that nursing home you guys took over. You know, the seniors around here are always looking for ways to help folks. I was wondering if I can get a group together to carpool over there once or twice a month, if there's any way we could help. I hate to admit it, but the thing that drives my askin' is that, well, what would you think about us making sure everyone's registered to vote, and then we could make a point of helping get them to the polls~But we'd like to help in other ways you can think of."

David laughed. "Yes, and they can take part in your email brigade, too. I'm not sure if I ever slowed down enough to thank you and your crowd for intervening in Tucson that night! To keep Amelia from going into the CPS system! And then when we ran into the problem in Saudi Arabia~"

Sunday morning under the 'Big Top', as David affectionately dubbed the temporary church facility, the first service opened with prayer, followed by a mini-concert! Emotions ran high! As the favorites flowed outward through town, the police dispatcher received complaints. "It's so early on Sunday morning! They're disturbing the peace. I have my radio all the way up, and I can still hear it."

The rehearsed response was that the CO would be approved Monday morning, no matter what!

Of course, there were others who approached curiously, enjoying the surprise concert. Many sang along with the more familiar selections. Whether it was an ache created by the area's spiritual emptiness, or mere curiosity, about three hundred people assembled!

David looked out and registered surprise at seeing William Stringer, his neurosurgeon, in the front section. Little did he realize that the doctor was lauding himself for David's fine motor skills, allowing him once more to play his violin! But if the doctor thought that, the others knew the One whose touch remained in evidence!

Following a few announcements and the offering, Billy Blaire rose, taking the pulpit, to spit and scream about hell for the next thirty minutes. Uneasy, David thought it was the most artless sermon he had ever heard. Still, as the message wound down, Mallory moved to the keyboard to play the invitation. *So Little Time* by John R. Rice flowed from her fingertips.

"Ah, very good, Sister," Billy approved from the mic. "Sing it for us; would you please?"

Mallory shot him a panicked look, which he either ignored or missed. David joined her, figuring she didn't remember all of the lyrics. He joined in, forgetting his stage fright as an almost soloist, thinking about helping her and bailing the service out. He was amazed as people poured to the makeshift altar.

As lunch wound down, Diana piped up suddenly. "Well, everyone here knows my feelings about Sunday afternoon naps, but I was thinking; while we're all here together, what about going to the nursing home and holding a service?"

"Brilliant!" Mallory agreed. "I wish I'd thought of it!"

"David!" Mallory's delighted voice, as she took in the changes wrought at *Shady Grove.*

He was pleased at her response. "Okay, well, the inside still looks mostly miserable. It's a little slower with having to work around the patrons and staff."

She nodded. "I'm sure, but still-"

"Well, yeah, and a lot of it's, thanks to your mom and all the flowers. Except one of the species they put in wasn't doing real well. This lady named Myrna said the ground's too alkaline. So, we thought of adding the flower boxes, to try to save them. They're coming back, too. She wasn't sure how they'd transplant; I think she must have done CPR on them."

"Well, the flower boxes look amazing! So it turned out really well. And all the little bird houses and hummingbird feeders, too"!

He nodded. "What do you think about a fountain and a Koi pond? Not to disguise a diamond dyke, but to actually be able to put water and fish in!"

She laughed at the inside joke; then grew serious. "You know what; this is kind of a surprise visit for the staff. Why don't you call and give them a few minutes heads-up?"

Chapter 7: GOSPEL

David and Mallory were astonished at the heart hunger surrounding them in the Arizona foothills. "Wow, everyone has seemed so lost and mean and angry." Mallory remarked. "It's another proof of the veracity of Scripture. The harvest fields really are ripe. And, did I tell you what Dana Ames told me?"

David caught her in his embrace. "I don't think so; we've barely been able to gasp out hellos and goodbyes. Let alone more meaningful dialog. What did she say? More about what a miracle it is that I survived?"

Mallory met his eyes and hugged him extra-tightly. "As a matter of fact, she starts every conversation with that, but then, she told me that the reason she always works weekends, is so that families can have a chance to be together. She didn't know the way to Heaven, and hasn't been convinced that both Heaven and Hell are real places! But she figured just in case there was a Heaven, and you needed to rack up good deeds, her being nice to work every weekend would help her case. She's single, so she doesn't really mind the shifts, but since she received the Lord, she's grateful for Sunday and Wednesday night church. I've never really considered that angle of good reasons for having church more than simply Sunday mornings. Churches that have adopted that schedule haven't regarded shift workers."

"That's true," he considered thoughtfully. "I'll mention it to my dad, and he can add it into his drumbeat. Just teasing; it is a good thought. And, I didn't know she got saved." He laughed. "And these people think Pastor Blaire hung the moon."

"Yeah; the first sermon was a no-punches-pulled Hellfire and Brimstone, and the next week tithing! That's what I liked about his and Katy's dad."

"You really don't care for a smoother approach?"

"I do! I think the world of Pastor Ellis. He still takes a firm Biblical stand, but he's learned that tact and finesse work in the Dallas market. And your dad has mellowed, too. And I don't in anyway infer any criticism. But Billy's barebones approach is working with these bared-boned people. And the nursing home patients are hungry for any attention. It's amazing how you've lifted their spirits. And you were only thinking about giving them something, and not getting anything back. It's amazing how the Lord honors that. We stand to bring in a healthy revenue stream, even with the added expense of benefit packages and the remodeling."

"Well, the improved pay for all of the workers is raising morale. You could place bird nests and flower gardens around all day long, but if the helps' frustrated and mean-"

She nodded. "And the deal with Kerry and Tammi, too-"

"Mmm-hmmmm, the Lord's been pouring it on. You're right about all of the miracles there. Well, Tammi's surrender to the Lord in time to save her relationship with Kerry-I mean, I'm glad the Lord used what happened to me to get her attention-"

"Yeah, and I was sweating how much cash we'd need at closing. After my expensive night of shopping-"

He shrugged. "I thought you were wrong; but everything you ordered has paved the way for expansion. And then, when Kerry started looking into *Shady Grove*, and took note of the potential, and convinced Tammi-"

"They were eager to waive the research and legal fees, and bring cash to closing for a share of the profit." She pulled from his arms, still holding his hand. "I suppose we should go get the girls and get some dinner. Oh! But something else first! Do you remember mentioning to me that you'd like to have Rudy Sunquist's old beat up pickup? Even after it nearly pounded your brains out?"

"I remember; what about it? And it wasn't the truck's fault. It would be so cool restored!"

"Well, I asked Kerry about the possibility of suing Sunquist's estate for damages! Believe me, both of us endured plenty of pain, anguish, and suffering as a direct result of his actions!"

"Yeah?" David's eyes shone. "What did he think? Might it really get us the truck?"

"Well, he was kind of caught off guard by the question, but he gave me the name of a Phoenix attorney. I contacted him. Well, they make a percentage of what they recover-"

"So, he's taking the case?"

"Yes, and while he's looking into everything, he's considering cases against the other two estates; the policeman and the assayer. The thing is, they both have widows and family-"

"Okay, wow; that's a tough call! So let's not you and I make it. We can leave that to a jury."

By humility and the fear of the LORD are riches, and honor, and life. Proverbs 22:4

Mallory passed the attractive Scripture plaque, almost without noticing. Her key to the penthouse office suite was ready, but the door was already opened. "Marge, you're in early," she exclaimed. "Did you know we were in town?"

The taciturn receptionist responded flatly. "No, I just come in and try to keep things going from this end. Actually, Dr. Wilson needed some information about your father's foundation. I think some mid-level Nigerian government officials are trying to shake down American interests. I knew where the paperwork is, so I've tried not to bother-" She broke off as she saw David emerge from the public elevator with both girls. Emotional in spite of herself, she even managed to give him a quick hug. Although the girls had both grown exponentially and looked adorable, she ignored them.

"We came up the main elevator so they could both get lots of turns pushing buttons," David explained.

But after her initial show of emotion, she snapped back to herself. "I've kept up with everything the best I've been able to, but I'm afraid that both of your in-boxes are running over. Gina's actually a good worker, too, so that helps. Are you staying in town long?"

"Not too long. I'm checking on my building, and Mallory has an appointment with her doctor. Two or three days, and then we're going to the *Ranch* for a week."

"Oh, that's good. Deborah Rodriguez must call here three times a day asking if you're in. Should I just tell her that you're going to be there?"

David ignored that, taking both girls to the play area through his office, and leaving Mallory to get the word about Deborah! Deborah knew both of their cell numbers, so if there was a problem~"

Amelia giggled with excitement. "I haven't seen these toys in a long time! Come on, Avery~" Releasing her carved papoose toy, she sprinted to the toy box. She looked back to check her baby sister, and frowned. "That's mine, Avery!" She dropped her Tupperware®, shape-sorting toy, to snatch at her newest prized possession!

"Okay, Amelia, don't grab things away from her. You put it down. Let her see it a minute."

"No, she bites on it! See her tooths marks? Right dere?" She showed the damaged place.

"Don't tell me, 'No'. Avery, don't put stuff in your mouth!" The only reason he didn't laugh at how much he sounded like his dad, was that he was trying to keep a stern face for dealing with his kids. "Amelia, she really doesn't hurt anything, and Mr. Charles can smooth those places right out. There's a toy-store full of toys here, so play nice and get along."

Mallory stared at her desk top; well, the margins that were visible. A 'full, in-box' didn't begin to describe it! For some reason, the sight flashed her back to her first morning on the job. "And I think I felt less daunted then, that I do now." She buzzed Marge to bring her coffee before attacking the stack.

Mid-morning, she buzzed David. "I'm actually making headway; how about you?"

"Yeah; great, actually! Mr. Ames wants to buy us a steak dinner tonight. He gets frustrated with Zeke, but they actually ironed out the problem and work's going better than ever. I'm still eager to visit the site! I can take the girls along. Are you thinking about lunch?"

"Mmm-hmmm, starved. Let's go to the Mezzanine and eat. And then I'll bring the girls up and put them down for a nap. You can go on to your skyscraper. I'm eager to see it, though."

"Well, you've seen the most recent pictures~" David's sudden self-conscious tone.

"Yes, but I'm sure they don't do it justice any more than five by seven post cards do of *Half-Dome*! We can swing by together on the way home."

Tammi grabbed David, sobbing, as they entered the café. "Sorry to be emotional. The building gossips are buzzing about you guys' being back!" She relinquished her brother to smile at her nieces. "So, Kerry called me, and I came to meet him for lunch, hoping to get to see you."

"Yeah, you look great!" Kerry extended his hand. "We wondered if you have time to go out to dinner tonight! Our treat"!

"I just made arrangements to go out with the real estate investors. Maybe Thursday night?" David settled Avery into a high chair as he spoke.

"Okay, David's going out with the investors," Mallory corrected. "I'm not tackling an elegant steak place with these two!"

"Oh, let me take them!" Tammi beamed at the prospect. "Actually, I can take them with me when we finish lunch! We can have a great time! Actually, they can spend the night!"

David considered. 'Wow, so far, so good with the new Tammi!' "That might work. Mallory's appointment's at ten, so we can pick them up about nine in the morning. I'm not sure we brought enough baby food and diapers for an overnighter."

"No problem. We can go to Wal Mart on the way home and shop for what we'll need, and you can pick them up tomorrow after Mallory sees the doctor. Put your money away," as he offered a twenty. "I'll get it."

Mallory finished applying subtle touches of green around her eyes. Gorgeous in a peachy hand-crocheted lace dress, she strapped on matching leather sandals. Lip gloss over pale peach color and shimmering powder. Fastening on her Shamrock jewelry set, she turned to David.

"How do I look?"

"Dazzlingly beautiful"! He stood behind her studying both of their reflections multiplied in sparkling mirrors. "Incredible! You can be positively elegant, but then-" He paused, remembering something. "But then, you're cute with your hair just pulled into a pony tail. You always wore it that way whenever you visited me-"

She turned to face him. "You knew I was there?"

He shrugged, uncertain. "I guess-on some level. It's hard to believe I lost four months!"

"David, I'm so sorry I messed everything up so much-"

"Whoa; don't cry; you'll mess up that perfect cosmetics' job. You didn't mess anything up; if this is heavy, maybe we should continue later. I'm hungry for that steak!"

She nodded, still somber and subdued. "I didn't know what to do, except come after you, myself."

"I know, and am I ever glad you did! Look, I shouldn't have gotten upset with you for riding to my rescue when we were first married. And I know that this time, you didn't have a chance to find someone to leave the girls with-"

"You-you haven't asked about Mocha-"

"Because, there's no need to ask! I never shod her, because I didn't know she'd end up making a strenuous trail ride; and Amelia's special saddle-chair was pretty heavy. I figured she was a casualty of the day like the dog. Amelia hasn't said a word to me about him. Mallory, nothing's your fault! It's the fault of the bad guys, and they are 'no mas'!"

"I didn't know you were injured so seriously; well, I didn't know for sure you were alive. And shooting the wasp nest seemed like a good idea at the time! I had no idea that they'd swarm around for hours on end so no one could come for you! Your condition got even more severe due to the delay."

He shrugged. "Mallory, your actions went above and beyond the call of duty. I have a problem not being bitter with the Forestry guys. Trent told all of them to make calls about the best way of dealing with the wasps, but they were spinning their wheels, worrying about grabbing gold nuggets. And then, the one bug specialist who was most helpful told Trent it's a miracle the wasps left me alone. That they have a sense of living threats. Maybe I was close enough to dead to trick them, but I more think that's another miracle of the day. I love you! I'm glad you rode to my rescue. I could hear Sunquist and the other two talking, so I knew when they saw you on that mini-cam. I was praying for a way for you to help me without being captured, too! Shooting the wasp nest was the only answer! And it was brilliant!"

Kerry took a bite of pizza before Amelia pulled him towards another game. Laughing, Tammi helped Avery at the little rides and games.

"I always loved this place when I was a kid," Kerry confided. "The girls are so cute that they make it even more fun. What do you think?"

Tammi laughed. "I think they're wearing me out! We never did anything like this when I was a kid. I grew up in Murfreesboro; remember?"

"Well, yeah, I grew up on an apple orchard, but we went to Spokane occasionally."

"Well, going to Hope was our idea of a big time. And that didn't happen often. We didn't even go to Little Rock or Dallas because gas cost so much. I was always bitter. And then, when the Lord turned things around for us~I don't know~I guess I still always had a problem with Mallie. 'She read her Bible, she had a good attitude, she got good grades.' I always knew my dad wished Mallory was his daughter instead of me."

Kerry grinned, his infectious grin. "Your dad always thought you hung the moon! All of those other things, well he was I guess, trying to wake you up, not to be another Mallory, but to be the best Tammi!"

She nodded before jumping up to pursue her busy charge. As they loaded into the car, exhausted, Tammi caught Kerry's hand. "Look, Kerry, I know this makes you want kids even more than ever~"

"No, Tam, listen. I want your happiness! That's what I've wanted since the first time I saw you! I think you were really sweet to keep the girls so David and Mallory could eat dinner and go to her appointment. And you are good with kids."

He didn't say it, but her recent resubmitting to the Lord was a huge answer to his prayers. And God could give them children when the time was right; His time!

"Your head hurts worse again this morning; doesn't it?" Mallory could tell, and she worried.

"Little bit." He kissed her forehead and reached for a freshly brewed cup of coffee. "I think maybe changing mattresses and pillows, affects me some way."

"Okay, well, which ones seem best? We can throw out the others and get all the same?"

"Well, that's sweet, but I'm not positive that's a factor. Do you mind dealing with the girls? I mean, we can stay in."

Mallory's alarm heightened. David never suggested staying home from church; especially when they were at the *Ranch*. "No, I'll get them both. I better get in gear."

"Girls, mind Mommy and help her get you ready for Sunday School." With that, he turned on the fireplace and kicked the recliner back.

"How's your head?" After church, Mallory fastened Amelia's car seat as David secured Avery. "You want me to drive?"

"No, I'll drive!" His voice and expression were both tense. "Maybe it's just tension from being around my dad. I think it's easing off."

"Okay, because Hal's baked chicken and stuffing sounds really appealing right now." Her eyes glowed.

When he didn't echo her enthusiasm, her spirit dropped. Usually, he was passionate about food! When he felt better! As they neared the lodge, he grinned at her and winked. "Beautiful offertory! And I love the arrangement you wrote using *So Little Time.*"

"Did it sound okay? I planned to run through it some more before we left for Sunday School."

"It sounded great! Sorry I wasn't more help-"

"That's okay. You always do so much." She smiled her brightest, trying not to think about how she might manage three little girls if he didn't spring back. She pushed the thought aside, reminding herself that at least she wasn't a widow.

At the table, with beverages before them and orders placed, Lana turned to her firstborn. "Honey, you look just awful! Daddy and I think you're trying to do too much, too soon!"

David didn't respond, instead, helping his girls with drinks and complimentary biscuits.

"You know, Mallory, I always took care of the kids so John could be free to pastor!"

Mallory fought tears, forcing a smile. "Yes, Ma'am, you guys have been an amazing team." She tried to change the subject; "I really enjoyed that message this morning! Just what I needed"!

"Yeah, Dad, it was good!" David's response as he increased his attention to his daughters. How he and Mallory divided up their responsibilities was none of their business! At least, now he was pretty sure why his head hurt more. "Okay, 'Mea, don't put your drink where you'll knock it over." He set it farther back.

"I like it where I can reach it." She moved it back.

"Amelia!" Her grandfather's voice made her jump with alarm. "Mrs. Tate told me you talked back to her in Sunday School-"

Her little face set defiantly. "I did not neither talk back to her!"

"Okay, Dad, please-"

"Well, David, you need to deal with this."

"And I do, and I will! Just back off, Dad- Can we just enjoy a meal?"

"See, David, you're so cross because you're so stressed. Running all over the countryside chasing dreams-" Lana's assessment again.

David forced a smile for the server who appeared with the girls' plates. He cut Amelia's waffle and warned her about its being hot, while Mallory blew on French fries and broke them into bites for Avery.

"What did you think of Mallie's offertory? She wrote the arrangement, herself!" For some reason, he thought he might salvage the situation.

"Well, I wasn't going to say anything; but it didn't sound the best!" Lana's opinion! "Maybe the piano needs to be tuned again. And I don't know that we need, 'arrangements'. It sounds like you're showing off rather than just trying to be a blessing like you used to be when you played! I'm concerned, Mallory! I just think that the love of money is pulling you away from the Lord, and you drag David along-"

"Like what? A rag doll"? David could hardly believe this was happening! "Why are you both so determined that we aren't in the Lord's will? It's your will that we're not in!"

"David, don't take that tone with your mother."

"Okay, sorry," he mumbled. Getting the server's attention, he requested his and Mallory's meals be packaged to go. "Okay, girls, finish up, so we can go!"

"Mine's still pretty warm." Mallory opened the Styrofoam to expose her baked chicken with dressing, mashed potatoes, and lots of gravy. "Are you going to eat?"

David smiled suddenly. "Yeah, it does look and smell good. Hey, Baby, I'm not sure what put such a burr under their saddles!"

She nodded. "Yeah, they can really hurt my feelings. They're the two people I so much never wanted to disappoint~ I think even more than my dad~"

He took her hand. "Let's pray." He blessed the meal and chewed and swallowed the first bite before gently disagreeing. "No, you always wanted to please the Lord! I care what my dad thinks, too! Still! But it's a lot easier to please God than it is him. Well, in fairness to him, he worries. He doesn't want us to get drawn away, and end up ruined and breaking our kids' hearts. But, ay-ay-ay! I think that his and mom's way of dealing with us is counter-productive!"

She savored a bite of the gravy-laden potatoes and stuffing. "Well, let's don't let it be. Remember when Lilly took Cassandra?"

He laughed, and the tension left his features. "Yeah, I hear you were hoping she'd come get our two. Don't try to deny it~"

She laughed, relieved that his pain seemed to flee with the tension.

"Okay, not confirming or denying~but, I was trying to make a point. Daniel and Diana prayed together until they knew it was the right thing! To let Cassandra go! But, they also knew they would be misunderstood and maligned. We need to make, sure, David, that we're right, that we agree, and that we have the Lord's favor! Then we won't be so thrown by the opinions of others!"

"Well, I wouldn't say I'm thrown by their opinions; but there's no sense in their being mean to you and the girls!"

She nodded. "Amelia does talk back, though!"

"Yes, and we work on it. But I'm not snatching her out of a high chair in a restaurant and marching her out for a spanking just to impress my dad! 'Witch Tate' told me about the deal when I got her from junior church. Evidently deciding I'm an incompetent dad, she mentioned it to my dad, too. And, by now, probably everyone else in the county"!

Mallory shook her head sympathetically. He was right. Mrs. Tate always seemed to hate the Calvary Baptist kids, way back when she and David were smaller and beneath her jurisdiction. And she was a gossip!

"Okay, I shouldn't have called her a witch."

Mallory shrugged. "Yeah, it's amazing, that she hates the job and hates kids, but she won't quit and let anyone else do it!"

"Yeah, that's church work; and my dad wonders why I don't want to pastor. I mean, we've done a lot of soul-searching- Mallory, I'm so happy doing what we're doing! I love our life! I love sharing responsibility for looking after the girls; I love the business and phone-calling. I love running job crews! And traveling and seeing new places. I never told you, but you used to get on my nerves quoting that poem about:

All I could see from where I stood,
Was three, long islands, and a wood."

She laughed. "You're wrong! I think you told me all the time! I just quoted it anyway because that was how I felt! The Lord has opened up the vistas. I never want to stop giving Him the glory! Do you really think that my piano playing-"

"It's beautiful, Mallory. I'm sorry that dumping the load of getting the girls ready made it so you couldn't run through it again this morning. But it was flawless. And the piano is in tune. My mom's so tone deaf she doesn't know if it is or isn't, but she's going to address the way you play! Consider the source and don't let her get to you!" He regarded her pensive expression. "I know; easier said than done!" He rose, changing the subject again. "That was good; want some ice cream? Are you going to nap?"

She hopped up. "Yikes! No! Deborah's coming! Something she's been worrying about and that she wants to explain face-to-face! I guess your parents really got to me; they made me forget to worry about whatever Deborah's hitting me with!"

Mallory hugged Deborah warmly, then pushed her away to regard her in wonder. "You look adorable! Come on in. Coffee or pop?"

"Maybe water! You look great, too." Deborah accepted the water and followed Mallory to chairs facing the fire place in the great room. She fidgeted nervously.

"Well, the reports and numbers look great! Wh-what has you concerned?"

"Okay, well, we did something-uh, I guess to see if we could-"

Mallory frowned in puzzlement. "Okay, who do you mean by we?"

"Tia Rose! Uh, she wanted more pay, and I tried to tell her-and so-"

"What? She quit? You gave her too much? Are you in tax trouble?" Mallory fought panic.

"No! None of that! We should have told you, but it worked so easy~and then with David~"

"Okay what worked so easy?" Mallory couldn't imagine; drugs? embezzlement?

Here! I am telling you. My aunt Tia, she want more money, and she doesn't like the sewing. And so I thought of this plan! And it went like clockwork. Except I meant to tell you and Mrs. Diana about it right away, and then~ But Tia and some of the others like cutting out the pieces, and so, when, you know, woman, minority~"

Mallory nearly went limp with relief. "So, you helped her get a loan and start her own corporation; and her company does all of the cutting~ That is amazing! I'm so proud of you!"

Deborah sat up straighter. "Yes, we were proud that we could do it. I had a problem with Tia then, because she wanted to make a bigger profit by cutting a little off-grain to get more pieces cut. But I refused the poor quality pieces and she had to take the loss for messing up. She got mad at me and Mama. But Mama just told her, we make nice things and we don't cut corners. And she can cut off-grain, but we won't work with her. Now she is being careful to fill our orders correctly."

Mallory breathed a sigh of relief. "Yeah, family's hard to stand up to. Glad your mom had your back! Deborah, that's incredible, though! And hey, about those two VIP cruises you finessed your way into?"

"Yes, I'm glad they worked for you. My family enjoys the Caribbean because they like the Latino cultures and they can sometimes meet with relatives for shore excursions. You gave the trips away?"

"Yes, and they got us lots of mileage with our nursing administrator at *Shady Grove*. She took her mother with her, and they're of Norwegian descent! Ella got to meet relatives she never expected to, and her mom was thrilled to see family after so many years. When she got back, she asked how we knew to put together a Scandinavian trip. We didn't! The Lord did it! Of course, her pictures turned out so gorgeous, that now we all wish we hadn't said, 'Scandinavia? Eh?'"

Deborah sighed loudly with relief. "Well, I've been so nervous~"

"Well, you're just amazing to have handled your aunt like that~ I'll call and tell Diana, but she'll be amazed and delighted, too. Are you heading back to Texarkana this afternoon?"

"Yes, I think; but you must come and see how everything is now, sometime. I know you are very busy, and we are so relieved about David!"

"Would you like to stay the night in the guest cabin?" Mallory's sudden inspiration. "We're leaving for church in a little while. In the morning, I'm not sure what David's plans are, but I can come see the operation. Chow hall serves sandwich makings on Sunday afternoon, but you're welcome to eat down there. Actually, you're invited to go to church with us, too."

"Uh-I don't know. I am Catholic."

"Well, no pressure. I'll get the cabin key and the key for the golf cart!"

"Hello, Mallory, where are you this week?" Diana's voice cheerful, as Mallory answered her phone.

"Arkansas! We spent a couple of days in Dallas to dig out some of the paperwork there, and for me to go to the doctor. Then we came on to the *Ranch*. Are you in Tulsa?"

"Actually, we're nearly to the *Ranch*, too! Honey Grove went to two morning services; we go to the early one. So, we decided to head that direction. The kids are excited that you're there. Actually, Cassandra is making a recording Tuesday morning. We're flying Phil in to handle the session."

Mallory disconnected as their vehicles paused for the gates to admit them. She grabbed Cassandra as soon as the girl crawled out of the back. "You're making a CD?"

"Yes and would you pray that I sell some? I kind of got in trouble."

"Oh you did?" Mallory waited for details, but they didn't come. "Well, you look really cute. Love your new hairstyle; it makes you look grown up."

"Look, Mom, Deborah's here!" Alexandra waved eagerly, and sprinted toward the guest cabin.

"Is everything okay with the Rodriguez'?" Diana's expression showed concern. "They've acted stand-offish."

"Yeah, guilty consciences! They spun her Aunt Rose off into her own corporation; got the minority-woman business loan all on their own, then rented and renovated two more facilities, in both Miami and Texarkana, to specialize in cutting out the garment pieces! They did a stellar job; I'm going to Texarkana with her in the morning to look it over. Well; depending on what David wants me to do. If y'all are hungry-sandwiches-"

"Yes, and we're wandering that direction. How's David?" Daniel's words of greeting!

"Better! I think; I hope! But today he woke up with quite a bit of pain. He's not sure if it's the different pillows and mattress! Or the ever-present tensions with his dad. We invited his mom and dad to join us for lunch at Hal's, and it didn't go well! I'm not sure if he's even planning to go tonight! I'll go wake the girls up and join you for a sandwich. Hey, I invited Deborah to church; why don't y'all ask her, too?"

John Anderson sat in the church office gazing out at the quiet little street. After finishing lunch quietly with Lana, he dropped her at the house and sought the solitude of his office. Of course, her tendency was to blame Mallory for David's anger at them. He sighed deeply, then rose to pace. "Lord, this has been a torturous year! Thank You for bringing David back, when they said-" He didn't bother mopping at tears. "It's easy for me to be against what they're doing. Because it scares me; not being in control! Maybe I'm even a little jealous that a goofy kid like Billy Blaire-okay, not goofy, but definitely a kid-okay, so none of them are really kids anymore. He has a place to minister and people are getting saved- Father, please let me see someone saved tonight! Maybe that's what's frustrating me! And I did take it out on them! I'm accusing them of getting cold, and being drawn away; I guess it's me!"

Chapter 8: GEOLOGY

David slanted a glance toward his gorgeous wife. "Why do you always have to have such a great spirit?"

Mallory laughed. "Well, thanks, but I don't always, and I don't now! You were really planning on not going tonight, weren't you?"

"Yeah," he admitted, "until all of the planets aligned and I was outnumbered by myriads of Super-Christians!"

"Yeah, the Faulkners' showing up and Deborah's decision to attend! Well, I knew we needed to go tonight, even before Deborah and the Faulkners showed up! My faithfulness is to the Lord, and not to your mom and dad! I mean, David, they were so instrumental in my being where I am today! And yeah, they kind of hurt my feelings, but how often I grieve the Lord with my carelessness!"

He laughed. "Okay, don't preach! We're on the way to church, and I'm sure I'll be dead in my dad's sights!"

"Okay, let me tell you something amaaazinnng!"

"Amaaazinnng? Okay, I'm all ears!"

"The reason we haven't heard much from the Rodriguez' is, that first of all, they're always afraid they're bothering us, or they'll wake the girls! But even more so recently, was because Deborah's Aunt Rose came to her, wanting to do only cutting out and no sewing! And demanding more money-"

"Yeah? I hope Deborah told her to hit the road!" He caught her look. "But let me guess, using amazing tact and diplomacy, she saved the day!"

Mallory pretended to pout. "Boo! You figured it out, and ruined my story!"

"Yeah, Erin! I always could read you like a book! But, I can tell you're dying to fill me in with the details!"

She directed her gaze out her window. "Not really! You're the one who's dying to hear them!"

"Hmmmm, no, you want me to guess! I'll play! Something big they were afraid to spill to us over the phone while my head was cracked open! I concede defeat!"

"You do? Your head still hurts; doesn't it?"

"It feels better. I'm just giving in because I can't guess and I want to know!"

He nodded approval as she finished the narrative and they reached the church. "That is amazing! Of course, she learned from the best! Employees who make waves usually have some leadership qualities, and if you can work with them, and salvage them, it's usually advantageous on both sides. Let's say a quick prayer for Deborah to hear and accept the Gospel. Maybe with a first time visitor, my dad will home in on her, and save his salvo intended for me for another day!"

"You always have such ulterior motives!"

He shrugged. "What can I say?"

"Ms. Diana is upset." Deborah's voice showed anguish. "She shook my hand and said she's happy I trusted Christ, and then she took off. She doesn't even want to go have dinner together with me!"

Mallory hugged her friend. "That isn't it at all. Don't get paranoid. What you've done is astounding! Simple! So simple we never considered it, but now we see how profound it is!"

"You have done this before; making good employees incorporate–"

"Right! But, Diana rushed back to the *Ranch* to make some calls to her garment manufacturer. You and your Aunt Rose know how crucial the cutting process is!"

"Sure, Ms. Diana drill that into us!"

"Yes, but the way Amber has always run Diana's factory was by having each employee take each garment from the beginning phase to its completion. Consequently, the same seamstresses always turn out the same quality of finished garment. And the problem is that a few of them have a tendency to get in a hurry with the layout and cutting. You know how cutting even slightly off-grain makes the entire garment out of whack!"

Deborah, nodded, catching on to Mallory's line of reasoning. "So she is separating out cutters, who know what they're doing and like that job the best!"

"Mmm-hmmm! Well, we've had an escalating problem with shrinkage in the inventory. Not the fabric's shrinking, but theft! Well, we assumed it must be theft!"

Deborah nodded eagerly. "Just, lots of goods damaged by hurried and wrong cutting! Maybe you can always rip out stitching and sew again. But once the fabric is cut, mistakes can't be undone! Still, Amber should track and report ruined yardage!"

"You're good! Come on, lets' go eat. I'm starved. I always miss Diana too, but this was too big for her to wait on! It's already well into Monday at the factory, and she was going to make lots of related calls! Maybe she'll be finished in time to go to Texarkana with us in the morning!"

A church crowd settled in around the big table at Hal's. "Where's Jer?" Daniel's surprised question to Alexandra.

"He went with Mom. Sometimes he helps with her business calls."

"He does? Why have I not known that?" Handsome features showed displeasure at the new revelation.

"Not sure, Dad; just sometimes Mom thinks that a deep masculine voice is more effective. Mom always deals with Amber, but I guess she was going to contact the landlord and also an air conditioning guy."

"Yeah; why?"

"Well, I guess Mom was talking to Amber about the best way to up benefits, and Amber said everyone would be happy just to have the factory air conditioning working again! But then it turned into a mumbo-jumbo, that the air conditioning people need the landlord's approval! Which, since it's his building, he actually should keep the systems all working! But I guess he's throwing a monkey wrench into Mom's being able to get it done! I think he's trying to raise the rent as kind of extortion for letting her fix the air!"

Daniel's scowl deepened. "Your mother and I may need to go over there and pay a visit in person!"

"Well, maybe so, but Jeremiah's pretty smooth."

Well, let's get our food ordered and eat kind of quick. I didn't realize your mother was dealing with that kind of junk!"

Alexandra laughed. "Well, sure, but we do it all the time!" She reached a bejeweled, manicured hand into the fragrant basket of rolls.

Diana finished the Skype sessions and sat regarding the blank monitor. Frankly amazed, she chuckled delightedly. "I think I should probably pay Tia Rose a finder's fee!"

"Yeah, maybe so," Jeremiah agreed. "I mean we follow the mandates of *The One Minute Millionaire*, to take a minute of time here and there and think of improvements and minor adjustments to what we're doing, that will make dramatic increases farther along the continuum. And yet you could puzzle and puzzle, and not come up with this new angle!"

"Yes, that really isn't a new angle at all! Division of labor! I mean, Mallory just did it effectively at the *Enclave* with the chow hall and child care. Letting people specialize in what they like and are good at, and freeing others to work within their gifts. I never considered, though, dividing up the tasks of garment construction. I mean, I know it's a process used in mass production!"

"Yes," Jeremiah inserted. "But our line is too special for mass-production! We incorporate far more workmanship and artistry! But that's no reason not to step up the process where we can without reducing quality! Aunt Rose was right. The workers who enjoy the laying out and cutting do a better job than the ones who whack it up so they can get to the part they enjoy the most! Well, what do you think Dad will say about our new negotiations? And who exactly do you have in mind to renovate the two new sites?"

Diana laughed. "Not David, you'll be surprised to learn. But I've learned some lessons from his and Mallory's experiences in Arizona!"

"What? Not to import labor to places that have high unemployment rates?"

Diana laughed. "Yes exactly! I'm thinking about Deborah's cousin, who is so good at fine finish work. If I can help get him set up with his own business, he could go over there, and all of his expenses would come out before taxes. He could hire a crew among locals. I think he'd be a good manager with his Latino background of being in less of a hurry than we are!"

"Okay, so you're thinking he'd be just laid back enough to understand the slower-than-a-turtle-mindset, but still get some productivity?"

"Wow, were you aware that the field of Geology was started by this Hutton guy for the sole purpose of challenging 'Creation'?" David's eyes met Mallory's across the master suite at the *Ranch.*

She couldn't resist digging back. "Uh-Yeah! First day! First chapter! The same as you"! She laughed. "The incredible thing is, that the reality dispels all of the 'old earth theories' they so desperately espouse, and backs up the Bible! The beginning course is annoying though, because it's all that Geo-babble of naming layers by Jurassic Park sounding names. I wish the discipline would deal with facts and leave the unobservable, hence the unsupportable, to the Philosophers!"

He laughed in response. "Yeah, it should just lead us straight to the Diamonds."

She nodded enthusiastically. "Don't laugh at Diamonds."

"Oh, I wouldn't. And besides that, there are lots of other treasures down there."

"Well, I disagree with Marilyn Monroe about 'Diamonds being a Girl's Best Friend'! Jesus is my best friend; and then you. I do laugh, though, that I found that big pink stone one day when I was out in dress clothes and high heels. And the Forestry guys laughed that Nan Burnside prospected in high heeled boots. I've decided that maybe Diamonds decide to show themselves to girls who know how to appreciate them!"

"Well, did my mom and dad apologize to you? Not to change the subject! And it's amazing about Deborah!"

"Yes it is, and that's what matters. The devil wants church members at cross-purposes so the Gospel gets side-tracked. But I keep thinking about what your mom said about the piano needing to be tuned. It's okay, but, do you think they're in a money crunch? That might make them on edge."

He frowned. "I wouldn't think so. The board voted to raise their percentage of what the ministry brings in. They should be in better shape than they've ever been in their lives."

She nodded, returning her gaze to a catalog layout. "Unless, maybe the ministry has taken some kind of a hit"! She blushed laughingly. "I never check the site anymore. I used to access it all the time so I could see you."

His tickled giggle erupted in response. "Did you really? Why didn't I ever know that?" A couple of bounds plopped him on the bed beside her.

"Then Sam put a click counter on it, and I tried to be cooler! I wonder if Sam keeps it up-"

"Yeah, because I haven't been! I'm checking it right now. Anyway, my dad apologized, so I felt a little better. Except he still told me we need to deal with Amelia."

"Well, we do. But like you said, we try to chasten her for her benefit and not his gratification."

David's only response was to glance up sharply.

"What? Has it been hacked?"

"You're not kidding! It's awful! I'm shutting it down and calling Erik and Sam! It's-uh-pretty sophisticated-"

Diana joined Mallory and Deborah in the chow hall. "How was dinner last night? I'm sorry I missed it, and Jeremiah felt brutalized. But we accomplished so much! When Daniel got home, he suggested we go straighten things out in person, but between Jeremiah and Skype, we really dealt with some obstacles. While we're in Texarkana today, is there a chance that your talented cousin could join us?"

"Yes; maybe! Which one? You are not taking my workers to your other plant?" Dark eyes snapped.

"Whoa, wouldn't dream of it. I meant your cousin who helped with the housing remodels! Really good, and he gave David his card."

"Yes, but then David never called to give him any jobs. Why do you need a carpenter for your garment businesses?"

Diana laughed at the suspicious attitude. "Well, when I spoke with Amber about improving the benefit package for the workers, she informed me they've been weeks without air conditioning! The landlord hasn't taken her calls, and then when I tried to talk to him, he wanted to raise the rent before he would even give us permission to replace the air conditioning."

"Well, if he is the owner of the building-"

"Yes, but it isn't like it is here, and I forget. Well, the place has gotten rundown, and he refuses to make any improvements. So, we went to an agency and leased two other buildings in the same area. One will house the layout and cutting, and the other will be where the garments are assembled. Both spaces need major renovation, and the new landlord promised remodeling supplies if we provide labor."

"So David is going, and he wants Jorge to work for him finally?"

"Well, actually, Deborah, how good is Jorge? David has so much going on; too much maybe, after such severe injuries. I was wondering if Jorge might start his own business."

"Well, he has passport for going between Honduras. I guess, maybe. Can he get start-up?"

"Well, he isn't a minority woman; but I think he probably still can." Diana laughed. "I'll have my dad start working on getting him a visa to run the Philippines job. He might bring another good worker or two with him, but we're thinking that beyond that, he should hire local labor."

Suddenly excited Deborah pulled her phone free. "I am calling him now!"

David looked up as Mallory peeked into his workshop. "Hey! How was Texarkana?"

"Running like a sewing machine," she quipped. "We're excited! New designs, gorgeous fabrics, growing customer base! The Miami sites are incredible, and Bryce and Lisette are finally getting their heads above water and growing again."

"That's great! Did the girls give you any trouble?"

"Just the usual when they're around Deborah. She picks at them, and then they kind of get out of line-"

He nodded knowingly. "Yeah, they're both so cute she can't leave them alone."

She tiptoed in to better survey his latest project. "That's cute!"

He grinned at the praise, holding the piece up for better inspection. "Just more junk"!

"Seriously, you should mass produce those!"

"Well, the books are copyrighted, so I'm not sure about that-"

"Yeah, but-"

His latest Western-themed project was amazing. Old Western paperback books stacked rakishly, topped by a rusty stirrup; poly-coated to form a lamp base. Coordinating book ends formed of polished cedar and more books completed a set.

"I just made them for my office at the *Enclave*. I read that Geology textbook until my eyes crossed, and then I came out to put the finishing touches on these."

"Hmmm, interesting"! David studied the puzzle pieces on Mallory's desk. "Are you trying to support the 'Continental Drift Theory'?"

She studied her 'Continent' pieces, traced from a Geography book on onion skin paper, then cut out, before responding,

"I'm pretty sure it's already been established beyond reasonable doubt. And it's another thing that backs up the Bible. Where it says in a couple of places that in Peleg's days, the Earth was divided! I'm studying where rich Diamond deposits are known to be. See where the western coast of Brazil would have fit against the eastern African coast? And then India fits up in here, too? I mean, it's a theory; I'm not sure it's viable. Maybe Diamonds are just everywhere. I'm not supposed to be looking, anyway."

"Pretty interesting"!

Lilly scurried from the suffocating confines of her office. Her feelings for Cassandra Faulkner, unbelievably strong, she headed toward Caesarea. Walking along the coastline always lifted her spirits! Well, there was no reason for them to be down. The bad news for Lilly was Cassandra's determination to study nursing. The good news was that Cassandra had accessed her money without her parents' consent to fund some courses. Consequently, she was making a CD to recoup the spent money. Now, Cassandra was determined to choose Christian music rather than classical selections. Lilly didn't know if that was good or bad. Or why she so desperately wanted Cassandra to be a violinist above all. Maybe it was still Lilly's own pride at stake! That she had made a spurious move on the young prodigy. And she wanted the move to play well to the world that was aware of her actions. As she strolled, she admitted that she didn't really know what would ultimately be best for the girl, and she should leave it to the Lord to sort out. Feeling somewhat better, she purchased a gelato.

"Lilly!"

The voice made her jump!

"Benjamin! What brings you out here?"

"And what do you think?"

"Spying on me?"

He laughed. "So suspicious, Lilly! To say that I am looking out for you sounds so much nicer. A storm is coming."

She nodded, aware of the increasing wind, rising swells, and dark clouds. "I love storms on the sea."

He laughed. "Still, we should watch it from inside."

Within the protection of a small café, he took her in with an amused gaze. Taking a sip of strong, hot coffee, he directed his attention beyond the plate glass at the barreling storm's approach. "You may be surprised, my Dear, to learn, that I was as surprised to see you here, as you were, me. Although we both like to come here when we need to think! Why would I spy on you? If there was ever a devoted Israeli, Lilly, it is you!" He held up a hand so he could continue. "Yes, I know that your detractor's try to use your conversion against you, and it plays well with many Israelis! When the national stance is still that of vehemently denying Jesus as Messiah, your turning to Him makes you suspect! But I know better! I know it has made you better in every way! And my prayer is as yours, that our nation would turn to the One Who gave Himself for us! Sadly, our people will suffer very many more terrible atrocities before that day!" He sighed heavily.

Not sure how to respond, Lilly licked at stray rivulets of gelato.

"You have not asked me what heavy thoughts brought me out here for a walk. You are not even a little bit curious?" Serious eyes probed hers.

"The task you have set for yourself is daunting. The question would be why you are not out here more often." She wearied of parleying with a mind far more brilliant than her own.

"No!" His forceful voice made her jump. "My daunting task, I hit head-on day after day! I know what to do, and I do it! And we are making headway, Lilly. Although, if I had heeded your words years ago, the problem would not have reached this scope! No, what leaves me puzzling-" his dynamism flagged as he fought sudden emotion, "is how to undo what I did to us."

Some strange force of physics caused the gelato to propel itself from her hand into her lap. He held such a strong sway over her, still. She struggled with tears and profound embarrassment.

Then, suddenly, he was beside her, retrieving the cone and wiping at the mess. On one knee, his eyes met hers. "Lilly, would you honor me by at least considering-" His voice trailed away. "Please, Lilly. There would be no reason for you ever to forgive me-"

"Well, there's nothing to forgive. Just, we were incompatible, is all!"

"Yes, we fought about everything. And for the longest period of time, I thought that Michael was the only good thing to come of it. I was arrogant, unforgivably arrogant, and I was a sexist, refusing to acknowledge your wisdom and intellect! I thought I knew all; and that you knew nothing! And treated you accordingly! The best gift God ever allowed me, and-" He fought ravaging emotion as he knelt there, clasping her hand.

"Look what came!" David's voice was jubilant as he waved a handful of official looking papers.

"The permits from the state of Louisiana? Or another refusal?"

"The permits! Where are we starting?"

Doubt clouded Mallory's countenance. "Good question. Maybe I should reanalyze the data."

He nodded, trying not to show disappointment. They had studied and studied the data before beginning the expensive and time-consuming task of getting the drilling permits. He didn't want to be hasty, but neither did he want to suffer from paralysis of analysis. "That's a good idea. Anything I can do to help?"

She studied him thoughtfully. "Do you want to help me study the images?"

"Yeah, but we really need to upgrade our equipment. We need a big plasma monitor and we also need to be able to receive well logging readings right here in the office. Stuff, which I know costs; but is it costing us more by delaying the inevitable?"

"What kind of cost are we talking about? Ballpark figure! You know cash flow as well as I do."

"I can call Sam and get a better estimate. Maybe he has an inroad for a discount, too. I don't mind helping you look the images over on this little monitor, magnifying section by section. But what if we overlook something significant by doing it that way?"

"I know you're right! Why be stone age rather than cutting edge? Let's go for it. If Sam can get right on top of helping us upgrade, fine! Otherwise, you know enough to do it."

She laughed nervously. "Okay, uh, Lord, did You hear us? We're going for it. You instruct us to move forward in faith-"

David frowned. "Okay, Sam's phone went to voicemail; I'll leave a message."

Suddenly decisive, she shook her head. "No; let's just do it! ASAP! These permits are a miracle, and they don't test the limit of what God has for us. Remember *John 16:24*?

> *Hitherto have ye asked nothing in my name: ask, and ye shall receive, that your joy may be full.*

Lord, we need more operating capital to move forward. Thank You for helping us to get the permits. We're taking that as a sign to move forward. We really need some cash to flow in that we aren't aware of."

David disappeared and then resurfaced in her office forty minutes later. "Okay the new components are ordered to be installed in the morning. Let's go eat lunch in the mezzanine and head home. Want to invite Herb and Linda to join us?"

Bright eyes showed her agreement. "If they can break away on such short notice, I'd love to see them."

David buckled Avery into a high chair and hoisted Amelia onto a booster seat. Mallory waved at her aunt and uncle. "Awesome to see you"! She hugged them both and David shook hands.

With orders placed, Mallory addressed her aunt, "You look fabulous! What's new?"

"Well, just what you know. We've had a good year and orders are growing. Are you planning to go to the Gem Show in New York?"

"That's entirely up to Alexis Elle. She should make her appearance well before that time! I'm not sure how much I can accomplish-"

"We can accomplish whatever we need to," David asserted!

Mallory's phone rang as they finished praying for the meal. She frowned. Lilly! Usually, she wasn't particularly talkative; maybe she already knew about the Louisiana drilling permits. But Diamond exploration wasn't the sole thrust of that. She started to refuse the call, then, thought better of it.

"Hello, Lilly, how are you today?"

"Hello, Mrs. Anderson!" The booming voice alarmed her. "This is Benjamin Cowan."

"Oh, Mr. Cowan; is Lilly okay?" Mallory couldn't imagine why the former Director would call her from Lilly's phone.

"Yes, I think she is fine! She has something to tell you, and then I must speak with you of a business matter! Here is Lilly!" His voice resonated so that the entire group could hear him. Mallory thought he hardly needed the phone.

"Hello, Mallory; we are being married."

Lilly's breathless announcement confused the young executive even more. At a loss for words, she gasped out, "Uh, is that a good thing? I mean, we haven't had a clue-"

"Yes!" Benjamin back in charge of the phone! "Lilly is surprised, too, although I have been pursuing her again for months. She will be very happy!"

By that, Mallory couldn't tell if the powerful Israeli intended to make Lilly happy by the ordinary methods, or if he was just telling her, 'You will be happy!'

"You should congratulate us!"

She found her voice and parroted, "Congratulations!" Then, "Would you like to talk to David?"

"No! Not really!" His bluntness was typical. "I want to talk to you about something you found several years ago! Don't say it! I am interested in acquiring something very special for my bride-to-be-again. Give it to Herbert Carlton because I am calling him next! He will know what I want done! I'll pay top value! Do you trust me?"

"Yes, Sir; I guess so! If Lilly does"!

A quick laugh and he disconnected.

"He's marrying Lilly?" David's voice mirrored her startled expression. "That could cause fireworks!"

"Yes, it did very much with their first go at it." Herb got that revelation out before his own phone vibrated. "It's him," he mouthed as he rose to take the call privately.

Mallory helped both daughters in between her own mouthfuls. She tried not to let her mind and the short talk with Benjamin Cowan carry her away. Still, if he knew of a way to purchase the large pink from her without blowing the secrecy-it would obliterate cash crunches for a good long while. She could hear the murmur of Herb's voice intensifying. Herb would be afraid to cut the stone. Well, she would be afraid to let him. Although, if the Cowans owned the diamond, it would be their call! And evidently they felt Herb was the man. She surfaced from her thoughts to realize Aunt Linda was talking to her.

"Is he talking about what I think he is?" Linda's carefully arched and made-up brow shot up.

"Whatever it is, don't tell anyone!" Mallory knew her order sounded terse. Linda was aware of the extreme confidentiality they all demanded in their businesses. At least Mallory had kept from saying, "Don't tell my Mom."

David was puzzled but refrained from saying more than a few instructions to the girls.

Herb returned to the table with a worried frown. "Will you hire an armored car?" His voice was a whisper, but Mallory felt as though every conversation at the surrounding tables lulled at once.

"That's probably a sound suggestion. I'll take care of it. Not to change the subject, per se, but, how are the jewelry courses going?"

"Very well! The Texarkana classes weren't full last term, but they were so successful that now there's a waiting list. Deborah is enrolled, and very excited to start. A couple of community colleges and one of the universities have invited us to teach courses through their extension outreach. Neither Davis nor I have time to work that in, but it is very nice to have that recognition. Do you remember Candace?"

"Yes Sir, the registration secretary at *Gemhouse*? I only spoke with her a time or two, but I was pretty impressed. Is she a jeweler?"

Herb rocked his hand to indicate 'yes and no'. "I think her administrative skills are her strong point. She's Intermediate, should we say; and so Davis is pushing her in to teach beginning level."

David frowned. "Merc or Samuel can't do it?"

Herb put his index finger to his lips mischievously. “I have them both very busy already.”

“Ah, yes, let’s not jeopardize what’s going on. We don’t want our orders to backlog.” David laughingly turned to wipe a couple of pairs of grimy little hands. “Yikes no! Don’t touch me!”

Both girls laughed and tried harder.

Chapter 9: GEMSTONE

"Thanks!" Mallory disconnected and dropped her head into her arms on her desk. Tense morning! "Thank you, Lord," she breathed. She still felt a heavy concern. Armored cars never pulled up at *Carlton, Corporation*, and as far as she was aware, few people knew that the plain warehouse-looking facility stored vast quantities of valuable materials. Of course, there were state-of-the-art security measures in place. She just wished Herb hadn't brought up the subject of an armored car in the busy café. Her preference would have been to leave the rough Diamond wrapped in the paper that stuffed the toe of one of her shoes. Walking into his business with a shoebox beneath her arm wouldn't have sent out shock waves like declaring value of the Diamond for the armored carrier. The value rendered was a low estimate. She really didn't know the value! Lots! She hoped! She wondered vacantly if Benjamin was aware of the gem's size and clarity. He must be! Because Lilly had seen it, and she knew Diamonds like no one else Mallory could think of. Strange, to think of Lilly's being married. Mallory was unaware of the formidable woman's previous marriage. Always assuming she was a spinster. So, Lilly would end up getting the Diamond she craved! So like the Lord to do things like that for His children. And it would certainly help *DiaMo*! Well, that is, unless it blew the cover and sent hoards of rumor-crazed prospectors tearing up western Arkansas!

Such a delicate balance! She admired Lilly for achieving it. She buzzed David.

"Hey, you hungry?" came his response.

She laughed. So like him; his head seemed much better for the past week. Maybe he was healing up, "Getting that way! I buzzed to tell you that the 'robin egg is in the nest'."

He chuckled, "Duly noted down into my Audubon Society log book! I'll gather up the girls. The tech guys are on their way now, too!"

The intercom buzzed and Mallory disconnected from David's extension. "Yes, Marge; what is it?"

"Uh, there's a court officer out here to serve you with some papers."

She forced her upbeat tone. "Okay; I'll be right out." She checked her reflection before hurrying to the reception area. Smiling, she accepted the documents and made her way quickly back to her sanctuary. "Okay, this probably isn't good from my vantage point," she confided to the Lord. "But from Your viewpoint, I know there's a reason." She split the envelope adeptly and scanned the writ. She frowned. Evidently she was being sued for trespassing and drilling illegally on someone else's property. She hadn't a clue how that could be, until she returned her attention to the injured parties.

"Okay, Lord, this is nuts! We've had things in position for weeks, to sink a borehole here. Pritchard and Halsey have intentionally purchased and taken possession of this land; and made sure we haven't been notified!" Of course, the damages specified are astronomical! If she could beat it, it would cost a lot in court costs and legal fees; and if she couldn't~ And they had an army of slick attorneys and all she had was Kerry! "Oh, yes, Lord, and You, too! It's so easy to forget and start trying to figure out how to fight my own battles!"

The tech team appeared, and she relinquished her office to them, hurrying to find David.

"Are you hungry? Why don't you call Kerry to join us at the café? We got served~" She proffered the documents and went to round up the girls while he made the call.

"Have you had a fun morning?" If the litter of toys was any indication, they should have been having a blast. She helped find shoes and get them on.

"Mommy, I miss my fwiends in Awizona. When can we go back?"

She hugged Amelia and kissed her bright curls. "Soon! We can talk to Daddy about it tonight maybe."

"Or, at lunch! I'm hungry! I want pancakes!"

"Well, they don't have pancakes."

"I want Awizona pancakes. Let's talk to Daddy at lunch."

"Well, Uncle Kerry's joining us for lunch, and Daddy and Mommy have important stuff to talk to him about!"

"You always have important stuff to talk about! My stuff's important!"

"Amelia, don't stamp your foot at me! I want to go back to Arizona, too; before the new baby comes. We'll work on it; don't talk back!"

"I wasn't!"

David crossed the room in a bound and scooped her up. "I'm pretty sure you were! And you are important, and what you have to say."

Finding a balance between 'Children should be seen and not heard'; and letting them take over, was challenging!

Avery jerked at his trouser leg and he bent and scooped her up, too. "Yep, you two beautiful girls are important to Daddy. And, I guess we all miss our friends in Arizona! But who do you miss most? Mr. Charles? I thought I was your best boyfriend!"

Amelia's blue eyes grew serious in a cute, puzzled expression. "No! You're not my boyfriend! You're my daddy!"

Kerry looked the papers over briefly. "So, you're saying that Halsey and Pritchard found out where you were planning to drill, and they secretly bought that parcel, just so they could sue you?"

David nodded; certain of the fact! "The property's basically a swamp along the Atchafalaya. The property owner makes the guys on *Swamp People*, look like high society! We paid him a fee for the easement and got the permit from the state of Louisiana. We barely started yesterday afternoon. They were ready with these papers before our crew set foot on the place!"

Kerry frowned and swirled his iced tea glass. "So, has your schedule been delayed?"

"Our schedule always seems to get delayed!" Mallory's frustration registered in spite of her attempt to stay calm and trust God.

"Well, that may be in your favor in this case!" More ice swirling, and then Kerry drummed on the table edge. "Have you contacted the drillers and told them to stop until further notice?"

"Uh, no-" She dug for her phone. "I should have thought of it." She made the call and returned her attention to the attorney.

"I'm going to get with Carmine and Jacobson, but I think we can prove their malice in this unethical action."

"Well, yes, and actually, we've always tried to be nice to them, even when they were undercutting us."

Kerry nodded. "You should have sued them before. They don't have the capacity to understand your ethics and mind-set. To them, you were just willing to pay to avoid trouble. That's what they want here, too. For you to settle out of court! They seem to think you're made of money and you're a soft touch. Sometimes-"

"You have to play hardball," she finished for him.

Mallory snuggled next to David. "So, what do you think about making a quick trip to the *Enclave*?"

"Well, if it were a quick trip, I'd be all for it; but it's quite a drive!"

"So, let's fly!"

He laughed. "You're so smart! Why didn't I think of that? I guess I was thinking about needing my truck when we get there!"

"Well, let's get another truck and leave it, so we have one at both places!"

He pulled her close and kissed her lingeringly. "Okay, I'm all for it. I'll go see about booking tickets reasonably on the spur of the moment."

Herb gazed in awe at the stone which rested before him on his workbench. In spite of Benjamin and Lilly and their jibes, he was not touching it! It was going to Tel Aviv where it could be properly assessed and handled by cutters at the top of their game. His having cut and polished *Radiant Dawn* seemed foolhardy in retrospect. To his surprise, Linda agreed.

"Well, I know little about any of it, but your strength is in jewelry design; utilizing gemstones that are already cut and polished to their most advantageous. Let the others do what they do, and free yourself for what you do best! That's what Deborah Rodriguez and her aunt figured out, even within the field of clothing manufacture."

Herb nodded. "Well, I couldn't agree more. And one of the reasons Benjamin has been pushing me is that I'm in Dallas and so is the Diamond.

Now, they agree that there's no rushing such a perfect stone! They are marrying now and getting the ring in its proper time-frame. Actually, they are married in Israel. But because their American friends could not get there quickly, they are coming to the states for Pastor Anderson to perform a Christian ceremony."

Linda considered briefly, but then curiosity got the better of her. "How much is the Diamond worth? And how is Benjamin paying for it? I thought from Lilly's carping that Israeli civil servants earn small salaries."

"The walls have ears," Herb warned. He hoped Lilly didn't mind hearing herself referred to as a 'Carper'. He shrugged, remembering a saying that, 'People who eavesdrop never hear good things about themselves'.

"We can talk later," he mouthed.

"Jason isn't picking us up." David wasn't happy with the development, and Mallory's frown indicated she wasn't either.

"What are we supposed to do?"

"Little Feather is coming. He wanted to show us a surprise."

Amelia's features lit up, "And Mr. Charles"?

"Okay, you'll see him soon enough, Amelia." Mallory didn't mind the bond her daughter felt to the Navajo statesman.

"I'm not Amelia! I'm Fire Spirit!"

David rapped her lightly on the head with a couple of fingers. "Watch the backtalk."

Blue eyes widened, but amazingly she made no come-back.

"Mr. Anderson!"

They turned toward the voice and smiled to see Little Feather accompanied by his grandfather.

"So you got the job of picking us up? Thanks!" David extended his hand toward each man before turning back to gather up kids and paraphernalia. Actually, the fact that they had duplicate baby stuff at the *Enclave* uncomplicated some of the struggles involved in traveling with a growing family. "There are five of us and our luggage! I hope you came for us with a U-Haul truck!"

"No!" Little Feather motioned proudly as they exited the terminal. "*Arizona Quad-county Transport, Incorporated*! At your service"!

David and Mallory exchanged delighted glances. "Wow! Look at y'all! What-"

Crazy Feather sat in the driver's seat, grinning happily. "We also got a minority loan to start a business. As you know, I have driven school buses for fourteen years. And, I am a good driver: easy on engine, transmission. So, when the school district upgraded the fleet, we bid on a couple of the buses being retired."

"It's beautiful! Little Feather, you did the artwork; didn't you?"

The younger man nodded modestly. "Yes, and already we have a good ridership. The men working at the quarry now park at the *Enclave* and all ride together to the work site! And we are establishing other routes. Many people hardly have one car that works well, so this helps them while also proving to be profitable."

David laughed in amazement. "So, you got the loan; you've incorporated; you have insurance and everything?"

"Yes, Sir"! Crazy Eagle rose from the driver's seat to make way for his father. "As you know, I lost my position driving the school bus due to my drinking problem. So, I administrate our new company, but I lost my CDL. Our costs would be lower starting up, if I could drive, too! But that's what happens when you mess up! I'm amazed things are not much worse!"

Herb and Linda sat together on a bench at the Dallas Arboretum. "This is a nice get-away." Linda's remark reflected her puzzlement at the atypical outing.

Herb chuckled and kissed her. "You are wondering if I have you confused with your sister. Truly, she is the flower lover. Take some pictures to send her if you'd like. We should get something from the hefty admission price besides a private place to talk."

"Oh, so you didn't forget that I asked about the value of that Diamond, and how Benjamin Cowan can afford it! I mean, stones like that are usually jointly owned by investors; aren't they? And worth millions! And how can Mallory receive that much cash without a tax hit?" Her words were reminiscent of Mallory's refusal and inability to accept lavish gifts from them.

"Both very good questions! To begin with, Benjamin is a brilliant man; and then he is also privy to so much information! I wouldn't say he's an 'inside trader', but he's in a position to know things and seize upon opportunities. He would be foolish not to. As to your second question about cash like that flowing to Mallory; she and David have been investing so heavily in all of their businesses and projects, that a great portion of the money has already been reinvested, even before they receive it. You might even say that they've been out on the proverbial limb! I'm not sure what kind of pickle they might have gotten themselves into-" He paused, shrugging. "Many people think that they are loaded with money! And of course, they appear to be so. And they could sell off assets to get cash if necessary. They walk by faith more than anyone I have ever known!"

Linda nodded thoughtfully. "That all makes sense."

He laughed. "I still haven't told you the value of the stone! I don't know, and I'm sure it will be a closely held secret! It's the most beautiful thing I've ever seen!" He sighed, then thinking quickly, added gallantly, "Present company, excepted, that is!"

"Oh, you're so nice! You know, when I think how close I came to refusing Mallory's invitation to visit Turkey with everyone-" She dabbed at sudden tears. "And she kind of hurt my feelings and made me mad! She was just a seventeen year old, and I barely knew her; I was never close to Suzanne and they lived a long way away!"

Herb nodded. "Very lucky for me that she shook you loose from your rut! I was in something of a rut myself! Mallory is truly a remarkable young woman. The wonder is the way she allows God to use her. She was the catalyst for us coming to the Lord and meeting each other."

"Yes, and then even when the trip was over, she brought me up short for trying to 'play it cool' with you! Frankly, she thought I was too old, and you were too good of a catch, for me to risk such childish games!" She laughed self-consciously.

"Well, to a seventeen year old, perhaps, you might have seemed old; but I have felt like a cradle robber for marrying you. You make me feel younger and fuller of life than I felt for many years!"

Mallory's phone rang as the *Quad-county* bus neared the gates of the *Enclave*. It was word from the local attorney: there was no response to the notice requesting information on any of Rudy Sunquist's possible heirs. The truck and the cabin were David's as soon as he paid taxes and court and attorney fees. She thanked the receptionist and disconnected, hoping the antique truck was worth as much as David thought it should be.

"Okay, once we pay up with court and legal fees and taxes, the truck and cabin, and the contents of said, are yours. Since Rudy was a squatter with no title to the land, the acreage doesn't transfer."

"I'm surprised we get the cabin."

"Well, probably because it's an eyesore; they're probably hoping we tear it down."

"Which we will, but, eyesore or not, there's a thriving market in used lumber." He smiled satisfied. "So did you get an inkling of what the bottom line's going to be? Maybe we should hold off on buying a new truck; and I can fix the transmission seals, and drive-"

"M-mm-m; it's just got the one bench seat! No place for the girls at all. Besides, don't you mostly want to restore it as a trophy? We still need to bite the bullet and get something nice and adequate for when we're here."

He nodded. "Any idea of when we'll see revenue from the 'robin egg'?"

"I wish; but still, we need the truck!"

Benjamin faced his new wife across the table at their favorite sidewalk café. "The stone should give a high yield of gem to discard. It literally presents no problems for the polishers."

"I've known you long enough, to be aware when you're reneging on what you've said." Lilly's tone didn't challenge; she was simply stating a fact.

He shrugged, meeting her gaze ruefully. "The fault is mine! You described the Diamond to me, but it's been years since you saw it, and I thought maybe in your mind it had grown larger and finer than it actually was. Once again, I underrated you and your assessment of a situation."

She nodded. "You assumed that it would require cleaving into two pieces. Most large stones include flaws that require them to be divided up in cutting. I thought-was afraid-from the moment you suggested it, that it wasn't really workable for a ring setting!"

"Unless you want a ring that is beyond ostentatious"!

Lilly laughed. "Well, ostentation wouldn't bother me, but the proportion would be-not even artistic!"

"I wanted to present it to you in a wedding set, Lilly. My love and appreciation for you~"

"Yes, but it won't work! It's far too large for a ring, and it would be a crime to reduce the size to make a ring setting! And, it's still such a problem. Mallory is counting on money coming in for it, but if we try to put it up for auction, we have to prove its origin! And if word gets out that Arkansas produces such stones~" Her countenance was troubled. "Thank you for loving me; I trust you to present me with a very nice ring, but we cannot~"

He nodded. "And you are right; we cannot auction the *Lilly Rose.* To prove that it is not a conflict diamond, we would have to prove its origin in the US, and that would be unwise. But we cannot simply ask Mallory to take it back and stash it forever in her shoe. She has been so reasonable, and such a friend; I credit you with that, Lilly!"

Lilly burst into laughter. "Maybe you should credit it to our Messiah! I waded in and made a mess with everyone involved!"

He joined in the rollicking laughter! "Yes, that's right! Barging in and grabbing Cassandra! For who knows what reason? And then tangling with Trent Morrison for trying to help the Faulkners, which involved your also pulling tricks on Simon Cohen here! On second thought, how did they all become your friends?"

Lilly sobered quickly. "As I was saying, I praise God for how He has worked things out for my good and His glory. You were saying that we can't leave Mallory hanging with her diamond back and no money."

"Yes, we will personally purchase the diamond from her and keep it in a safety deposit box, maybe in London. We can front two million into one of her corporations and then continue adding installments annually. The diamond will still be yours, Lilly. And I have named it the *Lilly Rose.* And I have purchased us a property in London. Your position as head of our Diamond agency could be better served by more of your presence there."

She nodded, enchanted at the idea of owning Benjamin's Tel Aviv home and another in London. The Lord really did bless! And not only the beautiful and charmed Mallory O'Shaughnessy! But plain, drab, little Lilly Cowan, too! "Yes, that would be very nice," she managed.

He nodded and pulled a box free. "Thank you for understanding my changed plans." He opened the box and she gasped in wonder.

"Oh~Benjamin~"

"Cassandra, you look so grown up! And so gorgeous"! Mallory hugged her 'little sister' before pushing her away to survey her again. Cassandra sported a cute new haircut for a polished look on her CD cover photo. Now as Lilly's bridesmaid, she wore a touch of lip gloss and mascara for the special occasion. "I think these dresses are the cutest things your mom has ever designed to date! And I love your CD!"

Cassandra beamed. "Yes, now please pray that they sell. Daddy thought classical music would sell better. But I think that there are too many classical violin CDs made by far greater violinists! And, don't misunderstand; I love the classics. But the CD is my heart!"

Mallory nodded. Cassandra's latest was not only Christian music, but strongly missions themed. She wondered if Cassandra was entertaining thoughts of becoming a nurse and surrendering to the foreign mission field.

"You gave me the idea of the CD's title, when you pulled out that song by Dr. John R. Rice to play for the invitation at the new Arizona church."

Mallory blinked back tears, "*So Little Time*! It's a great reminder! And then I love the final song, too, that y'all sing: *The Time Is Now.*

THE TIME IS NOW

The time is now; please do not say,
"There are four months 'til reaping day."
The harvest fields are fully ripe.
Lift up your eyes to fields of white!

There really is no time to waste;
The time is now for urgent haste.
Too few have heard My pleading cries
As all creation groans and sighs.

The time is now: lift up your eyes,
As even now, a lost soul dies.
Please hear My heart, beat for each one.
The race is on! It must be won!

A race to make the message clear,
To souls far off or very near.
Make haste! Make haste! Please don't delay!
To work, to win, to watch, to pray!

Stanza

The laborers are very few.
Lord, please send workers, good and true.
Help us to feel the awful plight!
The time is now! Fast comes the night!

And *So Send I You* has always brought tears to my eyes! Just great selections!"

"Thank you, Mallory. I wish you were in the wedding party."

"Thank you, but I'd rather play the piano, and sing the duet with David. I guess Lilly plans to stay out of site until she walks the aisle. Maybe I'll get a chance to talk to her later. I hope."

"Yes, Michael's escorting her up the aisle!" Cassandra's face flushed as she spoke.

"Michael? Uh, Morrison?" Mallory couldn't put together in her mind why Michael Morrison would perform that duty, but he was the only 'Michael' that came to mind.

"No! Lilly's son, Michael! And Mr. Cowan's son, too, I guess! Michael-is awesome!"

Mallory chuckled at the poised girl's suddenly seeming flustered, "Yeah, awesome how? Tell me more, Cassie! Why don't I know any of this? Lilly was married before! And now she has a son?"

Cassandra laughed. "See, that's what happens when you're so above a little friendly gossip. I wouldn't know about him, except that he used to come to Lilly's apartment in the late nights, when they thought I was asleep. They argued a lot!"

"So, how old is he? Methinks thou hast a crush."

Cassandra blushed again, "Maybe, a little! He's like, maybe thirty-five."

"Thirty-five"!

"S-s-s-hhh, Mallory, keep your voice down! It's you he liked, and he used to fight with Lilly about that; and most everything else!"

"Me? Why would he like me?"

Cassandra laughed. "I guess because you are very beautiful and exceptional!"

"Who is that? Do you know him?" David's stunned whisper as they made their way behind a lattice screen covered with fake flowers.

"Do you?" came Mallory's retort.

"I asked first," he challenged back

"I'm not at liberty~" She took her place on the piano bench and began playing love songs.

"To be continued," he mumbled in her ear.

And then, for Mallory; something even more disconcerting! When Lilly and Benjamin exchanged rings, Lilly's rings were stunning! Stunning *Canary*!

Mallory's heart sank. "Okay, Lord," she prayed silently. "Your power to help me doesn't rest in the pink stone, or in Lilly and Benjamin! Or anything else! There is no searching of your understanding! Or of Your ability to strengthen and sustain! You know the situation~"

Chapter 10: GALVANIZED

Alexis Elle put in her appearance right on cue, and Mallory cuddled her youngest before handing her to David.

"She's beautiful!" He regarded the baby lovingly before snapping several pictures to send to waiting friends and family members.

They were both exhausted. If this was supposed to get easier each time, they weren't seeing the difference.

"Do you still want to try again? For a boy"? Mallory's tearful voice!

"Uh, we don't have to decide that right this minute! As a matter of fact, deciding that now would be a 'snap decision'. Something you usually try to avoid."

She laughed through the veil of tears, relieved by his light-hearted reminder.

"Besides that," he added, "you still have that long list of names; we've only made it through three."

Mallory blushed. David loved teasing her about that! "Well, since I was an only child, I thought it sounded romantic and easy to have a big family."

"Well, as we're learning; nothing in life that's worth having or doing is particularly easy. Yeah, I know; I sound like my dad. Get some rest."

Jay and Sophia were not surprised to lose their lawsuit with the Saxons estate. Undeterred, they filed another suit claiming different damages. The Vincent's assumed the Anderson's suit would probably win them a substantial sum. Sophia was contented to air the truth about Robert John and Bobby Saxon, Jr. And of the many journalists who had given the proceedings some coverage, one was intrigued at the plight of prisoners/slaves being held world-wide. That was gratifying, in and of itself.

Following an early church service they met Uncle Adam and Aunt Barbara for brunch at the country club.

"I do declare that there isn't a speck of justice left in the world!" Aunt Barb's indignation matched the fire in her eyes. "You were up there, with your vision stolen from you, baring your soul-"

"An army of slick attorneys, Aunt Barb," Vincent agreed. "Oftentimes truth, justice, and the American way seem to be trampled in the dust. At least we've made a case that might assist others in being freed."

"Yes, or prevent their being kidnapped to begin with. That's my hope," Came Sophia's fervent words. "I can only do what I can do, and I trust the rest to the Lord."

Adam frowned but refrained from rebuking his niece.

"Wow! You look exceptionally gorgeous! Is there a special meeting today, or something I've forgotten?" David racked his memory.

"No, I just need to look sharp to promote the line." She smiled sweetly.

He nodded understanding. "Ah, with the proverbial wolf at the door, we need to maximize profits. Good thinking, actually. This may not be all bad, if it forces us to think and then do a better job."

Mallory shrugged. "I guess; I just wish I'd hear what's up with my diamond."

"Well, agreed. But since you're dressed up extra-special, we should go out-of-house for lunch. Everyone that eats at the mezzanine café knows about our designs."

"Yes, good point. But at least they're kind of used to the girls and our three-ring-circus. I'm not ready to venture into a nice, new arena of lunchtime-fare until we're more accustomed to dealing with three."

"Let's invite Kerry and Tammi to join us. They both enjoy our girls, and Tammi really has a gift with kids."

"That's kind of sneaky." Mallory's wide ingenuous eyes at the thought of trying to use people, only served to make David smiled evilly.

"Yeah, payback time to the biggest sneak of all times!"

"There's Heather Clark." David sounded tense, having spotted their former employee as they entered the new eatery.

Mallory nodded. "Well, we're committed." She followed the hostess and Kerry and Tammy to a table, holding firmly to each daughter's hand. Amazingly, they all settled in in a fairly orderly manner and Amelia and Avery went to work on coloring sheets.

With orders placed, Mallory rose. "Let's go talk to her. Seeing her gives me another idea."

David followed, a little less certainly.

"Hi, Heather," Mallory began. "How are you? We haven't heard from you in a while."

"Doing well! Gina keeps me in the loop about y'all." She paused before adding, "Somewhat."

Mallory laughed easily. "Meaning she doesn't violate her CDA? You know more about our business than she does, anyway. Listen, it's been a while since we went through our accounts for fraud-"

The other young woman's suspicion seemed to melt. "You're probably right. We can save you some money. I'll revisit your previous contract this afternoon when I get back to the office. Great-looking suit! Can't tell you just had another baby"!

"Thanks, you're too kind." Mallory's ripple of laughter was natural. "How would you like to represent the clothing and jewelry lines again?"

"Are you kidding me? I'd love it! I hear you even send some of your reps on cruises."

Mallory's features set into marble-like perfection. "Occasionally"!

Heather laughed, rising to the challenge rather than backing down. "We'll find a way to save you five thousand a month, gratis."

Mallory shrugged. "Not, 'gratis', exactly! A trade"?

"Seem fair?" Heather questioned.

Nodding agreement, Mallory proffered the most recent design catalog. "Choose five sets of coordinates."

"Wow! Gladly"!

Heather's party arrived and she introduced David and Mallory around.

"They have more business going on than I can keep up with." Heather's awed voice carried. "This is the latest from their fashion lines." She held up the glossy magazine.

Although the newcomers seemed politely interested, Mallory didn't press her business cards on them. But David was right. More exposure didn't hurt.

"Are you planning to tell me the deal with Lilly's son?" David's question erupted, taking Mallory by surprise.

"David, I don't have a 'deal' with Lilly's son. I didn't know she had a son!"

"Okay, I'll buy that. But there's something you're not telling me."

She regarded him steadily. "Yes, and something I can't tell. I'm sorry. It was a long time ago, and not anything romantic or relational at all."

"He's who helped smuggle you back into Turkey." David's perceptive guess! "That would make sense. Bransom and Ahmir have been amazed that anyone could get you spirited, not only back into Turkey, but into Bransom's hotel suite, right under all of their noses. An Israeli operative could possibly have accomplished that-"

"David, I'm not at liberty-"

He sighed. "Have you seen him again since Lilly's wedding?"

"David!"

"Well, where does he live?"

"David, I don't have a clue! My guess would be Israel. Ask Cassandra. She seems to have the inside track-on second thought, don't ask anyone. Just-leave it alone."

He smiled. "Yeah, you're right. I don't need any trouble with Lilly and the Israelis. But, he doesn't live in Arkansas?"

"David! I said, 'I don't know'! At least give me credit for being truthful with you. Why would he live in Arkansas? To keep an eye on the diamonds? I think Lilly does that via satellite."

"Well, maybe so, but I ran into him right after we got married, on the trail to the diamond dig."

Her features reflected genuine puzzlement. "Maybe he was sent because he knew about the joint agency operations going down in the National Forests. Maybe he came to hide evidence of Arkansas diamonds from the gang elements. That would kind of make sense. Okay, so you've seen him before, too. Is that who sent you out with the diamond parcel?"

"Yeah, maybe he was trying to get me killed so he could have you. He seems to be Johnny-on-the-spot whenever you're in a predicament!"

"You think so?" She was amazed at that assessment. "Where was he when Sylvia Brown threw me into the mine pit to freeze to death? Or when Bobby Saxon kidnapped me and Amelia? I don't think he's about me at all! He's an Israeli operative, but not limited to diamonds. I think he was in Turkey, searching for that smuggling route. I'm sure it was being used to route nuclear materials into Iran, which has sworn to annihilate Israel. David, I've only ever wanted you."

"How's the most gorgeous woman in the universe?" Daniel spoke as he approached Diana's studio.

"Oh, you're so nice! I'm actually doing even better than usual!"

He leaned into the space, "Yeah, how so"?

"Well, it's like sales have received a B-12 shot! You know, we used to barely stay up with orders. Then, we increased our manufacturing capacity; well, it seemed like sales were waning some."

"Yeah, between Deborah's company and ironing things out in the Philippines, we have greater production ability. Without adding in a great deal of extra cost! What do you attribute the jump in orders to?"

"Mallory, of course! She's busy revisiting everything to maximize income. One of her ideas was bringing Heather Clark back on-board." She nodded at his frown, "My thoughts, exactly. Of course I don't have quite as big of a problem with Heather as I do with-" she paused, frowning.

Daniel nodded understanding. Nanci Nichols was a sore subject between them.

"So, are they going to be at the *Ranch* any time soon? I know you're dying to see the new baby." He tried to make the change of subject smooth.

"I guess not! Arizona's on their agenda ahead of Arkansas, these days. We could still go, though." Her tone was hopeful.

He considered. "Yeah, our place is amazing. There's no use in not enjoying it, waiting on them. Of course, they always make things fun. Let's go first thing in the morning!"

"We want to go," Mallory insisted.

"Why? It's cold and windy. I'll be fine. There's no point in risking the girls' getting sick."

"We'll all bundle up!"

"Well, are you sure? I'm going because I have stuff I need to do."

"I know! I can take care of the girls; we won't get in your way."

David relented, not particularly happy with the situation. Loading everything necessary for a day trip for a family of five was challenging and time consuming. "Maybe you'll hear something from Lilly about the diamond."

She met his gaze determinedly. "Nice try, David, but I'm tired of waiting for a call that doesn't come."

Suddenly she felt like crying. David's day tearing down the Sunquist cabin would be long; he'd work until dark before even starting back. She didn't feel like being cooped up at the *Enclave* all day with the girls. And Katy was in Nebraska visiting her parents.

They rode in silence. Even the movie went through the girls' headphones.

"How much do you think the used lumber will bring?" she questioned; not only trying to break the silence, but because they needed the revenue.

"Not sure," The noncommittal response.

"Are you going to fill up the truck?" She strove to sound casual.

"Uh-no! There's a half tank. Plenty to get up there and back"! He frowned. "Let me guess! You're planning on staying in the truck all day with it running!"

"Well, it occurred to me for part of the time. We can watch another movie."

"The gas station's five miles the other way, and it'll cost half hour to go fill up. Why couldn't you just do what I asked?"

Tears escaped.

"Ah, don't cry! It's just, everything's comfortable at home, and I really have a lot to do. You just asked the value of the wood, and I won't know until I get a chance to pull the place down."

Trent Morrison studied his facts, chewing his lip in concentration. Maybe some of his Forestry LEI Agents should be fired and replaced, but the job applicants seemed even more dismal than his current guys. He stepped into the outer office looking for a bracing cup of coffee. Just the usual cold dregs!

"I can make a fresh pot," Came a cheery offer. "Maybe you should get one of those single cup deals."

He shrugged, "Maybe so! In the meantime, there's always Starbucks. You can reach me on my cell." He retrieved his files and clattered down two flights of stairs.

At the popular coffee place, he purchased his Americano and found a table. Rather than studying his information further, he sat people watching. The subjects at hand made him feel more morose than ever. If he didn't already know America was in trouble, which he did, this would be a wakeup call. Call him old, but they all looked like a bunch of freaks. Maybe it was the city, and if he canvassed small-town America, he could locate some grass-roots people who aspired to better things in life than outdoing everyone else for weirdness. His phone buzzed. Bransom!

"Hey, Erik, what's up? Is everyone okay?"

The FBI Agent rasped out a laugh. "Yes, actually; as far as I know! Amazingly, this is a phone call of a social nature."

"No kiddin'; that's good, I guess. No calamities going on at the moment and you have time to chat."

"Meaning you don't?"

Trent laughed. "Sorry! I guess I do. I always feel guilty leaving the office and hate to chat on the Government's time."

"Well, I'm not a real phone chatter, myself; but Suzanne and I are in DC for a couple of days, and we'd like to take you and Sonia out for dinner. How about that steak place at seven-thirty??

"Wow, Erik. That sounds great. I'll call Sonia, and we'll look forward to it." He disconnected to call home. With that done, he refocused his mind on the hiring problem. If he tried hiring guys, uh people, he knew from church-well that would be politically incorrect. Not totally legal. Hopefully Christian people would make better Agents. Maybe he should try what worked for Mallory. Cull his high school for graduates that he could train with some values. Although that was a thought, it seemed to him that values should be instilled, already. And high school and college graduates should be applying to him! Well, many young people were disenchanted with the US; and Government jobs equated with Big Brother. But the US Government agencies needed the brightest and the most principled. Otherwise, how could situations like David Anderson's not be repeated? That men scrabble for gold nuggets while someone depending on them dies!

"Lord, we really need a revival," he whispered inwardly. "And I need to know what to do in the meantime." Even as he completed the thought, inspiration seized him. He called to reserve an airline ticket to Arizona, and then made it for two. Even buying on short notice, he found a deal; why not bring Sonia?

In spite of a biting wind, Alexandra, Jeremiah, and Cassandra made a bee line for the tree house, including Zave, Nadia, and Ryan without being reminded. It was fun with all six of them anyway.

"Okay, well, don't get too cold," Diana cautioned. It was amazing that the kids didn't tire of this escape. She and Daniel carried Elysea and her paraphernalia into the comfortable cabin.

"You were right, Di! I'm glad we came. I'll keep up with her for the first shift." He followed resolutely as his youngest began busily exploring the area.

Diana nodded agreement. "Okay I'll put the groceries away. Do you want me to start-"

He grinned easily, "Nope! I hear the chow hall calling!"

Mallory fought tears that seemed determined to surface. Whatever David's problem was, he needed to get over it! She looked around, desperately! She figured he would have a construction shack on site. If she had known there wasn't, she would have stayed home. She was left with few options: their pickup, low on gas; or Rudy's truck; or the cabin-which was to be demolished. Doubts charged into her brain, unbidden. 'Maybe seeing Heather again and being nice to her wasn't such a good idea!' Morosely, she wondered if David's plan for today was really to come up here and tear down the cabin. Maybe that was his cover story, and she had forced his hand'.

She remained in the passenger seat, changing Alexis' diaper and starting her on a bottle. When the movie ended, Amelia passed her a DVD case, indicating her next choice. Mallory twisted to address the girls,

"Not right now; I don't want to drain the battery"! She turned the key off completely. "You guys can unbuckle and play together back there." She pulled out a few toys.

"But can we watch a movie while we play?" Amelia's request was either reasonable, or she was trying to get the last word again, rather than obeying. Mallory was never sure which.

"No, Amelia. I said, we can't run down the truck battery. Just play together! There doesn't always have to be a movie on!"

Sonia nodded and offered her hand as Trent introduced several couples from the Southwestern Division. The atmosphere was tense, in spite of his offering to treat his men to fine steak. Maybe this was a bad idea. Usually, he was tight with government money, earning awards for frugality! But most of DC was about partying, boozing, entertaining. Even now, he felt the resentment when he nixed beers as beverages of choice for his guests. Maybe they could even get him into trouble for imposing standards on them that few people recognized. That by not paying for booze, he was pushing his religion on them. He felt like Wile E. Coyote, holding onto the bomb, waiting for it to blow up in his face.

As if reading his mind, Sonia tucked her hand into his elbow and leaned into his ear. 'Bee-beep!'

He dissolved into gales of laughter while the other couples stared at them in perplexity. Still, she brought back his equilibrium. When the bread arrived, he passed the baskets around, and the tensions broke.

"Inside joke," he apologized.

As the guests busied themselves with passing butter, placing napkins, sweetening beverages, Trent and Sonia bowed for a prayer.

The hum went dead! Twelve eyes stared at them like they were Martians.

Sonia reached for the basket and placed a roll on her bread plate. "So, we have four kids: from twenty-one down to twelve! Uh, this is our first time to leave town without them. One of our reasons for feeling the necessity to pray"!

That brought a few smiles. "Yeah, raisin' kids these days isn't easy," one of the guys agreed.

"Yeah, so-why don't you stay in DC and keep tabs on your kids? We take care of our Division business!" Rob's hostility, uncurbed.

"Well," Trent's drawl was a measured response. "Because the Federal Government doesn't pay me to watch my kids"! He lifted his coffee cup and studied the wisp of steam before sipping thoughtfully. "They pay me to police my policemen. Which, I like to think y'all don't need a lot of my hands-on oversight. I-uh-try to trust my personnel."

Addington dropped his gaze guiltily. "Yeah-uh-a few of us kinda blew it that day!"

"Yeah, you did!" Trent's eyes snapped. "I got called on the carpet while I was trying to decide how to deal with the problem. Which, when you work in DC, you stay on 'the carpet' and in the 'hot seat'! Look, I want to be fair-"

"Yes, Sir, we can tell that." Dean Schaeffer spoke up softly. "We appreciate it, too. Listen, we all like what we do; we get along with each other. Maybe too much, why we're worried about you cannin' any of us! And you and your wife are real nice to bring us out for dinner." He turned his attention to Sonia. "We have three children, Ma'am. Dixie, our daughter's in third grade. And then, Kasey's in kindergarten and Max is almost three, our sons."

David moved throughout the cramped cabin, studying it carefully. He really needed a ladder and couldn't believe his poor planning now that he was actually here on site! He could try to blame his recent brain injury. Or the fact that Mallory and the girls' joining him changed his focus about what to bring. He scoffed to himself bitterly. Except that this was kind of the story of his life, even before the injury. And the whole place gave him the creeps. As he moved out through the back door, the incident with Sunquist and his two partners in crime flipped on is'his mind like a movie projector. The leaking truck sat in the same ruts, and the scraped ground that refused to become a grave seemed to mock him. 'Wow, they planned to bury me alive!' He trembled! From sudden emotion and cold! He moved quickly back to the interior, but didn't escape the eerie sensation. Suddenly he was glad not to be up here alone! He was deeply grateful for Mallory's insistence on coming along! If only he could accomplish a little bit now! His assemblage of tools seemed all wrong! Well, for one thing, he hadn't brought a hard hat! The continued tenderness in his head made them unbearable, and so for that reason, he had avoided jobs where they were necessary. But to start pulling boards apart without head protection seemed ludicrous. Even as he surveyed the structure, the wind rocked it. Common sense would seem to indicate pulling it down from roof to floorboards, but now it seemed to be so flimsy, that moving one piece from anywhere seemed almost a guarantee that the whole thing would implode.

"Mommy, it's cold!" Amelia put a cold hand on Mallory's cheek as she spoke.

"Yeah, here, put your hood up." She yanked the garment into place and pulled the drawstring. "Sit tight, while Mommy checks something!" She was cold too, and rubbed her hands together to warm them up. She pulled David's keychain from the ignition and felt gratified that the old key to the Sunquist truck was there. Maybe it had some gas and a good heater! Sadly, the battery was dead. She returned to the new pickup. No choice but to start it up long enough to warm up! David was right. They should have all stayed warm and safe at the *Enclave*. The truck was warm and she was pouring cocoa from a Thermos® when David jerked the door open, startling her!

"Sorry! Sorry!" He apologized. "Wow! Hot chocolate! What's up? Partying without me?" He mopped good naturedly at a small spill.

"You want some?"

His earlier bad mood seemed gone.

"Uh-guess not! Look; let's just forget this for now! I didn't even think about bringing a ladder, and I should really start at the roof. The whole place feels like it's going to blow over. I can come back another day and bring a crew."

When Mallory's face set obstinately, he could tell she was thinking about the money they needed.

"I didn't even bring a hard hat! It's too dangerous!"

"Well, do you really have to take it down one board at a time?"

He shrugged noncommittally. "I don't know! Why? I'll need a ladder if I'm going to pull it down two boards at a time!"

Her eyes flashed with sudden inspiration. "Okay, when you tore my old house down, you did it piece by piece to retrieve the diamonds. Will it ruin the value of the lumber if we just attach a chain and jerk it down with the truck?"

"Hm-m-mm, you're pretty smart for a girl; did you know that?"

"Daddy?" Amelia's voice from the back seat! "You better be careful what you say about girls."

He laughed. "You're right, 'Mea. I'm seriously outnumbered."

Trent sat on the sofa in the hotel suite, watching a few football scores. "Well, was that the fiasco it seemed to be?" he questioned when Sonia emerged.

She snuggled affectionately beside him. "Well, let's say, it was real different. I believe you're right about them; all being basically good guys. They seem like they're probably more adept at chasing felons through National Forests than they are eating in a nice restaurant. They were uncomfortable socially."

He put his arm around her shoulder, pulling her closer. "What was with the 'Bee-beep?"

She pulled back slightly to meet his gaze. "I knew you wouldn't get it, but you just had this expression on your-"

His smile spread slowly. "Oh, I got it! Sometimes it's scary to me how you read my mind!"

She smiled mischievously. "Oh, it's simple!"

What's simple? My mind? Or reading my mind?"

She laughed. "Yeah"!

The sun was low and the rain which had threatened all day began pelting down. Both truck beds were loaded with lumber and other finds of the day. David grabbed his wife and kissed her lingeringly. "Good plan you came up with there. I'll lead and you can follow me in case this clunker doesn't make it."

Mallory nodded. "I hope you don't get stopped for the plates and inspection. Uh, it doesn't have liability on it yet, so don't get in any-"

"Ah, good thinking. I'll call our agent as soon as we get where there's reception. And, you can calm down. I think we're out of our hole."

She nodded. "Yes, but we're supposed to pray like it all depends on God, and then work like it depends on us!"

David laughed his unreserved cackle. "Well said, Pastor Anderson. And you have worked hard! So have the girls. I think we all deserve pizza. Pray we make it without incident."

Chapter 11: GUIDANCE

I Timothy 6:10 For the love of money is the root of all evil: which while some coveted after, they have erred from the faith, and pierced themselves through with many sorrows.

"What's going on?" Diana was immediately aware when Daniel's response to a phone call was one of controlled panic.

"No one's been able to contact David or Mallory all day. Katy and Jason are in Nebraska, and~ Well there hasn't been any alarming news, but~well, Erik gets concerned."

Diana's eyes deepened in alarm and she pulled out her phone. Nothing! She pushed Mallory's speed dial, and when it went to voicemail, she spoke. "Well, I'd say we should at least pray~"

Rob Addington glowered! "How long do I have to sit here and listen to the same thing over and over?"

Trent squared his shoulders authoritatively. "You can get up and walk out any time you want. But when you do so, you terminate your employment."

"Hey, my record's been spotless. You haven't been able to~" the Division Head included some unsavory words about Morrison's lacking backbone to terminate him.

"Your record's been a blank slate! Fourteen years, and you haven't made any major boners to come to anyone's attention in DC. While on the other hand, you've hardly distinguished yourself, either"!

"Yeah, but you know there's nothing to back you up on firing me. I can dispute. I have my men against your word about what happened up there that day!"

Trent's frown deepened. "Meaning they'd be willing to lie for you? Because you messed up! And you held a man's life in low esteem while you plucked your pretty pebbles from the earth!"

"One time! And you won't let it go! I've told you over and over, the guy's boot wasn't moving. Everyone thought he was dead!"

"And it's still no thanks to you that he isn't! And I'm going over and over it again for your benefit, to try to wake you up to the consequences of wrong actions!"

"You wanted all of us calling people for information on dealing with wasps. We did that! We all got the same information!"

Trent rose, bending forward! "Yeah, what if it had been your kid up there? Would you be happy if someone made one half-hearted phone call before giving up? To grab gold nuggets! If your kid lay in a coma for months, with no hope of a normal recovery, would you be all right with public servants' being so lackadaisical?"

"I didn't give ten minutes to the gold up there that day, if you'll admit the truth."

"Why don't **you** admit the truth? You quit gathering because I ordered you to quit, and then, you still stalled about calling and continuing with the calls! And, yes, you're a leader to your men, and they were all following your bad example; accepting your evaluation that if Anderson wasn't dead, he soon would be; and why risk being stung to death? Your wrong actions led to your division following your example, condemning David Anderson to further pain and suffering."

"You just keep harping at me!"

"Because, you don't get it! You know, the Bible says that a man can't serve two masters."

"Don't use your Bible on me. I have a spotless record with one little glitch that you seem determined to hang me over! I've been a good Agent with a spotless record. You haven't tried to fire me yet because you're afraid to! You can't make a case against me."

Trent settled back into the chair, calm and serene. "I don't have to. Your actions have brought another government agency to bear on ours. I've been trying to save you. And I must say, I've worked harder at rescuing you than you did rescuing Anderson that day! That's all. Turn in your resignation."

Mallory laughed at her reflection in the rear-view mirror. Grime, with gilded edges, described her face. Her muscles were tightening up, and she was eager for a hot bubble bath and the promised pizza! Not necessarily in that order. So far, Sunquist's truck was still moving. The question was whether the transmission fluid would all leak out before they reached *the Enclave.* She studied the vehicle before her as David eased it over the rough terrain. Criss-crossed bungee cords held the load in place, seemingly securely. She checked her rear views again for the treasure she hauled. All seemed okay~

Trent sat in the empty office, revisiting his stack of prospects. He pulled out his cell and pressed a speed dial button. When Bob Porter didn't answer immediately, he went to work. Pulling the liner from the trash can, he began emptying Addington's personal belongings into it from the desk drawers. The guy seemed to have little. Suddenly curious, Trent went to the outer office and pulled a drawer open on an unlocked file. Not much paperwork! Strange for an arm of the Federal Government that still had a penchant for reports on reports submitted in triplicate! He shrugged, pulling open more drawers and leafing through more filing cabinets. Wow! No wonder they were never happy to see him! He remembered a managerial quote from one of David and Mallory's training sessions. *People don't do what you expect! They do what you inspect!* So much for trusting! He checked his watch. There should be time to call his secretary to schedule trips to the other divisions. There was no answer. Annoyed, he called her cell. She answered immediately stating that one of her children was throwing up at an after-school pep club meeting.

Apologizing for the call, he asked her to work out some airline reservations for visiting all of the divisions without giving any advanced warning. He felt extremely foolish for not giving her the benefit of the doubt. From habit, he found a set of keys and locked the nearly empty filing cabinets. He needed to straighten out a bunch of messes, evidently. He silently prayed that all of the Divisions weren't in such sad shape.

Mallory sucked in her breath in amazement! Not fifty yards after entering the county highway, a sheriff's deputy pulled out behind David with flashing lights. She struggled with panic and indecision. She thought the officer was waving her over, too, but she sailed past, pretending to focus attention on the girls. She bore down on the accelerator and set cruise control before fishing her phone free. Usually atop the next hill was when phone service kicked in. She knew David hadn't had a chance to contact the insurance agent. Forgoing the insurance agent's number, she scrolled contacts for the Phoenix attorney. The hour was late, and as she was about to disconnect a receptionist answered breathlessly with the names of all the partners.

"Hello, Hillary, Mallory O'Shaughnessy-uh-I mean Anderson. I was hoping to reach Mr. McManus. I'm afraid I might be calling too late."

"As a matter of fact, he got back from a deposition just a few moments ago. He has a moment for you."

Mallory felt relief, although she figured the attorney's fees would add up quickly.

"Mrs. Anderson, how may I help you?" Steve McManus settled in behind his sleek, ultra-modern desk, listening intently.

He responded, "Okay, well, I'm sure the sheriff's office will be reasonable and give you and your husband a chance to have the vehicle registered and inspected. Truthfully, you shouldn't have turned it onto the highway without all of that business cared for."

"Yes Sir! Of course, you're right, and so will the sheriff's department be. Except, it seemed like they knew we were coming, and were just sitting there waiting to nail us. David's head's still-uh-I think they were arresting him without giving him a chance to do much. Can you recommend anything to me?"

Something in her tone caused the attorney to forget about the lateness of the hour and the rashness of the young couple's actions. He felt a sudden concern. "Okay, Mrs. Anderson, actually the county attorney out there owes me a favor. Maybe I can get him to step in. Otherwise, your best course of action is to go bail your husband out. If you get the problems with the vehicle resolved, a judge might reduce the fines."

"Okay, thank you very much. Will you let me know what your friend says?"

Receiving a half-hearted agreement, she hung up to call Erik, bursting into tears at his voice. The story poured out through wails and lots of tears. "None of these guys ever hassled Rudy Sunquist for driving the truck with the seriously outdated plates and sticker! And yet, they waited to pounce on David the moment he entered the highway. It's like someone in the county's been watching us; someone has it in for us. They had David out of the truck, spreading his feet, searching him; and his head-"

"Okay, Hon; okay-I'll see what I can find out!"

Mallory pulled through the electric gates and watched as they closed behind her. Jason and Katy's place was still dark, and she wasn't sure about confiding anything to the Blairs. She pulled as close as possible to her and David's temp home and unloaded the girls.

"Sh-h-h," she held her finger to her lips. "Go in and go potty. Then you can play."

"What about-" Amelia started to ask a question, and thinking better of it, refrained.

Mallory grasped the infant seat and pulled it free, reminding the other two to keep quiet! Which wasn't working, because they were all hungry! Trying to hold herself together, she mixed a bottle of formula while she searched fridge and pantry for something to hold Amelia and Avery. Hmm-m, a shortcoming caused by having a chow hall, was that she didn't have any groceries stocked. She was hoping against hope that David would pull up outside the gate and honk to be allowed access. While her three exhausted, hungry, dirty little girls joined in a mass chorus of despairing howls, she sent a blanket text to everyone on her list that they were okay. Erik, of course, knew a little better!

A knock on the door sent alarms jangling along her nerves. Her pistol ready, she peered out. Johnna! She opened the door to admit the pastor's wife, whose arms were laden.

Johnna Blair pushed past to deposit her burden on the kitchen counter. "Macaroni and cheese, and fresh-baked cinnamon rolls. Not exactly nutritionally balanced"!

"Thanks, Johnna; you're a life-saver. They turn their noses up at nutritional stuff, anyway."

She nodded, then demanded, "Where's David? Are you guys okay?"

"Well, I guess. We won a settlement against the Sunquist estate and got that old truck and cabin. But when we got to the highway, uh-the expired-uh-no insurance! He got stopped by County immediately."

Johnna nodded sympathetically at the incoherence. "Yeah, I think I understand. Look, let me feed and bathe the girls. Do you need to go bail David out of the hoosegow?"

Mallory smiled weakly. "At least make some more calls. I already phoned the Phoenix attorney and Erik. I thought I might try Trent Morrison and the Neurosurgeon, too."

Johnna shrugged, wondering if Mallory's plan made total sense. Still, she agreed, giving Mallory a gentle shove. "I'll take care of this; go make your calls. Maybe Hanson and his email brigade; have you tried him?"

"Good thought. Again, thanks. I'll go call from David's office." She grasped a set of keys from a hook by the door and hurried to the nearby building.

Red Radcliffe sprawled at his desk as one of the deputies shoved David past him. "Okay, Anderson, two violations push the envelope, but three big no-no's equal an arrest! In this county, anyway"!

"Yes, Sir, I understand that. I have a credit card. Can I just pay bond or the fines and get home?"

"You rich people are all alike in your disregard for laws and the legal system. I'm afraid we run things by the book around here. You'll be booked in, and we'll see- Where did your wife go?"

"Probably home to get the girls fed and bathed and put to bed."

"I motioned her to pull over, but she kept going." Deputy Adam Burch explained to his boss.

David said nothing, but there was no reason why the deputy should have pulled Mallory over, too. The truck she was driving was brand new, with fresh inspection sticker and valid dealers' plates. Strange for the sheriff to ask where she went. The inexplicable actions deepened his dread. It seemed that there was more to this than the stated violations.

Radcliffe frowned at both David and the deputy. "Have a seat, Anderson; we'll book you when we get to it."

David obliged. Having an arrest on his record was the last thing he wanted. They could take all night. Except that he had a family to get home to. The small county facility wasn't set up to deal with volumes of crime, so David was relieved at the laid back lack of a good system. He leaned back and closed his eyes, but relaxation eluded him. It was so odd, that the deputy was right there! Where they would enter from the Sunquist cabin and before phone reception became available. He was lost in thought, not realizing how quickly business was picking up around him.

Suddenly, Radcliffe's voice split the air and brought him back to reality.

"Deputy, cut Anderson loose! He got a signed note from his doctor that his nut's still cracked! Anything happens to him in our custody, and his attorney says we'll be liable! Just shut down the computers and ignore the emails! Anderson, you're free to go-for now!"

Without a word, David grabbed his proffered wallet, keys, and phone; and hustled toward the exit. Light rain fell as he jogged up the highway, hoping Sunquist's truck would be where he left it. He gauged it was probably a good four miles. And if it was still there, would it have enough tranny fluid for him to nurse it to the *Enclave*? He slowed, breathing evenly. He wasn't aware of any calls from either the sheriff or the deputy about taking the vehicle into impound. Strange! Did they know about the golden bonanza? Or didn't they? His assumption had been that that was what all of this was about. He pulled his phone out to call Mallory before entering the dead zone.

"Hey, Baby, you and the girls doin' okay?" His tone anxious as he heard her voice on the line!

"Yes, fine. Where are you?"

"Thanks for making all the calls to get me sprung. When they sent me on my way, I headed back to the truck. I hope it'll be there, and that I can get it wrangled home. I'm about to leave phone reception. No, don't try to come for me! Just stay in! And keep the girls in. Promise me. I'll call you again as soon as I can with an update."

Trent was still up when Erik called him. He answered with some trepidation. Odd, not to be on the FBI guy's social radar, until just now when the FBI and their phone taps had nosed into his division, and- "Trent Morrison." He tried to lay his suspicions aside as he answered.

"Hey, Morrison, uh; you're still in Northern Arizona, aren't you?"

"I am. I fly out tomorrow for the Northwest and Sonia goes back to DC. I guess I should spend more time with my boots on the ground." He figured it was no secret from Erik about his personnel, so he gave grudging admission.

"I think you do a great job. You've sure been-" Erik paused and cleared his throat. "Listen, can I ask you a favor?"

"Well, yeah, sure. Put it on me."

David shivered as every footfall seemed to drive bamboo shoots up through his brain. It couldn't be too much farther. The night was dark, and it seemed that he and the road and the black sky were the only things around for miles. Maybe he should have let Mallory come for him. 'How dangerous would that be for her to-' Confused, he brushed his face with a soaked shirt sleeve and plunged on.

Lights coming from behind alarmed. No traffic had passed him on this road that yielded few savory destinations. More fearful than hopeful, he dropped out of sight, waiting for the vehicle to pass.

'Maybe-maybe they did know about the gold. And freed him, only to come run him down out here, alone! Maybe they had already raided the *Enclave*-' He waited warily until the halo from the headlights disappeared up a hill beyond him. Once more on the road, he poured on all his reserve. He was nearly to the marker- He dropped once more as the dark, sinister vehicle made its way back toward him. "Help, God! Please help me, God!"

Down a small embankment from the shoulder, on his face; he waited interminably for the big SUV to get back past. Maybe someone was out here, just lost! That would explain turning around and coming back! It was crawling! It wasn't the deputy's vehicle, just a big dark car in the dark night! Hunting him down! Like some sadistic sportsman! If Rudy Sunquist's truck was still just up ahead, and if it had been left alone, his gun- The SUV stopped, idling softly, rain bouncing from its hard smooth surface. Nerves straining, David watched as it performed a tight u-turn!

Exhausted and sobbing, David felt around him for some good rocks to lob at anyone who might accost him. With the vehicle out of sight once more, he crossed the dark, asphalt ribbon and walked heavily forward. Almost there! Almost there! Almost there! The driver of the mystery car must have decided on a course because no headlights made their way back toward him. With a little cry of joy, he spotted the object of his quest! It was there, maybe a hundred yards beyond him, tires still on-maybe-

☐ ☐

Mallory paced! The girls were sound asleep, thanks to their exhaustion and Johnna's help. She gazed at the clock, trying to figure out when it would be time to worry. David thought he had to run or walk about four miles. How long that would take, she wasn't sure. And then, if the antique truck wasn't still there- Restored it would be worth a lot of money! But restoring it would require a lot of money before any could be made on it. So assuming the truck wasn't stolen or impounded, David was worried about the transmission- A fresh thought struck her. She had tried to start it earlier-was that only today? And it wouldn't start! Not until David jumped it and let it soak up juice for quite a while! She paced more frantically. She had promised to stay! And not go search for him! But he was probably stranded someplace with no phone reception! A dead battery- and if he got it running and tried to drive it on the roads again, could they arrest him again? Surely they wouldn't! Even though it was late and she knew she'd wake him up, she called the insurance agent to make sure the insurance was in place.

☐ ☐

Click! Click! David pumped the gas pedal furiously, although he knew flooding the carburetor wouldn't make up for the worn out battery! He couldn't guess how much the seals had leaked; the truck sat in puddles of rain water. He sat, dead tired, weighing his options. "Okay, Lord, I'm so tired, and Mallory and the girls-please-" Filled with hope and faith, he turned the key again! Nothing! Frustrated, he sagged back against the ragged upholstery. He wasn't sure how he could have dozed, but a vehicle with beams on bright suddenly filled the wide, old, rectangular rear view mirror. Same guy! David's hand closed over his pistol and he watched, tense, trying to penetrate the dark and rain and haze with tired eyes. As it had all night, with its cat and mouse tactics it crept slowly toward him. Every muscle strained, he struggled against the shakes. The car pulled over and stopped behind him.

꙱ ꙳

Trent pulled his sat phone out and contacted Bransom. "Okay, I'm at the old truck. The weather's deteriorated until it's like trying to see through pea soup. I think someone's in the driver seat, but I can't tell if it's David. Are you sure you can't contact him? I have no desire to get shot."

"Mallory says he's in a dead area for reception. I don't like it that they go up there where they're cut off-"

"Okay, well then, I'm going in."

"Yeah, stay on the line," Erik instructed.

On proverbial pins and needles, Mallory waited, moving often to peek through the blinds at the new truck and its load. Unable to sleep, she considered unloading it, but where to unload! The *Enclave* would be overrun before daylight with work crews showing up for breakfast at the chow hall. The clouds parted suddenly and moonbeams shone on the gilded tarp. At least it seemed that way to her over active imagination. "Lord, I don't know what to do," she breathed in the stillness.

David crouched as low as possible, keeping eyes trained on the rear view mirror. He clasped both his pistol, and the largest rock, waiting. Surreptitiously, he eased the handle up to release the door. He needed to be ready to make his move! He had no desire to hurt a 'good Samaritan', but the dark vehicle seemed to bode no good.

Waiting was the hardest part. Why didn't whoever it was, make a move? Then a horrible thought occurred to him. He had thought the driver was on the phone, but puzzled how that could be, with no cellular reception. But maybe, it was someone in possession of a Sat phone, and they were now waiting for backup. He wondered if he should make his move before reinforcements arrived. Or wait to be outnumbered.

With a swift motion, he was out of the truck with the pistol trained on the driver of the SUV! When he drew no fire, he was relieved. Advancing cautiously, he made a motion for the driver to emerge. The car door opened, flooding light on the threat.

David's hand dropped to his side as he nearly went limp with relief. "Mr. Morrison-"

⁂

Morning light at the *Enclave* brought an extra flurry of activity. Erik and Dawson, and Dan Wells, in charge of the Phoenix office, all listened somberly to the young couple's story. Trent had already heard it from David as they drove to the *Enclave* together, and he was already gone, and on the warpath! He made call after call, barking orders. Enough was enough! Still, the question nagged at him! Should he fire everyone who was in defiance? They certainly deserved it! Or could they come out of it learning something, and being better than a bunch of green, new, hires? This was unconscionable, though! They should be fired and sent to jail! But-

⁂

Refusing breakfast, Erik was grim-faced as he left. "You two should probably get some rest."

"You're right, we probably should. Erik, uh-we're sorry! We're definitely upgrading to Sat phones. Maybe we should order Life Alert® jewelry." Mallory's attempt at humor brought a grimace of a smile.

"Maybe so, and get another dog, and let someone know your plans once in a while!"

Exhausted and still covered with grime, Mallory fought tears at the rebuke. Their plans always seemed sensible enough until they ended in catastrophe. She closed the door behind him and turned to face David. "Quite the twenty-four hours, hunh?"

He nodded, practically numb! "I'll run to the chow hall and fill us a couple of plates. You get in the tub, and I'll bring your breakfast. Then I'll clean up. We need to do what we're doing! Quickly"!

⁂

Trent met eight guys from the Southwestern Division at the same spot where he had rescued David a scant few hours earlier. He was almost sad about Addington's resignation, in light of the most recent facts! He wished he could give him one further piece of his mind, and then fire him! Practically the only legible incident report in the files was one where Addington and the rest of the unit followed his orders to come out here and search for any human remains. The report went on to summarize that there was no evidence of anything suspicious within the radius.

Totally false, according to David and Mallory's frenzied tale! And he tended to believe them! Bransom and the FBI would be on site soon, and he planned to ask to join the investigation. So, his thoughts were in turmoil. Obviously, his unit did mount a search, utilizing government resources for a couple of extensive eight hour shifts! But in his heart, he knew they went back for the gold! While the environs of the cabin concealed some grisly gore they missed in their 'search'!

"Well, I'm so relieved they're all okay!" Diana moved out to the front porch with a baby draped on one arm, and carrying a cup of coffee in the other hand. "Get some coffee and tell me the details."

Situated next to her, he began the narrative. "Well, to begin with, I didn't realize they've been a little strapped for cash. It's been ongoing for several months, I find out now. They thought sending the diamond to Ben and Lilly would bring in lots of cash, but-"

"They haven't paid for it yet?" Diana's tone was incredulous.

"I guess nothing so far. I mean, Diana, it's really valuable! But exactly how valuable is open to speculation! Literally! I don't think Mallory's worried about it, except-that they needed the money! In the meantime, they sued the estate of that Sunquist guy-"

"You're kidding! He had something to sue for?"

"Not that much! As far as anyone knew! But David kind of took a shine to Sunquist's old beater pickup truck! I mean, restored, it might be cool! Standard transmission, with a stick on the floor! It would be fun to drive-"

Diana laughed. "That must be a guy thing! I'll take an automatic any day of the week, but the story-

Daniel sipped thoughtfully. "The state gave notice for anyone who might be an heir to Sunquist's stuff to come forward. When no one responded, the state awarded it to David for damages Sunquist inflicted on him. That included the truck, and for some strange reason, the cabin, because Sunquist possessed some type of squatter's rights."

"Squatters have rights?"

"Yeah, not the acreage, just the structure"! He went inside, returning with a print-out of the small frame structure.

"Bear in mind that the kids are kind of desperate for cash, so David wanted to hurry and dismantle the place for the used lumber. That was his agenda for yesterday, but then Mallory insisted on taking the girls and going along. Now, he's glad she did. He thinks having her along, and that she didn't stop when the deputy tried to get her to, saved him."

Diana's eyes widened, "Really"?

He nodded seriously. "Of course, Erik and Dan Wells, and even Dawson are delving into the whole thing. Actually, Erik's call to Trent Morrison-well, that's another amazing story."

"What do you mean?"

"Okay, when Mallory got back to the *Enclave*, she called the Phoenix attorney, David's neurosurgeon, and Steb Hanson. All of that caused the Sheriff to release David."

"That's good, right?"

"Yeah, except that then David decided to hike the four miles back to where he left Sunquist's truck. There's no wireless reception up there, and he thought someone was following him. Then, Trent showed up just in time, and David apologized for hiding from him each time Trent passed. Except that Trent said, he wasn't the one who had been circling around!"

"Wow! Thank You, Lord! People who don't believe in miracles should follow David and Mallory around for a day or two!"

Daniel laughingly agreed. "Well, Mallory had the idea of chaining the cabin to Sunquist's truck and jerking it down. Not a bad idea, so then, they all worked, pulling nails and loading the wood! There was a fortune in gold stashed there."

"Stolen?" Diana's eyes danced at the mystery and surprise twist.

"Maybe, or mined from the area! A great while ago! Longer ago than Sunquist, by far! Maybe dating back to the eighteen hundreds"!

"So, will it belong to David and Mallory?"

"Legally, the chances seem good. If they can keep from being killed for it before they can cash it in!" His face clouded. "Just as they were finishing the demolition and loading the gold and lumber, they discovered a body-or parts thereof"!

"No!" Diana gasped with astonishment. "A body-like-the old prospector? From the eighteen hundreds"?

"No; a young woman! Probably not dead for very long, not as long ago as the day the three nabbed David. I guess it was horrific to behold."

Chapter 12: GLOW

Mallory sat facing Lilly at a coffee shop on Oxford Street in London. She drew energy from the vibrant street, and Lilly seemed transformed. "We have not forgotten you," Lilly's assurance the moment they met.

"I didn't figure you did," Came Mallory's earnest response. "I'm learning that not only do things take lots of hard work, but they can also take time. Sometimes waiting is harder than working. I figured there would be hurdles about the stone-"

Lilly nodded. "Of course, but now the transaction is complete. Is your CPA prepared?"

Deep green eyes sparkled. "As ready as he can be. And we found the gold to help us through until the diamond sold. I'm pretty sure we'll be paying a hefty tax bill!"

Lilly nodded brightly. "There could be worse problems, I suppose." Her face clouded. "You are aware of Michael's recent marriage?"

"Yes Ma'am. Uh, you weren't happy about it?"

"Well, yes, Mallory, of course, very happy! But, uh, we decided on a very small guest list-"

"Well, that I understand, and I haven't been offended in the least. Believe me, I know how you can start to plan something modest, and then it takes on a life of its own. I heard it was a sweet blend of cultures-"

"One can hope the blend will last. You were smart to marry David when you think alike."

"We like to think so. Our relationship still takes commitment and work, though."

"Are you going to shop when David and the girls meet you?"

Mallory considered as she watched trendy Londoners scurrying by with shopping bags bearing expensive brand logos. "I'm not sure! We may window shop for amusement. With the exchange rate of Dollars to Pounds, it strikes me as being foolish to purchase here what's available at home. Most of this area is clothing, and I go with our own designs."

"Perhaps the theater"? Lilly suggested. "Or going for a nice dinner?"

Mallory laughed, "Or going back to see the Crown Jewels again! That's my idea of a tourist site! I like London. It's big and full of energy with a mass transit system to emulate. But the food's tasteless overall, so we may eat at Burger King™ and go to the zoo."

Lilly made no effort to hide her distaste for that plan. "Fish and chips, at least you should have!"

"All right; I'll take that under advisement then." Mallory's line from the movie *Horton Hears a Who,* and the joke, were pretty much lost on Lilly.

"Here comes David. It's always such a pleasure, Dear"! Lilly rose, planting kisses on each of Mallory's cheeks. She slid a bank book into Mallory's handbag and moved toward the door. With a curt nod at David and the girls, she hurried into the bustling foot traffic.

"That was weird," David observed as they paused in front of a shop. "At least, I guess she doesn't feel like talking my ear off this time."

Mallory's expression questioned. "She never does."

"Ah, so you have noticed! So did she have something to tell you about the diamond? Or why exactly we're here?"

They made their way into more of a sheltered spot as Mallory fished for the small booklet and an umbrella. She gasped in surprise at the one entry! "Why would she deposit the money into a bank here? I told her the CPA's ready to shelter the money as much as he can."

David emitted a low whistle in spite of himself. "Well, we do own a property here; maybe-we're legal residents and-"

Mallory stared at the staggering figure and the prospect of being international. She softly quoted part of a stanza from *Renascence*

All I could see from where I stood,
Was three long islands and a wood.

David pulled her close and kissed her lingeringly. "You're incredible, Mallory O'Shaughnessy Anderson!"

She lingered in the delightful circle of his arms until rain pelted harder. Laughing, they both moved into action to tie hoods and zip the plastic cover of the double stroller. "I guess it's going to be too rainy to visit the zoo," Mallory lamented.

"Yeah, and we don't have any exotic animals to contribute to it, either!" David's deep eyes met hers seriously. "I'm thinking we should go back to Victoria Station and catch the night train to Scotland. While we're up there, we can capture Nessie and bring her back to the zoo!"

Mallory laughed. "Night train! That sounds like a fun plan. And that's something we can't do in the States." She laughed delightedly as his words soaked in further. "Scotland sounds like fun, but I'm Irish!"

"Oh, how could I forget? Erin go bragh! Okay, let's take the night train to Scotland and tour up there for a couple of days? And then we can either fly across to Ireland, or take the ferry across the Irish Sea to Dublin! Looks like we're moneyed up enough"!

"We should have flown non-stop to Dallas," David observed as they awaited luggage at the Phoenix airport.

"Maybe so," Mallory concurred. "Except, then we'd be in Dallas, and we have the most to do here. And you have a medical appointment." She knew what David meant though. The three girls had done great through, England, Scotland, and Ireland, and then slept on the flight from Heathrow to JFK! But from the layover at JFK, through the domestic flight to Phoenix, something evidently had occurred to turn the adorable children into Gargoyles. The hour was late with no sign of Jason.

"Can that conveyor possibly go any slower?" David's tolerance was thin, and as he spoke, the luggage halted with a grinding thunk.

"See, you jinxed it," Mallory's voice was tired.

"Did not! We don't believe in jinxes."

"Oh, yeah, I forgot."

She surveyed her phone at the marimba tone; an Arizona number, but she didn't recognize it. Guardedly, she answered. "Hello! Mallory Anderson."

"Oh hello, Dr. Stringer," She felt like she must be both jet-lagged and exhausted because she couldn't put together in her tired brain, why the neurosurgeon was contacting her cell phone. If it was something alarming about David~but he hadn't seen him yet~

"I'm sorry," his jovial response to her confusion! "This may be rather of a late hour for making a social call."

"Oh, well, we're still awake"! 'A social call?' She still associated the doctor with panic and David's life-threatening injury.

"Yes, my wife and I have wanted to take you out to dinner at our country club. Your Dallas office said you were returning to this area today, and so we wondered if we could arrange something."

With an ear-splitting screech, the conveyor restarted, and suitcases began thumping down onto the carousel once more.

Mallory moved where she could hear better, "I can't tell you what the invitation means, and we would love to join you and your wife. Is it okay if I wait until David and I can talk and I'll call you back?"

"Welcome back."

Trent grinned and nodded at the receptionist. "Thank you, Maureen; it's good to be back. I'll get unburied, and then I'm out to the two remaining divisions. Anything else I should know about?"

"Just what I told you! Rob Addington calls for you every day! Wanting his job back! He keeps telling me he learned his lesson, and because of it, he'll be a better agent than ever."

He nodded thoughtfully from the doorway to his inner office. "Yeah, that's one I'm still mulling over."

"I'll bring your coffee."

He took his place at his desk and clicked his computer on, going to the on-line applicants. Every other application was from Addington. Trent shook his head wonderingly. Maybe finding gold nuggets wasn't as easy and lucrative as Rob had assumed. No surprise there. He looked up as Maureen appeared by his desk with the promised brew.

"Contact him back and tell him he's rehired at entry-level if that's what he wants. It's the best I can do. Maybe I can salvage his previous years of service toward his government pension."

Years of practice almost helped her mask her surprise. "Yes, Sir"!

Davina Stringer leaned back, dabbing her mouth with a delicately tinged damask napkin. "I'm not sure I follow the logic of the Sheriff's department out there. Why did they arrest you?"

"Well, thanks to your husband's intervention, I was never actually booked," David clarified. "I was guilty of the three violations. Or 'Big No-no's' as the sheriff tried to break it down for me. I guess since I'm brain-damaged, he wanted me understand the scope of my misdeeds."

They all laughed at his modest humor before the doctor grew serious. "Well, it's amazing, your level of recovery-" He paused, trying not to use the words miraculous or supernatural. The body is just such an amazing piece of machinery; sometimes it does a better job of repairing itself than other times. You are a lucky young man, retrieving all of your motor-skills. You suddenly regained consciousness, ready to charge the world again! Without a moment's time in physical therapy! I must say, I've been amazed that you can still play the violin!"

Mallory didn't want to be reluctant to give God the glory to the skeptical doctor and his wife. But for some reason, she took another tack. "One of the things that has amazed me, was your willingness to come to that small-town hospital. You put your life at risk for us, and so did Dr. Hammond! Anyone less in the trauma center that day, and I'd be a widow."

David nodded agreement. "That's true. We can never thank you enough."

The doctor shrugged, elegantly nonchalant. "For the life of me, I can't explain what came over me. I've never done anything like that in the past. Whatever the reason, it did work out well for you. But, it hasn't hurt my career, either."

David and Mallory nodded agreement, each wanting to mention the way God works things out for good to those that love Him.

"You mentioned that it was my email as well as others that made the sheriff release you. I know who blankets this state with email campaigns!"

David nodded. "Yes Sir, Steb Hanson." He wasn't sure that the doctor felt favorably about the Arabian rancher, but David and Mallory loved the things Hanson and his group accomplished.

"Which brings us to the subject, Dear-" Davina arched one of those looks at her husband, so he cleared his throat and proceeded awkwardly.

"Yes, well-uh-er-uh-it's our understanding that he sold you guys an Arabian mare-"

David and Mallory exchanged pained glances. As they both struggled for composure, Davina went on. "Did he cheat you? Did he sell you a genetically weak horse?!" Her carefully moderated voice turned suddenly strident.

At last, David found his voice. "Uh-painful subject! Mallory and I can't even talk about it."

"But, we've never felt like Mr. Hanson cheated us," Mallory responded slowly. "We don't talk to him about it either, and he never brings it up. It's just one of those sad things that happen in life. It hurts, but it's one of those things. Really no one's fault! But I guess in a way, it's my fault."

David shook his head. "See why we don't talk about it? Do you mind telling me why this matters? Have you ever dealt with the Hanson Ranch?"

The doctor leaned forward. "No, we've heard about him by reputation only. A spotless reputation, too, as far as we can tell! Except we felt there was a big question mark about the horse he sold you."

"You would have had to see her." Mallory's eyes brimmed with tears as pride and passion infused her voice. "She was something-truly special-" Her eyes sought David's and he nodded unspeaking agreement. "She possessed more heart and spirit than she did physical stamina. The Arabian industry-" She couldn't finish.

The Stringers nodded understanding. "Well, we recently finished building a country place." Davina attempted to mask the pride she felt. "And it's always been a dream of ours to own Arabians. Hanson has seemed like a lonely voice against racing them."

"Yes, Sir, so we understand," David came in smoothly. "He was under a lot of pressure to breed *Sugar*, her name in the Association. Some of the experts felt like she would reproduce her own classically beautiful lines in stronger stock if sired correctly. Mr. Hanson thought she was too fragile, and so he sold her to us as kind of a rescue attempt. We paid more money than we could afford, but nothing like what she was worth! It hurt us both in so many ways to lose her, and we know the Hanson's hearts broke over her, too. Like Mallory said, 'She was special!' Something hard to describe! In answer to what I think you're getting at, we think Mr. Hanson is highly ethical. We would buy from him again, but we really can't afford-"

The doctor motioned to the server to bring coffee and the dessert tray. "We're impressed by your ethics regarding her."

Mallory's hand trembled as she doctored her coffee and stirred it. "Our ethics? About, *Zakkar*? I'm not sure I follow you."

"You wanted the horse put down, even though the vets fought you on it."

Mallory pulled a tissue from her bag and dabbed her eyes. "Well, we thought they stood to make money on trying to save her, and that that was their basic underlying motivation. They didn't seem to mind that her suffering would continue on, and she could never be-" She paused. "That may be unfair. But then the specialist from Louisville started asking permission to take tissue samples, live tissue samples. I didn't know if they wanted to clone her. My mom's husband thought the plan might have been to harvest ovum. Whatever! I just wanted her to die in one piece with some dignity!"

"Okayyyy," David sipped slowly. "So, Steb Hanson is as straight an arrow as they come! If I were in the market for an Arabian, I'd go to him again in a heartbeat. And you might be able to get some good deals. I think he'd be ready to sell out and retire if he met some principled buyers. Although, maybe I shouldn't have said that! Can we change the subject?"

"Certainly! We hear you just returned from the UK. We love it over there." Davina's enthusiasm was genuine. "What did you see?"

"Harrod's Department Store and the Crown Jewels! And we tried to see the changing of the guard, but the girls got too restless waiting. We ate at a bunch of McDonald's and Burger Kings, with one stop for Fish and Chips on another tourist's advice. Then, we took the night train to Scotland. We saw Glasgow and Edinburgh and Loch Ness! The only Loch Ness Monsters we saw were the ones in the gift shop."

The other couple laughed. "Did you rent a car and drive on the wrong side of the road?"

Mallory shook her head vehemently! "I wasn't up for that at all. We took trains and taxis, and Amelia liked riding the double-decker buses in London. Although getting up and down with three girls and all of our stuff got daunting!"

"Did you do any shopping?" was Davina's question to Mallory as William asked David if he had golfed St. Andrews. The conversation divided up as Mallory went through her deal with the exchange rate. "We did tour a couple of china manufacturing places at Stoke on Trent. I sent some Wedgwood pieces home for me, and then I bought my friend Diana, an awesome Royal Albert china set! The Pink Castles! And then when we visited Ireland, I contacted some of my Grandmother and Cousin's business associates. I found a few nice woolens and pieces of Irish linen, mostly to use as samples for our businesses."

"The outfit you have on is extremely charming. I've been envious of you since we first met. I find it difficult to find nice things anymore. The price tags are high, but the quality–just seems to be gone. And I probably have two hundred pair of blue jeans, and I mostly live in them–but sometimes–"

Mallory was sure her jaw dropped. 'Two hundred pairs of blue jeans?' Trying to mask her astonishment, she led the conversation toward the clothing and jewelry lines. Without the slightest hint of pressure, Davina Stringer was hooked!

"This is amazing to me! I'm not sure whether to share this information with my friends, or let them eat their hearts out wondering!"

Trent met Sonia for lunch on his way to the airport. "Hello," she greeted, teasingly good-natured. "Should I know you from someplace?"

"Hey; hey! I just took you with me a couple of weeks ago."

"Mmm-hmmm," she agreed.

"And then I pretty much left you to your own devices. Sonn, I'm sorry!"

She laughed. "I'm just kidding. I think it's my hating to let you travel when you really needed to, that made these guys think they could get by with so much."

"Yep Sonia Morrison! It's all your fault that hundreds of men around the country are drawing their checks while getting by with doing as little as possible! That's a stretch. The problem rests with my being trusting! Brings to mind the old adage, 'Trust but verify'! It's like every business and industry. Most people have to be helped to stay honest. I think that there are charactered people who can police themselves, but that's not the norm. I've learned some hard lessons, if none of the others do. I guess I had the feeling that since I'm at the top of this chain, I have nothing more to learn. This is an eye opener. Although, how we as Christians can go through life with our eyes closed to such glaring problems–"

She nodded, picking through her salad. "Well, yes, but in fairness to you, many of these guys have gone to great lengths to hide the truth from you. So, the human remains at that cabin in Arizona? Were they left there after your division followed out your orders to search for more bodies?"

"I'm pretty sure they never conducted the search. Sonia, there was hardly any paper work verifying any of their activities for the past three years. But then, there's the report on their search, filled our completely in triplicate with the copies duly filed! In other words, there's no paperwork on what they do, and a thorough report stating they did what they didn't do."

"And you're rehiring?"

He paused, frowning. "And you know that how?"

She smiled nervously. "You must have told me."

"I'm pretty sure I didn't. You talk to Maureen?"

She feigned innocence. "Am I not supposed to?"

"Well, I guess she's entitled to her opinions, but not to express them to me unless I ask! Which, I don't think I've ever asked her opinion on anything more than office supply requisitions! Sonia, he keeps reapplying, saying he realizes now, the mistakes he made. If so, I'm ahead of the game with him over somebody just stepping from the college classroom. He's hired at entry level, and as soon as all of his paperwork's in order again, I'm transferring him here. I can keep an eye on him, and prospecting for gold in his spare time will be a challenge! Unless there's a deposit of the stuff in the Potomac I'm not aware of!"

Chapter 13: GHOSTS

Bloodcurdling screams from Amelia brought Mallory from her bedroom in a panic! She seemed barely able to move as the screams intensified. At last, she reached the living area of the modular home, a scant few feet, to see her daughter doing a terrified dance as the piercing screeches intensified. She couldn't imagine what the problem was! A beesting? Ant bites? Maybe even a snake?

"Amelia! What happened? Calm down, and tell Mommy."

Crying and gasping for breath, the toddler pointed a trembling little finger at the TV.

Mallory stared at the screen, unable to grasp the situation. ESPN broke for a commercial. She and David usually tuned in to sports broadcasts when they could. Maybe it wasn't the TV. Maybe Amelia was pointing at something else.

"What, Honey? Did you see a bug? Did you get stung? What made you scream? You scared Mommy practically to death!"

"Aaah! Ah-h-h"! The wails began to abate. "I sawed-the mean man! You told me he burned all up, but I sawed 'im."

The words weren't making sense to Mallory, but alarmed, she went for her pistol, releasing the safety. 'Was it possible? That Bobby Saxon escaped death twice? First, from Jennifer's gunshots and then the fiery jet crash'? Mallory couldn't imagine how that could be. Because, not only was the plane on fire when she and Amelia were sucked out through the open door, but Saxon himself was aflame. Placing the weapon within reach on the kitchen counter, she gathered Amelia into her arms.

"Okay, where did you think you saw him?"

"I did sawed 'im. He talk like this, 'R-rrr-r rr-rr'."

Her face twisted as she imitated the terrifying felon, which always creeped Mallory out to no end! Just when the trauma seemed to have worn off~

"Okay, was he like, looking in the window at you?"

Fresh terror crossed little features and blue eyes widened to enormous as they traveled to the small kitchen window.

"Where did you see him, Amelia? Tell Mommy!"

"On the telebision! You said he died, but he was on the telebision. I sawed 'im."

"On this channel"? She watched until the commercial break finally ended, but then it went to a story about one of the NBA teams. She searched the images carefully but saw no one that remotely resembled Bobby Saxon. Maybe Amelia was more traumatized, still, than they realized, and her imagination was conjuring things up. Mallory was certain the man in question must be dead! Erik had called her with the coroner's report. Still rattled, she told Amelia to go play and dialed his number. By the time his voicemail came on, she almost felt foolish leaving the message. But by now she needed further confirmation! For her own piece of mind, as well as her daughter's. She retrieved her laptop from the bedroom and set up where she could keep an eye on the larger plasma screen. Gradually, she calmed down and refocused on her task, by now questioning the wisdom of her call. The NBA story ended and an interview with a pro football player came on. But as that feature ended, and before the commercial break, a baseball teaser appeared. She scoffed softly. Sadly, baseball season was months away. But as *Take Me Out to the Ballgame* played on a calliope, footage played of fans making their way into various ball parks. She recognized Fenway, thinking she needed to call her grandmother. As she studied the faces of the fans entering the old Boston ballpark, the idea occurred to her that maybe one of the earlier blurbs had indeed, been of the Ballpark at Arlington. And maybe Bobby Saxon was on film. By the time her phone jingled with a call from Erik, she no longer felt foolish at all.

At Hal's, David and Mallory waited for Erik and Suzanne. Puzzled, Mallory asked David, "Does Hal seem bent out of joint with us, or is it my imagination?"

David shrugged. "He's always resented us; my dad's stance against alcohol goes against his grain. His daytime restaurant business seems better than his late night bar crowd; and by daytime crowd, I mean the group largely made up of church people, most of whom don't drink. Of course, my dad has tried to win him to Christ, to be cussed out royally."

Mallory sighed, and David turned his attention to the object of their discussion. Usually the lodge owner at least acted jovial and tolerant on the surface. "Sumpin' up, Hal?" he queried.

"What are you trying to do to these parts, Anderson?" Hot-blooded color rose in the restaurateur's face. "There aren't enough ________ running over our borders, breaking laws, and taking jobs? Gettin' on welfare? Without you importin' 'em?"

"Are you talking about the Rodriguez?" David questioned innocently. "They're legal. And they're good paying customers when they frequent your place. Most of the time they're all down in Texarkana, or else in Miami! And they're not on welfare. Why would you rile yourself up over that? You look like you're ready to stroke-out."

Mallory was shocked by the response, but David wasn't surprised. He knew that Hal was one to lean toward White Supremacist thinking. He listened intently as the man spewed statistics about demographics and racial balance, and the seeming doom prophesied for white people.

Mallory was horrified, but David decided to feed the monster. "Yeah; and here's the real kicker, Hal, nearly fifty six million Americans have been slaughtered in the past forty years, most of whom were white!"

Hal's eyes narrowed to mere slits. "If you're talking about abortion, I think a woman has the right to choose what happens to her own body!"

David shrugged. "Just sayin', Hal. It's a procedure that's tougher for minorities to come by. If you're so interested in trying to keep the US population predominantly white, these casualties should matter to you."

The guy scurried away muttering at the logic.

Mallory's eyes met David's.

"What?" his tone striving for innocence.

Always a sucker for him, she couldn't help smiling. "Just don't make him so mad he poisons our food. I guess it never occurred to him that if we knew any white people who are willing to work at garment production eight hours a day, we might hire them. It would be cheaper and easier than getting visas for foreign workers, and moving them here. And, we wouldn't fight the language barrier."

"Yeah, these guys could care less about logic and reason. I wonder if he's KKK. My dad has wondered-"

"David-"

He shrugged. "Well, why is he so stirred up about the Honduran people? None of them are ever here! It's because he attends meetings with other guys from the state! Be willing to bet."

"Maybe, but that would be so counterproductive and such a waste of energy-"

Hal returned with their beverages, smacking them down so hard that they sloshed all over. "You're making a lot of people burned up besides just me. And having them ________ in my establishment has hurt my business. I bet it's fallen off by twenty percent."

"Well, do you know that for sure? That your business has fallen off?" Mallory, the businesswoman, questioned his words. "What kind of records do you keep to quantify that? And if the lodge really is in decline, serving minorities might not be the reason. At least, not the only reason"!

He slammed the empty drink tray down on the next table! "What do you mean by that? Yeah, that's the reason. Folks around here like to be with their own kind, if you get my meaning!"

"I'm afraid I do, but you have this blind spot keeping you from seeing the forest for the trees. From our observation, it looks like your clientele is pretty loyal. But Hal, people mostly come here because there aren't other choices nearby. Your food isn't as good as it once was; sometimes it's cold; the help's rude! And you haven't done anything to the place in twenty years! It could use some serious freshening up."

"Sorry to hear you feel that way! Why don't y'all beat it on out of here, then?"

"Calm down, Hal," David's demeanor unruffled. "Tell you what. Since you're a leader in our community, and your restaurant is a local and tourist landmark, why don't you let me bring a crew in for a facelift? Besides, here comes Erik. Don't make me have to tell him you're a 'White Supremacist'.

"I'm not! I'm just a patriotic American that hates to see our country going to the dogs!"

David let it go. He hated to see the country 'going to the dogs', too. But he knew minorities weren't the problem, and racism wasn't the solution.

As the Federal Agent settled in at the table, the lodge owner turned into sweetness and light, making David more convinced than ever that his dad's suspicions might be on the mark.

"Brampa," Amelia turned long-lashed, bright blue eyes on Erik.

Melted, he responded, "What, Darlin'?"

"Brampa, did you ever find my boots?"

"Um, I guess not. Did you lose some boots?"

Her expression clouded. "Yes, them bad mans took 'em."

He was still mystified. He was aware of evidence gathered by agents from the warehouse where Amelia was first taken on the night of her abduction. But, he couldn't recall that there were any little girl's boots.

"Amelia, when did you start worrying about the boots?" Mallory shoved a cup of milk in front of her daughter. "Your feet have grown a lot since that night. Those boots wouldn't fit by now, anyway. Daddy and Mommy will get you some more boots."

"Brampa wants to hear about the boots," Erik responded. "What color were they? Who took them off of you?" Erik ignored Mallory's pleading expression.

"Dey was brown. And the Rr-rr-rrr mean man taked 'em off, and he telled da guy to put 'em in a trash bag and throw 'em in the dumpster."

"Really"? Erik's question prompted more story!

"Uh-huh, and da guy, he says to sell 'em cause they're real nice. And da real mean man, he say some bad stuff-and, 'There ain't no time to go sell junk'-"

Erik smiled, knowing Mallory was dying to straighten out the child's grammar and diction as well as prompt her to say, 'Yes, Sir', rather than 'uh-huh'. He shook his head at her. Amelia's words were very important, just as they came out. He wondered vacantly who won about the fate of the boots. Saxon! Undoubtedly!

Dean Schaeffer moved into the recently vacated office with some plants and pictures, aware of disapproving scowls from the other guys in the division. Shoving the door closed behind him, he arranged his items and settled behind the desk. Not too bad. Maybe a coat of fresh paint wouldn't hurt. He turned his computer on and addressed the schedule. Monday and Tuesday of the coming week were blocked off for orientation and in-service. He needed to establish himself as boss in Rob's place, a task he knew would be challenging. And lay out some new rules and groundwork. He braved the scowling countenances and went back to the outer offices looking for the big Federal guidebook. The only one he could locate was three years out of date. He considered going on line to requisition a current one, then changed his mind. No time like the present to cross the guys.

"Bill, call HQ and requisition a current guideline."

"Why? No one goes by it."

"Well, we might give some thought to that. Unemployment lines aren't all they're cracked up to be. Actually, you should be glad I want it. It will probably give you more leeway than you'd get from me without it. Before I crack the whip, I want to make sure I'm not overstepping. Get right on it, please. Maybe you can get it downloaded to my computer."

"Addington's going to bring Morrison down!" Bill Baines blustered. "And Rob'll be back, and you'll be out of here."

"When that happens, you'll answer to Rob again; but until then, my name's on the door. Trent Morrison still seems firmly in control, and it's Rob and his family that are having a tough time of it."

"Yeah, thanks to Morrison for treating him mean."

"Aye-aye-aye! I can't believe I'm hearing this! Rob's having a tough time and dragging his family through Toughsville with him, because of his own mistakes! It's not Morrison's fault! It's Rob's fault! He brought it on himself."

"Why, what's happening to Rob?" one of the other guys questioned.

"Well, he got transferred to DC with his pay cut to entry level." Baines was glad to fill everyone in on the struggle. "DC's lots more expensive to live in than out here, so Rob and Marilyn and the three boys are all crammed into a tiny apartment! You know how those three boys are used to roamin' freely out here-"

"That's the thing; if Rob had it made being Division Head out here, and his kids had it made and were happy, that's something he should have thought about that day when he disregarded Morrison's orders. We all have it good, too. Why jeopardize it? Once you get me that procedural manual, you and Cramer go into town and get paint, ladders, cleaning supplies. Everyone come in tomorrow in grubby clothes you don't mind getting paint on." He made his way back into his private office and started making some phone calls.

Erik sat at his desk, going through every report he could locate on the human trafficking cases. He had to assume that Mallory had been a target since very early on. Beginning with the Boston mob and her Uncle Ryland? Maybe, and yet Merrill Adams had been hired by Ryland O'Shaughnessy to kill both her and Suzanne. Okay, because he personally hoped to inherit Patrick's estate with Mallory and Suzanne out of the way? But was he off track from what he should have been doing? Decidedly! So, Mallory's abduction from Turkey! She thought she had seen one of the Melville twins above her at the Pamukkale site. Who later proved to be a local Turkish thug, wearing a hat and pair of sunglasses such as Oscar Melville favored. That had scared her, causing her to fall. But, what if she hadn't caught a glimpse of the guy? Would they have nabbed her right then, if she had approached nearer to their position? He sighed, finding it difficult to connect the dots into a cohesive plot. Maybe they were all separate incidents. The attempt to blow up the tour buses! He shuddered, considering how that might have ended far differently. He tried something he hadn't tried in a long while and placed a call to the Turkish colonel.

David arrived at his skyscraper site ahead of schedule. His appointment with Willard Ames, the spokesman for an investor group, wasn't for another forty minutes, but he liked to have the RV in place and set up with refreshments. With everything in readiness, he made his way to the site to check on progress since his previous visit. His other architectural project, the mansion in Tulsa, was ahead of schedule, to the owner's delight. He snapped a couple of pictures and sent them to Mallory who was spending the morning working from the Dallas office.

Her response was proud and enthusiastic, and he gave her a quick call. "Hey, is everything under control there?"

"I think so. Actually, Rhonna called me. She wants to take me to lunch, so she's helping me with the girls. We're going to a new Thai place." When there wasn't a response, she questioned. "Is that not a good plan?"

"I'm not sure. You know I worry about security. Maybe it would be better for today if she joined you in the Mezzanine. Please? Why did she call? What's the latest with Jim?"

"She didn't mention him. I was just excited to hear from her."

"I know. Okay, go ahead and stick to your original plan. I'm sure it'll be fine."

Mallory disconnected, figuring David was right. And even with Rhonna's willingness to help with the girls, the in-house restaurant would be both simpler and safer. She needed a balance of going out of house to expose the designs to a broader customer base, while at other times the building's café was expedient. And Rhonna was fine with the switch.

"Well, how's everything going?" Mallory questioned, once pleasantries and small talk exhausted themselves.

"Girl, you wouldn't believe! Well, you keep track of the company growth-"

"Well, David does; I don't," Mallory inserted. "I mean, I've assumed it must be okay, since I don't hear word to the contrary-"

Rhonna's expressive features glowed. "Yes, it's amazing. Real solid and steady. Mr. Whitley, well sometimes he reverts back to the old Jim. But for the most part, he's a different man. He won't say he's saved, but-"

"Well, I wish he would get saved and admit it openly. If he's reformed, I'm glad. That's hard to keep up. We both know he needs to be transformed."

Rhonna nodded uncertainly. "Well, I'm a pretty new Christian, and I get confused-"

Mallory nodded. "I think I know where you're going. That a guy like Jim can turn around by the strength of his own will and personality, and Christians so often never utilize the transforming power of Christ to change their lives. It's an indictment on the state of Christianity in America as a whole, I think."

Rhonna frowned, ever so slightly. "Well, you and David are good role models for Jim and Jamora both. And their following your parenting skills is making a huge difference with their boys."

Mallory laughed. "Thanks, I guess. I'm not sure we have parenting skills for anyone to copy. You know, it seems so cut and dried before you actually have kids. And suddenly, you have this huge responsibility staring you in the face- Well, enough about Jim, what's going on with you?"

"Well, I'm dating this guy-"

"Oh yeah? Tell me more! Where did y'all meet?"

"Well, at a training convention. Luke and Damon held one in Saint Louis. I took about fifteen of Jim's new hires, and Alan was there from Springfield, Illinois with new employees from his company."

"Good guy?" Mallory helped the girls while she waited for Rhonna's response. "Does your hesitation mean you aren't sure about him? Is he saved?" Mallory was flooded with concern as she prayed for wisdom.

"I'm not sure. I think so. He's-uh-white."

Mallory glanced over sharply, forgetting the 'wisdom and treading softly' thing.

"What!" Rhonna bristled defensively. "You don't think I'm good enough-"

"Whoa! Rhonna, you're good enough; and too good, for most of the men in this world! It's just that, when you worked for *DiaMo,* you couldn't get comfortable with the other girls, or they couldn't adjust to you! And you still like working for Jim and his predominantly black staff; even though you earned a lot more and had more upward mobility with us. I'm just saying, think long and hard before you jump into a world that will make you more unhappy than you can imagine!"

Tears sparkled in the other girl's expressive eyes. "I thought you would understand."

"Well, Rhonna, I don't! But whether I understand or not, is relatively unimportant. What does God want for your life? If Alan is God's will, He can help you with the obstacles and hurdles you'll face."

"What makes you so all-fired sure we'll face obstacles and hurdles?"

Mallory leaned back, exhaling softly. "Because, Rhonna, that's what life is made of. There will be plenty of problems without deliberately taking on more. I'm not opposed to interracial marriage, but the world's full of radicals who are. Which if you choose to go against the current-never mind! But whether or not he's saved is something you can't stick your head in the sand about. That's the crucial issue."

Erik was buried in paperwork of cold abduction cases. Surprisingly, Amelia's line of questions had him pursuing some new 'rabbit trails' as Dawson called them. But if Dawson truly thought it was a waste of time, he'd call a halt.

Caroline Hillman complained, "This is really a lot to investigate so long after the fact."

Erik agreed. "While you're delving into it, why don't you also write a new recommendation, making this a part of every investigation from now on"!

"I'm sorry, Erik, but I don't think anything will pan out from it."

"Well, keep at it, anyway. I'm getting you more help. And maybe nothing significant will materialize on the old cases. But I'm convinced it'll turn up leads in years to come on new ones."

"And the idea came from Amelia?"

"It did. Two of her captors wasted time arguing about her expensive little boots. Saxon was right! Disposing of them where they wouldn't be found was the wisest course. But you can always count on some of these guys getting greedy for more. Maybe pretending to follow orders, but then retrieving them to sell online or at a kiddie resale shop. They always want a few bucks more. Remember what helped us capture some of the terrorists in the first attempt to bomb the Twin Towers?"

A smile played on her features against her will. "Guess ya got me with that one. One of the not-so-bright terrorists returned to the rental agency where they initially rented the truck they turned into a bomb. He tried to get a refund for the four hundred dollar deposit."

"Exactly! Everyone he implicated by that trick is still doing hard time! They slip up. And that's why I want a search made for Amelia's boots." He sorted through case photos of other kidnap victims. "This girl was carrying a new designer handbag. Look at this gal's wrist watch."

"Well, yeah, we always look into fences that would help move jewelry."

"We do! Initially! When the cases are fresh! But if these guys wait until the heat dies down-"

"So, canvas the pawn shops again, the consignment stores, and the online sellers?"

David felt pleased as Willard Ames and another of the major investors painted rosy forecasts for the new office/retail complex. David was gratified by the initial interest of prospective tenants, but his approach was cautious.

"We need to be leery of guys that say they want to lease and move into our building as soon as their current leases end. Some of those are three years out. There's no telling how many newer and more exciting properties will have entered the market by then. I mean, you tell your friends about our building, and what are they supposed to do? Act like they aren't interested? I'm just thinking we need to take it all with a grain of salt."

Ames slapped him on the back. "Come on; don't be such a pessimist."

David shrugged. "Well, you're the one working to get investors. But the way the economy is, it just seems speculative to assume a high occupancy without hard deposits. As the old saying goes, 'Talk's cheap.' If it fills up to that percentage, then it might be wise to consider erecting a second."

"Well, you and your guys have been paid your fees. Are you telling us you don't want any more work? Have you run that past your guys? I'm pretty sure Zeke Allen and John Smith don't have rich wives to keep them afloat while they pick and choose."

David regarded the two men levelly. "My rich wife and I do have to consider staying afloat. And that depends on having a good name. You're telling investors questionable facts, as if they're absolutely true. It's their money you seem eager to risk."

"I don't see a risk."

"And you may be right! I'm glad there's a lot of good, exciting buzz regarding our property. But I think rallying investors and drawing more plans so soon is premature."

David watched as Mallory smeared sticky cream on her scars.

"I'm not sure this is making much difference," she observed. "I think they all fade with time, anyway."

He sank down next to her on the sofa. "Hey, if Diana thinks it's good stuff, keep using it. It's sure not doing any harm. So, Erik confirmed that Saxon died on the plane that morning?"

She nodded. "Yes; and the agents went back through the ESPN footage and found what Amelia saw. It shows Bobby and that other guy from the baggage truck watching us and talking about us. That's evidently what made Amelia remember about her boots."

He rose and paced. "You know, I can hardly forgive myself for that whole incident."

Mallory regarded his anguish steadily. "It wasn't you! It was the bad guys, and their pre-meditated criminal activity."

"I know-it's-just, I spent the whole night praying and searching for both of you, and then I didn't even recognize my own little girl!"

"Well, that's part of how they get away with it. They drastically change the kids' appearances."

He paused, and his dark, tormented eyes pierced her. "I mean, I'm driving down that tarmac like a mad man, not knowing how I can get the two of you freed before the jet explodes. And here's this kid that looks like an orphan with cancer, running up out of nowhere. And I'm thinking, what's that kid doing there? He's gonna get hit by the firetrucks! I don't have time to stop and grab him, because the plane's-And Avery was awake again and screeching in the back seat. And this little kid on the runway-I look in the rearview mirror and he's crying and holding out pleading little hands. Like Amelia does, but I still can't even realize- And I'm thinking the ambulance drivers and sheriff can keep from running over-But then, it seemed too late about the plane anyway-and I circled back-and this little waif was calling me, 'Daddy' and I'm wondering why this kid thinks I'm his-"

"I can't imagine how surreal all of that was. And how exhausted you must have been! And it sounds like it was a tough call, and you did what was right. Now, if Amelia and I can get over the nightmares we keep having-"

He pulled her up into his embrace. "Well, the nightmares are hardly surprising in light of the events. I'm glad Amelia saw that footage, even though it shook her up again. It gives us more of a chance to talk it over with her, now that she's a little bigger and understands more. And it gave the Feds more evidence and insights. Branson's even assigning agents to delve into more film archives for Dietrich, and also the late Undersecretary."

"And see which of their associates might be implicated, too," she agreed. "And which of those might link to Jennifer's artwork."

"The nooses are inexorably tightening on these people. We need to talk to Jay and Sophia about what their PI's are finding out, and we need to bring pressure to bear on the headmaster of that school. It's real strange how he manages to divert attention away from himself."

Mallory pulled free and made her way into the bathroom to cleanse her face, "Well, yes, and the members of the school's board of trustees. It seems that if allegations like these have been raised about their headmaster, why would they not want to get to the bottom of it, for the safety of their students and the reputation of the institution? But they seem to be covering for him, instead."

"Hm-m-m, now that's something I was unaware of."

Chapter 14: GAMBIT

"Hey, Dad, can I come in and show you something?" Alexandra used the intercom as little as possible when she was in the *GeoHy* office. Her dad didn't mind her interruptions, but she tried to avoid resentment from long-term, *GeoHy* staffers.

"Absolutely! Care to join me for lunch?"

"I'd better not. It'll just take a minute to show you something intriguing. I've actually just started on a project, and I brought a lunch."

"Okay, I'll stop by your desk on my way down. I'll be right there."

True to his word, he appeared immediately and she turned her laptop so he could see her monitor. "This is a surprise to me; were you in the loop?" Her question accused.

He grinned infectiously. "Nope! Surprise to me, too! Mallory's been full of surprises since the first day we met her! Uh-we don't own her, Al. She doesn't have to run everything she thinks about through us! This is a good idea, though! Wish I'd thought of it!" He straightened, turning his gaze from the screen to his daughter's frustrated expression; then pulled a chair into the cubicle and sat next to her. "What else does it say?"

She scrolled and Daniel whistled softly, amazed. "Nice site! I wonder if David built it, or they hired it out." He shot Alexandra a sideways glance. "An E-zine! The subscription isn't expensive, but it'll still give them a good stream of revenue. Savvy! Give 'em credit."

"Well, there are all kinds of Geological periodicals, hard copy and electronic! How can they compete?" Alexandra continued to be miffed.

He shrugged. "Well, the domain space doesn't cost that much. This isn't like a brick and mortar company with a lot of overhead! And she's raised curiosity all over the country with her drilling and keeping her data so confidential!"

"So, why tell any of it on-line? If she's found stuff that's so world-shattering, why doesn't she go for it?"

He stifled a laugh, suddenly realizing all ears seemed tuned toward Al's cubicle. "By mining; you mean? Al, she is mining, in a sense; without all of the red-tape and high overhead involved in starting up a mining operation. She's placed herself as a middle man, gaining information to pass along to established mining companies. It's quite a remarkable niche! Subscribe to it! I'm dying to see what the first issue has to offer!"

"She could have at least given us a subscription."

His voice turned firm. "Get over it, Alexandra! They've given us so much! I think we can come up with twelve, ninety-nine per year! As a matter of fact, this first issue-how did you find it?"

Eyes still resembling gray storm-clouds, she confessed. "I was researching; looking for an ailing business for us to take over-"

"That's great, Al! That you were searching for a way for *GeoHy* to ramp up revenue! I think you found it! Subscribe and make me a hard copy of the issue. I'll set up an early afternoon meeting with the head Geologists!"

"Do you really think there'll be any information to jump on?"

He rose, grinning, "What do you think?"

"Okay, keep an eye on 'em," Erik had listened patiently to an agent from the New York office fill his ear with information on Jennifer and Sophia. His understanding was that Americans were still free to choose which funerals they chose to attend. He assumed the women's reasons for going to such lengths to make it to Robert Saxon, Jr.'s memorial service, wasn't their devotion to him! But, as long as they didn't make a scene and break any laws, what could he do? Off the record, he admired their spirits! From what the agency could surmise, Sharon Saxon seemed to have been quite in the information loop as to the origins of her and Robert, Sr.'s fortune. If she wanted to try to paint her son as saintly within their Connecticut enclave, Jennifer and Sophia knew better! Their appearance would be enough to create a stir, without their doing anything! At least, he hoped they wouldn't put themselves in legal peril. Even as he worried, he knew they would tow the mark! Sophia possessed the counsel of a bevy of top-notch attorneys and private investigators. Her intention was to make the Saxons look as bad as they were; not to tarnish her own reputation further.

Roger and Beth listened to Cade and Catrina sputter about David and Mallory's new E-zine, *Drilling Platform.*

. . . . "I don't understand why you're questioning their ethics," Roger finally asserted with his usual voice of reason. "They financed your start-up, and they've sent their core samples and paid for your analyses. Their doing that, and the response from others, has proven the industry need for more independent labs. What they do with the information is their business."

"Well, yeah, technically; I guess you're right~" came Cade's grudging words.

"Well, I can see why they feel like they do," Beth spoke up.

Roger shook his head mildly. "Believe me, I've been the victim of businesses that were unethical! David and Mallory are as above-board as you can get. Simply because they took the data and went a different direction than you anticipated~" He paused, grinning broadly! "Have you subscribed? I'm not sure why I'm sitting here! There's probably data that can boost *The Sanders-Chandler Corporation* along!"

Sharon Saxon, with Robby in tow, took in the scattering of acquaintances. Few people were in attendance, and she felt profound disappointment! Of course, she was relieved that her ex-daughter-in-law Kayleigh wasn't there, or any of Kayleigh's family! But, what about friends from the city council and country club; or Bobby's clients? Of course, this memorial was somewhat after-the-fact! Bobby's unrecognizable body had been cremated immediately. So several months later, his memory seemed already to be fading. But still, his friends and colleagues could come and show some respect!

The minister cleared his throat and she glanced at her watch as a few last minute attendees took their places. She stiffened!

Mallory watched interestedly as her counter pegged the hits on the *Drilling Platform* site! Subscriptions were being processed, and as money rolled in, so did criticism. Nothing new there! As usual, Dr. Phelps Hensley was vocal, again challenging her credentials and mocking her for claiming to be a Geologist! Nate Halsey set up a site, attempting to draw off her following. To be expected! But, despite the nay-sayers, her information was both enlightening and irrefutable! Some subscriber stood to make a fortune on the contents of the periodical, and this was only the first issue! She sat back, satisfied. Somewhere, opportunity and jobs should spring up, presenting opportunities for those poised to seize upon them! "Lord, You are so amazing and vast," she whispered.

"You asked to see me?" Rob stood nervously in the doorway of Trent's office.

. . . . "Have a seat," Trent carefully closed the file before him and asked via intercom for coffee. Settled in with the coffee and the door closed, Trent began. As he expected, Rob's entire demeanor screamed resistance.

"Are you against Americans' right to bear arms?" Rob's tone went beyond belligerence, but Trent sat calmly.

"I guess it depends on what Americans plan to use their arms for. Realizing I can't always predict the outcomes of gun possession and use, I'm in favor of caution. Sadly, all guns are not used for self-defense and sport!"

"So you're saying you feel threatened by militias? I know lots of guys that take part in week-end games."

Trent sighed, "Yeah, Rob, I know you do. But look; we work for the US Government. I still believe in the US. That doesn't mean I agree with all that goes on, politically and in our society! But I still think the political process is effective, and I'm not for week-end games that practice fighting us! Hey, if guys want survival skills and paramilitary training, that can be useful. Most American men used to be rugged, tough outdoorsmen! I guess my concern isn't what people are doing, as much as why! Why should these guys use the National Forests and Grasslands the Government protects and provides, to practice a coup? You know my opinion! That, real men have their families in church on Sundays, and that they pray for a restored and blessed nation!"

"I don't agree with that!"

Trent grinned. "You don't have to! That's the beauty of America! Look, Homeland Security and the FBI have the most radical groups on their radar. My concern is what goes on in my area of responsibility. Just as we don't want innocent campers and hikers hit by stray bullets from hunters, we don't want them caught in the cross-fire of militia groups. I'm asking you to head up a task-force to visit each region and make sure we keep our extensive house cleaned out of all illegal and/or dangerous activity!"

Alexandra tried not to worry! Odd, that her mom showed up and was behind closed doors with her dad. She jumped when her extension buzzed from his office. "Yes Sir!"

"Mom's here; can you join us, please?"

She scrambled up, trying to think what she might have done to be in trouble. She paused and tapped lightly.

The door opened. "When I tell you to come in here, Al; you don't have to knock!"

She slid in past him. "Yes Sir!" Her alarm rose. "Uh, what's going on?" She settled into a chair next to Diana.

"We've been talking." Daniel's decisive voice!

Alexandra nodded. He had been, anyway! It looked like her mom was mostly crying.

"Is this about Mallory's new magazine?" Her mind sought an explanation of the strange scenario. "Did you see the copy I made you?"

He nodded slowly. "I did! I've gone over it quite carefully! What about you?"

"Uh-not yet! Was I supposed to? I've still been going through stuff on-line-"

He laughed good-naturedly, slightly alleviating the tension in the room. "See, Al, a good Geologist stops drilling when he finds treasure! When you found *Drilling Platform*, you discovered the proverbial gold mine! Instead of scrolling past like it was nothing, you should have delved into it!"

"Okay-uh-I guess I still have a problem with it. You kinda told me to get over it, but sometimes it takes me a while-"

"Well, look at it now." He shoved the document at her when all she wanted to know was why her mom was crying. She looked up, frustrated.

"Mom's fine. Read over the magazine and tell me what you see!"

"You know what I see! I see that Mallory broadcast all this important stuff instead of mining!"

"Yeah, that's the broad overview! First impression! Look at it again, Al! If you were going into the mining business, which item would interest you the most?"

"The silver in Colorado," she decided at last.

"And why?"

She returned her attention to the black and white copy. "We should get a color-copier."

"Mmm-hmmm, changing the subject is always a good dodge."

She laughed. "Yes, Sir; I thought so. Okay, why Colorado? Because it's the least impressive, and it's listed last in this issue! Big international companies with lots of capital will be all over the tops of the list headers. And while there's always more talk about gold prices, silver prices are tied to gold-" she paused.

"Go on. What else?"

"Well," she laughed with delight. "There's silver here, but like you said, 'It's a Proverbial gold mine'; isn't it?"

"Why?"

"It's a working cattle ranch; so if someone acquired it, it would provide revenue from the ranching side, while they got a mining operation underway!"

"Bingo! And while you were continuing aimless research, I investigated this a little further. Since Mallory drilled and pulled off-site, this rancher has passed away. His widow-"

Alexandra leapt to her feet in excitement! "So, you're purchasing it, and you're going to open a mine?"

"Not me! I'm less interested in mining than David and Mallory are!"

"Oh!" She settled back, dejected. "I guess you lost me then!"

She sat regarding him curiously. "Well, I can't do it! I wish I could, though!"

Diana spoke for the first time. "I thought we tried to instill into you, not to say that, Alexandra!"

"Not to say what? What did I say?" The emotional energy of the interview weighed on her as she replayed in her mind. "Oh! 'I can't'! We're not supposed to say, 'I can't'; unless it's a moral or legal issue!" Her eyes widened. "Oh, so that's why you're crying?" Tears welled up, and streamed down her cheeks as she hugged her mom. "You're crying because I'm about to launch!"

"Mmmm-hmmm, I'm excited for you, Sweetie! It just seems so soon! It seems like I just brought you home from the hospital-"

"Well, staying for church tomorrow night could work, I guess." Mallory was eager to be in her Dallas office Monday morning. That was the office where the logs fed from the drilling sites. "If you don't like Faith, we could visit other churches in Dallas."

"Well, I like it; it's just-" David's frustrated sigh.

"What? That same guy that always waylays you about a job?"

"Yeah; the one that I tell every time, to email me a resume and go on-line to fill out our application. If he's too interested in short-cuts in the job search process to take those steps, I'm pretty sure I can't use him."

"Well, if you've told him that, and he won't do that stuff, just brush him off. Wherever we go to church, we'll run into that, I'm afraid. It goes with our territory."

He nodded, growing silent.

"Okay, so what else?" She grew more perceptive about him with every day.

"Well, Pastor Ellis suggested I give him a shot! Told me what a hard time the guy and his family are having, and about our responsibility to the household of faith!"

"You're kidding! Pastor told you that? Maybe we should take them out to dinner again. We haven't in quite a while. And we can explain to him that the guy makes a bad impression when you tell him what needs to be done, and he refuses to do it."

"I tried to explain that! He just said that people do get tired of the application process and all of the rigmarole!"

"Well, there's always the Serenity Prayer, about changing what you can and learning to live with the rest! No matter how much you hate the paperwork, it's part of it! He's not doing well being a lone wolf going against the flow. Maybe there's something in his background-"

"May be! But I'm the guy known for hiring people with dishonorable discharges and felony convictions. At least they're humble enough to ask for jobs and follow simple instructions. Joe Hamilton could have been earning a good salary for the past eight months, but he's decided he's the exception to the rule!"

Mallory nodded agreement. "I'm surprised Pastor put pressure on you about it."

Bransom shared Sharon Saxon's disappointment at the low attendance for Bobby's memorial service! That none of the partners in crime seemed eager to associate themselves publicly! That was okay! He and other agents were on the trail of plenty of culprits in the expanding investigation! He punched a button on his phone and Jay Cox answered on the second ring.

"Hello Agent," he greeted amicably. "How can I help you?"

"I was wondering if Sophia saw anyone~"

"That's the problem, Agent! Sophia can't see! If she sensed any 'presence', she didn't mention it! Brandon saw a guy lingering by the mausoleum that put him in turmoil! Guy got in a Bentley and was chauffeured away~Look I should have called you~"

"You're doing great! An agent's been tailing the guy you just mentioned for a couple of weeks~"

Norma Engels parallel parked her big Chevy and cut the motor. She was tired, tired and old! On the brink of doing something that she at one time, had sworn she would never do! "Times, they are a-changin" she sighed to the haggard face in the rear-view mirror. Since she was early, she refilled the Thermos™ lid and sipped cautiously at the hot coffee! Well, she should be happy! Happy and relieved! To be out from under the old place she couldn't afford or manage physically! To get her asking price without a lower counter-offer~ The money sounded like a good bit~long as she didn't have to stretch it out too far before 'kickin' the bucket'! She watched the analog clock on the cracked dash click to eleven! This was it!

"Has the man taken complete leave of his senses?" Lilly spluttered around the airy London flat!

Benjamin regarded her steadily over his reading glasses. At least her twentieth time to pose the same question! At last, he responded, figuring anything he said would draw her wrath.

"I think *the man's* judgment has been called into question since he first allowed you to spirit Cassandra away! At least, Alexandra's eighteen!"

"Well, Cassandra isn't! And she's going, too! First the nursing-"

"If I didn't know better, I would think that you are fretting, Lilly! Faulkner's idea is astounding! Give him credit! I guess you perceive him as your rival for Cassandra's talent! Parents must help children discover themselves!"

Lilly glowered!

He laughed. "With all of your twenty-first century technology, you think you are in the loop enough to keep from these surprises!"

"Cassandra is a violinist!" The force of Lilly's words startled even her.

He shrugged. "Of that, my dear Lilly, there is no question! Because Faulkner has allowed the child to accompany her sister on the adventure; is no reason for you to drop the ball on your end! Have you broached the subject of another concert series?"

"Well, no, Benjamin! She is studying heavy nursing courses while she's barely in middle-school! And she doesn't practice, even as much as her parents would wish!"

"Why should she practice? She's already better than the norm and better than their church performances demand! Maybe she needs the impetus and challenge that you bring to the table!"

Her expression was horrified. "And why did you not say that to me before this has happened?"

He shrugged. "You're just mad that something got by you! This new decision by the Faulkners in no way changes your relationship with your prodigy. What can change it is your backing off!"

Dr. Darius Warringon still held onto a vestige of hope that he could beat the charges against him! His pompous denial of reality began to deflate as he entered the court room! Meeting Jennifer's Mo'a'aloa's contemptuous gaze, he appeared shaken for the first time! Shock waves tore through him as the blind girl took her place in the gallery! He was the nice guy; why was he here, standing trial alone?

The proceedings were a blur! In spite of all of his attorneys' motions to suppress much of the incriminating evidence, any vestige of respectability he clung to, tore away. Stunned, he realized he was finished. No more protection! No more shelter by the AMA! His silence, refusing to incriminate anyone else in the crime ring, had only allowed his survival long enough to face the criminal justice system! In spite of his efforts to remain aloof, he trembled violently! After a few obligatory 'Objections', his team of attorneys seemed to concede defeat!

After a day and a half where the prosecutor triumphed at every turn, the jury was sent to deliberations! Enraged, Warrington spoke with his chief counsel. "What about an appeal?"

"Okay, they don't have a conviction yet! It's too soon to worry about an appeal! You might still beat this!"

The surgeon could hardly fathom the strange words! Beating all of the charges with the evidence presented against him-and yet, the attorney seemed to be in the know-

Alexandra's eyes danced with anticipation! "You ready?"

Cassandra nodded. "I am if you are!"

Alexandra went through her paperwork once more! Her first time ever closing on a property! She kind of wished her dad-but if he was that confident in her- Not comfortable with parallel parking on Main Street, she parked at a lot at the end of the street. They could walk back to the title company.

Alexandra extended her hand to Ray Meeker, introducing herself and her younger sister.

The attorney looked them over perceptively. A couple of blonds; young, and out of their league-maybe. He turned to greet Norma Engels with a broad smile. "You ready, Norma?" He drew her to the conference table and made introductions before checking out the seller's stack of paperwork! Without so much as offering coffee or any hospitality, he shoved the purchase documents at Alexandra to sign. When she began to study the paperwork thoroughly, he grabbed a pen from the center of the table and pointed Alexandra to the purchaser's signature line!

Resisting pressure to hasten the closing, she met his gaze, troubled. “This is different. Why is this changed to deny me mineral rights?”

“Why do you care if you're buying a cattle operation?”

“I was under the impression that I'm purchasing a ranch! The whole ranch, including all that's on it”! Alexandra's voice was cool.

“Well, perhaps you should have told Norma your real reasons for buying her place.”

Alexandra studied the elderly woman with interest. “I did tell her my real reason. She's selling a ranch, and I'm buying it for the price she asked.”

Norma spoke up, “That's right, Ray! Let me see what she's balking at.”

He covered a nervous cough. “Miss Sweet-cheeks here forgot to mention to you that she's a Geology major and doesn't know the first thing about cattle!”

Alexandra felt her face flush.

“Okay, hold on, Ray. The young woman's name is Alexandra, and she does have a sweet countenance! If she thinks there are minerals on my place, I'd doubt it. But if it helps me sell, her thinking so, then I'm glad I let that company come drill the sample!” She returned her attention to the contract. “Nice, Ray, I see you've tried to make yourself custodian of the mineral rights!”

“Well, to protect you, Norma!”

She eyed him coldly. “Look at this face, Ray! Do I look like I was born yesterday?”

“Uh, no, but you do look lovely today! That color-”

“Can it, Raymond! I hired you to oil this through, not to throw a monkey wrench in the works! Fix it like it was when Miss Faulkner and I came to an agreement! I'm paying a lot for your service! And you're trying to step in and hijack mineral rights for yourself!”

“Come on, Norma; you've known me for a long time!”

“Yeah, you're a shyster and getting worse!”

Another self-conscious cough, “I just thought that she misrepresented herself by not telling you about the Geology-thing.”

“And I didn't ask her anything about herself because all I care about is if she has the financing so I can get my money! Since Mort died, I don't care what becomes of the place! If she sells off the herd, if the herd dies off, if she rips up the whole place looking for some pie-in-the-sky kind of fortune! Change the contract back; I'll be out in my car!”

Darius Warrington felt as though his heartbeat reverberated throughout the entire chamber. Surely the short jury deliberations meant a conviction! Somehow he managed to rise in unison as the judge took the bench and the jury foreman stepped forward to hand the verdict to the bailiff!

Then, the doctor was pounding his lead-counsel on the back and shooting a vicious glance at the stunned women in the front row of the gallery! 'Innocent on all charges'! He didn't know how! He didn't care how! He was a free man! He couldn't wait for a celebratory drink and meeting a lady somehow. He hadn't forgotten his old pickup lines!

Norma poured more coffee! Scoundrel of an attorney! Maybe Raymond should have told her about the Geology and mineral deal, before closing was arranged. And without making himself the benefactor! She watched as the Faulkner girls emerged and crossed the street to a café. At least they seemed to be sticking around in town; maybe they didn't mind waiting to try again. Her mind went back to the attorney's attempt to pressure the girl! She fought tears. Evidently, with her desperate need to sell, and the young woman's eagerness to buy, Ray considered himself in a prime position to take advantage of a situation! Sad! Everyone out for themselves! Even when she thought she was paying him to be in her corner; at least a little bit! It all served to deepen her sense of loss for Mort!

David was more than a little shocked at Mallory's lunch time news!

"The Faulkners hit on the Silverton deal? That's a shocker!" He waited until she returned her attention from Alexis to him. "Are you surprised at that?"

Animated, she glowed! "Blown away amazed! But then-" Laughing she slowed down to explain. "Well, I never figured anyone at *GeoHy* would see the issue. Unless another Geologist saw it, and happened to mention it to Daniel! So, I'm surprised about that! Uh-I've been worried though, about Alexandra! How long can you sit with your siblings in a home school classroom? I mean, I know the kids have friends and all kinds of diversions, but still. And Alexandra has experienced frustration working for her dad, because the other employees resent her inside track. I know I felt like none of it was real until I did some Geological field work! Dr. Higgins led it-it was tough, though! Some of the guys-"

"Yeah, I've always been afraid to ask you how that went."

She shrugged. "Probably about like you'd expect! Dr. Higgins was good enough friends with Daniel at that time that he ran quite a bit of interference for me! But you wish you could be a colleague without all the junk, without needing someone to run interference for you." She sighed. "I know; I could stay home and bake cookies!"

He made a face. "Yeah, but then I'd have to pretend that they taste good. But face it, you'll never just be one of the guys!"

Her turn to grimace! "Don't remind me! It ruined my baseball career, too!"

"Well, we're not doing so badly with the gender and career that God put you in. I'll admit, it was confusing to me when you turned into a girl from being one of the guys!"

She blushed, "Don't remind me."

Darius Warrington sat on a park bench in Santa Monica, watching sunbathers and water sports enthusiasts on the beach below and in the surf beyond! Southern California! And Erik Bransom's efforts to lock him up and throw away the key had backfired! Warrington figured jury-tampering, but the 'how' was immaterial to him! They owed him to get him off! He grinned up at white puffs sailing above. Freedom felt good!

Nick watched Jennifer as she surfed the internet. He figured she must feel bitter disappointment at the outcome of Warrington's case. She didn't mention it, but he figured it was a safe assumption.

"Anything interesting?" he questioned.

"Yes! As a matter of fact"! The glow of her countenance shot joy through him.

"Great! Anything you can share?"

"Yes, thanks to Sophia and her endless dedication and money supply! Of course, Dr. Warrington only got off with one of the murders! So, the FBI is bringing up new charges to arrest him again! And of course, Sophia's after his jugular about his botched surgery on her eyes! Her attorneys are ready to serve papers in a civil suit! In the meantime, he's been in touch with someone on a burner phone, who has scheduled him on a flight to Caracas! According to the PI! Now, that's a country that won't extradite him, so they may be sending him there so he won't face further prosecution! But also, and Caroline Hillman is investigating, that may be where the illicit surgeries are performed.

"Why would rich people be willing to go there? It's pretty dangerous."

"Because it's a last resort to save their own lives, or the life of one they love, with a new organ! Desperation! Many of them are so well off they have their own security, anyway! And, they know they're breaking American laws by going off-shore! Some of them think laws are made to be broken! And there's something else. Do you remember that Mallory shot the nanny?"

A heavy sigh, "How could I forget? What an awful night!"

She twisted her face contemptuously. "Yeah, I missed Bobby's heart! But about this nanny! I figured Mallory shot an innocent in the melee, but I just saw her photo for the first time!"

"And she's someone you knew?"

"No, Nick! I didn't know her! But I saw her several times. There were two main groups of us! Those of us originally from the US were kept in Europe; and the European women were sent to the US. I guess less chance that way of any of us being recognized!" Her expression grew somber as she struggled with emotions. "But this woman, whom Mallory knew as Glenna, was getting old! And so they made a big story up for us, that she married a Caspian Oil Baron who fancied her! Now she's rich, happy, and respectable! But really, she was still under their thumb, playing Nanny to help them kidnap Mallory and Amelia! When I thought I had learned not to believe a thing they told us, I still fell for the story-How stupid-"

Nick moved to her side! "You had to believe it, Jen! It kept you functioning; kept you alive that there was hope!"

"False hope, Nick!"

"But still, it kept you going until the day you found Mallory and she introduced you to the real Hope! But now you know the truth, even about this, and it should be liberating!"

Tears filled her eyes as she melted into his arms. "You're right, Baby! It is liberating!" She pulled back to search his dark eyes. "Nick, I'm so sorry!"

"Get out and open the gate!" Alexandra's crisp order to her passenger!

Cass gave her sister a dirty look. "Is it safe to turn loose?"

"Whatever Cass; I'm a good driver! Just open the gate!"

Slowly, Cassandra followed the order, pausing to kiss the ground in the process.

Annoyed, Alexandra honked the horn, making her sister jump involuntarily. Then, she was further miffed when Cass decided to walk up to the house rather than getting back in. Guiltily, Alexandra remembered promising not to fight, if Cass could come with her. Well, she needed to mend the fence with her sister, even before she began the huge task of mending fences on her new ranch. She carefully placed the transmission in drive and surveyed her prize with an overwhelming sense of possessive pride!

Chapter 15: GRUMBLING

"Good to see y'all". Pastor Ellis' voice conveyed warmth and concern.

"Thank you. It's good to be back." David tried to match the tone! 'Well, being back was good. Amelia and Avery both liked their classes, teachers, the other children. Amelia talked non-stop after each service about a Veggie-Tale™ pirate ship she loved to play with.'

Of course, that had made David want to buy her one of her own, but Mallory's caution; that for now, that was one of Amelia's motivators for being in her class. And that if she owned one, she wouldn't play with it any more than she did her other toys.

When David laughed at the argument of a shallow reason for church attendance, Mallory laughingly admitted that at one time, her primary reason for attending, was usually to see him. "Right or wrong, I still heard the stories and songs and sermons! And they're still helping me," she reasoned.

"I thought I'd see you guys last Sunday night." Ellis' words brought David back to the conversation; the words barely softening a probing question.

"Yes Sir. The afternoon just got away from us so we went to my dad's church and drove back late." He hated to mention the troublesome job seeker. "If y'all don't have plans for after the service, would you like to join us for dinner?"

With the pastor's hearty acceptance, David made his way to the nursery wing to check Alexis in.

"Did you go to church this morning"? One of Daniel's first questions when the Skype came on through the sat link!

"Yes Sir. A little one up in Silverton! It was real different. Loud with a praise and worship team and one of the girls in the team had a bare midriff with a ring in her navel." Cassandra could be blunt.

"Well, there's not a lot of choice up there. I'm sure they're people who love the Lord, and emphasis is often different from one ministry to another. And you two can set a good example; but please do it in a humble way. So, Al, you're a proud property owner!"

"Yes Sir. After a couple of wrinkles"!

Daniel laughed, aware of the mineral rights dispute. "Good job, holding your ground; not to use a pun!" Both girls winced visibly, and he continued. "So, no one's bothered you; and you feel pretty safe?"

"Except riding with Speedy Gonzales® down winding mountain roads"! Cassandra's eyes grew enormous, remembering.

"Okay, well remember the two of you promised to get along. Cass, you can start learning to drive on the ranch property."

"Really?" She screeched in delight.

"Where's Mom?" Alexandra was surprised Diana wasn't on the camera.

"Well, she'll be along! She has four little ones to get ready for bed."

Cassandra fought tears. "I miss everybody. Is Xavier okay?"

Daniel fought tears. "He is! Well, we've all been in the doldrums a little bit! Yeah, Cass, he goes from your room to your place at the table, and back. Like when you were gone helping Mallory, he was the same way. The little ones all miss both of you. So do Mom and I. We feel like this is good, though."

To Alexandra's surprise, she was suddenly homesick. "Dad, what if I can't do this?"

"You know the answer to that. You're on a great quest that you can't possibly handle!"

She nodded. "So, pray! I have been! We have been!"

Diana's face appeared on the monitor. "That's what I like to hear. We're praying God's wall of protection about you. What have you been doing to keep busy?"

"We-elll," Cassandra's tone turned doubtful. "This house is pretty smelly and dirty, but we don't know what to do with this stuff. Was this lady supposed to move out before we closed and she gave us the keys?"

"Well, bag it all up in trash bags and store it in the garage or someplace for thirty days." Daniel's quick judgment!

"Dad, trash bags are so expensive!"

Daniel laughed. He was pretty sure this was Al's first experience controlling money and caring about the price of things. "One of those expenses you have to bite the bullet on, Al. You know, you still have the job as Mom's assistant if you want that salary to keep up."

Her eyes widened and she struggled for composure. 'Uh, keep up her schooling, keep up her music, keep us with Cass, keep up with the ranch, start figuring out a way to locate the silver deposit- "Yes, Sir! Have her email what she needs me to do!"

When the session shut down, Alexandra felt a sense of elation, despite the load! Her mom and dad trusted her, and she was on her own!

David and Mallory, with girls and diaper bags in tow, waited in the foyer while the pastor visited with stragglers!

At last, he headed their way! "Hey; sorry to keep you waiting! I took the liberty of inviting Joe and his family to join us. They already headed to-" and he named a restaurant the Andersons didn't try to frequent with their small children. "He's getting a table for everyone. Y'all can go on, and we'll be right behind you."

In the car, Mallory was silent. She figured David was fuming and didn't blame him. At last she ventured. "So, even if we don't want to hire Joe, we're still going to end up buying his dinner. We can call Pastor and tell him it's late, and the girls-"

He giggled his funny staccato. "And you accused me of trying to take evasive action."

She shrugged. "Well, let's just say, I see your point now! So, let's just pay for our family, and pastor can spring for his own guests!"

He shook his head. "I guess we're hung in this. I'll buy and then we won't offer any more-for a long time!"

Trent tiptoed through the quiet house. Unusual when he couldn't sleep. Maybe he was getting too old to drink real coffee in the evenings! But no;

there was a great deal on his mind! He turned on a lamp in his office, and debated between turning the computer on, or opening his Bible. He opted for the computer!

He sat up suddenly! Wider awake than ever! 'What in the world could Faulkner be thinking?' He logged into his Forestry Service account and pulled up a map of Colorado.

Megan's timid bed-time prayer request, was that Alexandra and Cassandra would be safe on some old relic of a ranch where they planned to open a Silver mine! His first awareness of the situation! So, Jeremiah stayed in touch with Megan! There was a shock! And then evidently Faulkner felt that Trent and the Federal employees he commanded had nothing better to do than baby sit a couple of clueless little girls who should still be his responsibility! He massaged fingers through thick waves of hair, trying to corral his frenzied thoughts. Okay! He guessed he owed Faulkner his stable marriage! The guy was a great guy! But what a judgment lapse! He couldn't imagine how Alexandra could have wheedled her way from 'no freedom' to taking the world by storm with no restraints! Okay, he didn't know the details! Maybe it was all blown out of proportion! And he was upset that Jeremiah and Megan had a thing going on behind his and Sonia's back. He scrolled the map, having a hard time discerning where this alleged ranch might be. He frowned. As he thought! Fairly well surrounded by National Forest! He smiled suddenly. Maybe it was time for another family vacation! It could be fun, and he could get to the truth of the situation first-hand.

The meal was a fiasco! Evidently, Pastor and Mrs. Ellis figured if David and Mallory could see firsthand, the plight of the unemployed man, they would change their minds.

Joe clapped David on the shoulder like a long-lost buddy. "I'm sure glad for us to get a chance to get acquainted."

"Yeah, we're divided between here and Arkansas, so we haven't gotten to know people here very well. I've known the members of my dad's church nearly my whole life."

That was true, and Mallory was proud of David for trying. Then, Joe ordered first, opting for a sirloin.

"Excuse me, Joe; usually either ladies order first, or the gentleman orders for them." David didn't add that business etiquette suggested following the host's lead in ordering. For example, if the host ordered a burger, you went in the same price range. Unless the host said to order whatever you want! As the host, David hadn't offered Carte Blanche, and it was Hamilton's faux pas! But that was only the beginning of his obnoxiousness!

Strangely, the Ellis's seemed clueless that their scheme was backfiring!

"You should really find a place for Joe!" Mrs. Ellis's countenance glowed with the assurance that she was right."

"Well, that sounds nice, Mrs. Ellis, but a place for him doing what? He hasn't filled out our on-line ap or sent me a résumé. He has refused so steadfastly, that now, I feel like he's a rebel, and I don't want him. My Bible says that the rebellious dwell in a dry land! He can rebel about the way things are done 'til the cows come home. I just feel like if he ignores everything I say about getting hired, he'll ignore what I say as his boss. I don't need that!"

Hamilton lashed out, "Says the greenhorn kid married to the rich wife! The only reason my kids aren't starving to death is because we qualified for food stamps!"

Determined, the pastor's wife pressed, "Why can't you just see that someone in the household of faith needs your help?"

"I guess we're already helping! We pay the taxes that provide his food stamps!" Mallory's words shot past her lips, and she immediately knew they were too hard! "Okay, back up; with all due respect, Pastor and Mrs. Ellis, we can't afford to hire Mr. Hamilton."

"Oh? Don't tell me this economy has hit y'all in the pocketbooks, too?" Pastor Ellis sounded almost fiendishly gleeful, and David frowned. Before he could speak, the other man continued. "Aha! So y'all are mostly a front! All show?"

David caught the grin fighting to free itself on Mallory's lips. 'Yep, she was right! As usual! He should have canceled instead of seeing this through.'

"Well, if you can't keep up your mission commitment, I understand." The pastor's tone, sympathetic!

"We can keep our commitment. That isn't a problem! God has blessed us for stepping out in faith~"

"Okay, well that's good, but I should probably tell you that our budget's in the red in this economy, and with summer vacationers and the corresponding dip in the offerings, we're writing to tell our missionaries we'll try to pick their support up again in the fall."

Silence dominated for several seconds. "Okay, that's odd," David's voice struggling for control. "You have foreign missionaries that work hard to share the gospel, and you don't care if their kids go hungry~and yet, your heart bleeds for a lazy guy that fills out barely enough aps to keep his unemployment compensation up. I'm sorry, but missionaries don't have the option or the luxury to qualify for food stamps. Our church never had much and we didn't support as many missionaries as my Dad wished we could! But we would have all done without, before he would have stranded a missionary!"

Mallory's heart surged with pride. That was quite an admission from David, who had resented doing without what they did! His pride in his dad's ministry seemed to grow daily.

"You know what? We're pretty tired," she apologized. "We've had a busy week, and we're hitting it early in the morning. We're probably pretty frazzled, so before we say any more, we're just going to take our food with us. Pastor, we'll be out of town next weekend and possibly the next. "Y'all stay and enjoy your meal."

They paid and were gone.

Norma tried to relax in the Ouray hot springs pool, hoping the minerals' supposed healing properties would soothe aching bones and joints. And a ravaged soul! Now, she was beset with doubts! Strange that the ranch was listed for more than a year, and not one inquiry! But now, with the deal done, she was getting buyers offering double! Maybe she did make a mistake! But how could she know other offers would pour in? Maybe there was still a lot of silver up there. Sadly she thought of the two purchasers. Geologist! Hunh! Didn't look like she could find her way out of the beauty parlor! They were out of their element! But as her thoughts tumbled in the agitator of her mind, she realized that she had no plan. Once again, she felt betrayed by her late husband.

Still toweling her hair, she unlocked the old Chevy and slid onto the warm bench seat. Turning the key, she went through the usual babying maneuvers to coax it to start. You just had to have the deft touch~ But then, fighting tears, she realized deft touch or no, the engine wasn't turning over.

Feeling more morose than ever, she slid out and relocked it; then jumped with alarm as a giant loomed above her.

"Sorry! Didn't mean to startle you"! A dazzling smile and proffered hand reduced her caution slightly before her defenses came back up. This kid was probably some bushwhacker who knew about her cashier's check and was here to con her out of it!

"She won't start? You think it's just the battery? I can try giving you a jump."

Her suspicion shot up. Maybe he had loosened a wire while she was in the pool, to show up now like a knight in shining armor! "Thanks anyway, Son. Guess I'll go call my husband and have a bite of lunch while I wait for him."

David was loath to give up. "She's a beauty. You think he might be interested in selling?"

"I'm sorry! Who? Sell what?"

"Your husband; selling the car?" David wasn't sure what he was doing! He hadn't even started restoration on Sunquist's antique truck. Of course, that was partly because Amelia had formed an affinity for playing in it! From Mallory's gene pool, who had spent her life bonded to a junky, old tractor!

Norma bit her lip, filled with uncertainty. "I haven't seen you around before-"

"That's because this is my first time here." He beckoned for their convoy to slow, and Mallory leaned out the window of the RV.

"What's going on? Hey, aren't you Norma?"

Astounded, the older woman nodded. "And you're Mallory, the one that contacted me about drilling on my ranch. I looked you up online after you first phoned me."

Mallory nodded. "Let me go find a place to park this thing, and I'll be right back. We're blocking traffic."

David watched the procession follow her to turn right at the next corner. 'So, you're really a widow, and your husband won't be here to help with the car? That's a good idea, though, to say that! My name's David."

Norma, nodded, embarrassed by her flawed subterfuge. "So, you here to drill more places"?

David couldn't tell whether she was antagonistic or curious. "No, Ma'am, we came to help Alexandra and Cassandra set up. How far are we from the ranch?"

"Not that far actually! Less than twenty-five miles! Over the famous Million Dollar Highway across Red Mountain Pass! Road's better now than it ever used to be. And summertime isn't so bad! Is your wife coming back?"

He grinned. "Yes'm, I think so. Once she parks, she has to pack up the stroller. We have three little girls."

"Oh, that's a lot of trouble!"

"Well, we're getting used to it, and we kind of have a system. Here she comes!"

Despite Trent's best sales pitch, none of his family seemed thrilled at the prospect of another Colorado camping trip. Rob Addington was no fonder of the plan, but Trent pulled rank on him. Whimsically, he wondered if it might work to try pulling rank on his family. He grinned to himself. Well, they were all growing up with plans and responsibilities of their own; truth be told, he couldn't ask for better kids. Rob was a mystery to him! Begging for his job back, willing to come back, nearly starting over, and still maintaining a belligerent attitude!

"We're packing in there? Just us two?" Addington stared at the map, wary. Out in the sticks, just the two of them, Morrison could really bear down on the religious thing!

The Director shrugged casually. "Yeah; unless you know of someone else to join us"! Then figuring Addington would want to include drinking buddies, he hastened to add, "What about your sons?"

Cassandra slid behind the wheel against Alexandra's wishes. "Dad told me I can learn!"

"Well, he didn't say first thing!"

"He didn't say not first thing!"

"Okay, well, we have lots to do! We should start by fixing the fence. Why don't you get that wheel barrow and start filling it with gravel and rocks? We can prop the fence posts back up by piling rocks around the bottoms."

Cassandra scoffed. "That won't make them stand up. They look rotten and broken." Annoyed, she strode into the house to find the car key.

Frustrated, the older girl went for the mentioned piece of equipment, dragging it to a gravely patch of ground. Her sister was supposed to be here helping her! Hardly deterred, though, she began scooping up the loose stones.

"Does this gauge work, or is this thing really out of gas?" The younger girl's question carried in the clear air.

Dismayed, Alexandra strode to her sister's side. That was something she had never considered! Fighting tears, she took in the quivering needle. There was sure a lot involved with being 'On her own'! "Okay, I've heard that you can really save on gas by coasting in neutral-"

Cass sprang out to face her, "Oh, no, no, no, no, no-no-no! We are not coasting in neutral! In these mountains"!

Al's face twisted mockingly, "Okay, better plan?"

"Maybe walking and bringing back a gas can? I think I'll go call Daddy."

"No, Cass, please?" Al turned from sarcastic to pleading. "I have to do this. Let's just try to think. I know!" She jumped up jubilantly. "I saw a gas can in the barn; I think it has a little bit in it!" She broke into a run and was back immediately with the red, plastic container. "It doesn't have much."

"We should call home. We don't actually know what that stuff is. If it's not unleaded, it'll mess up the engine."

Alexandra's expression darkened. "You don't know what you're talking about!"

"Why take a chance? There isn't enough in there to help much. And it took a huge chunk of your loan money to buy this place. Why risk ruining an engine the first week?"

"Okay, how about this? Let's call Roger Sanders and ask him if there's a way for us to tell if this is leaded or un-"

Cass's turn for sarcasm! "And he'll give us some data to run a chemical analysis, but we forgot to bring our 'la-bor'-a-t'ry'!"

Alexandra couldn't help laughing at the phony British accent. "Okay, remember what Dad said?"

"Probably to watch the gas gauge! He told us lots of stuff!"

"He told me this is too big for me to do alone, and I need to pray."

"Well, yeah; but we should still be smart. I mean, we've run out of gas up here a long way from any stations; and we bought microwavable food, but there's no microwave." Cass paused at Alexandra's defeated slump. "But, praying's probably as good of an idea as we've come up with. Uh-you start."

With the brief prayer meeting ended, Alexandra stomped back to the wheelbarrow and shovel, attacking her task furiously. If two people had to be in agreement to get their prayers answered, they were stranded up here indefinitely!

Riding point, Trent reigned in, motioning silence to those behind him. Sadly, silence wasn't one of the boys' strong points! Scowling, Trent dismounted, pulling his mount back and getting Rob's attention.

"What's up?" Even the cautious question seemed to echo!

"Trip-wire! We need to high-tail it back. I know stuff like this can happen, but I wouldn't have brought your sons along-"

Face tense and white, the other man nodded, pulling his mount around. His children, picking up on the fear vibes, fell silent. Both men, rifles across their saddles and side arms ready, seemed almost afraid to breathe until they made it safely back to the ranger station.

One of the rangers emerged, grinning. "Short camp out! City sli-i-i-ckerrrrs"!

Not amused, Trent silenced the guy with a look. "You have someone cultivating a cash crop about an hour up the trail! They have the forest booby-trapped. I saw a huge spider building its web on the tripwire, or no telling-" his voice trailed off. Guardian angel on duty today, for sure! He presented his badge, and the ranger snapped to.

"What do you need me to do?"

Within an hour, Rob and his sons were headed home, and a task force surrounded Trent!

Convincing Norma to go with them took a while! First Mallory, and then David, pled and cajoled. David's attempts to jump her engine and let her take off on her own, didn't work; so at last she was left with her only viable option's being to hop on board the convoy! Mallory wasn't sure if it was a good thing. Norma's language wasn't the best, and David's requests for her to be careful what she said around his kids, fell on deaf ears.

"She's a bad person! She talk like the mean mans-" Amelia's whisper carried as her expression imparted extra meaning. After another rest room break and snack purchases, the caravan proceeded out of town.

A beep at the gate made Alexandra jump, startled to see a car seeking entrance to her remote property. Keeping a tight hold on the shovel, she moved toward the vehicle. When one of the visitors waved brightly from the open window, a relieved Alexandra recognized her as one of the members of the praise and worship team. She was aware of Cassie's approach from the house as she drew near the visitor.

The passenger opened her door and eased out. "Hey, it looks like y'all are busy, but I wanted to come say, 'Hi! I'm Kendra Meeker. My uncle served as Norma's attorney in the sale of this place. I'm his paralegal, but I still didn't put together who you guys were until you came to church! You guys made me so nervous! Here I'm up singing, and you two are serious musicians! You must have thought we were so hick! This is Natalie, and we know your names! Oh my word! I can't believe I'm actually talking to you guys! Thank you for coming to our church. There aren't too many of us teens and young singles, but we're grilling burgers and hot dogs and having a singing out at our place Friday night! Do you think maybe y'all can come? Well, I'm on my lunch break so we can't stay, but call me." She thrust a business card into Al's hand and they circled around and headed back toward town.

"You could have said something," Cassandra suggested as she fanned at the cloud of dust enveloping them.

"Well, she kinda did all the talking. What was I supposed to say? We're out of gas; can you spare us any?"

Cass shrugged. "Well, the visit and invitation were nice. You suppose Dad and Mom will let us go?"

"Maybe! I'm sure Dad'll have Erik and the FBI check their story first."

Cassandra bravely fought tears. "Well, we're really okay for now, anyway. We can cook our food on the burners, and maybe-there's no place we need to go for now."

Daniel deplaned and gave Diana a call as he waited for a rent car. "So far; so good! I told Al I trust her, and now here I come to check up on them before it's been a week. I mean, they've said they're fine-"

"Would you quit worrying? We are still the parents! Just tell them I've been in panic mode over them, and blame it on me."

He laughed. "That was my plan, but it's great to have your permission. Is everything okay there? As soon as I see the lay of the land, I'll head back day after tomorrow as scheduled. Love, you, Beautiful! Call if you need anything!"

He disconnected to do the rent car walk around, then slung his bag in the trunk and headed toward the small tourist, almost, ghost town, of Silverton.

"Okay, right at the end of this road cut, there's a county road," Norma hated coming back here. She wasn't sure, but she thought she might get in legal trouble. Sell the place and move on down the road! Her plan gone amuck already! "You'll turn left; watch for traffic coming. It moves fast, and ya can't see each other-"

David jammed the brakes on his pickup and Mallory nearly rear-ended him with the RV! An eighteen wheeler barreled past, sounding an aggravated blast of the air horn. "Okay, yeah, Norma; no kidding! I see what you mean."

"Bad intersection! No telling how many fatal accidents-"

David looked askance! Cars and trucks continued to materialize suddenly, making him wonder if anyone ever survived the intersection! While he hesitated, Charles hopped out of his truck and approached his window.

"Crazy Feather's going to walk up and stop oncoming traffic."

"Hence the name 'Crazy Feather'! Tell him to be careful." David rolled his window up and turned toward Norma. "How much farther?"?

"Four, point two miles! On your left hand side"!

Painful blisters forced Alexandra to give up with the shovel! Sinking down wearily on the front step, she stared around, fighting feelings of hopelessness! She guessed the cattle were doing okay. It was past calving season, and there seemed to be enough pasture for them to graze. Her concern was the broken down fence; the one Cassandra wasn't helping her to repair. Well, it hadn't gotten in such bad shape overnight. She felt suddenly exhausted and hungry. She studied her palms. If they could ever make it back into town again, work gloves would be a good investment. Looking up beyond towering peaks, she breathed another prayer!

Chapter 16: GLIMMERS

Jeremiah 33:3 Call unto me, and I will answer thee, and shew thee great and mighty things, which thou knowest not.

"Wow, Lord!" Alexandra's barely audible words, as a choking dust cloud revealed a stream of vehicles halting before her sagging gate! Not totally sure what to make of the procession, she was pretty sure it was the great and mighty deliverance she was despairing of. She hopped up and moved toward the entrance, but David was already swinging the gate wide to grant entrance to the assortment of cars, trucks, and RV's.

Cassandra was out of the house and ahead of her, hugging Mallory wildly as Mallory hustled Amelia and Avery from the RV, her arms loaded with Alexis, a diaper bag, and her hand bag!

"You didn't think I could do it!" Alexandra's tone was more hurt than defiant.

"I absolutely knew you could! But you know me and synergy! What one can do, many can do better and faster!"

"Look, there's Daddy!" Alexandra and Mallory both turned at Cassandra's exuberant announcement.

"Okay, don't tattle!" Alexandra was unsure her warning was even heard as Cass flew across the yard.

Mallory grinned. "She won't. This place is ama-a-zz-zing!" Her voice turned breathless as she took in the stunning panorama.

A concerned Daniel freed himself from his emotional daughter and closed the car door. "Hey, hey, everything okay? I told you to call us if you needed anything. Why're David and Mallory here with an army? And y'all called Trent Morrison?"

"Well, no, Sir! Not exactly! You just told us we would face huge challenges, and we'd have to pray! Uh, so that's what we did, and we weren't sure God was listening-but, apparently-He was!" She surveyed the chaotic scene. "I'll never doubt Him again!"

Daniel nodded. "Until next time; if you're anything like me." But, he too, gazed around in wonder at the measure of response! He felt somewhat ashamed of himself, talking about 'trusting God', like that was just empty words Christians said.

"But you didn't help Him out by calling Mallory?" Maybe his faith was weak.

"What do you need me to do to help?" Mallory appeared at David's elbow as he directed set-up tasks.

"He gave her a quick kiss! "Nothing! Just keep the girls corralled so they don't get run over by all of the vehicle's jockeying around. When things are farther along, there may be some jobs you and they can do."

She nodded. Her job sounded easy enough, but- Inspiration seized her. She pushed the partially loaded wheel barrow toward the porch, with the idea of emptying it, and giving rides.

Amelia was beside her immediately with Avery tagging at her heels. "Can I help move those rocks?" She was already daintily picking them up and lining them along the porch. Mallory stared amazed. Since Amelia liked the new rock game, Avery was immediately on board! Quite the little copycat of everything big sissy did! Easy enough! She hoped it would last as she perched on the edge of the porch, bouncing the baby!

"Look, Mommy. Here's a little, baby, shiny one."

At first, Mallory paid little heed. They both said 'Look, Mommy,' from morning 'til night, and it grew hard to feel their wonder at every little thing.

"Mommmeeee"!

"What, Amelia? Don't whine! Mommy's kinda frazzled from driving all day!" That was the truth. Barely used to driving, she had maneuvered the RV all day, through mountains for a good bit of the way, and tending all three little ones, solo!

"Look, at this little, shiny, bitty, baby rock!"

Sighing, she held out her hand. Then she did a double-take, sensing weight compared to size, before studying the metallic object, trying to be certain of her identification in the purple twilight!

"Wow, Baby, that is a pretty one. Why don't you and Ave'y keep looking for more like it?"

Diana made her way to the design studio. She was exhausted, not realizing how much she counted on the two older girls to help with the little ones! Finally, all four were in bed and asleep. Jeremiah was busy at the computer. Not sure anything creative could happen, she still settled in with some new fabric samples and her sketch book. Maybe working would pass the time until Daniel phoned her with a first-hand report on Alexandra and Cassandra! She was surprised at not having already received an update.

Darius Warrington pulled into a space in remote parking at LAX and pulled his carry-on bag from the Porsche. Freedom! And his finances were about to swing back into the black! He checked his jacket pocket for his passport and e-ticket. He was good to go. Just as he approached the line to clear security, a uniformed officer approached.

"Darius Warrington, M.D.?"

He started to deny, then thought better of creating any questions before boarding.

"Yes, but I have this flight-"

Before he could finish, the constable served papers. With a smile, he accepted. A couple of hours, and he would be on his way to where the American courts couldn't touch him. "Thanks, have a good evening", his voice dripped sarcasm.

When the court officer disappeared from sight, he trashed the documents. That's when he caught sight of Erik Bransom and Jed Dawson! Heart sinking, he knew his gig was up!

In interrogation, bravado fled. Using information supplied him by Missy, Jennifer, and Sophia, Erik rattled the doctor to his core, convincing him that others high up in the organization were crumbling and talking!

"Is everything okay?" Diana's voice sounded both concerned and aggravated.

"Yeah, Beautiful! Sorry time got away from me! The girls are doing great, but there's been lots of excitement! Good excitement!" he added hastily.

"Okay, why are you calling me from the sat phone? It's late, even there. Are you not back in Durango yet, at the hotel?"

"Uh-slight change of plans! I arrived up here in conjunction with David and Mallory and their sizeable crew. Then Trent Morrison showed up in a Forestry Service vehicle! So, the change in lodging is that the girls and I are bunked down in one of the Andersons' RVs. The girls want to talk to you!"

"Well, I want to talk to them, too, of course! But, did they send out an SOS?"

His laughter carried through the confines of the vehicle. "They did! To heaven! Well, I'll be having a visit with our eldest son!"

"Well, he's been beside himself with worry!"

"Mmm-hmmmm, but maybe he should try prayer too, rather than making contact with Megan Morrison!"

"Megan Morrison, that's what brought Trent there? Oh my-"

"Welllll, Trent's story is that he's spending more time in the field, checking both on his employees and for signs of illicit activities. He asks the Lord to direct him, and Megan's tip sent him here, to the San Isabel National Forest. He barely saw a trip-wire in time to avoid it; so he and another guy from his agency, with the guy's two oldest sons went back an hour along the trail to a ranger station to muster a larger contingency of law enforcement. By the time they returned, the area was cleared out!"

"Please tell me that wasn't near Alexandra's Ranch!"

"Very near, but it's routed out for now! Let me tell you the good news! No wait; Al wants to tell you-"

Diana listened, amazed at the torrent of information!

"Platinum"! Diana's voice echoed her daughter's word in awe! "The babies discovered nuggets? Platinum nuggets?"

"Yes, Ma'am, and Mallory was so exhausted that she didn't pay any attention at first! To the girls and their shiny pebbles! My wheel barrow also held some sizeable quartz chunks, and Daddy and Mallory agree with me that they're flecked and veined with visible traces of gold! Well, I was suspicious of what brought Mallory and her entourage up here! She's the one who put this site in her e-zine. If she wanted it, why did she wait until I closed, to beat it up here?"

"Alexandra, you don't think the Andersons are trying to undercut you; do you?"

A self-conscious laugh, "I guess it entered my mind! Or that they didn't think I'm capable! Which, come to find out, I'm not! Not as much as I thought! Well, Mr. Meeker, the attorney, who tried to sabotage my purchase, showed up with three others guys offering to pay once and again what I bought the place for! I would have been really tempted-"

"You know, maybe you should consider it!" Diana was sorry to sound so hopeful, but the deal sounded sweet to her. Her daughter could pay off her loan, pay taxes on the gain, pocket a chunk of change, and come home as if nothing had ever fractured the family!

"Nice try, Mom, but Dad and David invited Mr. Meeker and his associates in, and we've loosely cobbled together a consortium! Mr. Meeker is drawing it up according to what we voted on, then Dad will have our attorney look it over, and David and Mallory will send a copy for Kerry's approval!"

Diana stifled her temptation to reprove Alexandra for using Kerry Larson's first name, but Alexandra was suddenly moving comfortably into the adult world. Struck by nostalgia, she was forced to admit Daniel was right, and the butterfly was emerging on schedule!

"Wow; that is an exciting evening! Good excitement just like your father told me!"

Silas Remington viewed the printed matter spread across his handsome desk, dazedly, as if trying to shake off a horrifying dream! How could this be, after so long a time? He was an esteemed educator, long time headmaster of this prestigious academy! Caught in the under-tow of a couple of injudicious decisions, he could hardly fathom where the journey was now taking him, and at warp speed!

Just look the other way, then claim the girl was spoiled and unhappy; be convincing about the runaway notion! That would cancel the debt with no further blackmail demands! And, they had been true to their word! Someone had even aided him several months previously, when authorities were preparing to arrest him and the media got wind of the scandal! Maybe the magician and his mirrors would intervene again! One thing he knew for sure! Former student, Sophia Marie Cox Vincent was back! And with a vengeance!

Pastor Paul Ellis sat at his desk, his thoughts in turmoil, even after spending the past hour in his Bible. The sudden buzz of the intercom made him jump! Trying not to be annoyed at the interruption, he pressed the button. "Yes, what is it?"

"Pastor, John Anderson is on line one."

Struggling with dread, he picked up. "Morning, Pastor, what can I do for you this morning?"

The other preacher's voice came, convivial and relaxed. "Well, Lana and I drove over here to Dallas for a quick getaway; we would love to take you and your wife to lunch. I mean, I guess this is short notice, so if tomorrow would work better-"

Ellis figured Anderson was upset about the after church dinner fiasco with David and Mallory. He assumed the young couple wouldn't be back, and he was thoroughly aggravated with himself.

"I think Mary Beth is on campus someplace here. She's just finishing up a meeting with the head nursery workers. What time, and name the place."

"How about twelve-thirty"? He named a steak place.

"It seems like they're committing themselves heavily in Colorado."

Benjamin looked up at Lilly's worried words. "It's simmering, Lilly; relax!"

"Are you certain?"

He chuckled, "Yes, why aren't you?"

"Because, she has her finger in so many pies"!

"When we think she's only about Diamonds, we get nervous; and then when she is pursuing everything else, we also worry. God is on the throne,

Lilly. If David and Mallory are not the ones to do this, He can bring the ones who are; in His timing!"

"But think about the significance of this! For Israel! It's our history! It's who we are!"

He sipped at strong coffee. "Yes, you are right, Lilly. It is part of who we are!"

"What it would prove to the world; Dir-Benjamin! The veracity of-"

He waved thick hands. "It would support, Lilly! Support the Biblical story of our people as they left bondage in Egypt, led by the literal Moses! It wouldn't prove it! People can overlook facts and logic to believe what they choose. What is coming to light, in this age, gives support to the ancient writings! But God has ordained that people still make a choice-to believe or not!"

"I just wish that Mallory was not putting so much energy-"

He shrugged. "They have energy and money to burn, Lilly! They reduced their tax liability for selling the pink by plowing it into further exploration! What happened to them, being seized unlawfully from Cline's ship in the Strait; that rattled them! Sad that it didn't rattle the rest of the world as much! Israel is criticized by world opinion for every breath she takes-and yet episodes like that one-Is buried the next day! (The world treads softly with the Saudis for the oil!) But, Mallory is very fascinated by the venture! I'm certain she is working on it, if only in the back of her mind! In the meantime, our enemies will bar them from exploring, if they think Israel is working by proxy! I am impatient also, to know, Lilly! But it is the Lord's work."

"Well, the story of the Exodus has come to be rejected because nothing of archeological significance has ever been found at the traditional Mt. Sinai! How could millions of people have camped at that site for forty years, and not left a scrap of pottery?"

"So, because they are searching the wrong place, they reject the entire event as mythical! Why can't they think, 'Maybe this is the wrong place? This location doesn't make sense, and nothing has ever been discovered here!' But Satan has blinded our eyes, and the eyes of most of the Gentile world! This recent emphasis on crossing at Strait of Tiran and wandering in Arabia makes far more sense. If our forefathers were in the present day Sinai Peninsula, for the entire forty years, they would never have needed to cross the Red Sea to begin with, or the Jordan River, for that matter! They would already have been on the West Bank!"

Mallory was up early, checking e-zine subscriptions! To her surprise, they chinked in steadily. She figured interest would wane after the initial issue, until excitement was regenerated by the next month's news. She smiled, amused yet aggravated at colleagues within the industry. At the end of each drill site summary, the e-zine suggested contacting *DiaMo* for a more complete dossier! The e-zine articles were a treasure map, of sorts, but gleaning further information never hurt. She was aware of one company's mad dash with thousands of dollars of equipment, to the first bulleted site on her first issue. That meant they were paying through the nose for information she already possessed and was willing to reveal! For a price! But not nearly so much as their further exploration cost them!

Then she was aware of real estate speculation. She frowned, thinking of Alexandra's purchasing here, and then people coming and offering double-and more than double!

"Steak? For lunch? Are you sure they're treating?"

Paul Ellis squeezed his wife's hand. "We can hope! I do have a credit card with me that can handle a little more, if it turns out to be Dutch treat. Just-can you kind of let me lead out in the conversation?"

She looked hurt. "Don't I usually? But I thought David might at least give Joe a shot-"

He nodded. "That was David's point. They did give him a shot! And another shot! And another! Every time he told him to fill out the on-line ap and turn in a résumé, it was opportunity for Joe! If he's that lazy, or belligerent, or whatever- In hindsight-" He sighed, "Tough summer!"

"I know. I've felt bad for antagonizing David and Mallory, but they miss so much-"

"Well, they don't really miss! They're extremely faithful for such a young couple! They're just on the go! I'm afraid we'll lose them, and it's been a tough summer."

"Well, when David said how they would have gone without-"

"Okay, Sweetie, don't get started crying! No one knows we've cut our salary; you've been a trooper! I mean; maybe we shouldn't have. The

Apostle Paul wasn't sure he did the right thing by not taking a salary from the church at Corinth-"

She wiped daintily at her nose. "And we've done the right thing! The Lord will turn this for us! He always has. I was listening to the song about God's being on-time every time; even though we sometimes start to despair."

David wasn't sure what to do with Norma, exactly! He went in search of her.

"Oh, there you are! Can we talk a minute?"

Her anxious eyes returned his gaze. "About? You seem to be busier than a one-armed paper hanger."

He laughed. "Yeah, but if I'm not being too bold, do you have a plan for getting your stuff moved out? Or do you need help?"

She shrugged, defeated and uncertain. "What does it say I have to do?"

"Do you mean in your sales contract? I guess it says you're moved out, Alexandra has the keys, and the place is hers."

Fear showed in dark, trapped eyes. "So, do I have to get all this junk cleared out for her?"

"Okay, hold on. A lot of it's junk; but some of it's new that's never been unboxed!"

"Yeah, that was Mort, always buyin' stuff and then more stuff. Now I never had a penny to call my own! And the junk's not necessarily new anymore. Like that microwave-big as a kitchen! And I never wanted it nor knew what to do with it! Why the man couldn't get me what I wanted-"

"Well, what did you want?"

"This is a waste of time!"

"No it isn't! What do you want now? You have your cashier's check; are you buying another house? One in town? Where are you going? Once you get your car running? Do you have kids or grandkids? Travel plans?"

"What difference does it make? I guess I'll just hang onto the check for security."

"Okay, well it has an expiration date on it! You should really deposit it in a bank, or invest in something. What did you want that your husband-"

"You'll laugh, but I wanted to sell cosmetics around town and the county. It's a pretty good drive for people around here to buy that kind of stuff. Used to be even harder to get good stuff without going to Pueblo or someplace! You can go ahead and laugh now!"

"It's a pretty brilliant idea! I was thinking, this stuff will sell to someone for some kind of price! Maybe we can rent you one of the empty stores in town and you can hold kind of a flea market until it all goes! That will clear it out of here while earning you more revenue. And you can look into the cosmetics companies to see who you want to rep for."

"Oh, I already know!"

His laughter reflected delight. "Well, all right, then! What are you waiting for?"

Usually, John was able to carry a conversation, but the Ellis seemed tense and barely communicative. After several stabs at small talk, he plunged ahead!

"Maybe I should come straight to my point. There is more purpose to our invitation than simply social." When silence reigned, he continued. "David felt bad for sounding off to you the other night about the missionary support. I'm not here to apologize for him, though; because he needs to do that. He mentioned that the church has been going through a tough summer, servicing the debt and staying current."

Ellis nodded slowly. "Yes; sadly! Usually summer creates a pinch. But I guess this year has been a perfect storm! Between the economy, the grumblers, and church tramps moving their letters from place to place around the Metroplex~ I mean, we keep encouraging one another that God is faithful." He exchanged glances with Mary Beth. "And I've been beating myself up for antagonizing great members like your son! I'm not sure where my head was! I'm the one owing an apology! I guess we both allowed Joe's side of the story to cloud our judgment. Joe forgot to tell us the part about repeatedly refusing to go through the preliminaries. Well, he did mention to me that the routine of aps and interviews was getting old; and I commiserated. But believe me; I didn't know he was being so high-handed with his demands to David."

Anderson nodded thoughtfully. "Every church has members like that! People with few social skills running people off that have good sense. What can you do? You have to make a place for everyone! Jesus did it! But trust me, every day, I realize how far short I come of being like Him!

Pastor Ellis finally relaxed enough to laugh, then sobered quickly. "So; what? Joe's behavior coupled with our equally tactless conversation-is-uh, running your son and his family back to Arkansas to stay?"

John chuckled. "No, their business demands keep them on the move, but they'll be at your church as much as possible, like they've been doing! This is awkward, but *Anderson Ministries* oversees a ministry fund. Usually, the board votes to help smaller struggling churches and the starting of new ones. I'm the Chairman, and I've been in contact with the guys. They agreed to a gift of fifty thousand dollars, as well as reimbursing your salary that you haven't been drawing. I'm sorry David never gave you the benefit of the doubt!" He laughed. "He's a fine one to talk! He always resented what he perceived as 'doing without' for the sake of our ministry!"

"Well, usually the worm turns when school starts and people start making their way back into the routine. We can probably pay back-"

"Hey, whatever comes in, just squirrel away for next summer. This is a gift. Sorry I didn't know sooner how tough things have been for you! David regrets what he said to you, and you've been sorry for the incident. But once again,

> *Romans 8:28 And we know that all things work together for good to them that love God, to them who are the called according to his purpose.*

bears out. Because of the dinner conversation, the Lord caused our *Ministry* to be aware of your need. We also arranged a trip for you and your wife to visit Israel. Unless you've been there before and would prefer a different destination!"

"Thank you, Pastor; we're truly humbled!" Paul Ellis' emotion-charged voice! "We've talked and dreamed for years of visiting the land where our Lord Jesus walked! He's so kind and good, I'm not sure why I allowed myself to become so doubtful! Tell the other board members we are truly grateful!"

"Well, we're all grateful for other good men and great ministries around the nation! We all need one another. It seems like we're losing out in the battle against Satan! We sure need to strengthen one another! Now! Let's order so we can eat! I'm starved!"

Mallory stood breathless, taking in an emotion-charged atmosphere!

"Come on, Mommy! Play some more." Amelia pulled at her hand.

Dying to get in on what was coming down, she allowed her daughters to lead her away, instead. Her thoughts whirling, she hid her eyes and began the count to one hundred!

Alexandra was acutely aware of Mallory's disappearance, forsaking her to deal with some super-handsome guy standing at her gate, by herself!

"Well, Ma'am, may I leave my résumé?"

Somehow, her hand managed to reach for the proffered folder. Impressive! Thick and complete, pages encased in plastic sleeves.

"You said that you recently graduated from the Colorado School of Mines?"

"Yes'm, that's right. A bachelor's degree in Mining Engineering! I'm going to work on courses toward my masters! You're probably looking for someone who already has an MS or PhD; plus years of experience! Who's in charge here?"

She drew herself up. "I am!"

He nodded, "Thought so! I've been following the *Driller's Platform e-zine*! I thought the dope on this area was impressive, so I followed the purchase. You're Alexandra Faulkner, aren't you?"

She nodded, extending her hand and loosening the latch on the gate with the other. "And you're Jared?" She read the name on the document she held. "Please come on in!" Her thoughts in turmoil, she noted him as he regained his pickup and eased it through the opening. Squeaky clean, until he hit the dusty stretch of road leading to the ranch! Impressive guy! She wasn't sure what to do with him! Not that she was interested in him! But she guessed someone with a degree in mining engineering might be a boon to her!

"Have a seat on the porch," she urged. "I'll go in and get a couple of drinks. Coke? Dr. Pepper?"

He shrugged. "Just a glass of water would be fine!"

"Who's that?" Daniel joined her in the kitchen as she struggled with the strange and ancient lever on an ice cube tray.

"His name's Jared. He has a BS in Mining Engineering from the Colorado School of Mines. I guess other places he's applied want advanced degrees; and experience, to boot! He came here because he's been following Mallory's online magazine! I don't think I need him. Do you want to tell him?" She pressed the résumé at him, meeting his eyes hopefully.

His cold gaze met hers, and he made no move to accept the document. "He's a gift God dropped on your doorstep, Al! Why in the world would you say you don't need him? But if you didn't, you do your own dirty work of honestly confronting people and telling them 'No'! Have we not taught you anything?"

Cassandra's voice preceded her popping into the space! "She's worried what Tommy will think!"

The 'killer look' from Alexandra confirmed the theory!

"Conduct the interview, Alexandra. Make sure you make an offer he accepts, and arrange for him to start as soon as he can. We'll talk later!" A stern glance caught Cassandra by surprise. "And you, too!"

David's head pounded! It often did, but maybe the times of relief were lasting longer. He hoped so. He struggled to find level enough ground to place the assorted modular buildings scheduled for arrival. The flat ground in front of the ranch house, though dry now, seemed to be a flood plain. Sometimes a creek ran through, but with the semi-drought condition, it was dried up, revealing the alluvial gravels! With spring run-off from the mountains, there could be a torrent. Water damage of the house testified to that fact! And although a bulldozer made valiant attacks, he was dealing with bedrock! No wonder many local builders created split-levels, building with the steep slopes rather than fighting them! He either needed tons of fill dirt, or dynamite to blast with! He was accustomed to dealing with problems, but this- He sighed.

Dr. Paul Ellis watched as his bank account balance popped up on his monitor! All of his forfeited salary of six months! Replenished! "Thank you, Father," he breathed softly. "I couldn't see a glimmer of hope to get through this time!"

As Alexandra took her place across from Jared on the rickety porch, pieces fell into place in her mind! She needed to get over the teen-agery thing of running her life by what Tommy would think! He needed to be mature enough to realize~ She met Jared's gaze confidently. "Could you please tell me a little more about yourself?"

Chapter 17: GRIT

"Is everything good in our world?" David grinned when Mallie jumped, startled by his sudden presence!

"As a matter of fact-" She turned her attention to a spreadsheet on her monitor as she responded, "Motoring along on all eight cylinders! Frankly, I've been amazed at the hasty investments some of these businesses are making based on the ezine reports alone! They're reluctant to pay for the in-depth reports, although the information is still a bargain! Well, I think so. Their own exploration will cost much more! How are your pads for the temp buildings?"

"Suddenly great! As soon as Al hired Jared, I approached him about obtaining dynamite, and doing some blasting! We need at least three acres of fairly level ground for the housing and mining operations."

Mallory whistled quietly in amazement! "Dynamite"!

"Hmm-m, kind of the same response I got from the new mining engineer."

Mallory gave her full attention; "So are there any other options?"

He laughed. "Of course! To quote a wise woman whom I quote often, 'There are always options! We just need to find them'!"

"Well, sometimes I'm guilty of, 'easy to preach it and hard to live it'! Seriously, David, those buildings are scheduled for delivery the first of next week!"

He bent and kissed her. "Yes, we could actually benefit by having them yesterday. Anyway, the new mining engineer noticed a property between here and Silverton with signs posted that grazing land's for lease. We drove down and called the number: since we actually don't want to build our little village on leased land, we offered to buy!"

Mallory nodded. "Is Alexandra on board with it? I'm not sure the bank lent her enough. She's seriously undercapitalized."

"Yeah, since she isn't a minority woman, but a rich kid, Daniel had to cosign for what the bank did allow! Uh, I was thinking-"

"That we should buy it?" she finished for him.

Hands thrust into jeans pockets, he watched her response keenly.

"Well, I wouldn't' mind doing that," her measured response, "but I don't want it to appear as if we're trying to undercut Alexandra or the consortium! I guess we should begin by letting Alexandra, and Daniel, and Mr. Meeker into the loop. We need to act quickly and discreetly, though! The owners of the property doubtless already know about the ezine report and Alexandra's mining intentions. I'm sure they'll inflate their asking price! If that's a good location for the modulars, you're right! We needed it yesterday! You can handle everything; I'm behind with these reports. And I'll keep up with the girls!"

Shay O'Shaughnessy fought terror, pale freckles standing out against paler complexion! The road they were on wasn't the most notoriously dangerous on the South American Continent, but the ribbon of crumbling asphalt snaking upward into the higher reaches of the Andes, wasn't the safest, either! With a cliff rising dramatically on the opposite side of the road, and a steep drop-off, without benefit of a guardrail, falling dizzyingly beneath the windows of the hired car, there was no place to pull off! No way to accommodate Emma's morning sickness: actually more of a mysterious malady prone to hit at any inopportune time, seemingly not limited to a particular time of day! With a panicked, pleading look, she lost the battle; and her stomach contents launched.!

Craning his neck around, the driver issued a string of rapid Spanish which Shay figured wouldn't bear repeating, let alone interpreting. Nevertheless the earnest interpreter also turned his attention to the back seat.

"Yeah, I get it," Shay gasped, fighting his own battle with his stomach! "Just tell him to turn around and watch the road! We'll take care of cleaning the car up! We'll pay!"

Davis Hall studied final entries in a Jewelry contest! They fell into three levels of expertise; Beginning, Intermediate, and Advanced; with each level further divided into classifications; Best Utilization of Metal, Best Use of Gemstones, Best Overall Technique, and Most Avant-garde! He felt proud of his students and his accomplishment as the CEO of this division. While he studied the pieces, judging forms before him, he was joined by Herb Carlton! With past animosities in the past, he rose and shook the other man's hand!

"Well, nothing to compare to the master! But all in all, not a bad lot, either."

Herb looked the glowing display over thoughtfully, nodding modestly at the admiration.

"I figured to eke out a modest living for the rest of my days in my pawn shop." He removed his glasses, wiping his eyes, and then the lenses, while he struggled to overcome sudden emotion! "And then this one fateful evening-" He broke off. "I have probably told you this story many times! When you get old you start repeating yourself!"

Hall chuckled. "The most amazing part of it to me is, that Linda knew you liked Suzanne first, and she still married you!"

"Yes, or that she married me for any reason!" Herb reached for an entry from the Beginners' category and ran his hand expertly but reverently across it. "Our Deborah Rodriguez displays quite an alacrity for this."

Hall agreed. "It's more nicely done than some of the entries from the Advanced school!"

"So, what do you think? Do you think she will sell off her business and focus on this rare gift she possesses?" Herb's winsome tone revealed that he hoped for an answer not forthcoming.

"Well, she has a lot of value in her company already. She could basically sell and invest herself totally in the creation of beautiful jewelry and objets d'art! Her best bet would be to sell to family members, none of which possess sums of money to invest. Any other investor in the IPO wouldn't care about her family or her nurturing of minorities! I think she'll continue to do both! Like Faulkner and Cassandra with their gifts as violinists!"

David felt a pang of anxiety! True, he was usually more of a hard-nosed negotiator than Mallory! But the trump in negotiating was the ability to walk away from the deal! And they needed this acreage! The sellers had him over the illustrious barrel, and they must surely be aware of that fact! Still, he felt a certain pride in Mallory's confidence in him! When he began being ribbed for being Mr. Mom, she did the parenting duties, proving to the mockers that she and David were partners who got along, enjoying the challenges of balancing family and business responsibilities. Of course, she was still coaxing the girls to scour the gravel deposits in the yard for additional Platinum nuggets!

He pulled up before an address in the small ghost (tourist) town. He loved the place! Nestled at nine thousand feet, the little hamlet came alive when the Narrow-Gauge train disgorged its passengers! Then, after scurrying around for lunch and souvenirs, when the tourists re-boarded, or headed back to Durango by an alternate route, the little berg fell asleep once more! He took note of the turn-of-the-century, Victorian architecture! A real gem of a property, fighting against the onslaught of time! This one seemed to be winning, but others in the neighborhood seemed to be faring less well. He rang, and heard the chimes bong musically.

"David Anderson, please come in; I'm Hallie Pritchard." She stepped back so he could make his way into the narrow, polished, front hallway. David was enchanted in spite of himself. The place was an absolute doll house! And Hallie looked amazing!

"Ma'am, pleased to meet you!" He offered his hand, feeling suddenly bashful and out of his league. Mallory should have been the one to come! She would adore this woman! And vice versa! As if reading his thoughts, Hallie peered into the street behind him as she pulled the door closed. "Mrs. Anderson didn't come with you?"

He shook his head regretfully. "No Ma'am, we have these three little girls-"

She shook her head mildly. "Please, come in. Norma and Ray are here. My husband, Russell"! She indicated the group assembled at the kitchen table.

Perplexed at the group, David suddenly wondered if Alexandra and Daniel should be here. Alexandra, at least!

Russell rose and held out a well-manicured hand, meeting David's gaze at his own level. Sharp guy, wearing a Nautica polo shirt and knife-edge-creased twill slacks. The older guy laughed, "I guess we're both discombobulated to meet eyeball to eyeball with anyone else. Have a seat, Son; you intimidate me!"

David seriously doubted that, but with a relaxed laugh, he obeyed.

Norma sprang up to help Hallie serve broad slices of deep dish apple pie and tall mugs of coffee!

"Cheese or ice cream"?

David opted for ice cream, as did Ray Meeker. The other three went for thick slices of cheddar. David was so impressed with the Pritchards that he decided he must definitely give cheese with apple pie a try some time!

"Okay, now that you're here, you might as well make your offer!" Pritchard's pleasant countenance disappeared behind a stern poker-face, leaving David feeling at a distinct disadvantage.

Hallie swatted her husband's ear playfully as she topped off mugs. "Cut it out, Russ, and behave yourself!" She turned bright eyes to David! "He still enjoys playing the game, even though we're theoretically retired!" She once more addressed her spouse, "You know we're as eager to unload those acres as this young man is to acquire them!"

"Ah Hallie!" He sighed and pretended to pout before opening up! "We planned to build a prestigious log home up on the site, but then Hallie fell in love with this place! We run like rabbits to Florida with the first prediction of snow. Do I think there are valuable minerals up there? Yeah, probably, if you can find it and extract it while the price makes it worth it! Between blizzards and rock slides! I've admired your wife's reports on her ezine! Quite a clever way to deal with the information she has assembled."

"We've been accused of being naïve and foolish!" David's comment interrupted.

"Sadly, that's the thinking of so many! If you can't use the knowledge to extract every penny possible for it, just sit on it. My grandfather used to quote this little rhyme. I think it better describes American business now than it did then!

Get all you can!
Can all you get!
Sit on the can!
And poison the rest!

Your generosity with what the drilling has gleaned is incredible to Hallie and me! We-uh-have a slight accumulation of wealth! But we see the government trying to hamstring any mining and drilling operations in the US, choking small businesses, and wanting to tax us when there's no industry, no production, no jobs to stimulate the sluggish economy! The fence up there is in a sad state of repair, not because I don't keep it fixed, but the snowfall and wind give it a perpetual beating! If you can use it and keep it up, it's yours for a percentage of the mine profits."

Mallory struggled to hold herself together as Erik broke the news to her over the phone.

"Is Grandmother-"

"Yeah, she's holding up! Of course, I'm sure she's terrified for them! Right now, we're trying to dissuade Sanders from launching out on his own, looking for them. You just sit tight, too! The State Department-"

"Okay, but Erik; isn't The State Department who was supposed to help David and me when we were held in Saudi Arabia? Maybe I should contact Sam- Well first I need to go to Boston and be with Grandmother! When-How did we find out they're missing? What happened? Is anyone demanding ransom?"

"No contact from anyone that we're aware of! But they never showed up in La Paz for their flight home, and there's no answer on either of their phones. Just, promise me you won't do anything until David gets back-and then that the two of you won't do something stu-ill-advised!"

"I promise!"

"Okay, I'm holdin' ya to it! Go ahead and call Delia! I think you can help calm her."

Mallory sat staring at her phone! How could she help calm anyone when she was in the grip of paralyzing terror?

"Oh, Lord," she moaned. "Not Shay and Emma! Dear God, please no! Please watch over them and keep them safe-"

At Daniel's prompting, Alexandra readily agreed to granting the Pritchards a stake in the mine in exchange for the much-needed acreage! Disconnecting from the conversation, she was forced to once more be in awe at the scope of answered prayer within the past few days! "Well, the Lord is really opening doors and steamrolling this along! And Mallory and her synergy- Of course, my money's going fast! I was relieved when David and Mallory wanted to make the offer to the Pritchards, or have the consortium as a whole, acquire it-" She paused as her dad's serious eyes met hers. "What?"

"Well, your money is drying up, but there's still one big item you need to acquire!"

She stared at him. "Like a bulldozer?"

He laughed. "I'm sure David has a line on leasing heavy equipment-"

"Okay, are we just going to play a guessing game, then?"

He shrugged, knowing she was annoyed about the bad news of another major expenditure. "Only a guessing game if you refuse to engage your mind and think!"

Struggling against frustrated tears, she sat regarding him in silence, considering his words about using her brain to think. At last she nodded, breaking the silence, knowing the right answer, "Mallory's in-depth report! I should have already-"

"Unh-huh, Al, you shoulda!" Even as he spoke, he was amazed by her resolve! She was going to do this!

Shay and Emma huddled together in the scant shelter of a crumbling mud-brick shanty. As he tried to reassure her and dry her tears, regret filled him! So much for the idea of traveling and working together! Especially with a new little O'Shaughnessy baking in the oven! "Okay, okay, we haven't thought to pray!"

"Well, I have been, but I'm still so scared, and it's really cold! Shay, I'm so sorry-"

He hugged her more tightly. "Hey, it isn't your fault! I think they were already abducting us, anyway! Maybe Grandmother and your dad, and everyone, can meet their demands. I can pay them all back; it just may take-what do you think they want?"

Her terrified eyes searched his, "I have no idea!"

While Shannon awaited an evening flight to Boston to be with his grandmother, he paced Roger Sander's office with him.

"Why are you sure anyone will call?" A veiled challenge to Roger's reasoning for staying at *Sanders*. "But if they do, they can probably reach you at home as easily." Although not admitting it, Shannon was aware of Emma's concern for her parents' relationship. He couldn't imagine why Roger and Beth would want to endure this ordeal separately.

"Not that it's your business, but I told Beth to come in here! I don't know why she's such a hermit!"

Shannon nodded; but in his heart, he knew the executive knew the reason better than he knew his own name! His wife's weight battle! When Suzanne appeared with a fresh pot of coffee, he jumped to help her. "Thanks, Aunt Suzanne! Is Erik in town? He can't really do much, can he? Since the kidnapping went down in Bolivia?"

She mopped at tears. "Well, he's always as involved as he can be! Lending suggestions and expertise, trying to keep pressure on the State Department! Hey, do you know any details of the trip? If Delia has any details, she's so distraught~ I'll call him and maybe you can add something~"

Before Shannon could object, she acted, and her cell phone was at his ear. Reluctantly, he accepted the device, moving out of earshot!

Roger's attention followed the young man, and he frowned! If Shannon knew something, he good and well better~

"Hey, Shannon; ya got something for me?" Erik's gruffer than usual tone let him know that the agent was no more eager to talk than he was.

"I'm not sure if I do or not. The alpaca king he deals through's, name's Enrique Cisneros! Shay likes him; he seems to be a pretty good guy! The authorities have probably talked to him already. That contact is no secret. Grandmother would be aware of that."

Erik frowned. "And what else?" His voice was a demand.

"This was Aunt Suzanne's idea for me to talk to you!"

"Mmm-hmmm; and her ideas are usually stellar! So talk to me! What are you holding back?"

"Well, first; what are you holding back? Who do you think grabbed them? Local thugs, or associates from my dad's past?"

Erik suppressed a groan. "I haven't a clue! What's your take?"

Shannon frowned as Roger Sanders and his aunt closed in on him. Oh well, the secret was going to be exposed anyway. With no further attempts to keep his voice low, he spilled a confidence.

"Well, about a month ago, Lawrence Freeman, Grandmother's friend and attorney invited Shay and me to lunch. We figured he wanted to marry Grandmother." Shannon's face twisted with pain. "But that wasn't it; it was something he wanted us to be aware of. I think he basically wanted us to tell Grandmother so he wouldn't have to-"

Erik listened to the back story, desperate to hear the point!

"Uh, some woman has crawled out of the woodwork, or from under a rock, claiming to have had an ongoing relationship with our dad. Has a kid and the whole nine yards."

Erik winced at the pain in Shannon's voice, but questioned if this revelation could tie into the young couple's disappearance. Still, it didn't seem fair to add more to the two boy's burdens; or Delia's! "Okay, well, I'll see if I can contact this Enrique Cisneros. Tell Roger I'll keep him in the loop with every scrap I can get!"

Mallory sat on the front porch watching the girls play. They were coated with dirt, and she figured Diana would be horrified if she knew! She nodded as Alexandra neared and sat beside her. Mallory figured Al's reddened eyes were about Shay and Emma.

"They'll find them; they'll be fine," she encouraged, trying to lift her own spirits as much as her friend's"

"Find who?" Alexandra sniffled. "I mean, 'whom'," she corrected herself.

"Shay and Emma! I thought that was the reason-"

"No, we're all in a lot of trouble! Uh, my dad and Mr. Morrison have been comparing notes! I've had a Facebook account-"

Mallory's eyes widened. It was news to her, too! She hadn't been friend requested!

"Alexandra, what's the matter with you? Why would you do that? Oh, so you and Tommy-"

Alexandra's blubbering turned suddenly cold and crisp! "No! Tommy hasn't gotten a friend request either! If I had tried to friend him, he wouldn't have accepted. He's still trying to undo the Paris debacle with Daddy!"

"Okayyy, so I guess it's good that someone wants to keep things above-board!"

"What did you need to see me about? Shay and Emma are missing?"

"Yeah, they missed their flight out of La Paz, Bolivia! They never returned to their hotel for their things! There haven't been any ransom demands-why open Facebook? Is he making you go back home?" Mallory's mind was in turmoil, evidenced by her confused conversation! 'Yikes, Daniel wouldn't pull the plug on this; would he?'

Alexandra wiped her nose another swipe and steadied her voice. "Okay, I don't have many friends, mostly Madeleine and Megan Morrison. You didn't know Jeremiah liked Megan? A lot?"

Mallory forced a laugh, trying to lighten the conversation. "No! I thought he still liked me! My heart's broken!"

Al's gray eyes reflected pain. "Don't I wish! He asked me to do it, because he knew she has an account, and he worries about her asthma! Well, any word about the Morrisons always kind of filters in slowly in bits and pieces."

Mallory frowned, "So did your dad buy that story?"

"Well, he isn't demanding for me to come home! If that's all you're worried about"!

Mallory shrugged. "It isn't all I'm worried about, but that's a biggie!"

Alexandra turned to face her, "You're right! You guys have been phenomenal! No, it's just that Megan's so juvenile, and Jeremiah's so serious. I'm really sorry about Shay and Emma, Mallory. I'll pray, too; but I think they'll be fine. Now, why did you call?"

"Maybe we should discuss it when we're both in a better frame of mind!"

Alexandra squared her shoulders with a new confidence and determination. "My frame of mind is great! This is something that's going to cost me more money?"

"Yeah-uh-cost all of us a little! I think you should give Jared some shares in the mine!"

"Why?" Alexandra's eyes shot sparks. "I'm breaking my bank for him already with my package!"

Mallory grinned. "Great! You just answered your own question so I won't have to!"

"I've barely held onto controlling interest as it is! Are you engineering a hostile takeover?"

The barb hit Mallory's heart. "No! But Jared's a great guy, and the Lord dropped him on your doorstep when he's discouraged and desperate!

But give him a couple of years here, and a Master's degree, experience, and success! And the tables'll be turned! He'll be ripe pickings for any of the huge mining companies, and they'll be able to offer more salary and perks! And he'll be gone!"

"Maybe not; and how do I know for sure that he'll work out anyway? I'm sorry what I said about your trying to take over."

"Thank you! Apology accepted. Don't you see, Allie? It's a Biblical principle! You can't buy loyalty! When all's said and done, people are loyal to themselves! And, you really can't blame them! Remember the words of Jesus about the two types of shepherds? The ones who own the flock; and the hireling? The owner stays and fights because it's in his own best interests! The hireling flees because it isn't! If you don't give him some ownership-"

Shay stumbled away, aware of Emma's distress at being separated. She was at least being moved into the house where presumably, it would be warmer! Maybe they planned to hold him and release her! He prayed hastily to that end, as winded, he clambered upward along a steep trail, a pistol jammed between his shoulder blades!

Trent Morrison disconnected from a three-way conversation with Michael, Madeleine, and Megan, shaking and fighting sobs that fought to erupt from deep within his soul! Struggling for control, he punched Sonia's speed dial.

She answered immediately, breathless! "Trent?"

"Yeah, did the kids already call you?"

"Mmmm-hmmm; Michael's holding on the other line! They were just starting-I'm on my way home!"

"She's starting with that asthma-thing again?"

"Well, it isn't a 'thing', Trent! It's a serious illness, and stress triggers attacks!"

Tears flowed against his will. "I know, Sonn, but we have to be able to deal with her! If Faulkner hadn't-"

"Look, I'm as shocked at the Facebook thing and her chats, as you are! But the wheezing ties me in knots! I'm just a few minutes from home, and I can handle it! You don't need to rush home!"

Her words jolted him, but rather than unloading on her, he backed off. "Okay; well, keep me in the loop!"

He barely ended the call when his phone buzzed with a call from his eldest. "Dad, you're not coming home?"

"Well, if you can keep a confidence, I'm coming home as quick as is feasible from the Colorado high country! I guess I need to pay a surprise visit to your little sister so she doesn't have time to work her symptoms up to critical level!"

"Yeah, Dad, it's a good thing you ended her chat session when you did! How did you know?"

"Daniel Faulkner told me! Which, is the last way I like to find out what's going on with y'all! I'm out here because I've been led to believe he's a senseless parent, throwing Alexandra and Cassandra to the wolves! And he has everything under control, as always-" his voice broke! When he could force words out again, the anguished question erupted, "You're sure she didn't send the guy the pictures he was after?"

"Yeah, Dad"!

David was relieved when Daniel handed Jared the thick report, making the engineer call it quits on helping him with the pads. Maybe now he could get something done without hearing a better idea every time he opened his mouth! He hoped the know-it-all was as good at mining engineering as he thought he was about all other issues! Crazy Feather walked up, grinning!

"If you can keep that guy out of our hair, we can get this staked this afternoon. That way, when the heavy equipment gets here in the morning, we can start moving dirt. The septic system's the big thing! Being ready for the deliveries on Monday shouldn't be any problem. You're getting ready to leave?"

"Yes, I think so! I'm depending on what you just told me. If Harrelson shows up on this site again, let Alexandra know! She can deal with him."

"Yes; or Mr. Faulkner!" Crazy Feather suggested.

"He's heading out, too! Alexandra's in charge!" He took in the other man's shocked expression. "I know, she's a girl, and she's young; but she's the boss! Don't ever doubt it!"

A few more upward lunges and they were on a grassy plateau! A brutal gust of wind snatched at what breath Shay had left, and whipped at his alpaca sweater! This couldn't be happening! He scrunched his eyes closed against stinging particles, feeling the grit in his teeth! If there was anything in the situation to be grateful for, it was that Emma wasn't out here, exposed like this! As they made their way, perhaps an additional half mile through high, thick grass, Shay noticed grazing Alpaca, and hopefully, more civilization!

A car swerved in toward them from a faint track; the aged Mercedes from the previous day! Shay couldn't imagine where they planned to take him! Fear gripped him afresh! Not so much for himself-but for Emma! And their child!

Jared viewed the thick paper dismally! It looked like a lot of material to wade through! And he needed to get on it! But first, he needed to call Abby! He checked his cell! No service up here. He wavered between driving down to town, or wherever there might be a couple of bars of reception; or asking to use the sat phone!

Deciding on the independence of not requesting favors, he eased his truck carefully across stones and ruts toward the gate. Concern filled him as Alexandra indicated that she would get the gate! He wasn't sure what to make of a woman getting the gate for him, or the whole thing of working for a female Geologist as her mining engineer. He guessed he wasn't chauvinistic; more worried what Abby would think about him being around a group of gorgeous women rather than the men's world he had assumed and consequently painted for her.

She forced the grudging barrier open and then smiled as she motioned for him to lower the window.

"Mallory and I have a couple of more things to discuss with you, but they can wait if you're in a hurry somewhere." She hoped he wasn't, because David and Mallory were preparing to depart.

"Nothing major; just trying to find good reception so I can call my girlfriend and give her an update"! He didn't want to seem hen-pecked by Abby, but he wanted to set a boundary that his heart was spoken for! "And I thought the Andersons were getting ready to pull out for a few days!"

Alexandra smiled. "Yeah, what we need to discuss shouldn't take long! And you're free to come and go; but the sat phone is available, and you can use it in privacy whenever you need to!"

He nodded, "Yeah, I might do that! Until I have a chance to get my own. May take me a paycheck or two~" As he spoke, he fell into step next to her, heading for the house!

"Okay, before you do that! I should have already equipped you with one! And with a laptop for mine business! Mallory always does that for her workers; I'm~um, a little green at this! Where does your girlfriend live?"

Mallory appeared, followed by David, who offered a six pack of cold Dr. Pepper cans!

Jared twisted one free appreciatively and sank onto the edge of the porch. "Is this the place where the meeting's to be convened?"

The others lowered themselves into positions along the splintery porch.

"Until our village arrives! Then, there'll be a mine headquarters and housing, including a chow hall," David announced quietly.

"What kind of housing?" Jared was mildly curious.

Mallory took over, "Well, a double-wide for Alexandra and a double-wide for you, for right now! Plus, a complex of buildings for the mining operation, and a new barn for the cattle! David's helping clear out some of the major junk in this house and the garage, and Norma's going to live in it again, once we update it! State of the art fencing and security measures are top priority, too! I know Alexandra left your start date up to you, but as soon as you can start, we're ready! Now, all of that could have waited, but~" she sent a signal to Alexandra who deftly picked up the conversational baton.

"Well, we recognize the fact that you wanted to start with a major mining company; not a fledgling operation owned by a girl. And, Mallory pointed out to me, that in a couple of years, as you get an advanced degree and some experience, and success, because this mine is going to be legendary; that you'll get offers to leave us that I can't compete with! So we've factored in, to present you with three percent of the mine's yield! From the actual profit"!

A slow grin spread across his features, "Wow! I thought you already had me motivated-but that amps up the motivation exponentially." His face clouded, "How much will the housing cost me? I might be able to rent an apartment-"

Alexandra nodded, undeterred. "The property across the road that you noticed, now belongs to the consortium, and David and Mallory own the buildings they're bringing in. You'll have the use of the double-wide, but you'll need to treat it with respect, as part of your salary package! Utilities will all be on one meter, and David and Mallory provide a back-up generator, so utilities are provided also!"

He nodded, more than pleased, but he pressed, "And you said I'd have insurance?"

"Yes, good medical as well as life insurance. My dad is the expert in that area, and he's already called our insurance agent. You're my first hire, and you and I need to work out together, compensation packages to offer other hires. Do you know anyone who can start right away?"

Before he could answer, racket filled the air! They all watched, transfixed as an amazing helicopter lowered beyond them, and settled in puffs of dust on the new land.

Mallory's eyes riveted on David, who suddenly sat silent with a satisfied grin plastered on handsome features!

"Da`vid"! Mallory's eyes shone with wonder! "David, we-we need that-wow-what a -what a surprise!"

He opened his arms and she flung herself against him. "We do need it," he agreed, "and it should pay for itself with the time it'll save-" He pulled her back. "I'm just so sorry about Shay and Emma, and what a pall that casts over-"

She laughed through tears. "I know! Sometime, you'd like to give me an 'up' when there aren't any 'downs' going on! It's still gorgeous! I love it and it definitely brightens my day! Who did the art work? Little Feather?"

He nodded, extremely pleased with the appearance of the chopper! "We need to get gathered up and head out!"

"Eeeee-eeeh!" her joyous screech was ear splitting! "We're-we're going in that, instead of driving?"

David laughed. "Yeah, I thought we might as well!"

He drew an envelope from his pocket, turning toward Jared. "Thanks for the sharp eye noticing the signs. We customarily pay finder's fees to people-"

Chapter 18: GIVER

The interior of the chopper was cute, too, featuring David's whimsy with the kids in mind! This must have been in the works for nearly a year, and she never sensed- She watched as David secured the girls and plopped next to her.

"Rhonna's trying to book you a flight to Boston from Albuquerque. Morrison's flying back to DC from there!"

She turned toward him, "I really appreciate your thoughtfulness, but we can't afford the time for me to go to Boston right now! You have a high-level meeting about your building! I've talked to Grandmother, and I can't help Shay and Emma any better from there! Shannon's there; and he can stay several days." Her expressive eyes deepened. "This may be a siege!" She dabbed at tears. "When Shannon has to leave, I may go! Mom's really worried about Beth and Roger."

David nodded, speaking softly in spite of the noise of the rotors, "Have you heard anything weird about them?"

Mallory didn't like gossip, "Anything worse than just their strained relationship? David, I'm tired of hearing weird stuff!"

He grinned at her. "Well, weird stuff happens! In fact, it happens so much, that it almost loses weirdness!"

Instead of laughing, she stifled a sob, which caught Amelia's attention! Assuming her sternest expression, she shook a little finger authoritatively, "No fighting"!

That did make Mallory laugh. "We aren't fighting! But that's a good rule!"

"Okay," David's word barely above a sigh, "What's going on, that I don't know about?"

"Well, I haven't had a chance to tell you, and Shay and Emma are more important-"

He slid his arm around her shoulders the best he could with the seat backs as they were. "What else?"

Wishing for better chances for long talks and lead-up times for subjects, she blurted out her distress! As usual, it was now or never!

"Oh wow! That is craziness! So Shay and Shannon know; but Delia doesn't?" He reached for a fresh tissue, dabbing tenderly at spilling tears!

"Well, they haven't told her yet, but if I know Grandmother-" She straightened determinedly! "Thank you for listening, but you have more to do than dry my tears; and I have more to do than sit here crying! Is that a useable phone?"

"It is! If you're sure about not going on to Boston-I'll call Rhonna and tell her to cancel flight arrangements; although she was having trouble booking with short notice-"

Laughing, Mallory unbuckled and launched upward, "A likely story! I had first dibs on the phone! You didn't want to use it until I wanted to-"

David was on top of her. "My call's the most important!" Using an old line from a *Patch the Pirate* children's CD, *Kidnapped On I-land*!

"NO!" Mallory's screech imitated *King Me-first*, as she struggled against his greater strength! "Mine's the most important! Me First! Me First"!

Amelia scowled, but Avery broke into giggles, at which juncture Amelia whispered, "Don't laugh! It'll just make 'em worse!"

Jared studied the check for long moments, comprehending; but yet, not fully! One of his favorite verses came to mind:

> *Isaiah 41:18 I will open rivers in high places, and fountains in the midst of the valleys: I will make the wilderness a pool of water, and the dry land springs of water.*

This is what you did for me today, Lord!" his voice barely audible in the wondrous moment of worship! "This morning everything seemed as hopeless as things have all summer. No one hiring! 'Need more advanced degree! Experience! And then we have a string of applicants longer'n your arm, ahead of you, that have all that'! This morning, paying back my student loans and ever hoping to marry Abby seemed utterly impossible."

Punching the latch to the glove compartment, he pulled out a dog-eared jewelry catalog! 'Wow! A job with a fair compensation package, plus free housing and utilities! And this check'! He pulled the finder's fee from the envelope, gazing at the figure once more! 'Enough to start the loan payments, buy the wedding set that just this morning seemed so far out of reach! Maybe take a small honeymoon-' But, he was getting ahead of himself. First, he needed to call Mr. Hampton and ask permission to propose to his daughter! He hesitated, wishing he had his own sat phone! This was important, and he hated to take up someone else's line, who might overhear, even after telling him he could have privacy! And it might take some convincing, with both Abby's father and Abby! Well, he knew Abby wanted to marry him! She just wanted to wait until the engagement was official, sealed with the customary diamond ring, before beginning plans for a lavish ceremony! With the sudden new developments, a job in hand-well he wanted to marry her and be done with it without all the hoopla! He sighed. Still, if it meant a lot to her-and he was sure it did.

He was aware when Trent Morrison, a Forest Service guy, but not a Ranger, plunged past the gate of the ranch and moved rapidly to the waiting chopper! Amazed he watched it rise and bear southward! Sweet bird!

Mallory was aware of Trent's emotion-ravaged countenance as he hopped on, buckled up, and the helicopter rose! Figuring he wasn't that distraught over Shay and Emma, she was pretty sure she was afraid to ask! She couldn't bear the thought of anything's being wrong with Sonia or his kids! Maybe it was just about Sonia's elderly parents; not that that would be good. Somehow a verse occurred to her about trials coming to make you able to succor (comfort) others. If that was really the case, maybe the sooner she succored him, the sooner Shay and Emma would be released! Unharmed! Considering it worth a try, she unbuckled with the purpose in mind of offering sympathy, assistance, or whatever.

David caught her eye, shaking his head negatively. Finishing the conversation with Rhonna, he turned the phone over to her. Evidently he knew what was going on with the Morrisons! She had plenty on her plate with Shay and Emma; the sudden appearance of a cousin, and Beth and Roger Sanders!

David was aghast when he realized she was calling Delia's attorney. He winced, and she turned her back to him.

"Hello, Mr. Freeman! Mallory O'Shaughnessy, here! What information can your give me on this woman? And her supposed son! Is she trying to cash in on my grandmother? Why is she just now crawling out into the light of day?"

David cringed, as all of her emotions from the day boiled over. For one thing, she was Mallory Anderson now! And not O'Shaughnessy!!

"What do you mean, 'You can't divulge that to me!'? Surely you're not representing her, whatever her name is! What is her name? Just her name and current phone number? Isn't your protecting her a conflict of interest with my grandmother as one of your long-time clients?"

David tried to make sense of the patient-sounding reply. Freeman wasn't representing the woman, but what she had divulged, he was obligated to confidentiality!

Frustrated, Mallory backed off. "Okay, Mr. Freeman, thank you! But I'm equally obligated to my grandmother and my cousins." She disçonnected and phoned a private investigator!

David's eyes shone with loving humor. "Feel better?"

She nodded, belligerent! "As a matter of fact! And I've solved Roger and Beth's problems, too!"

"Just like that! They'll be glad to know!"

She jabbed her elbow in his ribs and he yowled in mock pain, evoking another giggle from Avery and another disapproving look from Amelia! He unbuckled to fix a mug of hot chocolate and offer something to the others. Grasping Alexis, he checked her diaper and returned with her. "So, what's the solution for Beth and Roger? I think he's tried everything!"

"Spoken as a member of the good ole boy club?" She arched one brow as she responded, before softening. "David, Beth has too much time on her hands!"

"Supposing you're right; she's too well-off financially, for us to hire, if she even has a skill set!"

"Oh, she has a skill set! I need to get Diana on-board, too, because she's brooding over Alexandra's leaving home!"

"Well, what I understand, Beth really has a problem with her!"

"With Diana? How could anyone have a problem with Diana? You must have misunderstood!"

David sighed. "Roger told me, himself! Beth's just so self-conscious about her weight, that she's totally unreasonable! It's like God has put slender, happy people on this earth for the sole purpose of making her more miserable! Which probably means; you're low on her list of people to like too!"

Mallory blinked tears again. "Well, right now, I'm sure her focus is on Emma and the baby. But-uh-when this resolves, and they're back home-okay-" she couldn't finish!

Tears sprang into David's eyes, too. "What baby? Emma's pregnant?"

Daniel realized when the new mining engineer wasn't able to make contact with either one of his calls; leaving messages that he would try again in the morning. He watched him make it back to the seclusion of his pickup, wondering if the kid planned to sleep there! All in all, not a totally dreadful situation until the mining village was set up! His head still spun slightly at the rapid development! David and Mallory to the rescue was a good thing, but he admired Al! She was going to do it! Even as he thought about her, she emerged from the small bedroom at the far end of the RV!

She stretched her arms around him and gave him a peck on the cheek! "Thank you for waking me up about the rest of the *Drilling Platform* report!"

He grinned. "Anything useful?"

"Oh yes, virtually eliminating guess work. The silver mines up here actually didn't shut down because the silver was exhausted-"

He nodded, "Yeah, the government enacted a bill that manipulated the price. When the price dropped, nearly everyone pulled out! And history can repeat itself! Flying high one day, and then the next-"

She sank down across from him. "Yes Sir! But there's a lot more up here than the silver! And in the samples reflected in the report, there wasn't any Platinum! I mean, I've studied Geology enough to know that where one of the noble metals is present, the chances of one or more of the others' being there is fairly good! But the new discovery of the Platinum puts things over the top! I mean, Platinum is really great stuff! And for more than jewelry"! Her exuberance faded and a somber expression took its place. "Mallory thought I should give Jared a percentage of the mine, too! Now, I barely own a majority!"

"So, have you said anything to him about it? Maybe major decisions, you should still bounce off of me."

"Well, it's hard to exactly repeat what Mallory told me, but it made a lot of sense! I'm just saying, 'please don't offer anyone else a chance to buy in'. I mean the deal with the Pritchards was a have to, because we needed that acreage! And the deal was better for the moment than more outlay of cash!"

Trent acknowledged the ride as he exited the chopper and jogged briskly toward the terminal. Checking his cell, he was alarmed at a string of missed calls. He pressed Sonia's speed dial as he tried to get the automated check-in to accept his driver's license!

"Hey, I've been in a chopper for the past two and a half hours. I'm in Albuquerque; what's up? No reception! The Andersons chopper had a sat phone, but I didn't know you were trying to reach me!" His words tripped over themselves! When he paused for breath, Michael spoke,

"Dad"!

"Where'd Mom go?"

"Dad," Michael tried again. "Dad, she's in with Meggy! Why are you in Albuquerque? You need to get here!"

"What's going on?" Trent forced himself to be calm as he moved to a different kiosk. Voila! The plastic disappeared into the slot and the screen changed. "What's going on, Michael? I'm trying to get there! But it's a long ways!"

"Dad, Megan's really critical!"

"Critical-" he echoed the word numbly, "Critical! Megan? His stomach churned as he listened for further word, automatically responding to the check-in screen. "Michael, is she so I can talk to her?"

"Who; Mom, or Meg"?

"Yeah, I guess! Sorry! Not thinking straight!"

Trent could hear a voice on the other end telling his son, "I'm sorry, Sir; you can't use your cell phone-"

Michael's eyes shot a pleading look at the no-nonsense head nurse, and he walked past her. Handing the phone to his Mom, he said, "It's Dad! He's only in Albuquerque!"

Trembling, she reached for it. "Trent! Trent! She's bad! I shouldn't have told you not to come; she wants you! I mean, she knew she was in trouble-"

"Okay, she's not in trouble-" His mind was so numb he could hardly focus. "Let me talk to her."

"She-she's not responsive! She's on life-"

Fresh terror shot through him! He wasn't going to make it! No way he could get there in time! "Okay, will you put the phone to her ear? I promise not to make things worse!"

"Okay."

Sonia's voice gave way to the gurgling sound of the respirator.

"Hey, Meggy, Baby, Daddy loves you! I'm on my way home, but this flight doesn't even board for another twenty minutes! Meggy, Daddy loves you! I'm praying for you to get better real quick-"

He fought overwhelming defeat and the desire to crumple in total despair, right there!

Sonia's voice came from the instrument he still held numbly. "Trent! Trent, are you still there? Hurry home, Babe! We need you! Lots of people are praying!"

Emma sat against a chilly, stained wall in her new prison! Oh, there were no gates and bars, or even restraints! The women went about their tasks as though she were not there, and she was tired of responding to the gazes of curious kids. Both hungry and thirsty, she fought despair! Maybe she could rise and run! She wasn't sure if the women would even try to stop her! But where would she go? This room lacked amenities, and she couldn't feel warmth from the hearth at all! But it was some shelter from the brutality of the unforgiving mountain range. Maybe they would come back soon, with Shay! She tried again, to pray; for Shay, for the child she carried, about her concern for her dad and mom's relationship! Tears rose once more.

Daniel glanced at pages as Al finished with each! Suddenly, he was filled with wonder at the treasure trove he sat atop! If she could get it going, if the kid mining engineer knew anything at all, if~ He scrunched his eyes closed; the print was small, and as he sat there, the strains of Cass's violin floated from the back of the RV!

"I'm a blessed man," his emotion-charged voice directed at his first-born. Then noticing the time! "And if I want to stay blessed, I'd better call Mom!"

Just as he reached for the sat phone, it buzzed. He took note of the number from the Colorado area code. Must be Jared's call-backs!

"Good evening; Daniel Faulkner!"

Daniel listened as the caller identified himself, asking to speak to Jared Harrelson. Catching his daughter's eye, he sprinted toward the pickup to turn the device over to the kid!

"Four hundred dollar"!

Shay assumed they were demanding that amount for the cleanup of the ragged, old car! He was pretty sure it had seen worse messes! And wiping it down with a strong cleaning agent and cleaning the carpet didn't seem as though it should take that amount of money! Still, if he could be certain that he and Emma would be released and returned to La Paz, it would be a fabulous deal. Problem was, he didn't carry cash!

"Speak English?" His hours of being with them made him pretty sure they didn't! The demand for four hundred dollars was the first thing that had made sense all day!

"La Paz! And I give four hundred dollars!" His face was a study in anxiety as he spoke slowly.

"No! No, La Paz! Four hundred dollar"! A rise in volume alarmed him. If he was going to negotiate, he didn't want to make them mad.

He nodded, "Okay, okay! No La Paz!" He reached cautiously for his wallet as they scowled threateningly! "No four hundred dollars!" he showed the empty bill section of the billfold. "ATM? Bank? We go! I get four hundred dollars at bank!"

They exchanged confused glances, and then the driver shook his head vehemently! "No! No go bank!"

He tried again, "No dollars! Look! No dollars"! Showing the empty wallet once more, he pulled credit cards and the ATM card free. "I get money! I give you! For car! Bank"!

Hard countenances made his stomach squeeze. If they were aware of ATM cards and getting cash on credit cards, it wasn't evident! But maybe they did know, and didn't want to take him to a populated area where he might get help! Or have a traceable electronic transaction.

"Four hundred dollar! You pay!"

The second man leered. "You pay four hundred dollar for señora!"

"Okay, but I don't have cash with me! No money!" He pulled his pockets inside out! "I hope you're taking it easy on my wife. Baby! Uh-bambino-I pay four hundred dollar!"

A sarcastic laugh issued forth. "Four hundred, usted; four hundred, señora; four hundred, bambino!"

Shay strove for calm in the face of deteriorating negotiations. "Habla Ingles? Interpreter! Where interpreter"?

"Muerte! We kill!"

"No! What point will that serve? I can get money! I get dollars! Many, many dollars! And you free my wife and me! We go! No toubles! We give money; we go back to USA! No police!"

The hour was late when Trent raced past baggage claim without stopping, and ran out to greet Michael. His son's face, ashen and ravaged, he figured that answered his question about how Megan was doing. "Are you guys and mom doing okay"?

"Not really, Dad! Dad, it's all my fault-"

"I'll drive!" Trent shoved his way into the driver's seat and Michael complied. "Whatever happened, Son, it isn't your fault!"

"Well, see; when you called and we stopped her from sending the pictures-uh- we just all kind of ganged up on her! We were pretty brutal. Dad, I called her a brainless dimwit!"

"Well, your sister isn't brainless, but the stunt she was about to pull, was! Michael, what you're describing is typical brother-sister love talk! Whatever happens, Michael, she's in the Lord's hands! Promise me you won't put more of a load on yourself than this is already!"

Accelerating up the ramp onto the freeway, he didn't make further conversation!

Ned McAllister dreaded this talk! After listening to Jared's message and the assurance that he would call back in the morning, McAllister decided there was no use in postponing the inevitable! Now his reasoning was further supported by the fact that the number seemed to be some type of party line! And the guy, who owned his daughter's heart, didn't yet even possess his own phone!

"Hello, Mr. McAllister; this is Jared! Thank you for calling me back!"

"Well, Son, you won't be thanking me once I get finished!" When shocked silence was the only response, Abby's father plunged ahead! "Listen, I've undoubtedly spoiled Abigail! She's my most prized possession and she's so very gifted. And I was worried about her when she went to Aspen to further her music studies that summer! It concerned me that she feared nothing, and picked up with some friends in the drug-hippie culture! I was almost relieved when she had her religious experience-"

"Well, yes, Sir!"

"Don't interrupt me when I'm talking! I've spent a good portion of the evening trying to surmise a reason why you should be in contact with me! The only thing I can think of is that you're hoping to borrow money! Surely you wouldn't ever presume to think I could consider you a suitable contender for my daughter! You do realize that the only thing you have in common is the religion thing! And lately I'm trying to dissuade her from that!"

"Well, have you ever thought of asking Abby what she wants?" The words sprang from somewhere deep in Jared's soul!

"My daughter's name is Abigail, and what she wants is a vocal career! I know that you're backed into a corner! A worthless degree that you're in hock for up to your eyeballs! How about if I settle out your student loans, and then you never contact either my daughter nor myself again?"

Jared's voice came, soft and composed. "I'm sorry to break this to you, but borrowing money from you wasn't the purpose of my call! I guess it's your worst nightmare! I got a good job today, and it holds a lot of promise! I actually have received an unexpected sum of money-"

The line went dead!

"Shay and Emma are in my country, Agent Bransom? Are you sure of your facts?"

"Well, if they aren't there, then no one has a clue where they are! Mrs. O'Shaughnessy's last contact with Shay was prior to his boarding a flight into La Paz." Erik thought the Bolivian businessman sounded sincere.

"Well, yes, and that is what I think! I think they are coming here! And I send my driver for them-he come back, saying they-no come!"

"Well, trust me Mr. Cisneros, they were on the flight and they deplaned and checked into a hotel near the airport! They spent the night and headed out yesterday morning. A desk clerk remembers seeing them leave, but they've never returned to their hotel, nor do they answer their phones. We've reported them missing to the state police!"

Erik listened, concerned, to the other man's voice. After waiting in the hotel lobby for two hours with no sign of the American, his driver had called to ask him what to do. When Cisneros tried to contact Shay, he got no answer either, just surmising that O'Shaughnessy had changed his mind about the trip, and now refused to answer his phone to give an explanation.

When the hour got later and later, Daniel finally sent Diana a text message!

The new Engineer's using the sat phone. I just wanted to tell you I love you all, and I'm heading down to Durango now, to catch an early flight out! I'll call you from Denver, but then I'll head to the office to get a little bit done there! I hope there's good word about Shay and Emma!

Diana read the message forlornly! Why did things like this happen when she most needed to hear his voice? Not only was there no encouraging news about Shay, but the word about Megan Morrison was even more heart-rending! And Jeremiah was beside himself over her! She texted back:

Call me tonight when you can get good reception, even if it's late! I'll be up!

But the message wouldn't send!

"Jeremiah, Jeremi-you need to try to get some sleep!" She tried to use her most authoritative yet compassionate nurse-tone! Wow, while they worried about Alexandra and her thing for Tommy, Jeremiah's affairs of the heart had never entered their mind! He was smitten! And Diana wasn't the least impressed with the little girl! "Good-night, I love you! Wake me if you need anything."

After checking on the sleeping little ones, she closed the doors of her master suite behind her. Getting her Bible, she turned a lamp on above the Chaise Lounge and hunkered down. "Lord, You do this! Sometimes, You cut me off from people in my life to force me to turn to You! I-I'm-uh-really sorry if I haven't been heeding You! Lord, about Megan; I don't even know how to pray! Please give me wisdom, and Jeremiah, too! I thought he had his head on straight! But then, he convinced Alexandra to go on Facebook against our rules, so he could keep tabs on Megan and all of her silly little boyfriends she 'goes out' with! And it all shoots daggers through his heart!" Tears poured down her face and she reached for the tissues! "I guess because he's grown into a man's body, and he seems to single-mindedly desire to serve You, I've lost sight of the fact that he's really young and naïve!" She stopped short of asking God to take the other couple's child, but it kind of seemed like it might do Jeremiah a favor in the long run. Thinking that sounded cold, she paused to explain her thinking to the Lord. "I don't want any of my kids to choose the wrong spouse and end up being miserable, or divorced! But Lord, with Jeremiah's wanting to enter the ministry-it's extra-important-"

She paused, engulfed in silence and an awesome sense of His being there!

The next thing she knew, the phone was jangling over on the nightstand! Amazed, she launched toward it, aware of bright light trying to fight its way into the suite around heavy, silver, velvet drapes!

She fought off the fog as she gasped. "You-you're already in Denver?" The clock by the phone reinforced that that was probably the case!

Megan was basically already gone! Kept on life support until he could get there! Papers forced themselves into his line of vision! Permission to harvest organs~ In profound shock, Trent stood there, listening numbly and dumbly to the plans for his youngest child! How could this be? How~

At last words sprang to his lips! From a wellspring of rage! After a cursory and insincere, 'Mr. Morrison, we're terribly sorry for your loss~' they had launched into a memorized speech of signing the permission, contacting a funeral home: and, 'oh, and did they have a church affiliation?'!

"Okay, just~just stop with all this!" Eyes ablaze, he flung the clipboard onto a chair in the corner of the ICU cubicle! "Get out! I need to talk to my little girl!"

They started over again, patiently telling him that she was basically totally unresponsive by the time the EMT's drove away with her in the ambulance! And the respirator was a courtesy to him to give him time~

Still, through the stupor, the fact wasn't lost on him that the heroics were also partly to preserve her organs until his arrival; when he and Sonia together could give permission to pull the plug and begin harvesting! He was just so shocked! He wasn't ready for this! He could never be ready for this!

Rasping sobs rose; he guessed from his own chest. "Please," He strove for patience. "Please, can we have some time with her privately?"

The charge nurse, not easily deterred, opened her lips.

Ignoring her, Trent tenderly moved his little girl over and sat down beside her, pulling her partially into his arms. No response but the eerie gurgling of the equipment! His tears covered her face as he pressed his lips to soft skin. "Meggy! Meggy? Baby, it's Daddy! Hey, you've beaten this before! We have! With the Lord's help! We can do it again! Daddy's been praying, and we'll get a prayer chain started around the country! God has other plans for you than calling you into His presence right now! Meggy?"

He trembled, and kicking his shoes off, pulled his feet up onto the bed! He wasn't moving! He was going to stay here and hold her~and hold her~and hold~

Jared tried again and again to get Mr. McAllister to pick up! What kind of a man hung up and wouldn't even allow him to present his case? Frustrated, he didn't know what to do. He and Abby both desperately wanted his blessing! They were both of age, and Ned couldn't stand between them, legally! Although undoubtedly, he possessed enough clout to cause them problems! But with their commitment to the Lord, they wanted to be especially considerate. Abby's prayers for five years had been for her unbending father to receive the Lord! With communications with him at a standstill, he wasn't sure if he should even call Abby and explain. While he considered, she called him.

Overjoyed, he answered. "Hey, how did you get this number?"

"Well, I came home for a few days for a visit and to get more of my stuff. I thought it was you who called earlier. Do you have good news?"

"Well, I thought so! But then, I kind of got my parade rained on. I'm sorry, Abby; I shouldn't have said that! The Lord swung a door wide open and then the honey has continued to drop! Suddenly, I feel like I'm in a great position-but then your father knows I have nothing for you like you're accustomed to! And yet, I think there's more to it than that, his reason for not liking me!"

"Agreed! It isn't a personality conflict; it's a philosophy conflict! He wouldn't mind our being Christians if we more fit his definition of the word! But you sidetracked me; what did you mean by 'in a great position'? Did you get a job? What honey dropped? I mean I know the passage of Scripture you're referencing! Is the job like anything near your major and what you want to do?"

"I think it's tailor-made for me-" he paused, not certain how to proceed. He so much wanted her dad's blessing-and besides, he didn't want to propose over the phone-Especially since Mr. McAllister was probably listening in. "I'm chief mining engineer at a startup mine near Silverton-"

"Not working for Alexandra Faulkner! Please Jared, tell me you're not!"

He felt pure joy ebbing away, as he remained silent so she could explain herself.

"Jared! Jared; are you there?"

"Yeah, Abby; I am! I'm sorry; what's wrong with working for the Faulkners?"

She started crying. "Okay, don't try to play games with me, Jared! Alexandra owns the property! I know all about it because I saw an ad online for a job that I thought you might be interested in! You'll be working for her, and she's beautiful; it's just the two of you alone up there-"

"No, you're wrong! We're strictly professionals. Norma, the lady Alexandra bought the ranch from, is going to keep living in the old house for a while! I'm calling my dad tomorrow to hire him first! Abby, I only love you-"

"Well, maybe you think so, for now! But if we have to wait a long time, and she's just right there-"

"Listen to me, Baby, if we have to wait forever, I'll wait for you! I don't cares who's closer or who else is available! I don't want to ask you to marry me over the phone, but will you marry me? I mean, the job's good enough we don't have to wait! I just figured you wanted time to plan a nice wedding, and your dad would want to put on a big shindig!"

He paused, knowing she was crying, but unsure of why! "Wh-what's the matter?"

"Um-uh, you asked me-a-question-uh-do you-want an answer?"

He was totally frazzled. "I did? What did I ask? Oh! I asked you if you'll marry me! See, I wanted your dad-"

"I know, Jared! But he totally doesn't get us! I don't want him to throw me a lavish wedding! We'll fight over it every step of the way! I know you've told me not to argue with him, that we'll never win him that way-I don't know what to do! Can I just come there and be with you?"

Chapter 19: GRIMNESS

Jeremiah's appearance shocked Diana! "Why didn't you wake me? I didn't intend to sleep so late! Thank you for helping with your brothers and sisters."

He sank wearily at the kitchen counter. "No problem, Mom! I still wish Cass was coming home and not going to Israel!"

She sank beside him, waiting for a cup of coffee to brew, and patted his arm tenderly. "That makes two of us, and not just because she's such a help with the little guys!" She sighed. "I guess I knew this day would come-it's just taken me kind of-off guard!"

Jeremiah nodded absently.

"Milk, or juice?" She forced her brightest tone.

"Neither Mom; thanks! When's Dad getting home?"

"He's on a flight from Denver, but he's going to the office; things are behind there! Jeremiah, I wish you'd drink something! Did you sleep any?"

"What do you think? No, I didn't sleep! And you haven't even asked me if Megan's doing better! Can I go to Washington, Mom? Please?"

"Washington-" she echoed the word blankly. Maybe she was having a hard time clearing cobwebs after sleeping so late. "DC?"

Jeremiah's brown eyes registered anguish. "Yes, Washington DC, where the Morrisons live and Megan's on life support! Mom, do you care about me at all?"

"It just so happens that I do! That's why I'm insisting you take in some fluid!"

"Okay; sorry Mom," his words were a mumble as he grasped the juice glass and headed toward the stairs.

Mallory placed the phone receiver in its stand. There was still nothing definitive about her cousin and his wife! At least Shannon planned to stay in Boston indefinitely! Thinking of Shay and Shannon reminded her to call the private investigator, who was looking into the woman's claims about a relationship with Ryland. With a laugh, he asked her to give him time, and she disconnected without asking him if he ever traveled abroad looking for missing or kidnapped victims! Maybe she should seek out someone tougher! Ex-military! Erik probably wouldn't approve of her hiring a mercenary, but proper channels were doing nothing! And, he would throw a fit about her planning to go herself! That's why it would be best if he didn't know!"

David listened with a heavy heart to the news about Megan Morrison! Trent was such a super guy. "Lord, please turn the situation around! I know she's bad by the doctors' standards, but You can do miracles!" He rose resolutely from his desk to go find Mallory with more bad news to break. Hearing her on the phone, he realized his timing was perfect!

"You are not going looking for Shay yourself!"

Expressive eyes turned their most luminous and pleading expression on him.

"No, Mallory! Absolutely not! Cancel! Cancel now!"

Reluctantly, she shut down negotiations with the ticket agent.

"Okay, Mallory, don't forget that when we pray, God sends forces into the battle! Sometimes prayer is the only thing we can do, but it's also the most powerful thing we can do! It isn't the same as doing nothing! Listen, I know that your riding to the rescue for me, has made the difference, and both times, you put yourself at risk! But I just can't fathom allowing you to go to South America by yourself-"

"Well, you could come-"

"I know, but we have kids to think about! I don't want them growing up without either one of us! I sure don't want them orphaned! Listen, I think that Lt. Atchison resigned or didn't reenlist! Maybe he's looking to~we'll talk about it! Okay? Actually, I nearly forgot my reason for coming in here. Megan Morrison~uh, she's really critical~with her asthma!"

Mallory dropped her head into her arms and sobbed! "Well, why didn't you tell me before this? That's what was wrong with him the other night!"

"No, he was upset about a stunt she pulled, or was trying to pull! It could've been disastrous. But then whenever Megan gets into trouble, or thinks she's going to, she starts her asthma symptoms, on purpose, to manipulate the situation! So~" He stood watching her miserably

"Hey Beautiful! My dad and I are onto something really great! Can I call you back?" Daniel Faulkner's voice radiated excitement and joy as he answered his cell! "The next ezine edition just popped up, and I spotted something simultaneously with Dad! We nearly collided in the outer offices~"

"Daniel! Jeremiah~"

"Huh? What about 'im, Honey?"

"I think he~he~he ran~away!"

"Well, Honey, Jeremiah's not a runaway type kid~"

"It's about Megan Morrison! He asked me if he could go to DC~and he's been fasting for her; but now I'm worried about him! I just insisted that he drink some juice~I~I don't know why I wasn't listening to his heart!"

"Okay, maybe he's just out in the yard, having some quiet time; to think!"

"No, uh~he took a couple of my credit~cards, and left a note under the full juice glass that he's sorry! Daniel, he's really dehydrated and he hasn't had any sleep!"

She could hear him still talking to Jerry about whatever the deal was, then he came back on, "Okay, I'll be home as soon as I can get there!"

"No-oo-o! You need to get to the airport! And if he isn't there, you have to follow him to Washington! Make him drink something! Or he's going to be on the critical list, too!"

"Listen, Di~I don't think he can pull something like that off! I mean the credit cards are in your name, and he doesn't look like a Diana~"

"You have to find him!"

Trent relinquished his daughter for some daily ministrations. For the life of him, he couldn't get hold of himself! Well, he didn't agree that there was no mental function. He sensed that Megan was afraid, taking comfort in his holding her and talking to her! The medical people all turned into talking bobble-heads about the financial issues with keeping the life support going! Part of him was terrified by the financial crisis it was causing! But! Meggy! How could he not sit and hold her when she was afraid to die? And he was afraid to let her die! The thought haunted him: 'What if she isn't really saved?' If she were saved, would she delight in bringing on her symptoms to order her own spoiled world? Would she be on a face book account she wasn't supposed to have, messaging to boys no one knew,-and-It was his fault! Stymied at being unable to discipline her and make her do like he did the other three-had he just abdicated? But what could he do? Every time things nearly came to a showdown, and Megan gasped for breath, Sonia intervened! And, why not? She was a good mom who loved her kids! But still, he should have done something-anything-to keep from ending in a situation like this!

"Hello, Mrs. Morrison?"

Sonia looked up at the sound of her name, to see another white-coated apparition! A different face, but she knew the mission was the same! To explain to her Trent's loss of ability to cope and face reality! Their terminology for his continued refusal to sign the papers halting the heroics! Their new game plan was to try to prove he wasn't competent; and if a court would declare him incompetent, then she could sign the paper! Her mind shrank from both trying to undercut her husband, and being the one to end her daughter's life! Which, according to them, basically ended before the paramedics arrived at the house! Sitting down without invitation, he once more directed her attention to a clip board where daily costs were broken down! If he intended to terrify her, it was working! She fumbled for her phone. "I-I need to have my son come-"

He rose. "Well, there's really no need for that! Mrs. Morrison, I know this is a tough call, but it rests with you!" With that, he left rather hastily.

Sonia stared after him as the tears flowed again. 'That was his job? To come put the thumb screws to her? When Trent wasn't with her; or even one of the boys? They were saying now 'that it was too late to harvest any of Megan's organs; so they had no agenda but the overall well-being of the rest of the kids-' She just didn't know-

⁂

Jeremiah made reservations in his name over the phone, using the credit card number! Not a hitch! The cab ride to the airport was expensive, but he used some of his cash! Cab fare would be high from Dulles to the hospital! His stomach was in a knot! From lack of nutritional intake? Doubtless! But mostly about Megan! Of course, his conscience was eating him up! But he was disappointed that after being gone for a week, his dad had opted to head straight to the office rather than coming home! Sometimes it seemed like they weren't there for you when you needed them!

When the flight left on time, he sighed with relief; and when it was permitted, he started his iPod playing the Psalms through his ear phones. Never intending to fall asleep, he roused with a start when a flight attendant shook him awake to turn it back off! Frustrated by the weakness of his flesh, he asked the Lord to forgive him for sleeping and not watching unto prayer! Finally making it to the jet way, he broke into a lope, navigating by signs for ground transportation. Seeing policemen made him nervous! Doubtless his mom and dad knew by now that he-

The cabbie motioned for the wild-eyed kid to hop in and Jeremiah fidgeted nervously through the forty minute drive through traffic, pulling up at last to a daunting hospital complex! No problem, though! The printed off schematic rested in the front pocket of his backpack, but he had it memorized! A quick jog and he gained the elevator, expecting at any moment to be arrested!

Then, he was at Pulmonary ICU where he buzzed to gain admission. He watched as the doors thonked open automatically, then tried to enter with an assurance he was far from feeling!

"Jeremiah Faulkner! I'm here to visit with Megan Morrison!" He extended his hand toward the head nurse who made no move to reciprocate the friendly gesture!

She studied him with an unyielding frown. "How old are you, Jeremiah?"

"What's the visitor age-limit?" A well-known parry his parents used on him when they preferred not to give a straight answer!

A smile tugged at the corners of her lips. "Why? If I say it's twenty-five, are you going to try to convince me-"

"No, Ma'am, and it wouldn't be twenty-five. I'm fifteen, and I thought if the limit's sixteen, I might be able to fudge a little bit. Could I please see Megan?"

"I haven't seen you here before! Unless you're family, there's really no reason-"

"Mrs. Schmidt, please-"

"Okay, Jeremiah, but you need to be prepared-"

"Yes, I know-" His pleading eyes pulled at her emotions.

"But first, I'm getting you a Sprite! When you down it, I can let you-for a second-"

He nodded assent! Fasting or not, this woman was no one to argue with!

Emma forced down a doughy thing and some runny beans, determined to survive this ordeal and get back home! She hoped Shay was okay; no sight of him! And if the women knew any English, they weren't conversant with her!

Mallory met Rhonna with a hug as they met at the in-house café. "You look great," she complimented! "How did you escape Jim's oversight to meet me for lunch?"

"Yeah, that's a good question. Hey, any word on your cousin? I've been praying! I did have to promise Jim I'm not trying to come back to work at *DiaMo*!"

"No new updates on Shay and Emma. Thanks for praying! I know it makes a difference! David was nearly afraid to let me come meet you for lunch! I want to go look for them myself, so bad! So, tell me about your romance!"

Seated, Rhonna's dark eyes met Mallory's "There is no romance! I could just tell that his parents were dead-set against me. Uh, he had told me they had some reservations; understatement of the year! But then, guess who called me?"

Mallory thought briefly. “I don’t know; Carm?”

Rhonna laughed ruefully. “Did you put her up to it?”

“She’s one busy woman! I never can catch up to her! Why’d she call?”

“And why would you think?”

“Uh, I guess to help bind up your broken heart! Rhonna, I can’t stand to see you hurt, and his parents; well, you’re their loss!”

“Well, thank you; uh-Caramel gave me a lot of insight! I was amazed when she called. She’s kinda been my hero! Well, I have lots of heroes! I didn’t know she knew I was in the world! For her just to call me up-and say-just the right words-”

Mallory’s eyes welled up. “The Lord always does that! Sometimes He uses His Word, and other times he sends us other people to help salve our wounds! Rhonna, do you have any vacation time? Would you like to go on a cruise?”

“What? A cruise? You and David going?”

“No; we can’t get away right now-”

“No matter! Yeah, I want to take a cruise! Maybe I’ll fall off the edge of the world!”

Mallory reached across the table, patting the other woman’s hand! “God has someone better!” She proffered a glossy catalog. “Pick a wardrobe and a destination!”

Trent retreated with his Bible to the heart-lab waiting room while the hospital staff worked on Megan. He was clueless about how to comfort other members of the family, and unwilling to listen to their opinions on the future- He sank down and let his Bible fall open! His vision clouded by tears, he dashed at them angrily! When he could focus, he noted with hope and amazement, the passage before him:

> *Matthew 9:23-25 And when Jesus came into the ruler’s house, and saw the minstrels and the people making a noise,*
>
> *He said unto them, Give place: for the maid is not dead, but sleepeth. And they laughed him to scorn.*

> *But when the people were put forth, he went in, and took her by the hand, and the maid arose.*

"Okay, Lord, I believe this story, and I believe you performed this miracle when You walked on earth as a man; but how many other Christians have lost children, and begged for this? Lord, I wish You would-uh- I just wish I had assurance about her salvation, and seeing her again, in Your kingdom! I mean, they laughed You to scorn! That's what I feel like they're doing to me! I feel like they think I'm a pervert to sit there holding my child who's afraid to die! I know they're putting pressure on Sonia! Well, it's on me, too! Lord, You know we already can't afford what this has cost- I see bankruptcy-if we pull the plug this afternoon! But how can I just decide? Nothing makes sense! They say there's no brain activity, and she's gone; but then they keep medications going to alleviate suffering! How can she suffer if she's not in there? There's just this huge area that seems like gray area between life and death! Maybe Sonia and I can't care for her if she'll never be right-and I don't want to saddle the other three-with debt and guilt-how can I know? I'd let them put me in a straightjacket and have Sonia sign, but when it comes down to it; I don't think she can do it either! And then-I won't be able to be with my child when the end-comes!"

Sobs racked him! Probably they were finished with Meggy, and he could go down and resume his vigil, but he stayed, wiping away tears of hopelessness, reading the miracle story again, and then skimming ahead to read a verse he especially liked as a Numismatist:

> *Matthew 17:27 Nothwithstanding, lest we should offend them, go thou to the sea, and cast in a hook, and take up the fish that first cometh up; and when thou hast opened his mouth, thou shalt find a piece of money: that take, and give unto them for me and thee.*

Grinning sardonically, he pulled the last few coins he owned from his slacks pocket! Maybe a '43 copper penny would magically appear- Not that he didn't check every coin that ever crossed his palm! Occasionally, he would find a nickel to sell for eight dollars or so! Sonia would laughingly remind him he spent more than he ever gained by his hobby, on the books and magazines!

Thelma Schmidt ushered Jeremiah into the small ICU room, surprised when Trent wasn't already back in his place! Jeremiah stood beside her silently, taking in the still form, the only movement being those that were mechanically generated.

Struggling for composure to speak, he questioned, "There's really no chance?"

"Jeremiah, I can't discuss her case with you. I really figured her dad would be back, and if he was okay with your visit~you really should go now!"

Since he could hardly bear seeing her like that, he nodded willingly. "Yes, Ma'am; but I'd like to pray for her!" Without waiting for permission, he stepped forward and covered Megan's hand with his own, bowing his head, and beginning, "Please, heavenly Father~"

Before he could go any further, she choked and gasped, trying to sit up. Weird sounds fought their way from her throat, and the nurse sprang forward, pressing the call button and ordering Jeremiah out! Horrified, he watched from the doorway as other members of the medical team rushed in, injecting more medication into the IV and easing her back into calm! Catching Nurse Schmidt's warning glare, he turned to make a retreat! Spinning dizzily, he hit the floor!

Daniel raced through Dulles, also without luggage, and hailed a cab! No sign of Jeremiah!

"Lord," he pled, "please let me find him! Please forgive us for not listening to him! He's such a great kid, and he never~Please, protect him, and please heal Megan! Even if she isn't the one you have for Jeremiah, and we kind of hope she isn't~But for Trent and Sonia's sakes~"

The cab pulled up and he stared at the complex dismally! "Do you know where someone with asthma would be?" He handed his credit card, including a nice tip, but the cabbie wasn't any help about where Megan might be! And consequently, Jeremiah!

With directions from the information desk, he located the correct hospital, stepping from the elevator in time to have Sonia Morrison throw herself into his arms! Not sure what to do, he patted her shoulder awkwardly, as he freed himself! He and Diana should have already been here for their friends. Guiltily, he stepped back. His purpose for showing up now, was Jeremiah!

He stared helplessly as Sonia began a tearful revelation that was hard for him to fathom! Something about having Trent certified as incompetent! Surely that wasn't what she was saying! If Trent was incompetent; where did that leave the rest of them?

Seeing Michael, he made his way toward him. "Hey, Michael, we're sorry to hear about Megan! Where is your dad?"

"Thank you, Sir! Thanks for coming! If he isn't in Meg's room talking and reading the Bible to her, sometimes he goes up to the heart lab waiting room! It empties out in the afternoons~and he has some place for quiet! He isn't crazy! That's what they're trying to say, so they can get a court order to stop life support!"

Sonia interrupted hopelessly, "Maybe you can get through to him!"

Daniel nodded mutely! How could he try to convince another dad to terminate his child's life? Striving for nonchalance, he directed his question at Michael. "Hey, you haven't seen Jeremiah anywhere; have you?"

Jeremiah struggled weakly, trying to figure out what was happening! His stomach squeezed and he dry-heaved painfully! "Wah~" A weak moan and he sank backwards on a gurney! Surely he couldn't have passed out~ Schmidt appeared at his side, intending to start an IV! He waved her away, guiltily realizing he should have listened to his mom about fluids, and probably he had made a mistake by coming here without their permission! Now he was running up a hospital bill, and things were spiraling out of control.

"No! No, Ma'am! You don't have permission to treat me; do you? I'm a minor! Is Megan~"

"The same"! She folded her arms importantly across her chest, frowning at him from what seemed to be her perpetual expression! "I have some crackers and an apple sauce! Then you should probably be on your way!" She watched as he polished them off before offering a hand. "Okay, got your legs under you? Take it easy!"

Escaping her line of vision, he pulled his diagram free, checking the best escape route where he wouldn't run into the family! He needed to find a place to gather his thoughts, maybe read his Bible! And he needed to call his parents and apologize!

Daniel fished his phone free. "Yeah, Dad"! He answered his father's call. "How does it look? You need to call David or Mallory and get the complete report! Yeah, okay, I can do it! Yeah, something's come up-uh- just go ahead, Dad! Come on; you can do this! You were doing it before I was even born! Just take it and run with it, Dad! We have to beat everyone else to the draw! I'll ask David if, when we buy the full report, they can hold off for maybe twenty-four hours before they release it to anyone else! Not that I'll blame them if they tell me, 'No'! Yeah, Dad, whatever you need! Whatever it takes! I trust your judgment; you don't need to check out every detail with me! Okay, love you too!"

Before he could slide his phone back into his pocket, Diana called. "Hey, Baby! I'm still hunting for him! This is a huge place, so maybe he hasn't found the right hospital!"

"That isn't it! I checked his search history, and he checked out the hospital before he left here! At least that confirms that that's where he went! He must be there somewhere! Is there any change with Megan?"

"No; I guess she's on life support, and the doctors are trying to divide and conquer Trent and Sonia to pull the plug! It's convoluted-I'm looking for Trent now! Maybe Jeremiah's talking to him!"

"May be! Keep me in the loop! If he's still keeping up such a rigid fast, he might be passed out somewhere! If Trent has any medical questions, call me!"

Trent studied a text message from Sonia. Faulkner was here somewhere looking for him! He guessed that was a good thing! Although, he really didn't feel very sociable! Faulkner was the one who, by way of Alexandra, had learned what Meg was up to, precipitating the present crisis! Not that it was Faulkner's fault! But-Meggy! He was immersed in thought when a voice made him jump!

"Sorry to startle you, Mr. Morrison." Jeremiah stood hesitantly at the doorway.

"Well, that's what they're saying!" His voice, brittle with tension! "That my nerves are shot! I guess they are. Where's your dad?"

"Uh, I'm not sure! I came here to see Megan and pray with her."

Trent closed his Bible, rising. "Thanks, Jeremiah! You look awful! Are you okay?"

"I think so!" Jeremiah moved toward a vending machine. "I think I'll have a juice; would you like something?"

"No thanks, I'm on my way back-"

Jeremiah nodded, relieved. That was what he thought Megan was had tried to convey to him! That she wanted her daddy to come back! He slid a five into the machine and change clunked down as the bottle of juice delivered.

Trent started to say, "Congratulations, Jeremiah; it sounds like you hit the jackpot!" but before he could utter a syllable, Faulkner was there!

Trent met the other man's gaze through red-rimmed eyes. "Hey, I was just on my way down to see if they're finished with my daughter! Thanks for coming, though!"

Daniel extended his hand before giving the other man a supportive hug! Jeremiah hung back, hoping his dad wouldn't dress him down for his stupid stunt in front of Megan's dad!

"Yeah, I understand you wanting to spend time with her, but what's going on?"

A broken man sat sobbing and trembling helplessly. When he could speak, the story issued forth! "Her lungs shut down! Even the paramedics couldn't get oxygen to her! They hooked her up; just to give me time to get here! Since then, they've just-put pressure on-They said she's gone! No brain activity! Now her major systems are shutting down! Which, if she's been gone all week, why are they just now-none of it makes sense! I guess it does to them! I feel like Megan's afraid-and I just want to hold her and comfort her, what little I can! I've failed her so completely! Nothing like trying to make up for lost time after it's too late! Surprisingly, Sonia understands the logic better than I do! I mean this thing has already buried us-" he wasn't sure why he was admitting this to Daniel Faulkner of all people! He tried to push his way past.

"Okay, time out! Sit back down here and talk to us!" His eyes met his son's. "You too, Jeremiah"!

Jeremiah complied hastily, but then jumped back up to retrieve a penny from a corner. With a clatter, he released the new prize with the vending machine change, and uncapped the juice. "Would you like one?" He offered.

"Coffee"! Daniel's voice carried an extra air of authority! "Trent, can he get you something? You should have something! Candy bar; juice? You need to keep your strength up!"

Jeremiah reached for the pile of change, and Trent stopped him, stretching out his hand for the coins! Agonized thoughts tormented him! Here he was, praying for the miraculous coin! And who should get it, but the Faulkners? Why did everything always come to them? Not that he wanted money! He wanted Megan back, and to be out of this latest yawning chasm!

"Don't spend these, Jeremiah! Put 'em in a safe place! Really, thanks, but I just need to get back-"

"Well, if they're valuable, would you please take them? I would never have known the difference! I was just ready to feed them back into the machine!" The young man's face was a study in earnestness!

Daniel wasn't surprised when Trent refused! The man was a study in character that he deeply admired. He caught his son's eye as he tried to insist.

"Where's your pastor? What has he advised?"

Trent patted Jeremiahs' shoulder heavily. "He's on vacation with his family!"

Jeremiah was horrified. "Well, does he even know?"

"I'm thinking he must not, or he would have called me and offered to come back! We don't need him to do that! He needs rest and recuperation, the same as everyone else; and so does his family! Christian people are praying!" He straightened with determination. "Thank you for coming; it means a lot! But go home!"

Daniel watched the other man's retreat with a heavy heart!

"Dad, why wouldn't he even take eleven cents? If it can help Megan-"

Daniel choked back a sob! "Jeremiah-you need to brace yourself-eleven cents won't make any difference. I think he made the decision to sign! If the coins are worth ten thousand dollars, which I doubt, he'll be forced into bankruptcy anyway! The costs are just too exorbitant!"

"Dad, she moved! She tried to sit up and ask for him! But she has that tube down her throat and they injected more meds-"

He shook his head, doubting his son's words; Jeremiah was in denial, too!

"Dad, I felt bad, because I thought I scared her and upset her, by being there when she wanted Mr. Morrison! And the nurse acted mad like I did something wrong! They said it was spasms and reflexive stuff-but I think she was cognizant and far from brain-dead! And I've been thinking about the money-remember when Lisette gave Katy the ideas for raising money to help Tim Baldwin?"

"I remember! Son, but this is beyond help by a couple of pancake breakfasts and a chili dinner at the church! We're not talking about a few gallon jars filled with pocket change! Even if someone combed through every coin, looking for collector's pieces"!

The teen nodded, spinning the dime absently.

"Jeremiah, they told Trent that all of her systems have shut down!"

"I know, but that catheter bag; Dad, it was-" He paused embarrassed. "Her kidneys are working! And so is her brain!"

"Me of little faith; huh? I hope you're right! Even if she doesn't survive; if he can get assurance that she's received the Lord-" He pulled his phone free and dialed Hanson's ranch.

Instead of Steb, he got Lilly Cowan's weird son! "Hey, Michael; is Steb available?"

"He went to an Arabian show! Do you have his cell phone number?"

"I'm not sure I do; maybe you can help me!"

"I'm happy to try! What's the problem?"

Daniel quickly hit the highlights, then asked about the mission statement of the *SOC Foundation*! If there was any leeway for diverting funds for a family with their daughter on life-support!

"I don't think that is possible," Came Michael's quick response! "But maybe we can start a new foundation, for that purpose! You say the hospital seems eager to end the life support, and they are putting financial concerns on the front burner for making this crucial decision! That should not be the main criterion!"

"Well, I'm not certain that it is! From a medical standpoint-the only thing creating any semblance of life-"

Amazingly, it was like Cowan hadn't heard a word he said. "Yes, we will name the new charity, *the Children In Peril Foundation: ChIP,* for shortened! Upper case *C*, small *h*, and upper case *I* and *P*! What will be your donation, Mr. Faulkner?"

Daniel laughed tensely, hoping Trent's assessment on the value of the two coins was in the ballpark! "Forty thousand"!

Chapter 20: GRATITUDE

David fidgeted nervously! With another promise not to leave in search of her cousin, Mallory had gone to meet Rhonna for lunch. Seemed liked she should be back. He buzzed reception and Gina answered.

"Hey Gina, is Mallory back from lunch?"

"No Sir, not yet! Would you like me to order you something sent up?"

"Guess not; thanks, Gina! If Rhonna was stirred up about something, I may be having lunch with Jim! Any calls I should know about?"

"No, the phones have been quiet. My sister's out here wanting a quick word with you-"

David frowned, not sure what Heather could want. "Okay, couple of minutes. Send her back!" He rose courteously and indicated a chair as he repositioned across his desk.

The former employee sprawled back languorously and crossed her legs, revealing plenty of thigh!

He frowned. "Time's running out! What do you need? Maybe it's something you should run by Mallory!"

Shiny black nails picked through file folders in her unzipped case.

David didn't care for black nails! Too Goth for his tastes!

With the correct file located, she smiled a weird smile! If she was trying to be enticing, she was only making him nervous! And annoyed!

She handed him a file, and he noticed her hand shaking. He glanced up sharply as he took in the top page! "Let me guess! You're here to borrow money! Good grief! How did you get in so much trouble?" He glanced at page two. "Playing Russian roulette with the IRS doesn't generally work; even for smart people! You know, what, Heather? We're not a bank! Maybe you just need to turn the car back in and downsize! Looks like you've bankrupted a viable company!"

His cell buzzed and before he could reach for it, she struck like a viper!

"David's phone; this is Heather!" Her voice purred as he grasped for it back!

"Daniel Faulkner!" She leered as she handed him the device!

"Okay, Heather! Get out! And don't ever come back!" He buzzed Gina! "Yeah Gina? Call building security up here to see your sister out!"

Trent resituated himself in the hospital bed and pulled Megan back into his arms! As usual alarms and beeps from the various monitors went crazy! One of the reasons they didn't like him to hold her! He didn't care! This was the last time, anyway! He watched them as they readjusted everything before he spoke softly. "I'm ready to sign now!"

Schmidt nodded and sent someone scurrying for the paperwork.

While they waited for the medical team to assemble, he spoke softly to his baby girl. She lay limp and unresponsive, the only other sound that of the respirator. With his lips to her ear he began singing a little song that she had sung in a little girls' quartet at Bible School. He sang the verse, surprised the lyrics came back to him so easily. Fighting for control, he started the refrain:

How shall I fear?
Jesus is near~

She trembled slightly and he looked into deep, quizzical, brown eyes. He kissed her forehead as tears flowed down her cheeks!

"Meggy? Can you hear Daddy?"

Nestling harder against his chest, she nodded; a barely perceptible movement! Then as terror gripped her, she began gasping and wheezing, her panic tearing at his heart strings.

"Okay, Baby, don't panic! Try to breathe like they teach you! And try not to cry! That makes it harder to get breaths, remember?" He sat coaching her breathing like he so often heard Sonia doing, unaware that the medical people assembling were staring in total disbelief!

The Chief of Pediatrics recovered himself first; astounded, but ready to take control! With a few barked orders, he wheeled and walked away! 'Evidently he had been misinformed on the patient's condition'!

"Okay, calm down, Megan!" Schmidt stepped forward to reassure her frightened patient and follow the new set of orders. "We're happy that you're breathing on your own, but let the machine help you!"

Trent was dazed, "She-she's breathing on-her-own? But what-about?"

Daniel Faulkner listened to the craziness reaching him from David's Dallas office! At last, David's rattled voice- "Okay, you're never going to believe this-"

"Well, I might! Try me sometime! Right now, I have a couple of urgent things to run by you-"

David sank back into his luxurious chair, still shaking. "Okay, I'm listening!"

"Well, first off, about that oil discovery written up in the ezine! My dad's on-site there, and we need the detailed, follow-up report! I think we have twenty-five grand in-" and he named an account!

"Okay, well don't put yourself in a bind. You can stretch it over three payments!"

"Oh that's right! I forgot you offered Al that option! For her, I thought getting it paid for with her loan capital was wisest! But, yeah; three months will work better for us!" His sigh of relief was audible! "And could I ask a favor? I've-uh-made an unexpected detour to DC, and my dad's-kinda rusty-"

David actually enjoyed the moment of hearing Faulkner stutter and have a hard time getting to the point! 'Oh, DC must mean the sadness going on with Megan Morrison.'

"Anyway, once you send me the report, can you give me twenty-four hours before you sell it to anyone else?"

"Well, we'd be happy to wait; except once someone purchases the report, they own it!"

Daniel was quick to grasp the news! "Oh, well, that is good news, then! What a relief!"

David listened, glad to have clarified the report purchase, "I get the sense there's still something else on your mind."

"Yeah, this deal for Trent Morrison; he's buried financially."

"Will he let us help him? I admire him, but still-"

"No he won't, and that was a problem! But then Jeremiah and I came up with an idea. So I tried to call Steb! He wasn't there, and I got his new son-in-law-"

"Bummer"!

Daniel laughed, "My sentiments exactly! Except that getting him instead of Steb got really fast action! He set up a Foundation, like right then and there. *Children in Peril Foundation*! Or *ChIP Foundation*! It's amazing! Sending donations to cover Megan's costs at the hospital"!

"Wow, and maybe it shouldn't matter, but will our donation be tax deductible?"

"Another plus I never considered! Can you and Mallory help them out?"

"Be glad to; is she any better?"

Faulkner hesitated. "No! He's ready to sign the papers, stopping life-support!"

Mallory frowned, puzzled! From her place in the café, she had taken note when Heather entered the elevator! Now she watched as building security escorted her out!

"Wonder what that was about!" Rhonna's words echoed her thoughts!

"I'm not sure, but she wrecked one of our nice dresses! Maybe I should call Diana and we need to reevaluate letting her represent our line!"

"Yeah may be! Looks like a do-it-yourself job of hemming it up shorter! Like she didn't cut it down! It was just all bunched-up lookin'." She shuddered dramatically before hugging Mallory! "Hey, thanks for listenin'! Thanks for the prospect of a fun getaway! And I won't mess up the pretty outfits! I promise!"

Diana frowned when her caller ID indicated a call from Mallory! She was hoping no one would find out about Jeremiah's crazy stunt! She forced herself to answer brightly!

"Hello, Mallory! Is there any word on Shay?"

"No Ma'am, not yet! But I'm working on a plan! It's not that good of a plan, so please keep praying! But, whenever they do return, that's when we need to be ready to ambush Beth with our 'Intervention'! I'm putting more details in as ideas come to me! What's the latest with Alexandra? Did Cassie get to Tel Aviv okay?"

"They're both doing great! Thanks for asking!"

"The main reason for my call is about Heather! I just saw her downstairs, and she hemmed the gray silk paisley way short! It looked hideous!"

"You have got to be kidding! She can't be a rep for the lines if she doesn't understand them any better than that! Maybe we should put something like that into our contracts-"

"Well, let's just tell Heather she's done! We'll leave the contract as is unless this becomes an ongoing problem! I've tried pretty hard-"

"I know you have! Listen, she heard the Gospel and she's made a profession of faith! She needs to allow herself to grow in grace! If I were you I would have pulled away from her before this!"

"Yeah, I still-well, you're right! I guess I'd better check in with David before he thinks I took off for Bolivia! Catch you later."

Daniel frowned! Diana was on another call. Before he could pocket his phone, it buzzed. His heart dropped! This was it! Trent was- No! This was Alexandra's sat phone!

"Hey Al, everything going okay, there?"

"Fabulous! I mean, I wish things were even faster, but all things considered- I'm calling because you were working out Jared's health and life insurance!"

"Yeah, he's covered! Why, has something happened to him?"

"No, Sir, just that he's getting married right away, and he wants to add a dependent now. Will that be a problem? He didn't mention it earlier because he didn't think he was going to be able to swing getting married for at least a year! But with the perks-"

"That's great, Al! I'll get the coverage changed!" With a few more instructions and pleasantries he ended the call! So the mining engineer was getting married! That was good! He couldn't help being concerned about Alexandra and a single guy working up there together in close proximity!

Jared seemed like a really great guy and getting married should settle him down even more!

Trent's mind was slow to absorb the change! Sleep deprivation, little nutrition, lack of faith! He couldn't figure out why the clipboard was so slow materializing now that he was braced and ready to sign! If they didn't come soon, he was afraid he couldn't go through with it! The wheezing always grated on his nerves; he couldn't understand why she was wheezing again-

A respiratory tech appeared with a breathing treatment and Schmidt added more medication into the IV drip.

"We're trying to get her breathing a little better before we start to wean her from the respirator, Mr. Morrison. Megan, can you hear me? I need you to breathe this in for me! Can you wiggle your toes?"

Her eyes drifted open and then closed again, as if weighted.

"She's been pretty heavily sedated. We'll let some of it wear off before we try to evaluate exactly where she is! Kidney function's back; we'll see-"

Sonia and the other kids huddled miserably in the waiting room. Too numb to visit, or even pray any more, they waited for word. At first they had all gathered around Megan, dreading whatever happened when death cast its shadow! Though they were all saved, knowing that the curse of death was defeated with the resurrection of Christ-that was something to talk about in Sunday School and church; not something to experience with a little sibling! And the questions raised about her salvation added an extra pall! When Trent had noticed Maddie couldn't stand it, he had excused her, then the two boys, and finally asking Sonia to join them.

"Mom, we'll be okay! Do-you-you want to-go-uh-tell her-you know-good-bye?"

Sonia's head shot up! Dry eyes angry! "Of course I don't want to tell her good-bye! I don't understand why we have to do this now!"

Michael and Matt exchanged helpless looks. She was the one originally caving to the pressure! Talking about how their dad couldn't face the facts! Making him ready to sign so he could at least be with Megan at the end, rather than in a mental ward! It wasn't just hard to grasp that Megan was dying, but the dynamic ripples through their family, their parents' relationship!

"I'm sorry, kids! I know I should go-how can I just stand and-"

Michael steeled himself as the head nurse approached.

Sonia dropped weakly to a plastic sofa, head in her hands, dreading the finality!

"Mrs. Morrison, Uh-we don't know how to explain it, but-"

Sonia's nerves were shot! "But what"?

"Well, we were prepping her and waiting for the paperwork and the team-and she started breathing! On her own! Still very asthmatic-and of course, we've been keeping her in a coma, so she couldn't fight-Now, we're giving some time for the drugs to leave her system so we can evaluate where she is! She was without oxygen for quite an extended period, so she may require a lot of rehab- She seems to understand and respond somewhat-"

Sonia stared at her, trying to comprehend.

"You can all go in and see her now! Mr. Morrison's still in with her! Where did Jeremiah go?"

"Jay, will you check emails, please? It may be something vital to our cases."

He rose and checked. "Sorry Sophie! Just looks like spam!"

Her face twisted. "I'm sure you're right, Jay? But please open them and tell me what they say, anyway?"

"Are you sure? Sometimes they can cause a virus!"

"I know-"

He laughed. "That's right! I keep forgetting that if we need to, we can buy a new system! Sometimes it's hard for me to rewire my thinking. Okay, a mortgage refi offer; electric cigarettes, and a *ChIP Foundation*! Claims to be raising money for children in peril"! He read the contents mockingly! "A way to help families of critically ill children who have astronomical expenses! Everyone has a scam of one kind or another."

Sophia smiled patiently, but held her ground. "Jay, you know that children in peril resonate with me! Is there anything to lend credibility?"

"There's a link to a web site! Accessing now! Oh wow! Sorry for laughing!"

"Well, you're right, Jay! There are so many scams that legitimate causes hardly have a chance! What? What does it say? Is it a real deal?"

He drew her into his arms! A very real deal! It's endorsed by Steb Hanson, established by his new son-in-law! People who have donated and asking for additional gifts are the Faulkners, the Andersons, Delia O'Shaughnessy, and Roger Sanders! Wow! Donovan Cline just dropped a big chunk of change!"

"Why would it list the donors, Jay? Every organization, real and imagined will be on their door steps!"

"I think we're getting a private showing to get us on board! Realize it's sterling people! Soph, what I haven't told you is what motivated the foundation!"

She paled. "Who is it, Jay?"

"Megan Morrison! The monies collected will pay off the Morrison's medical debt first, and then additional funds will go to families approved by the board!"

"So, one of Trent Morrison's children is critically ill? Jay, isn't he the one that rushes to everyone's rescue? Why would God let his child get sick?"

"I can't answer that, Sophie! And she isn't just sick! She's on life support, but-"

Daniel faced his eldest son across the table in an exclusive DC steak place. It was time for a talk!

"Dad, you told me you're not still mad."

"I'm not! But you said I never listen and we don't talk! Are you sure that's all my fault? Is a relationship a two-way street? Without a lot of convoluted guessing games? Jeremiah, I'll take responsibility for my failures, but you knew you were doing the wrong thing! Am I correct?"

"Well, the person I love is dying, and I needed to talk to you, but you were just going with Grandpa, all gung ho! Chasing another deal"!

"Well, Grandpa and my chasing deals has provided pretty nicely for you, the which I hear few complaints about! You didn't call me; you didn't text! You just hoped I'd come home ready for a chat with you! How often, of all the times we're together, have you ever said anything to me about a love interest? When I try to talk, you're often the one who won't meet halfway! You've kept your feelings for Megan, not only silent, but covert! You convinced your sister to go behind our backs!"

"Before we leave town, can we go back to the hospital? Dad, I helped come up with the plan about the foundation!"

Daniel sighed. "Yes, Jeremiah! You're a great kid! You're bright and innovative! We're proud of your calling to the ministry! The foundation was a good idea! Your immense capacity to share and care, but you lost perspective, Jeremiah"! He was at a loss!

"I know, Dad. Good things don't cancel out bad! So, tell me about this new deal! I'm sorry for being ungrateful and finding fault with you! You're right!"

Daniel leaned in, "A sizeable new oil deposit! You haven't lost track of those coins have you?"

Jeremiah's eyes flashed. "Why? They're supposed to go toward Megan's bills!"

Daniel laughed! "They already did, before we've even received any of the money from their sale! Now I need to sell them to replenish the account so we can pay David and Mallory for the report!"

"Why can't they just give it to us, Dad?"

"Jeremiah"!

"What, Dad? Why can't they?"

"Better question: why should they? Jeremiah, they're in business! But they're in fair business. I assumed that the second in-depth report would be available to anyone who wants it and can afford to pay! So, you'll be glad to know I asked a favor of David for friendship's sake! I asked him to give Grandpa and me a twenty-four hour head-start before they sold to any competitors! But they don't operate that way. The report is for whoever asks first and has the money for it! We paid for the information and now we own it!"

"Won't people show up from the ezine article and create challenges?"

"I'm sure they'll try! That's why we're still rushing there with equipment and man-power! With moving in fast, and the extra knowledge, we possess a double edge!"

"And my stunt could have botched it up!"

"I didn't say that!"

"You didn't have to, Dad!"

David forced his eyes open, aware of the bright Arizona sun's determination to push its way into the room despite dark slatted blinds and lined draperies. Stretching and moaning, he sat up on the edge of the bed, habitually reaching for a bottle of aspirin! Strangely, though, his head wasn't throbbing! The pain was in his neck and shoulders, doubtless from swinging a hammer all day the previous day for the first time in weeks. He was usually awake before Mallory, but seeing her Bible and journal missing from their place by the bed, he assumed she was up and having her quiet time! Everyone was near panic mode about Shay and Emma! He stretched again and massaged his neck with both hands, trying to resist the beckoning analgesics! Miraculous, for the ever-present head ache to be gone! He grinned. To quickly be replaced by other pains! He must be getting old! Still, he was filled with sudden wonder! A miracle! And besides that, Megan was scheduled for release from the hospital later today. And although Trent wasn't aware of it yet, he was going to learn that Megan's stay was paid in full with surplus to help many other children! He tiptoed out to find his wife.

"Mornin'; you're the early bird this morning!"

Her smile brightened the room. "I guess I was just wide awake, and didn't want to bother you."

He started a cup of coffee. "You never bother me! I'll get my Bible and join you."

"Well, with the usual craziness, I didn't get a chance last night to ask you how the wall is coming along!"

He stretched his neck, still massaging, "Kind of discouraging! It looks pretty rustic and stupid and out of place! I didn't rip it all back down! Yet! Mostly, because it took so much work to put it up!"

"So that begs the question; if it's such a pain to do anything with, is it really treasure?"

He sipped carefully, "Good question. I'm still mulling it over."

"How's your head?" She tried not to ask the question too often because it sometimes made him frustrated with her!

"It's great! Pain free! I'm stiff from lifting and stretching and hammering yesterday, so I started to take my usual handful of aspirin! I think I'm going to install pulsating shower heads in all of our places."

"That's a great idea. I love the Jacuzzis when I'm stiff! Since you're more of a shower guy; that might be good"!

"Yeah, I've tried them in some of the hotels! I'm not sure why I've never thought about putting them in! Easy deal"!

She nodded. "So specifically, what's wrong with the lumber?"

"Okay, you remember how bad Rudy's shack looked? That wall now looks the same way!"

"Oh!" She sighed, "Really, that bad?"

"Yeah, and we worked so hard trying to get all the gold dust out of every board!"

She laughed. "Yeah, we did!"

"We smacked it around, and rinsed it, and used a scrub brush, and tried to recover every speck of the gold, but so much is just trapped in the wood grain! But then yesterday, every hammer blow brought gold sifting down! It's still all over the floor. I just locked the doors and came home because I was too tired to deal with it! It was all in my clothes and hair again."

She tried to frown. "Really we have such serious troubles! Remember when the Tates used to whine? And we thought if we had as much as they did, that we would never complain?"

He squeezed beside her. "I remember!"

Shay ate the meager portion they brought him, hoping they were treating Emma better! His stomach was in turmoil and he hoped he didn't have a parasite or something from the water! He tried not to cough! That didn't help with his other problem! They came and went without speaking, and never brought the interpreter back! He wondered if his captors had demanded ransom, and that was what they were waiting for! And if their demand was still for twelve hundred! Surely Roger would fork that over for Emma and the baby! That didn't help his state of mind! Maybe he had; and Emma was back in the States leaving him to rot here!

Scared and bored beyond belief, he had already prayed for everyone he knew and quoted every Scripture he could think of! He knew a story of a Viet Nam POW who spent every day of his captivity playing an imaginary round of golf, going through every drive and putt; and finally emerging from his confinement to play perfect games of golf! Sighing, he decided he didn't possess the same mental stamina military men did! He tried not to nod off because the nights were endlessly long and lonely as it was. Still, he must have dozed because he roused, thinking he was hearing car doors and voices! Cautious and wobbly, he rose and made his way to a window! Any glass that might have covered it was long gone! Cold air struck him forcefully! Only silence and the sighing of the wind came to his ears as he strained hopefully for any hint of rescue! Figuring it was a useless exercise, he moved deliberately anyway, pulling the scant few objects below the opening! If he could stack up some debris that would support his weight, and he heard something again, he could check it out!

Forlorn and surprisingly exhausted at the exertion, he returned to his rumpled pallet. Shivering, he drew his knees up to his chin, tucking his arms in for warmth! Never one to have much meat on his bones, the damp chill penetrated to his core! They only came morning and evening to check on him! If he escaped, they probably wouldn't realize it for hours! But he didn't know where he could go to find help that would be sympathetic to an American! And he didn't know where they were holding his wife! So he stayed!

Trent and Sonia returned home with a fully-recovered Megan, aware of the miracle from the hand of the Lord! The three older kids were gone, back to their usual routines, and Trent felt oddly out of place! With traffic heavy at all hours of the day, trying to get to the office in time to head home seemed pointless! Sonia scurried to her office to check and respond to emails! Megan punched the TV remote. Looking up and catching his gaze fixed on her, she set the remote down.

"Is it okay if I watch TV?"

"Oh-uh-yeah, it's fine!" He couldn't believe how stupidly awkward he felt with her. "You need anything? Can I get you some ice cream?"

"Yeah, do we have any?"

He forced a smile. "I'll check! If not, do you want to go to the store with me?"

"I don't know! I look awful!"

He struggled with a lump that seemed to be a permanent fixture in his throat! "You look beautiful to me! If you want to fix up a little, there's no rush! Or you can just tell me what kind, and I'll be right back!"

She punched the television set back off and popped up! "I wanna go! Wait for me! Can we get two gallons! And can I get a candy bar?"

"We can get ten gallons and ten candy bars! I'll check the score of the game while you do whatever you need to!" Usually, he tried to help her with her weight! The constant steroid treatment for her asthma made her on the chunky side and always hungry!

He spent a magic hour with her at the grocery store while she filled the cart up with everything she'd always wanted! They got lotion, and mascara, and hair removal cream, and head bands, and pony-tail holders, and a popular scarf style, and a new curling iron, and the highest price shampoo and conditioner on the shelves! Nail polish and remover, lip gloss! Being a woman wasn't easy! Or cheap! He followed her around like an obedient little puppy! So glad for her sheer aliveness! "Oh Daddy: I've wanted to see this! Can I get this video? And let's get some popcorn to eat while we watch it; want to?"

'Did he want to?'

She paused surveying her choices. "Is this too much? I can put some stuff back! Can we still get ice cream?"

He laughed. "Oh yeah! Ice cream! I forgot what we came for! I should call Mom and see what else we can pick up to save her a trip!

Toilet paper, laundry detergent, trash bags, paper plates, always milk~no wonder the money went and there was still never anything around to eat!

"You know what? I think we need another basket! I'll go get one! Start picking out the stuff y'all like to snack on~"

At the checkout, she slid her hand into his! "Thank you for all the stuff, Daddy! Are you sure about everything? I don't really need ALL of it!"

He squeezed the trusting little hand. "I'm sure! The only thing worse than spending money on you, is losing you, and not being able to spend money on you, ever again! Thank you for coming back to me, Meggy! What a brave little fighter you were!"

"Will the hospital and doctors cost a lot?"

"I've turned you into quite the little worrier! When I went to the hospital business office to sell you as a slave~they wouldn't take you~"

"Daaaddy"! She slapped at him, and they both laughed.

"Seriously, every cent was paid in full! By a new foundation begun with you in mind that will help countless other families after ours! I still would have thought that God is good, Megan! Even if He had chosen to take you from me! And even if we were strapped by debt from the medical costs! But, I'm so glad for His mercy and His grace~"

Tears filled her eyes. "And I would have gone to Heaven. Sometimes I've doubted my salvation, but not anymore. Daddy, I'm so sorry about the Facebook and the way I've done to get my own way!"

He nodded. "We better get in line before the ice cream melts!"

⊰ ⊱

"Señor! Señor O'Shaughnessy! Shay! Señor Shay!"

Restless sleep turned into panic! Inky darkness and frigid air! A nightmare! 'What? Huh?' Shay fought stupor as footsteps ground in the gravel approaching the derelict building! He cowered back, terrified! The footsteps paused.

"Señor O'Shaughnessy, are you here? Can you hear me?"

Shay strained his ears in the darkness! Afraid to answer and afraid not to!

The voice lowered from calling his name to conversing in rapid Spanish with another man.

Once more, he heard car doors; and the sound galvanized him. Whoever it was, he couldn't survive another night like this! This was the coldest yet! Panicked, he sprang up and dashed from his meager shelter.

"Here! I'm here!" He stumbled toward the retreating vehicle, a shiny new Mercedes! Waving frantically, he staggered onward, aware of the lengthening gap. "Here! I'm-"

He dropped into a sobbing heap! At last, he caught his breath. 'Maybe it was just as well-'

⊰ ⊱

Mallory swept at the defiant gold dust! It was both fine and heavy, and it kept drifting down from the extremely rustic wall! David's original plan for the used wood was to straighten it up, sand it down, and use it for floor planking! But that was before their demolition had permeated it with gold dust! Now he figured sawing and sanding would further disperse the valuable golden metal! Amelia and Avery swept at the 'mess' as Amelia termed it, with their little brooms. Alexis watched from her swing.

David entered and surveyed it critically. "Do you have any suggestions?"

"Well, I'm not sure; but maybe! Have you seen those waterfall, fountain, walls?"

"Yeah, cute idea, but won't it wash the gold away?"

"Well, not having the water actually coming into contact with the wood. You know, two pieces of plexi-glass, with the waterfall streaming between them? And illuminated! Maybe we can still see the glow of the gold, but things won't look quite so rough?"

He considered. "Let me think on it! It sounds pretty, but the actual mechanics may be daunting; but then again, maybe not!"

He fished his phone free and terror filled his expression. "It's Shannon!"

Chapter 21: GENIUS

"Hey Shannon! Any word"? David's voice, tense and low, as he braced himself for the worst, hoping to shelter Mallory from heartbreak!

"Yeah, great news! You guys are the first to get it. When Erik finally convinced Mr. Cisneros that they were down there somewhere, he conducted his own search with his people! It was a close call with Shay by the time they found him, but he's in a hospital now, being treated for hypothermia, dehydration, and an infection. Emma got checked out and put on antibiotics, but she and the baby are fine! She's a guest in the Cisneros compound until Shay gets released. Hopefully, they'll be home by this week end. Did you put me on conference, Dude? And is Mallory listening?"

"Yeah, that's great news, but she's still crying!"

"Trust me! I know the feeling! I think that Grandmother and I couldn't have cried any harder if the news had gone the other way! Anyway, gorgeous cousin, Shay said he had plenty of time to do some deep thinking about the sudden appearance a new brother."

"Oh yeah"?

Shannon laughed at the reserved response. "He wants to meet with him and welcome him to the family! Based on the way you always make room for people! We know you love Grandmother, but you can pull the PI off and send him snooping somewhere else!"

"Oh, I'm glad to hear he's been subtle, Shannon! Thanks for calling! Let us know when they're coming back and where! We want to be part of a big welcoming reception!"

"What are you girls fighting about?" Trent didn't normally try to settle disputes between his kids. Working things out and learning to compromise at home were lessons that would stand them in good stead, for when they entered the work world and had to get along with people with every issue imaginable!

"I just want to borrow a pair of her ponytail holders! She isn't wearing this color; she doesn't even own anything this color!" A frustrated Madeleine knew she couldn't usually win out over the baby of the family!

"Okay, Meg, isn't that a package of forty? She can't borrow two?"

"Well, I guess she can, but she piles so much hairspray on, that they'll never be the same! That's why she never has her own! They all get yuck!"

Trent considered both sides. Megan was right! Maddy was the hairspray queen!

"Okay, Meg, let her wear them, and-"

She slapped them down with attitude.

"Would you give me a chance here? Let her use them, and tonight, I'll take her to the store and let her shop for some things! We'll get her a set of these, and she can pay you back out of the new set!" He thought his response was nearly as wise as that of Solomon with the baby, but they both huffed away without bestowing boatloads of respect on him, or even a thank you.

He paused in the kitchen to fill his travel mug, and Sonia came in, apologetic! "Of all the groceries you got the other night, everything's skimpy now for making you a lunch!"

"That's okay! I feel like eating out anyway!"

She gave him a surprised sideways glance and he met her gaze as he tightened his lid, checking for leaks in the seal! "I told Maddy I'd take her shopping tonight for some of the same bits and pieces that Meg got the other night! But sometimes I've noticed in the laundry, that you girls all need some new apparel items! You suppose you can find a good sale?"

She laughed delightedly as she reached for the credit card. The lines of care from the past days of torment fled, and he kissed her warmly! Finally she pulled free and met his gaze; "How can you not be furious with me?"

"Well, the doctors were right! And the mounting costs were-it's a vicious cycle. The impossible debt forces families like ours to declare bankruptcy every day! And that hits everyone in the pocketbooks! The care institutes; the care givers! It has to come to an end at some point in time! And you have to consider, not just the one lying in the bed, but the welfare of the whole! I couldn't face it! You were right! They were right! It was an ordeal I hope I never face again, but since we went through it, I hope I learned something. Speaking of-do you still want to go to Fashion Week? Is it too late to make arrangements?"

"You-you'll let me go? After what happened"?

He smiled grimly! "Yeah, even as old as the kids are, I've wanted you to stay home with them; stay home with them; stay home with them! And you're always home with them, except then the two hours a week that you get out, they crisis! That wasn't your fault, either! Anyway, Sonia, I'm so glad for who we are and where we are and what we have! I know you really wanted another baby there for a while!"

She nodded. "I thought I did, and if we had more, we could work it out; but I'm satisfied, too! If we can just keep Megan's asthma-"

"Anyway, if you want to go to Fashion Week, just you and Maddie, I can keep the rest of us functioning! But I thought it might be kind of fun for all of us to go!"

Mallory was shocked at the sight of Shay; wondering if his health would be permanently broken by his ordeal! She waited her turn among the jubilant welcoming detail, and finally gave him a lingering hug.

"What happened?"

He grinned, "Kind of a long and involved story! Meaning I'm still not exactly sure myself! Thanks for coming and thanks for praying. You can't do anything with the media, can you?"

She started to explain the impossibility of that request, but then aware of his fragility, she moved into action!

"He's back, but he's still unwell! Could you all please wait for a more opportune time?"

The gauntlet of cameramen stayed in place, snapping frenziedly, but the hail of questions actually hushed! With Delia's hand on Shay's arm, she propelled the hassled couple to the waiting Rolls.

Roger was relieved for the parting of the press and the kids' getting jostled along, but he had barely hugged his daughter. And his plan had been to escort them to his big SUV where Beth waited. She wouldn't be happy about this! He made his way to the parking garage alone.

"Where are they?"

Roger met her wrathful gaze, defeated! "There was a huge crowd, and a big media representation! Shay looked like he could use another month in the hospital. Somehow, the crowd opened and Delia was able to get them loaded into-"

She trembled with fury.

"Okay, Beth! Breathe! Emma looked good and she said she wants us to see the sonogram! And we will! We'll go to Delia's and I'll ask them to come out-if you'd still try to do something with yourself-"

"Like what?"

"Like getting dressed out of your robe and slippers and going to the beauty salon like you used to do!"

"Okay, Roger, I don't need this right now! You know how worried I've been-"

"Everybody has been! And they all fixed themselves up to look presentable to meet them at the airport!"

He gripped the steering wheel angrily and turned the key. "Everyone would like to demand a private 'audience' with them! This is all about you! Everything's all about you anymore! I heard Mallory ask Shay for the story! But he and Emma were both weak and exhausted before the eight and a half hour flight. Everyone will get a chance to be with them and hear the whole story! Let's just be glad that they're okay, and they're home!"

As usual, her only response was crying.

"David, where are we going? Let's give them some breathing space, and maybe Shay will be well enough to go to New York week after next!"

"I thought you were going to straighten Beth out!"

She scoffed. "I didn't say that! Sometime-"

He gave her his mock-stern look.

"I didn't even see her. Maybe she stayed home."

"M-m-m; doubt that! Would you if it was one of our girls? I'm betting she was hiding out in the car, and Roger was supposed to take the upper hand-Which means now they're forced to go to Delia's! Call Diana to meet us"! Serious eyes met hers. "This is at critical mass, you know-"

"You mean about my mom?"

"Sorta," he was surprised the naïve and trusting Mallory grasped that part.

"Yeah, the more miserable Beth is, the more miserable she makes Roger, making him spend longer hours at work confiding in Mom! And Erik's gone a lot, too! I know all that! Plus! I just feel bad for Beth! I'm just not sure this is the best time~"

He shrugged. "Maybe not; but there may never be another~"

Trent slid into a seat at TGI Fridays! Not his favorite, but convenient for meeting Michael. He smiled, trying not to swell with too much pride as his first-born approached. "Hey, how's your morning?"

"Pretty good! I got my grades! I worked really hard on a project for Real Estate Law and got a 'B'! Am I in trouble?"

Trent laughed. "Well, usually I eat a brown-bag sandwich at my desk, so I never invite you to join me for lunch! I thought this might have more appeal for you!" He leaned back to allow the server to place his ice water, cup of coffee, and spinach dip appetizer in place before taking Michael's beverage order! "Go for a soft drink!"

"Wow, Dad, still celebrating Megan?"

"Mm-hmm! And you, and my life in general! I probably won't ever turn into the last of the big time spenders, but I'm lightening up a little!"

"Well, I for one; am glad for fiscal responsibility! I think you've been a good example, and I'm thankful for it!"

"Okay, well, I appreciate that. And I want you to know how to handle money! More than anything I want you and your brother and sisters to be good, responsible, faithful, Christian citizens!"

Michael's turn to laugh! "Yeah, Dad, we may be slow, but you've managed to drill that into us! Are you seriously not furious with Mom for trying to undercut you about Megan?"

He met his son's expectant gaze. "Michael, I don't know if you're interested in anyone, but I hope you find a wife that's at least a fraction of what Mom is! Aside from my salvation, she's the best thing ever to happen to me! Followed by your addition to our home~and then the others! She didn't want to undercut me! Neither of us wanted to be in that place! With the grief and hard choices! Well, did your mom mention to you about going to New York City? Can you make time to come? Do you want to?"

"For Fashion Week? Are you kidding me? Uh-well, I try to look as sharp as I can, and I can always count on Maddy's catty remarks if my fashion fouls are too glaring-"

Trent laughed! "Yeah, she keeps us in line! Or tries to! We may not be fashion experts, but we could both use some new clothes!"

"Man, Dad; I just paid six months of car insurance and had to get new tires before I could get an inspection sticker! And now, I'll be paying for my next courses!"

"You do a great job! I meant on me! A couple of new pair of slacks and a sports coat? Your dress shirts are pretty frayed. Do you have time as soon as we're done eating?"

"Uh-yeah! I was going to show a house, but I'll call-"

"No, do your showing. What time is that? Will you be free after? Just let me know when you can meet." He named a store that made Michael do a double-take!

"Now you're wondering if Mom should have committed me, after all!"

Instead of his son's laughing, tears welled suddenly in his eyes. "I guess I've been bitter and angry-well at myself! I'm the one who actually precipitated Megan's recent attack! And I figured she died because of me, and we'd have insurmountable bills, and we'd never have a chance-"

"To have anything again," Trent finished. "We serve a great God!"

The Faulkner's arrival at Delia's coincided with the Anderson's! Both cars pulled into the broad circle to effectively hem Roger's vehicle in. As clouds stopped threatening and made good on their promise to cut loose, Mallory tapped at the rear window on the passenger side as Diana did the same on the driver's!

A confused Sanders punched the unlock button and both women sprang into the shelter of the dry back seat! A horrified Beth shot him a killer look

"What? You want me to make them stand out in the rain?"

Her angry gaze assured him she really didn't care.

"Okay, Beth; you're caught!" Diana's lilting voice! "And there's no point being mad at him! He didn't set you up-he's innocent! So, be mad at us; but listen to us first!"

Beth was so humiliated and angry she simply dropped her head into both hands! Like if she didn't look at them, they weren't really there!

"Okay," Mallory plunged in. "Your main problem is that you have too much time on your hands! Roger's gone for long hours as the CEO of a thriving company! A company that you've contributed to, greatly! It isn't your adversary! And we thought about a job for you there; but then we had a better idea!"

Roger sighed; glad for that!

"I don't want a job!" Beth's anger exhibited between gritted teeth.

"Well, no, not a wage-slave, plano, plano job!" Diana came in quickly. "Something exciting that you can't wait to get at each day! Something that challenges the brilliant, gifted woman you are!"

Anger softened slightly into puzzlement and then intrigue. She was hooked and Roger hopped onboard eagerly!

"Like what?"

"Something food-related," Came Roger's grasp of the obvious! To get a withering stare!

"Exactly! That's what Diana and I arrived at simultaneously; and see, Roger knows that's your strength and gift, too! You need to start up a food e-zine, blog, talk! It might make money, which would be fun for you; but even if it only helped people, you'd feel happier with a brighter outlook! We were serious about your having too much time to brood and eat out of utter boredom! We know you read your Bible and pray, which lifts your spirit! But then after a few soap operas and a couple of Judge Judy's, you get literally oppressed! And your misery with yourself is walling you off from all of us that love you and want admittance to Beth's world!"

Still suspicious, "How would I help people? You mean by talking up the latest fad diets?"

Diana's eyes were serious. "I mean, you could address that; and maybe you already know some recipes that taste delicious-"

"She does," Roger assured. "Believe me, she's at home in the kitchen, and the times she's tried to diet, she's come up with some pretty great stuff!"

"See, sharing things like that would be great, but you have a gift and understanding of, not only food, but gracious entertaining."

"Well, aren't a lot of other people already doing that? You mean on-line?"

Diana nodded, beaming from ingenuous, big, blue eyes! "Yes; probably thousands! That's what makes it fun! Other people own chemical companies, other people design and manufacture clothing, other Geologists delve beneath the earth's crust!" Her gesture included the three of them and their chosen fields. "You just elbow your way in and find your niche and do it with your whole heart! And ask the Lord to bless it!"

Beth nodded slowly. "Okay, you may have something! I'm not sure! But I'm not starting anything until after I lose fifty-"

Roger looked up miserably. "Beth, you're starting today; or I'm done!"

Daniel left the coffee bar with a venti Americano! A superb party, where Mallory actually had a Starbucks opened, as well as her usual provision of soft drinks and appetizers. After a couple of high calorie specialty coffee drinks, because they were gratis, he decided it was time to cut back. He frowned as Xavier neared the concession.

"Don't give him anything with caffeine! Or sugar!" he instructed. "Zave, tuck in your shirttail!" He patted his son on the back and then frowned as he took in a jarring note in the gracious affair.

Plastering on a smile, he made his way toward the misfit with outstretched hand. "Daniel Faulkner; and you are?"

"Delton Waverly! What kinda party is this? I had to go out and around the corner to find a beer!"

Daniel regarded the newcomer narrowly. "Well, I guess it isn't a drinking party; I'm pretty sure the invitation didn't tell you to bring your own!"

"So you're Faulkner, huh? I'm a Geologist, too; actually David Higgins' assistant! I know all about you!"

Daniel knew his body language was a give-away as he took a couple of steps backwards. The guy, evidently not the sharpest, seemed not to notice that the veiled threat hit its mark, whether he intended for it to, or not! As he sought for a smooth escape, they were suddenly joined by Cade Holman.

"Evening, Holman!" Daniel realized his voice was a little on the loud side as he heartily clasped the Chemist's hand! "How are things going for you? Meet-" Usually one to remember names, his mind was blank.

"Oh yeah; hello Waverly! Thanks, Daniel, but we've met before!" Holman's tone showed a hint of distaste for the new employee. "Waverly helps Higgins run the drill sites for Mallory!"

"Ah, I see!"

"Yeah, she wastes a lot of time and money, if you ask me!"

The other two men weren't sure if it was the beer, inebriation prior to this one, or if the guy was just a moron.

"We didn't ask you," Cade's swift repartee!

"That gal's runnin' us ragged all over the world, punching holes in the ground! And half of them are fruitless!"

Daniel frowned; sure both Waverly and Higgins were more than adequately compensated by Mallory for whatever was required of them!

"Notice what goes in her e-zine!" he continued. "Yeah, she's stumbling into something occasionally, but, pfft, mostly she doesn't get so lucky! And then she blabs it all around on that site! Makes ya wonder why people that clueless end up with so much money to burn!"

A swift, contemptuous look swept Holman's face before he regained control. Waverly missed it completely; but Daniel, from his bygone days of playing poker, couldn't miss the tel! He withdrew without so much as a parting handshake, head spinning with realization! He needed to find a secluded spot to think!

"Are you talking to your jewelry?"

Mallory jumped, startled. "Guess ya caught me!" She grinned, not totally self-conscious. "I'm talkin' to me da!"

David nodded at her brogue, not sure whether to tease, present a reality check, or drop it!

She moved toward him and he circled her with his arms. "Okay, I know me da's in heaven, and whether he sees me, or hears, or still cares is subject to debate."

He kissed her and then pulled back to gaze into her eyes! "Okay, whether or not he still cares about you, is not open to debate! His love for you is more perfect now, and more refined than ever! You were and probably still are all he talks about! Probably the angels run the other direction when they see him coming with that third grade picture!"

She laughed, suddenly overwhelmed with emotion. "I think it's the fifth grade one. In third grade, my mom still usually tried to do something with my hair, especially on picture day! By fifth grade I was on my own with it."

"Yeah, and you were more interested in baseball than anything else! He probably tells the angels all that, too! Uh, since we're on the subject; are you ready to get rid of all the rest of that garbage?"

She pulled free. "That's what I was talking to him about! I want to hang onto it, just in case there's more there."

"I think we've kind of mined it dry!"

Her eyes met his! "Good analogy! But when mines are depleted; are they really?"

"We've combed through it all, time and time again, until we located every anomaly!"

"Time very well spent, because every single lead, David-"

He nodded, amazed, as he gazed around their sumptuous surroundings with renewed wonder. "Yeah, you're right. Every single clue has paid off! But the rest of the bits and scraps are trash, part of the subterfuge to disguise the important stuff-"

"That's what I said! Because that was what I surmised! But I was wrong!"

He raised his fist playfully to her mouth. "Would you say that again, please, for the microphone?"

She frowned. "What? I admit it when I'm wrong!"

He shrugged, grinning. "Well, I wouldn't know about that, because you've never been wrong before! So for this rare occasion-"

She frowned at him and moved to her desk, picking up a tattered and faded receipt, "That's what I was asking him; 'What am I still missing'?"

"And what did he say?"

She held the leprechaun bracelet up to her ear, pretending to listen intently! "Reception must be bad! Mallory to heaven! Mallory to heaven! Come in, please! Hmmm; no answer! I guess I'm supposed to keep figuring it out!"

"Maybe you've figured everything out! There aren't any more spills, arrows, colored pieces. Look, this is just a receipt for one cup of coffee at McDonalds! He wasn't incorporated, so keeping this didn't help as a business expense! You were right about this all being stuff to sift through to find the pertinent stuff."

"No, I'm more convinced than ever that every scrap is pertinent! Look where this is from, David! Most of the address is torn off, but it's Florida! David, my dad never went to Florida! Look at the date. This was early spring of our freshman year! He had to fly there, and back, in less than a day! Why would he save a coffee receipt and not leave any record of an airline ticket?"

"An airline ticket would be a major red flag; if the McDonalds receipt means anything at all, it must not be significant!"

She sank down at the desk, pulling out a magnifying class to closely examine the fading ink.

"It's a credit purchase, and not cash. Daddy never used credit cards!"

"You thought! You didn't know he had a cell phone and a sophisticated office up in that shed! But maybe that's not his receipt; he never was in Florida, or used a credit card! He just picked scraps of trash up to save for you and keep you out of trouble while you went over and over them!"

She laughed, "Entirely possible. I can almost make out the store number."

"Why does it matter?"

"Because then I'll know exactly where he was in Florida and what he wanted me to find!"

"Where would be your guess?"

"I'm guessing Vero Beach; and I'll tell you why! If I'm right"!

Diana glanced up from a flat pattern, surprised Daniel was home. "Hi; are you okay?" As she eyed him swiftly and with a professional assessment, she guessed the answer before he uttered it.

"I'm fine! I've been puzzling over something since the closing dinner the other night!"

"Something related to Higgins' weird friend?"

"Did you meet him? Did he say anything off the wall, to you, Honey?"

"I met him briefly, not really to speak to! He wasn't invited and if he wanted to crash the party, he could have dressed to fit in!"

"Yeah; he came in carrying a bottle of beer, and then crabbed at me that there wasn't a bar provided."

Diana's beautiful features registered distaste. "Well, I hope you told him to check parties out better before he crashes them next time! What brings you home early?"

"Just kind of curious! Does Mallory ever tell you anything about the drilling and the success/failure rate?"

"No, we barely have time to discuss things pertinent to *DiaMal*! Why? Have the reports not been accurate? Alexandra?"

He sat down on the corner of her worktable, "Extremely, reliable. Cautiously underestimated, if anything! Okay, let me explain. Higgins' buddy Waverly went from crabbing about no alcohol, to blasting Mallory. At some point in time, Holman strolled over, and I thought I could stick him with the new guy and saunter away! So, I've been impressed with Mallory's successes! I've wondered how she can drill so many places, affording the expense of it, and finding so many promising sites! Waverly implied she's an idiot lucking into a few treasure troves, but being too free sharing the findings! He said half of the sites they've drilled haven't produced anything! Well, I would have fallen for what he said at face value! But then Holman shot him such a disgusted look!"

"Well, maybe he doesn't like Mallory's employees being disloyal like that," Diana suggested, thinking the same thing!

Daniel nodded. "What I was thinking; but, Holman's look spoke volumes more than just that! Remember, Holman oversees all the core sample testing! See, I've kind of surmised the same thing as Waverly! That when she hits, she shares! And when she misses; nothing said."

"Okay, is her professional dignity on the line?"

"Well, I'm trying to impress you that my years at the poker table finally paid off! Not that I'm taking poker up again-the look on Holman's face told me that what Mallory's carrying close to the chest, are the biggest and richest discoveries! Not failures! How does she know? Waverly was right in that the drill sites seem rather random-Do David and Mallory have money I don't know about?"

Diana laughed, "Maybe so! What difference does it make? But maybe we should caution people that their CDA's include; not only what they say, but what they telegraph!"

He nodded. "Yeah, Waverly missed the 'look' completely, but Holman saw my expression and already wished he hadn't given away what he did! This has puzzled me, though, for several months! Drilling exploration is unbelievably expensive! And then, finally, she puts a few results out on the web; sells the entire findings for a fairly good amount! But I don't see how that's beginning to cover what they're putting out!"

"So is this something else I'm supposed to worry about?"

"I guess not! Our oil operation is off to a promising start! And Al's doing great! Did I mention to you that the new mining engineer is getting married weekend after next? He hired his dad, a vet and a hard rock miner! Well, Jared's a Christian, but his dad isn't. He's a smoker, and Alexandra asked him to put out his cigarette! So, he put it out and lit up a cigar!"

"Well, that wasn't very nice!"

"Diana, we're talking hard rock miners! Alexandra debuted into the real world, and she mentioned the incident to me to let me know she's learning to give and take! Fix what you can, and deal with what you can't fix the best you can!"

"Well, how did she wind up there, dealing with coarse, unsaved men?"

"I guess when she wanted to be a Geologist! Remember, Jesus didn't ask the Father to take us out of the world, but to shelter us from its influences! We're supposed to impact the world for Christ! And not be the ones to be impacted by the world! Or hide behind monastery walls!"

Her face registered concern, but she refrained from speaking.

He drew her near. "You're wondering if Higgins' digs got to me, after all"?

She sighed, then, relaxed suddenly, favoring him with a glowing smile. "Maybe it occurred to me! But you're right! Alexandra's ready to leave the nest! I-I guess I've been taken by surprise!"

David sat next to Mallory as she did some quick searches on her most recent 'hunch'! His mouth dropped open in awe before she got very far!

"Wow! Shipwreck Alley! And a lot of the treasure has been recovered! But those gold coins washed up on the beach just within the past few months? I never saw that story!"

"I saw it once on Facebook, but I never saw it on the mainstream news! I kind of keep an antenna up for anything that relates to the Atocha recovery and the Mel Fisher family! Family members still expect to find the stern castle of the wreck quite intact and laden with valuable cargo! And they may, but divers have searched the area time and time again since the discovery came in 1988! I'm thinking the storm must have demolished it, and before that-Well, the two stories related in the Bible, of ships caught in storms-what was standard practice?"

David shrugged, noticing the lovely light of excitement and discovery on her features. "I guess ya got me! Uh, try to avoid getting caught in storms next time?"

"No! Well, probably that, too!" She laughed! "Consider the stories of Jonah and the Apostle Paul! When the ships were in dire distress, the crew started pitching cargo overboard!"

He nodded, unconvinced! "Yeah, but it doesn't say they threw out silver and gold and emeralds!"

She nodded seriously. "Of course, they didn't throw the valuables out at the first stiff wind or the first raindrop! But that stuff is heavy, and she was way overloaded with more gold and silver contraband she picked up in Havana! When they feared for their lives-and fierce hurricanes spun them endlessly and helplessly, cargo was disposed of! That's why divers continue to find rich, rich artifacts, somewhat randomly throughout these search grids. Tides and currents continue to wash wealth ashore after storms."

"So you're thinking of a dive boat?"

Eyes resembling the waters and emeralds being discussed, met his. "What do you think about a dredging/drilling operation?"

Cade Holman studied Cat across coffees.

"You're sure that creepy Waverly didn't notice?"

"Yes; He's more of a rock than the ones he's drilling through!" Cade's thoughtful response. "It's Faulkner I'm concerned about! Because he picked up on it like radar! I'm not sure how much of David and Mallory's business he's privy to, but I could see light dawning; and also I'm not supposed to disclose anything; verbally, but-"

"Well, Waverly and Higgins both have such great jobs because of Mallory; why can't they give her the benefit of the doubt? Or just hush! Maybe you should call her, and explain the whole incident to her. Maybe she can tell Waverly to keep a lid on his opinions. And tell her you didn't intend to divulge anything-"

"Congratulations!" Mallory regarded the document behind plastic proudly.

"Thanks; but what's a Bachelor's degree to someone who's nearly a doctor?" David's deep eyes shone with humor.

"Well, I'm proud of my Architect, but actually, I think Mechanical Engineering is even more you! Our patents are saying the same thing!"

"Well, a very wise and frustrated young woman once informed me that it's impossible to learn knowledge or any course of study that won't at some point stand me in good stead!"

She flushed. "Yeah, well I was so crazy about you! And your balancing act made me a nervous wreck!"

"Because you were so worried what Faulkner thought of me"!

"Well, he took over in Daddy's place; did I ever tell you about Proverbs nine and my wild ride with my dad? About life in general, but about you in particular, I think!"

"Uh, no; you asked me once if he ever took me on a drive all over western Arkansas. And I was curious when you referenced it that one time, but then I forgot about it."

"Well, Proverbs nine wasn't my favorite Proverb, and I made the mistake of telling Daddy that! He started a lecture that it's about the two paths! The one of wisdom and right choices leading to happiness and success; and the one of living foolishly and making bad choice after bad choice! So, I tried to tell him that I was helping you- Well, the next morning he woke up in a really jovial mood and said he wanted to take me to Little Rock and let me shop! We never went to Little Rock! Or shopped! So, I'm elated, and then he took this crazy exit! But I thought maybe there was construction or some reason to take an alternate route! Well, to make a long story short, he took one bad turn after another-an object lesson of sorts for Proverbs nine! We never got to Little Rock, and I was so mad at him-"

David grinned. "Well, it made you back off from me! I never appreciated you that much when you were trying to be my conscience, anyway! But you really kept your distance while I decided which way to go."

"My dad kept my distance through the proxy of the Faulkners!"

"Well, Romans 8:28! Where did he take you?"

"Where didn't he-" she broke off. "That ride that day-it seemed random-"

David grinned good-naturedly. "Let me guess! You want to try to retrace that route!"

Chapter 22: GLAMOUR

The *DiaMal* and *Rodriguez-Reynosa* delegations arrived at the Manhattan Marriott Marquis resplendently outfitted. Deborah's eyes glowed with anticipation! No room for fashion fouls this year! For arrival and check in, she opted for violet tweed Eisenhower jacket, featuring violet velveteen self-covered buttons and elbow patches atop coordinating knee-length tweed skirt. Metallic silver, high heeled pumps matched her handbag and emphasized an attractive hammered silver brooch, adorned with scrumptious, big, purple amethyst cabochons! Another of her own creations!

Diana wore an adorable fitted dress of sky-blue, wool flannel, accented with woodland-themed brocade piping inserted in princess-style seams! Soft mustard, kid shoes picked up the delicate autumn foliage in her brocade handbag. Her jewelry sent sparkles in fourteen karat yellow gold foliage studded with blue and yellow topaz, peridot, and smoky quartz! Her signature, gemmed sparrow perched on a golden branch, centered at her slender throat! At her side, Daniel stood out powerfully in brown silk suit with some understated slubs running throughout; perfectly dimpled, mustard, faille silk tie; and impeccable white French-cuff shirt fastened with yellow topaz cuff links. Of course, their kids were perfectly turned out, as well.

Mallory appeared in a dusky, sandstone-red suit, the slim skirt ending at mid-calf, and the swing jacket lined with a panorama of Arizona scenery. Her shell coordinated, a fine silk in the dusty red, printed with sage green Saguaros and bleached cattle skulls. Her handbag was an adorable box, crafted from camel bone, fitted with gold-tone hardware and lined with the same print. Matching red leather pumps completed her look! She actually sported very little jewelry! Her wedding set, the sensational ring from her dad, and her gold Rolex! David appeared in a charcoal, muted glen-plaid suit; white dress shirt, and dusty red and ivory diagonally striped silk faille tie. Mont Blanc cufflinks secured his cuffs.

As each family checked in, they accompanied the bellmen to their suites, freshened up, and regrouped in the lobby-to network with each other and with other representatives of the fashion business!

Filling a larger and larger section of the elegant lobby, they exchanged hugs and welcomes, bestowing extra affection on Megan and Shay and Emma! They contributed their own special élan as the group grew, networking with other convention delegates as opportunity permitted.

Daniel was quick to notice when a string quartet arrived to entertain in the lobby bar. Enthralled, he found a seat as near as possible, smiling at the cocktail waitress who appeared immediately, and ordering coffee! If he had to order five dollar cups of coffee for as long as the gig lasted, he would do so; although he might 'nurse' each refill.

Cass suddenly took the seat next to him on the settee, and he stared at her, dumbfounded! Not just that she had flown alone from Israel; that didn't scare him as much as her making it from JFK to central Manhattan! Without a spoken word, both artists turned their attention to the hired musicians.

Daniel had wondered absently if his presence made them nervous; then decided that was foolish. But with Cassandra seated next to him, he decided that the violinist was definitely abashed! He sent his most reassuring smile and the group commenced, presenting easy-listening romantic numbers from several past decades. Daniel lost himself in the entertainment, although the *Theme from Moulin Rouge* brought guilty and unwanted memories of Nanci Nichols to his mind! Things she had repeatedly accused him of-*Your lips may be here, but where is your heart?* He gave himself a mental shake! 'In the past! Don't go there!' *Unchained Melody, Music Box Dancer, Wind Beneath My Wings.*

When the musicians put their instruments down and not away, Daniel was glad. 'Taking a break, but not finished.' He shoved a ten dollar bill into their tip glass and encouraged them to 'hurry back'.

"What do you think, Cass?" his question erupted as soon as they were out of hearing.

Her gaze met his, "Well, over all, not too bad! What are those songs?"

He placed his arm over her shoulder and gave her a squeeze, amazed at the question. Cass knew the range of classical music and myriads of pieces from the realm of Christendom! Popular, she seemed totally in the dark about! Well, and older numbers, too!

"Popular music from way back, but classics of the genre!"

She nodded, "Some very pretty melodies! I think you're making them nervous, though."

He grinned. "Well, trust me, it got worse after you joined me. Your concerts have been great!"

Cassandra's turn to laugh, "You mean the Israeli Orchestra Summer Concert series! Yes, they have been sold out! They always are! Israel has a great appreciation of the arts, as well as the sciences!"

He agreed with her assessment, glad she realized that the successes of the season weren't all about her; although he felt great pride in her accomplishments. She ordered a coffee, too, pouring half of it into his empty cup to make room for the entire contents of the cream pitcher and several packets of sugar. Just as the quartet returned, Zave pushed his way in between father and sister. He and Cass adored each other, but Daniel figured his fidgety son wouldn't be the best at listening attentively. To his surprise, Cass got up and wandered away, while Zave sat, transfixed.

When the foursome broke again and started stowing instruments into cases, Xavier whispered so softly that Daniel wasn't sure he heard him correctly. "Why can everyone else do that, and I can't?"

"What? Play an instrument?"

Xavier nodded earnestly.

"Well, it's something you have to learn to do, and practice at."

"Well, yes, Sir; I know that-"

"Are you asking why we haven't insisted on your learning?"

A barely perceptible nod!

"That's a real good question! Al, Jer, and Cass had no choice. I guess when *the Maestro* passed away we kinda dropped the ball with you little guys."

A frustrated expression flitted across handsome features as Zave spoke under his breath, "Yeah, I guess you did, and I'm not a little guy!"

Daniel dressed for dinner as Diana scurried around, dressing the youngest children to the nines! With that job completed, Al took charge of making sure they were entertained in such a way as not to destroy her efforts. When she emerged, ready for the evening, Daniel let out an amazed whistle! "Wow, Di, you look-" he fumbled for words, something rather rare for the man who always had a line- "beautiful, amazing, fantastic! I guess I don't know the dinner plan-I hope we can afford it!"

Diana's expressive eyes met his. "It's been kind of hush-hush! I guess it's David and Mallory's deal! I can't believe how hard it's raining! So much for cute new shoes"!

He surveyed her again, her slim form draped with teal blue rows of diagonal ruffles which swirled around to be a bejeweled clasp and swished into a short train. Matching leather high heeled sandals with smaller jeweled adornments completed.

"Yeah, what ever happened to the concept of galoshes? Fashionistas should devise a new, more stylish take on those."

She refused to take his bait, answering evenly, "Just so you know; they have! Especially for teens, tweens, and children! They haven't addressed an 'evening' version yet, though, sadly."

"Well, the limos can pull under the canopy out front here, and hopefully, wherever we're going will have a porte cochére! Did you bring your coat?"

"No, it's just September! It's considered gauche to pull furs out too early in the season! It's still in cold storage."

He nodded understanding, glad for her grasp of the industry, but proud of acquiring the full-length sable coat for her! "I need to take you more places where I can show you off in it." He stood back, a happy pride surging through him as his family preceded him into the wide corridor.

"Okay, hotel etiquette! Absolute silence in the hallways, and I'll push all of the elevator buttons!"

By six-thirty the lobby bustled with guests from as far away as Spain, Israel, and Jordan. Soft, excited murmuring, as friends admired friends and the lobby ambience.

Roger Sanders made a bee line for Daniel and Diana, dragging a reluctant Beth with him. Diana hugged her warmly assuring her she looked fantastic!

"Do you know where we're going?" Sanders' whisper!

Daniel shrugged, realizing that neither of them, as executives, liked being out of the information loop! As he took in the growing size of the crowd, he was hoping fast-food if *GeoHy* was expected to pay for part of the dinner.

At seven minutes before seven the elevator doors thumped open, revealing the Andersons! A stunning Mallory stepped off! The bodice of her gown featured a Saguaro cactus and Arizona bluff, barely discernable against a deep, dusk sky punctuated by stars, many of which twinkled with diamonds. A silk satin sash emphasized slender waist, and created a large bow at right front. A sweep of black skirt swayed prettily when she advanced toward the group! She held Amelia and Avery by their hands, and David emerged in black and charcoal tux, carrying Alexis. Amelia was dressed in a gown of leopard print velveteen trimmed at cuffs and hem with narrow lines of ranch mink. Avery's empire-style, silk crepe in deep maroon swept down to little maroon Mary-Janes. Alexis wore pale tan lace, the skirt caught up into puffs by deeper tan satin roses and ribbon nosegays; with the deeper tone satin piping embellishing the waistline.

David took charge, noting that most of the guests were assembled. "Follow me!" Aware of the seating for seven o'clock, he took long strides. As the group waited for 'up' elevators, he instructed, "Go to three and then find the F bank of elevators. Then take one of those up to *The View Restaurant* on the forty-eighth floor! The maître d'hôtel will assist you in finding your places."

Using a hand held mic, David gave instructions. "If you can get seated, we're under a time constraint here. We want plenty of time to enjoy the meal! Servers are moving around now to take orders for tea and coffee drinks, as well as soft drinks. Sorry, folks, no alcohol"!

Ned McAllister's head shot up and he gazed at his daughter in astonishment! "Does he mean no wine with dinner? I'll call for the Sommelier and we can have a nice glass all around."

The six people at the table eyed one another warily. Jared gave his dad a warning nudge, and Abigail frowned at her father's plan. John and Lana turned their attention toward their eldest as Master of Ceremonies~and their three bewitching granddaughters! To Jared's relief, his dad seemed too awed to run his mouth about drinks or anything else! Although as a mining engineer, he was familiar with the use of explosives, he was pretty sure he was nervous in this volatile situation!

In response to David's instructions, tables filled quickly as efficient wait staff appeared with the beverages, appetizers, and bread. Donovan Cline appeared, and to Mallory's delight, Carmine accompanied him. The Prescotts, Shay and Emma, and Delia and Shannon appeared with the newly discovered family members. The Sanders shared a table with Cade and Cat, and Brent and Connie. John envied Sanders the comfort of sitting with family! Jeff and Juliet joined Tammi and Kerry and Janni and Melody. Deborah Rodriguez took her place with Davis Hall, Herb and Linda, and Blythe and Samuel. Nita and Manny Rodriguez chatted sociably in Spanish with the Riveras and Enrique Cisneros. Trent and Sonia Morrison sat with their four kids! Lilly and Benjamin Cowan found their places by Michael and Missy, Cassandra, Xavier, and Steb and Christine.

And the kaleidoscope of colors and the symphony of hushed conversation lent the elegant restaurant yet more of an aura.

"Wow! Look at everyone!" Diana's whisper in Daniel's ear! "She's filling up the whole restaurant with a private party. In answer to your question the other day, about whether they have money we aren't aware of~

"I hope so"!

They said the last phrase in unison.

From a lifetime of privilege, even the accustomed Daniel Faulkner admitted this event was special! He relaxed about the cost, realizing David and Mallory wouldn't count on his picking up part of the tab without working it out down to the letter in advance. He needed to purposely savor the moment, with Diana at his side, his kids in attendance, and surrounded by amazing friends and colleagues. Still, guilt and worries nagged at the edge of his awareness! Tommy Haynes had waylaid him earlier in the afternoon, requesting a time to talk to him. And he didn't want to talk to Tommy! He was secretly amazed at the kids' tenacity and commitment to each other, but Al was still barely eighteen! The most crucial time for establishing life-time patterns, and meeting other singles! And although Al had been afraid to express her concern, he had immediately known her reservation about interviewing and hiring the God-sent mining engineer, was her worry about if Tommy would be upset if she hired a handsome, young, single guy! Teen agery! But why not? She was a teen ager! He wasn't ready to bestow his blessing on anyone for Al yet! And he was still rattled by Jeremiah, his 'thing' for Megan Morrison; his running away. From his Head-table position, he kept an eye on his two oldest kids; and their heart interests!

His thoughts returned to the string ensemble; always a special treat for him! But the old love songs now filled his mind with memories and guilt! Memories and guilt he tried to escape on a daily basis! He roused himself to greet people who sought a word with him and Diana, or David and Mallory.

'Lord, I'm so blessed! Why do I have such a sense of oppression?' He strove to shake off the eerie feeling, to realize that Diana was speaking to him.

"I'm sorry, Di; what were you saying?"

"Do you feel okay? You seem distracted! I asked Alexandra is she's paying for her employees, and she told me David-"

A forced smile as he patted her gem-sparkled and manicured hand! "Yeah, still a lot on my mind, I guess! Tommy Haynes asked for a chance to talk to me; I'm not ready for this, Di! And I know Jeremiah- Like, I should go speak to Morrison, but I don't know what to say-"

She nodded. "But that isn't all-"

A deep sigh, "No, but the rest I can't even formulate into cognizant thought for myself, let alone explain to you-especially in a crowd! Di, I love you; I love the Lord: I'm the most blessed man alive." He paused to order from the course selections. He laughed as he perused the dessert choices. "New York style cheesecake; what other choice could there be? Oh absolutely, with the strawberries!"

When David asked him to bless the food, he rose and prayed.

When Mallory returned to her place, the wait staff moved forward with skill and precision.

"I hope the seating's okay!" She placed her napkin across her lap and signaled Amelia and Avery to follow her example! "I agonized over it! It was David's idea to stick his dad and mom with Alexandra's miners and his fiancée and her dad."

"Well, both Jared and Abigail's fathers need the Lord," Daniel agreed.

"Yeah, but maybe Dad would like to enjoy a meal sometime without having a little flock to shepherd." Mallory; always thoughtful!

David grinned. "He couldn't handle it! If we forbad him to try to take oversight of their souls~"

"Mommy; what's this picture?" Amelia interrupted, referencing the napkin.

"It's a map baby; it shows what sights you can see out the windows while the restaurant turns around. Look out the windows; isn't everything pretty?"

Her little brow furrowed and she frowned. "No, it's raining outside!"

"Well, rain's pretty! The clouds look awesome!"

"No they don't!"

"Amelia!" David's softly spoken warning carried authority.

"Mr. Charles likes rain," Mallory tried; to get a frustrated glance from David.

"I don't think so!" Amelia, ready for her habitual arguing! "He says he does! But then he stays inside! I don't like staying inside! I don't like rain!"

"She'll argue as long as you'll argue with her!"

Stung, Mallory turned her attention to Avery. Maybe an elegant, full course meal, that included babies, was a bad idea.

To brighten the pensive tone, Diana leaned past Mallory. "Amelia, your dress is beautiful!"

The pout evaporated into a smile! "Thank you, Mrs. Diana! I like it a lot! It has real mink on it! It can come off, but I didn't want it off! Cuz I like it on there!"

Diana laughed. "I hear ya! I love the mink trim."

"And I have new shoes, and I got my ears pierced, and I have on earrings!"

Diana laughed at the conversational girly talk. "Wow! Earrings and all! Your hair looks pretty too! And I love your mommy's hairstyle!" True! Mallory wore a particularly sophisticated arrangement of asymmetrical wrapped braids from a diagonal part.

"Cassandra helped me with it! Speaking of; I think that she and Xavier and Benjamin and Lilly are all chattering in Hebrew and leaving the Hanson's out! I should have put Benjamin and Lilly with us, anyway~"

"Everybody's fine! You worry too much!" David already felt bad for rebuking Mallory, at any time, but particularly around the Faulkners! "Look! There she is!" David sprang up in such haste that his chair rocked, before deciding not to topple!

"There who is? Who is that?" Diana's whisper in Mallory's ear!

"A long, and incredible story! To boil it down, she's pastor's sister! Kind of long-lost, black sheep, bleak life! Somehow, she got wind of Alexis' looking like her; that Pastor and his parents couldn't get over it! I mean, the Senior Andersons still haven't warmed up! David and I have tried to keep in the loop with them since they attended our wedding! Anyway, her name's Celeste, and she's a little younger than Pastor! She hitchhiked into Silverton and found David when he was helping get Norma's things-that's another long story-we need to get together more and stay caught up-"

Mallory stopped her rambling to take in the emotional scene as John and Lana and the senior Andersons rushed toward the long-lost family member.

As the hubbub died down, guests began eating, to the soft music of clinking china and silverware, and subdued conversation.

Mallory started to relax and focus on New York landmarks surrounding her, as well as the attractively presented appetizers.

And then! Horror grasped at her! This couldn't be-

Chapter 23: GAFFE

Realizing she was gaping stupidly, Mallory assessed the situation unfolding before her, aware of Diana's horrified gasp and accusation! Thoughts spun through her confused consciousness. "Something the cat drug in," came to mind! Except that was a trite saying! And there was no such verb as 'drug'!

There stood the threesome of her hires! Purposely omitted from her guest list! Nanci Nichols, Dr. David Higgins, and Delton Waverly! Drenched and dripping, they stood as a stark antithesis to the seated guests! Before she could recover, Waverly began ranting!

It boiled down to 'They were not pleased at being excluded'!

"With a soft, "I'm so sorry," flung over her shoulder toward Daniel and Diana, Mallory raced toward the newcomers. She felt trapped! What could she do but include them? Since they were here, demanding inclusion! Turning a pleading look at the maître d'hôtel, she asked if three more place settings could be squeezed in.

Horrified at having to refuse, he pled the strict city code. They simply could not make exceptions and overcrowd the restaurant.

Mallory made a quick, helpless decision, realizing whatever she did would be wrong to someone. Without hesitation, she rushed Benjamin, Lilly, Cassandra and Xavier to the places reserved for the girls and herself, and ushered the soaking newcomers to the places they vacated.

Loaded with Alexis, the diaper bag, her evening bag, and grasping both Avery and Amelia by their hands, she whispered frantically to David. "We'll be fine! Make sure everyone has fun!"

David felt a certain envy as he watched his four girls make their exit! They would be fine! His orders sounded daunting! He thought about dumping MC duties on Faulkner and following his family! But seeing the other man's careful attention to the table cloth and place setting before him, he knew that was out of the question!

"Okay, thank you all for coming; please continue with your meal."

The only response besides polite attempts to carry on and be normal was Waverly's continuing rant! To the professor and Nanci's credit, they seemed embarrassed by their companion and his continued barrage!

"You knew!" Diana sent an accusing whisper at her husband, despite the presence of their children.

He scowled at her! 'How crazy was that? If he had known, he would have given David and Mallory a heads up and asked hotel security to ban the unwelcome trio! How could Diana even surmise that?'

Miserable, he kept his gaze downward and forced down the food that deserved better enjoyment than he was bestowing!

"Mommeee, where are we going"?

"Okay, Sweetie, we're going back up to our suite to wait for Daddy to be finished."

"Finished? With the very nice party?"

"Mmmm; that's right!"

"Were we being bad? You and Daddy said if we be'd good-"

"I know! It was those big people that were acting badly! So then there weren't enough places for everyone! We'll get some good supper brought up to our suite!"

The little girl burst into disappointed tears. "I want to stay at the party! Everybody didn't get to see me in my pretty dress! And my mink"!

Mallory couldn't help being both tickled and heart-broken by Amelia's dilemma.

"I know, Baby; sometimes things don't work out how you want them to! There'll be other nice parties and other pretty dresses-"

She was so confused she couldn't think! Daniel and Diana were mad at her because she had promised them that if she hired Higgins and Nichols, their paths would never cross! And she felt equally bad for omitting her drillers, and one of Deborah's best division leaders! When she desperately needed everyone in her corner, things were coming apart at the seams! No pun intended! Or trite expression!

"Okay, let's sit down here for a second and think!" She needed to balance her load and talk Amelia into cooperating! With a sigh of relief, she sank down onto a sofa in the lobby. Scrambling for a tissue she dabbed at tearful eyes. "Amelia, please don't cry! You were being good; very good-"

"I'm sorry I said the rain wasn't pretty!" A sob issued forth with the apology, and her little lower lip trembled pitifully.

Mallory hugged her. "I have an idea! Let's go in this restaurant and have our own party! And then, when the upstairs party ends, everybody can still see how pretty you look! But you have to keep being super-good! Stop crying now; it ruins your pretty face."

Amelia's response was a serious nod.

"Hey, Dad; do you mind checking on Mallory?" David whispered the request as entrees arrived. Not surprisingly, his dad pulled his phone free and sent a text!

"Says she's fine"!

David strolled around, pausing at various tables to engage in pleasantries. He could have sent a text! Still, her response back to him might have been less positive! Maybe having his dad do it was savvy.

Back at his table, he was amongst the frosty Faulkners! Their attitude was starting to annoy him! It should be obvious to anyone that the three had crashed a party they were not invited to! Why be mad at him and Mallory?

He rose when the executive chef and hotel general manager approached, offering a handshake to both men. "Hey, trust me; I understand building codes! We're fine-"

"We could have ushered out the uninvited guests-"

"Yes, Sir," David acknowledged the manager's suggestion. "I guess that's not what my wife wanted to do! It's kind of a convoluted story-we're fine! Everything is ideal."

"Your wife and daughters are in the other restaurant, which offers a more casual menu! But we are serving *The View* menu items to your family, Sir! Compliments of *The View* and the hotel"!

"My name's Christine."

Steb frowned at his wife's civility to the uninvited clowns at their table.

Her laughter rippled in response. "At least they speak English!"

Steb regarded Waverly, hunched with a protective arm around his plate, shoveling mashed potatoes into his tater-trap with a spoon!

"Yeah, sadly, I can understand every stupid word he's uttered. I think I preferred the Hebrew."

Ivan Summers emerged from a mangle of aluminum and cables, aware that his cloud of bubbles announced his presence, if anyone cared what he was doing! With a strong kick of his fin, he propelled himself into shadows lengthening in the dusk! Filling his lungs, he unfastened his air tanks and let them fall away, trailing a dwindling bubble stream. To his absolute terror, a shot rang out, the shell cutting through the water toward the target just shed. He forced himself to be calm, swimming underwater, staying in the shadows! At last, with no choice, he surfaced, gasping air desperately before swimming toward a thick tangle of wood and foliage! Whoever took the shot would doubtless be waiting for him, and the brush looked like a haven for snakes! To his amazement, he managed to clamber upward across the mud, falling exhausted beneath the shelter of a rocky embankment!

The evening air presented a sudden chill and he shivered! From nervous response, too; he was sure! He strained his ears for any sound; sounds that should be filling the twilight! Frogs, crickets, and birds! The heavy silenced filled him with dread! Someone else was here; someone listening and watching! Someone aware of his snooping around the scuttled luxury yacht at the bottom of Lake Ouachita!

Diving without a buddy was foolish, especially with added danger of the criminal element! But the Arkansas agent didn't know who to trust! He couldn't find anyone who wanted to learn to dive on their own time and at their own expense! And he had mentioned this phase of an investigation to Agent Bransom! But Bransom didn't seem to think it would yield enough new evidence to make any difference! Now, Summers not only thought that he knew better! He knew beyond any doubt that he was right! The problem now was safeguarding his findings and staying alive to share what he had!

"I'm out of here! Get the kids rounded up and to the suite!" Diana brushed past Daniel with the whispered order.

That was fine with him! He freed Elysia from the high chair the second Cass finished wiping her hands and face, making a beeline for Ryan! "Zave, Buddy, stay with Cass! We're heading straight to the suite! We can regroup there and figure out what we're doing!" Reaching the elevator ahead of the crowd, and urging the kids to hurry, he shoved the 'close' button and descended to the third level! As they awaited the other elevator, members of their group began catching up.

"Hey, Faulkner"!

Of course, it was Higgins! Nearly the last person on earth he wanted to talk to at the moment! Scooping Ryan into his other arm, he sprinted from the crowd gathering at the elevator door, figuring there had to be other elevators, or a set of stairs! Always responsible for his family's safety, he realized he should be more cognizant of evacuation routes!

Higgins and his loud voice pursued. "Faulkner! Daniel, hold on just for a minute! Daniel, for ___________, will you hold on?"

Another bank of elevators, and the doors sprang open at the push of the button! As Daniel stepped in, a force hit him, nearly bringing him to his knees! Shocked, he found his legs, readjusting his balance and tightening his grip on his two youngest!

"Somebody's trying to talk to you, you high and mighty"-followed by a string of profanity!

Aggravated, Daniel shook free of Waverly, not certain why these two clowns didn't think they'd already created enough of a scene for one night!

"Come on! Fight me! What kinda guy hides behind a couple of babies?" Waverly lowered his head and attacked again, to be sent sprawling by a defensive kick! The elevator doors closed and the car shot toward the lobby!

"Look, Dad, he ripped your sleeve!" Jeremiah's voice as he emerged from shock at the whole episode!

"Yeah, just try to get to the other elevators to get to the suite! Stay close! They're mostly all mouth! Maybe hotel security will deal with them if they try to hassle us in the lobby!"

"I can handle him, Dad!"

"And what, go to jail for assault?"

"Oh, I never thought of that! But they started it, and everybody up at *The View*~"

Daniel smiled grimly. "I know you think you could win, but you don't know if he has a gun; I think Cowan figured he didn't. But I'd lay you odds he doesn't run his mouth like he does unless he carries a knife! Son, when you think you can keep a situation in hand there are always variables you can't anticipate!"

Mallory and her daughters attracted interest from diners in the restaurant, but not because the girls were acting up in David's absence. For some reason, they seemed happy and engaged in their own little games. Mallory took advantage of the situation to follow emails and reports on her smart phone! Everything was so exciting! If she could prevent an all-out war between factions!

Occasionally, men would stop to ask her for information! One asked for the time; but most wanted directions, or information on theater showings, or clubs, or other dining. Mallory assumed they were too cheap to tip the concierge, so her standard answer was becoming, "I'm sorry~I'm not local! You really should ask the concierge!"

After listening two or three times, Amelia took over answering the queries: "I'm sorry! I'm not loco! You should really acks the cone-see-erge!"

David appeared just in time to overhear.

"I'm sorry! I'm not loco! You should really acks the cone-see-erge!"

With a laugh, he scooped Amelia up as his eyes met Mallory's. "I take it you've had quite a few guys hitting on you! I thought you were going up to~"

She sighed. "I don't think anyone's been 'hitting on me'! I think they're just too cheap to tip the concierge, or they're not aware of the service! And I was going to the suite, but Cinderella wasn't ready to relinquish her ball gown; or the ball!" Her gaze rested on her eldest child.

"Yeah, not everybody seed me in my dress!"

David laughed and nuzzled her before putting her down so she could pirouette.

"You do look mighty pretty! Have you been good for Mommy?"

"Yes Sir, except about the rain!"

David nodded and met Mallory's gaze, "I'm sorry for fussing at you! Just the start of the night's not going as planned!" He handed her the credit card receipt for the lavish event. "I wish I could have come up with a better plan than letting you leave!"

She shrugged. "Well, there wasn't anyone else there to ask if they minded-so what all happened? Especially, with your aunt"?

"I don't know! I don't think I pulled off restoring the evening to a good time! Waverly kept on and on, mumbling and muttering! I'm pretty sure Higgins and Nanci were embarrassed to no end by the whole thing!"

"Well, they all showed up together! He didn't have a gun to their heads! The whole fiasco's my fault! I didn't think they would ever know the difference. They knew we were coming to Fashion Week, but they didn't know everyone else was invited for parts of it! Especially about the dinner! And they should have been included! They're really critical to what we have going on! So, I risked having them quit, because I didn't want to make Daniel and Diana mad! And they're still mad-sometimes things seem kind of hopeless!"

She shook her head bemusedly, but she didn't really seem that down about the turn of events; which was always a huge relief to him!

Diana locked herself in a stall in the nearest ladies' room, relieved for the completely enclosed privacy. Pulling loops of toilet paper from the roll, she allowed the tears to come! Anger, jealousy, and fear took control of her thoughts! Anger at Mallory for breaking her promise; anger at Daniel for everything; anger at herself for not maintaining better control! Jealousy of the other beautiful woman who still seemed to maintain her hold on Daniel; jealousy of Mallory for her youthfulness, prosperity, getting a gorgeous dress made on her own-well, as long as she was getting it out of her system- And fearful of getting old and losing her looks, of losing Daniel, of the older kids' spreading their wings!

At last, she blew her nose and drew a shuddering breath. Enough of a pity party! She accessed the Bible ap on her phone and scrolled for one verse to give her strength and faith for the moment!

Isaiah 41:10 Fear thou not; for I am with thee: be not dismayed; for I am thy God: I will strengthen thee; yea, I will help thee; yea, I will uphold thee with the right hand of my righteousness.

Whatever happened, she was the child of the King! No reason to fear or be dismayed when she owned His promises of help and strength! She blotted her makeup one more time, freshened her lipstick, and surveyed her wavering smile in the vast bank of polished mirrors. "Okay, Lord; more help, more help! That won't fool anyone!" Pasting on a high-wattage smile, she emerged, softy singing the lyrics of an old hymn, changed for the moment from third person to second: *You will take care of me! Through every day; o'er all the way~ You will~*

Concern and aggravation overtook Daniel when Diana wasn't in the suite ahead of them.

"Where did Mom go?" Jeremiah's question, innocent, but worried.

"I'm not sure! I hoped she made it here ahead of us~"

"Uh, are you in trouble with her? You didn't know they were going to show up~"

"No, I didn't; but just her being in our radar is upsetting!"

"And yet, you don't think I should like Megan!"

Daniel strove for calm. "I'm sorry; we can have a discussion about that sometime! But it has nothing to do with the moment!"

Jeremiah bristled, "But you won't discuss it! Not really! You just brush me off about being too young~"

"Because you are too young! And you're right; Mom and I are not impressed with the girl right now! And we're not impressed that you stole and lied and took off across the country on your own mission, fueled by emotions you're not ready to handle!" So much for staying calm!

"Well, she's a lot better than that Nichols woman you picked!"

Daniel took a purposeful step! "You know, Jeremiah; it took all my restraint not to deck Waverly! This is not the time and place for you to persist in this!"

"Well, you made some real boner mistakes, but you've turned out okay~"

Daniel's probing gaze pierced his son. "Seriously, does this look okay to you?" Tears started. "Jeremiah, I don't want you to make 'boner mistakes' and have to fight every day, just to hold your head up and go on!"

Michael shed his coat, and untying his shoes, pulled them off. A deft jerk loosened bow tie.

"It's kind of early," Missy suggested cautiously.

He surveyed her seriously before smiling suddenly. "I guess you're right! Dinner seemed like an all-nighter, but it was actually just a couple of hours. What did you have in mind? A carriage ride in Central Park? Listen, if you don't mind, why don't you see what your mom and dad are up to while I check on a couple of things? Your dad might want to watch the baseball game, but your mom loves New York and bright lights. I'll call you and see where you are and join up later."

He opened his arms, and she moved into his embrace. "You are very beautiful; did I tell you that?"

She met his penetrating gaze. "I think several times, but I don't mind hearing you repeat yourself! It was amazing to see Megan, wasn't it?"

He pulled her closer and nuzzled his lips against her ear. "You look very beautiful! You look very beautiful! You look very beautiful!" He pulled back with a rich laugh! "And you give me undeserved credit about Megan and her miraculous recovery! Faulkner had the idea about raising money; I simply answered the phone and was by my laptop when the call came in. You better hurry and leave before I change my mind about letting you go." He kissed her long and hard before releasing her reluctantly.

Summers huddled for endless eons of time, watching and listening. He was certain his adversary hadn't given up, but natural noises were cycling up in the cool night air. The shooter must know that no blood stained the water following the shot! Whoever was out here was deadly serious, and what Summers had in possession was too important for him to take any unnecessary chances. He figured his car was disabled, his phone and gun long gone! Scary to so underestimate the adversary! But, if they thought something incriminating-why not send divers down in the intervening time? Maybe they wanted to leave the secrets lie, unless someone like him came nosing around. But who was keeping them in the loop? Was someone from the Arkansas Park Service on their payroll? Sad, but not totally unthinkable!

Remembering a story of David Anderson's, he scanned the trees in close proximity; for one that could hide him and bear his weight! And one climbable for someone who hadn't attempted tree-climbing in decades! Eyeing a possibility, he hesitated! A sliver moon cast a rippling reflection on the breeze-stirred arm of the lake; deer and nocturnal animals should be venturing out! He was uncertain if he was the only presence causing caution, or if the adversary was still out here! Wearily, he knew they were!

"Hey, Honey; I've been worried about you." Daniel turned his attention from arguing with Jeremiah, to Diana, as her keycard granted access to the suite.

"Sorry!" She forced a bright voice. "I'm not sure if it was something I ate, or nerves, but-the ladies' room beckoned! I'm fine now! What's going on here?"

"Jeremiah and I were having a talk!"

She nodded, striving to keep up her brave front! "So how did your coat get torn?"

"It's kind of a long story. Let's talk in the bedroom. Big kids, watch the little guys; we won't be too long." With that, he propelled Diana into the master bedroom and closed the door.

"You didn't really mean what you said to me up there; did you?" He demanded softly. "That I knew party-crashers were going to ruin everyone's evening?"

Her smile sagged in sync with her heart. "Honestly, Daniel, I don't know what I think! I believed Mallory when she promised- And-and-you were just acting so-uh-off-all afternoon and evening! And you said you couldn't sort out your own emotions-" Tears started.

"Okay, the emotions 'I couldn't sort out', aren't about if I want Nanci Nichols. Diana, I don't! And I didn't want to see her or Higgins! And where in the world they ever picked up that nut-case Waverly! He's who tried to rip my sleeve off! It started-"

"Because I've been sad and moody about the miscarriages, and I haven't been a fun companion!" Her words spilled out in a rush.

"Diana, there's more to us than fun! And you are fun; but hey, life's a battle at times! It's the miscarriages, and Al's leaving home, and Jeremiah's escapade- but this afternoon, when I listened to the string quartet-"

She nodded. "They were kind of bad."

He laughed and became immediately intense once more. "Some of those old love songs did conjure up memories I try every day to outrun! Not memories that are pleasurable! The lyrics-it all just reminded me again of what a scum-! What-a reprehensible-

Your lips may be near;
But where is your heart?

She knew that about me! She knew she didn't make me happy! That I was always roving and wandering, restless! All the guys on campus-" He stopped, anguished. "I never knew happiness and satisfaction-and thenl I loved you so! Adored you! And yet I put you through a miserable-I never wanted to be married to her, to anyone, until that day I regained consciousness and looked into your eyes! I knew I loved you and wanted to keep you forever! And I still do! But your value isn't in producing babies. If it isn't God's will for us to have more; and if the loss makes you sad, and I don't know how to comfort you, you are who I want! This is what I want! What I have is what I want; and what I want is what I have!"

She stood several feet away, listening, fighting for control over the tears. A fight that twisted her lovely features heartrendingly! He reached for her but she backed away, throwing her head back slightly in a characteristic way that he loved. Catching her breath in little puffs, she clasped her hands like a European performer, beginning her own trip down memory lane:

It was fascination I know
And it might have ended right there at the start-

He stepped toward her but she shook her head, backing a couple of steps, her lovely, controlled voice pulling his heart out through his heaving chest! 'How could she love him? What could have been 'fascinating' about a gangly, feverish, hemorrhaging guy at death's door? How could she have fallen for him? How could she continue such steadfast love? How could

God have loved him, to reach down-' He focused on her as she continued without missing a syllable. Transfixed, he didn't move again until the last note died away. Then he stood, hoping she would make a move toward him.

Michael sank down in front of his laptop and entered a code to open it! Once again, he had some new reality to absorb! Once self-possessed and smug, having all of the answers, the facts, rationale, he now marveled at the ways in which God continued to work him over! Like his marriage to Missy! A smile crossed features neither handsome nor homely! He had his reasons for the match! A match which Lilly had resisted! Of course, the story of his life had been fighting with Lilly! So, what was one more battle? He never referenced her as 'Mother'. He scoffed even now at the term. Lilly Cowan and Lady MacBeth could coauthor a book on being the antithesis of motherhood! He remembered actually feeling pangs of envy when Lilly latched onto the little American violinist! Until he realized Cassandra didn't receive any more nurturing than he ever did! And yet, there was an affection there! Of Cassandra for Benjamin and Lilly; and she for them! He never called Benjamin his father either! Just no warm cozy emotion, sentiment! That was great! Making him able to calculate coldly and do what must be done!

'And then-Messiah-' tears flowed from eyes new to them! 'Chasing down first Lilly, and then Benjamin, and him last of all, ripping to shreds the rationale and dogma he clung to! 'Like, the operation to free the slaves held at the Moldavan orphanage! His argument was the difficulty of extracting the victims! Transporting them over borders and across the ocean! His suggestion was to gather the criminals together through infiltrating their communications, and blow the place, taking out the captives and captors together! And why not! These pitiful, abused slaves would never make any contribution to society! They could only live to be bullies, perpetrating the same atrocities on others, that they experienced day after day and year after year-' He slapped at tears with the heel of his hand. 'But they were survivors, and more than that, conquerors! His case in point, Sophia! Hopelessly blinded and tormented (he didn't know about the Diabetes and kidney removal at the time of his argument), but now a blossoming woman, an heiress, fighting a crusade! Mostly losing, but fighting all the same! Married, straightening out the warped kid she called Brandon. And Sophia, the one he assessed in his own infinite intelligence, as being incapable of ever making any positive contribution to society, donated enough money to the *ChIP Foundation* that Morrisons were out of debt, and several other families were already reaping the benefits of her generosity! She had looked ethereally lovely at the dinner, on Jay's arm! Jay, who looked much better except for a few residual bruises left from corrective surgery!'

He studied his screen and made a couple of terse responses before returning to his musings. 'Still, his proposal to Missy began in rationale! She stood to inherit Hanson's ranch, and having an American wife could serve his purposes well~very well!' He sighed and then smirked at his own devious intentions! He wasn't sure when he ended up so hopelessly in love with her, but it didn't take long!

He longed to go back out and have fun with her, but the Waverly character put his discipline to the test! As if the moron hadn't spent the night tap dancing on every one's last nerve, he launched into a diatribe about Jews and Israel that was quite challenging to ignore! Not that that was anything new to Cowan! Sometimes, though, even with his disciplined training~

"Are you ready to go up?" David addressed his question to Mallory.

"You know what? I'm going to meet with those three now, up in the suite! Why don't you and the girls stay down here? I shouldn't be too long, and I'll be back."

"Why leave me out of the meeting?"

She smiled disarmingly. "Because I can handle it, and you guys need to be a presence down here! We have all this cash outlay in these clothes, to show what we're about! No one will see them without some exposure!" She rose, giving him a kiss! "And speaking of 'being hit on', just remember that girls have cooties!"

He laughed, but Amelia's head snapped around and she responded indignantly, "No we do not have cooties!"

Mallory joined the three red-faced employees at the dining room table in her suite. They were subdued, and she plunged in. "Okay, for starters, I really owe you all an apology! I hope you'll trust me that my rationale for not having invited you was sound! But the way I handled it was pitiful! I've learned a lesson, and I hope you can forgive me!"

"Are we fired?" The question burst from Higgins! He pretty much hated his job! Still preferring the classroom where he didn't battle elements every day! Until it was suddenly at risk! It was a great job, and the pay~

Her laughter rippled, "Absolutely not! Please let me finish with my apology and explanation!"

They laughed uneasily.

"I've been really busy and really pumped about everything that's going on! And I knew I should have come to each of you, and just worked out something, to let you know how crucial your are to what we have going on, and ask what I could do for you in lieu of not being invited to tonight's event! But, I buried my head in the sand, simply hoping you wouldn't know the difference! I guess I insulted your intelligence! So, now I'm here to eat crow! And although, I don't consider myself in a position to ask favors of you right now; I need to ask each of you to do me an immense favor!"

They exchanged glances among themselves without responding.

"Okay, Nanci, you actually work for Deborah, and you're doing an outstanding job! She will never forgive me if I lose you due to my carelessness! She didn't realize how many people I was inviting and how personal your exclusion would seem; or she would never have allowed it to happen."

Nanci nodded, swiping at tears.

Mallory continued, trying to tread softly. "You know the reason why~"

She nodded, "And so does David," she added.

Mallory expelled her breath slowly. "Tomorrow night is another corporate event where we hand out bonuses and awards and clap and cheer for one another! But I'm asking the three of you to leave town tonight!"

They nodded, already aware no rooms were reserved for them in the solidly booked hotel.

"I made reservations for you at a nice hotel in Newark, Delaware. You can all fly out of Bradley, International tomorrow afternoon. I'll reimburse your transportation costs both ways!"

They nodded, relieved not to be dressed down for showing up uninvited and making such a scene. The generosity to pay for the unauthorized trip was a relief.

"And I want to give each of you a cash bonus; the problem with that's being your tax bite! If you have a tax advisor, maybe you can find out the best way for me to structure the bonus to your advantages."

Higgins and Nichols exchanged glances again, but Waverly started his mouth!

"I'll just take cash, right now! Thank you very much! I'll worry about the tax later!"

"Okay, well calm down! I don't have cash; I can wire-transfer-"

"That'd be just fine!"

Mallory forced a smile! Waverly could be hard to take, but she had things rolling and going; and he was good at what he did!

"David, y'all load your luggage into a cab and find the nearest car rental agency. Here's the confirmation for the hotel reservation! Again, I'm sorry for making you feel like you don't count! Because you do! Big time"!

"I'm sorry for taking it out on you!" Diana's apology as she allowed Daniel to pull her close! "But, Mallory sort of gave her word-"

"Well, yeah, and, Honey, you know her word's her bond! I'm not sure she could help it if social baboons show up, totally uninvited and unplanned for-"

She nodded, "But still-"

His phone buzzing in his trousers' pocket interrupted. "Hey, Dad; what's happening?"

He listened, thinking the connection was poor! Which shouldn't be a problem with the sat phone!

"I'm sorry, Dad; I'm having a hard time following you-"

"Yeah-uh-guess-I'm emotional! Uh-I've been at this for a long time-"

"Well, yes, Sir; but if there's a problem, put it on me! Problems are bound to arise-"

There was a long pause, making Daniel worried about what could be that bad! Diana's worry evidenced itself as she strained to make sense of the one-sided conversation.

"I've been at this, for~a~long time~Son! And I've never seen anything like this! Uh~we have~uh~an honest-to-goodness~

Daniel sank onto the bed, suddenly woozy from a frenetic several hours! "Dad, are you positive?"

Chapter 24: GUSHER

Daniel sat dazed, tears pouring down his face! What a day of emotional extremes! Joy filled his voice! "A gusher! You-hit a gusher? What, exactly- uh, you haven't been able to cap it yet?" Laughing through tears, he gave Diana an exuberant thumbs-up, patting the bed beside him for her to sit down! His arm circled her waist and he gave her a rib-crushing squeeze!

"Yeah, Dad, believe me; I'm glad you got to see it, too! Hearing about it second-hand isn't too bad, though! Wow! Wow! Dad, that's-that's just-stellar- Yeah, send footage! It's-uh-kind of hard-uh-to grasp! Yeah, Dad, I'm booting up my laptop so I can see the images better! Hang on a sec-" he indicated for Diana to assemble the kids! They needed a lift too, after the crazy earlier events!

Mallory reached the lobby restaurant as the Faulkners appeared. "Hey, I am so sorry- Uh-what happened to your sleeve?"

Daniel shrugged, "Guess they don't make 'em like they used to."

Diana swatted at him for his inference that her company's goods were inferior. Not that she really minded! She wasn't sure exactly what the oil discovery would translate to in dollars, but from Daniel's reaction, it must be something big!

Mallory remained concerned about the ripped tuxedo, hoping if Higgins or Waverly were the ones responsible, that they were on the way out of state and wouldn't be arrested for assault! Not that it wouldn't serve them right-but they were so crucial-

"We have something to celebrate! And we would like for you guys to join us!" Daniel's voice literally rang with excitement!

"You already know; don't you?" came Diana's question.

Mallory's eyes shone and she shrugged. "I may have a pretty good idea! Where do you want to celebrate?"

"Well, there's a coffee shop down a block and a half, and the rain has stopped, at least for the moment! We can walk! Shall we invite some of the others?"

David laughed. "They're probably mostly there ahead of us! But if they aren't, we can discuss your news better!"

Daniel caught his breath, staggered. "There's more?"

"Just in case we don't get an opportunity; would you care to continue the ball in our suite, après? Our little belle isn't eager to give it up!"

Ivan hugged his knees against his body for warmth to his core! At least he was dry by now! The lake was engulfed with silence, and pinpricks of far distant stars provided little light! He sat motionless, except for an occasional shiver; thoughts of surveying the area better from a higher position forsaken as he continued to sense the pervading danger! He couldn't guess the time; just that it seemed endless. 'When he didn't appear on time for work', the idle hours filled with supposition, 'would anyone have a clue where to look for him?' He possessed skills as a law enforcement officer, but unarmed against at least one marksman with a rifle? A determined one, with a lot at stake!' He cursed his own bravado! 'Well, at the time-'

The coffee shop bustled with activity, as though the entire neighborhood emerged with the final rain drop! David was right about a good representation from their friends and associates being there ahead of them! Not a good chance to visit about the new bonanza! But there would be time! And for now, the atmosphere was convivial. Other people involved with the 'Rag Industry' showed up, too, exchanging business cards and engaging eagerly about a common passion! The impromptu coffee event seemed like it might be more productive than all of the scheduled appointments!

And then, Deborah appeared, eyes flashing warningly! "What did you do to me, Mallory?"

Mallory desperately attempted to free herself from a banquette, where she was hemmed in. "Take it easy, Deborah! I think I employed sufficient damage control!" Finally gaining freedom, she urged the other executive to a far corner.

"You're right to be upset, Deborah! I should have explained everything to you, but at the time I wasn't sure it was 'need to know'! Bad judgment error! I see now; in hindsight!"

"Why would you invite everyone who works for me; if they barely run for notions for the seamstresses-"

"Okay, that's what I need to explain! Nanci and Professor Higgins have ties to Mr. Faulkner-uh- going all the way back to their college days at Tulsa University! Uh-fraternity/sorority stuff! But then, Mr. Faulkner met Diana and received the Lord and went a different direction, but-"

Deborah's eyes shone with unshed tears! "Okay, enough! I get where you're going with it; but still, her feelings must have been hurt-"

"Well, yeah; Waverly spun things his own way to both her and the professor; that they were supposed to be invited, but-something happened and their invitations never arrived! At least that's the story they were agreeing upon a couple of hours ago! Now, Nanci and David are pretty embarrassed! I sent them all to a hotel in Connecticut to clean up and get some rest before they head back to their respective places. I'm paying for their out of pocket expenses to come, and giving them a cash amount! I didn't treat them with the respect they deserve for what they contribute!"

"But what about Nanci? She doesn't work for you!"

"No, not technically, but I'm the one who created the offense, causing you a problem you don't deserve! So, I'm trying to make it right! Deborah, I apologize! I'm pretty sure she's okay, though!"

Proverbs 22:3 A prudent man forseeth the evil, and hideth himself: but the simple pass on, and are punished.

At breakfast, Nanci asked to join the two Geologists, who were more than pleased for her company. "Do either one of you know what to do to protect the bonus money from being eaten alive by the IRS?"

"Well, obviously, the rock scientist here doesn't," came Higgins' teasing response! "And I'm not up on him by much, except that I know a couple of professors in money management accounting at TU! I tried to reach Terrence Dover late last evening to explain the situation! Hopefully-"

Before he finished the sentence, his phone jangled. Nanci ordered coffee, trying to listen in on the conversation.

"Hey, thanks for your time, Dover! Yeah, I'd like for you to do that, but I'm not home much! I'm headed to Florida and then through the Caribbean, Panama Canal and the Pacific Coast of Chile! No rush; I can delay receiving the money until I can meet with you to set it up. Yeah; it's turning out good! Sometimes I still miss the hallowed halls! Yeah, you know who Nanci Nichols is; she's interested in having you set her up with an account, too!"

He disconnected and turned his attention to the stunning woman. "You want him to be your retirement banker, too, don't you?"

She sipped thoughtfully. "I'm not sure! You've heard the story about investment bankers who were showing off their yachts at a yacht show?"

He squinted shrewdly, "I'll bite!"

"Yes, the yacht salesman asked why all the people whose retirements they planned, weren't there buying yachts, too!"

Higgins chuckled, as Waverly began another rant! "I'm just telling you, my account isn't showing any wire transfers! That dame better come through!"

"Nichols laughed, "She probably did and the IRS already siphoned it all back out!"

"Well, the evening ended up being really fun!" Diana's eyes sparkled with new delight!, "any more word from your-" she hesitated.

"No, but it's the middle of the night there! Wish we could've gotten together with David and Mallory, but we do all have early appointments!"

David snuggled Amelia, burying his lips in soft, bright curls as she sobbed heart-brokenly.

"She's exhausted; so are we!" Mallory's tender words! "Let's just get ourselves all put to bed, and things will look brighter in the morning!"

David nodded. It was hours beyond his little 'Belle of the Ball's' usual bedtime, and yet the tears were not simply from exhaustion! Her feelings were decimated; her heart broken! "Yeah, I agree," he assented. "But I still want to comfort her a little."

Not happy, Mallory changed Avery and Alexis into pajamas and fixed a bottle! Blessedly, Avery fell asleep instantly and Alexis' eyelids fluttered sleepily as she downed the formula. Tasks completed, Mallory swiped at make up with a cotton ball! She felt sorry for Amelia; but a little more pragmatic, she realized hurts just come! David seemed to be taking the offense more to heart than Amelia was; if that were possible! With a sigh, she moved to the edge of the king-sized bed! Finally out of the dog house with Daniel and Diana about Nanci Nichol's uninvited appearance, she didn't want to create a new rift with them because Ryan told Amelia her mink liked like a 'dead kitty'! They were both babies and they could work it out and be friends again in a heartbeat! If the parents didn't get sucked into a major dispute!

She stacked pillows behind her and reached for her Bible! 'That was it! The reason for the entire evening of fiascos! Marvelous and exciting things were happening! Things that made her heart race and her spirit soar! Things that were bringing honor and glory to the Lord in a marvelous way! Of course, the devil wasn't pleased with that! And just as she prayed David wouldn't take the issue up with the Faulkners she knew that she shouldn't tie in with David about his response to this now! God wasn't the author of confusion! It was Satan who wanted them all at each other's throats!' She opened to:

> *MalachI 3:8-11 Will a man rob God? Yet ye have robbed me. But ye say, Wherein have we robbed thee? In tithes and offerings.*
>
> *Ye are cursed with a curse: for ye have robbed me, even this whole nation.*
>
> *Bring ye all the tithes into the storehouse, that there may be meat in mine house, and prove me now herewith, saith the LORD of hosts, if I will not open you the windows of heaven, and pour you out a blessing that there shall not be room enough to receive it.*

And I will rebuke the devourer for your sakes, and he shall not destroy the fruits of your ground; neither shall your vine cast her fruit before the time in the field, saith the LORD of hosts.

She studied the beloved text wonderingly, not certain that with their influx of wealth, their giving was keeping pace! She smiled! Not a bad problem to deal with! But what she specifically sought was the added promise, that with being a faithful giver, God Himself promised to deal with the devourer! "Yeah, Lord, he sure wants to get into our vineyard and wreak havoc! Thank you for David, and don't let us get crossways-"

He appeared in the doorway, looking wiped out, carrying his limp daughter!

Mallory laughed! "What's the deal with that?"

A tired smile shone through thick, past-mid-night stubble. "She still wasn't ready to take the dress off, and I was trying to convince her to put on her nightie-uh-by showing her the cute outfit she has for tomorrow-"

"Oh, I see! So, she bonded with the cowgirl boots, too! You know, she's going to end up sleeping between us! And she kicks like a mule-without the boots-" Still, her heart melted at the little tear-stained face, the sobs still easing off as slumber deepened. The incongruity of the fur-trimmed formal with the western boots!

He began emptying his pockets. "I'm sure you were right about not indulging her!"

"Not necessarily-a little TLC always goes a long ways! I was being like my mom and you were being like my dad!"

He nodded, motioning for her to scoot so he could sit beside her.

"Well, in all fairness, you weren't being like your mom! You always did have your dad wrapped around your little finger, though!"

"We understood each other!"

He laughed. "I guess her tears shocked me, because I didn't know how much girls-I-I made you cry; didn't I? When we were in high school?"

"A few times," she admitted. "I was so sappy over you!"

"No wonder your father took issue with me! Man, I can't stand having her cry like that! I mean, it wasn't just that she still didn't want to take the dress off and go to bed-"

Luminous eyes met his. "You're right! It would be funny if it weren't so sad, how much she wanted Ryan to see her all dolled up, and have him say something nice-I thought she wanted people in general, to see her! Theyre'-they're so little-"

He leaned over, pressing his lips on hers, and she circled his neck with both arms!

An exhausted Summers shivered and shifted uneasily! Surely he hadn't dozed off! He gazed around in alarm! This wasn't good! In fact, it bode ill-Tense, he strained senses! Obviously his adversary possessed resources not at his disposal! Reinforcements! The sound of voices pierced the pervasive darkness; then powerful flashlight beams pierced the night around him! Terrified, he shrank back into his meager shelter, trying to think of a way to stash his evidence before surrendering to whomever it was- the shrill howls of search dogs! Feet pounded past him, within twenty feet! Fired shots! Muzzle flashes! The thrashing through the underbrush beyond him, ceased! Obviously somebody nailed somebody! Then a chopper clattered above him; good guys to the rescue? No one knew he was out here, pinned down! No, it must be them! The bad guys continued to grow in numbers and sophistication! But a chopper was beyond the reach of most-wasn't it?

"Agent Ivan Summers! This is Ward Atchison! Your partner sensed you were in some kind of predicament; when the Little Rock office wasn't convinced, he brought us on-scene! Come on out, Summers; it's over! Let's go get a hot breakfast and let you get dressed for work! When you walk in like normal, you'll prove they were right!"

Summers laughed! 'Wow! Hot breakfast sounded great!' Still cautious, he jammed his treasure into the most hidden spot he could find and moved forward, hands high!

Mallory appeared at the restaurant in stunning gray monochromatic! Navajo rug design scaled to elegant alpaca/wool jacket proportion featured deep red diamonds in the traditional pattern. Ankle length solid charcoal skirt in the same nubby texture swirled to be met by charcoal western style boots. Amelia wore a miniaturized version, containing more of the deep red tones; and her boots were red. Avery and Alexis matched one another in a different theme! Diana assumed Mallory and Amelia's ensembles were not *Rodriguez, Incorporated*; the wool/alpaca was indicative of Shay! At any rate, that petty stuff wasn't on her mind! A gusher! *GeoHy* hit a gusher!

"Would y'all care to join us? Maybe we can talk a little before everyone else descends!"

After settling in and ordering, they quickly got to the pressing issue! "Word will spread like wildfire!" Mallory's softly-spoken warning. "I'm sure it already has! We actually own the surrounding land! We had that in place before releasing the initial report! We plan to farm/ranch it; but it's also a training facility for security personnel!"

Daniel and Diana exchanged amazed looks and he laughed exuberantly! "That's awesome! I've kinda been worried about my dad-"

David's serious gaze met his, "Rightly so! Even with the security training and armed personnel, some of these big oil companies run rough shod over whoever can't stand up to them! That means legal maneuvering and using the law when it's advantageous-"

"Yeah, and abandoning what's legal and right when it isn't!" Daniel finished. "So you're warning us of legal manipulation as well as the possibility of criminal incursion?"

Mallory shrugged. "Of course; if you have anything at all, someone will be after it! So the easy course is to not try to have, or to do, anything! That's why I love what God promised Abraham in:

> *Genesis 15:1 After these things the word of the LORD came unto Abram in a vision, saying, Fear not, Abram, for I am thy shield and thy exceeding great reward.*

God planned to bless Abram very much in a material way, but before He did so, He created a shield around him! First came the shield, and then the reward! And not just a reward, but a great reward! And then, not just a great reward! But an **exceeding great reward**! More and more I'm aware that I need the shield in place, even more than I need exceeding great reward! But God is so abundant in granting both! More and more David and I see the need to begin each day pleading His protection over us and what we do! And then, we have the security people on-site, too!"

Daniel nodded, "being as wise as possible and doing all we can, but realizing we need the Lord in all we do!" His expression grew serious. "Really; you guys plan to be farmer/ranchers?"

"Of course! Farming brings treasure forth out of the earth, too!"

Diana's brow crinkled, and Mallory laughed! "We're not going to live there part of the time, though! We're spread thin between Dallas, *The Ranch*, and *The Enclave*! We haven't been to our church in weeks, and we need to get back! We kinda had words with Pastor Ellis. He'll be thinking we got mad and left!"

Diana looked surprised. "Really, what about"?

"It's my fault," David confessed cheerfully. "It's the kind of stuff you guys deal with on a weekly basis! We're just not as seasoned at 'fielding the ball' as you are! This same guy tries to hit me up for a job every time he sees me! For example, every church service! And every time, I tell him to go online-"

Daniel shrugged. "Yeah, that's what we tell people! But it's amazing how they usually won't do it, and then the next time you walk in the door at church-" He paused laughing. "Maybe we're not better at 'fielding the ball', after all. But we figure that's just part of what God has allowed us-so, what; this guy got Pastor Ellis involved?"

"Yes, and Mrs. Ellis, too," Mallory inserted. "She acted like his kids were doing without and it was our fault!"

They all nodded and David continued, "Then, Pastor Ellis just started talking about the tough economy in general, and how that has affected the church and offerings this summer! That's when I stepped out of line! He mentioned dropping support for some of the missionaries-"

Diana spoke from experience as a MK. "Yeah, if churches go under and close their doors, they can't come back another day and resume support! But by the same token, missionaries really work under-supported and under-funded! When you figure exchange rates for their currencies, and cost of living in some of the countries-"

David and Mallory nodded and he continued with his narrative. "Anyway, I mentioned Calvary's crunch to my dad, and he got authorization to alleviate the situation from *Anderson Ministries'* funds. He told me to apologize to Pastor, which I've done! I mean, I was in the wrong! We just need to get back and resume normalcy and the relationship!"

"What does the guy do who wants a job?" Daniel's idle curiosity.

Mallory chuckled. "Good question! Maybe we should find out! He might be one of those treasures that you brush aside in your quest for treasure!"

David shook his head. "Says he's an insurance agent! That's what all guys try that can't make it at anything else! I mean if his license is current, why isn't he with an agency? Handing out business cards, and at least trying? And why buttonhole me, since insurance isn't our major thrust?"

Mallory started a cup of coffee upon entering the suite! "Would you mind handling this next appointment? The girls are still feeling the effects of late night and then early morning; and I could really use some time to study this map and make a call or two!"

"Great plan! You sure you don't mind?" He figured the girls were too out of sorts to take with, and allow them to accomplish anything; but usually Mallory liked taking care of business better than she liked dealing with them alone.

She laughed. "I don't mind, if you don't! You already have a great relationship with this company-"

He nodded. "No problem! Why don't you give up on the Louisiana drill site? It's actually the first unsuccessful-I know! It wrecks your dad's batting average!"

She nodded stubbornly! "I'll check all the data once more; and then, if there's still nothing, we withdraw! Deal? And I have a couple of calls to make!"

"Okay, but you know as soon as you start on making calls, they'll start acting their worst! Why don't you get them down for naps first?"

As soon as the door closed behind him she dialed Calvary's number and asked the church secretary for Joe Hamilton's number. 'Insurance'! That gave her an idea! She dialed the number and Joe answered on the first ring!

"Hello, Joe; this is Mallory Anderson! Did you ever complete our online application? David said something about your being in insurance? Could you do me a huge favor and complete it? It's only a couple of pages? Is there a reason why you've hesitated about it? A felony conviction, a problem with being bonded?"

"Nothing like that! It just seems like an exercise in futility! To fill in all the little blanks and know it's hitting the circular file before you get to the elevator!"

"That won't happen! I'll be watching for it eagerly!" Even as she finished the conversation, Amelia and Avery started fighting! Amelia wanted to play Sunday School teacher and Avery was building with blocks!

"Come on, Avery! Let's play Sunday School! You have to stand up and sing with me! Let's sing, *Deep and Wide*! Put the block down so you can do like I do with the hand motions!" When there wasn't compliance, Amelia grabbed the block away and grasped her little sister's hands, to force her to motion 'deep'!

Avery screeched in protest as light dawned on Mallory!

"That's it!" Her eyes danced at the revelation! With Avery screeching and Amelia loudly singing the little chorus, Mallory placed a call to Higgins!

"Yes, Professor; hey hold off on pulling the Louisiana drillers off-site! I want to expand the exploration! Order them to go deeper and wider!"

Trent and Sonia drank coffee at Rock Center Café as the kids shopped in nearby stores at Rockefeller Center. Sonia looked stunning in brown wool herringbone skirt topped with solid brown fine-gauge sweater set! A silk twill scarf, arranged bewitchingly beneath her chin, was an elegant print of elk among late autumn foliage! Brown tights, and high-heeled pumps with matching handbag completed the ensemble! "You look sensational, Sonia! Like, how much would that outfit set me back if the Lord were not on my side?"

"Thanks! A round figure would be right at a thousand! Diana and Mallory try to keep their prices down! That wouldn't include the jewelry."

He gulped at hot coffee to keep from spewing it all over!

Her lovely features were serious! "Trust me; the prices are great! Some vendors would price the handbag alone at five hundred!"

He shook his head, still trying to absorb it all! "Well, if a woman pays five hundred dollars for a purse, how will she ever have any money to put in it?"

She laughed. "Handbag! And trust me; there are lots of people with huge discretionary incomes!"

"Well, I do trust you! Although, with my upbringing, it's hard to grasp! Why don't you make your way to the ladies' room so you get more exposure? Maybe someone will stop you and ask-"

She nodded; his plan wasn't bad! He always seemed to be nervous about her representing the lines when there were no definitive results! She rose! So, maybe she could get a 'definitive result'!

David took in the sight before him with wonder! Blocks and toys were strewn everywhere! Alexis slept in the crook of Mallory's arm; who was also sound asleep! And Amelia and Avery were doing their own thing!

"Daddy, will you tell Avy to play Sunday School with me?"

He pulled off shoes and jacket, loosening his tie. "Just play nice unless you want to take a nap! Daddy's going to close his eyes for a few minutes, too!"

Hot breakfast and getting to work on time, although very appealing, were put on hold! Summers, with the Arkansas State Parks personnel, investigated the shooting as rays of sunlight shot across the lake! With the body on the way to the morgue, Summers and Haslett retrieved the evidence from its hiding place, and headed toward headquarters to turn it in!

"Kind of taking casual day to a new level, aren't you, Summers?" his superior questioned. "Sorry for not believing Haslett when he tried to raise the alarm! I just figured in the middle of the night, that you didn't owe it to anyone to take calls!"

"Well, as a general rule, no one calls me in the middle of the night! So I would be concerned enough to answer! I'm not sure how he knew I was in trouble!"

"So, what's Atchison's gig?"

"Aside from saving my life, I'm not sure!"

"Do you consider the use of deadly force necessary?"

"That guy shot at me last night, just as I began to surface!"

"Well, you say that someone shot at you! I'm not sure we're searching the lake bottom to look for a shell! And you don't know who it was-"

"Well, when you find out what they did with my car, maybe there will be evidence there!"

"It's our car, Summers! And we're trying to find it! The agency's in a budget shortfall, and you misplace a vehicle?"

"I told you where I left it, and reported my service revolver and cell phone stolen. Everything was out of sight and the vehicle was locked! I was pinned down all night! It's a good thing Haslett kept after it."

"Well, we don't need any renegade paramilitary organizations taking the law into their own hands around here. Tell Atchison not to go far while we sort it all out!"

"Is everything okay?" Cat Holman noticed immediately as Cade's expression registered alarm in response to an email.

Worried eyes met hers. "I hope so! Uh-I might have messed up-"

"What? Let me see!" she grabbed for his device, but he shook his head warningly.

"No, this may be something else that violates my CDA! I told you about telescoping that look to that idiot Waverly. I thought only Faulkner picked up on it, but something Waverly said to me at *The View*, about my giving him a 'snotty look' and his thinking later about its significance, has worried me!"

"Well, if Mallory's companies stop using us, can we still survive long enough to rebuild our customer base? What did you do? What's the email?"

"Well, I don't know! First off, the last thing I want to do is violate her and David's trust! And they can sue or prosecute for violations- What I did was come here for this week in response to her invitation! Most of the test data goes securely to her. But a visual inspection of a core sample-" He studied the email image again. "Usually, you don't see anything significant-it's the analysis that tells." He responded to the email.

"Got it, delete your picture and anything else related! Put the entire sample back in the box and lock it! And put it in my office and lock my office! I don't have to remind you to keep quiet, but KEEP QUIET!"

"Maybe we'll have to try again later on the carriage ride-" his apologetic look really unnecessary for Catrina's understanding nature.

He forwarded the email to Mallory.

Chapter 25: GROWTH

"How was the Big Apple?" Rob, exhibiting his usual attitude!

Trent got it! The former Southwestern Forestry LEI division head was casting aspersions on his manliness for joining his friends and colleagues for Fashion Week! "Great trip! Sonia loves it! And there's no lack of things to see and do! Our family has never been to the Statue of Liberty before! Sonn attended some meetings and there were the usual awards banquets for the company performers! One evening was a fabulous dinner at *The View* in Manhattan. I never in my days figured I'd go where I've been able to go, and see the things-" He cut himself off, not wanting to sound like a braggart! "God has blessed me beyond-"

"Yeah, no kiddin'! Megan still doin' okay?"

"As if it never happened-"

"Yeah, bet it ran up lots of bills though! I feel sorry for you!"

Trent frowned. His leadership style was strong, always avoiding whining and trying to garner sympathy. Part of his management philosophy formulated when he taught a Bible series on King Saul! When God departed from the beleaguered king, and things spiraled downhill for him quickly, his authority ebbed away! A lesson in submission! Strong leaders are always also good submitters to the authorities over them. At one time, as King Saul's army dwindled, and he trembled with fear and indecision, his son, Jonathan, had crept out with one of his servants and defeated a Philistine garrison. Instead of rejoicing, Saul whined to the loyal men still with him that 'none of them felt sorry for him to tell him Jonathan-' Like, why would soldiers feel sorry for the king?

Trent directed his focus back to the other man. "Well, thanks but send your sympathy elsewhere! Like I said, God looks out for me~"

'Hmmm, better not admit anything beyond that! The debt's being expunged might look to someone like an influx of cash to him! Like taxable income!' He grinned grimly! In that case, he might need sympathy~ He didn't want to be proud, but~

"So, Dad, what do you want to do?" Jared's question as they headed to JFK. "Do you want to go home until spring in the Rockies? There won't be much actual mining once the snow falls, starting any day now! But you can come to Colorado anyway and spend the winter, helping me order equipment and be ready to go the first opportunity."

'Pick' Jameson considered, amazed this kid continued calling him, 'Dad'. Christened Peter Wells Jameson, he had grown up hard-scrabble in a Philly suburb where he got a neighbor girl in trouble and married her producing a daughter they named Tara Marie. Although, he doted on her; marriage, fatherhood, and holding down a job proved too much! He and his spouse, both substance abusers, fought and clawed like everyone else in their complex! With the fighting in the Balkans, he sobered up enough to pass the physical and join the U.S. Army! GI Bill, or no, when he returned, injured and shell-shocked, he figured he wasn't college material! Figuring his spouse was not much of a loss, he made a few meager attempts to locate his little girl! Never did find her! And then, yeah, he messed around, moved around, finding one dead-end job after another~mining jobs, where his military training with explosives stood him in good stead! Then finally between VA benefits and Social Security disability, he attempted to disappear without a trace into his neighborhood saloon! That's where Jared found him, claiming to be his kid! That was follwing the kid's first year of college, making Jameson really question if he could have a true genetic link with a college kid! Must have gotten his brains from his mom, whoever she was~maybe she looked a little familiar! He wasn't sure.

"Come to Colorado, then!" Jared's urging at the silence. "I figured you were dead set on going home, but if it's taking you this long~"

"You're getting married~"

Jared squeezed Abby's hand. "Yes Sir! We sure are! If you come now, you can be at our wedding! You can even be my best man! I'm not sure why that just occurred to me-uh-we're keeping it small and simple, without a big wedding party-"

"Yes, we are," Abby leaned around Jared. "But having you stand with him; that would be awesome! Please come to Colorado! They're putting in bunk halls and a chow hall! Lots of activity, in spite of snowfall, and being unable to mine immediately"!

Pick nodded thoughtfully, considering. The two kids seemed as legit as anyone he had ever been around. "Your daddy; he don't think too well of us?"

A troubled expression crossed Abigail's sweet countenance. "I know his feelings were obvious! Which I thought was impolite for a man who prides himself on having gracious manners! I've done some things I'm ashamed of, but it at least broke me from the country club snobbery. What should I call you? Pick, or, Mr. Jameson?"

"Or, you could call him Dad," Jared suggested.

A sardonic grin twisted hardened features. "Ya might as well; this kid does."

Joe Hamilton exhaled a disgusted puff! This was unbelievable; for the Andersons to have so much! And lead pastor to believe they were having as tough a time as everyone else! And more information continued pouring in! He painstakingly did as Mallory requested, although, from the outset, he could tell he was wasting his time! He didn't know of a way to beat the rates she had, by a large enough sum to make it worth her while to switch! Halfway through the afternoon, he paused to send an email: "I don't think I can find much better rates than you have already!"

An email shot back! "Price isn't the only issue! Could you please put all the policies together for me to compare?"

He studied it gloomily! Wondering why price wasn't her issue! The coverages were neck and neck- Still, he continued doggedly, not sure why! Unless she bought all of these policies from him, there was no commission or payday in sight! Good grief! Property and structures and vehicles and equipment! Policies added one at a time for the other insurance company; not the headache for quotes like Mallory had dumped on him! He guessed he kept at it to be vindicated with Pastor and Mrs. Ellis! That he did seriously try! At last, he completed the spreadsheet and whistled in amazement at the total! Wow, the insurance coverage for owning lots and lots wasn't cheap! No wonder people whined to him about being insurance-poor! The Andersons' net worth must be staggering; something tough for him to contemplate! If she and David purchased many policies and stayed with them, his residuals would come in handy! 'Don't get ahead of yourself, Joe', he warned himself morosely. He emailed Mallory, announcing he was finished.

"Can you and your family meet us at the Chick Fil-A near the church in an hour or so?" came David's response! "Our treat! Great job"!

"No problem," was his response. Inwardly he raged! 'They didn't have any intention of switching! They were just using him to make sure their current rates were the best! And why not? With so much to insure! You'd think they could at least spring for steaks rather than fast food!"

The Hamiltons watched the young couple unload girls from a large SUV! Not brand new, but new enough! Good tires! Nothing so flashy as to holler out their bottom line! They all managed to get shuffled in the door, and David nodded. With the little one buckled into a high chair and the two toddlers scampering to the playground, Joe joined David in line to place his family's order!

"Bet you're hungry," David noted good-naturedly! "You did a lot of work today!"

Hamilton shrugged, trying to cloak his annoyance.

"How long will it take to get all the new policies into effect?" David's logical question took the agent off-guard.

"Excuse me?"

David laughed. "Yeah, Hamilton; we're trying to buy! Let me guess! Sales isn't your long suit! You're a good bean counter, though!"

"What do you mean?" Joe was honestly baffled at the assessment!

"I mean, we've given you openings all day, to close a huge sale! You run from it! That isn't a bad thing! It just means selling isn't natural for you."

"Well, it seemed like a hassle for me and for you guys to readdress your insurance when I couldn't save you that much! Why bother?"

"We never asked you to save us money. That was your personal frame-of-reference. We all come complete with a frame-of-reference that colors everything we do. We met this woman named Norma out in Colorado, and her lifelong dream was selling door to door cosmetics! She-uh-doesn't look much like a cosmetics type woman! I don't think she's ever used any makeup until she signed up as a rep; and she looks kind of clownish now!

But she's such a natural saleswoman she astounds me! Like this one old guy, a local rancher, came into a store that's-well, that's another story. Anyway, Norma was filling out an order for his wife and then she sells this guy a bronzer! Like, get this, his skin's is leather! Like he never spent much time out of the sun! The last thing he needs is-"

David stopped laughing; besides not being a salesman, Hamilton wasn't much fun-

"Never mind! If you have to explain a joke, it loses something-"

They balanced trays stacked with food to the tables nearest the playground, and David prayed before Mallory began cutting up fruit and chicken pieces for Amelia and Avery. David slid bits of waffle fries to Alexis as he continued. "As I was asking; how long will it take you to get new policies in effect for us? Our six month premiums are due the end of October and we'd like to have the new policies overlap!"

"You want double coverage?" Suspicion shone in Hamilton's expression.

Mallory met his gaze, laying knife and fork aside. "Okay, we might as well explain the story to you! In answer to your question, we don't want double coverage; but neither do we want any of the policies to lapse in the transition. Now, to answer your burning question as to why we want to switch when it's a pain to do so, and we aren't saving any money-"

"Maybe even cost a little more," Joe interrupted seriously.

David shook his head bemusedly. He was for honesty, but this guy was enough to put George Washington to shame!

"Yes," Mallory continued, giving David a warning look, "here's our reason for wanting to go to a different carrier. We had a nice cabin in Colorado, but it was burned to the ground by an arsonist! We reported the loss to the adjustor, and figured we would get the claim settled right away! Well, they came up with this scenario that David and I burned it ourselves, or hired it done! We didn't! The sheriff's department told us they're working the case! Which that only means they haven't closed it! Our caretakers barely escaped with their lives! If they had died, the case would have gotten more urgency, but blessedly, they made it out! So, since the case wasn't being solved and we couldn't get the insurance money, we hired a private investigator-"

"Can you do that with an ongoing investigation?"

"Not supposed to, but anyway, our PI led the sheriff's department to a person of interest in that, and several other cases! His-uh-name was Rudy Sunquist-"

"And you killed him, so now he can't clear things up with this insurance company?" Joe was familiar with the aspect.

"Well, because they grabbed David! He nearly died!" Mallory fought frustration that Joe knew that part.

"Well; how do you guys have so much money? I mean, are you even twenty-five?"

David did a slow count! Hamilton had a problem! Not writing up the policies as fast as he could without so many questions!

"Not by fraudulent insurance claims! Which isn't your worry! You're an agent; not a claims adjustor!"

Mallory nodded agreement at David's answer before continuing calmly. "We've tried to get the adjustment, all the while, adding additional policies as we've acquired more properties and equipment! We've had some theft and damage we haven't made claims on, trying to establish a good name! But they keep smearing my name! Evidently to avoid paying this claim! And our reason for changing isn't vengeful, it's just practical! What if we're paying all of these policies, and they plan to use their same 'out' that they've devised for the cabin? For any claim we may make in the future? I've acted in better faith than they have! It may all be money down the drain! If we don't have insurance we can count on."

"Most people sue; have you talked to an attorney?"

Mallory remained calm. "No, I guess the claims adjuster has run our claim through their legal department, in case we did. He already taunted me that I can't win, and a trial will just certify me as unstable. Which David and I have both bent over backwards to stay reasonable, and give things a chance to resolve~"

"What happened to the woman you took hostage?"

"A good salesman stays on track, and doesn't let his prospect chase rabbits! You're muddying the waters for your own sale! It isn't our fault~" David was more annoyed with the guy than ever!

"David's right! If we're able to pay the premiums, that's usually all you need to write the policies." Mallory's voice came extra-gentle. She didn't want Hamilton worried that she was going to grab him and his family as her next hostages! She caught the twinkle in David's dark eyes.

"Well, there are a lot of people wondering about it," Hamilton defended himself, "so while we're out together~"

"You thought you'd question us, and report back!" Mallory's tone turned decidedly crisp! "Minding other peoples' business while your own is in a sad state of affairs is really fruitless! Unless someone in the church is willing to pay you for your gossip! We didn't meet with you so we could satisfy your curiosity or set yourself up as judge, jury, and executioner! Is your license current? And, can you write these policies?"

Totally disgusted, Joe's wife answered for him!

"Hey Bransom, good time in Little Rock"? Dawson's frosty voice! "Want you back here at one o'clock for a budget meeting."

Erik made a face! "Budget meeting! Not exactly my forte! Summers dive netted a treasure trove of info-"

"Yeah, leave it in the capable hands of the Arkansas Bureau! Let their labs and experts sort it out!"

Erik looked at him sharply! Budgets are one thing; but this investigation crosses state lines! What if the state lab misses something?"

"That's why you need to be in the budget meeting! You can help us balance our budget instead of always spending!"

"Pretty sure I can't help balance any budget," Bransom grumbled.

"Why not"? Dawson annoyed with the attitude.

"I just gave my genie the rest of the week off!"

Un-amused Dawson shot back. "Don't give anyone time off without checking with your superiors first! Got that?"

"Yeah, I got it! Look, I'm not the one that's costing the money! Treat me like I'm the bad guys here! Crime is surging, and criminals aren't cutting back on any of their operations! I understand the Federal Government's being in a jam; but easing off on crime, because fighting it costs? That just doesn't make sense!" Erik sat through the meeting and discouraged, escaped to his desk! Everyone wanted a balanced budget, order, and advances up the pay scale; but no one was willing to bite the bullet and cut back! 'Let everyone else cut back!' seemed to be the hue and cry! He checked emails and was glad to see some things that were helpful. Ivan Summers, Colonel Ahmir, and Delia O'Shaughnessy! He squinted at Delia's short missive, wondering why he hadn't considered what now seemed obvious! Ryland O'Shaughnessy's last love interest!

Trent arrived home with a gallon pickle jar under his arm! The thing was heavy!

Sonia greeted him with a kiss and a puzzled expression!

"From the office!" he explained. "To help us with Megan's bills"!

A worried face popped around the corner! "I thought you said everything's taken care of!"

Trent's resonant laugh filled the space. "It is! Good thing! Although this was sacrificial-uh-it wouldn't go far toward what the costs were! Also, I'm not sure it's okay for me to accept!"

Sonia laughed. "But you couldn't resist bringing it home to examine every last coin!"

He shrugged amiably.

"I wish I could help," Megan's earnest expression. "I guess I should get interested so I know which ones are valuable."

Trent's eyes met hers! "Well, I have quite a few books and magazines on the subject, whenever you're serious! If you really want to help, you still can! You can help me turn them with all the heads up!"

Rather than drifting back to the TV, she scooted up to the table as he dumped the jar's contents. He marveled as nimble little fingers attacked the coins!

Magnifying glass first for a casual once-over; then anything interesting or worn, received further examination beneath a loupe. Megan watched, fascinated, as a small but separate pile built up.

"Okay, now I'll check all the tails." He glanced at her apologetically, but she was already turning the coins. His magnifying glass moved slowly as he pulled one batch closer for examination and pushed those already checked out of the way! "Ah," a sudden sigh escaped.

"What? What?" Megan launched from her chair to peer over his shoulder.

"Double stamped quarter! Old too, silver! I'm wondering if an area collector died, and the collection fell to family members dumb enough to dispose of the coins at face value! I was shocked to find two very rare coins in Jeremiah's vending machine change!"

Megan's face glowed at the mention of the name. "Do you mean last week in New York?"

Trent frowned as perception grew. "No, actually, Jeremiah and Mr. Faulkner came to lend us moral support at the hospital! They didn't really stay! Just popped in! But it meant the world to Mom and me!"

Tears popped into expressive eyes. "I thought I saw Jeremiah, and that he was praying for me! But then-I figured-I must have been-dreaming-Wow, it means the world to me, too!"

Trent bit his tongue, but Megan picked up on it. "What? I'm not going to start wheezing if you tell me not to set my sights so high!"

He laid the quarter and magnifying glass aside and met her fearful eyes. "Okay, that's the last thing I'd ever tell you, Meggy! I want you to set your sights higher than that! You deserve the best!"

She flushed and lowered her gaze. "Spoken like a good dad! I-I'm so embarrassed-I don't deserve anybody even decent!"

His heart broke at her self-condemnation! And although she had stopped purposely bringing on her symptoms, he worried about how the emotion might affect her breathing!

"Well, I'll say this, although, in your heart, you already know it! God is too gracious and kind to give any of us what we deserve! Megan, everyone makes mistakes, and when they come to themselves, they wonder what possessed them-"

She nodded, lip quivering, and he reached for her to pull her close! She melted against him and the healing tears broke free!

At last, he pushed her away to meet her eyes. "Okay, stop crying! You can't cry and breathe at the same time!"

She caught a shuddering breath and moved to the paper towel roll to wipe eyes and nose. When she returned, he chose his words carefully. "Megan, you're so young to be so caught up with boys, and whether you have a lot of admirers! I mean, there's so much pressure not to enjoy being a little girl!"

She nodded. "Yes, like you barely have a grasp of."

He nodded seriously. "Old people have a better grasp than you give us credit for! But you're right; I can't walk in your skin to experience your personal peer pressure! Let me show you one verse, and then we'll finish so Mom can set-" he looked at his assorted piles. "Let's go out for dinner! You pick where! And the verse is:

Isaiah 55:9 For as the heavens are higher than the earth, so are my ways higher than your ways, and my thoughts than your thoughts!"

She nodded. "That means that if I relax and leave the choice to God, He will provide me with a better mate than I could ever choose. I'm going to memorize it!"

"Good, and don't expect Him to put him on our doorstep this year!"

Tears dried, her eyes sparkled impishly! "Okay, but by the end of next year, I want to know who-"

He gigged her in the ribs!

Roger sank into his recliner, weary, but pleased with the numbers for *Sanders-Chandler's* previous quarter. Beth flounced in haughtily, ruining his moment of joy. Figuring he was hung whether he pursued the problem or let it ride, he opted for the latter!

'Dumb, Roger!' he castigated himself silently! Never the right choice in thirty years of marriage!

"What'd I do now?" Not that he wanted to know! And not that she'd tell him without hours of wheedling and pleading. He felt for his car keys! Maybe it was time to walk away!

She turned around, exploding with hurt and frustration! "Not once, since I've tried to change, have you paid me a compliment! You didn't like it when I didn't work on myself! And-"

He rose to face her, silencing the *Braves* game!

"You know what, Beth? For thirty years I have worked on complimenting you! Who you are! And all you do! And how you look! And I've been as sincere as could be! Look, I know I spent a few years putting everything in jeopardy-but even in that time, I honestly loved everything about you! I-I realize I'm still 'Paying the piper' for my past indiscretions, but I'm just so tired of it-when I say nice things to you-things from my heart, you act like I'm lying! You accuse me of lying! I guess I'm worn out with trying to convince you of my love and admiration, if you insist on hating yourself! I have noticed the hair styles, and make-up, and cuter clothes than ever! I'm sorry if it just seems more prudent for me to say nothing than to get my head chopped off! I can't say the right lines with the proper inflections!" Misery twisted his features, but before he could continue, the thought struck him of what walking away would cost him! With startling truth gaining clarity, he backed cautiously from the figurative precipice he teetered on!

He opened his arms and she moved toward him. Although still miffed at the entire conflagration, he closed his arms around her! How much would he finesse a client, to get that one lucrative contract? How would he make phone calls, and follow-up emails, business gifts, and expensive meals? Whether he liked them or not, was beside the point! Their money was a part of their make-up that he did like! Sadly, he viewed reconciliation with his distant mate as good business sense, rather than even as the way for a Christian man to act! Whatever the disparate motives, they had him double-timing along a singular course of action! With millions on the line, Roger Sanders could come up with the right lines, properly inflected, to be convincing!

He squeezed gently. "It may be too late, but I have noticed! Maybe I've been afraid to break the magic spell Diana and Mallory put on you! Uh-" he hesitated. This one could really be dynamite! "You've lost some weight, too; am I right?"

She relaxed in his arms before meeting his gaze. "Twenty-five pounds, and, I haven't been trying that hard! Just staying busier! I really love the blog, and it's actually growing a following!"

Something about her shy admission tugged at his emotions and he nodded. "That was something, your getting that interview with that big name chef in New York!"

She repeated the unpronounceable name musically, and he laughed.

"Yeah, exactly! That's the dude I meant!"

David placed a call to Mr. Prescott, to follow up on an email! Not to pay the insurance renewals! They couldn't afford paying overlapping premiums, but neither did he want any coverage to lapse.

Preston's bass laugh rumbled through the air waves to David's phone! "Wow! You switched every policy? That must have been a pain!"

"Not too bad," David responded. "We found a licensed guy who wasn't doing much anyway; he did a great job getting us switched over."

"You're not saving that much." Prescott's words were cautious, not wanting to sound like David was inexperienced, and that he had all the answers. "As a matter of fact-"

"It's actually costing us more," David finished for him. "The other company still hasn't settled our claim on the cabin, and they actually impugn Mallory's integrity every time we bring it up! With all of our policies at their mercy, we're not sure they won't use their same unfounded accusations to weasel out of other claims! We're tired of what we pay, to get nothing!"

"They still haven't settled that? Even after you guys found out who set the fire?"

"Yeah, they basically accused us of murdering Sunquist to prevent his denying setting the fire! And also, they bring up the other shootings in the Tucson hotel and the incident with Mrs. Allenby-"

"Hmmmph! Surprised you didn't shop a new carrier before this, in light of all that! Does Daniel know?"

David grimaced. "I'm not sure! No reason why he should, either way! Since you handle our books now! We're not a couple of cry-babies!"

"Well, no, but Daniel's putting a rider on his current policy with them, for the new oil drilling operation-"

"Well, do whatever you think's best about mentioning it to him. We're not trying to be vindictive with the company or persuade anyone else away from them. We just need to do what we feel is right for us!"

With another hearty laugh! "I understand. I'll make sure the automatic draw gets cancelled. The new policies are already-"

"Yep! Premiums paid for six months! Full coverage in effect as of yesterday! And the old is still in effect until the end of next month! We should be good to go! Thanks! Appreciate all you do!"

"Roger, why did you get me a ten pound box of chocolates?"

He grinned! "Why do you think? Because I love you! Did the flowers come?"

"They are beautiful! And not fattening!" She turned serious. "Thank you for being so thoughtful!"

He nodded, grateful for any brownie points he could muster.

"Which of Beth's famous recipes are you planning to whip into dinner?" He fought annoyance as he took in the kitchen, sparkling clean, without a hint of food prep! Images of money bags with $1,000,000.00 stenciled on their sides, inserted themselves into his mind! (Not exactly noble, but whatever maintained his poise) "Well, you know what; you look absolutely fantastic! Why should I hide you away in the kitchen, when I can be seen with you on my arm? Eat your heart out, world! Let's go to Little Rock for a fabulous dinner! I can make a reservation during the drive! Bring that box of candy and I can turn it into a five pound box faster than you can say, 'Five pound box'!"

She giggled.

Nanci packed a bag for a day excursion! The previous day, she had visited major tourist sites in Athens, feeling strangely lonely and unsettled! Kind of a first for her since starting her job with Deborah! Maybe it was seeing Daniel~she sighed! What an idiot Waverly~she fought tears, trying to forget the humiliating ordeal of crashing the corporate event at *The View*! Neither Mallory nor Deborah had given her a chance to explain, but at least she still had the dream job! She wasn't sure the explanation was plausible anyway; probably just come across as a lame excuse! She fought the vague sadness as she stepped onto deck into a puddle of weak sunshine! A little chilly; she pulled an adorable sweater jacket free from the bag and tied it carelessly around her shoulders!

"Oh, my," a pleasant looking fellow cruiser sighed admiringly, "wherever do you find so many cute things? I wore Harry out dragging him all over creation trying to find a wardrobe for this cruise."

Nanci smiled her warmest at the couple! "Well, out of sympathy for Harry," she drew a glossy catalog free and extended it.

Bright eyes met Nan's gaze. "Thank you! But I like to feel the texture and try things to see how they look on me! You've such a school girl figure~"

"I don't blame you," Nanci commiserated. "But, I'd like to suggest that you at least give us a try! If you'd like made to order, you can fly in and have a dress form fitted~and then any of the styles that come out, you can call and get them custom-made! They're slightly more expensive that way~"

An arthritis-knobbed hand with bright red nail polish grasped at the jacket, and scrunched a handful of fabric.

"See! No wrinkles!" Nanci didn't mind the hands-on prospect. "Our companies always use the finest fabrics and workmanship! And we have a very reasonable return policy, although we have a high percentage rate of customer satisfaction!"

"Okay, just take the book, Maggie! We may give it a try! What do we have to lose? Thank you, Ma'am! You have a pleasant day!" Steering Maggie by her elbow, he maneuvered toward the gangway where other cruisers jostled one another to disembark.

"Hey, Cade; what's up?" Mallory hoped for good news as she listened, perplexed, "Of course! I always keep my emails checked! I'm in business! I haven't received any-"

Frowning, she clicked her computer screen to bring up the internet, "From several days ago? I can check my trash, but I never delete your emails without reading them. What was it about?"

"The sample from the Atchafalaya"! His voice dropped to such a conspiratorial whisper she could barely hear him.

Mallory's grin spread as the image came to mind of Amelia's forcing Avery to play Sunday School! 'Ah, the *Deep and Wide* drill site.' "Whadya find?"

She clicked as the email resent!

"Oh, you have got to be kidding me, Cade!"

Chapter 26: GOALS

Stupefied, Mallory recovered enough to hit the intercom! "David, can you come in here a sec?"

Startled at the unexpected summons, he jumped and ran to the opposite office suite, appearing anxiously in her doorway.

She motioned him in. "Shut the door."

Complying, he crossed the office in a few long strides to gaze over her shoulder at the screen. "Uh-is that what I think it is?"

"Isn't it the most beautiful-" her awed voice died away!

He straightened. "Not next to you! You eclipse everything around you!"

She smiled. "Cade said he sent this email last week! Then he wondered when he didn't get any feedback from me-believe me, if I'd seen it, he could have heard my feedback from here! I wonder how I can let Lilly know! Then I should delete-"

"I'm guessing Lilly knows!" David's measured response! "Hence, why you never saw the first email!"

Her startled eyes met his! "Uh-yeah-that would explain it; wouldn't it?" She nodded, "So delete-" Still, she paused to examine the photo again in wonder!

Trent and Megan replaced seventy-one cents in change, worth twenty-four dollars to collectors. Not bad! He put it in the office kitty for flowers for funerals or fellow employees who were hospitalized, then returned the jar of change!

"You sure go by the rule book," Rob gritted.

"Okay, come in my office for a minute, would you, please?" He led the way and closed the door. "Look, Rob, I don't pretend to be perfect, but I've found that going by the rule-book has stood me in pretty good stead."

Addington sank into a chair opposite the big desk, taking in a few of Trent's personal items, even though the government office was rather bare-bone! Pictures of smiling family, handsome blotter set on the desk, model trains, the leather attaché case featuring the raised railroad design.

"It's just a jar of change, for-" he let an oath slip. "Surely you have bills from those days of Megan's being on life-support-I mean, I'm sure it's hardly a drop in the bucket! But it's a way for us to show you we care!"

"I know, and I appreciate the kindness, but I do live by the rule book! Oh, and not just the one for federal employees-I try to live by the Bible, and when I obey the Lord, He blesses me."

"Then why does Megan even have asthma? I mean, how can you buy into this God-business? And you're not supposed to haul me in here and preach at me-"

"Sorry! But I did get a miracle and got Meggy back! The reason-you're not a happy man-"

"Like you know anything about me, Morrison! Yeah! I hate DC! Whose fault is that?"

Trent shrugged. "I don't know! Whose fault do you think-"

"Yours! You uprooted me from Arizona! We were so happy there!"

Trent's level gaze held the other man's.

"Okay, then why did you make the grab for gold nuggets when we were supposed to be working? If you were happy and contented, you would have been happy doing your job!"

"You keep bringing that up!"

"Sorry." Trent rose dismissively. "I won't bring it up again! You're right; I've beaten that horse to death! Why don't you take the afternoon off?"

Nanci strolled at a leisurely pace, taking in the sites of Volos, Greece with little real interest. It didn't matter; all she needed to do was stroll around in the cute clothing, offering business card or catalog when someone commented. It wasn't like she had to write the places up-

She caught herself up short! 'Duh! Nanci'! She slid gracefully into a scrolled wrought iron chair at a cute sidewalk café to allow her lightning bolt realization to sink in and assume a more concrete form! She smiled to herself! Everyone around her was inventing and reinventing themselves, almost on a daily basis! And she remained stagnant! Maybe still too caught up with Daniel Faulkner, while he was moving on! She sat, stunned, startled by where her thought-trail might lead! To a summit somewhere! Her eyes riveted on Mt. Pelion! 'What had always been her goal? Not having Daniel, so much as having money! A goal which never did work; selling herself short to men who had no intention of marrying her, or sharing what they shared with their wives! Tears wanted to come, but she forced them back! 'No time now for poor lil ole me'. Those plans were daydreams, stupid and naïve, even as she'd grown sin-hardened. For the moment she forgot how lovely she must look, dressed in her favorite hot pink, sliding beneath an umbrella of the same bewitching hue, her hair ruffling gently in a capricious breeze from the harbor!

She castigated herself for not having a notebook with her! 'They' always carried notebooks, in one form or another! Mostly electronic now; another way to announce they'd arrived! To capture the ethereally fleeting wisps known as ideas. Her lips parted in silent laugher at herself. 'No one had ever accused Nanci Burnside-Nichols of being a thinker, or having any good ideas! And her idea now was far from original! But, still-"

The possibilities infused her lovely features with a new glow! 'A travel blog! And why not?' She loved that this job entailed exciting destinations! Destinations that she at one time figured could only be reached by snaring the right man with her feminine charms!

'I can do it without a man.' The thought was so revolutionary to her that she feared to speak audibly, but then as the truth dawned, "I have been doing it without a man! I can do this!" She sipped a latte as she scribbled on cute paper napkins. Now she needed to locate an internet café and contact Mallory! She sent a long email!

Dear Mallory,

Thank you for overlooking our faux pas at The View and being so discreet, sending us on our way! We deserved to be fired, I guess! Rather than a bonus! I know David's getting with a financial structure guy he knows from TU, but as I've strolled around Volos,

Greece, a thought occurred to me, that I might incorporate and write a travel blog! I love the travel involved with my job, and the pay's great, but-this idea has captivated me-So, I've wondered the best way to approach using the ten thousand dollar bonus to incorporate! Buy a web-site, a good camera, and a laptop? I felt confident about it until I started trying to sell you on the idea-maybe I should just be happy with what I have! That's more than I ever hoped to have, and certainly more than I deserve! If it seems like a bad idea-

The response came so fast that she was scared to open it.

Dear Nanci,

We didn't know you didn't have a laptop! Your idea is outstanding! Get a laptop before you leave shore, courtesy of DiaMo. Then once you're set up for emails, I'll have our attorney send you the forms to incorporate! Do you not get emails on a smart phone? Get a good phone, too! And the camera! Save receipts! They're life-savers at tax time! We will reimburse for the laptop and phone; the camera is on you. But I would get that immediately, too, so you can shoot several pictures of your present locale! It's such a great idea to fit hand and glove with your job! I know you spend a lot of time just at sea-I'm sure the water all starts to look alike! And working on a blog during those times; well, why not? Just be sure you don't hibernate in your cabin so no one sees the clothes! Sheer genius, Nanci! Here's Sam's email; I recommend his company to design your web page! Give it plenty of thought so you know exactly what you want! Check out the competition so you have an idea which names are taken! Excited for you!

Mallory

Dazed, Nanci paid to have the missives printed out, then gazed at the proprietor in consternation!

"Pro-blem'"?

"Uh-yeah-a little"! She smiled. "This looks like Greek to me!"

With an apologetic smile, he punched a button to print in English, and charged her again!

"Ciao! Have a good one!" She left without arguing! The Greek economy was in the tank, and she had too much to accomplish!

The port didn't have much to offer in the way of electronics, and she made her way back to the cruise ship slightly disappointed, but buoyed up by her blossoming concept!

Alexandra looked up to see a tall, lanky frame looming in her doorway! "Welcome back! You missed the first snowfall!"

"That's what I hear! My dad told me things are progressing here. Hope he's behaving himself! Abby's settling into the house, and I thought I should come over and report in!"

Alexandra nodded; hoping the new bride with the long pedigree could adjust and be happy in a double-wide trailer with few near-by amenities. She expressed her concern to her mining engineer, and he grinned. "You're doing it!"

Her head bobbed up and down eagerly! Yeah, and she loved it! Her only hope was that Abby would too! "Well, chow's five to seven! And you're welcome any time!" She blushed as she mumbled something about the newlyweds-

"Pretty sure we'll be there! Neither of us are your gourmet chefs!"

"Just so you're warned; chow hall fare isn't exactly gourmet, either!"

Rob Addington headed toward the Pentagon Mall, then, changing his mind, pulled his phone free to call his wife.

"What happened," she demanded! "I tried to reach you at the office, and they told me you'd been sent home for the afternoon! Rob-what is it with you?"

"Just dumb, Baby! I'm sorry! It won't happen again! I promise!"

"Are you fired?"

"No, it's just for the afternoon, and I've already gotten some clarity!" Since he was busted, he was glad he had decided to call her! "Why don't you go pick the boys up early and I'll be to the apartment in an hour to pick you all up! I've been so bitter about the city, instead of Arizona I haven't even considered seeing the sights! I thought we could drive to Philly tonight, get there in time to see the Liberty Bell; then drive on to New York City in the morning, see the Statue of Liberty before heading back! It'll be a quick trip, but maybe fun!"

A pause! The plan did sound fun; except if he really was just sent home for the afternoon~

"I'll call Trent and ask if I can have tomorrow, too!"

"Okay, I'm on my way after the boys! Are you sure the car can make it that far?"

David regarded Mallory, glowing with a barely bottled-up excitement!

"Tomorrow! Finally!" He forced his voice to sound like what he hoped matched her enthusiasm, but she still shot him a concerned glance.

"Has your head been hurting again?"

"Nope! I'm great! I guess thinking about what I need to accomplish before we leave~"

His shaky smile in pallid face belied his words, and she thought the work was pretty well cleared for their pending departure.

"Okay, well if something's wrong; you'll tell me?"

"Yeah; like I said, tension! Everything's finally on go!"

Still, despite his reassurances, he could see her glow fading into doubt.

She finished dressing in an amazing suit fashioned from white wool knit! Slender skirt topped with a fine knit, screen printed sweater of a stark, wintery aspen forest! Ghostly pale trees with a few defining lines of deeper gray-brown, snow-covered. The scrumptious swing jacket revealed lining repeating the sweater design. Shoes and handbag in the gray-brown pulled everything together. Usually, David raved about her ensembles, but this one stood out! She hoped he was okay, as she tried not to fret about possibly ruined plans! Well, at least delayed. "Lord, please let him be alright," She pled.

Nanci changed into dressier wear, and strolled along the deck while she awaited her dinner slot! Excited, she was still frustrated about not being able to acquire the necessary electronics! The shopping aboard the cruise liner was paltry as well. Evidently the merchants assumed travelers would arrive well-supplied with electronic gadgets! She paid too much for a laptop! But she needed at least this much, just to start! Mallory had offered to supply that, but she hadn't said pay the most you can! She frowned. Ten thousand dollars, which sounded like a lot, seemed to be dwindling fast! Maybe she should change her mind and let Higgins help her invest~and it wasn't like she needed the money! This was a very good job~And she was disappointed not to have gotten any pictures, of either the Greek town, or the sensational sunset other people on deck had been snapping happily away at! She was fairly certain what she planned to name her blog: *At the Seaside, With Nanci Burnside*! She wished she had a photo of the phosphorescent pink ball of a sun sliding into the Mediterranean, staining the swells and gilded clouds with the same spectacular hue!

Barely settled behind her desk, Mallory checked her phone! Deborah! Usually, Deborah tried not to call, so she felt a certain alarm! Was everything lining up to put a monkey wrench into her long-awaited plan?

"Hey, Deborah; what's up?" She attempted to infuse her voice with a gaiety she was no longer feeling.

"Like you do not know what is up, Mallory O'Shaughnessy! Why do you keep messing with one of my best employees?"

Distressed, Mallie strove for calm. "Do you mean Nanci? I didn't mess with her; she sent me an email about the blog that sounded like a good idea! It won't affect her productiveness! It will actually give her the illusion of being busy and productive in the public spaces, rather than like she's just hanging out to get noticed! She's hoping to earn extra income from it, and I hope she can! As you've realized, there's only so much we can do for our employees~"

"Why did she not contact me? I have helped my aunt to incorporate and get set up in business! You are not the only one who knows about these things! And you are trying to get her from me for *DiaMal*!"

Mallory put her phone on conference on the desk before her so she could grasp her head in frustration with both hands. If Deborah only knew how much Diana did not want Nanci for *DiaMal*, she could relax! And it was a good thing Nanci had approached her; Deborah would have led Nanci the bank loan route! Nanci's previous fraud and monetary mismanagement wouldn't look good on a loan app! All information not necessary for Deborah to know~

"Okay, Deborah, I understand why you're upset! But the way things are working, it's really for everyone's best! Tell me; when have I ever tried to hurt you, your feelings, or your company? I'm an ally! She loves what she's doing, Deborah! Working for you! But this plan of hers is a perfect match, to supplement her income dramatically, and~" She paused. "She'll be wearing your designs on the blog; so they'll garner even more attention! She can actually add links~" Mallory paused, enchanted by the perfect plan as it expanded before her.

Deborah was quick to grasp it also, and she quickly apologized, laughing with delight at the prospects! "Oh, yes; a whole new world of contacts opening up to *Rodriguez, Incorporated*! If this blog is successful, imagine the increased exposure to my beautiful products!"

Mallory's frustration evaporated, too, at the inspired direction the business plan was going. "Uh~yeah~I guess then it's in our best interests to help her make sure it's successful!"

She closed the call, thanking the Lord for helping turn an explosive situation into more potential for earnings!

Nanci lingered on deck, taking in the inkiness of sky and water; differentiated by stars in one, and ripples in the other! Far off, she thought she could make out a ribbon of light, indicating some city or hamlet on shore. She studied her itinerary and the scant information on Volos; well, not scant, but barely the high-points for the day excursion! Untypically for her, she researched on her new laptop, to fill in more information for the first edition of her blog.

She emerged from her study to notice they were navigating from the Aegean Sea into the Dardanelle Straits; which would lead to the Sea of Marmara, up the Bosporus, before finally entering the Black Sea! Never a noted scholar, she was suddenly filled with curiosity! She needed a printer, too; to run off all of her research results! For the present, though, she simply scrawled the high points down as fast as she could!

"Why so engrossed?"

She jumped at a sudden presence behind her, and he laughed, pleased with himself for startling her.

The guy was good-looking enough; a little on the paunchy side. Exuding self-confidence that his advances would be welcome, he grinned! "Why are you working so hard? Thought cruises were supposed to be vacations! Would you care to join me for a drink?"

Not a teetotaler in the least, she considered the offer! "Thanks anyway; maybe another time? I'm on a roll here! I guess I'll keep at it for the moment."

A hard stare, followed by an indifferent shrug told her 'maybe another time' wasn't her call! 'Whatever! Men, like buses, came along every few minutes!'

He strolled away; then seemed drawn back. "Are you into a project of your own? Or do you have a really mean boss?"

"Actually, a project of my own"! Just saying it and savoring starting up her own company flushed her with confidence.

Ah! Self-employed! I see!" His respect seemed to climb, so she confided, "Yes, my job entails traveling, so I'm starting a travel blog-"

"Oh-ho! A blog! A travel blog-" the respect's morphing into his treating her like a joke, rankled!

Yeah! She knew everyone was doing this gig! She just planned on doing it better! And she needed some pictures! Overlooking the intended insult, she extended her hand. "Nanci Burnside! You took quite a few pictures today; didn't you?"

"I thought you were watching me," he gloated.

"I couldn't pull my gaze away," she played along. Actually, everyone on the shore excursion had been taking pictures; everyone but her! "Do you mind showing me your shots; in consideration of allowing me to use them in my first edition"?

"Ah! First edition! Good to know you're so seasoned at this, too! What would be in it for me; letting you see my pictures?" he winked meaningfully.

Not a novice at the cat-and-mouse game, she came back swiftly. "If you have anything useful, I'll credit you for the photography! If you have a company I could plug-"

He moved closer, and she smelled bourbon, even as she backed away. Unflinching, he leered, "I have an advertising budget bigger than your annual salary, so I don't think a plug from your unviewed blog holds much incentive for me! What else do you have to offer?"

"There you are, Dear! We've been looking for you! Oh, my; are we interrupting?" Maggie hurried toward them as Harry hung back.

"Not at all"! Although Nanci wasn't frightened of the admirer, she was glad for an escape. "Harry and Maggie! Why have you been looking for me?" She recognized the couple from the morning and wasn't surprised by their response!

"Well," Harry began, "Maggie really does enjoy shopping, getting out with her friends, going to the stores! And I think it's good for her! But she does come back sometimes, disgruntled at not finding good quality, or clothing that fits! I took your catalog this morning-"

"To be nice and escape from me," Nanci finished the sentence good-naturedly. "And then, even if you were interested a little bit, you didn't want to carry anything extra around with you all day! So you trashed the catalog at the first bin!"

"You watched us?" Maggie was embarrassed.

"Yes'm; it happens all the time! I usually don't try to hand them off to people at the beginning of the day, but you guys stopped me, and so-no problem! Would you like a replacement?" She did a good job masking her horror at being without a copy! Note to herself, not to get so involved with her blogging that she failed to keep up with her paying job! "I'll dash to my cabin and get another and meet you at the coffee shop in thirty minutes?"

"Well, do you have time, dear"?

Nanci couldn't help squeezing the sweet lady warmly. "Yes'm; I think I have another ten or eleven days! Did you guys get any good pictures of the excursion today?"

Mallory buzzed David's office. "Hey, did Alvie text you, too? That she's sick?"

"No, but when she wasn't already in, I wondered," he responded. "The girls'll be okay! I can keep an eye on them."

"Well, I can bring them in here with bunches of toys! No problem! You said you have lots on your plate-"

"No, they're fine! They obey me better!"

Annoyed, she did a slow count! 'No need to growl at her; he was the one who said he had so much going on! And she could make the girls mind!' "Okay, buzz me when you want to go eat!" She disconnected.

Rob was barely surprised when his boys grumbled non-stop throughout the trip! The historical stuff was 'bor-ing'! They were cramped in the back seat! Even what he thought would be a particular treat: a night in a motel was source for more whining. He couldn't get away from Trent Morrison's words, about being an unhappy man! Maybe that was what his boys were learning from him; to be unhappy, no matter what! Silent and thoughtful, he refrained from reaming them out! Still, when they arrived back at their apartment, the kids attacked the luggage, hauling it to the second story and cleaning up old French fries and fast food cups!

"Dad, I never knew that about the Statue of Liberty! Can we do this again sometime? I have an assignment for History, so now I'm going to do it about the Liberty Bell! Because someone else already picked Lady Liberty"!

Rob tousled his hair and loped up the flight of stairs to help start laundry.

Mallory fidgeted! With her desk cleared in preparation for this trip, she was basically marking time! When the intercom buzzed, she pressed the button quickly. "Everyone in there hungry"?

There was hesitation, and then after an interval, Amelia's tearful voice! "Mommmeee, I think Daddy's day-ud!"

Mallory could hardly process! 'Dead! Was David teasing? Scaring them, to be funny?' She froze, unable to get her legs under her, to launch from her chair and across her office! Stricken eyes met Marge and Gina's as she plowed past them, out of the suite, past the Aviary where purple plumage fluttered at her sudden appearance, and through the opposite suite! She stood, horrified, gasping for breath~

Harry and Maggie sipped at coffee beverages as Nanci scrolled through their camera! "Wow, you have some amazing shots! I'm just getting my blog underway, and my budget is limited-"

"Well, Dear, if any of them are something you could use-" Maggie's offer was sweet, but Nanci caught a fleeting expression cross Harry's face.

"Well, thank you for your kindness! You two don't even know me, and you certainly don't owe me anything-" Even as Nanci spoke, she was amazed at herself! That was a switch from her ordinary stance of feeling that she was owed. "So, I was saying, I'm trying to get up and running with as little cash outlay as possible! That doesn't mean I expect you to turn your pictures over to me just because I want a few of them. I was thinking about offering some cash and some credits for the pictures, and if you would be interested in advertising-" She was hesitant to try the approach again after the reception she received from the 'buy you a drink guy'.

Harry's body language sprang to life! "Yeah, whatever your offer is, count me in! I've spent my life with photography being my hobby! I've sent pictures to contests and magazines, to have them rejected! It would just do my soul good to finally make anything on my pictures!"

"Okay, well I don't want to take advantage of you, but what about five hundred dollars for ten pictures? That's only fifty dollars per shot, but then like I said, I'll mention your name in the credits, and-"

"Young lady, consider it a deal!" He pulled a cable from his camera bag. "Just tell me which you want and I'll transfer then to your laptop right now! Do you mind telling me exactly how it is that you're setting yourself up in business?"

"Well, I recently received a ten thousand dollar bonus, but the person paying it out suggested my not receiving it until I could shelter it! So a guy was going to help me invest with another guy-" she paused with a self-conscious laugh. "But yesterday, it came to me that since I travel for my job, starting the blog would be a natural business. And incorporating somehow helps with the taxes! I'm sorry I don't understand it better. Anyway, this attorney, Kerry Larson, is doing my simple S-corporation paper work for a thousand-although, maybe if I recommend him in my blog, he might take fifty dollars or so off! Just thought of that"!

Maggie and Harry exchanged meaningful glances. "A thousand dollars is all?"

Nanci looked confused. "I think so; I mean maybe Mallory got me a deal! Here's the attorney's phone number and email! Like I said, I've never learned some of the things I needed to. So now I'm on this advanced learning curve to catch up!"

"Well, Harry, maybe we should do that, too!" Maggie's tender expression as she addressed her husband made Nanci's throat constrict! 'Would she ever be in such a loving relationship?' Maggie turned her attention to Nanci. "I hate to let you pay us for the pictures! I wish we could just-"

Nanci laughed, fighting tears. "It's okay, Maggie! If five hundred sounds agreeable; I'm delighted! It helps me forge ahead, and-who knows?"

"So with the five hundred we receive for the pictures, and if we take five out of savings, we can swing it-" An eager Maggie!

Harry tried to exercise caution amidst the risk of being swept up in emotion. "Okay, well, that's *if*, maybe a big *if*, we can get the paperwork done for a thousand! I always thought it cost a lot more!"

Maggie released a laughing 'harumph'; she was always the one fearful of his photography dream! Suddenly he wanted to drag his feet? "Call the number!" An impatient red fingernail thumped at the business card.

"What if he laughs?"

"Okay, don't give your name; just ask if a thousand is in the ballpark! If he laughs, we can hang up! This may be the answer-"

"That we've prayed for! Oh Harry of little faith"! His eyes alight, he pulled his phone free!

Grabbing the phone, Mallory dialed 911, telling about David before explaining about the exclusive parking area and express penthouse suite elevators.

"Okay, help's en route, Ma'am. Stay with me! You said he's breathing?"

"Um-uh-yes, Ma'am; he is! He's out cold, though! Uh, he said his head was-well, he said it wasn't-uh-but-uh he had a head injury before! Should-uh-I call our doctor in Arizona? It's okay, Amelia-Daddy's not dead! The doctors are-Uh-yes'm! Uh, almost twenty-six-okay-Amelia, calm down; you didn't-uh-yeah, there's a little blood! I think when he fell-Uh-yeah, hey, Diana-it's me-uh-can you come? Yes, Ma'am, he's still breathing! I'm-uh-talking to my little girls-uh-and calling-Hey, Pastor-" Mallory dissolved into tears, unable to speak!

A car from building security and an Addington patrol car waited as Mallory made her way to the parking space with all three small daughters! Tears rolled as the ambulance roared onto the toll way with the ladder truck right behind! She didn't have keys! They were in David's pocket!

"Mrs. Anderson," the security guy. "We called the police and they sent a patrol car to escort you. Let me help get the girls buckled-"

"I don't-uh-no keys-"

"Okay, get in! You didn't see me do this-" He scrabbled under the dash until he located the wires he sought! "Hey, why don't you let me drive you?"

"No, you have your job-"

He opened the passenger door. "This is my job! I'll call and let 'em know what's going on!"

"Kerry Larson, how may I help you?"

"Yes Sir; my name's Harry Willis! I'm aboard a cruise ship!"

"Lucky man," Kerry quipped, wishing the guy would make his point.

"Well, I consider myself blessed! We were speaking with a young woman I believe you are familiar with, Nanci?"

Kerry combed his mental contact list! Quite a few Nancy's, but then he put the cruise with the name! Ah yes, one of the three interlopers at *The View*! The one he was currently working on incorporating! And this guy seemed to be a Christian, correcting *lucky* to *blessed*! "Ah yes, Miss Burnside! How can I assist you, Mr. Willis?"

"Okay, well, Miss Burnside was telling us about her business getting started up, and she said she was getting incorporated for a thousand dollars! Uh, is that a special rate, just for her?"

"It's actually a special rate for Mallory Anderson, my sister-in-law! What type of corporation are you interested in?"

"You know what; I've probably already taken more of your time than I can afford to pay for-"

Kerry's laugh rolled all the way from Dallas to the Sea of Marmara! "Okay, I don't actually charge by the minute, Mr. Willis! If you're talking a straightforward S-corporation, I can extend my special sister-in-law rate to you! Give me your email address and a receptionist will send you the necessary paperwork! Print it, fill it out, get it notarized and sent back as soon as possible! Meaning a reasonable time frame! By all means enjoy the rest of your cruise."

Dazed, Harry gave the email address with a heartfelt, "Thank you for your time, Sir!"

The building security officer, Curt, pulled into a parking space designated for Emergency Room patrons! He pulled the wires apart and the engine stopped. "I'm helping you," he insisted. Hopping out, he released Alexis and Avery as Mallory pulled the still-sobbing Amelia free.

"Amelia, you didn't hurt Daddy! His head already hurt this morning!"

"I did hurted him, and he said, 'Ow, Amelia! That hurt! Just stop!' and then he flopped back!"

"Okay, well you just usually wrestle, and you couldn't know-just-you have to walk; stay right with me-"

Mallory couldn't remember feeling this lost since-well, since David had first been hurt! She tried to shove the memories and accompanying dread aside as she dragged Amelia through the automatic doors! She didn't have keys, or the diaper bag! Or her cell phone-She needed to send Curt on his way, but his help was reassuring-"

And then, Marge and Gina were there! With David's wallet, her handbag, the diaper bag, and both of their cell phones! And she could fish the car keys from David's pocket-

"I phoned Dr. Stringer," Gina's greeting; "and he said to have the ER physician call him! Once they make sure David's stable, he wants him moved to Baylor where one of his most respected colleagues is chief of Neurosurgery-" Gina reached for Amelia, swinging her up into her arms against her protests!

Kerry buzzed the receptionist about getting Harold Willis' incorporation underway, trying to decide whether to be pleased or irritated! The thousand dollar fee hardly lined his pockets significantly! There was the research and fees! He sat bending a ruler back and forth, recalling Mallory's pie-graph from a previous corporate meeting! Maybe this Burnside woman could help him make his 'pie' bigger! When her completed application hit his in-box, he used one of her answers as an excuse to phone her.

"Hello, Mr. Larson, did I make a mistake referring you to that couple?" Nanci's alarm! "I'm just so excited-"

"No, listen I appreciate the referral! If you run into any additional would-be entrepreneurs during your travels, I'd appreciate it if you mention me again."

"Or, I could include advertising on my web-page," she suggested eagerly.

"I'm not sure how that would fly with the partners, but an occasional mention in your text might be extremely beneficial. More subtle than a link"!

Nanci got the gist of what he was saying, although she didn't necessarily grasp the semantics!

Even as Kerry engaged in the conversation, mental wheels whirled. 'If he helped corporations get started easily, offering a reasonable fee, who would the same corporations be likely to call upon when further legal questions surfaced? Maybe not all; but surely some! He could give the idea a try, and if it didn't pay out in a reasonable time period-'

While Gina and Marge corralled the girls, Mallory raced to be with David! There was the usual confusion about having all of the insurance info down in black and white- Marge took that over smoothly, leaving the girls to the more capable Gina!

Tears streamed down Mallory's face as she took David's hand and stroked it gently.

His eyes fluttered open and he gazed at her through his haze of pain. "Hey, don't-cry-"

She nodded bravely and wiped her nose and eyes. "Dr. Stringer wants us to get you stabilized here and then transport you to Baylor! He said he knew he left a bone fragment- Why wouldn't he have mentioned that before now?"

David scrunched his eyes closed against the pain. "He did! I've known about it-"

Mallory fought for control, "But you didn't want me to worry-"

Dark, guilty eyes met her steady gaze.

"Yeah-uh-sorry for messing-" his speech slurred, but she knew he referenced the planned trip.

"Don't worry about anything! I'm just glad this didn't happen when we were a million miles out at sea! I mean, believe me-uh-I wish it wasn't happening-

A barely perceptible nod, and then a rally: "Where are the girls?"

In the waiting room with Marge and Gina! Daniel and Diana are coming and so are your parents."

As medical personnel assembled in greater numbers, Mallory eased out to give them space to work! She sagged, scared, but thankful for his regaining consciousness! Although that didn't guarantee anything!

A nurse popped out! "We're on the way for x-ray and MRI, but he says he wants to see his little girls? Here's a bag for his belongings."

Mallory accepted the bag and went to get the girls.

Chapter 27: GAIN

James 4:13 & 14 Go to now, ye that say, To day or to morrow we will go into such a city, and continue there a year, and buy and sell, and get gain:

Wherefore ye know not what shall be on the morrow. For what is your life? It is even a vapour, that appeareth for a little time, and then vanisheth away.

With the ER head trauma resident thoroughly annoyed at the transfer, he thrust the permission form at Mallory, assuring her that she alone assumed responsibility, if the transfer~

"I'll sign!" David reached for the clip board, infuriated that anyone would try to make things more difficult for Mallory to cope with! Still, after the forms were signed, it seemed to take an eternity longer. At last they kissed goodbye as the ambulance doors closed and Mallory's support group arranged who would ride where for the jaunt to Baylor.

Frenzied with worry, Mallory still needed to take care of some phone calls! Marge had cancelled the flights, but Mallory needed to contact the others involved! Privately!

David Higgins' annoyance melted away as Mallory explained the reason behind the canceled flights. "Oh, anything I can do to help?"

Mallory forced her voice to remain steady. "No, I guess not!"

Since Dr. Higgins was unsaved, she didn't request his prayers. "Just take some much deserved time off! We have airline miles accumulated if you'd like to go somewhere-"

"Like?" He hated to jack her up when she was in the midst of calamity, but-

"Like! Lots and lots of miles racked up! If you're thinking international, you might as well-this other thing is going to be on hold-uh-indefinitely." Even as her voice caught, she realized she was doing the right thing, giving her hard-working, though unwilling, head driller, time off now! As she finished the conversation, she knew that Higgins was still strongly pulled toward Nanci! She felt sorry for him; it reminded of all her years being so smitten with David! Maybe he could help with the new web site and blog set up! It seemed like Niqui was picking up Diana's gauntlet, not wanting Sam to help! People and their little grievances-still, some of the challenges, you just had to work through, or around, or whatever!

With a couple of additional calls completed, she returned to the waiting room, where the others kept vigil. The girls were exhausted, and Alexis was asleep! Avery whined, but at least Amelia was busily playing with Nadia and Ryan.

"How could the other doctor have just left a bone fragment?" Lana exclaimed as the waiting grew more and more tedious.

Mallory didn't know! The first surgery with the scrambling through David's brain tissue had left him at death's door; with survival and recuperation looking extremely dim! At least by Dr. Stringer's quitting when he did, she and David had been allowed a little more than another year together! Wonderful times! She couldn't even conceive of continuing without him. Her gaze traveled pensively to her first-born, who was certain that disobeying and tackling her daddy had put him into the present crisis! Mallory's words to the contrary were met by a hard stare from big blue eyes! Big blue eyes that said, 'I'm not allowed to talk back! But I hurt Daddy, and I know it's my fault! No matter what anyone says'!

Mallory returned her attention from her inner musings to Diana's gentle attempt to explain the medical implications to Lana! John rose and paced! Mallory figured they were inwardly blaming her; but at least, they weren't saying so! She quoted a couple of verses to herself from the book of James, about making goals without considering God's will! She fought tears! She felt like she and David did seek God's leadership before each step! It was true though, about life's being so fragile! A vapor! Someone like David, so young, and seemingly so strong! She suddenly wished she could bring Rudy back, to be stung eternally by swarming wasps. She sighed! He was doubtless enduring far worse torment than that! What might the outcome have been, if she had witnessed to him? When he told her 'everything belongs to the good Lord', why hadn't she responded, 'Yes, let's talk about how good He is! He died on the cross for our sins!' Would he have listened? Would it have changed the outcome of their kidnapping David? She wasn't sure if she drifted off, but she snapped to attention when the surgeon appeared, smiling!

David Higgins sighed, cramped into a crowded flight in the airline miles seats. 'I don't look very good', he realized glumly! Not that he usually did! But he had no 'good' clothes with him, whatsoever! He was packed for the work trip that had been scheduled for the past couple of months. Nothing for him to impress Nanci with! Oh well, Yalta would be a sight to see, a pleasant and interesting way to spend a day, even if she told him to get lost! It was amazing to have caught the flight at the last minute.

Kerry finished such a grueling afternoon in court, that the incorporations and new client base slipped his mind! He turned on his phone as he headed toward the parking lot, and saw the message from Tammi about her brother. He called her.

"Hey, sorry to hear about David! What happened-"

He listened to angry, tearful words about a bone fragment- "Okay, well, I just finished in court! Are you at Baylor now? I'm on the way! Praying! Can I bring anyone anything?"

With assurances that there were restaurants and vending machines all over, he sped toward downtown!

Mallory smiled for the first time in hours! To the amazement of the chief of neurosurgery, the fragment lay right on the surface of David's brain, near the site of his original injury. The doctor told them the procedure couldn't have possibly gone any better! And that David was in recovery, and as soon as he came out from the anesthesia, Mallory and John and Lana could see him.

The relief mixed with exhaustion made her giddy! He was okay! It wasn't going to be the same ordeal over again! The trips to the nursing home; the hopeless days and nights! Maybe, a month or so, to fully recover, and the plan could be back on go! If it was the Lord's will! She was sorry, but she hoped it was!

Ryan conked out on Daniel's lap, and Mallory explained to the unreasonable Amelia that Daddy was out of surgery just fine, and as soon as he woke up a little, they could all see him! Comforted, Amelia fell asleep! But still, no one appeared to give the word that David was awake!

Diana was nodding off, too, so Mallory refrained from asking her how long the recovery should take. She waited, and waited!

"We're going to go look for something to eat," John whispered. "That'll probably make them come."

Mallory nodded, hoping so!

Benjamin and Lilly Cowan both leaned back, astounded! "Her daughter sings a Sunday School song, and she is led to such a gem!?" Benjamin's soft, awed tone!

Lilly laughed, not a pleasant sound, but he was accustomed to her. There was more to it than Amelia's singing *Deep and Wide*, but still an incredible method Mallory used to discover treasure-troves with remarkable accuracy!

"Do you remember when Patrick's will was read?"

Benjamin shrugged. He did and he didn't, he guessed.

"On Friday, April 13; if you remember, I was aghast that it worked out that way! Not that I've been superstitious, but I didn't want any force of any kind working against me. With the uncertain weather in Arkansas that week, I hoped it would be postponed! However, looking back, the date has become important in that it portended incredible good. Because before the proceedings began, Mallory opened her Bible for strength for whatever~ I can't imagine how she must have felt; but even so young, her trust in Jehovah and the Messiah was rock-solid."

He nodded, not minding the narrative! There would be a purpose to the story!

The first verse she read that morning was:

> *Proverbs 13:1 A wise son heareth instruction: but a scorner heareth not rebuke.*

She was prepared to follow Patrick's wishes, whatever that should mean!"

"Yes, and she continues to listen to him through his trail of mysterious clues! His premise was that Arkansas diamonds eroded from the dikes and were washed down the Little Missouri into the Ouachita, and then into the Red River, the Mississippi, and the Atchafalaya! She wanted permission to drill in the Mississippi Delta, but it's a wetlands habitat, and already busy and heavily industrialized."

Grasping the stone securely she surveyed it once more through her loupe! The blue was lovely and even; no broken edges, and no major flaws. Trigons confirmed the identity of the seventeen carat stone.

Mallory looked up as the door to the surgical wing opened. She slipped silently toward the medical person who emerged.

"I'm Mallory Anderson-" She extended her hand automatically, and the nurse introduced herself in kind, "Melody Craft".

"Mrs. Anderson, I'm afraid we're having a hard time getting your husband to respond! The cranial pressure is still down, and the surgery went smoothly; Dr. Rivers is aware of the situation! It's really rather mysterious-and, we have antibiotics going, of course. There's really no reason we can see for his coma. He seems to have hit the side of his head when he fell; that's the source of the blood that you noticed! It shouldn't-"

Mallory backed against the door frame for support! 'It couldn't be happening again; could it?' She forced her knees to support her. "So, what? Uh-just-wait and see?"

"For now, that's really all that I can tell you. Can I get you anything?"

Shaking her head negatively, she moved away. Her voice wouldn't come! She needed to find Pastor and Lana and tell them the latest! She dreaded bearing the news, but they deserved to know!

"Sit down, Mallory, before you fall down!" Pastor crossed the café in a couple of bounds and slid a chair behind her. From her expression, he was afraid to ask.

Her voice came out in a weird squeak. "He-uh-he isn't waking up like they-uh think-uh-he should!"

John's immediate fear was that David was gone, so Mallory's words caused relief to resonate in his voice! "Okay, he came back to us before, when the brain trauma was a lot more severe! It'll be okay, Mallory!" He patted her shoulder reassuringly as Lana stared numbly!

"Wh-what exactly did the doctor say?" Lana's brown eyes against pallid face indicated her terror.

"I didn't talk to the doctor again. I think he's gone home. It was a recovery room nurse, Melody Craft. She seemed real nice; they don't know why-just we need-to-uh-wait and see. Hopefully-uh-he'll come back-before the hospital boots him-if I have -to move him-I don't know-here-Arkansas-"

"Okay, breathe! You're getting ahead of yourself! I'm getting you a cup of coffee, and you need to eat something!"

John Anderson felt curiously lighthearted! "Let's pray; I almost forgot!" He said a quick prayer and rushed to the line for sustenance for her.

"Good job, Summers!" Erik updated the Arkansas Agent on the latest news about David, but then he pursued some case news. Arkansas was going full-steam-ahead with tracking down and arresting the culprits implicated by Summers' dive on the yacht! Although the evidence lacked chain of evidence and wouldn't be admissible in court, it opened up lots of leads in the investigation! Considering the budget woes at the federal level, he let it rest! As long as someone was on it! Not that each state didn't have money problems-at least this was on go for now! "Keep praying for David, and I'll keep you posted on his condition."

"Soph! Look at this!" In Jay's exuberance, he forgot his wife couldn't see what he brandished.

"The newspaper, Jay!" she recognized the unmistakable smell of the ink. With a laugh; "What does it say?"

"Oh, sorry! Uh-the front page headline says that Silas Remington, long time headmaster and esteemed citizen-blah-blah found dead on the grounds of a hunting lodge in Canada!"

She sank onto a dining room chair, unsure how to respond! The man's behavior at the time of her abduction was strange; she wasn't sure it meant he was involved. She thought he was! Sadly, she wanted answers more than she wanted to hear of his demise. She sat, breathing rapidly, trying to grasp the implications! At last, she rose. God knew! She was working on leaving things more in His hands! She didn't feel like Master Remington's death was divine judgment; more likely he knew something that someone didn't want brought to light! The Canadian Mounties were investigating, and the paper said they had a lot of leads to pursue.

"What shall we do today, Jay?"

Mallory sipped the coffee gratefully, although forcing the breakfast sandwich down was harder. "I'm going back to the waiting room. I hate to just assume someone will keep an eye on the girls."

"Yeah, go ahead. I'm gonna get a bunch of sandwiches and coffees. People will be waking up."

"Should I go with-" Lana's indecisive question! "No, she's okay! Stay here and help me carry food."

Nanci wrote and rewrote, remembering Mallory's drumbeat about never getting a second chance to make a good first impression! Not original with Mallory, but an important fact! If Nanci hoped to prove to 'Mr. Buy You a Drink' that she was an entrepreneur, her first offering had to be good! Outstanding! Something to set her apart! Fortunately, Harry's pictures were first class! She berated herself for being behind! In owning the usual array of electronics, and in technical expertise! Sam Whitmore didn't seem too interested in getting her up and running. She tried to decide what to do if he didn't come through! She hated to tattle to Mallory, and Deborah would worry whether her fashions were going onto a back burner. She was wishing this idea had occurred to her a day earlier when she was in Athens. Oh well, Athens wasn't that far removed from her Istanbul home; she could write it up when she had more experience. Maybe the lesser known site would be interesting, with fewer travel blogs to compare the coverage with! She sighed, feeling strangely lonely, but glad she had resisted the drink offer and where it might have led. She needed this time to focus on her concept. A yawn and she decided she should try for some sleep. With one more scan through the pictures, she retired. There was one shot of her so perfect that it couldn't be more ideal if she had hired a photographer and posed for an entire afternoon!

Mallory noticed that Daniel's place on a sofa was empty She settled in while everyone else, including her daughters, continued sleeping! Exhausted, but her mind wouldn't still itself! Every time she tried to pray, her mind focused only on the four month ordeal of David's being in a coma; with the prospect that he would be a vegetable beyond help, even of a bevy of therapists! She didn't know if the same specter hovered in reality, but it weighed on her. She started awake, not aware that she dozed, to face Melanie, shaking her gently.

"Mrs. Anderson," her whisper was so soft Mallory couldn't understand what she said. Fighting the haze of sleep, she focused on the clipboard and the restraint the nurse demonstrated. "Mr. Anderson is restless, and the doctor doesn't want to sedate him if he can avoid it-"

Mallory straightened up stiffly. "You want me to sign to restrain him? Can I see him?"

"He's just out of it, Mrs. Anderson; and you know, he's a pretty big guy-"

Mallory made her way to the doorway with Craft trying to overtake her, warning, "I don't think he's up to a visitor!"

But Mallory's mind was made up. They weren't tying David down unless she thought it was necessary-as a last resort! Yeah! She didn't want him sedated either, when they wanted him to wake up-

"Okay, just for a second!" Craft complied, not seeing an alternative. "Don't get too close, or you might get clipped! This way"! She led the way to a cubicle in recovery.

Mallory stood, watching David pitch and moan. "Is he in pain?"

"I don't think so; he's too out of it-"

"David!" Mallory's soft voice barely carried, but the thrashing ceased. "Hey, Babe, it's Mallory! Can you hear me?"

She and the nurse watched as he forced his eyes open. He struggled to speak, past a dry mouth and drug-thickened tongue.

"Where have you been?" he rasped. "I've been calling and calling for you!"

Mallory shot an accusing look at the nurse before the fact dawned on her that David might have thought he had called for her; he was loopy!

"I've been right here! Out in the waiting room! You had surgery again! Do you remember passing out in your office?"

His eyes were opened but she couldn't tell if he heard her. Then a wince and a slight nod! "You didn't go?" speaking was still a struggle.

"Go?" she echoed, confused. "You mean go on the trip without you? No-no, I've been right here."

Before they could say much more, the doctor arrived, and a relieved Mallory announced to the concerned friends, that David was awake and aware of his surroundings.

Mallory's phone buzzed as waiting room friends began stirring. Cade! She moved to the empty corridor. "Hello, Cade; what's going on?"

The chemist and Catrina were both concerned about David, but the urgency of his matter prompted him to address it first! "Mallory-uh-I'm not sure how to-uh-break this-"

"Let me guess!" She cut to the chase. "You've had a break-in! Have you called the police?"

"Well, I'm not sure about a 'break-in', but it's gone! The case, the sample, everything! And, with the way the sheriff's department-"

"Yeah; I'm glad you haven't reported it! I'm pretty sure it's fine! Don't worry about it for now! I mean access back there is limited to a privileged few, so-I doubt there's any evidence left, anyway. It's like the whole thing never happened!"

"Oh, okay!" Cade was so relieved and perplexed he forgot to check on David's condition!

Catrina's face a study in worry, she asked, "Was she mad?"

"Not really. She was almost like she was expecting it-"

Mallory disconnected, annoyed at the strong-arm measures, but at least she didn't have to wonder if Lilly knew! She pushed a speed dial, international number, speaking when Lilly answered, "Hello Lilly, would you tell Cassandra that David's better, but to keep praying"?

"Oh yes," Lilly's solicitous voice. "And so you know, I've been rather blue about the whole thing."

"I never questioned you, Lilly! Ciao!" She disconnected, hoping funding of the stone would kick in soon! "Lord, You do all things well! Thank You about David; please don't let him have any more set-backs." Tears of gratitude broke free and she reached for Alexis. "Let's change your diaper, and you can see Daddy!"

With a couple of hour layover at Paris Orly, David Higgins checked out the shops. He opted for a masculine, brown, hooded sweatshirt embroidered with matching thread. A low key 'Paris' souvenir and nicer looking than his ragged, soiled work jacket! He thought now would be a good time to get his head examined! Nanci still seemed to think she had a chance with Faulkner! Why did he entertain the thought he might ever have a chance with her? With the exchange rate to Euros, the thing set him back a hundred bucks! Of course, he had more money on hand than at any time in his life! A hot shave and shoe shine, and it was time to board! What was he thinking?

Mallory reappeared briefly, all three girls with her. Then a circus of visitors paraded through. At last, the nurse ran everyone out and administered additional pain medication. With the silence, David's self-castigation kicked in! Tears welled up and ran down his face onto the pillow case! He felt like a big, dumb oaf! The bull in the china closet that always got yelled at! He could hardly believe he had fussed at Mallie for not being there for him; because, of course, she had been! Always doing everything just perfect and right! While he was a disaster! How could he have messed up the voyage she was so keyed up about? If he healed rapidly, he wasn't sure how long it might take to put all the pieces back into place. Some of the drilling and dredging permits were for specific dates and time frames!

Mallory always did things for other people, and then when it was her turn-Well this proposed venture would still help a lot of other people! Mallory's chief thrill was discovery! That and proving that Patrick was right!

Nanci moved around Yalta, in and out of shops! A couple of cameras seemed nice, but their cords and plugs were geared toward local current and outlet configurations. She purchased a set of post cards, thinking she might use them, but the picture quality was poor. Copyrights aside! 'Well, Rome wasn't built in a day,' she reminded herself! She was on an adventure; but it was in its infancy! It would come; if she just stayed at it! Too late, she realized she should change her habit of wandering alone, and stick with the guided tours! If she hoped to learn about these destinations and share them with others! She sank down onto a harbor-side bench! With so much food available twenty-four seven aboard the ship, she hated to buy and consume extra! Keeping her figure was challenging, but something she worked at, nevertheless!

The strange feeling invaded her solitude, making her restless and uneasy. Pulling a jacket from her bag, she draped it across her shoulders. A picture she kept trying to push from her mind! Of Daniel Faulkner, children in tow, trying to escape the craziness of Delton Waverly after the debacle of crashing the New York party! How handsome he still was! What a good and devoted husband and father. She felt pangs of loss, not sure why! She had never owned him! And if she had, the man that then was, wasn't a shadow of who he had become! She didn't want to go as far as admitting that Diana Prescott had been good for him! Just, he wore the maturing process well! A pensive sigh freed itself!

"Daydreaming about Faulkner?"

The unexpected voice made her jump. Caught, she blushed. "David, what brings you here? A drilling job?"

"Drilling locations are confidential." He felt foolish for just showing up at such an out-of-the-way destination! Where she just happened to have a shore excursion! "You didn't answer my question."

"My daydreams are none of your business," she responded tartly. "Nice sweatshirt!"

He stood, facing her awkwardly. "Uh-you heard about David Anderson; right?"

Alarm showed on her exquisite features.

"Guess he's doing great now; but he had problems with one last bone fragment loose in his noggin! So, our next jobs got postponed. I've been hitting it pretty hard, so the Andersons gave me some vacation time in the interim! And some airline miles! Nice place!" 'Dumb, Higgins', he thought to himself. 'Not such a nice place it would have beckoned him of all the cruise destinations in the whole world!' "Have you already visited where the treaty was signed?"

Not sure what treaty he referred to, she played along. "Not yet; you?"

"Nah, I just got here? Want to check it out?"

"Sure; why not?"

Roger buttoned his top coat; something seldom necessary in Hope! Boston was a different story! He followed Beth and Emma around Quincy Market! This trip was Beth's idea, and he was still hanging in, daily fighting the urge to throw in the towel on his marriage! Maybe there was just too much water under the bridge! Too much baggage for him to surmount! Yeah, he had created the original problem, but when was enough, enough? He was tired of coddling her through her issues! He was nearly to the point of filing and letting her 'take him to the cleaners'. Even as the grimness of that prospect clutched at him, he sighed. "What price, peace?" Maybe too high!

For the zillionth time, he murmured a prayer, "Lord, Ya gotta help me here! I'm thinking life's too short to live out the remainder of my time with an unreasonable grouch!"

His phone in his breast pocket vibrated and he pulled it free, reminding Himself that the Lord didn't need a phone. Still, he stared at the notification, puzzled. An email! From Trent Morrison! He barely knew the guy! Kind of a friend of a friend! He eased onto a bench, to be surrounded by pigeons! He flapped at them, annoyed, to drive them off! Didn't think he was to the point yet of sitting on a park bench and feeding the birds. He opened the email, and laughed. Morrison's words were offered in genuine sincerity:

> *Hey, Roger, you asked me about this a long time ago, and in the craziness, I forgot all about it! Guess I'm as derelict as the butler was with Joseph; huh? Anyway, this is the gist of Faulkner's marriage*

seminar talk! I reference it quite often, but it's still never occurred to me that you wanted it! Good stuff! Again, sorry for forgetting!

Trent

Sanders sat, transfixed, trying to convince himself, that the long overdue email came to Morrison's mind now, after all these years, and that it was pure coincidence! Nothing to do with the desperate prayer he didn't expect an answer to! And certainly not such a dramatic answer! He deleted it. The last person he wanted to hear from right now, was Daniel Faulkner! Or Trent Morrison either, for that matter!

His face lit as Emma made her way toward him, scattering the pesky pigeons as she neared. She was beautiful, and his heart lurched at the agonizing days when he couldn't find out where she was! Wondering if he would ever see her again! He scooted over and she started pulling her newly acquired treasures out to show him. Her earnest excitement took him back to the days when she was a small girl; hard to believe she was married and expecting a baby in a few months! He forced a smile through his misery.

"Daddy, are you okay?" her excited chatter faded as she surveyed him carefully.

He gave her a squeeze, "I'm fine," he assured.

"Mom seems happier," she tried hopefully.

Roger's steely eyes traveled to Beth who was moving toward another shop. "Think so? That's good."

Emma fought tears at her daddy's flat, disinterested tone.

"Is there someone else, again?"

His temper flared and he responded, "Uncalled for, Em! No, there's no one else! Look, I don't expect you to understand-"

She popped from her place next to him, facing him, eyes blazing! "Good! Because I don't"!

Mallory returned to the hospital, relieved for a chance to go home and clean up! At Tammi's insistence, she was keeping all three girls. She glanced around the neurosurgical waiting room! A new set of anxious faces, awaiting surgical outcomes! Although strangers, her heart went out to them, and she breathed a prayer for the surgeons and patients, alike!

She knew David was gone for further tests, strictly precautionary, after which, he was going to a room. She nodded at an interesting-looking woman who had put in an appearance the previous evening, taking a seat across from her.

"You are wearing another marvelous ensemble!"

'Thanks to Diana,' Came her disjointed thoughts. With David in crisis, the last thing on her mind was what to wear. "Thank you! My friend is the designer and we're in business together! When she sees me, she'll probably fuss at me for picking this one today, since it's so similar to what I wore yesterday!"

'Yes, and no,' the newcomer continued running an appreciative eye over the details. The suit style was similar, but different, too; this one executed in soft aqua green crepe, the lining displaying muted beach scene of blues, greens and aquas of sky, palms, and ocean! "Lovely fabric; is it actually woolen?"

Mallory nodded, "Actually, one of Diana's absolute favorite mediums to work in! Wool crepe! It is dreamy! Uh~are you here with your~husband?"

"No, with a fellow employee! We are both here from Spain as guest professors in the DU World History Department! Frederico received head trauma in an automobile accident yesterday. Luckily, his prognosis is good. He will require some therapy for motor skills! We barely know each other; our ties to Spain what we have in common! He is young and impulsive; he's like dealing with my son all over again. And, you? Your husband? He is patient?"

"Yes, Ma'am; his surgery went well, and they're moving him to a regular bed when he finishes undergoing some tests! I had a scare in the night, when they couldn't get him to respond. All of our friends who were here with us are real prayer warriors, so I credit David's condition to the goodness of God and their combined prayers. I'm sorry; my name's Mallory Anderson!" She drew a business card and a gospel tract from her bag and offered them.

"Ana de Castille." The woman drew back visibly, standoffish from the pamphlet.

Mallory let it drop easily. "My friend Diana and I traveled to Spain! Our trip was for business and was way too short! So much to see with so little time"!

"Madrid?" The woman's tone remained icy, although her curiosity was piqued by the conversational turn.

"Initially! I was in a motorized chair at the time, so the travel arrangements were somewhat complicated. We flew from Madrid to Seville where we began working in tandem with the Rivera family for our leather goods. Then, one of my school friends from Arkansas, with ties to Honduras-" she paused with a laugh! "Long story! But we concentrated on the southern part of the country and visited Gibraltar! I got to see the monkeys!"

She nodded again; still stiff. Mallory knew that there was contention between Spain and the UK over possession of the territory! Whatever, it was a super cool place to have seen!

"Wow! Wow! You are some kind of gorgeous!" David was propped up in front of a late breakfast tray. "Where are my other three little beauties?"

She kissed him lightly. "With their Aunt Tammi"!

"Ah, that's good! That'll be more fun for them. Listen, about the trip-"

"You need any help with your food?"

He shook his head, and pulled a cover off, surveying it. "Have you eaten yet?"

"No, but I will! About the trip, I wanted a chance to talk about it before everyone shows up again! This is such a relief that it happened where and when it did! Think if we'd been thousands of miles out in the ocean!"

He considered her words. Good point! He still felt bad about it, though.

"It's made me really think about a lot of stuff! I've been in too much of a rush! Oh, I forgot to tell you the latest about the email Cade sent me."

He stared at her blankly.

"About drilling on the Atcha-"

"Oh, yeah; that email!" his face lit up and he smiled broadly.

"Well, it's been stolen!"

"What?" His expression aghast!

"Relax! In this case, it was a good thing! And a good thing Cade doesn't trust the county sheriff!"

He laughed lightly. "Ah; I follow you now!"

"So we have more capital, and I think we need to trade the bucket of bolts back in favor of a newer ship!"

He frowned. The one they owned was old, but a friend of his who was a marine architect had looked her over from stem to stern, pronouncing her seaworthy, if she wouldn't win any beauty contests!

"Hear me out! It doesn't even have an infirmary; and it needs to! Hopefully, not for your sake! But good sense dictates it! And then, in addition to lifeboats, it needs a motor launch and a chopper and pad on deck!"

He considered! What she suggested would definitely cost!

Deborah frowned when her phone interrupted a meeting with her parents. "Good Morning! *Rodriguez, Incorporated*!" she smiled when the caller spoke with rapid Spanish, listening intently.

"Yes, this is Deborah," she responded in her first language. Expressive eyes widened in astonishment. The caller, Señora Ana de Castille,·related her story of admiring Mallory Anderson and conversing briefly with her in one of the Baylor hospital waiting rooms. She was actually familiar with the Riveras in Seville.

Deborah responded animatedly, although the Spanish varied slightly, and was sometimes tough to follow. But within half an hour, she had a new friend, an order for some of the garments from the newest *Rodriguez* line, and an addition to her mailing list. Señora, you should really check out the *DiaMal* web site as well, since you so admired Mallory's suits! They are lovely and high quality! No use limiting yourself because we are Latino." Then an idea occurred to her. "We do not discount or mark down our clothing, however, if you are able to represent my line, I will discount your order! By that I mean, that if someone compliments an ensemble, you simply give them a small catalog; or at the least our business card. In your classes and with the faculty at Dallas University, you will expose my lovely garments to people I will never cross paths with."

Señora de Castille ended the conversation by informing Deborah, that even the European market that she frequented, didn't feature anything comparable to what she was seeing! She eagerly took the young entrepreneur up on the deal! She knew people who would welcome the lovely styles eagerly!

Chapter 28: GLIMPSES

The voice in the earphones ebbed and flowed in Nanci's consciousness. Hearing the details of the Yalta Conference brought back vague high school recollections. President Franklin D. Roosevelt, Winston Churchill, and Joseph Stalin, dividing up the post WWII world! Her thoughts returned to Daniel Faulkner, remembering conversations when he chided her for being shallow! Looking back, she could see his point, which at that time, he wasn't much farther along the shallowness scale than she was! Oh true, he wasn't caught up like she was, with her appearance; but other than partying, his main obsession was money! Economics! Banking! Things she still didn't grasp! She was only interested in money as far as his understanding it well enough to keep them both supplied! Now, he seemed to have more than ever, but that was no longer his major thrust! She sighed and followed other tourists as they placed the head sets into baskets and filed toward restrooms, gift shop, or the exit!

Following a visit to the gift shop, they exited into pale sunlight. "Whatever your plans were, do you mind if I tag along?" Higgins figured he seemed pathetic, but he was committed this far.

Nanci slanted him a strange glance. "I'm happy for your company. You have a camera."

He nodded, "Yeah; you don't?"

She laughed ruefully! "No, I don't, and I had this idea I bounced off of Mallory; she liked it, and I've shopped for a camera since then! But they're all for different; they won't work at home!" She paused, confused! Because home was now Istanbul and this stuff might work there.

"Well, mine has a fully charged battery and empty memory stick. What do you want pictures of?"

"Well, right here at Livadia is very picturesque!" She paused in the garden to pose with the imposing structure behind her, but he was snapping away every other direction. "David, do you mind getting me in one? I'll pay you for any I like!"

He blushed. Taking her picture was what he wanted to do! He wouldn't mind having thousands of her! He was afraid of making her mad. He focused on her, but she looked too stiff and posed. "Okay, turn your head slightly, relax your face, and then smile!" He snapped and captured her at her most charming. "Just let me know what you need pictures of, okay? And you don't have to pay me!"

She smiled. "Okay, let's go to the embankment! I won't pay for your pictures then, but I'm getting hungry. Can I treat for lunch?"

He told her, yes, but then he slid his credit card when it was time to pay. "So, what was your idea that you've been looking for a camera for?"

"Promise you won't laugh!"

Her serious eyes met his, and he glimpsed something in her he had failed to notice before! An appealing vulnerability! Why would she care whether he laughed at her, or not? He wasn't a blip on her radar screen!

"If Mallory thought you had a good idea, you must have had a good idea! Whatever it is, I can keep a confidence!"

She considered before bubbling enthusiastically!

Erik followed the Canadian case in the death of Silas Remington with interest! Remington was neither a hunter, nor a guest at the hunting lodge! No record of his leaving the US! No passport stamp at customs! The Philly PD seemed slow to concern themselves with when and from where, the victim disappeared. Bransom suspected a red truck emblazoned with *Rasmusson, Refrigerated.* Since there was no proof yet, of a kidnapping, Dawson told him to stay out of it! Still, he wondered if he might leave an anonymous tip at either the PD hotline or that of the Mounties! This was why inter-agency cooperation was such a good thing! Oh well, maybe if the suspects thought they got away with it~

Selling the battered ship and locating what they wanted in a newer, larger vessel was proving time-consuming! David worked at it from his hospital bed between visits. He hoped to be discharged soon! He set his phone aside and closed his eyes, to be awakened an hour later by Tammi and his daughters.

"Hey, come on in!"

Tammi eased in, whispering to Amelia and Avery to sit together in the large chair. She toted Alexis, and he reached for her, snuggling his cheek against her soft skin. She jerked back from his stubble and he laughed. "How's everything going?"

"Good! For us! How you're doing is the question!" Tammi fixed him with her sternest look; which never had fazed him!

"I'm fine now, thanks!" he directed his attention to Amelia, struggling to control the chair and how much she wanted to share with Avery. He patted beside him on the bed. "You two better come over here where I can thump you!" Avery scrambled down without waiting for a second invitation; Amelia dropped her head on her arms and started to cry.

"She thinks this is all her fault," Tammi explained. "I guess she-"

David nodded, remembering the scenario. "Yeah, my head kept hurting worse and worse. The door to the nursery was open because Alvie was sick, so I was supposed- Anyway, I tried putting my head down on my arms, but then I felt like I was still going to pass out-"

"But you didn't call Mallory, or 911?"

"Nah, I thought putting my head between my knees might restore my equilibrium, but everything I tried intensified the pain! So, I decided to just get down on the floor, so if I lost consciousness, I wouldn't have as far to fall-"

"And usually, when you get down on the floor, it's to play and tussle like Daddy always did!"

He nodded. "Yeah, she nailed me with a tackle from out of nowhere! I started to scold her, and that's the last I remember! I don't know how long it was before Mallory found me; must have been lunch time!"

Tammi gathered her niece into her arms. "Actually, this very smart little girl knew how to use the intercom! She buzzed Mallory-"

He laughed in amazement as he extended his arms. "Really! You knew how to call Mommy over for me?"

"I thought you was day-ed! I called Mommy and told her you was day-ed! I didn't obey about staying in the room and playing-"

He wiped away tears and pulled her close! "Shhhh-hh, it's okay! It's okay! Everything's okay now! Stop crying for Daddy, and let me see that pretty smile!"

Pastor Ellis watched the church parking lot from his office window, taking note of each family by car make and model. He was surprised to see the Anderson's SUV in the car queue for the nursery drop-off! It looked like David was driving! Guilt pangs attacked! Of course, he had heard about David's brain surgery, but since he hadn't seen them since the after church meal which had kind of morphed into misunderstandings, he wasn't sure they considered themselves members; hence, he hadn't made the hospital visit. Now in retrospect~ He moved to a better position to see Mallory unload the girls while David went in search of a parking space! He sighed. After John Anderson's coming to the rescue for Calvary's financial dip~Not usually one to want to hide from his members, he considered just staying put here until the last minute~He answered a light tap at his door, and there loomed David!

"David, come on in!" He stepped back, indicating a chair.

"No thanks, Pastor! I know Sunday mornings aren't times when you can sit and visit! I just wanted to apologize that we've been out so much! Not out of church, but out of the Dallas area! We really miss being here. Well, looks like a crowd's assembling, and I know everybody else wants to shake your hand! I better find us some seats! We're leaving for Arkansas right after church, so our schedule's still a little off-kilter!"

Nanci wakened early, sensing that lonely feeling again. What was it? Saying good-bye to David? His unexpected appearance had made the previous day's excursion fly by! Oh yes, his promise to email her his pictures! Hopping up, she opened her laptop! True to his word, a file full of pictures! She could look at them at breakfast; giving her something to do while other tourists ate as couples or in groups. She watched as rain spattered against her cabin window. She was still going ashore! The thought occurred to her, from she wasn't sure where, that she might find a church~

'Why not'? She could add a charming, aged cathedral, and include it in one of her blogs on Odessa! She selected a silk dress created in a delft pattern reminiscent of China dishes! The drape around her was elegant and flattering, and a solid blue coat repeated the dress fabric in the lining! Very lovely with her blue eyes and raven hair! Twists of gold and pearl jewelry lent their charm, and black wedge heeled pumps seemed the best choice for walking in the rain. If she needed to go any distance to find a church, she could hail a cab.

She noticed Harry and Maggie in the group waiting to debark. But as the wind increased and the rain slanted in sideways, she noticed the group going ashore dwindling.

Religion wasn't her thing, and now that she was ashore, she wasn't sure why! Although her umbrella was sturdy against the wind's onslaught, the gusts of rain were soaking her, and inevitable puddles soaked her shoes. She sought solace at the first crowded coffee shop, grateful for a hot latté while she sought information from the locals!

Church? At which a leering, evil-looking man invaded her space, offering her a ride. Terrified, she declined, remembering that Eastern European gangs were notorious for enslaving women! She fought tears, longing to be back in the comfortable ambiance of the ship! Of all the stupid days and crazy places to decide to try the religious thing~

Gradually, she calmed down, and with the mug drained, made her way back onto the street! Maybe just going from coffee shop to café to tourist booths could fill the time! As she forgot the church attendance goal, she suddenly noticed several local people streaming along! Mostly elderly and with the women all wearing large head scarves of various brightly printed designs, they seemed to be headed for worship. She followed curiously to where they entered a magnificent cathedral. She followed diffidently, and was stopped by a dower-looking man in religious regalia, who evidently didn't understand or speak English, motioning why she wasn't wearing a scarf! She was confused, not sure but what she was actually in a mosque! She had never heard of Christians being required to cover their heads~ with an uncomprehending shrug she pushed her way past and sank onto a back bench. Others making their way forward, stopped as they entered, kneeling, or lighting candles~ She wasn't feeling any peace in her quest, but weirder and more out of place than ever! So, even though she didn't 'know the drill' this should count for something, shouldn't it? Providing there was really a God, and that He cared what people did! Which, if there was, and He did, she was probably doomed, anyway! Sudden shame brought tears to her eyes! Very disconcerting, because she was always determined not to care what anyone thought! She sat miserably through incantations and rituals that were meaningless to her, puzzled why the devout around her seemed so helped and at peace!

'This isn't what Daniel has! The churches where he performs music are bright and cheery, and the songs make sense!' She only ever watched bits and snatches, not wanting to see Diana and his kids; and certainly never watching the videos until there was a sermon~now she realized that was the answer! Pastor John Anderson and the Faith Baptist Website!

She rose and slipped silently past the frowning doorkeeper and onto the street!

David Higgins parked the tiny, low-budget rent car and headed into the Villa Pinia Hotel. More than seven hours driving, to show up at the next cruise port of call! How crazy was he? With check-in complete, he made his way to his room for a shower! Crazy weather; she probably never even came ashore! Not much luggage, so he donned clean underwear and put the same pants, shirt and sweatshirt back on. Usually not one to go for cologne, he suddenly wished he had some! And some more clothes! He shaved and checked emails before heading back to the lobby.

His phone rang, and he noted nervously that it was David Anderson.

"Higgins, where are you, and what are you up to?"

"Why? Mallory said that everything's been delayed, and this would be a chance for me to take some time off! I'm~uh~in the Ukraine! Where do you guys need me to be? It's good to hear your voice; how's your head?"

"Uh~screwed on straighter than yours is, evidently!"

"What's that supposed to mean?" Higgins growled, to get a chuckle in reply.

"Hey, I'm just on bed rest and bored out of my mind, so I've been tracking your credit card! You're stalking Nanci Nichols?"

"She decided on Burnside because it rhymes with seaside for her blog, and I'm not stalking her! She needs my pictures and tech help to get her new idea up and running! It's what she decided to do with the ten grand~"

"Well, all that's great! She needs help! But~"

"She uses people to get what she wants~yeah; I've known that for more years than I care to~you telling me to back off? Or just trying to cushion me from getting hurt?"

"Hey, neither! You're a grown man! Like I said, I'm a little bored. But, incidentally, you can book a flight from Odessa to Constanta and save yourself a rugged drive to the next port! The flight actually only goes between the destinations three days a week, but this is your lucky day! Want me to book you? We have the free miles!"

A suspicious, "Why would you do that?" brought a considered answer.

"Because her travel blog's a great idea, and you are the help she needs! We appreciate it; I just hope she does!"

Higgins laughed, "Yeah, I hear ya!"

Nanci nearly ran from the oppressive feelings of the cathedral, and hailing the first cab that passed by, questioned, "Shopping?"

With a nod, the cabbie hit the accelerator and never slowed until he reached a charming retail district! He glowered at the proffered credit card, and directed her attention in no uncertain terms to a money-exchange kiosk! Hardly the best place for a good rate, she was sure, but she offered her credit card and received a fistful of whatever the local currency was! It all baffled her. She held it toward the driver who helped himself smilingly!

"Tip?" she questioned.

The smile nearly split his face, and he grasped at more of the paper currency.

"Thank you! Four o'clock?" she held up her watch and he grinned again, nodding eagerly!

"Four o'clock! I come get~"

Roger disconnected from his conversation with David Anderson. Yachts, he knew! The kind of tub the Andersons sought, he was less sure of! Which he had explained! Still, the offer and request intrigued him! "I'll see what I can find." He placed a call to Cat, who was less than thrilled to talk to him! Well, all the kids seemed to be on Beth's side. He guessed Cat was also worried about violating her CDA! He was just curious as to where David and Mallory planned to dredge, drill, and dive! His immediate impression was the southern or western coast of Africa! That was where diving and dredging for diamonds traditionally took place; and where he might locate a boat outfitted for that specific purpose! Cat wouldn't tell him if the main exploration thrust was for diamonds! Staying home in Arkansas seemed like it could provide plenty for them, as he understood it! If he could get more of a grasp on the situation, he could have a better starting place. Still, he called an acquaintance who was a yacht broker.

"Roger, you know I don't deal in commercial, exploration ships."

"Yeah, but I thought maybe you know who does! And I'm talking about a small start-up operation and not a battleship!"

"Mmmm-hmm and when do you need this vessel?"

"I dunno! Last week? Find me something, and I'll treat you right!"

"In that case, I'm on it!"

David walked around the bustling shopping area, noting many of the same stores prevalent in the US. He headed into one, relieved he might actually be able to find some jeans in his size. A couple of shirts caught his eye, as well as another sweatshirt! He tried to contain his excitement! If he couldn't find Nanci here, maybe he could tomorrow, in Constanta! And catch a flight, rather than more exhausting driving! He grinned. It was hard to put anything over on his employers; but they were so savvy in every way! Rather than blasting him for the charges on the corporate card-they were actually glad for his presence to help with the travel blog! That would almost sound plausible for an excuse for why he was stalking-er (following her around the Black Sea)! Relieved for the painful experience of shopping to have gone so smoothly, he headed for what he hoped would be a food court, with something American, like maybe KFC!

The Faulkners showed up at Faith slightly ahead of David and Mallory! Seeing the advantage of the situation, Jeff sprinted to his dad's office to fire off an email! Christians should esteem being in church for the fact that it was the right thing to do, the commanded thing to do! And they should value music in its proper place, as preparing hearts to hear the preaching of God's Word! Preaching! The Power of the Gospel! The Dynamite of the Gospel! But hearing that the Faulkners and Andersons would present a Christian concert always brought people in! People who were too much infants in their Christianity, to have priorities straight! But you had to baby them along; sometimes they grew and matured in their faith; often, they stayed stuck and miserable!

And then Deborah showed up, too! Which Mallory figured Deborah needed the grounding in her faith that Pastor could give. Sadly, she felt that Deborah's appearance was to talk to Diana and get Diana into her court against Mallory's newest brainstorm! Ignoring the huddle and the injured looks shot her direction she and David discussed the impromptu selections with Daniel!

And there were serious holes in the group. Of course, Cassandra always charmed, but even more than that, was Alexandra's piano accompaniment! Of course Diana was an excellent pianist, but she preferred not to play the piano and sing, so she usually opted for vocalist! That left Mallory on the piano, but she and David had worked up a beautiful number in which they sang, and then played a violin duet. Usually Daniel could be a hard sell on a song he wasn't familiar with, but he quickly glanced over the music and liked it. He figured Diana could sight read it admirably to add to the evening's repertoire. He turned to see the tête-à-tête at the back of the auditorium. "Calling Mrs. Diana Faulkner!" he intoned.

She responded, but her expression wasn't the happiest.

"Okay, lots to do to pull this together! Can you accompany David and Mallory on the piano?" He held up the music, and she took it reluctantly.

"Look, go tell her that we don't conduct business meetings on Sunday, and when she has an issue, she can call you during the week! She doesn't need to show up at church with some agenda that sours the atmosphere and quenches the Spirit!"

Diana took her place on the piano bench, castigated. Her husband was right! What slick ways the devil used to slip in and wreak his havoc. She caressed the notes as she took in the lyrics: *An angel from long ago stepped down to earth below!* And then the chorus which was also the title: *Cherish That Beautiful Name!* The song wasn't new, but the lovely combination of lyric and melody washed across her, dispelling the remainder of her attitude and humbling her heart.

"You're not sight-reading! You know that one! And you've been holding out on me?" Daniel's voice a laughing challenge!

"Try not to get a bad attitude right at church time," she chirped cheerfully.

The rain ceased; although the wind remained sharp! Beginning to give up on the idea of bumping into Nanci, Higgins focused on taking pictures for her of the prevalent tourist sites! Although Odessa, Ukraine wasn't a top destination, it did have the common sites that everyone posted pictures of! He needed something different-more sensational! And then, as he stood poised at the top of the Potemkin Steps overlooking the busy harbor and the Princess cruise ship, a double rainbow emerged from the mist! Stunned at the sudden granting of his wish, he captured several stunning shots!

"David?" An amazed voice at his elbow made him jump.

"Hey! Nanci! Having a good day?" He was going to explain that David Anderson wanted him to help her with the blog startup, but he noticed tears.

"What's wrong? You okay?"

"I'm fine! Guess the rain just made me feel a little blue! Are you on this same cruise?"

"Uh-no-I rented a car and drove here! I have this vacation time, and you're trying to get the most, bang for your buck with the ten thousand dollars! I've been racking my brain how I might do something similar with mine! That wouldn't create a conflict of interest with The Andersons! Wanna sit down and see the pictures I've taken this afternoon?"

She shivered, making him long to slip his arm around her. Instead he suggested finding a nice restaurant, where they could be warm, see the shots, and discuss the venture. "A crucial part of travel is the cuisine; you should include that."

She sighed. "I suppose you're right! You know, I used to like the Travel Channel when it was actually about travel!"

He laughed. "Yeah, I feel the same way! It's gone totally to being about food and not travel destinations at all. You know, another thing people always want to know about in depth is night life! I guess one of the best clubs in Eastern Europe is right here! Want to check it out?"

"I'm not sure. I feel cold and wet and bedraggled! I'm thinking more about cuddling up with a book! And the best in 'Eastern Europe' doesn't impress me that much! I guess I'm kinda homesick!"

"You look as beautiful as always! It'll be fun! You love to dance! You're a great dancer! We can take some pictures and that'll really help hook followers!"

"No, I'll miss my boat! It's a long swim to Constanta then!"

"Stay the night! We can book you a room in my hotel; if there's much night left. And you can fly with me to Constanta in the morning!"

"Flights don't always-why are you going to Constanta?"

"Anderson wants me to."

"You sure you don't want to get back into choir?" Beth moved coffee cups from the sink into the dishwasher. "We're starting to work on some great new music! And the men's section sounds weak. I'm not sure you realize what a leader you are, and-"

Roger battled the chronic annoyance. "No, I'm fine! Guys miss more during hunting season. Just go enjoy yourself and I'll see you at church. I can cheer on my team for another forty minutes! 'Go, Hogs'!"

"Just for that, I hope they lose!" Evan clattered an empty pie plate into the sink, directing his remark toward his dad. "I'll go with you, Mom! I've been thinking about starting in choir. Wanna ride with me?"

Beth summoned a smile! "Sure; why not live dangerously?"

"Oh, I'll be careful with you, Mom! You're my favorite baker!"

Arm in arm, they made their way to the garage, both aware of what Roger didn't say: "You better be careful of your mother for more reasons than that!"

Still, Evan was a pro at getting smiles from his mom, and a couple of his antics even brought a slight laugh!

Nanci watched as travelers scurried aboard and the gang plank started up! She thought missing David Higgins was the cause for her doldrums earlier, but now he was mostly a pain! She still wanted to access the Faith Baptist website; she didn't know why! And usually she loved the night scene! Even with a hick like Higgins! She would go off and do whatever she wanted and leave him sitting and drinking alone! "I'm sorry; what?"

"What will be best for your blog? One of the finest restaurants that gets touted in every review? Or an out-of-the-way spot frequented by locals?"

She shuddered. "I don't know! I'm not in favor of braised goat tails! I like to know what I'm eating, and I've never been sure what 'braised' means exactly!"

He laughed. "Good point! The restaurant at my hotel looks nice, and we can make sure we can book you a room! We'll be out so late that you can just crash with me-"

She ignored the suggestion, watching the oily gap widen between the dock and the security of her ship!

"I don't have anything with me! Clothes, cosmetics"! Her voice sounded panicky and he felt guilty.

"You worry too much. Let's find some dinner. No use arriving at the club too early! This way-"

She kept up with him easily! Stubby legs, short gait! Why did she compare everyone she met with Daniel Faulkner? And David Higgins was a far cry from her ideal! Just as they reached the hotel, an angry cab driver cut them off from the entry.

Higgins uttered a furious oath as the cabbie sprang from his seat and made his way toward them.

"Take it easy, David," Nancy cautioned softly. "This is my fault! I arranged with him to pick me up and bring me back to the harbor; and then forgot!" She stepped forward. "Hey, I'm sorry! I probably cost you a fare. How much do I owe-"

Higgins grasped her arm firmly. "Don't worry about it! I'm sure it happens all the time! Part of the hazards of the job! Get lost, fella, before I call the cops!"

Mallory settled the girls in at Hal's and placed orders for their beverages. David was talking to Roger Sanders about locating a new boat, and by now Pastor and Lana made her nervous.

"Did the doctor say it's okay for David to come this far?" Lana's concerns echoed Mallory's; but stopping a locomotive was probably easier than stopping David when his mind was made up! How people could say she ran him was beyond her comprehension!

"The doctor told him he can do whatever he feels up to doing!"

"Well, is he okay? Why doesn't he come in?"

"She said he's on a phone call," John reminded. Then turning his attention to his daughter-in-law, "Who's he talking to? You know, Daniel got onto Diana for conducting business on the Lord's Day!"

"Well, yeah, and maybe you can get onto David about it! You usually climb his clock about everything!" She couldn't believe she said it, and tears stung her eyes!

Amelia's big eyes took the incident in seriously before she spoke in a stage whisper, "Mommy, don't talk back to Grandpa! He don't like it!"

"Why didn't you just let me pay him?" Nanci's alarm increased. "You talk about calling the cops like they'd be on our side! We're not in the US, you know! I have no desire to get into any kind of trouble-"

"These people love American tourists! They need our money! Come on, you worry too much! What happened to foot-loose and fancy-free Nanci?"

"You're quiet!" His voice challenged as they were seated in the upbeat space. "I'm buying!" the announcement sounded grand and she refrained from scoffing aloud. "Beer"?

"Uh-no thank you. I'll have a Perrier," she graced the server with her winning smile!

Higgins' countenance turned furious! "Oh, 'scuse me for offering to buy the lady a beer! I guess you think you're a class act like Faulkner! Would you care for a glass of wine?"

She struggled for composure, "Look, my ship sailed without me, so let's make the best of this! I should call Deborah and let her know my change of plans. She actually pays me for cruising! I love this job and I don't want to jeopardize it! And I don't want to get thrown into a Ukrainian slammer! Order me this salad; this place looks crowded; I'm going to check on getting a room!"

He watched her march toward the long queue at reception, sorry for ruffling her feathers. She was beautiful and he watched as a desk clerk with a clipboard hurried toward her to expedite her check-in! Then, the clerk shook his head regretfully!

Higgins managed to remember his manners enough to rise when she returned to the table. "Booked?"

He expected a tirade, but she simply nodded silently before making a valiant effort to establish a status quo.

"So, David, tell me about yourself!"

He laughed at her effort to save the debacle from further deterioration.

"Okay, enough about me," he laughed uneasily. "Tell me about yourself! Have you ever considered getting married?"

A wounded look flashed in deep blue pools before she recovered to answer candidly. "I don't seem to be the type that men want to marry!"

He released his soup spoon into the cup, focusing on an opportunity. "Well, don't sell yourself short! You go for the ones who are already married! If they wanted to marry you, there's just~divorce, hurt kids, it costs~"

She forced the quiver from her voice. "Who are you to judge me?"

"Oh for ________," a string of epithets, and she winced. "I'm not judging you! I'm just sharing my perspective that what you've tried hasn't worked. And in that case, trying something different, does"!

"So, you're telling me to set my aim lower!"

He shrugged miserably, "Or higher! I guess it depends on your perspective!"

She stabbed at a piece of onion and shoved it aside as if it were the enemy! This seemed like the perfect ending to a crummy day! "What about you? Have you ever considered marriage?"

"Why are we trying to act like strangers? You know I always wanted to be a cool bachelor, wooing countless beauties to my pad! Stuff that never worked for me, either! If there's anything I envy about Daniel, besides your undying love for him, it's his kids!"

She rocked back, shocked, a bubble of laughter rippling suddenly. "No kidding! Rug rats! You! Well, maybe stranger things have happened!"

Chapter 29: GRABBED

Erik sat once more across the table from Darius Warrington! Combing through additional archived news items, yet more men had come to the attention of the FBI! Associates of Wilhelm Dietrich, Robert and Bobby Saxon, Mel Oberson, Ted Coakley, Carson Felton; even the Arizona former sheriff, Roberson. But Warrington clammed up; grinning at what he felt was his upper hand in stymieing the ongoing investigation and arrests in the seemingly endless list of implicated people! Erik didn't care! Just keep pluggin' and reelin' 'em in one at a time!

"So, tell me the names of some of the other quack doctors out there, 'Cosmetic Surgeons'? Isn't that what you call yourselves? Lot of vain people in the world you ply your craft to?"

Warrington never could resist taking Bransom's bait! "I could make great improvements, even to that homely mug of yours!"

"That so?"

"Yeah! Surprises me people don't run when they see you coming!"

Erik chuckled. "Actually they do! I thought it was because of their guilty consciences! Never considered the possibility they might not like my face. Now I'll probably develop such an inferiority complex that those of your ilk can prey upon me, too! Tell me; do you ever encourage any of your victims to develop their inner person and not to put so much emphasis on phony externals?"

"See, you're so dumb you're hardly worth my trying to talk to you! They are patients, and I resent your referencing them as 'victims'! And with the truly beautiful people, appearance is very highly rated! What good does it do that someone's smart or clever if he can't make it in the door?"

"Yeah, you're right! I'm pretty baffled all right! Help me out! Who do you mean by 'The Truly Beautiful People'?" He held up the photos! Coakley! Felton! Saxon, Sr., Wilhelm Dietrich! "If these are 'beautiful people', I'm on a personal crusade to stamp out beauty! These guys are nothing but creeps and common thugs!"

Warrington made a couple of additional jibes about the agent's facial features, to which Bransom laughingly sang a jingle that surfaced from somewhere in elementary school days:

I know how ugly I are!
My face it ain't no star!
But then I don't mind it,
Because I'm behind it!
'T's the feller in front gets the jar!

Erik had no illusions that he was particularly handsome; but he looked okay, and the jingle further annoyed Warrington. At which point Erik made his move for the figurative jugular, by raising a photo of Cy, Warrington's nephew!

"See, you did all this work to make this ugly kid into a 'Beautiful Person'! He was a sadistic creep, and by now the worms have eaten off, all the pretty exterior you worked so hard to craft!"

The surgeon shot upward against the chains restraining him. "He pretty nearly got your li'l Darlin' now! Didn't he?"

Bransom hardly flinched. "My 'li'l Darlin'"? Guess ya lost me again! Try to remember how dumb I am! Oh, you're referencing Mrs. David Anderson? Yeah, she was quick to see past Cyrus' perfect features and memorized lines!"

Warrington shrugged indifferently. "He did misplay his trump card! Sadly there was only so much I could accomplish with him! In the meantime, since you've brought up the subject of the lovely Mallory, perhaps I should warn you that she's moving past her prime! And all of those ugly scars-" He shook his head in mock pity! "I could make them go away; that might restore some of her value, before it's too late!"

"Wow! You could do that? You must have a heart of pure gold!" Bransom's mocking sarcasm caused the pulse at the doctor's temples to throb, revealing the turmoil he strove to mask. "I'm pretty sure it's you and your dumb cohorts that created her scars, and she's plenty valuable to all of her friends and family just the way she is! People don't age past their value, except in a false economy! Hey, have you heard about some of the things Steb Hanson and his friends have accomplished? Hey, do you remember Danay Livingston and Jack and Estelle Norman? They put a dent in Mel Oberson's plan; didn't they? Yeah! Yeah! Lots to be said in favor of the over twenty-five crowd! Incidentally, how old are you? And can you not do anything to help your own ugly face?"

Bransom paused, wondering if his new revelation was a stretch, or a perfect fit! Justine Martine; Sylvia Brown; the Malovich twins; the Turkish abduction-with Dietrich and the other lineup of dastardly characters! Even Anson Bennett and the yacht at the bottom of Lake Ouachita! And for that matter, Dietrich's yacht scuttled at the marina in Marseille? The common denominator seemed to be Mallory! Keeping his own emotions veiled behind his best poker face, he rose slowly and buzzed to exit the interrogation cell!

Mallory fought her way from the grips of deep sleep, gazing around the darkened suite! Everything was quiet. David slept next to her and no sound came from the girls. She forced herself upright on the edge of the bed, trying to escape the eerie sensation! Something she heard-maybe-her phone? She sank back against the pillows listening. If so, and someone needed her, they could call back-but maybe not! She remembered her own short window of time to phone Erik when she and Amelia were abducted from the ball game. Breathing a prayer for a wrong number, or its only being her imagination, she made her way through the blackness to the bathroom! A missed call from an international number! Something must be wrong! With either Nanci or the Professor! Mallory guessed the latter, as Nanci should be safely on the liner! With dread, she listened to the voicemail! Tears filled her eyes! It was from Nanci-with men's voices shouting in a foreign language, and Nanci speaking urgently "Help! Help us! I'm so scared-" Another wrathful masculine shout, and the connection ended!

Without hesitating, she called Erik, knowing by his alarmed tone that he was afraid she was in trouble once more. "No, we're fine," she assured. "It's Nanci Burnside that's in trouble!"

Erik's silence told her he was weighing Nanci's past infractions. Finally, he spoke! "Okay, call the cruise company and see if she's on board, and ask them what it might mean! The Ukraine's pretty far out of my jurisdiction~"

"Yeah, but what about Colonel Ahmir? Maybe the same people that grabbed Nanci are linked~"

"Yeah may be! I'll give him a call! It's at least day time in Turkey!" Even as he spoke, he remembered Warrington's words about aging, and who the cartel considered valuable targets! Burnside seemed beyond their targeted age range, if she did still look pretty good! "Yeah, Ahmir's as good of an idea as any in that part of the world!"

"Yeah, I'll call the cruise company and then the local police there! Then, maybe Steb and Sam! They helped get David and me back from the Saudis! Oh, yeah; the State Department, too! I guess they didn't do so much~"

"Yeah, Hon, well, we'll be praying too! That's what does the most good! Look, just be sure you don't try to rush to her rescue in person! Promise me!"

"Okay, well, it depends on whether I can accomplish anything by phone!"

David's head throbbed and he shivered! Fighting waves of nausea, he forced his eyes opened and took his surroundings in, terrified! "Ah," moving gingerly, he scooted to where he could hug a yellow girder! He literally had a bird's-eye view of the Black Sea! Well, except for the fog! His clothes were in shreds, feet bare, and he hurt everywhere from the beating~ Nanci! Keeping his white-knuckle grip on the metal beam, his eyes sought for her as tears seeped from swollen eyelids! They must have taken her with them~

Mallory broke the news to Deborah, who went into an angry tirade. Mallory disconnected! Not her fault and she was doing everything she could think of! No point in mentioning it to Daniel and Diana. She forced a smile at David, who took in her pallor and fighting Irish eyes as he appeared questioningly at the bathroom door!

"Can't locate Nanci or the Professor," she acknowledged through clenched teeth. She pushed past him to go to her office to work on her search and rescue efforts. Any more attempt to explain, and she'd go to emotional pieces! She needed her laptop anyway, rather than just her phone!

"Harry!" Maggie's voice came out aghast! "Look at this! I knew I was right when I begged the Captain not to sail without her!"

Harry gazed at the email alert from Steb Hanson! They followed *The SOC Foundation* avidly, and this was cause for concern! "I thought they rescued children; what they're about-but, it's sad! The Captain has a ship to be responsible for and a schedule to keep!"

"Yeah, and he has some responsibility to locate this young lady! I'm paying him a visit! I'll be nice, but we can show him our pictures from yesterday! She was last seen with that sleazy-lookin' fella-" She paused and grabbed his forearm in her pincers!

His shocked eyes met hers, "Yeah; and I didn't get a picture, but there was that really freaky guy who said something to her first thing, in the coffee shop! It looked like he gave her cause for alarm!" Horror crossed his face at the memory. "Maybe we shouldn't get involved-I can email what we know to Hanson, and he can disseminate the information as he sees fit!"

"Okay, well I'm calling this company she reps for! Maybe they'll pay ransom or whatever-she was really exceptionally pretty; you know?"

He pulled her close and they trembled together. "Yeah," he acknowledged, "Very pretty! It may not be about ransom money, at all!" He sighed. "That would explain *SOC's* involvement!"

Higgins sat frozen! Both with terror and from the icy wind blasts that tried to pry his fingers from their hold and hurtle him into murky swirls lapping ninety feet below! He tried to scream, but no sounds came! From his vantage point, he couldn't detect anyone around to hear him, anyway!

Trent Morrison dashed through Atlanta Hartford International Airport! He halted, annoyed, and Addington nearly sent him flying!

"Go home! You're headed for the wrong terminal!"

"Unh-unh! I'm comin' with-"

"No! You're not! I'm heading far from our turf; I'm just not sure where exactly!"

"Well, your flight's to Istanbul!"

"Yeah, which is kinda expensive! It kinda tapped my credit limit! If I get close to where they're holding them, I'll be facing danger!"

"Yeah! That's why I got your six! You can trust me; I won't get sidetracked again!"

Trent muscled past him; he needed to keep moving! They could argue on the move! "Look, I have vacation time, and I'm on my own! Agriculture isn't going to back me or fund me! This isn't my job! But it's something I gotta do!"

The stubborn expression he was accustomed to in the other man set defiantly. "Then you can understand that this is something I gotta do, too!"

"Look! Prove yourself to me some other time! Some other way! If you're just assuming Mallory will reimburse your expenses-"

He shrugged. "Never occurred to me! I'm comin'!" They reached the ticket counter together.

The rain started! Higgins, terrified to move, was suddenly galvanized! Where there was rain, lightning was likely! Some huge crane jutting upward from the Black Sea was the last place he wanted to be! Especially in an electrical storm! Despite the pummeling wind and rain barrage, he inched toward center, and what he hoped was a ladder!

Nanci stirred weakly, moaning! She was in a dark, cramped space with no windows! From the violent rocking, she assumed she was on a ship! Longingly, she thought of the luxurious cabin on the cruise ship! Where she should be! She sensed burning thirst, and tasted blood. "David," the barest whisper received no response. She closed her eyes, relieved for the solitude, then decided to take whatever action she could! Their plans for her were dreadful beyond comprehension! She couldn't be idle and let it happen without a fight! She forced herself painfully to her feet, then, was nearly toppled back to the concrete as a forceful wave rocked the vessel. She moaned again, reaching for the wall to steady herself! A thick slime made her gulp against nausea! That didn't matter! Mold and slime were the least of her worries at the moment! Listening intently, she moved around the perimeter of her prison! A small space and she tripped over obstacles a couple of times!

"Hey, take it easy! Screaming at people isn't going to help!" David's gentle words as he tried to pry Mallory's phone from her hand.

"The Odessa police-" Her eyes were dry and the hot color burned on her cheeks! "They won't-"

He tried to pull her close, but she resisted, rigid! "You don't know what it's like! She's in the trunk of some car, headed, 'who knows where?'" I can't just wait for a bunch of cops to finish their tea and crumpets-I'm not sure any of them understood English-"

"Daddy, this looks like something!" Missy's voice sounded hopeful. Emails deluged the site with well-meaning followers stating they were praying, or even trying to mention tips.

Steb looked over her shoulder! An older couple on the cruise sent a picture of Higgins as the last person they saw Nanci with before they boarded. They also mentioned a terrifying wacko who had approached her earlier in the morning. They hadn't noticed him again-"

Hanson was interested in the second part; Higgins was gone, too! He was considering how he might get the tipsters linked to a sketch artist when he noticed Missy's stricken appearance!

"What Darlin'?"

"Wh-where did you say they were when they dis-appeared?"

"Way up on the Black Sea! Some Russian resort area-Odessa-Why? Here, sit down! Christine!"

Missy straightened determinedly, shaking off the dread in favor of action. "I'm all right, Mother! We just figured this thing out!"

Christine stood in the archway anyway. "Oh, is that good?"

Missy squinted at the missive through narrow slits before answering softly, "Yes, Mother, very good."

Chapter 30: GRACE

Jennifer grabbed Jason and passed Nick on her way to the bedroom. "Let's go someplace! Want to? I feel like the walls are-"

He followed her and stood regarding her as she flung assorted apparel items into a suitcase.

"Okay, maybe Honolulu?"

Her gaze flitted across his wide face and earnest eyes. "You're not going to try to talk-"

He shook his head slowly, taking an opposite stance from his normal. "No, I'm with you! The walls have been closing in on me here, too! My family has never seen Jason; and it isn't your job to find this Burnside woman! You've gone above and beyond! I'm not sure this incident represents any fresh danger for us! But the goons all know where we are, anyway!" He pulled his own suitcase out, laughing when Jason crawled into it to play! He went to the bathroom to pack his ditty bag before getting his laptop to make flight arrangements! With the flights booked, he placed a call to his mother!

"Want me to go to the bank and withdraw some cash to start out with? I can take Munchkin with me so you can get everything together!"

"Yeah sure! That'll be great! You're really serious? About going"?

Nick laughed an exuberant, light-hearted laugh! "I am; you figure out what we'll need for ten days! I'm good with trunks, sandals, and a couple of Hawaiian shirts! We can use my mother's washer and dryer!" With Jason in tow, he made his way out the back, whistling *Tiny Bubbles*!

Jennifer's heart took wing at the prospect of an Island getaway, but rather than continuing with the packing, she pulled out a sketch pad and pen and ink!

'Odessa'! And he had Nanci tightly in his ferocious grip! With trembling hands, she made several deft lines before casting the work aside! She paced! Maybe it wasn't her job to rescue the other woman, but she had some responsibility before she could take off with Nick and Jason for carefree fun! Steeling herself, she picked up the unfinished portrait! The eyes! They were the worst; and she wasn't sure she could do the evil in them justice with the present medium! She got it close enough to be disconcerting! Fighting literal illness, she snapped an image with her phone and emailed it to Agent Bransom!

Higgins appearance at the base of the rig was met with befuddled stares from local fishermen! He knew he was a sight in shredded clothing and bare feet, with black eyes and an arm which hung painfully at an odd angle. They began to barrage him with questions in whatever the local lingo was! He was just eager to get to the hotel and try to get word about Nanci! They deposited him on the dock. Although he shrugged and mumbled 'English', they seemed determined to hold him! Too weary to argue, he followed their pointing and charades. Sure enough, a polizi car showed up and two burly guys strode toward him! Cold, exhausted, and hung over, he regarded them glumly! The biggest one thrust a photo of Nanci in front of him, speaking loudly and excitedly; just not in English!

"I don't know where she is; sorry, I wish I did."

With the pain in his shoulder, he convinced them not to cuff him; maybe at the police station someone would speak English. At least maybe he could call the embassy! Self-incrimination hammered with the other hammer in his brain! To his surprise, the car pulled up in front of his hotel and they ordered him to get out! The language was still unintelligible but their body language made their meaning clear enough. In the room, a couple of guys rifled through his and Nanci's belongings! A hotel manager appeared to interpret, not necessarily voluntarily. Higgins was surprised to see his laptop and camera, along with a crudely framed note: 'We're letting you keep your pictures, Sucka! It's the last you'll ever see of your girlfriend!' His empty stomach knotted and the two police officers continued screaming questions at the interpreter, who formulated them to English to the best of his ability! He seemed scared and nervous, too, and Higgins sympathized with his plight.

"Do they have to let me contact my embassy?"

He blinked behind his glasses and then looked away before continuing, "How you climb crane, drunk?"

Higgins tried again to give his statement. "We went to the club! For a few drinks and some dancing! This dude: uh-weird eyes-really creepy-like those strange contact lenses do at Halloween, but his eyes didn't focus the same direction-uh-black, slicked back hair-uh-I think he scared Nancy earlier in the day! At the club, he asked her an off-the-wall question-about-if she found a-church? Nanci doesn't go-"

The hotel employee and the older of the two policemen exchanged significant glances! Higgins was certain the looks were significant! He just wasn't sure why! His tormented brain told him the local law enforcement would doubtless frame him for Nanci's disappearance before they tangled with a local criminal boss! He hardly cared. It was his fault, after all!

David fixed toast and a fresh mug of coffee and took it to the office.

Mallory's features contorted with torment, but she forced a grim smile. "Thanks! That looks good! I'm-uh-not getting anywhere with anybody."

As he sank down on the corner of the desk, his phone rang. He pulled it out, and his startled eyes met his wife's. "Higgins!"

"Hey Professor! Where are you?" His anxious voice cut straight to the chase. His expression turned puzzled as he listened. Then the call disconnected.

"What?"

David looked disgusted. "Slurred, still drunk, he said they're not taking the flight to Constanta; they're driving the rent car, to view and photograph the scenery!"

"Okay, are you sure it was David's voice? Anyone could claim to be him, slurring, and- They have his phone! And they don't realize Nanci was able to make a distress call- They think that by making us think Higgins and Nanci are taking a long car trip together, they can buy more time!" She consulted a map. "Call back! I'm sure they won't answer, but leave a message to stop at Viziru and take pictures of some monastery ruins there. Tell him that we're working Nanci's travel blog from this end and to text us the pictures."

"Okay, write it out! How do you know that there are monastery ru-"

She smiled mischievously, a first for several hours. "I don't! It just sounds like what we'd tell them! Like we believe they are on the car trip! And like we're into the blog as if nothing's amiss"! With that, she returned her attention to the map as though he were no longer there. He made the call, and sure enough, there was no answer. He left the dictated message before interrupting her.

"Okay, I'm eating right now." She emerged from her map-trance guiltily, and he laughed.

"What did you see on the map?"

She lowered her voice, her eyes huge and luminous. "Look at the driving route, David! It crosses right over the southernmost tip of Moldova! Isn't that where-"

He paled too! "Yeah, where the orphanage was, and-maybe Lilly's all over this-"

"Why would she be, David? I don't follow you."

The cold, dark box pitched with extra violence, and Nanci groaned. Dread gripped her, and tears streamed freely! Maybe, if she hadn't run from church-was God angrier than ever with her for doing that? Snatches of arguments with David tripped through her mind! He loved the seamy club while she felt like she could jump clear out of her skin! He was annoyed that she wasn't still her former partying self! When she refused alcohol, his taunting was that she could try to reform as much as she wanted, but Daniel would never have any use for her again! She closed her eyes! That was the thing! She wanted to be held in regard by him, as well as the Andersons and the other successful people now surrounding her! But whether David Higgins believed her or not, she had other motives! In the lonely darkness, with her future in jeopardy, she was afraid of God. When she had expressed that motive, Higgins had quickly reassured her there was no such entity! That only foolish, uneducated, backwater folk bought into that! And maybe she wasn't the brightest, but Higgins and Waverly seemed to be the uncouth, uneducated dolts; while those that espoused God and the Bible led orderly, successful lives!

"Dear God," her whisper seemed to reverberate in the small metal space, and terrified, she softened her speech so that her lips moved, but the murmur didn't carry. "I don't know how to pray. You know all about my father and mother, and their divorce; and that none of us ever went to church! I guess I can't blame~I mean, I've been grown~with a car~and I still never~I was starting to search for you~even~before I ended up here~wherever here is~do You even~really know~where I am? Why would you~care? I have done bad~things~I guess, trying~to be a~home wrecker~I'm sorry~and I'm not just~because of this~I'm scared about hell~and that I've laughed about~it!" She paused, wiping her nose and eyes with the heel of her hand. "Please, if you~could~help me! I didn't want night clubs on~my travel blog~I know the Andersons~wouldn't~Please, God~"

Disheartened, she rose and felt for the heavy metal of the door! She wanted to free herself before that dreadful guy~ More desperately than ever, she clicked at the door latch. It actually seemed to latch from within! Like slamming it, made the bolt drop down and catch! With a metallic click, it released and she swung it open gingerly! The blackness lessened slightly with light entering weakly through grimy portholes. Sounds assailed her ears! Bilge pumps laboring to stay ahead of incoming seawater; groaning stressed metal; and chittering of myriads of rats! Not a fan of rodents of any kind, she hoped that their presence meant that the old tub wasn't in imminent danger of sinking!

To her left, a stairway led to the deck above. Consequently, she stepped over the hatch and eased right. Revulsion; as her bare feet plunged into icy water and more slime! The ship's roll, combined with the unsure footing, caused her to proceed with extra caution!

Erik studied his most recent gift from Jennifer grimly. 'Odessa'! Another 'O' name to add to his list! Not the suspect's real name, but the name associated with the city whose underbelly he controlled. He studied it in light of David and Mallory's most recent discovery, that Odessa was eerily near Moldova and the now obliterated orphanage! That was the thing with these people: run 'em out one place, and they cropped up again, somewhere else! Knock out what you thought was their front line, to see eager and ambitious foot-soldiers step into the coveted positions, a rung or two up in the organization!

"Okay, Lord, don't let me be overwhelmed, but take one step at a time! Getting Nanci and Higgins back"!

Following a couple of hours of being harangued by the two police officers and the hotel employee, Higgins was in jail! No embassy! They just wanted a confession from him of what he did to Nanci, and where her body now was. He made motions for tablet and writing implement, and to his surprise, they were provided immediately. Guess they thought he was ready to write out his confession! Instead, he began recording snippets coming back to him of the events of the past twelve hours! Arguing with Nanci! Dumb! She said her reason for not drinking was because he was getting so lit; she wanted to drive back to the hotel without any fender-benders, or anything else to land them in legal trouble before they could get out! He was the one super-imposing Daniel on top of her every action! So, they weren't at the club long before the weirdo approached them about if Nanci had managed to locate a church! Higgins remembered telling him belligerently to move along! Oops! His night club! That response and Nanci's beauty together marked them! But, they had made it back to the hotel~and he argued with her again when she refused his advances! Then, there were intruders~and she made it into the bathroom, locking the door! He couldn't remember anything past that, until he wakened high up on the girder! And then, back at the hotel, the bathroom door removed from hinges, and their stuff in disarray! Well, what little bit they had with them! So, they knocked him out and injured his shoulder some way!

David grabbed a bottle of water from the fridge and followed his ears into the great room where Mallory pounded frenziedly on the baby grand piano! A song he hadn't heard in a very long time! *The Children's Assurance March*! He wondered if her move from the office to the piano to play this particular selection meant that she had received some type of assurance from the Lord about Higgins and Burnside! In the meantime, it was amazing! Playing totally by ear, she ran through it a couple of times plain and straightforward. And then, she began adding embellishments, making an awesome arrangement of her own! He needed a way to record it so he could feed it through some music software that translated it onto paper.

"Don't stop," he encouraged. "It sounds awesome! I'm trying to save it; you should do this for your next offertory!"

She stopped anyway! "I wish we could hear some good news. Nothing new on your phone?"

He pulled it free to show her, and was surprised, "A text, actually! From the professor's phone"!

She studied it at length before handing it back! "It's the bad guys! Higgins can't spell!"

The content of the missive was ambiguous: that there was no sign toward the requested ruins as they passed through the small town~really due to the length of the trip, they needed to keep moving so Nancy could resume the cruise by time to board at Constanta! Spelling Nancy with a 'y' was a further proof that someone other than Professor Higgins was in possession of his phone!

Diana's prayers revealed as much confusion as her intercession with Megan Morrison's asthma attack! She certainly held no love in her heart for the woman from Daniel's past! But surely no one deserved the fate Nanci Nichols faced at the hand of her current captors! And, the woman did sell clothing! Since receiving the news, Daniel had maintained his poker-faced demeanor! Diana hoped he didn't care what happened to her! She sighed, reminding herself that the important issue was Nanci's standing with God! Maybe through this trying ordeal, she would see her need to confess to being a sinner and invite Jesus into her heart! Diana knew she needed to deal with her own heart, for at least that much! Besides, being rid of one adversary was no guarantee of her husband's continued faithfulness; or even her own! Their strong marriage was a gift from God, for which He was worthy to be praised, and His strength claimed against temptations that could undermine it! She felt better that the Holy Spirit indeed ministered to her confused and troubled heart!

Something sharp cut into Nanci's bare foot as she eased forward through the muck and sea water. Numbly, she tried to remember when her last tetanus shot was! With eyes and ears trained on the stairs, she reached a wooden palette which elevated wooden crates out of the water. She sank down onto one of the crates to examine the cut! The engine changed sounds, like power cutting back! Terrified, she prayed that they weren't at the destination! That she would continue to be left alone down here while she figured out a plan. "God, please, there's no reason why you should help me-" Even as she spoke, she noticed a crow bar behind her, on the edge of some of the highest crates. She grasped it! Hmmm, might at least cave one of their heads in-hopefully the ugly, scary one most in her face! She could do it, too! She was that resolved, that if anyone was going to be a victim it wasn't going to be her!

"Look, Rob, this is where you see about catching a flight right back to the good old USA!" Trent's attempts at dissuading Addington from sticking with him! "I'm not sure why I'm here myself!"

"To rescue that woman"! Addington looked like an overnight traveler: beard growth, blood-shot eyes. But his upbeat humor surfaced in spite of the lengthy flight, cramped in unmercifully!

Trent laughed, hastening his pace as they strode along the jet way at the Ataturk Airport in Istanbul! "Yes! Thank you for the amazing clarity! I'm saying I don't know where she is, and I have no plan-"

"You were going to call a guy you know in Romania?"

Trent sighed, "Men's Room! Then I'm not sure my acquaintance can actually help! I was studying the map in the flight magazine, and Nanci's last know location was in the Ukraine. That's a long ways from Bucharest and Constanta; even farther from here! That's why I said I don't know what I'm doing here-"

"Well, don't you usually pray then- I mean, you started this venture because you thought it was the right thing to do-"

Maybe it was jet lag, but Trent was the one who was supposed to remember to pray, not Addington. He laughed, "Men's room and then coffee! Maybe I'll call my friend then and see if he has any suggestions or any contacts farther up the coast. And, I have been praying-"

"Mr. Morrison!" a voice behind Trent startled him as he made his way across a crowded café with coffees and croissants.

"That's me!" Trent paused to survey someone who appeared Turkish military; imposing, with thick, black mustache! "Are you Colonel Ahmir?" he ventured a hopeful guess.

Strong teeth flashed, contrasting sharply beneath the black bristle! "Ah, so you know of me!" He seemed pleased at the recognition. "Please, bring your breakfast and follow me!" with a smart heel click, he did a military right face, striding quickly and authoritatively!

"Does this mean trouble?" Rob panted in his ear as they double-timed to keep pace.

"Either that, or the answer to my prayer!" flung over Trent's shoulder.

David engaged in chores to keep himself busy, pausing often to check his phone or return to check on Mallory and the girls. They were all doing as well as could be expected! Mallory pored over her Bible between phone calls and checking her laptop! At last Erik got word that Higgins was banged up, but alive, his release gained in the Ukraine at the insistence of the Embassy! Receiving medical treatment, he was bereft over Burnside!

Addington's pinched face stared straight ahead as two black Mercedes swerved through Istanbul.

"Breathe, Rob!" Trent's cheering voice from the seat beside him.

Addington's terror remained unabated. The Turkish Colonel's brusque demeanor and no explanation frankly rattled him. Trent just took in every bend and landmark through steely eyes hidden behind sunglass lenses. He trusted Ahmir! Up to a point! But his trust was in the Lord; and then, coincidentally, this powerful acquaintance of Mallory's group, showed up to provide transportation? He smirked! And with brand new Mercedes, at that! "Thanks, Lord," he murmured. "So far, so good"!

The two cars bore down on accelerators on a straightaway where water sparkled ahead! Then, they braked so suddenly, Trent was flung forcefully against his shoulder strap! "Guess that means we're here!" His features reflected good humor as he reached for the door handle!

Courteously, Ahmir's aide beat him to opening the door, standing back for both Americans to clamber out! Ahmir remained seated in the passenger seat of the other car. The aide pointed to a peeling door in the side of a long warehouse.

"Please, you will wait in there!"

Without a backward glance or further talk, Trent complied.

"Now what"? Addington's turmoil reflected in his voice.

With a shrug and a broad smile, Trent responded, "I guess we wait here!"

Hungry, Nanci wondered curiously if the crates contained anything edible. Wielding the crow bar, she pried a board loose! It groaned as long nails pulled loose, but the droning, clanging pumps seemed to cover the sound! She stared in horror at the contents of the crate! Guns! Then, wonderingly, she considered the possibility of using one of them! Not savvy about a lot of things, guns were a real mystery! A terrifying mystery! The men she had known liked war movies and shoot-em-ups! That was the extent of her familiarity with weapons. Being terrified by the growing gun crimes in the US, she tended to buy into the rhetoric for stiffer gun control! Now she simply stared, curious as to where these came from, and where they were going! Doubtless, not to deer hunters! She knew the top weapon was an automatic rifle, but it didn't seem to have any bullets loaded. She applied the tool again and another protesting lid lifted! No bullets! Just stacks and stacks of bound hundred dollar bills! The third crate yielded ammo for the automatic weapon, some grenades, and a really big gun! From somewhere in her movie experience came the expression, RPG! She studied the grenades. Maybe, if she could find a life jacket, she could use a grenade to blow a hole in the ship, and she could float free!

The boat stopped so suddenly she went flying, landing on her backside with hands behind her in more of the sickening muck! Then the pump motors fell silent, leaving her dazed in the silence! Panicked, her eyes darted between the stairway and the crates with lids ajar! She couldn't decide whether to try to at least set the crate lids so they didn't appear disturbed, or simply run for her former prison! After all, it locked from the inside, and she thought she had figured out a way to keep her tormentors at bay! Then, noticing that water rose steadily, lapping over the elevated palette, she froze with indecision!

"Major William Salazar! United States Air Force"! The Major strode purposefully toward Trent and Rob. "What exactly is your plan?"

"Trent Morrison," Trent extended his hand, to receive a hard gaze with no reciprocal gesture. "Rob Addington," he nodded sideways at his partner.

"Nice of you two farm boys to show up and pay us a visit"! The hard expression belied the sincerity of the Major's words. "Again, I ask you, what exactly is your plan?"

Trent sighed, trying not to take offense at the slur to his position in the US Department of Agriculture! "My plan exactly is to find a couple of Americans that have disappeared, and get them home safe and sound! That's the big picture; I haven't got it broken down into specific operations yet!"

"That much, we've gathered. Nix, on involving your missionary! I'm not sure I get them, and why exactly they do what they do, but they're exposed, with their families, to enough danger without being involved in anything police, military, political!"

Trent removed his shades to make eye contact with the major, and the dim interior of the warehouse didn't merit them, anyway! "I don't have a plan." He felt more foolish than he ever had in his life, and that was saying something! Landing in foolish situations seemed to be his stock in trade! "Can you think of anything?"

Major Salazar broke his stony countenance to roar with laughter, a sound which echoed around the large, empty space!

"Well, he had a plan, based on the missionary guy," Rob defended feebly, "but since you told us-", he trailed off lamely before the reflective sunglass lenses and folded arms of the military man. A large bay at the watery end of the warehouse slid open and an ancient and battered delivery van pulled in. Trent watched with interest as the bay slid shut.

"Gentlemen-" The Major indicated them to join him.

Trent wasn't surprised when the interior of the van was new, glistening, and chock full of everything state-of-the art; whereas, Addington's mouth dropped with amazement! Different reactions not missed by the Air Force officer.

"Ah, you are not even impressed by my toy, Mr. Morrison!" Feigned disappointment!

"Well, very impressed! Just not totally surprised; because I heard a new, high-performance engine"!

A shocked officer caught the eye of an attractive, petite lieutenant seated at the controls; she nodded, "Making a note of that, Sir!"

Salazar's respect for the 'farm boy' rose. A very important detail in covert operations! If Morrison picked up on it, so might the enemy, putting lives in danger! The Air Force needed to work on a high performance engine that sounded like a beater!

Gingerly, Nanci fed a belt of ammunition into the automatic rifle. To her relief, it was kind of a no-brainer! She was puzzled! The ship rocked, but other than that, there was no movement! No forward momentum, at all! Galvanized by the rising water, she pushed toward the stairway! The water was cold, and up to her knees! She couldn't figure out a reason to shut off the pumps and allow the water to rise, inundating the valuable contraband! Maybe they knew they couldn't prevent her sinking, and had abandoned-but there were still rats down here! Maybe that was urban legend; that rats deserted a sinking ship!

A sat map flashed onto one of a dozen screens. "You're looking at the harbor of Odessa, Ukraine!" Salazar's flat voice intoned. "This is your geologist friend!" A pointer caused Trent to utter a cry of alarm!

"Yi! How'd he get up there?"

"Thought you'd never ask, dumb, farmer"!

Trent laughed tensely. He could tolerate teasing in exchange for the intel! He watched as the sequence reversed! The picture was grainy, of some tub plying through the water toward the towering structure! Even with the poor quality of the images, he could see as the tub anchored and began winching something upward! The boat rocked, and the cable swung! Whoever was delivering Higgins to the girder seemed to be risking a lot! Crazy! Nuts!

His face turned white as an inert man was deposited on a yellow girder, the other man returned to the deck of the boat, and the vessel hasted from the scene!

"Not sure if he was drugged in addition to plenty of drinking!" the Lieutenant took over the narrative. "I'm pretty sure they assumed he'd fall to his death! I can't figure out how he didn't! But he didn't! Inched down, even though later on, we can tell that he sustained a shoulder injury! Here's a fishing boat that picked him up and took him to the dock, where Ukrainian cops picked him up for questioning in Nichols' disappearance. They have reason to believe that a local criminal kingpin nabbed her, but apparently, they were content to blame your geologist, rather than messing with this guy-"

Trent and Addington gasped in unison as the evil and sadistic face filled the screen! "Yeah, I could see that," Trent agreed weakly! "I'd rather deal with Higgins than that guy, too! Send that to my phone, would you? I can get some masks produced before Halloween! That's what I call scary!"

"That's who you're dealing with! We don't know his given name! He operates a popular night club there in Odessa; and usually doesn't get so implicated. His attraction to your friend evidently made him throw caution to the wind!"

Trent stared! Wouldn't be the first or last time that a woman caused a man to lose all sense of reason!

Jen should have been enjoying herself, being with Nick and Jason in the mellow Hawaiian sunshine!

"I think I caught enough for dinner, even with all the cousins coming over!" Nick's voice was jubilant! "Whadaya think of this?" He shoved one of the flopping fish toward Jason, who clapped excitedly, but eased backwards.

Jen hugged her son, laughing at the antics. "Guess he's not sure!"

Nick shot her a perceptive glance. "You're not enjoying yourself!"

Forcing a smile, she sighed. "I am, Nick! This was my idea! And I'll enjoy everything for a while-" lovely features clouded and she fought tears. "As long as I can keep it all pushed back-but thinking about-her-with O-Uh-why Trent Morrison?"

A sigh in response! "Well, he's a good guy, and he means well! But it's not his job! He has no resources, as far as equipment and backup! Grabbing Americans used to bring more rapid response from our government! Now, with so many Americans traveling, and so many cautions from the State Department-"

"Well, yes," Jennifer agreed. "But on a cruise-"

"Well, what's considered safe for tourists in ports in daytime is something different than missing the boat and staying, drinking and partying! If Higgins wanted to dance and drink, there's plenty of that offered on-board!"

"Well, yeah!" she turned extra pensive and drew inward.

"What?" He probed cautiously.

"Well, Higgins wasn't on the cruise! He just had time off, and he-uh-kind of follows her around-like a puppy-She could do a lot worse, you know!"

He laughed at the defiant fire in her voice.

Trent wavered between snoozing and reading his Bible! With the croissant wearing off, his stomach rumbled hungrily! Grateful for the chopper transport, he was reluctant to mention chow! He rose and stretched!

"I hope you're working out a rescue plan." Rob's whisper, returned to its plaintive norm.

Trent studied the man for several seconds. His own opinion was that the Lord had a plan which was opening up like a rosebud! Skimming across the Black Sea in a US Air Force Blackhawk toward the vessel being tracked by satellite? So far, everything seemed better than expected. Besides, he had tried to convince the whiner to stay home!

A member of the flight crew approached to offer MRE's, and both Forestry men accepted gratefully!

"Sorry for the absence of amenities." The words seemed more jibe than apology!

"We're just appreciative of the ride," Trent rejoined, trying to bring levity to the challenge!

"Expensive ride! The taxpayers-"

"I can't imagine," Trent's quick agreement! "Taxpayers that will be my great-grandchildren, trying to unbury themselves from the National Debt"!

The airman strode away, evidently not worried enough about the rising debt to stay and discuss it!

Nanci studied her ominous-looking weapon in the gloom. It looked okay, but what did she know? She thought the 'safety' was off, but what if she charged up on deck and it didn't work? She was fairly certain her nemesis wasn't so enchanted with her that he'd overlook her trying to shoot him! She hesitated, although the rising water alarmed!

"There's your lady," The airman pointed below, and the two men squinted at the toy boat bouncing below.

"She's riding low! You sure you can't drop us on her deck?" Addington's voice changed again from dull to engaged! "She's not too long from going under! Wonder why-" Then the obvious occurred to him! "Contraband! She's overloaded. Guessing it's-There isn't time for you to drop us on-shore and us to hire a charter, and get to-where on earth is she headed?"

"My guess is the Danube Delta!" Trent's voice carried assured authority! "You're right, though! She isn't going to make it! Do your sat photos give any indication that they might have abandoned ship?"

Without permission, Addington opened someone's binocular case and scanned the scene! "She's adrift! Is there any Coast Guard in whatever country this is, that would field a distress signal?"

The airman shrugged. Their orders were to transport the two men to the opposite shore of the Black Sea, take a few recon photos to help justify the flight, and not engage in any battles: with other nations, or criminals!

"If you're right, and they are weighted by contraband, they might not try to notify authorities." Trent's voice as he extended his hand to borrow the glasses. After a few moments he observed, "No davits for a life boat! If they ditched, they used an inflatable! Hard to see it from this altitude; they may be long gone! Doubtless, they took Miss Burnside with them." His tone registered regret at the possibility their target wouldn't be as easy to locate as he thought.

Relieved at hearing The Professor's voice, Mallory's feelings dipped at his remorse and self-incrimination about Nan. "Okay, well, just a few hours ago, we were despairing of you; and you're okay! Everyone's praying for Nanci! It'll be okay!" She struggled to remain upbeat.

Higgins listened, skeptical, but afraid to argue. 'What if he was right and there was no god at all, listening to their impassioned pleas? He was free due to the American Embassy! That was just the way it worked! No miracle there! Although-' he remembered his pain and terror! 'Lucky that the State Department came through for him! That was no guarantee for Nanci,' and his insistence at going clubbing was the reason why she was gone!

Mallory tapped a key to brighten the large monitor, and a laugh bubbled through her discouragement! She called David, who appeared, feigning innocence!

"Did you do that?"

His gaze followed her pointing finger. "Oh, that 'Sign here' sticker? That's crazy! Why would anything need to be signed on a monitor? Looks like your dad's handiwork!"

She folded her arms and pressed her lips shut in disbelief! "I think it looks like David Anderson's handiwork! Trying to fake my daddy's MO"! She pulled the red arrow down! "You noticed too?"

He grinned. "No; I noticed that you noticed!"

Trent heard Major Salazar's profanity, though the earphones fit snugly on the first lieutenant who piloted the Blackhawk!

"I can rappel onto the deck; find out if she's out of fuel, why she's lost power!" Rob Addington's plea!

Trent could rappel, too; though he didn't care anything about it! And he had never tried it from a chopper onto a rocking and sinking bucket of bolts! Besides which, their presence wouldn't necessarily be welcomed. Because they saw no movement on deck wasn't proof that they wouldn't walk into live fire. He remembered from Addington's file that he had been accepted for The Navy Seals, but didn't complete the rigorous course! 'Washed out', was his self-condemnation! Trent filled with fresh amazement at God's hand in the rescue of Nanci Nichols! An almost Seal assisting him was amazing!

"She's not flagged at all; for any country! She's just bobbing and floundering in a busy shipping area!" The second officer relayed Addington's argument to base!

More highly unflattering references to them as the major gave orders for them to write releases, taking responsibility for their own actions! Trent wasn't sure how much that absolved the Air Force of responsibility, but he was praying fervently for no mishaps, anyway!

Nanci Burnside fought her way through deepening water sloshed back and forth by swells, finally catching hold of a metal railing of the stairway! Weapon ready, she popped her head even with the deck! No one in view, and she rose another step, heart pounding! They were all gone! Leaving her to die! She was horrified at how high the sea water rose! And to her consternation, the rats poured up the steps, dashing for higher ground. She suppressed a shriek! "Oh-oh-Dear God-I'm asking-I'm begging-for-for-another chance!" She turned her gaze imploringly toward the heavens, and deep blue eyes widened in amazement as the beating blades of a propeller brought a helicopter into view!

Chapter 31: GRANTED

"I'll go first!"

Trent stepped aside to allow Addington to make the initial descent! It affected his equilibrium as he watched! The boat was totally at the mercy of the swells, and it seemed like it kept bobbing away from the apparatus trying to lower onto it!

Addington released the harness as his feet touched deck and gazed around quickly! She was going down, unless-Getting his sea legs under him, he bounded toward switches that should operate the bilges! 'Unless she was out of fuel, maybe'- He stopped mid-stride and thrust his hands above his head!

"Who are you?" a wild-eyed woman questioned from the other end of an automatic assault rifle!

"I'm Rob; are you Nanci? Could you please lower your weapon, Ma'am?"

Instead, she raised the heavy piece slightly, finger poised on the trigger.

"I came with Trent Morrison," he made a ginger motion toward the harness which was supposed to winch up to bring Trent to the deck after him.

She raised her eyes and gasped with relief when she recognized Morrison, before dropping the weapon with a clatter. Rob sighed in relief when it didn't fire. "Okay, Nanci, I'm going to try these switches, and then I'm securing you for a short elevator ride to the top! Okay?"

She nodded affirmatively, seeming dazed and disoriented!

Addington felt pressure to take fast action, but he needed to keep the woman calm to ride up solo in the basket. Relief swept through him when the pump motors rumbled to life! "Where did you find the weapon?" he questioned as he indicated for her to take a prone position in the basket.

"Down the stairs; in a crate," she mumbled. "There's money, and radio-active-" She broke off, not being exactly sure what was radio-active!

"Okay, you're fastened in tight! You may feel the wind tugging this around a bit-"

She nodded. "Yeah, thank you! Rob, did you say? I-I'll be-okay."

He gave a 'thumbs up' and watched as she rose toward the hovering craft!

Roger Sanders frowned. 'Good grief! Beth and Suzanne going to lunch together'! He wondered what that was about! His cell phone interrupted his concern! The boat broker!

"Hey, Tony; what's up?"

He listened, frowning, to the broker's excited story. "Can you believe it, Rog? It's too good to be true!"

"Mmmm-hmmm! I'll say! They just bought it? Sight unseen! And paid cash! And they're taking delivery ASAP! That's amazing, all right!"

"Yeah," Tony enthused, and you know where they want her? The Black Sea! All I'm saying is this *Housinger International, Inc.* must have some deep pockets! Corporations usually finance so they can deduct interest payments-and, it seems like they'd shop closer to home-"

"Yeah, seems like," Roger echoed numbly. "Okay, close the deal and get the check payable to *Anderson Exploration*! They'll cut me a check and I'll take care of my end of the bargain with you!" He disconnected while Tony raved on about the incredible aspects of the sale!

Roger surveyed the parking lot beyond the riotously landscaped yard of *Sanders, Inc.* Whatever Suzanne and Beth's lunch was about, it was due for an interruption.

"Hello, Boss," Suzanne's usual, sunny, phone voice! "What do you need me to do?"

"I'm sorry to interrupt your lunch when you seldom leave your desk, but could you call Erik right away and ask him to be in touch with me?"

"Well, I'll try, but we just got word that Miss Nichols has been rescued, basically unharmed! Erik's working on learning all the details-" She was reluctant to add that when Erik was busy, he would be more likely to answer Roger's calls than hers.

"Well, this may be related to that," Roger's speech gained intensity!

In less than five minutes the agent called in response to Suzanne's text. "What's up, Sanders?"

"Well, David and Mallory are trying to sell their little boat so they can purchase a larger one!"

"Oh, I didn't know that!" Erik's voice showed his frustration with seeming small talk.

Roger laughed. "Getting straight to the point, then! Since I know the boat market somewhat, they offered me a commission to sell; and I passed the task along to a broker I know! He called, excited, that someone's buying! This *Housinger International, Incorporated*! Said company's turning over a boatload of cash, pun intended, not haggling, and not financing! And they're taking her to, guess where?"

"The Black Sea! That is interesting, Sanders. You done?"

"Guess that's it." Roger disconnected, hurt. Not that he ever just wanted to chat when he was busy! But it seemed like everyone was sympathizing with Beth and treating him like the bad guy! That took his thoughts back to the circle of why Suzanne and Beth were out to lunch together. He sighed, his mind traveling to Tony's call and the boat sale! He frowned, disturbed that nothing kept the bad guys from business as usual. Scuttle one boat filled with evidence; don't even stop long enough to cry over your losses! Had to hand it to the determination of the devil and his crowd! Christians seemed to spend most of their time, defeated, and mourning over their defeats, whining and crying around, accomplishing little! His startled eyes reflected back from a large mirror on the opposite wall!

"Lord, that's me; isn't it? Getting in this little tiff with the amazing woman you graced me with, and wondering why other Christians don't take my side! Trying to sidetrack all of us with pettiness; while evil never stops"! He crossed his office to where a large decorative globe in a stand lent to the masculine décor. Lifting it, he traced with a finger the distance from the berth at Vero Beach, Florida to the Odessa port on the Black Sea! Who would expect this criminal element to locate a new vessel so far from their base of operations? Clever, true; but they just never gave up!

"Lord, please forgive me! Help me not to throw in the towel and give up! On anything related to Your kingdom! With Your indwelling, I should have more grit than they do! I haven't been keeping close enough to the

Power Source of You, to stay charged up!" Silence filled the masculine space filled with all the trappings of success. "I haven't really wanted to come to You because I've been so far off-base with Bethy."

David exited the Ranch heading toward Murfreesboro, his violin case beside him on the seat! Kind of funny, really, when he got over his annoyance! He was finally on the way to the recording studio to begin taping the violin course for Tom Haynes! The project, stalled by a series of interruptions, was also off-track due to pettiness! Evidently, Daniel and Cassandra both felt they were too far removed from the beginning phases, to relate! So, they had asked him! Had to admit, that he was offended that they considered him to be an amateur! He smiled at his reflection in the rear view mirror! And the ever competitive Erin was more than slightly miffed that they asked him, and not her! 'Ha, at least it was good to know he was better than someone!' When he kissed her good-bye she was trying to say something about if she just had a better instrument-At least that was an idea for Christmas.

Rob Addington stayed with the boat, hoping that the water level was receding, ever so gradually! He was a little amazed that the felons didn't make use of one of the grenades to make certain she went to the bottom! Although, that would be unpredictable and dangerous! There was plenty of fuel on board, and he nursed her toward a rendezvous point. He was uncertain why they bothered to snatch the woman, only to leave her behind to meet a certain death! Then it came to him. She wasn't part of the carefully laid out plan! Odessa's infatuation deviated from the assignment; certainly he never anticipated the American military's intervention! And there wouldn't have been that, except for Trent Morrison's sense of duty! He had to grin, even as he improvised a system to bail water from below deck! And radio-active? That was interesting! Upping the ante considerably, even from drugs and arms and the slave trade! Oh, yeah! Odessa had made a huge blunder! Rob's guess was that he was dead somewhere, executed! And the woman who captivated him was just a problem for the others! Not that they didn't have an efficient method of dealing with problems!

Maybe the clueless Nanci was mistaken about anything nuclear~but why would she have said that~

He spoke through the comm to Morrison. "Hey, who are we rendezvousing with? Burnside said something about there being radio-active~are we just turning this stuff back over to more thugs? I mean, even government people~"

"Are probably thugs," Trent finished. "How far can she make it?"

Addington sighed. "Well, she leaks like a sieve, but the bilges are making headway! I've devised a way to keep bailing mechanically, too! Running out of fuel would be the biggest risk~"

The second lieutenant's voice filled Rob's ears, and he listened.

"I don't know," he answered, "and I'm not going down in that filth! Ask Miss Burnside to be more specific! I'm just saying if they were smuggling nuclear, how wise are we to turn it over to the Ukrainians?"

"Bulgarians," Morrison contradicted. "We're delivering Nanci to the cruise ship when it docks in Nessebar. She has a nasty cut on her foot, but the infirmary on board is probably her best bet! Not saying that Bulgarian medical care isn't up to date; I'm just saying I don't know that it is!"

Rhonna breathed a prayer of relief when she learned that Nanci Burnside was either already back aboard the luxury cruise ship, or at least nearly back! A matchmaking little imp perched on her shoulder, and with a delighted giggle, she succumbed to the suggestion. Although somewhat irregular, the cruise company agreed to take on a new tourist half-way through the cruise!

"That's cool, girl," she congratulated herself as she booked Higgins. "Now he can keep a better eye on Miss Nanci, and if he hasn't learned a lesson about partying, at least he can party on board! And he can keep the blog progressing along!" Hmmm, another idea; she dialed an Arizona phone number!

Maggie met the bedraggled Nanci as she boarded, hustling her toward her cabin where she could clean up! Trent lagged, discouraged. Two things he wanted to address before he snagged Addington and headed home! What Burnside saw that she thought was radioactive and a chance to witness to her.

A ship's officer approached to ask him to follow him for a word with the Captain. He complied, taking in the opulent décor and appealing provision of plentiful food; reminding him that the MRE was his only source of nourishment in the past ten hours. The captain thanked him for his actions, offering him a brandy.

With an appreciative laugh, he declined the alcohol! He was worried still, about Burnside's continued safety; and Higgins! And Rob's, for that matter! He argued with himself about the advisability of leaving his partner in the care of the Blackhawk and her crew! What if the bad guys decided they wanted their stuff after all, since they hadn't succeeded in sinking the boat with its hoard of evidence? Valuable evidence!

"How about coffee, then"?

"Huh? I'm sorry? Did you mention coffee-that would be fantastic-"

"I usually dine with a later seating, but if you're hungry-"

Trent met his eyes, startled. The Captain doubtless heard his stomach growling. "As delightful as that sounds, I'm a mess!" He viewed his clothing sadly wishing Nanci Burnside hadn't decided to demonstrate her gratitude with such a mucky hug! Stuff stunk, too!

The fastidiously attired officer nodded sympathetically. "A prime rib dinner, then, served in my office?"

"You have no idea how tempting that is, but my buddy's still out there somewhere trying to muscle that boat in-"

With a laugh, the distinguished officer shook his head. "I'm afraid your friend has been relieved of his command!"

Trent's empty stomach tied itself into a hard knot! "What's that supposed to mean?"

"That means that with the possibility of nuclear components aboard that ship, the free world isn't taking any chances. Your mission, unadvised for consideration of one woman, has actually become strategic: putting the right parties into the right places at the right times!"

Trent nodded as he considered the words thoughtfully. Meaning, Lilly didn't alert the Israelis and make a move toward helping Nanci-no, she wouldn't-her Cassandra connection was feathered by not crossing Faulkner any further-but mention illegal nuclear-and Israeli interests being on the line-maybe the larger scope of the criminal activities would keep his actions from being called into question in DC! But he didn't agree with Lilly, or with the Captain! One woman's life was worthy of a rescue attempt! And he still needed an opportunity to witness to her. 'The free world isn't taking any chances', the Captain's expression! That must mean Israel was rushing to the scene! Although Turkey was Nato, and her secular government tried to play by Western rules, the Moslem majority made it risky to trust the Turks with whatever Nanci had seen down in that ship's cargo hold!

Eric sat back, satisfied! Although digging through layers and layers of shell corporations, accounts, and assets, took several hours, the effort paid off! The tight, fast little boat escaped from its berth in Vero Beach, but that was okay! *Housinger International, Incorporated*'s sleek new purchase raced without being aware of it, into a Coast Guard trap. Sure enough, she set a course north and eastward! Now that the information search was completed and the issue temporarily in the hands of the Coast Guard, he took time to wonder about David and Mallory and the boat! 'What were those kids up to next?' Well, anyway, a good thing for Sanders' timely call!

> *Proverbs 3:3&4 Let not mercy and truth forsake thee: bind them about thy neck; write them upon the table of thine heart:*
>
> *So shalt thou find favor and good understanding in the sight of God and man.*

Mallory loaded the girls and made her way toward Hal's. Evidently, David's recording session was finished and getting some rave reviews! Consequently, an entourage was gathering for a celebratory dinner! Amazing that neither Daniel, Cassandra, nor Phil wanted to stoop to do the elementary level; but then they all showed up to offer their input! Kinda typical! She smoothed lip gloss and paused to admire her necklace! A heavy gold plaque bordered with 'wreathen work' as the Bible described the design used in the priestly Breastplate of Righteousness! Her thoughts wandered. An artistic design later utilized by Carl Fabergé, the imperial jeweler to the last Tsar of Russia! Anyway, the wreathen work bordered the centerpiece of her necklace, which featured a balance with *Mercy* on one side, and *Truth* on the other, reminding her to keep her Christian life in balance! The verse in Proverbs instructed to bind the two words, mercy and truth, around your neck, and to write them on the table of your heart! She knew the meaning was figurative, but she liked it when her jewelry was Christian witness! A smaller version dangled at her wrist, and earrings were delicate knots of wreathen work!

"Put your headphones on," she ordered Amelia and Avery! "Mommy wants to listen to her music." They complied, and she turned up her volume! What a relief about Nanci! Well, and the professor, too! "Thank You, Lord," she whispered. "What miracles! And Trent Morrison makes me ashamed that I didn't do~ well, thank You for urging him to go, and then that Rob Addington~You know I've still been really mad at him! And thank You that David's head seems better again~" A delighted grin spread across her face, chasing the tears away! "And thank You for showing me another map!" She laughed aloud at David's stunt of sticking the 'sign here' sticker on the monitor!

David Higgins took another backward look at the official from the embassy before joining the crowd of tourists waiting for the tender to return them to the ship following a shore excursion! Still clasping his small carry on, he sidled past the crewman who vetted the boarders.

"Welcome aboard, Mr. Higgins! We're glad you're joining our cruise!"

Relieved, he bolstered a smile. "Thank you, Sir!" Not sure what else to do, he pulled his camera out! It seemed like days since Nanci had sat beside him, laughing, admiring his pictures, confiding in him excitedly about her new venture! What a dummy to argue with her, to mock her religious search, to talk her into staying on-shore~ He shot several pictures, figuring they would do little to restore him to her good graces! He had caused her to miss the shore outings in both Constanta, and now Nessebar! Not a good thing, for either her job with *Rodriguez* or her new blog!

"Sorry for taking so long!" Suzanne's breathless apology as she settled in at her desk following lunch. "I hope Erik phoned you! I sent him a text, but he's-"

"Yeah, he did call me; thanks! Sorry to interrupt your lunch; and it's no problem about the lengthened lunch hour! Most days, you work through your lunch hour. Or go to the cafeteria where everyone brings you their problems. Was Beth okay?" He cringed at the pitiful stab at acting nonchalant.

"Yes Sir! Doing great! It's amazing how excited she is now, about her life! She wants me to submit for her blog, about flowers."

"Oh yeah? Well that's your long suit! But, uh-I thought her blog was on food!"

Suzanne nodded. "Yes, she wanted me to research edible blossoms, as garnishes for plates, and even decorating cakes and pastries with real flowers! But I didn't have to research it, because it's just interesting to me, so I already knew!"

Roger nodded. "Cool! Anything else I should know?"

Suzanne met his gaze with open candor. One thing Suzanne could not do, was keep secrets! Consequently, Beth probably didn't confide much to her! "Well, just how excited she is about going to Boston when Shay and Emma's-remember how excited you were about your first grandkids?"

He grinned. 'Yeah, Suzanne couldn't resist.' He nodded. "I do remember! Are you talking about that day I rehired you, just before Patrick's estate-Suzanne, I'm excited about Emma's baby-I've just been in a little bit of a pout! I can't believe Tony is so big already-the grandkids grow up faster than the kids did."

The meal at Hal's seemed to have an extra dimension of joy! Of course, with the Faulkners there, Mallory didn't feel free to say much about the situation on the Black Sea! Or the dramatic answer to heartfelt prayer. But the whole thing was incredible! And there was a sense of elation about getting the long-awaited violin course off the ground! Her eyes sparkled at the prospect of Nanci and the Professor completing the tour together. After an overnight in Istanbul, Nanci's current city of residence, the ship would continue on to the gorgeous, gorgeous Sorrento, Italy, offering excursions for Capri and Pompeii; and ending in Citavecchia, the port nearest to

Rome! Her hope was that Deborah's model and her Geologist's attraction to one another would deepen. And, then there was the Danube! She could hardly contain herself!

Toward the end of the entrees, Diana offered a compliment and ventured a guess! "Mallory, you are absolutely the most radiant I've ever seen you! Do you have an announcement?"

Mallory's laughter rippled, "Well, not about any new additions to our family! But, just the Lord is so good, and when I couldn't figure out what His purpose could be, I got another amazing revelation! Speaking of, isn't Alexandra incredible? Sometimes I wish I could be everywhere at once! Like! Sorrento! I know that as soon as the blog-" She clapped a hand over her mouth!

"Yeah, we know about the blog," Daniel's tone was matter-of-fact! "It's a great idea! Diana and I have talked about advertising on it! Nanci needs the advertising income, and it would give *DiaMal* some great new exposure, too!"

"And what were you saying about Sorrento?" Diana resumed seamlessly, "and being everywhere at once?"

"Yes, Ma'am, our next destinations are Durango and Silverton. We're buying an adorable old house near the Pritchard's. Since it's a historical district, David needs to get the guidelines for renovating! I haven't met Hallie yet, but David tells me we'll love each other; that the Pritchards are something else! And we're starting a gold mining operation there!"

"Really"! Daniel's brow crinkled in shock! "There's gold up there!"

Mallory's mysterious expression made her look like the proverbial cat that swallowed the canary. "Uh-yes Sir! There can be!"

That was kind of a different answer.

"So, our plans have gotten jumbled around; for the better, I can actually see now!" Mallory's gaze met David's! "We were planning a trip commencing in Florida, but then with David's sudden medical-well-sudden to me-uh that got put on hold-"

"Yeah, while you upgrade your boat?" The question burst forth before Daniel could stop it.

"Yes," David took over smoothly. "Our plan was to start in Vero Beach; that's along Florida's Gold Coast! Called that because treasure from sunken vessels continues to wash up there, some of which is over four centuries old! The prevalent ways of finding it are diving near the wreck sites, or beach combing with metal detectors-"

"But your sweet little rig was set up for either drilling or dredging-have you heard from Erik about who purchased it?" Daniel's update!

"Uh-oh! That doesn't sound good! We haven't heard of its selling, and Erik has a scoop on it? What has it been involved in?" Mallory dreaded the answer. If it was sold, they needed the money; hopefully it wouldn't be confiscated-

"Some international corporation purchased it, with a cashier's check! And they're taking it straight to the Black Sea! Or they were, until the Coast Guard got involved!"

"The Coast Guard!" Mallory's dread deepened!

"Well, yes the Coast Guard stays on the lookout for illicit drugs and other contraband, but Nanci said that one of the crates she saw was marked with a radiation warning! She said the printing on the crate looked like Arabic, but turns out, it was actually Farsi! So, nuclear materials either coming from or moving in to Iran has everyone's undivided attention!"

Mallory met David's gaze in confusion.

"Meanwhile, Tony the broker was quite taken with your little boat, himself!" Daniel shot David a significant look. "He told Sanders there are some mechanical-"

David nodded modestly! "Yes, Sir; they have international patent protection!"

Daniel nodded in amazement! Why would he doubt? "So, instead of Florida, you're heading toward Colorado first, to mine for gold! Winter and snow have Al's silver mine on hold!"

"Let me finish! We were starting at Vero Beach, and then I wanted to see the Space Center! I want a picture of our family on the lunar vehicle! Then maybe Disney! And then, we were going on through the Caribbean to the Panama Canal, to the west coast of Peru! I've always thought it would be cool to go through the canal and see how the locks work; but David's really hyped about it! So, that's our agenda, and now you know!"

"Did you know that Lilly's upset with the German's?" Cassandra questioned.

"Yeah, stemming from the Holocaust"!

"Well, that's not what this is about!" Cassandra's eyes flashed.

"Maybe not directly, but the Germans aren't doing things any differently than most of the governments where we apply for drilling permits!" Mallory's mild tone!

"What are y'all talking about?" Daniel couldn't quite follow.

David laughed. "Well, when we think we've located targets with drilling potential, we contact the governments for permits! Naturally, while the requests are tied up in red tape, they send their own national geologists, or the big companies operating in said countries, to beat us out!"

"Well, that isn't very nice!" Diana's opinion!

David laughed. "When there's money involved, people are often 'not nice'. But then when their exploration doesn't turn up much, they assume there's nothing of value so they're ready to take our money for issuing the permits!"

"And then you drill, and find what you targeted?"

Mallory nodded, "Yes Sir, that's right!" With a smile and no further elaboration!

Chapter 32: GRADIENTS

David squinted at a text from David Higgins! Crazy! And actually, technically, he worked for Mallory. Still, he grinned as he replied:

In regards to-

I'm happy to send you the ten thousand! Congratulations, man! We wish you the best! Well, I do, and so will Mallie when I tell her! She and Diana are together in the first design brainstorming session they've had in months! I disagree with you! I feel like getting married is a great investment! Proverbs 18:22 states that: Whoso findeth a wife findeth a good thing, and obtained favor of the LORD.

Wiring to you now!

Relieved, the professor made his way from his small cabin to the ship's infirmary! "We're all set. Looks like the IV's almost done! You're-you're-sure?"

She nodded; deep blue eyes bluer than ever against the white pillow!

Higgins' head spun! Maybe still some vertigo from being stranded atop the girder; or the movement of the ship as she left anchor toward open water; maybe the narcotics for his shoulder pain; or just being so much in love! Maybe it was all the motions and emotions of the past few days all rolled together! 'Ew'! Don't say 'motion' or 'rolled'!

"Are you okay? Are you thinking about backing out?" Beautiful features crinkled in concern.

"I'm fine!" Higgins' voice betrayed him, coming out as a high-pitched yelp! Why couldn't he be more like Faulkner?

The nurse shot him a professional glance. "Maybe you should sit down! You wouldn't be the first groom on board, ever to faint! What are you taking for pain?"

Dumbly, he produced the small prescription bottle.

"How is your pain?"

"Great!" he knew his grin looked stupid! A cross between elation about Nanci, and the drug!

The nurse shot Nanci an amused glance. "Oh, he got it bad!"

She just nodded.

"I want to know what was on that boat!" Rob's features, taut from exhaustion and frustration!

Trent nodded agreement, stretching long legs in relief! First class, going home!

"We may find out; we may not! All Nanci could tell was that it was the circle with the three arms in it, like you see in hospital sections that use radiation."

"Maybe it was just medical equipment!" Rob deflated visibly at the thought!

"What if it was? These criminals do these organ harvests and transplants; all kinds of black market medical treatments! Anyway it's always in Israel's best strategic interests to keep tabs on what the Iranians are up to! If you didn't save the whole world from a nuclear attack, your actions were commendable! Thanks for insisting on coming!"

Addington grinned at the respect! "I don't suppose you're interested in what happened?"

"What, with the SEALS? It's just tough, isn't it? Anyway, it's in the past! And I figured that your employment by the government for law enforcement shows it wasn't for anything criminal! I'm just glad you were good at that dangling from a chopper over a bobbing boat! And, if I had rappelled onto her successfully, I didn't know the boat stuff you knew, to keep her afloat!"

"Yeah, and then you're the one who got the big hug! What do you think your wife will say?"

"Thanks, Rob! I was feeling sleepy! Now I'm wide awake! What would yours say?"

"Oh, she'd just bat her big beautiful brown eyes at me, and moan, 'My hero!'."

"Right, wish she had hugged you, then! I threw my clothes out, they stunk so bad!"

"Yeah, so what did you say to her? Why we ignored three warnings to go ashore before being thrown off?"

"I showed her the plan of Salvation!"

The other man flopped back disgustedly into the leather seat back! "Do you ever give that stuff a rest?"

"Well, hold on! You asked me what I was talking to her about! And she asked me about getting saved! She said that she tried all week to access Faith Baptist's web site; she even tried a church in one of the ports on Sunday morning! But it was real formal and not in English!"

Frustration filled Rob Addington! "The story of my life with what little church I've tried! It's formal and doesn't make sense! So, how can you, when you're not even trained in the clergy, boil it down, so that some cute but dopey woman can get a handle on it?"

"Because it really is that simple! Jesus explained that it's so simple a little child can understand it! It's adults that complicate it! Or who stumble at its simplicity! Jesus did it all when He died and rose again! It's a free gift that we have only to accept."

"It isn't easy! I can't be like you! I enjoy partying and having fun!"

"Well, you don't have to change yourself or your lifestyle to get saved. You simply ask the Lord to forgive you of your sins and come into your heart! When you do that, the Holy Spirit comes in and indwells you! He works on you gradually, making you ready to relinquish some things in order to take hold on better-it's joy like it's hard to describe-"

"Well, I've tried a lot of stuff! Guess I'm ready to give your angle a shot-uh, do I have to bow my head?"

Trent glanced around the first class cabin. Other passengers slept, watched movies, worked on laptops! Who would even notice a man with head bowed?

He grinned, laughing softly. "No, that's a tradition about praying; we teach it to our kids; 'close your eyes; bow your head; maybe even, fold your hands.' The reason for that might be to block out distractions–but it isn't essential. Prayer is an attitude of the heart. People can pray while they drive or do myriads of tasks. Just ask Jesus to come into your heart right now! You don't have to ask aloud. It's not for me, anyway."

Addington's hard gray eyes drilled into him and his jaws clenched! And then suddenly, tears started and signs of tension fled!

David halted, awed! With news of Higgin's nuptials, he had dashed up to the master suite! But his lovely wife was in a world of her own, ear buds attached to her iPhone! Curious about what was so transfixing, he hesitated. Then, tears began pouring from beneath closed eyelids, and her mobile features reflected a mixture of joy and turmoil! He was undecided whether to interrupt and make her aware of his presence, or tiptoe out–before he could decide, she opened her eyes, seeking the replay button.

Flushing with embarrassment, she pulled the buds free and straightened up. "Diana gave me the latest CD! There's a violin duet by Daniel and Cassandra playing *It takes a Storm*! It's always amazing to me how powerful an instrumental version of a song can be! If you know the lyrics, your mind fills them in! This–is–so beautiful–like, do you believe what we've been taught about sympathetic vibrations? Anyway, my mind ran through the major storms God has seen me through!" She proffered the earphones diffidently. Even though David was her best friend, they didn't always share experiences the same way! And sometimes one of them would be blessed by a song, when if didn't resonate with the other.

He listened to the entire selection before speaking softly! "No wonder they sent me to teach the beginners' course! They are both really exceptional!"

She nodded, "Yeah, I think I'm gonna stick with piano!"

David's inborn mischievousness took over! "Excellent! Does that mean that you forfeit the game?"

Her face set resolutely, and her eyes shot lightning! "I hate that word! When have I ever forfeited a game?" She slung a cushion at him!

His giggle erupted! "Hey, hey, hey; can't blame a guy for hoping! Scoot over! I actually came, baring amazing news! And you're right; the Lord has seen us through some major storms! But the strange thing is that though we've gone through the same storms, our experiences have been different!"

She nodded. One of her worst storms was the four months he spent in a coma; he didn't even remember most of it! "What's the news?"

He studied his chronometer and then grinned. "Your chief Geologist and Deborah's most valuable model have tied the marital knot aboard the cruise ship!"

Her mouth dropped open and she regarded him in wonder! "No way! David Anderson, are you kidding me?"

He assumed his injured expression. "Would I kid you?"

She laughed, flinging herself across him and kissing him hard! "Yes, you would! But that's legit! Aboard the cruise ship?" Her delighted laughter rippled! "That is so awesome! How do you know? Who told you?"

He explained, with the disclaimer of her and Diana's first chance at a design session. "He finished weakly: "So, is it okay that I wired the ten grand?"

She sprang up, infused with energy! "Yeah-it's great-but-but, they'll need more!"

"Wait! Come back! Are you going to finish what you started?"

She planted another hard kiss! "Later! Come with me!"

"What now?" David Higgins' perplexed question as the short wedding reception, provided in the wedding package, came to an end.

She shot him an amazed look! "Well, if you don't know-how about dinner? I was so hungry-"

He laughed, "Well, you might be surprised, but I do know!" His expression burned into her limpid pools of blue. "However, dinner sounds like an excellent suggestion-"

She nodded. "Are you having second thoughts?"

He didn't answer. "I'm new to all this! Where's the best place for us to eat, that people won't be congratulating us and wondering why we haven't yet done the traditional honeymoon disappearing act?"

"Well, maybe on deck; the stewards will serve dinner privately. It costs-"

He smiled through tense features. "Lead the way."

She took the lead, limping gingerly.

To Trent's amazed relief, Sonia did swoon, "My hero!" And he was ready with a good defense, too! Almost a pity he didn't need it. "And Ms. Nichols and Higgins were going to get married as soon as the ship was well out of port!"

She nodded. "Tell me more about the cruise ship! Was it nice?"

He was jolted! 'Was it nice? Uh-yeah-but where was she going with this?' He answered, "Yeah, it was the last word in lavish! Pretty to see; I wouldn't want to live there!"

Her features were real cute as she considered how much to pursue the topic.

"You wanna take a cruise?" He could hardly believe he was opening the door for her to walk through-

"Well, do you?"

He laughed. "Uh-to be perfectly honest-the thought never crossed my mind!" Well, that was true: golf games, hunting and fishing trips-had a lodging place in his brain! He preferred towering conifers to chandeliers and clinking china!

"I wonder how much it costs-" her tone was so wistful. Trent was surprised that cost hadn't occurred to him first!

"Well, maybe *DiaMal-*" he stopped! Whoa, the last thing he wanted was for Sonia to take a cruise! Everybody on board would hit on her-

"That's a good idea; I'm just not sure how I could approach it-"

"Okay, well hold on. What are we even talking about? A cruise, where? I've had enough of the Black Sea for a while!"

She nodded. "I know! And that's what I've always loved about you! The way you see what needs to be done and just get busy on it! Whether anyone agrees, whether anyone helps you-"

He nodded. "I was a jerk to Rob, but it was just so perfect, the skills he has-but we were talking about a cruise! I know!" Inspiration seized him. "How about Alaska and the Inside Passage? Some of the Christian groups-"

She nodded, slowly, "So you can see more of your National Forests?"

He laughed, "Well, that's not all! We can look at the water, too! See the icebergs calve!"

A soft sigh told him that was not what she had in mind.

"In answer to your earlier question, No, I haven't changed my mind! I can't even remember how long I've loved you-" A jumbo shrimp plunged beneath the surface of cocktail sauce! "I guess, I'm just a little leery of what your angle is now!"

She chewed her lip enchantingly. "You're still mad about the Estes Park deal."

He exhaled softly. "No, I'm still mad because you love Faulkner! Always have; always will! If this is some elaborate scheme to make him jealous, I doubt it'll work! It'll backfire, and you're stuck with me then!"

She grinned. "Well, maybe I don't think that's so bad! But that's not what I'm doing! You're the one who's still so taken with him that you superimpose him onto everything!"

He scoffed softly. "So, I'm just supposed to believe that you said 'Yes' because you love me!"

"That has been known to happen! I think that shrimp's dead; are you going to eat him, or can I have him?"

He chuckled and slid the appetizer across to her, focusing his gaze on the horizon where sky and sea melded in an intoxicating array of color and light! "I should get my camera! Don't go anywhere!"

"We need to get to Texarkana and look Deborah and her parents in the eye!"

David agreed! Mallory's sensitivity to people caused her to be preemptive! And Deborah was prone to get into dithers. "I'll get the girls and their stuff gathered up! You can access this map on your laptop while we drive! Showing her will help her to follow your brilliant deductions, my dear Watson!"

Mallory laughed, "Thanks, Sherlock! I need to fix my face, too!"

"My next task was to send money for the next six months' lease." Manny pulled out a list scrawled in Spanish and crossed off an item.

"Okay, well, that seems fortuitous!" Mallory responded. "How much notice does the landlord need? There are eight days until the end of the month. Well, make that a little over seven in Istanbul!" She studied her plan. "So, the newlyweds can spend the Istanbul shore excursion in Nanci's apartment in Beyoglu! Then they continue the cruise to Sorrento and environs, ending in Rome. Then they can actually honeymoon in Rome or fly to Venice! From there, I want them to take a river cruise on the Danube-" Mallory tried to downplay her desire, figuring it would conflict with Deborah's plan.

Deborah spread manicured hand atop the page, twisting it to view it better. "So, from now on, the consideration is of them as a couple, and you want Professor Higgins to be on this specific river cruise?"

Always the salesperson, Mallory enumerated the advantages. "You immediately save the amount of six months expensive rent! By the time they return from the honeymoon/slash river cruise, David and I will have purchased a house farther from central Istanbul, where they can live when they're there! We plan to contact the professor about selling his Tulsa house! It's run down, and I'm thinking Tulsa isn't big enough for them and the Faulkners! He'll receive the equity from his home for some additional cash."

The Rodriguez' nodded in unison, but they were savvy, not easily snowed. Manny blurted out the main concern. "Now that they are married, will the professor allow his wife to cruise alone? We assume that eventually, their careers will take them separate ways, at least occasionally."

"Well, it's hard to address the future with any measure of certainty," Mallory's truthful admission. "But they'll have a new dynamic in a new area! Nanci has worn the designs everywhere in the Beyoglu district since she started. A new neighborhood, new places to shop and eat, will bring fresher exposure! And she has the fresh perspective of being married. Sometimes people are suspicious of single women, especially in a culture that's basically Islamic. David and I realized the need to leave our office building for lunches oftener, because as lovely as the clothing is, we become ho-hum to the people who see us day in and day out! And getting out with the girls is harder than riding down the elevator! Would it be fair to ask you all to take one day at a time?"

"And *Rodriguez* won't be paying for any more of her housing?"

"No," David responded, watching the responses to his answers closely. "We'll own the house, and they'll live in it as part of Higgins' employment package! We'll cover the insurance for their belongings, as well as adding Nanci as a dependant to Higgins' health insurance!"

Mallory gave a silent cheer! Great sales point! "As to whether or not he'll be willing to send her on cruises without him, we can't say! We will try to facilitate her traveling to some of his job sites with him! We want her to travel, so she can keep her blog up, too!"

Deborah emitted a relieved sigh and a slight triumphant chuckle! "So, we are still dove-tailing! Were you surprised? At their elopement?"

David and Mallory exchanged glances, "Uh-yes and no!" Their response in unison!

Nanci read an email from Mallory stating that they needed to discuss some business items, and asking her to have Higgins call when convenient.

She responded that she would relay the message, and then expressed a concern.

> *I can't tell if he's happy or not! Or even if he really wants to be married to me-*

Mallory shot back:

> *Yeah, I hear ya! I call him Eeyore 'Iggins because he's always gloomy, waiting for the sky to fall! I'm sure he's elated! It's just always tough to tell! Like we could tell that you and Waverly were excited about the ten thousand; it just presented David with an extra worry! He always sees the glass half-empty!*

Nanci read the words with renewed hope! That was the right spin! And she was aware of it, if anyone should be! Tucking the laptop beneath her arm, she made her way to the breakfast salon! Mallory was right! Her buoyant nature would have to keep them both from going under!

After speaking with Morrison and Addington, Erik was hardly surprised to receive word about Odessa's body washing ashore! Single, high-caliber shot, execution-style! He rubbed his chin thoughtfully! Strange thing, Burnside agreeing to the hurry-up nuptials with the *DiaMo* geologist! Erik was tempted to send the bridegroom a warning text to keep his credit cards and accounts where she couldn't access them! The only reason he decided against it was her complaint that he had it in for her!

He studied the photo before him once again! Odessa, Moldavia, the orphanage, the Malovich twins! Billy Beauchamp! Everything that appeared isolated~wasn't really! The same people from the beginning, targeting Mallory! Ryland O'Shaughnessy involved, but low-level!

The agent's mind traveled back through time to an incident! Immediately following the Faulkners getting her relocated to her new home in Dallas! Home; more like a fortress! Because Patrick knew! Abducted Diamond miners; Mallory's miraculous evasion in the morning, to be accosted by one of the Maloviches at her Murfreesboro property later the same afternoon! The one whom she assumed was Oscar; because at that time, no one was aware of Otto! He cringed as his mind traveled backwards to the incident! Melville, or Malevich, had managed to practically strangle her! Could have been so much worse, if not for the fact that she had picked up that rock~ He sent an agent to round up the archived cases! Maybe it would be useful to re-interview everyone from the old cases. News footage and everything! He frowned, curious how much Shannon knew, from way back; and also one of Ryland's girlfriends who had recently contacted Delia! Was Shay right about his mother's death not being accidental? Of course, Ryland was dead and beyond the arm of the law, but who else might still be keeping on with the same-o, same-o? Time to make sure the crimes ceased! And ferret out those responsible for prosecution. Picking up his extension he barked a series of order!

David watched Nanci's approach along the deck. Heads turned as she passed, but she seemed impervious! Which kind of struck him odd! The Nanci of college days always noticed the stir she caused! Fed on it! Desperately needed it! She caught sight of him and smiled brightly, pulling a deck chair nearer his and snuggling in next to him with the laptop.

"You're never going to guess what!" Her enthused voice appealingly breathless!

Before he could answer that he hadn't a clue, his cell buzzed. David Anderson.

"Professor Higgins," his voice held a stiff pompousness.

"Listen, when you go ashore for Istanbul, Nanci's apartment is still available! But then the end of the month, we're not renewing the lease. *DaMal Properties* will buy a house out more into the suburbs! Her apartment has been rented furnished, but we'll see to moving her personal belongings. We-uh-wanted to ask you if you're interested in selling your house-"

Higgins tried to see the sour side, to keep his spirit from soaring! "Well, I'm afraid it would need a lot of work-"

"Our specialty! And you'll have the house there for your use, and *DiaMo* pays your expenses when you travel! Is there still any reason for you to keep ties to Tulsa?"

The geologist, sat, dazzled by brilliant sunlight reflecting on the ship's wake; and the delight flooding him at the prospect Anderson presented. 'Wow! Wow! If the residence could be unloaded any time soon, he could really use the equity! And his biggest monthly budgetary expense was his mortgage payment!'

"Hello-uh-did I lose you?"

"No, but-I'm not even sure how the market is-how long-"

Mallory's voice broke in, impatient with Higgins' misgivings! "We already have a buyer! We'll get you fair market value! Is there any of that stuff in there that you want? The house in Istanbul will be nicely furnished so you can have people over occasionally."

Regretfully, he realized he didn't own anything nice! "Well, all I have that's of any value is my booze!" Probably not the brightest point to make with the teetotalers, but he had money invested there!

"Okay, what's your estimation of the value-"

"Like maybe ten grand!" Higgin's voice held an edge that didn't invite argument. Still, there was a long silence before David responded. "We'll pour it out and give you eight for it! It's all been opened for a while!"

"Uh-okay-uh-"

"We'll wire the eight to the attention of the purser! It should arrive before you head ashore for the next couple of days-you should get your equity by the time you start the Danube cruise!"

Mallory gave David a happy kiss, and he drew her into his arms. "That was amazing!"

Her eyes glowed. "Yeah, it's the Lord. He leaves me speechless with wonder~"

He nodded. "Yeah, because it works out well for us, while giving Mr. and Mrs. David Higgins a fresh start! We need to get with the bank and title company so I can get Brad and a crew~"

She placed her hand laughingly across his mouth and then leaned her head against his chest! "Yeah, in the morning~"

⁂

"What's wrong?" Diana's troubled question!

"I'm not sure! I just can't sleep! Sorry to wake you~"

She reached for the lamp. "You didn't drink coffee~does it bother you?"

He smiled; "I don't think so! But, I figured if you woke up you'd wonder that!"

"Well, it must seem kind of different for you."

He sighed. "Yeah, that would be accurate! I mean I guess that David's reason for always bringing up her name, was that he was the one so crazy about her~"

"Kind of weird that she settled for him, though"!

His level gaze met hers. "Well, that kind of works both ways! I guess I worry about them; they're not saved~but I'm not so caught up with them and their chances of a happy home as I am about what Mallory said!"

Diana looked surprised. "Why? What'd she say?"

"About going to Colorado to open a gold mine! And I said, 'I didn't know there were any significant gold deposits there!'"

Diana nodded. "And instead of reassuring you that there are, she said, 'There can be!' I mean, it's there or it's not; right?"

"Seems like! And that's why I can't sleep!"

⁂

"What was that about?" Nanci's curiosity at the interruption of her exciting revelation!

"The Andersons want to sell my house in Tulsa! Well, that's what they said! But they're the ones actually buying it out from under me~"

She laughed. "And you think they plan to cheat you?"

"Well, they could! I mean, how would I know?"

Her eyes sparkled! "Okay Eeyore! If that's what you think, call them back and tell them you want to keep it! But, I've seen your place, and-uh-I'd rather not live there! I mean, how do you even attempt to keep it up long distance? I'm pretty sure Mallory wants us as far away from Daniel and Diana as she can get us!"

His expression remained troubled. "Why did you call me, Eeyore?"

"Because he's who you sound like! What do you want me to call you?" She didn't necessarily want him to know about her messages back and forth with Mallory about his disposition.

"Well, my name's David," he mumbled.

She pinched his cheek mischievously. "I'll call you '*Iggy*. Look, Istanbul!" Her tone subdued, as she indicated the panorama! "We're in the Strait of Bosporus! That's Asia to our left, or port side; and Europe to starboard! That series of buildings and ruins is the Fortress of Asia, with its counterpart on this side; the Fortress of Europe! That's the Dolmabahçe Palace! Do you want to tour it? It's amaaazzzing! And we need to visit the grand bazaar! The Istanbul grand Bazaar is one of the largest and oldest in the world."

He chuckled at her enthusiasm as he reached for her hand. "I'd like that! I'll have the most beautiful tour guide of any man in either Asia or Europe!"

Happiness washed across radiant features. "Oh, you're so nice! It's not long before we go ashore, and I need your help. Rhonna Abbot forwarded me this thing that Ella, the nursing administrator at Shady Grove put together from her Scandinavian cruise! It's perfect as is, and it's a great initial issue! I'll give her credit for it, but I'll pay her for her contribution!"

He reached for the laptop and melded the documents seamlessly, pulling her near so she could view the screen and approve it before he pressed 'Publish'.

Emotional, she nodded approval! "It looks good; doesn't it?"

Harry's lovely picture of her surrounded by hot pink at the bay in Volos, Greece, anchored one side of her banner proclaiming *At the Seaside with Nanci Burnside.* The other side showed the glorious rosy sunset taken from the tender at Yalta, as cruisers returned to the ship! Then the first entry featured narration of the delighted Ella as she shared her experiences of her Scandinavian cruise!

To David's surprise, he couldn't sleep! Insomnia never troubled him while Mallory's deep even breathing told him she was gone! Well, he had plenty to think about! The details for acquiring Higgins' aging home! Probably Gina could do most of the paperwork, and with a call to Brad, the renovation would begin. Moving to the Ranch office he and Mallory shared, he pulled up her map of the Danube! With his cursor he traced the route upstream from where the delta had snagged Mallory's attention during the search for Higgins and Burnside, up into the Alps of Bavaria at its source! Quite a trip! Amazing, that Higgins, with his practiced Geologist's eye, could pinpoint promising formations from the decks of the cruise ship! He studied Mallory's dropped pins, placed according to the gradients of the Danube's course! Coordinates where the currents slowed were prime targets for drilling operations.

Chapter 33: GENIALITY

Trent didn't expect a hero's welcome, so he was relieved not to be called on the carpet in response to his rescue mission. He sat, twiddling a pencil, immersed in thought! So, Nanci had eagerly received salvation, and then he and Addington were rushed ashore so the cruise ship could sail on time! The sudden shipboard nuptials shocked him a little! As a Christian, Nanci shouldn't have married the unregenerate geologist! But as a brand new Christian, there was no way for her to have known that. He breathed a soft prayer: "Lord, please help her to grow in grace, and help Higgins to find You! And-uh-thank you about-Rob's decision, too!"

Shoving the pencil atop his ear, he pulled the phone toward him. Sonia's immediate answer brought a smile to his face.

"Hey, what's up?"

He laughed. Once at work, he was usually too focused to call her until he was log-jammed in the commute home! "Nothing crazy, you'll be relieved to know! Hey, without mentioning it to any of the kids, why don't you start researching some cruises?"

Shocked silence before a tentative, "Like a few days in the Caribbean?"

"See, I don't know! That's not really what you were thinking, is it? Look, don't get too excited and worked up; just start checking into stuff; okay? Were you thinking more of the Mediterranean?"

"Well, I don't know, Trent! I imagine the cruise prices for that are higher, not to mention the flights-"

His heart did some acrobatics. That was something he hadn't considered. Flights to the cruise departure points! Still, he fought panic! "Like I said, I know it's confusing, all the different companies and what's included in packages. But if you can start to sort it out, it'll be fun to talk about and consider."

"Okay, I'll get started with the research." Even as she agreed, she knew Trent! Talking about it didn't mean it was going to happen! He'd talk himself out of it!

"Ah, the beautiful American lady has returned! And the gentleman; he is going buy for you, carpet?"

Higgins hoped Nanci was enjoying what he was enduring! The bazaaris were hard sell to the umpteenth power!

"Probably not today"! Nanci's manner, guardedly friendly! "I'm giving up my small apartment; then we'll be out of the country for the next two or three weeks. When we get back and move into a house, maybe!" She moved to a spot on the wall that continued to draw her like a magnet! One of the carpets; six by eight, woven of muted earth tones in silk! She fingered a corner lovingly, turning rapturous expression to her new bridegroom. "Isn't it beautiful?"

He didn't know silk from burlap, but her winsomeness pulled at him in the strangest way.

"You buy for her today!" The all-smiles merchant sensed the chemistry and pending sale! "She wanting it for long time! No worries! Today! We store for you free of charge while you away! Get house! We deliver!"

With Higgins' attempt at bartering, the price rose by fifty Turkish lira! Dazed, he stumbled from the store with a happy wife on his arm. They emerged to find a bench in Beyazit Square.

"I need to call Deborah!" Nanci was suddenly worried. "She tends to ruffle easily, and I don't want to lose my job."

"Well, then, wouldn't Mallory probably-" He broke off realizing her concern! 'Of course; Mallory's fashion business belonged by a majority to Diana Faulkner!'

"Hello, Deborah. We're in Istanbul for a night before the cruise finishes up next week! Uh-with things having been so crazy, I haven't really made many contacts with people about the styles for the past several days!"

"Well, yes," Deborah's tone showed no signs of wrath. "Again, let me tell you how relieved we are that you are both all right! How is your foot, and your husband's shoulder? And I understand why my clothing has been the last thing on your mind! Let me congratulate and compliment you on the launch of your blog site! I must say, I always have concerns that I get vocal about-but the site is so beautiful, and we have had a great day! With orders from people who visited your site"!

Nanci was stunned. "Oh, well then, I guess we're good then!" Happy emotion made tears well up!

"Yes, we are very good! Congratulations to you and your new husband! I am sending to you a wedding gift! Be happy and keep having fun!"

An ecstatic Nanci finished the call to receive a message notification! She hugged 'Iggy exuberantly! "She's good! Uh-loves the blog-orders coming in as a result-she sent us five hundred dollars!"

They sat there, laughing and hugging one another exuberantly, unaware of passersby who shrugged their antics off with the typical, 'Crazy Americans!'

So, in response to Trent's decree not to get excited, she wasn't! Everything was so expensive; even off-season! And he was right; it was confusing to sort out! She fought tears of frustration! He would take one look at it and tell her, 'no way'. Morosely, she wondered why she continued clicking from site to site! Annoyed, she pushed back and made her way to the kitchen for another cup of coffee! And there lay Maddie's prayer journal! With a sigh, she poured coffee and moved toward Maddie's room with the errant item! Maddie was prone to that! Leaving stuff where her brothers' curiosity got the best of them, and then freaking that they went through her stuff! She placed it next to her daughter's Bible, and then laughed lightly as a little figurative bell jingled in her mind! 'Why not'?

Getting her Bible and finding a spiral notebook with a few unused pages, she returned to her office! Mallory always journaled! A habit Maddie had gleaned from her! Sonia was forced to admit she hadn't paid much attention to the how-to's! "Okay, Lord, I guess I don't actually pray about much-You know, the stuff Trent and I pray about together; tests the kids are taking-trying to do the praying without ceasing throughout my days!" Tears started. "Lord, I am thankful for what we have-I would love to go on a cruise with Trent! But I don't know about leaving the kids-And the Mediterranean! Thank you for letting us go to England and France and the Holy Land! I guess if You could get us to those places, You can-if

You choose~if it~could please You~well, and thank You that Trent even is willing to consider~" she laughed through tears! "Thank you for our good relationship and marriage and that he's been a good provider! I guess You have made some adjustments in both~of us!"

Taking pen in hand, she wrote down a request: Mediterranean Cruise

"Lord, it's something that's really so unnecessary! No way it could ever be considered a 'need'! Aren't we only supposed to ask you for real necessities?"

Even as she spoke, a pair of verses popped into her mind!

> *Psalm 37:4&5 Delight thyself also in the LORD; and he shall give thee the desires of thine heart.*
>
> *Commit thy way unto the LORD; trust also in him; and he shall bring it to pass.*

"Is that true?" she questioned softly. That we can ask You for desires as well as needs? I've committed my way to You but I'm recommitting it now! Help me to trust in You and Your Word! Even when it seems too good to be true! Because it is true; isn't it?"

Beneath the request she wrote out the two verses, the prayer promises. With clarity of mind and a happy heart, she chose four options to discuss with Trent over coffee!

Nanci ran through an excited itinerary of sites to share with her new husband. He pulled her into his arms and kissed her. "We don't have to see the entire city in one day! You're limping more, and my shoulder's aching! Let's find a nice restaurant for some dinner, and then go home!"

She nodded agreement. "Since the carpet was kind of expensive, we can get really great kebabs at a kiosk I frequent. Then we can just sit on a park bench on the Golden Horn and eat while the evening deepens and the city lights blink on."

He took her hand and they continued in a happy fog of love and discovery! With food in hand, they found an empty bench and settled a scant few feet from the water's edge! David bit in hungrily, then paused awkwardly as Nanci dipped her head. He hesitated, "Were you praying?"

Even in the twilight, he noticed her flush of color. "Uh-yes, do you mind?"

"I-I guess not!" he stammered awkwardly. "Whatever floats your boat"!

"Breakfast at the Country Club in the morning?"

Beth looked up sharply! Roger's tone wasn't the recent condescending, conciliatory, make her happy enough not to leave; but rang with sincerity! And his anxious face revealed a certain vulnerability, that he was taking a risk with rapprochement.

She laid down her scissors and the coupon section from the paper to study him. "Sure, sounds nice! We haven't done that in forever! Are any of the kids joining us?"

"I haven't mentioned it! It's-just-a nice setting-"

She nodded. "It is-so-your boat deal fell through?"

"Mm-hmm, but Tony claims he made the sale so he still wants the commission-"

"Yeah, with the Treasury Department's grabbing it, it's a wonder David and Mallory got it back!"

He sighed. "Yeah, the thing is; they don't want it back!"

She shrugged pragmatically! "Well, it's better than being out the cash and the boat! Did you hear about their insurance switch?"

He frowned. Insurance was a subject he addressed as a necessary evil as a CEO, and as one who owned stuff, making insurance necessary. The topic didn't necessarily fascinate him. "Unh-unh! What about it?" He hoped she wouldn't fill him in.

"Well, when Mallory's cabin in Colorado burned, her insurance company considered her their prime suspect for arson! Well, it definitely was arson, and they assumed because the Normans weren't able to keep it rented to vacationers, that she-"

Roger sighed, "No kiddin'? Would a character witness help her case any?"

I guess people believe what's in their best interest to believe, despite evidence and facts! Since the Larimer County Sheriff's department was stretched too thin, to make the arson a priority, she hired a private detective! He tracked down Rudy Sunquist-anyway, the insurance company has continued to make the same claim, basically assassinating Mallory's reputation, with nothing but their repeated charges backing them up.

Roger sank onto a stool at the counter. Listening to somebody's long tale of woe, wasn't his favorite form of entertainment, but Beth was the most engaged-or maybe it was him-anyway-since she was speaking, he was listening. "So she changed companies?"

Beth's eyes grew enormous and vitality infused her features. "Yes, and try to imagine the assets they've acquired since the fire! A lot of new policies! But, she didn't rip all of her business away to get even! She was just afraid that would be their take on any future claim! That they had a loophole that they would use again! Why pay for insurance premiums, if your claims might all be turned down?"

Roger considered before nodding.

Beth continued. "So, the policy coverage overlapped by ten days!"

"Yeah, expensive, but you don't want any question on coverage-" Roger saw the wisdom of that.

Beth's throaty laugh, "Well, a guy from their church sold them the policies, and he was aware of what originally happened to David in Arizona; David was on the prayer list at Calvary the whole time! But then as he researched policies, that never occurred to him! And since David looks strong and healthy- So, I guess the agent is mad at David and Mallory-"

"Probably! He's doubtless been chewed out royally! Still, that would have been a huge job to go through all of their policies and then find something comparable-you-uh-got me thinking!" He laughed. "And the last thing I wanted to think or hear about is insurance. I might call David and ask what he thinks of the guy-if there's someone who really knows his stuff and is willing to dig down deep-"

"Di, Honey, what do you think? Should we send a wedding present?" A very hesitant Daniel made the suggestion.

"You know, I think we should! They neither one have much money. Mallory handed both of them, as well as Delton Waverly, ten thousand dollars for crashing her party and ruining a nice evening for everyone!"

Daniel shot her an amazed glance.

"But the professor spent his ten grand buying wedding rings aboard the cruise ship and on the wedding package! Nanci is using hers to start a travel blog. It would be a Christian gesture, and Mallory is still steering them way clear of us! She and David are buying his house here and sending him the equity, and when they finish the Black Sea Cruise, they're going to take a Danube River Cruise!"

Daniel shook his head in wonder! "Ah, a Danube River Cruise! You have to hand it to Mallory, once again, for sheer genius!"

She frowned. "I guess I don't follow! Nice, definitely; what's the sheer genius part?"

"Well, when Higgins and Nanci disappeared, everyone was accessing maps of the Black Sea region to figure out where they might be! Not normally a place on any of our radars. Of course then, the Danube Delta in the Black Sea flashed neon in Mallory's brain!"

"Okay, I hate to be dense, but-"

"Well, part of the way she works her discovery-magic is as a Geo-hydrologist! So, rivers scour out samples of rock as they flow downward from their sources-giving an overview in core samples, of valuable resources from higher elevations! She actually applies

> *Psalm 121:1&2 I will lift up mine eyes unto the hills, from whence cometh my help. My help cometh from the LORD, which made heaven and earth.*

Higgins can just float luxuriously along in posh comfort, and see if the Germans or the other governments of the region have rushed to drill the sites she's requested permits for. Her hypothesis is that King David lifted his eyes to the higher elevations because he knew that The God who made heaven and earth, had made them with rich supplies of natural resources. When you read what king David managed to accumulate for the building of the temple, billions of dollars' worth of silver and gold, as well as quarried stones and precious stones-it seems like her theory has basis in fact!"

"Wow!" She grinned suddenly. "You used the exprssion, 'posh', which is a colloquialism as well as an acrostic: P.O.S.H Port out; starboard home! In the eighteen hundreds, wealthy people making transatlantic crossings bought the more expensive cabins, which, pre-air-conditioning days, minimized direct sunlight and its warming effects! Port out from Southampton, and starboard side cabin on the return trip."

He nodded, "Interesting detour, Honey. As I was saying, we often look to God to give us warm-fuzzy feelings when what we need is solid help! And fast! And you know that Mallory always loved

Psalm 104:24 O LORD, how manifold are thy works! in wisdom thou hast made them all: the earth is full of thy riches.

even before the night when Patrick and Suzanne were both gone-"

Diana's eyes filled with tears. "So, have you figured out the meaning of her enigmatic statement about Colorado?"

He frowned. "Still puzzling over that one"!

"Let's go out and get a drink." Since Nanci's place was small with little diversion, Higgins suggested one.

She frowned. "Okay, this isn't like the US."

"Meaning?"

"Meaning the government is theoretically secular, but the population's Moslem! They believe alcoholic beverages are wrong, and they resent local establishments that cater to the foreigners about it. Now, if you want to go out for coffee and a pastry here, that'll work-please trust me! When we're back aboard the cruise liner, you can more safely imbibe. There really is wisdom about 'when in Rome, do as the Romans do'-"

He sighed, "Not even a beer?"

"Well, some places serve the non-alcoholic-"

A bitter laugh! "Well, I'll take your word for it; you were right about not going clubbing in Odessa-I should have-listened." He paled, remembering. "Let's just take it easy on your foot, and we can have another tea party."

With a laugh, she heated water and pulled out a tin of tea biscuits.

"Your phone just buzzed." She reached it and handed it to him.

Terror filled his eyes.

"What?" Alarm shot through her in response.

"Faulkner." His voice barely carried.

She laughed with relief! "Well, what? Does he say he's coming to kill you?"

"Don't laugh!"

She clapped both hands hard across her mouth, but her mocking eyes were alight "Open the message-"

"I told you I don't need to be on his bad side!"

"Come on, Eeyore; lighten up!" She grabbed for his phone and he pulled it back!

His eyes shot around desperately, "What am I going to do?"

"About what, David? For Pete's sake-calm down before you stroke out!"

"Okay-uh-okay, this isn't funny! It's serious-"

She nodded, trying to understand his concern. "Okay, 'Iggy, give me your phone!"

With a shuddering sigh, he complied.

She laughed again. "Oooooohhh, now you have me scared!" She pushed the button to open the message! "It says-" she paused for dramatic effect- "Congratulations, Higgins, Diana and I are happy for you. See attached-" she opened the attachment "A thousand dollars! Aren't you glad you have rich friends? Call him and tell him thank you!" She thrust the frightful device at him.

Sonia cleared breakfast things and made her way into her office! Since Trent's order for her to research cruises, there had barely been time for hellos and good-byes in the frenzy known as life! She plopped into her chair.

"Lord, I think he already forgot! I know he told me not to get my hopes up, but they were up even before I accessed all the pictures and diagrams!" She fought tears. "Okay, Lord, I know there are thousands of other people who never get to go on cruises! Please don't let me act spoiled because of the gracious things You've allowed us to do! Every day can't be about taking a trip-there must be ordinary days, to make the special happenings special! Rich people who cruise all the time must get bored with it! As a matter of fact, I could be sitting here right now in deep, deep mourning for Megan-I-I might have-even signed-how could I have even considered-" She sat there silently, her focus on a family picture. And even as she pulled her Bible toward her, a soft voice spoke in her heart!

"Don't fret! If Trent has forgotten, I haven't."

"Daniel Faulkner!" Daniel recognized the number. "Hey, Higgins; what's happenin'?"

"Well, we're back on board and headed down through the Dardanelles to the Med for the last two destinations in Italy! I'm calling to thank you for the gift! More than kind-"

"Well, we're happy for you," Daniel's words were genuine, although he was amazed at thanks from his former pal! In his years of friendship and being the one to buy and treat, he hadn't ever received much in the way of gratitude. "Enjoy your travels! Then I hear that the Danube is next! Kind of a cushy way to do Geological survey work"! Ooh, he knew that was the wrong thing to say-oh well!

"Well, trust me; it isn't always that way!"

Daniel strove to be sympathetic with Higgins' whining.

"Yeah, guess your work's really gonna be cut out for you-looking for gold in the Colorado high country-in the dead of winter!"

"Oh, yeah; that's not me! And it isn't mining or geology!"

"Yeah, that's what I heard; something like that!" Usually, Faulkner didn't have such a need-to-know.

"Yeah, it's more akin to manufacturing; or should I say, 'de-manufacturing'? Recycling gold from discarded electronics-sounds kinda crazy, if you ask me. But I try not to be too critical of their plans."

"Yeah, that's the best way to be! Well, happy sailing"!

Nick corrected Jason softly, wishing he had left his son with his aunt and mother. He knew Jen's reason for insisting, was showing him off! Sadly he felt Jen still possessed a mean spirit toward Sophia.

"So, Cousins, when did you get here? Aloha! Beautiful leis"! As a native islander, Nick was in the know! The orchid leis were part of the welcoming package of the Hilton Hawaiian Village where they awaited a table.

"This afternoon! We theoretically just lost another case!" Jay answered. "Meaning, that none of our accusations stuck enough that the defendant had to pay damages. Still, we made another community aware that many pillars of their communities have feet of clay! And it gets attention to the plights of the victims."

Jennifer diverted her attention to her son who fought having his freedom restricted. She felt that, no matter how reprehensible the Vincents tried to make the men look, the sagging moral values in the US tended to make people cluck their collective tongues sympathetically! And still do the classic act of blaming the women!

She curbed her desire to render an opinion with a weak, "Well, that's good! So, are you bringing a case here?"

"No, actually, we're taking a breather from it! Even though I promise Jay every time that I'll leave the results in the Lord's hands-"

Jay patted her hand. "It still gets to her," he finished, "An emotional toll for all three of us! So, even before this one went to trial, we booked this vacation-I guess you heard about Silas Remington's being found murdered in Canada?"

Sophia picked up on Nick and Jen's confusion at the unfamiliar name. "The headmaster of the private school I attended. His actions the day of my-abduction-seemed bizarre. The Philly PD recently began looking into his activities-but the Canadian Mounties say the 'execution' investigation has hit dead ends. Naturally"!

"Yeah," Nick's sympathy was genuine. "Jennifer and I comfort one another with the assurance that one day the Righteous Judge will put away all evil. Until then, He has daily loaded us with benefits!"

Sophia nodded. "Absolutely, and while we try to make changes, we should never lose sight of that! Thanks for helping restore my balance!"

"How are you aunt and uncle and grandfather?" Nick tried to keep the conversation moving, glad for the other couples' dinner invitation, although getting together brought a certain tension.

"Well, Aunt Barb and Uncle Adam still insist that Salvation's great for everyone except 'we Coxes' who are sinlessly perfect! Grandfather's doing well!" Sophia's musical laughter! "We plan to explore each of the islands, and then travel to Arizona next, to visit him. I don't want to make the assumption that he'll be around forever, but his condition is so much improved-What about you guys?"

Nick sighed. "We still can't decide what we want to do when we grow up! So, we've bounced between Jennifer's mother and mine! Which, they would both be tired of us, but Jason keeps the doors swung open-"

Jay laughed. "I can see that-uh-but have you talked to Risa lately?"

Nick frowned, "The FBI doesn't want Jen right down there on the Mexican border-"

"Neither do we!" Sophia's voice was so fervent that Jay was shocked.

"Well, Phil and Risa finally really have it going on!" Jay continued cautiously. "And Jack and Estelle Norman now run the Bisbee gallery full-time-"

Jennifer's breath caught! "Wh-what about-the Aspen-"

"Well, no one has worked out on a permanent basis there! If the Perkins hire someone who enjoys winter and snow, they usually want time off for skiing, snowboarding, or whatever! The people who don't like winter sports, I guess get tired of-"

"Well, Aspen's really expensive to live, isn't it?"

Nick could tell Jennifer was more intrigued about the possibility than about anything in a long time-

"Well, I think so; but it's a trade-off," Sophia responded rationally. "It definitely attracts customers with deep pockets! Although that creates drawbacks, it also presents opportunity. So it's a given with Phil and Risa, since they've been in this for a while, that the rent on their gallery is sky-high, and so must wages be!"

Jennifer's laughter erupted so suddenly that a startled little Jason jumped and started to cry.

When she could finally force words out, she turned to Nick. "I guess she's trying to tell me, that even if we live where there's a high standard of living, we'll make more than we do, doing nothing!"

Nick nodded. "Yeah, but you got habitually harassed, when you worked the gallery."

Jen blanched, remembering. "Yes, but it's been longer; and slowly but surely-"

"Well, if you want to talk to Risa-"

The Higgins sat in one of the ship's lounges, working on the next blog issue!

"Ella's opener was such a hit, it'll be hard to keep up-" Nanci worried. "I was concerned about having a slow start! Now I'm thinking that a successful jump start and then falling off the shelf will be even worse."

David nodded. "Yeah, let's just keep working on this and refining it. I got some good shots of the harbor and the Potemkin Steps! Having pictures is more important than a lot of wordy stuff! Plus, we can neither one spell or know the best grammar and punctuation! "One picture is worth a thousand words," as they say."

She watched as he manipulated photos into place, amazed at his sense of space and proportion. "That looks good! Shall we send it?"

He frowned. "I'd rather not, quite yet. Someone should proof the copy! Dumb people don't know or care when everything's correct; but sharp and educated people are turned off by haphazard stuff! We want followers from across the spectrum!" He pushed his unfinished libation aside. "Maybe we should go where people are," he surveyed the deserted space. "We can see where they're not! We need pictures of people, as well as the destinations! A balance! Where did your couple go that you were friends with early on? Maybe they know how to spell!"

She hopped up gladly. "Let's go look for them! Also, we should ask the Captain if he minds if we feature pictures from our wedding! That might generate interest and get us followers! I mean, I know that the cruise line uses the wedding-at-sea venue in their ads-"

"I'm running down to Hope to see if I can catch Sanders!" David popped in to announce his plan! "I have a couple of things to run by him! Shouldn't take too long! Will you and the girls be okay?"

"Yeah, sure; we'll be fine!" She smiled brightly! "Avery's napping; maybe you can tell me later about-what's going on to talk to Roger about? You mean the boat?"

His eyes danced mysteriously, and he grinned. "Yeah; that too! When Avery wakes up, just get chow hall lunch, and I'll be back by mid to late afternoon." He kissed her lightly. "Call if you need anything-"

She sighed as the door closed behind him, and after peeking in on Amelia and Avery playing peacefully together, settled onto the chaise with a book. Before she managed to read a page, Avery screamed, waking the baby! "What on earth? Amelia?" She bounded toward the playroom. 'How could everything be so smooth when David was around, and deteriorate so rapidly when he stepped out the door?'

"Avery tried to taketed my baby!" Amelia's eyes shot defiant sparks and she held the carved toy defensively!

"So, then, what did you do to her?"

"I didn't do nothin' to 'er!"

Mallory sighed with frustration and indecision. Avery did know the toy was Amelia's favorite! So then, who really started the fracas? She lifted

Alexis from her crib and cuddled her soothingly before returning to the play room where Avery rubbed her arm.

"Amelia, did you bite her? You told me you didn't do anything to her. Now you woke the baby and she'll be cranky, too!"

Amelia burst into tears, "But she taketed-"

"I know! And you don't say 'taketed'; you say, 'took'! You say, 'She took my baby'! Okay, Avery, you know that's Sissy's favorite toy; say 'I'm sorry'."

Avery did a quick subject change to avoid making the apology. "See book" She held up a fabric one, "Me a story?"

"Avy talk baby talk," Amelia grumbled, evidently resenting having her grammar corrected.

"Because she's a baby," Mallory retorted, realizing arguing with a three year old was counter-productive. 'Why was it easier to run corporations and solve business problems than it was to be a mom?' She remembered as a teen ager, being able to handle Sarah and Sammy Walters, when Janice couldn't do a thing with them! Where did her ability to deal with children go, now that she really needed it?

Chapter 34: GENEROSITY

Mallory surveyed gorgeous rows of 'Angel' sugar cookies, hand-embellished by the never-ending wonder of Diana's artistic hand! Well, to Daniel's credit, he had gotten in on some of the finishing details! Fine details!

"We should let the icing set longer before we distribute them!" Diana's knowledgeable and still upbeat voice.

"I should take a picture of them and send it to Beth for her blog." Mallory thought it was a stellar idea, but Daniel and Diana frowned at one another.

"What?"

"Well, they're just kind of roughed in, spur of the moment-" Diana's big blue eyes reflected her horror at being associated with such an amateur mess.

"Yes!" Daniel's definitive agreement! "We just worked these up with the decorating supplies we have on hand." He turned to the kitchen laptop as he spoke, pulling up a web-site of clever and elegant products for turning foods and pastries into the highest art-forms imaginable!

"I had no idea-" an awed Mallory.

"But it is a good idea, when we perfect the concept, to have Beth post them." Daniel's eyes ran over the treats again, and with a frown, he addressed Diana.

"Honey, what do you think about-"

"Fashion doll cookies, featuring our designs!" she finished jubilantly. She planted an exuberant kiss on Amelia's cheek and then smiled happily at Mallory! "I know you thought your day was such a disaster, but once again: *Romans 8:28*!

The idea was a good one, but Mallory wasn't convinced that the trials of the previous twenty-four hours were turned around for good that fast.

Beginning before lunch the previous day, when David suddenly announced to her that he needed to go to Hope to meet with Roger Sanders. At that moment, Alexis was napping and Amelia and Avery were playing together in the play room! And then, the second he kissed her good-bye and drove through the gate, chaos reigned! Avery made a move on Amelia's favorite toy; Amelia bit her; she shrieked; and Alexis was awake after a ten minute nap! And Avery knew she was supposed to leave that toy alone; and Amelia knew she wasn't supposed to bite; and they both knew better than to wake the baby!

So-in retrospect, she could see that her decision to load the girls and take them down to Sonic for lunch was a dig back at David for leaving her with them!

"Well, then, during the car ride, Amelia had once again gone into her creepy vocal and facial mimicking of Bobby Saxon! It was so disconcerting, that Mallory couldn't handle it! But her orders to 'quit' were as if Amelia didn't even hear! Again frustrating, because when David told her to stop, she stopped! Sometimes, all he had to do was give that look-that look that he had given Mallory; rather than their disobedient daughter. Disobedient? Troubled? Mallory found it difficult to affix a name-but the behavior rattled her to her core. Well, how would it be possible for Amelia to fall into the clutches of such pure evil, and not be affected? David just gave assurances that it was temporary, and with enough time-Mallory wanted to present the gospel and pressure her to get saved! After all, saved people couldn't be demon-possessed Just, oppressed?

Trying to interrupt the hypnotic seeming hold, she had pushed her CD case back and told Amelia to pick music! When she picked Christmas music, Mallory didn't even argue! And then, the music had reminded Amelia of spending an afternoon baking 'Angel' sugar cookies to provide special treats for bus kids at Calvary! Not Mallory's favorite pastime, but following the Sonic lunch, they went to the store and bought prepared cookie dough and some cans of icing!

So-that hadn't gone too smoothly either! Which, the next disaster wasn't her fault! The package directions said to bake at 400° F for 8-10 minutes! Then, it was her opening the back door to clear smoke that brought an inquisitive Diana up. "Oh, what are y'all doing?"

"Baking 'Angel' sugar cookies!"

"Oh, were they bad little angels? They look like they descended into the pit!"

"Ha, very funny! That's what the directions said. They are a little dark around the edges."

"Why did you decide to bake Christmas cookies?"

The unspoken parts of the question; 'when it obviously isn't your thing'! And 'it isn't Christmas time'?

"Amelia was doing that thing again, and wouldn't stop. But then, she wanted to listen to Christmas Carols, and that reminded her of baking cookies together before-"

Diana gazed around sympathetically. "Hunh; you've done this before, and she still had a fond memory?"

Ordinarily, that would have made Mallory laugh!

So, Diana had packed her and the girls up and insisted on their coming over so she could help! Which, with a big bowl, and an amazing array of ingredients, she created more dough to replace the ruined stuff! Then, it was into the refrigerator to thoroughly chill! One of the secrets of having them turn out successfully!

Of course, Amelia didn't want to wait for the chilling down, but seeing her daddy's approach, decided to comply.

Trent stared out the window. Although usually able to concentrate on the work at hand, he struggled. Not that there wasn't plenty to focus on! Travels to the other divisions caused his office work to backlog, and then with additional time off to fly into Istanbul-The other divisions varied along the continuum between the Southwest's being chaotic to Bob Porter's Southeast's being exemplary. Trent was planning his next surprise visit to the US Territory of Puerto Rico! By now, he was wishing he'd never mentioned to Sonia, the idea of going on a cruise! They were expensive; and although he'd been gone from the kids a lot lately; Sonia was with them! He supposed his kids should be old enough to fend for themselves if he and Sonn made a quick trip, but the thought made him queasy! So, what to do? Be honest and ask her to put the idea on hold for seven more years until Megan turned twenty-one? Or keep acting like he forgot about it, hoping she wouldn't bring it up? It was just that there was really no way-right now-

To Mallory's relief David wasn't furious with her for her reckless escapade.

"Yeah, everyone in Murfreesboro was calling to ask me if you were okay. So, I tried to call you to make sure, but you didn't answer your cell phone-"

She gasped in horror. "I turned the volume off so Avery could play a game."

He grinned before continuing, "So then I had to do what I hoped never to have to do-"

She paled. "Call Daniel," she guessed!

He laughed, "Yeah, and then actually it wasn't that bad. He could see you getting the girls out of the car-with all your dough-Well, he could see grocery bags; he couldn't tell you were loaded with dough!"

After that, he dealt with both girls, reminding them of the infractions! Avery was in trouble for two reasons regarding Amelia's wooden toy: the first one, that she nabbed it to provoke; and the second, that she chewed splinters from it which were bad for her tummy. Amelia was in trouble for biting and for doing her weird thing. And not stopping when Mommy told her twice. They both got their first 'pop' ever with a wooden paddle!

That was followed by a meatloaf dinner at the chow hall and back to the Faulkners to witness the next phase of the cookie-baking marathon! Rolling out the dough, cutting, and baking! Diana made it look so easy! None of the 'angels' misbehaved for her, as they had for Mallory! Sticking hard to the counter top and warping into short fat images as her struggle with the spatula disfigured them! No necessity to reattach dismembered heads!

Back home and getting the girls ready for bed, David answered a call from his dad.

"Hey, Dad, everything okay?"

David's features turned incredulous as he listened. "Really! Yeah, that's just fantastic! Well, yeah, Dad, but-"

Mallory listened from across the bed as David tried to insert an occasional comment! He gave her a thumbs-up, but she could already tell it was something good.

Blessedly his dad got another call, and David winked at his lovely wife as he disconnected. "Nanci got saved!"

Color infused Mallory's cheeks and her eyes sparkled. "Because of the web site?"

"Well, yes and no! I guess she's been seeking, and as she's obtained electronics to begin her blog, she's kept trying to access Faith's information! And then on a shore excursion in Odessa, she even went to a church! But it was very formal and the local tradition's that women wear head scarves! So between getting scowls and not understanding things, she was pretty disheartened. Well, then Higgins kept appearing, and he kinda mocked the things she confided to him about her quest! He's the one who convinced her to stay ashore and go clubbing~anyway, then when she was abducted, she tried to pray~"

Mallory's eyes filled with empathetic tears. "That makes me so ashamed I haven't tried harder to reach her~"

He sighed, reaching for her. "Well, we have tried to reach her; I think that's what got her started thinking about~"

She nodded, "Yeah, lifestyle evangelism; living your testimony out before people! Maybe we did impress her with a form of Godliness, but we didn't tell her what she needed to know! So she finally accessed the site to find the plan of salvation?"

His rich laughter filled their suite! "No, that's what my dad was lamenting! When she was back safely aboard and in the infirmary, Trent led her to Christ!"

Mallory joined the amusement! "Snatching the prize that rightfully belonged to your dad! Why doesn't he see that it doesn't matter? The main thing is that she found the Lord! H-m-m-m; if the professor and Nanci are going to make it, we need to help the professor see his need."

The dinghy bobbed like a cork as seamen attempted to navigate into the small opening of the Blue Grotto! Naples and the Amalfi Coast had been checked off the bucket list, pictures taken for upcoming travel issues! Harry and Maggie were disappointed at the prospect of being unable to enter the cave; somewhat of a lifelong dream! David just wished they'd shut up about it so they could give up and get back to the big boat before they all lost their breakfasts! And then drowned!

And of course, Nanci wanted the fabled site photographed and documented for her new venture. He scowled at her! Not only was she soaking up tons of religious garbage, but she had posted to a website about 'her decision'-and now her enthusiasm for getting to Rome, was as some sort of Christian pilgrimage! She frowned every time he ordered a drink, and he was getting the feeling that the Andersons were moving him to Istanbul because it was harder to stock booze!

Then, amazingly, they were inside the Grotto, surrounded by ripples and sparkles of blue brilliance! The water was calmer too, and he released his white knuckle grip, even managing a smile!

"I prayed we could get in," Nanci chirped happily.

Higgins suppressed an inner groan! Nothing to do with these guys who made this their livelihood! But because 'she prayed for it'! He studied his shoes as Harry snapped pictures.

"Thank you, dear, for praying for the water to calm." Maggie slid an arm around Nanci. "We've wanted to visit these sites for all the beauty God put here; but especially this! We hope to take more trips, but we'll probably not be back here! So it would have been disappointing, had we not gotten in! We've been Christians for forty-five years, and yet it never occurred to me to ask the Lord to calm the waters-"

Back in Diana's kitchen following chow hall breakfast, Diana assembled everything she could think of for icing and embellishing the lovely little 'Angels'.

"This is the part Amelia wanted to do-the fun part!"

Mallory's words were met with a short 'surely you jest' laugh and Diana pulled chairs up and arranged it so the girls could 'watch'!

"Wait!" Amelia's voice came in a screech, making Diana jump as she touched an icing tip down for the first stroke.

"What?" Her tone seemed a mild rebuke at the outburst!

"My song has to play! *Away In A Manger, No Crib for a Bed-*"

"Yeah," Mallory agreed, "that was part of our plan. I'll be right back!"

With the carol playing and replaying, the 'Angels' took on ethereal loveliness~with Daniel getting in on the act.

"Let's go into town for lunch," David met them on the path as they made their way home. "Are the Angels all done?"

"Yes, Sir," Amelia responded. "They looked very pretty! Later we get to take them to the poor children."

"Oh, that's nice! What poor children?" He grasped her and swung her up to his shoulders.

"Da ones that rides the buses~"

"No, Honey," Mallory corrected! "That's who we made them for before. We're going to take these and give them to the Honduran kids that work at Miss Deborah's company~"

"Oh~" with no argument!

"So, that means you're going to Texarkana?" David fastened Alexis' seat and buckled Avery. "Buckle in, Amelia."

"I want you to buckle me~"

He walked around and secured her. "Okay, Daddy's doing it, although, I didn't hear a 'Please'! And when Mommy tells you to buckle up for yourself, what do you do?"

She answered correctly and he kissed her. "How about it? Do I get a 'please' and 'thank you'?"

"Okay, for an update about Sanders! You've heard me mention inflating tires with Nitrogen rather than air?"

Mallory nodded. 'Mmm-hmm; didn't you say it makes the tread wear longer?"

"Yes, Nitrogen's less affected by temperature than air is, so tires tend to keep the same pressure whether it's cold or hot! I'm surprised the information hasn't disseminated more~"

Mallory laughed. "Yeah, you have to tell someone and then tell them to keep it hush-hush if you want to be sure it gets around! Not to change the subject, but Daniel got the professor to tell him about our plan to harvest gold from discarded electronics!" her eyes flashed indignantly.

He reached for her hand. "Yeah, he shouldn't have told! But you don't realize the forcefulness of Faulkner's persona!"

"I'm pretty sure I do!"

He laughed, rocking his free hand back and forth. "In a way! You do and you don't! Yeah, you were about as intimidated by him as you needed to be, for your Dad's plan to work! You're more intimidated by Diana!"

She sighed. Maybe he was on target with that assessment. "I'm sorry; I guess I changed the subject from Nitrogen and Mr. Sanders."

"Well, yeah, since he owns chemical companies, I figured he'd know a good source to supply Nitrogen and tanks, and we can start contacting some of the major trucking companies. Then, while we were talking about that, we got off on alternative fuels and making them more readily available! There are more and more places to recharge electrical cars, but not enough to make owning them practical! Well, not for any long-range trips! The same with Natural Gas and refueling-"

She nodded. Both potentially lucrative avenues to pursue! "Did he say anything about Beth?"

"No, but when I ran him down, he was at the Country Club! You know your mom; she told me 'to go ahead and track him down! It'd be fine'! Luckily, he and Beth were finishing breakfast, and my ideas caught his attention! It seemed like he and Beth were back to normal!"

"Wow! Wouldn't that be an amazing answer to prayer?"

"Trent Morrison," Trent tried not to be alarmed at Anderson's number on his caller ID as he answered.

"Hello, Mr. Morrison?" David had decided to be brash and call the man 'Trent'-until he answered his phone.

"Yeah, what can I do for you?"

"This is David Anderson, and the purpose of my call is two-fold; do you have a few moments?"

"Hung in traffic; what's up?"

"Well, first of all, that's amazing about Nanci Burn-Higgins-receiving Christ-"

"Yeah, the Holy Spirit had her ready! Nothing like staring down death to get you serious about it! Although, your friend the professor seems more hard-headed!"

"Yeah, rocks in his noggin," David couldn't resist the remark about the Geologist, hoping if Mallory heard about it, she wouldn't jump to the conclusion that he applied the slight to the entire profession "Uh-which brings me to the purpose for this call-"

Trent waited. Hung in traffic was true, but he was nearing home.

"Okay, and this is Mallory's idea, and we don't know if you have any vacation time, or if you'd want to-"

Trent pulled onto his block and pulled against the curb. Anderson didn't usually seem so tongue-tied, making him nervous about what the issue was! Provided he ever got it out-

"Okay" David expelled a breath and plunged onward. "The Higgins are taking a river cruise next along the Danube River. It starts in the Bavarian Alps of northern Germany and culminates at Budapest! Eight days! And nights"!-he cringed at stating the obvious, wondering why Mallory had put this sales job on him when she could do it better! And it was a good idea he was about to blow-

"Sounds really nice," Trent offered, trying to fill the awkward silence. "Please don't let Sonia hear about it; she's been dying to take some kind of trip like that!"

"She has?" Wonder infused David's response! "Is there any way you all could arrange to get off? It may be crazy, but we thought maybe-one of you-might get the opportunity-to talk to the professor-and it's somewhere else different for Sonia and Madeleine to wear the styles-"

"So, you're talking about Maddy, too?"

"Well, yes, Sir; the whole family! I know they stay busy going a thousand different directions at once! And with the flights on each end; we're talking about y'all being gone for at least ten days-just think it over and let us know-"

Delight shot through Morrison's being, an electric jolt of wonder! "Okay, well, we'll think fast and let you know before the evening's out! Don't offer it to anyone-I mean, thank you for thinking about us-I'll be in touch-"

"Sorry our date ended abruptly." Roger, home early, found Beth at her computer.

She smiled brightly, rising to move toward him! "Not a problem! Maybe we can try it again sometime!" she stretched her cheek upward for his kiss! "So, what was with David; anything you can share?"

He nodded, glad for the thaw of being allowed to kiss her soft cheek. "Let's make coffee! It's a-well you know the Andersons-mind-blowing!" He moved to the kitchen and began filling the carafe while Beth measured coffee. When it finished brewing, with two mugs poured, she sank onto a stool at the kitchen counter.

"Let's sit at the table so I can look you in the eye! Yes, I can share what David told me with you! You've always been able to keep sensitive information to yourself! Sometimes I neglect to tell you the specific things I love and admire about you." He smiled and patted her hand. "Of course, it's simply brilliant! Meaning so simple and sensible, you wonder why everyone isn't doing it! It's actually three-pronged, eventually! Phase one is being in contact with major trucking companies to present the benefit of inflating tires with Nitrogen, rather than air, and offering to set up and supply the gas and apparatus at their hubs! I mean, it's amazing, Bethy! It's a pretty low cost start-up for the savings it will provide! Not only wear and tear on tires, but also on fuel consumption! You get the best gas mileage when your tires are inflated properly! And it's less time consuming keeping the pressure constant! The other two things create more logistical problems, but not insurmountable! Providing Natural Gas and Electrical charging stations across the country, to make alternative fuel usage more practical!"

"No one's doing that already?" Beth's incredulous question!

"Not significantly! It's somewhat of a morass right now! The gas companies are afraid to commit enough to develop this at all of their stations, making the automobile industry crippled in its ability to market the hybrids more successfully!"

She nodded. "Still, they are catching on, and more and more people are placing orders for them?"

He nodded, "Barring anything unforeseen, this is the direction things are headed. We may not be in on the ground floor, but-we're in-"

Tears filled her eyes, and she scooted back to refill mugs and pull a pie from the refrigerator! Slicing expertly she placed a portion on an attractive plate for Roger and cut a small wedge for herself.

"So, that's my afternoon! Tell me about yours! Did you work on your blog? Delicious pie, by the way"!

"Thank you; an easy recipe and actually reduced fat! It's a recipe I worked out myself, and I've gotten a lot of positive feedback since I posted it on my blog!"

"What's positive feedback?" He had no idea she tracked visits.

"Well, I have about twelve hundred followers, and a hundred fifty people have responded about this recipe!"

Her answer so amazed him, that he choked hot coffee through his nose to keep from spewing it farther. "Twelve hundred! That's amazing! I mean, I guess I shouldn't be surprised-"

Instead of turning petulant, she smiled happily. "I'm pleased with the progress, and then, let me show you what Mallory sent me a little while ago!" She rose to retrieve her laptop! "Mallory pirated the picture from the Faulkners because they wanted to do a better job."

He surveyed the lovely, heavenly creatures in wonder. "A better job? Only the Faulkners! So-what are you going to do? Do you have to get their permission before you use it?"

She grinned mischievously. "It's easier to get forgiveness than permission! I already sent it out in a special edition! And now I have a huge spike in new site visits!"

Mallory listened, amazed, to the latest idea hatched in the devious brain of Lilly Cowan!

"Lilly, that is so perfect! Remember when you were 'out to get him'?"

"Well, I have occasionally made a mistake!"

Mallory laughed. "I hear ya! Haven't we all? Thanks; this makes me more excited than ever!" her voice rose, liltingly melodic!

Rome was rainy and windy, making the bleakness of the Coliseum and the Catacombs extra-depressing! They topped it off with a visit to the Mamertine Prison where The Apostle Paul was imprisoned prior to his beheading! (Because Pastor John Anderson recommended the prison site)! Higgins was tired of hearing Nanci quote that man! He endured the jostling in the Sistine Chapel as more religious nuts oohed and ahed over the masterpieces of Michelangelo. Although photography was forbidden, he was aware of surreptitious snaps. The old Nanci would have insisted on his breaking the rules, just for the adventure of breaking the rules! And she wanted pictures, which would be available in the shop! He was relieved that her religious bug curbed her irrepressible nature enough that she didn't challenge him to take pictures! He had spent enough time in a foreign hoosegow! His thoughts were a turmoil of panic and indecision! He needed a drink! And a chance to think through his hasty marriage! Yeah, Nanci was beautiful, and he had admired her from the first time he ever laid eyes on her! So, yeah, it was good, that she wasn't trying to get her hands on the wedding gifts, avoided the shipboard casino, wasn't flirting with every guy in the place-things she once would have done! Things like the quirky episode of her taking off in his car and stranding him in Estes Park! Still, he felt he would prefer to take chances with the 'old' Nanci than the new Bible-thumper!

His house was a done deal, the cashier's check delivered by courier. But maybe he could relocate somewhere besides Istanbul; maybe somewhere without Nanci. He was in a quandary! One minute, he loved her desperately, unable to believe they were together-and then the next beset by doubts! Doubts plagued him about her sincerity. All the religious garble being a cover for the fact that she only and always would love Daniel Faulkner! His thinking was to get out before she made him into a worse fool than he was already!

Chapter 35: GERMANY

Megan slipped her hand into Trent's as they joined other cruise members in a walking orientation of the ship! Excited, they had already checked her out online, and she was proving to be elegant and refined in reality, living up to the hype! Matt glared at Megan's monopoly of him and Trent laughed.

"You want to hold my other hand?"

"I'd rather be scalped and staked down on wet leather-"

With another laugh, Trent grasped his son in an affectionate but painful pinch on the shoulder.

"Dad, you're asking for trouble!"

"Come on, bring it!" Trent stopped, motioning mockingly with both hands.

"Trent; we're losing the group," Sonia's mild rebuke. "How can I make them behave when you're the one who's always trying to start something?"

He grinned at his beautifully clad and coifed wife. "I know, Sonn, but he started it!"

"Trent Austin! I'll hold your other hand, if only to keep it from getting you into trouble!"

"What a beautiful place," Maddy breathed, surveying the city of Nuremburg from the deck of the *Viking Aegir*. "It's exciting that we get to go tour it tomorrow."

Trent agreed: Sadly, the main sites were Nazi-related! The former Nazi parade grounds! And the Palace of Justice; home to the Nuremberg Trials, where notable Nazis were tried for the atrocities of their war crimes! Where, hypocritically, many of their compatriots were smuggled to freedom and positions in the Allied weapons and space programs! Evidently with the rationale that the 'ends justify the means'. Trent sighed wearily! His mind was too tired and jet-lagged to deal with that; it was in the past, anyway. He wondered idly how unsaved people grappled with the realities of life, not having the assurance that there is a Righteous Judge, in control, and able to make all of it work together for His good and the good of those who loved Him and put their trust in Him! Anyway, he was forced to admit, that though it was never a conscious wish to visit here, he was thrilled at the prospect! This was going to be a cruise with much more to see than simply ocean and beaches!

"Are we supposed to find the Higgins?" Megan's whisper in this ear!

"I'm not sure! I don't know if Mr. Anderson told them we're going to be on the tour, or exactly how we're supposed to play it."

"Well, I'm praying about it." Meggy's face was a study in sincerity.

The girls, bundled in adorable parkas and leggings, played in deep mounds of snow! Matching except for being created in different colors: from felted alpaca, embroidered ski caps; down to matching boots!

In Durango for the start-up of their gold mine! Special machinery from *South Houston* was well underway in the manufacturing process, and David was overseeing the retrofit of an old strip mall, getting stringent security measures in place well ahead of any deliveries. Mallory smiled as he bolted across the icy parking lot toward them. Handing her a stack of employment aps, he announced that she had plenty of work cut out for her.

She reached eagerly for the sheets, figuring they would probably start by hiring everyone! And keep additional aps that filtered in, assuming some of the hires might not work out! Usually, though, they did! "So, how's everything else going?"

"Good!"

She glanced at him perceptively, "Except for?"

"The city's not approving the chain link fencing! It will be an eyesore in the scenic wonderland."

She knew what he was thinking! The entire property was an eyesore! The retrofit to date made the unsightly complex look like the Taj Mahal compared to its former state. "Any chance of an appeal? Maybe if we plant trees"?

"I don't know! Trees are good; except from a security standpoint, they create blind spots! Cover for interlopers-kind of the reason chain link is good; the police can drive by and eye-ball the place-well, we'll see. I think there's time for lunch on the way to the airport. He scooped his protesting daughters from their snow bank and tucked them into car seats.

Mallory frowned. One reason for her being so enchanted with the prospect of mining gold from used electronics was her constant quandary of disposing of her own outdated equipment in an ecologically conscientious manner! Now as *DiaMo* conducted drives to collect and recycle, some people wanted to hold out! Okay, so they were relinquishing miniscule quantities of gold; but it wasn't like they could easily recover the metal from their discards themselves! It was quite a process! Still, the recovery rate of gold should be equivalent for *DiaMo,* to mines that moved the same tonnage of earth! "I really think that the best we can offer people is a tax receipt and the assurance that these tons and tons of outdated things don't end up in a landfill!"

David agreed. Their efficient process not only recovered the gold, but salvaged other materials for reuse as well. The surprise was that more companies weren't doing this!

"But about giving tax receipts. People can make preposterous claims to the value of discards."

"Yes, they can," she agreed. "But most people don't even bother. Unless they're incorporated and itemize deductions; and then they can't claim to have donated more than they ever purchased."

"Yeah, good thinking!" He paused to check a text message before winking at her. "Alright! The first semitrailer of used electronics is en route from Pueblo!"

Mallory's smile lit her face! "Bring it on! And then there's the amazing extra-that *Bendelson* has agreed to inflate their new tires with Nitrogen!"

"Yeah-" He sighed with wonder. "It's amazing the timing with that! We were looking for local truckers to haul from our collection hubs, and I found *Bendelson,* which was interested in the contract! And then we started up the Nitrogen just in time to mention it to the Operations VP! And they were approaching their annual new tire purchase! You know that's the Lord! You can just see His hand in the timing and giving us favor with these people!"

Mallory nodded. James Collier, the VP of operations at *Bendelson,* was intrigued, having heard rumors within the trucking industry. Unsure of the viability of the process, he was giving David and Roger an opportunity to test their facts with several trucks from the *Bendelson* fleet! Hauling through the Rocky Mountains, his trucks and their tires met the rigors of rapid fluctuations in temperature as well as atmospheric pressure! If inflating with Nitrogen rather than air, performed as claimed, he should see measurable results! Fairly rapidly!

"It's one of those industries that will probably get crowded with competition fast." David's deep eyes met hers, concerned.

"Well, if it does, then we can figure out what to do! Sell off as an IPO, or stay in and dig down to keep a market share? For right now, though, this is an open door! And it's giving people jobs while predicting a fair profit."

Trent sat on the sundeck watching the moon and stars float past, reflected in the rippled waters of the Danube! Silence prevailed; the hour was early, dark river banks barely discernable as the *Aegir* passed other river traffic in its down-river course. A great trip! Well, he wouldn't want to be like Nanci Higgins, doing it for a living! But for a week! Well, almost as good as a rail trip! But, not quite~ A staff member appeared, startling him, and receiving a start in turn!

"Good morning, Sir! May I get you something?"

"Well, a cup of coffee~"

"Yes, Sir, right away!"

Trent nodded. "I'm an early riser, and I didn't want to disturb my wife! And if I sit on a sundeck when the sun's shining, I just get more freckles!"

A courteous response, "I enjoy watching sunrises; would you care for a pastry as well?"

"May be just coffee! Thanks, though." He punched an icon to bring us his Bible ap and found his place in *I Corinthians,* reading until a verse caught his attention in a fresh way!

I Corinthians 2:12 Now we have received, not the spirit of the world, but the spirit which is of God: that we might know the things that are freely given to us of God.

He paused to meditate on the truths. Dealings of the Holy Spirit intrigued him in a new way. So, he needed the beauty of the Holy Spirit to replace the carnal, worldly wisdom that assailed his senses constantly. Part of the job of the Holy Spirit was to help him know with certainty, the things freely given of God! Gifts from God's hand, to Trent, in the here and now! That wouldn't be subtracted from his rewards in heaven some day! He considered a few of the things this verse might be referencing: things tangible, as well as intangible! Like the love and gifts of Sonia and his kids! Having Megan back from the jaws of death! Having a job he basically loved! Of course his salvation was pivotal to all of these other things! Sonia's position with *DiaMal*, including the houses they lived in, and the trips included!-The gift of a free and clear conscience-was huge-but Sonia had cuter clothes now than he could ever have provided, aside from God's freely giving- Hair appointments, nail salons, friends, the list went on! Things that he at one point in time, would have considered wrong to even ask for! He glanced up, expecting to see his promised coffee, to see Higgins approaching. He knew he needed to talk to the guy, but not now; not in this divine moment of solitude and revelation! He sighed, closing his ap, wondering how Higgins already had a beer in hand, and the coffee-

"Good morning, Professor! I guess you're an early riser, too?" Trent forced a smile and what he hoped passed for congeniality.

"Not necessarily!" The dour expression sent waves of aggravation through Trent! Why the sourpuss had to bomb into his space with his alcohol and hostility, was beyond his ability to fathom! Reluctantly, he admitted to himself that part of the Anderson's rationale in providing his family with this cruise, was to reach Higgins with the gospel! Besides that, he was cornered!

"Your coffee, Sir! Freshly brewed"! Presented with a flourish and fancy sculpted chocolate!

Trent straightened eagerly, taking a cautious sip from the steaming beverage. "Wow! That's good!" The compliment escaped involuntarily! "I mean, the first cup in the morning's always good, but-"

The crew member nodded, pleased with the praise.

"Viennese Roast, Sir! There is a remarkable difference, is there not?"

Wonder infused Trent's features. "I don't consider myself a connoisseur of coffee: it's all good compared to the cold, day-old dregs I consume at work! But–" He sipped again, relishing the flavor, rich without bitterness. "But, this is exceptional!"

"Thank you, Mr. Morrison! I am a native Viennese! We have graced the world with our music, our chocolates, and our coffee!"

Make-up people dabbed powder on Mallory as she smiled into studio lights! She wasn't sure why, but she had granted another interview to Carole Lee Whitfield.

"So, Mrs. Anderson, I understand that you have purchased a yacht, and you're taking a world cruise–"

"Yes, Ma'am; that's more or less correct! It's actually a work boat, set up for Geological exploration! We christened her *The Rock Scientist.* And for the time being, our exploration plans are limited to the Western Hemisphere. I'm sure you're aware that my husband developed a medical emergency recently, requiring immediate surgery! As far as we know, there are no more loose bone fragments, or anything to cause him further difficulties. But when that happened, I knew we needed a better vessel–one with better comms, a full infirmary; overall preparation for any emergencies. So we upgraded! Our cabins are very nice, although not as lavish as a yacht would be. Adequate and comfortable are what we strove for."

"Unh-hunh! I see."

Mallory smiled blandly! The news anchor brooked no clarifying of facts that she felt might hurt her sensationalist ratings! "So, as a soldier of fortune, how do you reconcile your life now with the idealistic Christianity you used to tout?"

"Uh–soldier of fortune–I thought that was a term used for mercenaries! I still consider myself to be very much a Soldier of the Cross! Now, if you mean that I'm a treasure hunter–well, I would be inclined to agree! I love the thrill of discovery–"

"Well, you must also enjoy the money it brings into your coffers! How do you reconcile raping and plundering the earth with your claims of Christianity? You don't feel any obligation to Mother Nature?"

"I think Christians should be good stewards; I'm sorry but I don't prefer the term 'Mother Nature'! God created the natural order in the beginning, as He claimed, and He is still in control of all of it! I believe in responsible exploration. Our drilling operations don't leave any noticeable footprint except that our equipment must burn fuel! We create far less of an environmental impact than your ordinary trucking company! And, as we require trucking companies to transport goods and services that supply what we need, while providing jobs, we must decide that they do more good than they do harm! While a changeover to cleaner, non-petroleum fuels remains in the works."

"I see you've given quite a lot of thought to justifying your actions! But do you deny liking the money?"

Mallory's expression turned droll. "Not at all! Do you deny enjoying yours? I feel like I use what God has given to me in positive ways-we further the cause of the Gospel; we provide jobs and opportunities; and we enjoy the fruits of our labors! The antithesis of what we do smacks of Socialism!"

"So, have you ever considered donating to charitable causes?" Ms. Whitfield's tone and expression grew snippier with each of Mallory's responses.

Mallory remained cool and patient. "Yes, Carole! I just told you that we further the Gospel! That is considered 'Charitable Giving' by the IRS, although they don't always allow us to claim the entire amounts we give for that purpose! And, I know what you mean; there are many good and noble causes out there! Some of which actually give the majority of the monies collected, for the cause as stated! But, I don't believe things like heart disease are going to be eradicated by research and treatment! When Adam sinned, death entered the world, and the Tree of Life was taken into heaven! Now, it is appointed that everyone will die! We will never eradicate the curse of death by human effort! The only thing that guarantees an endless life, is Salvation through the shed blood of Jesus! And it's the knowledge of Him that we invest heavily into sharing around the world."

The anchorwoman cleared her throat and straightened her shoulders importantly. "In a different vein; are you not expecting another child? This is what? Your fourth? You have a strange way of showing your concern for the earth and for society in general."

"Yes, we are expecting another baby! And we don't think we're doing the 'global village' a disservice by bringing more mouths to feed into the world! While the media tries to spread the ideas that the earth is overcrowded and natural resources are exhausted, we find the opposite to be true! That people are the first and greatest resource there is! And that aborting them is what does society as a whole, a huge injustice!"

"Okay, I though you agreed not to go there!" An angry hiss in a stage whisper Mallory was sure picked up live.

She laughed. "Okay, I'm sorry. I thought you brought it up! So to change the subject back to the abundance of wealth we're still finding-"

"To what do you attribute your astounding luck? is it true you attend séances to contact your father?"

Mallory sighed. "Okay, first off, I don't believe in luck; and secondly, I don't believe in attending séances or trying to contact people in the afterlife! We have a high success average in our exploration, I think, based on our world view-"

"World view?" An arched brow and sardonic grin!

Mallory nodded thoughtfully, knowing her response was important if anybody watched the interview. "Yes, Carole, our world-view is from a Biblical perspective! That the earth was created by God for the purpose of sustaining mankind! He created it to be vast and more than sufficient! In the Bible, I find the opposite of society's opinion! As I mentioned earlier in response to your comment about the size of our family! In God's omniscience and omnipotence, He created enough to last us for as long as time on this earth will last! So many people think that the United States Geological Survey is complete and conclusive about earth's natural resources. But actually, the earth's mantle is so enormous no one has even scratched the surface yet! One of the Scriptures that emphasizes this truth is:

> *Jeremiah 31:37 Thus saith the LORD, If heaven above can be measured, and the foundations of the earth searched out beneath, I will also cast off all the seed of Israel for all that they have done, saith the LORD.*

I realize the primary meaning of the verse is that God will never cast Israel off, but he used the illustrations of plumbing the vastness of space and the huge scope of the earth beneath our feet, as things that are impossible to accomplish."

"Okay, Bible lesson noted. You still haven't explained why such a high percent-"

Mallory shrugged, trying to be patient when she thought her meaning should be obvious.

"Because, I expect to find things! People who believe every vein has been discovered and tapped out, don't bother exploring-why bother? And in answer to your question about my Dad, I still learn from him; but not through seances! He left me clues and treasure maps that I'm still unraveling and making sense of! He was a true genius with an awesome sense of fun! I wish my kids could know him-" She broke off.

Higgins slumped into a deck chair next to Trent and ordered a coffee. "You heard any updates about David and Mallory and when they plan to launch the expedition?"

Trent frowned. "I seldom hear about them. Sorry; I'm not a good source of gossip."

The professor's gimlet eyes drilled into him furiously. "Just trying to get information! Wouldn't call it gossip! When you work for a goofy girl that doesn't keep you in the loop-"

Trent smiled past the professor at another cup of coffee, striving for a controlled response. "You're talking about Mallory Anderson? Why call her a 'goofy girl'? She probably keeps you in the loop as much as necessary!"

"All of my scholastic peers consider her a nut case and blight on our profession!"

Trent nodded, annoyed. If he was supposed to win Higgins, getting into an argument about Creation and Evolution probably wouldn't help-but then again-maybe that was the best approach-

"Di, Honey! Look what came in the mail-something from the *American Sheep Industry*"?

Diana reached for it. "Thank you! I joined! Out of interest in the wool industry in general"!

He studied her seriously. "Did you sign me up, too?"

Wide blue eyes considered the question. "Never thought about it! You're a member of lots of Geological clubs and organizations."

He nodded, not sure it was the same. Since she wasn't a Geologist!

"Well, it's no problem to sign you on; I didn't know you'd care! And we pay out a lot in dues and fees to organizations."

"True, but it's all tax deductible for us, and it creates more opportunities to network!"

"Okay, so not to be penny-wise and pound-foolish as the old adage goes-are you interested in attending a conference?"

"Absolutely, and I don't want you attending conferences without me!" He paused as illumination lit his handsome features! "We need to get everyone to join and show up in your gorgeous designs crafted from wool-"

Her face glowed! "And not only wool, but fibers from all of the 'small ruminants'!"

David stared gloomily at an email from James Collier, COO at *Bendleton Trucking*. The crux of it was, that the trial was so amazing, that *Bendleton* was in the process of switching their entire fleet to Nitrogen, but they were gearing up to do it themselves! And thank you for bringing the economical concept to their attention- He rubbed his head, fighting tears of disappointment!

Amelia rushed to him, asking if his head hurt again. He hugged her reassuringly. He needed to call Sanders-

"Hey, David; did you get the email?" Roger's tone was curious, but not livid!

"Yeah, that's what this call's about!"

"I see it as great news!" Roger's perspective took David off-guard.

"Well, yeah, it proved the feasibility-"

"Exactly! And they're big, so installing the equipment for making the change themselves makes sense! They could have at least sent us a box of chocolates! But not everyone will want to add this operation; they'll farm it out! I think we're still on track to make some good money! We need to get ads into some of their periodicals-I'll get Suzanne-"

"No, I'll do it! I had some artwork and copy ready, but then-I thought it was on the scrap heap!"

"Yeah, I don't really think it is-but-"

"Yeah, get these magazines contacted about placing the ads yesterday! On it!"

Trent drank in luscious colors as the sun peeked above the horizon, infusing the morning with glorious puffs and rays in hues he felt were probably not yet named!

"Pretty colors," he observed.

Higgins turned the air blue, making him wince! "Yeah, when I'm not toting my camera! I should be getting pictures, but if I go back to the cabin for it, the 'Old Lady'll' start in on me again!"

Coffee escaped from a shocked Trent in spite of his efforts to swallow it. He wiped fastidiously at his shirt, trying to come up with a response! He would hardly classify Nanci as 'the Old Lady!' Higgins literally did have rocks in his noggin! The question shot through his mind, how a class guy like Faulkner could ever have been this goofball's buddy! Before he had a chance to 'speak unadvisedly with his lips', the steward appeared.

"Sorry to interrupt, Mr. Morrison, but the Captain would like for you to join him in his office!"

Dazed, Trent sprang up. Must be his perpetual guilty conscience, but the questions flashed through his mind why he might be in trouble with the Captain! Maybe his kids hadn't followed orders regarding his curfew~

"On your six," Higgins' offered reassuringly as he fell in behind.

'Just to make things worse~' came a gloomy thought! 'Whatever Higgins had must be contagious!'

"Herr Morrison!" The Captain was a cute persona, and Trent extended his hand in return. "This gentleman, Herr Goldman, has joined us briefly to speak with you on behalf of the Israeli government! I shall step out and allow you some privacy!"

Still concerned, Trent turned to his shadow. "Guess that leaves you out, too, Higgins. Just go get the camera before the colors dissipate!"

Higgins shuffled awkwardly without taking the hint.

To be blunter," Mr. Goldman spoke up. "Your presence here isn't necessary, Professor! A good morning to you"! He strode purposefully to the door, using both body language and facial expressions to tell Higgins to get lost!

"Higgins, you're a rock! Get out!" Trent finally got action! 'Okay, this was going to be hard to get past in order to witness.' He sighed.

Higgins puckery face turned pink with indignation. "You don't have to get snotty with me!"

With the office door secured the Israeli burst into guffaws, holding his sides, and finally blowing his nose and striving for composure. "The purpose for my visit is to present you with a thank you from my country for your service!"

"Hey, thanks, but it was nothing! I guess it was just the Lord that prompted the entire thing! He truly does fight on the side of Israel. And the guy who was with me, Rob-"

The Israeli ignored the remarks about God, and cut in. "We are aware of Rob Addington's role in discovery of the contraband! However, it was your leadership-"

"Thanks, but I never could have made that descent onto that boat and taken the action to keep her afloat! God was in Addington's following along with me; although I kept telling him to go home! But, I'm sorry. I should at least allow you to finish!"

The Israeli opened a black velvet box, and Trent gasped in amazement!

"A wedding set for your wife! Congratulations on twenty-five years! Twenty-five years in spite of Ms. Cowan's messing with you! We thought this would be an appropriate thank you, but if you would prefer something diff-"

Emotion rendered Trent speechless as thoughts paraded through his mind! 'Yeah, Lilly's meddling! And what would the acceptance of the lavish gift do to his tax bill? And were they doing something for Rob, too, in light of his bravery and determination?'

He found his voice! "No! Nothing different! That-that's beautiful-" he reached for the box, still expecting there to be a catch. "Thank you." Gratitude, heartfelt and sincere!

"Thank you, Mr. Morrison; we remain in your debt! As for the details of your discovery, I am not at liberty-"

"I understand that, Mr. Goldman! I'm pretty sure I don't want to know!"

"Are you happy?" Mallory could barely word the question through tears.

David stopped mid-stride, turning to face her squarely. "Am I supposed to be? I'm never sure how to answer you! Especially, when you're crying so hard!"

"I'm so happy!"

"Okay, so I always thought smiling and laughing meant happy; and crying meant sad~" He pulled her into his arms! "I'm ecstatic!" He dabbed tears with his fingertips! "But I would have felt the same about another little girl~"

She nodded diffidently. "Well, I know you always say that~"

He laughed and kissed her. "Yeah, and I usually try to tell the truth and mean what I say!"

She laughed suddenly, pulling away teasingly. "You're just afraid he'll be like you and give you grief like you give your dad!"

Handsome features turned serious and he reached for her again. "Always on both of our minds about our kids! How do we keep them from getting rebellious and breaking our hearts? I'm not sure; just enjoy them and love them and train them to the best of our ability~"

"Your parents did that~"

He nodded, sighing. "Well, let's pray for the Rapture then!"

"We do that every day!"

"Well, we need to pray harder!"

She shook shiny strands of auburn, meeting his intense gaze. "That begs the question again of 'How do you pray harder'?"

"I still haven't figured that one out! I know how to kiss harder, though!"

Chapter 36: GLORY

Proverbs 4:18 But the path of the just is as the shining light, that shineth more and more unto the perfect day.

"What was up?" A frowning Higgins questioned, ambushing Trent as he headed toward the Explorer Suite he shared with Sonia.

"Nothing Higgins! Thanks for trying to be a help. Maybe we'll run into you and Nanci ashore." He scurried past-to nearly bowl Sonia over as she exited the luxury cabin.

"There you are!" She seemed a little miffed. "Have you eaten breakfast already?"

"No, actually, just a couple of cups of extraordinary coffee! I was awake early and wanted to let you sleep-come back in with me for a second?"

"Well, the kids are on the way to hunt you down and get into our seating-"

"Just for a second! You'll be glad-" Pulling her back into the suite, he drew the box from his pocket, opening it with a flourish! "For putting up with me for twenty-five years"!

Tears sprang up as both hands flew to her face! "Oh, Trent! Those are-" she spread her hand delicately to receive the beautiful set! "What a surprise; you must have been saving-oh, you are romantic-!" Her hands trembled and she flung herself into his arms.

"So, you like them?" he questioned lamely.

Mallory slit a thick vellum envelope deftly, pulling an elegant wedding invitation free! 'Really? Luke and Heather?' A great match, she supposed; just that she had no inkling! She punched her intercom buzzer. "Hey, Gina, what's with holding out on me with the romantic gossip?"

She heard a sigh from the outer office. "Well, since the day David had me phone security to drag my sister away-"

Mallory chuckled, "Oh yeah, that! So, what about you? Do you have anyone on the string?"

Embarrassed silence before a brusque response! "Not at the moment which will free me to help Heather with her plans! Our parents aren't exactly big event planners."

"True, but they're great people!" Mallory responded. "Let Luke and Heather plan their own wedding and reception! Luke plans events for a living! Listen, why don't you see if you can add in another air fare to attend the upcoming Sheep Industry banquet? I need you to join me as my personal assistant, and introduce you to some people!"

Stunned silence and then, "Yes, Ma'am, I'm on it!"

"Great and everything's put together for Trent and Sonia's day in Vienna?"

"Absolutely"!

"Well, I know last minute tickets to the Vienna Philharmonic-"

Gina laughed, and Mallory could picture the cute smile and deep dimples. "Yes Ma'am! I didn't say it was easy! I just said, 'I got it accomplished'. I had to go through every perk in your highest rated credit cards to manage-"

"And let me guess! It wasn't cheap! Which is not a problem," she added quickly.

"Professor Higgins!" Megan stood and waved frenziedly.

"What are you doing?" A frazzled Trent hoped to avoid the nosy, negative man until he had a chance to tell Sonia the story about the new Diamond ring set! He hated giving her the impression that he was romantic, when he hadn't given their coming twenty-fifth much thought.

"I like them," Megan responded. "And he was asking me all about if I think I really died; and I got to witness to him-"

"Was he open to the Gospel?"

"Well, let's say he's still shaken up about what happened to him. He's thinking, but it seems like maybe Mrs. Higgins is pushing too hard."

Trent pulled his legs in reluctantly so the other couple could join them!

"Wow, that looks elegant beyond words," Nanci complimented as she took in Sonia's ensemble.

"Thanks, one of the things Diana has noticed on European trips is the darling coats the women wear! Nice wool, tailored and with cute details. She thinks Americans wear too much puffy nylon stuff and not enough quality. One of her goals was to send me here with a coat from the US, to make European women take notice!"

Nanci nodded affirmatively for coffee and turned her attention to the kids. "So, what do you think about the Danube?"

"Well, I didn't know that we were going through a canal with locks!" Michael's face lit at the question and his delight at the engineering. "I mean, the whole thing's fun! Lots of history come to life! And scenic beauty-and the food's stellar!

"What about you, Madeleine?"

"Well, I'm really excited about Vienna, and the concert tonight-I wish I could play an instrument-the Faulkners and David and Mallory are so talented as well as being successful business people-"

Nanci nodded. "Well, it's never too late to start. What instrument would you play?"

"I wish I could get a piano and take piano lessons," Megan's voice broke in.

"Don't interrupt! She asked me!" Maddy's aggravation!

"Sorry," Megan muttered.

Trent stared around the table in wonder. Nanci Higgins was drawing intel from his kids, things he had no inkling of! And so far, Higgins hadn't spilled the beans about the rings!

"Okay, Mad, which instrument?" he prompted.

"I'm thinking!"

"Okay and Megan can't talk while you think?"

"Well, I can't decide! I wish I could play them all; I guess woodwinds, starting with an alto sax!"

"Matt, what about you?"? Nanci turned her high wattage smile as she asked.

"Hmmm, I was afraid you'd ask. I mean, I'm impressed with the Von Trapps, but I'm saving for a new hunting rifle." His tone bordered on defiance.

"It's okay to be your own man!" The professor's unsolicited opinion! "I'm glad we don't have to spend our evening listenin' to all that high-brow stuff! Truth told, you'd probably rather be in a sporting goods store, too; eh Trent?"

"Well, I like to think I've broadened my horizons a little beyond that!" Trent gazed from one kid to another around the table, feeling like a failure dad for not starting them in the assorted music lessons by the time each turned three! 'Yeah, soccer, football, volleyball, youth leagues, and church, of course'! It seemed like the time and expense of those things blinded him to polishing his kids in other dimensions!

"When the discussion waned, Nanci carefully drew Megan in once more, "Piano! Pianists are usually sought after. I have a piano! My dad dreamed of me becoming a classical pianist, but I wanted to be in a rock band from as far back as I can remember! I think I finished the first book of several different courses each time I started over. I'd like for you to have it!"

"Will your father mind?" Megan's eyes brimmed with tears!

Nanci's eyes danced! "Probably, but I'm used to fighting with him! I can always get my way! It's in Newport; I'll get him to ship to arrive when you'll be home."

The professor cleared his throat importantly and she turned toward him. "You okay?"

"Well, you know, you can check with me before you start giving our stuff away-"

Aflutter, Diana was everywhere at once! She always managed to keep her constituency well dressed, but her determination to attend the wool-growers convention with everyone dressed in woolen designs, added pressure!

"The plaids must match exactly! Press a knife edge into those pleats! Make sure the sleeves are set in smoothly! No, that buttonhole is off-grain!" She loved wool, though, and luxurious fibers from the fleece of other small ruminants, so she was up for the challenge; a new chance to shine! Not that any of the women's ensembles were man-tailored! She paused to caress a garment taking shape on a dress form for Gina! Rich raspberry red boiled wool sheath; the girl didn't have a waist to speak of, so the straight line would disguise that. And it would be topped with a gabardine coat of the same shade, complete with velveteen collar! Matching opaque hosiery with platform pumps would lengthen her silhouette! A sumptuous brooch of red raspberries carved of Rhodochrosite, and with leaves of Nephrite Jade on fourteen karat gold would grace the lapel and be repeated in silk twill scarf! Tears filled her eyes! Living her dream! She sank onto a stool in her studio and studied new fabric pieces carefully. She liked a chocolate brown and light pink buffalo print in a sumptuous wool/mohair blend! Definitely had Mallory written all over it! Coordinating fabrics were solid brown worsted; a brown and pink Donegal tweed, and solid pink mohair blend. She sketched, undecided if the tweed was too busy with the plaid, or edgy enough to be cute! She kind of liked it, but didn't want Mallory to feel obligated to wear something crazy! "Lord, what do You think?" She tried to make a habit of bringing Him into everything, but was still shocked when inspiration swept in!

"That's it!" Her hand flew across the sketch paper, and a dress emerged in the tweed, topped by hip-length swing-jacket executed in plaid. She colored in a generous silk twill scarf that was representational of the plaid, but edged with a representation of the tweed! Deciding against repeating the theme in the lining, she rendered it in pastel pink.

Pushing that aside, she began a deep blue coat with lavish, matching soutache trim! Oh! Cute; with Amelia's big blue eyes! The dress, matching in typical little girl style, featured short, puffed sleeves. Her eyes sparkled as her hand hovered. Avery! Little dress with gray flannel skirt, red velveteen bodice, and white cotton collar and puffy sleeves! Red, blue, yellow and green embroidered hearts and tulips trimmed hem and collar and outlined matching gray flannel coat! Whimsically, she drew bound buttonholes incorporating velveteen in the same colors as the embroidery and finishing with bright self-covered buttons! Alexis! What a little beauty! Well, Mallory's girls were all adorable~ Sighing, she rose to refill her coffee! Why couldn't she get herself out of the 'tan' mode and make something bright and colorful? She just loved Alexis's monochromatic, elegant coloring: olive-toned skin, tawny brown eyes, and honey-colored tresses! Amelia was Mallory made over; Avery, her Aunt Tammi; and Alexis, so much like David's aunt! She surrendered to her inner muse and drew a camels' hair coat, topping a camel and ivory hounds tooth, woolen knit dress! Little matching boots were the coup de grâce!

David approached Mallory with a good deal of trepidation! He wasn't concerned about making her angry, as much as disappointing her! She watched his approach, meeting his gaze steadily.

"I think I know what you're going to say."

He shook his head; "I doubt it."

"We're not sailing off on our great adventure-"

He sank next to her on the love seat in their master suite at the ranch. "Okay, so you do know! Hey, look, I apologize-I'm thinking we can do the front part, but-"

Deep hazel eyes sparkled. "Will you quit apologizing? It isn't like you wanted a bone fragment and another surgery! You mean you think we can do the Florida part from the boat?"

"Yeah; we can do Vero, and then on to Orlando for Disney and the Space Center! And then through the Panama Canal!"

She yelped with delight, flinging her arms around his neck and kissing him joyously! He laughed and pulled her close for a lingering kiss.

"You thought I'd nix the whole thing? That isn't necessary, I don't think. You're not too far along to travel; we'll be back by Christmas, though not by much! Then we send Higgins and Waverly to do the rest of the mapped out exploration."

"If it's dangerous for us, don't you think-"

He laughed. "What? It might be equally dangerous for them? Listen, I promise you, no one will kidnap them! But, if they do-"

Mallory's eyes glinted. "It will be like the *Ransom of Red Chief*," she finished, "and the kidnappers will pay us to take them off their hands!" She grew serious, "Still-"

"Look, for all their drinking and partying, I'm pretty sure Higgins learned a lesson in Odessa! And, actually, he told Megan the only thing keeping him from receiving the Lord is that he doesn't want to admit Daniel's been right all along."

Snow deepened as hired limousines approached the Denver venue for the American Sheep Industry banquet! The Faulkners and Andersons had attended sessions for two intense days, and now their guests were arriving for the final banquet, key-note speaker, and awards! Gina, in a salmon, wool crepe evening suit, clipboard in hand, directed the constituency toward the proper tables. She smiled brightly at Sonia and Madeleine whom she knew; before addressing Trent and the other kids. "Hey! It's great to finally put faces with the voices! Of course, I've seen your pictures!" She kept smiling although castigating herself for the dumb remark! Michael Morrison was a heartthrob! Struggling for calm, she studied her schematic; to be rescued by David!

"Hey, welcome! Did your flight have any trouble getting in? I'll show you to your places! You met Gina?"

They all nodded vaguely and David escorted them into the ballroom.

"Hey, David?" Michael's whisper stopped him. "What's with Gina? Where did she come from? Why have I never seen her around before?"

David bent in. "We usually keep her in the office, but she's filling in temporarily as Mallie's assistant!"

"Yeah; what else?"

"Uh, she's Heather's older sister-"

"Oh!"

"But entirely different! Hey, did you hear about Heather and Luke? They're getting married in June!"

"I guess I don't know Luke! Is he a good guy?"

"Yes, and I think Heather's getting her head on straight, too. She got saved, but then-for a while-"

"So what about Gina"?

David grinned. "Quiet and conscientious! Oh-uh-not dating anyone-she's heard the Gospel plenty from being around all of us, she's just so introverted-"

Donovan Cline strode up the embankment toward his Agaba, Jordan hotel! An extremely fruitful year in terms of gleaning knowledge and understanding! And now, suddenly, a monetary payoff! Not that there wasn't plenty of haggling going on! Egypt clearly was in the right concerning the ancient artifacts discovered on either side of the land bridge at the Straits of Tiran! Saudi Arabia was in the fray, because the loot strayed onto their side of the Gulf, as well! Cline secretly wished he could bequeath all of it to Israel! At any rate, he kept the rights to his photos. Each day as the thick layers of accumulated corrosion dissolved, the artifacts glowed more resplendently! Amazing the craftsmanship and creativity exhibited in the ancient treasure cache!

In the cool of the lobby, he ordered a coffee and pulled the photo file free! Herb and Mallory felt strongly that the Egyptians learned the jewelry craft from the Hebrews! That from Joseph's day when the Israelites were in great favor, until they became feared and subjugated as slaves, they were esteemed for wisdom, intellect, and creativity!

Now the recovery project was in the hands of Egyptian Archeologists, who excavated the waters carefully, reverent of the human remains! Cline's imagination took him to that long ago day of battle, when Pharaoh and his army, in pursuit of their millions of freed slaves, dashed their chariots into the opening of the parted waters! Of God's fearful judgment as the waters swept back into place! Heavy chariots harnessed to horses, and armor crafted to preserve the soldiers' lives, guaranteed no survivors in the depths. He fought emotion as the might and power of God settled around him in the quiet lobby!

Cinnamon wool crepe, fashioned with sweetheart neckline and long slim sleeves, fell to Mallory's knees, meeting sheer cinnamon hosiery that disappeared into shiny copper pumps! Gold jewelry and Diamonds lent elegance. She leaned toward Diana! "Look what the menu shows as the entree? I love rack of lamb! It takes me back to that Easter-"

Daniel leaned in, "When I scared you to death!"

Her eyes widened, and she felt suddenly breathless, remembering. "Uh, yeah," she laughed, "but the lamb dinner was before that."

Daniel laughed and his eyes twinkled. "I don't think I ever once managed to get a six month spread between you and David!"

"No, but the separations still always seemed so long-"

Diana patted her hand. "Your spirit was incredible! Your dad wasn't sure which Mallory we'd be dealing with; although, he thought you possessed Christian maturity beyond your years. Turns out, he was right!"

Mallory laughed. "I thank God every day for putting y'all into my life! It's been indescribable-"

"Look at these pictures, Lilly!" Benjamin Cowan's wonder-filled tone! "It's like Mallory pointed out! Nothing proves the Bible, or the Torah, as our nation-" he broke off. "But there are amazing happenings to support them for those who choose to believe!"

She nodded, studying each shot at length. "And yet, none of the world's museums are interested in exhibiting either the pictures or the reproductions of the artifacts that Mr. Cline is manufacturing."

"Yes, but he is a determined and resourceful man, Lilly! He is raising funds through gifts and investors to build a museum in Manhattan! New York is such a cultural mixture that he feels the exhibition will draw from Christians, Jews, Egyptians"!

"So strange that the Cairo Museum-"

He nodded thoughtfully. "Well, they will doubtless, in time, display the artifacts being retrieved. You just wonder what the spin on them will be! And a lot of the reluctance to get on board with Cline and other scholars who place the ancient Israeli crossing at the Gulf of Agaba, is because the Church and the Egyptian tourism agencies are so ensconced at St. Catherine's in the Sinai Peninsula! As you well know, people fight what hits them in their pocketbooks!"

Daniel looked around, frowning. A deviation in the guest seating brought a whisper in Diana's ear. She frowned too.

David noticed; one of those unforeseen things! The Faulkners would just have to be miffed.

Mallory suppressed a giggle. She wanted Michael Morrison to notice Gina! What she couldn't have guessed was that he would coax his little sister to sit by Cassandra so Gina could sit at his table! Bringing Megan into close proximity to Jeremiah! 'Oh well! C'est la vie!'

Nanci emailed a proof of her blog to Maggie, whose forte was proofing, and correcting spelling, grammar, and usage! Although, she thought she was getting better, the older woman still recommended a bunch of changes! Although Nanci had offered to pay for her skills, she refused, instead, forging a meaningful friendship! Nanci couldn't remember having a girl friend since early elementary! She enjoyed the respectability of marriage, even in a society that pretended not to care! And having a friend and confidante! Harry and Maggie were presently cruising Scandinavia, inspired by Nanci's initial blog edition compliments of Ella! Their next planned excursion was to take the Danube River Cruise, also at the recommendation of her site! 'Well, they might as well; rather than returning stateside and then having to fly back here for the next cruise! They were getting in on the Holiday Cruise where adorable German cities featured Christmas Markets!' "Tell Harry I'll pay him for pictures," she added.

The crowd murmured restlessly as banquet time came and the emcee was nowhere in evidence. People began moving around and Trent Morrison broke from his norm to approach David and Mallory's table. Mallory rose, laughing, "I've heard about Sonia's new rings! I guess I need to check them out!"

Trent slid into her place to speak with David. "Hey, thanks for bringing the Nitrogen thing to my attention! It seems like one of our cars always needs new shoes! The boys are responsible for maintaining theirs, but I always feel so sorry for them-hopefully, their tires really will last longer now. Maybe Higgins wasn't supposed to mention it to me-but after the concert in Vienna, we went to Hotel Sacher for dinner and the fabled Sacher Torte; and a General was there that I've seen around before in DC. Well, his wife complimented Sonia's attire, and well, I wondered if the Nitrogen thing was for real! I thought the General would probably know! He didn't, but the idea intrigued him. Nothing may come of it, but I gave him your contact information! And I'm sure his wife was hooked with the fashions!"

"Wow, Mr. Morrison, that's amazing! I mean, we contacted one big trucking company, and they tested the concept, liked it, and decided to cut us out by doing their own! I'm sure if the military is interested-"

Trent shrugged. "That they might do it for themselves? I don't have a clue, except that there are lots of civilian companies that hold military contracts!"

David's eyes widened. "Yeah, that's true."

⁂

With the banquet under way, Cassandra sipped a Coke before letting her curiosity get the best of her. "So, did you see Him?"

Megan laughed in spite of her awe at the accomplished violinist. "No, only doctors and nurses! They thought I was brain dead and couldn't hear-well, but I could!" Her huge eyes held Cassandra's. "I was terrified! And then, I saw Jeremiah, and he prayed for me!"

Cassandra frowned, "Well, a lot of people were praying for you!"

"Yes, I know! Wherever we go, someone tells me that! Anyway, I'm sorry I can't tell you that I was in heaven! I wasn't; I was still alive!"

"But you were a long time without Oxygen-" the little nurse in Cassandra persisted.

"So they tell me; I didn't say I can explain it! Did you see the rings that Israel gave my mom?"

"Hmmm-mmm; why did they do that?"

Megan shrugged. "Something about my daddy's leading the charge to rescue Nanci; she's nice!"

Cassandra froze! "Okay, so why would Israel give your mom rings because your dad rescued an American citizen?"

"Hmmm, I'm not sure! Anyway, Nanci was talking to all of us kids and asking us what instruments we would like to play, so I'm having a dream come true learning to play the piano!"

⁂

Nanci returned home from a photo-shoot! A very fun morning, modeling *Rodriguez, Incorporated's* latest creations: outside the Hagia Sohia, in the second courtyard of the Topkapi Palace, in the carpet section of the Grand Bazaar, standing next to the Baccarat Crystal stairway in the Dolmabahçe Palace, waving from a Bosporus ferry as it pulled into the terminal. She forced back tears, remembering how much she had to be thankful for. It was a dream! The job with *Rodriguez*, and her rapidly-gaining-popularity travel blog! The Turkish government begging her to use the famous landmarks for the *Rodriguez* catalog, and paying a modest amount to place them on her blog-site! All dove-tailing-well-miraculously! She folded the garments deftly for her cruise departure! An opportunity to wear the designs prior to the catalog release! She felt like David, or Iggy, was eager to have her leave. With a sigh, she turned her attention to emails. If the activity was supposed to take her mind off of problems with her marriage, it wasn't working! The first one she opened went wild about her shipboard nuptials~'The most romantic thing ever~yada~yada~'

The rack of lamb didn't compare to Daniel and Diana's, and the program grew lengthy and dull! And then suddenly, they presented Diana with an award! As a newcomer to the membership, but one with a passion for wool and its artistic possibilities, she was already distinguishing herself! The place came alive! And not only with Diana's close circle of associates!

Taken totally by surprise, she was overwhelmed! Mallory's tears brimmed for happiness at the recognition, and she resisted when Diana tried to insist she should receive part of the acclaim! Without Diana's knowledge and creative genius, there would be nothing for Mallory to partner in!

Finally, gaining freedom, they made their way out, to find the snowfall stopped, the temperature risen, and the earlier snow pack disappearing in slushy rivulets.

"Too late for coffee houses," Diana lamented as she checked a dainty watch.

"We can get coffee drinks at McDonald's drive thru and continue our party in the hotel lobby," David suggested. "I'm not sure why they close everything but the bar down so early~"

Daniel nodded agreement! "Their decisions are based on what their constituency wants! It's another sign that we've become a drunkard nation!"

Everyone around him nodded somberly. "But it doesn't have to rain on our parade!" Mallory reminded. "We just need to keep showing that Christians can have fun and enjoy life without substances! Well, coffee excepted!"

"Hey, don't get to meddling!" John Anderson's voice rang out!

"Yeah, let's hear it for caffeine!" Jeff's glance caught Juliet's. "Daniel, if you guys can get the girls back to the hotel, David and I can get the coffees! We'll just get bunches of everything available and drink it til it's gone!"

The professor checked an incoming call! David Anderson! "Yeah, what's up?" He moved from the noisy environment.

"Hey, Higgins, we're finally about ready. We're flying to Florida a couple of days after Christmas to meet *The Rock Scientist*. Permits are reissued for dredging/drilling. Mallory can oversee Waverly until we get through the Canal! Then you can take over and we'll fly home! Or actually back to Florida and do Disney on the way home! We've heard it's packed Christmas week!"

Higgins was silent, wanting to haggle his way in on day one of the excursion.

"Hey, great job on the Danube, by the way!"

"Okay, glad to hear it." Higgins disconnected, not sure how much his Danube River reconnoitering via cruise ship could have contributed. He rose unsteadily, hoping it was late enough that Nanci would be in bed and asleep.

"I'm still keyed up!" Mallory's countenance glowed with excitement and energy as she tiptoed from the girls' bedroom in the hotel suite! "Of course, downing three big coffee drinks at one in the morning-"

David nodded. "But you were right! We can show the world how much fun life can be-" he cut off, emotional. "You know, there was a time when I thought Christianity was corny and considered everything fun as 'forbidden fruit'! I thought I was missing out! I didn't know the pure joy in the Lord like you had! You were just so steadfast, and I-uh-I waffled-quite a bit-"

Her eyes snapped, remembering! "Yeah, tell me about it! You drove me crazy! First, with trying to convince Daddy that it wasn't-any big deal-and then-" Tears welled up, "and-then the Faulkners-"

He nodded, deep eyes meeting hers. "Yeah, and then by the time I figured it out and was trying to be on the straight and narrow, getting back in good graces with my dad-I figured Faulkner's liking me would never happen-that picture came through on the flight to Turkey!"

"Oh, yeah, that picture! Don't remind me of it, David!"

He grinned sheepishly, "Too late! And then, Sylvia turned out to be more nut-case than I ever could have fathomed! I still don't let my mind go back to~she pushed you down into that mine pit and left you to freeze~"

Mallory's eyes sparkled through tears and she laughed softly. "Yeah, and then she stole your horse and rode him right into town, wearing my clothes! Kinda gave her whole thing away!"

"Yeah, add that one to the list of dumb things criminals do! We barely found you in time~"

She laughed again. "Okay, enough trip down memory lane! The Lord has really been good to both of us! Your head doesn't hurt at all; you're sure you're telling me the truth?"

He opened his arms, and she moved into his embrace. "Head clear now, Kimosabe," he intoned dazedly.

She laughed, "Oh good, Tonto; just so you know who's boss!"

His laughter deepened and his mouth sought hers. "Don't make me have to show you who's boss!"

Both of their phones buzzed in unison. "That must signal disaster," Mallory gasped as she grabbed for hers. They both read the text message from Higgins at the same time, bursting into laughter.

Well, the old ball and chain finally nagged me into it!

"Well, that's the professor," David gasped out! "Overjoyed at being born again"!

"Yeah, that's the professor, all right!"